THE DAYS BEFORE TOMORROW

MARK HASS

The Days Before Tomorrow Copyright © 2024 by Mark Hass.

TheDaysBeforeTomorrow.com

Library of Congress Control Number: 2024903006

Second Edition, March 2025

ISBN: 979-8-9899094-0-7 (Paperback)
ISBN: 979-8-9899094-2-1 (Hardcover)
ISBN: 979-8-9899094-1-4 (eBook)

For Walter and Miriam Hass
May their memories be a blessing

"We shall not cease from exploration, and the end of all our exploring will be to arrive where we started and know the place for the first time." – T.S. Eliot

"Keep fire away from straw." – Ukrainian proverb

CHAPTER ONE

Mine was a place defined by war, but also by the hope war would someday end. I was born on one of those hopeful days.

My father, Marcus, joked that marching bands greeted me as my mother, Clara, brought me, her third child and second son, into a world emerging from the chaos of World War I and that was about to plunge into twenty-five more years of conflict and destruction. The people in my town and across the Ukraine celebrated what they thought was a momentous day, one on which their dream of living in a unified nation had been realized.

They were wrong, but they believed what they wanted to believe. The news from the capital Kiev was uplifting. A massive unification celebration filled the streets there, and newspapers heralded the noisy birth of a new nation. The dusty streets of our town were joyful, too. They writhed with euphoric drunkenness from the horilka being swilled by the men and the simple joy they got from taunting the Jews foolish enough to leave their homes. Yes, father said, it was a glorious day for some in our town, but dangerous for us. Tucked into the hills of Galicia, population four thousand, about nine hundred of them Jewish, a borderland, where control for centuries had shifted among powerful nations in a seemingly endless, meaningless battle between the armies of Poland, Austria and Russia, life in the place I was born was personal and local. Yet, it was stained by those bigger, outside forces.

"The first words she says to me," father recalled at the dinner table on my thirteenth birthday. "The very first words your mother says to me after you were born, 'The Golem,' she said. 'The Golem.' "

The room where we ate was not big, and we crowded around a small rectangular table, father seated near the oven, mother stirring a pot behind him on a coal-burning stove, and the three of us, my brother, my sister and me, arranged shoulder to shoulder just a few feet from them. Father, his long face beaming, his sharp nose and joyous eyes an oasis for anyone gazing at them, told this story as a means of celebration on each of our birthdays, recalling unique details when he recounted our births. There was one part each story had in common. He would raise his voice when he said the words, "the Golem," and they echoed around us. He liked a bit of drama when he told stories.

"The Golem was not something to fear, Wolchi," my father said to me, as he had on past birthdays, his voice lowered, almost a whisper. Pointing to a clay figure on a perch beside the front door: "No, what mama wanted was for me to protect you, as I'd protected your brother, Ira, and your sister, Leja, after they were born. So, I wrote your name on a piece of paper that I tore from our bible and placed it inside the hollow statue. That paper is there today, along with the names of your sister and brother."

Ira, 18 years old, thin and handsome, his head a riot of brown curls, looked at Leja and rolled his eyes; she stifled a soft laugh. I loved this story, especially because it was about me, and I sat rapt at attention as my father retold it.

A year after my parents' marriage, Ira was born. A year later, father was conscripted into the Austrian army and fought for two numbing years a war against Tsarist soldiers, men he might have otherwise shared a game of chess with or even a Sabbath table. Some were men he knew growing up. He lost his right foot in that war and now used a cane as he walked and also when he needed to make clear on the streets that he would defend himself if threatened.

"Papa, you know that Golem is just a lump of dried mud?" Ira said.

"Hush, Ira. Don't disrespect your mother," father said, pointing at my brother. "She believes it is more than that."

My father was not a religious man, nor was he a superstitious one, but he believed in the power of his wife's vision, her energy like a ray of sunlight that illuminated what he could not see. He believed in science, machines, the future, the absolute finality of death, but my mother saw something else, something ancient, and she taught us to respect it.

Superstition was one of two parenthood principles that guided my mother's interactions with her children. The other was food. On the evening of my thirteenth birthday, she served us chunks of sour black bread and steaming bowls of the dark mushroom soup she prepared for special occasions, each with two floating puffs of meat-filled kreplach. She stood behind my father as we ate, watchful that her expressions of love were being properly consumed. She rarely smiled or seemed happy. She also never ate with us. Only after she cleared the table would she sit, solitary in the shadows of the kitchen, and eat quickly while absent-mindedly sweeping crumbs from side to side. As she watched us eat, she reminded us that "a Golem had always protected my people, and it now protects us."

She fashioned our Golem from the mud of the flooded River Stryi in the autumn of 1913 after she and father were married. The river banks steeply up toward the dirt streets of the town, and the mud there is ankle deep in October, dark and cool. Everything near the river is wet after the autumn rain until the ground freezes in winter. The blue and yellow of the late summer flowers, the grey of the sky, the bugs swirling about her as she scooped the dark earth with her hands into a wooden pail – that's what she remembers and tells us about as we eat. We've heard it before.

Her creation, the ugly clay man now watching over us, reminded me of a fat brown bullfrog. She had hardened the soft mud in her oven and later carved three Hebrew letters across its chest –aleph, mem and tav – the first, middle and last letters of the Hebrew alphabet. They spelled truth and gave the statue its power, she said. Without the first letter, the remaining two spelled death. A Golem with that first letter obscured or removed is something to fear, a stark reminder of how thin the line is between sanctity and chaos.

"He is small, but powerful," she said, turning from us and returning to her stove.

Ira and Leja shared a meaningful glance, eyebrows raised. They wouldn't admit they believed any of it. It was like the wooden cross that guarded the entry to the Orthodox Christian church towering above the town or the Torah scroll the bearded, red-headed rabbi held high as he walked through the streets on the Sabbath leading a parade of his bent-back faithful. These were symbols of something that seemed to my older brother and sister of a time past, of a way of life that held no future for young people like them. I wasn't so sure. I was glad we had Golem and that father had stuffed tiny pieces of paper inside it with our names, and that mother seemed to understand the ins and outs of the whole Golem business.

"Remember when the Golem saved you, Wolchi, from the cemetery people?" Ira asked, his mouth wide in a grin and his hand messing my hair.

I loved my brother. He was gentle and said smart things, but he teased me too often. It was annoying. "Remember that night, Wolchi?" he continued. "There's nothing scarier than a monster you alone can see. Right?"

He was talking about the time I went lizard-hunting with my friend Ivan near the old Jewish cemetery by the river. The banks were dangerous in autumn, steep and slippery, a fast, straight slide into rushing waters. Towns people told stories about children disappearing from the muddy slopes after wandering too close to the river edge, their curiosity rewarded with a terrifying end in the cold inescapable currents. Mother insisted we stay away from the river after the autumn rains began, but that was where and when the best lizards, hidden beneath damp rocks and decaying leaves, could be found. So, that's where we went.

Ivan, three years older, was more Leja's friend than mine. They were the same age, shared a nascent interest in Ukrainian independence and the complex politics of the day, and sat beside one another at school. They liked each other and sometimes talked and joked during lessons. Even though I sat several rows from them near the back of our single classroom, I could hear them. So could our teacher, a scowling

Polish woman, who would yell at Leja. "Stop disturbing that boy, you dirty infected Jew." Leja, who prided herself on her appearance and her robust health, was not infected and rarely dirty. Still, she turned her eyes away at the teacher's rebuke, avoiding more stern punishment. Nor was she disturbing Ivan, a tall, confident Ukrainian kid, an instigator who loved to tease my sister and tell her silly jokes instead of listening to the yak-yak-yak from the Polish schoolmarm.

He hung around with me, too, and on an October evening when I was seven, just before dusk, with storm clouds darkening the sky ahead of us, we were returning home from an afternoon of hunting the small orange salamanders that lived near the river. I carried a wooden bucket with dozens of them, bringing them home for reasons I couldn't explain.

It started to rain, a drizzle at first and then a cold, angry downpour. We ran as the storm intensified, rain and then hail on our faces like the slap of tree branches. I heard thunder and felt the wind, so cold I knew it was from the other side, where my mother said the dead rose from their graves at night to dance and where malevolent spirits and dybbuks hid among them, the people so evil they couldn't cross to an afterlife. The trees of the cemetery on my left, already barren of leaves, swayed with warning against the grey and white sky. Wind lashed the brown grass between the fallen and broken headstones. Stars of David and the names of the dead carved in careful Hebrew letters were reflected on the wet ground. I heard the rapids on the river made angry and dangerous by the storm.

"I'll race you, Wolchi," Ivan yelled.

My head down, I ran toward the safety of home, with Ivan in front urging me to run faster. Faster. Lightning cracked across the sky in front of us, and the wind caught the cylinder of my bucket, filling it like a sail in a tempest, snatching it from my hand.

I stopped to retrieve the bucket and recapture the tiny orange lizards racing to safety, when I was enveloped by a dybbuk. Wet, white and snapping in the wind, it twisted around my legs and dropped me to the ground. On my back, fighting, I could feel myself sliding down the riverbank, could hear the rushing water becoming closer. The harder I fought, the more entangled I became, the wind so cold against me. Golem, I thought. Where is he? I called for him. Help. My mind raced with mother's warnings about the river. I sobbed. My breathing grew shallow, blocked by the dark force that had captured me. When the whiteness suddenly lifted, a grey shadow stood over me, its face dripping, its hand lifting me to my feet just yards from the riverbank. I saw ghosts everywhere, all the dead from all the generations of Jews who'd died in ancient pogroms. They floated in the trees, and I knew the dybbuk hid among them.

"Wolchi. Come on. Let's go," Ivan shouted.

I pushed past the shadow, grabbing handfuls of mud as I climbed the wet riverbank and ran, without stopping or looking behind, until I burst through our front door.

Leja, sitting near the warm oven with a book and Ira beside her, called for me. "What happened? You're covered in mud," she asked.

"I saw one, a dybbuk," I cried. "It caught me. I couldn't breathe. Golem saved me."

Ivan came through the door a moment later carrying my bucket and a dirty white sheet that had blown from a clothesline in a neighbor's yard beside the cemetery and which, he explained, he had peeled from my face and body.

"Maybe not the Golem," Ira said.

Leja wrapped me in her arms just the same. Still, I thought, maybe it was.

My fear that night didn't shame me, and Ira could joke all he wanted. It was nice, truthfully, to be the focus of his attention and his charms. Even though it was my thirteenth birthday, and I was a man in the eyes of the Jewish faith, with some emerging signs of adulthood on my face and elsewhere, I reveled in being the family's youngest and having Ira fuss over me and Leja hug and comfort me.

By the time mother served the special birthday honey cake, talk had shifted to more mundane daily matters, the likelihood of snow and the need to haul more coal into the house (father), the pretty blonde-haired Polish girl that Ira had his eye on (Ira), and the oppressive policies of the Polish regional governors and the emerging Ukrainian liberation movement (Leja).

"Mama, I think I'm in love with her," Ira said.

"I'm telling you to stay away from the Polish girls," Mother replied. "They will be nothing but trouble for you. For us. There are plenty of Jewish girls for you to be 'in love with.'"

"But none of them has her hair, so blonde and with so much flair," Ira said with a broad grin, his hands moving dramatically up and down from his forehead to his shoulders, combing through the imagined strands of his beloved. "Long blonde hair."

My mother turned from him in frustration, but Leja, shaking her head at Ira's performance, took up the debate.

"She doesn't even know you're alive. And even if she did, what would the two of you talk about? The best way to milk a cow? She's not the brightest firefly in your garden, you know."

Leja smiled approvingly at her witticism, as she watched Ira squirm while formulating a reply. And what better one than to turn the focus onto Leja.

"And what do you and Ivan *talk* about when the two of you are walking in the woods," he asked. "I've seen you."

Leja's face reddened, more embarrassed than angry. "That's not your business."

"I think the two of you will get married someday," Ira said. "Would that be okay, mama? A Ukrainian boy and Leja?"

Mother shook her head as she handed me cake, tension stiffening her face. Father stirred uncomfortably, searching for a way to settle his family and move the discussion away from this jagged terrain.

"Wolchi, can you help me bring in more coal after supper?" he asked. "It will snow tonight, and we'll need two buckets."

The room fell silent, everyone left to their thoughts. Ira resisted the impulse to have a last word. ("I love my family, so I'd best keep the peace among us.") Leja eyed Ira with that look she reserved for her older brother. ("Should I hug him or smack him?") Father ate his cake quickly. ("Delicious, mama.") Mother kept busy at the stove, moving pots about. ("What will happen to these children?") I watched them all, my gaze moving from one to the next, savoring mother's honey cake, bite after small bite.

"Honey will bring a sweet year to everyone who has a taste," my mother said. It seemed crazy, but I was wondering as I looked at my family whether the Golem would like some cake, too. ("It couldn't hurt.")

There was a lot I didn't know about my hometown while growing up, things I didn't learn until much later. Important pieces of history lived inside all of us, invisible, but defining. Our sliver of Eastern Europe, known as the Kingdom of Galicia, had Europe's most chaotic transition to modernity. Natural barriers, such as the Carpathian Mountains and the mighty Vistula River, sometimes defined its borders. More often, though, the succession of European powers whose armies gridlocked within Galicia's borders just kept what they'd conquered until the next war, redrawing the boundaries of the region. Some confuse it with a Spanish state of the same name, but my Galicia had a unique and colorful history that, even though it never existed as a nation, played a defining role in shaping 20th Century Europe.

It was a cultural center, where writers, professors and philosophers considered important human questions — the nature of freedom, the horror of war and the beauty of love — and where a Jewish population thrived in the large cities, Krakow and L'viv, and in hundreds of small towns scattered through the countryside.

It was part of Poland until it was annexed by the Austro-Hungary Empire in 1772, but Polish influence continued to dominate everyday life and sparked a nationalist movement to unite Galicia with the Ukraine, the Russian-dominated territory to the east. When the Austrian Empire collapsed in World War I and Poland re-emerged as a distinct nation, the ill will and conflict between Galicians of Polish and Ukrainian descent escalated.

In the 21 years between the end of the first world war and the start of World War II, Galicia would be punished by the rise of Nazism to the west and the spread of Marxism to the east. It was the place where those ideologies confronted one another in 1941, when the German and Russian armies divided it, and Europe descended into its most horrible war. Those years shaped and then nearly destroyed my family. When I tell our story, those times can seem cruel, but I recall them as wondrous, too, because so much that was lost from then still lives in me.

11

Chapter Two

The snow fell. When it snowed at night our town transformed. The mud in the streets froze and became blanketed with a clean cover that hid the evidence of commerce and personal grievance that dirtied the streets by day. The trees bare branches made a map of lines, whites and greys, against the ghostly sky. Everything became so still; it seemed the shape of each flake could be identified as it floated down and took its place among the others.

My father trudged in front of me as we circled the house to the coal bin. For an amputee moving on one leg and a wooden cane, his legacy of war, he made rapid progress through the accumulating snow. I carried our two coal buckets, stepping into each of his left footprints as I walked and placing my right foot onto the spot that would have completed his stride. From behind him, I could see the spread of his back and shoulders, still strong enough to operate the machines of his bookbinding and printing shop beside our house. Strong enough, too, to lift me in a morning ritual that I recalled from my youngest childhood. "Let me see how much you grew last night," he'd say placing his hands under my arms and hoisting me so my eyes could stare into his. "Ah, feels like ten grams, maybe." And even though the distance between his hazel eyes and mine was now less of a lift and my weight was a strain for him to move smoothly from the ground, our ritual continued on many mornings.

He slid aside the cover of the coal bin and took one of the buckets from me. He filled it using a square piece of wood that acted as a small shovel, and began to hum as he worked. I knew the song. A man in the town square who played guitar for coins from passersby would sometimes sing it. Mournful, eerie.

Ochi chornye, ochi strastnye
Ochi zhguchie, I preskrasnye
Black eyes, passionate eyes
Burning and beautiful eyes.

Black like coal, I thought to myself, as he handed me the full bucket and reached for the second.

"Go. Bring that inside," he said.

I made my way around the house to our front door and heard laughter and shouting in the distance. Probably some men outside the tavern celebrating the snowfall, or just another Friday night, with cheap horilka and glasses of the strong, warm beer brewed from winter wheat.

Inside, Ira helped me dump the coal into the bin beside the stove. Leja sat in a corner, her corner, with a book close to her face, reading in the dim kerosene light. I wandered to her, eager to spend a few more moments in the warm house before returning outside to retrieve the second coal bucket.

"What are you reading?" I asked. Leja was passionate about her books and magazines, some of which were gifts from one of father's distant friends and others which she bought from the traveling merchant who sold clothing, books, pots and pans, and even individually wrapped candies, from the regional capital in L'viv, where western ideas and merchandize began the journey to rural Ukrainian towns like ours. She hid them in a hollow behind a loose wallboard that she called her library. The wallboard was open when I sat beside her, and I examined the periodicals and volumes about history, and the novels by Joseph Roth, that filled the space.

Leja showed me a picture in a magazine of a crowd gathered outside a non-descript building flying the Polish flag, red and white stripes with a crowned white eagle.

"They are protesting against the government," she said. "They want us to be free from Poland and be able to choose our own leaders. Look at this."

She pointed to a close-up photo of a bearded, middle-aged man shouting with his arms in the air.

"He started a movement to unify us. He says we are the only country in Eastern Europe that was not given independence after the war. And Poland took people's farms and arrested anyone who fought back. Now, there are protests everywhere."

Ira turned toward them with a look of disinterest. "Not around here."

"Not yet," Leja shot back. "Ivan says there are many like him and me who think it's time to fight back against Poland. He wants to start a partisan group here. A lot of his friends said they will join."

"Ivan? Ira said. "Sister, is this about politics or something else?"

"Oh stop," Leja answered. But she smiled, and in that way acknowledged the underlying truth of Ira's remark.

Mother, standing across the room, couldn't resist joining

this discussion. She walked quickly toward them and snatched the magazine from Leja's hands.

"We keep to ourselves. You are not a Ukrainian. Not a Christian. The Polish will kill a Jew just for speaking about these things. Do you understand?" Mama asked.

"Mama, things are changing," Leja said. "We can fight for what we believe. Even Jews. We just want what every Ukrainian wants. We don't have to hide any longer."

All four of us then seemed to hear it at the same moment and turned toward the front door. Outside, the shouts and drunken laughter were close. Very close.

"Papa?" mother said.

I hurried back outside, where five men walked unsteadily down the road, singing, pushing one another, slipping to the ground in the snow, drunk, and armed with pipes and wooden handles.

"Zhidy. Zhidy. Come out of your hidey holes," one of them shouted. "Bring us your Zlotys, bring us your gold."

Nicholas Goreki stood at the front of the group, a boy Leja's age in our class at school. His father, Igor Goreki, was the town's largest landholder, a man of influence, who was deeded his property by the Polish government after the war. His farm, made up of smaller plots seized by the government from local peasants, was acre-upon-acre of wheat, rye and barley. In the summer, his melon fields supplied the wealthy in L'viv, and his apple trees yielded the best fruit for hundreds of kilometers. He was also the defacto representative of the Polish government and controlled thousands in government spending on everything from police uniforms to kerosene for streetlamps. He was very powerful, but most troubling to us, he was also a vocal anti-Semite, a loud, ignorant voice for pogrom.

Leja and Ivan joked about Nicholas. Despite the advantages of wealth and family status, he was as stupid as a stone, Leja said. Ivan added that he was also as dangerous as a rabid dog. I didn't interact much with him, despite sharing a classroom. But a few months before the snowy night, Nicholas stopped me as we left school.

"Hey, little guy," he said.

I was several years younger, but not much shorter than him. He was built like a boulder, though, square and beefy, his head the shape of a box and his arms dangling from his shoulders like beef on hooks in the butcher shop.

"You're a pretty smart little guy, aren't you?" he asked, pointing to the school books and papers I carried. "Let me see those." He yanked the books from my hands, spilling them onto the dusty street. "Oh," he continued, as he lifted one of the papers off the ground. "There's my schoolwork. I knew some Jew had stolen it." He slapped me hard across the face. I saw stars and fell to one knee.

"Jerk," I muttered as he walked away, waving the schoolwork above his head, his index finger touching his lips. "Shh," he said loudly.

It would have been bad enough that I was left that night to redo my work. But the next day at school, while the teacher graded those papers and the class sat mindlessly copying from the blackboard phrases celebrating "great Polish success stories," Nicholas again taunted me, silently now, index finger touching his lips. "Shh." When the teacher handed back those papers, Nicholas gleefully waved his (mine) and said loudly, "The top grade for me. An 'A'," and his friends, thugs that followed his lead because they feared his father's wrath, cheered for him. Written across the top of my paper was a red 'D-'.

So, when I went back outside that snowy night and saw Nicholas' drunken face at the front of a group of his friends, it wasn't fear I felt, but a foreboding. What did he want now?

I ran around the house to the coal bin. "Papa, let's go inside," I said, grabbing his arm.

"Wolchi, the coal. Take the coal," father said.

I lifted the overflowing bucket. Holding it with one hand and my father's arm with the other, I tried to hurry him into the house. He seemed unaware of the approaching men and looked at me with questioning eyes. "What's wrong?" he asked, just before a snowball struck his chest, then another struck his leg. And another and another. And then a stone.

My father turned toward the street and the gang of laughing young men. "You criminals," he shouted, waving his cane, steadying himself with a hand on my shoulder. "Your fathers will hear about this."

Nicholas and one of his friends, a man with a flat broad nose and a fish-hook-shaped scar on his cheek, ambled toward us, their faces turnip red, their eyes vacant and glassy. Without a word, Nicholas punched father, his full weight behind the fist, and father dropped to the ground. Nicholas turned toward me, smiling, and lifted his index finger to his lips. "Shh," he hissed.

I stared in confusion, at him, when a grimace crossed his face and he, too, fell to the ground. My father, from his knees, swung his cane, landing blows on Nicholas' legs. From behind, I was struck across the head. I tasted blood. Goreki's scar-faced friend dropped atop me, so close I could smell the alcohol and tobacco on his breath and see the decay starting to rot his front teeth. I swung my fists aimlessly at him, at anyone.

A piercing howl made everyone stop, and, in that paused moment, the flow of time halted. I saw and heard every detail around me as if I were staring at a photo from one of Leja's magazines.

Blood in the snow. The face of the drunken thug beside mine, his scar raised and knotted, hooking from below his eye to his lower lip. My father, trying to right himself, with Ira, holding his arm, steadying him. Chunks of coal scattered about. Nicholas whimpering on his knees, looking directly at me. His nose almost flat, his lips swollen and bleeding. My sister, holding the empty coal bucket, standing over him. She swung the bucket, for the second time, landing it squarely on his cheek, and he dropped to the ground.

Mother's voice broke the peculiar stillness, as she lifted me by the arm.

"In the house, right now. Go," she ordered.

To my father and Ira. "Go."

She took the bucket from Leja. "Inside."

In the doorway, I watched her. Her head was bare, exposed to the snow. Her back to me, she wore only the woolen gray shawl she favored for chilly evenings inside the house and a pair of unlaced boots that she'd stepped into hastily. She seemed powerful in that moment, mythic.

Pointing at Nicholas, still prone on the ground and moaning, she shouted at the scar-faced man and the three others standing around him.

"You. All of you. Take him home," she said.

My mother closed the door, gently took my face in both hands and examined my bloodied eye. I watched Golem behind her on the shelf, his aimless gaze fixed on the room, and I felt dizzy, as if adrift in turbulent water. My mother followed my eyes to the clay statue. She patted my cheek, kissed my forehead and nodded.

After that night, I got into the habit of touching Golem's belly before leaving the house. Like other Jewish families, we had a bronze mezuzah attached near the top of our exterior doorpost. It had a tiny scroll inside with the holiest Jewish prayer, the Shema, written on it. *"Hear, O Israel! The Eternal is our God, and God is one."* Jewish people were supposed to touch the mezuzah each time they entered the house as a reminder that home was a safe place, a holy place, and the outside world was not. Touching the mezuzah provided some assurance that the outside would not breech the doorpost and enter the home. I never touched it. No one in my family did, but maybe that's how I got the idea about Golem. It seemed to me that the time to engage some magical protection was on the way out. Golem was inside, beside the door and uniquely suited to the job at hand, so a personal tradition was born.

I also touched him before I opened the door to visitors. So, when the rabbi came the next day, knocking at our door late in the afternoon after the day's Sabbath services, I placed my hand on Golem's belly for the first time. When I opened the door and saw the rabbi's hand on the mezuzah, I thought there would be an especially strong force protecting our home this day, but I also worried he was visiting to chastise us for not attending services that morning. My parents no longer insisted that Ira and Leja accompany them on Saturday mornings to shul, but I was still expected to join. We would crowd into the airless wooden synagogue ten minutes from our house, the men on one side, the women the other and chant, sway and bow with the devoted for several hours, and then head home in silence for a meal of bread, salt and cheese.

It was a habit, something that connected mother and father to the town's community of Jews, which was important to them, but not a meaningful exploration of faith. My parents were unlike the others in that community. They had no slavish commitment to the ancient ways of Torah, or the impractical, unchanged rules that guided day-to-day Jewish life for centuries. My father kept his head uncovered except in the synagogue, his face shaven. I never heard him utter a prayer outside the walls of that synagogue. My mother rejected the stiff certainties of the rabbi's teachings, but believed the more unbelievable aspects of her faith. The Golem, the spirits of the dead, the incomprehensible forces that affected human lives. All of those made sense to her. The ramblings of the community's religious leader meant nothing.

So, when she came up behind me to the door, her greeting of Rabbi Breslov was formal and unusually stiff.

"Hello, rabbi. Can I help you?" she asked.

"I looked for you and Marcus at the shul today," the rabbi said.

"Marcus is not well. He's resting," she replied.

"Can I come inside?" the rabbi persisted.

She considered her response before stepping aside, allowing the black figure of the rabbi to stride into our home. Rabbi Breslov was a tall, red-headed man. His greying beard reached his chest and was so thick about his face I couldn't see his lips move when he spoke. He wore a stained prayer shawl over his shoulders, baggy flannel pants and wet shoes.

"May I speak with Marcus?" The words just floated from

behind the animal pelt covering his face. Without awaiting an answer, he walked past me and gently touched my head, studying the angry welt on my face and the bandaged gash over my eye. I stared at his round fur hat, beaver skin father once told me, all shiny with grease and sweat from the rabbi's brow. Ira said the rabbi never removed that hat, that rabbis were not allowed to. I suspected he was teasing me with this information, yet I couldn't help but wonder: Did he sleep with it, sitting upright to keep it perched on his head through the night? Did he shift it from one side to the other in the morning when he needed to rinse his hair and scalp? And what did the rabbi wear on his head before that beaver was trapped and killed to make the hat?

I smelled an odd odor as he walked past me toward father, who awaited him at our table. What was it? Old cheese? Old parchment? Coal smoke? The bits of butter and bread that dotted the facial hair near the rabbi's mouth? There were so many odd things about this man.

"I'm glad you seem to be well," the rabbi said to father. "When I heard about last night and didn't see you today in shul, I thought the worst."

"I was hit in the face by those thugs, and my head has bruises," father said. "Nothing more."

"They say the Goreki boy was not so lucky," the rabbi said.

"He deserved what he may have gotten," my father replied, his face reddening with anger. "Hooligans, drunks, no better than wild animals."

"The mayor came to warn us. Some of the Polish people want a pogrom for what happened to the boy," the rabbi said. "You know his father. He's always shouting for a pogrom. But this time he has gone to the priest."

"Nicholas Goreki is no boy, rabbi. He is stronger and meaner than any two men," father said.

"You know how these things are. You know what can happen," the rabbi answered.

"I was in the war, rabbi, side-by-side with the Austrians and the Poles. I know them. I saw what they did to the Ukrainian and Russian men they captured. Beat them for hours just for pleasure and then hung them in the streets where the wives and children could see them die. The Jews got worse. I lost this foot, for what? So their drunken sons could beat me when they choose, throw stones at my children in front of my own home? No," father said with anger.

"They want money. Or they will have a pogrom," the rabbi said.

"So, there it is. Money. Zloty coins. Pay us so you can live another day without feeling the harshness of our fists and sticks. Let a Jewish merchant deny a peasant a drink at the tavern, and Goreki calls for a pogrom. Let his son attack a crippled man who fought in the war, and that, too, is reason," father said.

"Marcus, you know what happened in Beryslav last Easter. My home. They killed many of the Jews. Robbed their homes. Burned businesses," the rabbi said. "This can't happen here."

My father's face turned stony, but resigned. His eyes bore down on the rabbi's until the holy man's gaze shifted to his hands. He fingered the fringes of the prayer shawl with his left hand and stroked his whiskers with the right.

"You know I don't have a lot of money," father said quietly. "Just what I earn binding books and printing, and my war pension. It's barely enough for food and coal."

The rabbi's gaze lifted. He breathed deeply and sat straight in his chair.

"We will get the money for this," the rabbi said. "The way we have done before. All of us together."

They spoke quietly for several minutes, before the rabbi stood and shook father's hand. As he walked toward the door, he again stopped and touched my head. "We'll see you again next Shabbos. Yes?" I nodded. His eyes were grey like his beard, but almost transparent. He stared at me, and what I saw beyond those eyes was some combination of wisdom and madness. I watched a single bead of sweat roll from beneath the brim of his hat onto the bridge of his nose. It hung there before dropping to the floor untouched.

"Shalom, young man."

———————◆◗◆———————

The slow tolling of the big bell at the small church that crowded the town square called the faithful Catholics to prayer the following morning. The trilling of many smaller bells, more distant, more melodious, filled the nearby forest and beckoned the Orthodox Ukrainians to their more ornate and timeless house of worship on the edge of town, atop a small, cleared hill. Every Sunday these sounds filled the air and competed for the ears of the faithful.

The Catholic church, built just a decade before when Poland assumed control of Galicia following the war, was squeezed into the town center, beside the government offices and across from the tavern, a place of prominence. It was too small to accommodate all of the worshipers who answered the call of the bell on Sundays. So, while the Catholic men crowded the spartan pews inside the building, their wives, daughters and children prayed on their knees on the ground outside, even on snowy mornings, with those far from the church door repeating the words and actions of those closer who could hear and see the priests inside.

The Orthodox church had stood for two centuries in a quiet meadow surrounded by spruce and ash trees. Its three ornate steeples were each taller than the next and covered by weathered wooden shingles topped by iron crosses, with the tallest circled by a dozen iconic bells. The Orthodox faith had survived in the Galician western Ukraine despite efforts by Polish Catholics to marginalize its priests and isolate its parishioners in everyday life. In my hometown hierarchy of influence, the Ukrainian Orthodox were a couple of places above the Jews, but not even close to the top.

My father rose early that morning, shaved and brushed thinning hair from his face and up over the top of his head in a way that made him look like a man of influence. He wore thick woolen pants, a white shirt, a heavy jacket and clean boots, an outfit he considered formal attire. Ira and I would accompany him to a parley in the town square, where the rabbi, the Catholic priest and the mayor would negotiate a resolution of the conflict over Nicholas Goreki's broken face.

Parishioners streamed from the Catholic church in the square as we arrived an hour later, the women peeling away from the gathering crowd, while the men, dozens of them dressed in Sunday finery, walked behind their priest and took up places between him and the doors of the church. The bells tolled. The priest was young and uncertain of his role in this unusual gathering. He fingered his wire-framed glasses anxiously and looked from side to side rather than making eye contact with

Rabbi Breslov and the small group of Jewish elders.

My father took his place beside the rabbi, with me slightly behind, his arm draped across my shoulders. Ira guarded my back. One of the Jewish elders moved beside my father, so that he was flanked by bearded men of God. The man held a Torah scroll adorned with a silver crown and a velvet sheath, the tintinnabulation of the tiny bells atop the crown barely audible above the bellowing coming from the church steeple.

It was still cold, and the Catholic men near us pulled their coat collars over their necks, stomped their feet slowly in the muddy snow, and watched with concern as a group of men, peasants more simply dressed, made its way down the hill from the Orthodox church and gathered in a close crowd opposite them.

Mayor Grygoriy Evanko walked with them wearing his military uniform, a badge and ribbons on the breast of his tan-colored jacket, a short tie knotted tightly at the high, stiff collar and his head adorned with an olive-colored, brimmed fez. When he reached the waiting priest, the rabbi and father, he shook each of their hands wordlessly, letting the grip linger just a bit when he held father's hand.

A commotion swirled from amid the crowd of Catholic bystanders, as a bald mustachioed man made his way toward us, pushing aside those in his path, walking regally and with disdain for those he passed. Igor Goreki. Despite the cold, he wore no coat, his starched white shirt visible under a thin jacket, his collar rising six inches up his neck, his face pock-marked and red like a wilting strawberry, his head shiny and white when he removed his black homburg hat to protect it from the jostling crowd. Everyone watched him as he stopped beside the priest, puffed his chest and announced his arrival.

"It's time we dealt with these filthy, diseased Jews who beat our children, who drink their blood on the Passover, who cheat us in their shops, who stain our streets with their very presence," Goreki said.

It was not clear to whom he was speaking, because he stared off into the middle distance as the words poured from him, loud, hateful and angry. "My son was beaten almost to his death, his face is broken, scarred for all time."

From the crowd of Ukrainian men a voice called out: "The ugly bastard. The beating was an improvement. Maybe his mother can finally look at him now."

Goreki turned to find the man who had spoken, defiant, but saw just a hundred hateful faces staring back. He then turned to look behind him at the men from the church.

"Haven't we had enough," he said speaking to them. "We cannot allow this man," pointing accusingly at my father, "to put his hands on our children. They must all pay."

"It was a girl that whacked your boy," another voice called from the Ukrainian crowd. "Dropped him like a little pig getting the hammer for a Christmas dinner."

This time laughter erupted from all around us, and Igor Goreki swung his eyes left, then right, then behind him in an effort to silence it. His head glowed redder than his face. Would it all pop in a bloody spurt?

Father held my shoulder more firmly, brought me forward and spoke.

"Mr. Goreki, I am sorry your son was hurt. But, you can see, my own boy was injured as was I, by the gang that attacked us at our home. They were drunk, Mr. Goreki, and they punched us and hit us with stones and sticks. If we did not fight back, one of us would have died."

Goreki stepped toward my father as if to strike him, but the mayor blocked his path.

"No good will come from more violence today," the mayor said. "I think the rabbi and the priest can show us a way forward. They are men of God and men of conscience, and they have a plan."

"Let me first offer my sincere regrets, Mr. Goreki, for your son's unfortunate circumstances," the rabbi began. "Every Jewish man and woman wishes him a speedy recovery."

"Maybe the girl can give him a whack on the other side of his face and push everything back into place," a voice from the crowd shouted. "Give the ugly pig a good whack."

"Give the pig a whack," the Ukrainian crowd chanted. "Give the pig a whack."

The mayor raised his hand. The shouts became murmurs. Then silence. "Rabbi, continue," he said.

"Every Jewish man and woman agree that we would like to make a nice donation to the church in your son's honor. Something that will benefit everyone in your community," the rabbi said. "The priest and I, we discussed this, and he also believes it is the best way."

Goreki looked down at the priest, who sheepishly nodded his head. Goreki turned abruptly, jammed his homburg firmly onto his head and walked away in the same direction he had arrived, knifing through the crowd, which parted as he approached like prey in advance of a wolf.

"Is everything okay, Papa?" Ira asked from behind me.

My father rubbed my shoulder and answered. "For today. It's okay, for today."

Chapter Three

"You should have seen it," Ivan said to Leja. "Every one of us was laughing at him. The whole crowd of men. You should have seen it."

"I wanted to see it, but mama wouldn't let me go." A glance to her right caught mother's stare.

"Was there a woman or a girl in the square while the men argued?" mother said. "Ask him that. Was I there? No. It was no place for us."

Ivan was standing beside Leja, seated at our table, with his hands on the back of her chair. He was Mayor Evanko's son and shared his father's plain peasant features, his narrow nose and flat broad brow. He had a uniquely infectious smile and a warmth that radiated from his blue eyes when he greeted you. Everyone liked him, except at this moment maybe my mother, who walked beside him and removed his hands from the chair.

Ira, Ivan and I had returned thirty minutes before, while Papa and Mayor Evanko lingered in the town square engaged in quiet conversation with the priest. Mother was waiting for them before serving lunch.

"There was nothing in that place to see," mother said again, more sternly. "Whatever happened we will learn when papa is home. That's it."

Her blunt statement clashed with Leja's evolving idea about the proper role of women in a modern society. The magazines she read portrayed a world in which women could be revolutionaries, leaders, even fighters in the forests where Ukrainian partisans elsewhere battled the Poles for control of towns and cities.

Leja knew her history. She knew that, after the war, Poland took control of villages and cities across western Ukraine. She knew that, despite words of reconciliation and good faith, they had exercised stern control and marginalized Ukrainian and Jewish people across the region. They seized land and encouraged Polish citizens to resettle, giving the new residents the best of that land. "The glory of Polish rule and the inevitability of Polish dominance," were ideas advanced by her teacher and the town's Polish leaders, but silently rejected by the thoughtful young people she knew.

She understood all of this better than mother, father, her brothers, maybe better than anyone in our town, and she chafed at the idea that she should be excluded from public life.

She was also a loving and dutiful daughter, though, who saw in her mother the strength and courage to protect her family in the best way she knew. Mother's beliefs and superstitions felt stale and incomprehensible to Leja, but she might never know her mother's true life, what forty years had taught her about how to survive another day. Mother had already lived longer than her own parents, had made a home for three children, kept them from the danger always lurking close by. Mother thanked the Golem for their well-being, but Leja knew the true magic resided in mother's stubbornness and determination, which deserved respect. Leja also knew she was her mother's daughter, and not so different.

So, she didn't argue when mother abruptly ended the discussion in the room and pulled a chair out for Ivan. "That's it. Sit, Ivan. Have lunch," she said. And, understanding Leja needed more than a sharp rebuke, she bent and kissed her warmly on the cheek, allowing her own face to linger for a wordless moment.

"Come Wolchi, Ira. Sit down for lunch," she continued. "Who knows when your father will be home?"

———◦•◦———

The midday sun shone brightly into the house when the front door opened and father and Mayor Evanko entered. Boots came off and joined the pile near the door; coats were hung beneath Golem's perch.

"Why are you late?" mother asked.

"The usual reasons," father responded.

This was how my parents always greeted one another at home. Mother from across the room, beside the stove, would ask why father was late or early for a waiting meal, and father would give his non-committal reply. It seemed to me there was no right time for him to return home from working or, on this day, from the confrontation in the town square. "Why are you late?" Or, "Why are you early?" Sometimes mama asked these questions in Ukrainian, sometimes in German, Yiddish or even Russian, but never in Polish. Papa's answer followed her language lead.

"Come sit, Grygoriy, Papa," my mother said to the two men hovering near the door. "There is mushroom soup and bread."

Evanko, or Grygoriy as mother and father called him,

squeezed between Ivan and me, while father found his spot near Ira and Leja. The men served together in the Austrian military during the late months of the war, and, despite religious differences that were a wedge between many Ukrainians and Jews, they maintained a deep regard and respect for one another. Evanko and Ivan sometimes spent Sunday afternoons like this one sharing our midday meal. Afterward, the men and Ira would play skat, a card game popular with soldiers to pass the long hours of inaction on the battlefront, while Ivan and Leja talked politics and taught me the meaning of exotic new words like boycott, liberation and revolution.

People said Evanko was a tough man, hard, someone to be feared. He had converted the largely ceremonial role of mayor, awarded him for his service during the war, into a position of action and influence.

Despite the hard, blank exterior, a different man emerged in our home on Sundays. His smile was warm and engaging when his mood was bright. Sometimes, though, sadness fell over him during our meals. He'd look at all of us, look around our home, and drift into a deep memory. Father once told me that, in those moments, Evanko remembered his wife who had died from a typhus infection in the otherwise joyous weeks after the war's end, just more than a year after Ivan was born.

Her death left him alone with his tiny son, whom he raised with help from my mother, who divided her attention among her wounded husband, the infant son of her husband's friend and her own infant daughter. My father struggled to work. There was little money. Hunger and disease were rampant.

Yet, when mother spoke of those times, she shared happier memories. She recalled that in the summer after the war, Leja and Ivan toddled together beside the pond that town's people used as a swimming spot on hot days, where Jews, Ukrainians and Poles sat together in the shared embrace of the Galician sun. She described carrying them in bundles wrapped across her chest, two dark eyes, two blue ones, watching her face intently like small buttons sewn into the fabric. There were also things she didn't say or even hint at, a secret she shared with Evanko that I learned years before and had, in confusion, buried in a place I hoped would be too deep to be recalled.

As Evanko and father joined the table that Sunday afternoon and mother served them bowls of soup, Evanko placed his hand on my neck and gently squeezed.

"How is that face, my boy?" he said to me. "It looks like you did some damage to someone's fist."

I shrugged, smiled. I suspect he meant to make me feel braver and stronger than I did, more capable of defending myself the next time I faced the hatred of a mob. But there also was something about his touch that stiffened me. It surely seemed to everyone else to be a gesture of comfort and concern, but to me his hand felt heavy on my neck, his grip too strong, like a vague threat.

"What will become of this business with the Goreki boy and his father?" mother asked.

"Money has solved it, for the moment," father answered. "We will give the priest one hundred zlotys to buy the peace. All the Jews in the town will pay something."

The conversation continued and explored the details of the deal. Who pays? How much? What does the priest do with the money? What guarantee exists that the pogrom wouldn't come despite the payments?

Then mother asked the question we all had on our minds. "And Goreki? Will he be satisfied?" she said.

"Goreki is a dangerous man who will look for a way to hurt us," father said. "We need to watch out and avoid his boy."

"But, papa, he is in our class at school," Leja reminded them. "He sits a few rows in front of me."

"Leave him to me," Ivan interrupted, lifting his arm to flex his bicep. "If I need to, that pig will get another good whack."

"I heard you in the square earlier," Evanko said sharply to his son. "You'll make it difficult for me if you are seen as confronting the Gorekis."

"It's time someone confronted them," Ivan responded with equal directness. "He and the others have stolen everything from us, and we still treat him with respect and fear his reprisals?"

"It sounds like you and Leja have been reading the same magazines," Ira said.

"He is an invader, and should be driven out," Ivan said. "In L'viv, the O.U.N. has formed to act, not talk. Goreki's time will come soon enough."

During previous Sunday dinners, Leja and Ivan talked enthusiastically about the Organization of Ukrainian Nationalists, a group created to fight against Polish rule and that advocated violence against the government as the best way to achieve independence. Mayor Evanko usually tolerated his son's politics, even though he was a mainstream politician himself who spoke to gatherings in the town square about peaceful techniques to expand the rights of Ukrainian citizens. I didn't fully understand most of it, but what I did made me worry, especially for Leja who seemed to believe deeply in the O.U.N.'s violent rhetoric.

Evanko looked at his son for a long beat before speaking. "Clara, the mushroom soup was splendid. The best in town. Thank you for sharing it with us today, but we should be leaving now."

CHAPTER FOUR

My father was a bookbinder and operated a small buchbinderei in an out-building beside our house. He used veteran's compensation from the Austrian government, payment for contributing his right foot to help prop up the failing Habsburg empire, to buy a small printing press, a type-case filled with lead letters, and the three modern machines that cut, laminated and bound loose sheets into the stiff-spined books that were highly desired possessions for many. Even if people didn't read the books, having them in their homes signaled sophistication and modernity.

Father had an emotional connection to those machines and exuded parental pride using and maintaining them. As a teenager, he learned the bookbinding trade from my grandfather, who relied on hand tools and crude, handmade wooden presses to sew and bind the bibles and prayer books that were his primary product. My grandfather died shortly before Ira was born, and he got grandfather's name and the honor of learning the bookbinding trade that was our family's birthright.

A key customer of the business was the Polish government, which printed posters and bound volumes touting the economic and political success in Western Ukraine that they attributed to their efforts. After our fight with Nicholas, Igor Goreki's influence had that lifeblood stanched. The only work left for the buchbinderi were small projects ordered by Mayor Evanko, and the occasional bible or prayer book for the local churches and synagogue.

Nonetheless, father and Ira spent the workday in the spacious workshop, as if nothing had changed. The room was well-lighted in the morning when the sun streamed through the eastern window, shadowy in the kerosene light of afternoon, and then relit through the western window by the setting sun. The machines lined the back wall, the paper cutter, its guillotine blade longer than a man's body, flanked by the laminating and sewing machines beside it, each with a heavy wheel to engage the operating gears. The printing press and its cases of lead type held a place of distinction in the room's center.

One afternoon, I joined them while they were tending to their daily closing tasks of cleaning and maintaining the workshop. My father let me sweep the floor while he lubricated the mechanical gears and used a coarse flint stone to sharpen the cutter's blade. Ira wiped the printing press free of dust and ink. Father, in a somber mood, moved slowly and uncomfortably as he attended to the machines.

The machines. They provided a key part of our family's origin story and occupied an outsized place in father's memories and self-worth. He liked to retell the story of the machines, and did so as we worked and the day's light dimmed.

It was an adventure story, he said, a recounting of the greatest and farthest journey of his life. He described it as a quest for something almost spiritual, a printing press and three machines engineered and cast from iron in a foundry a thousand kilometers to the west by the legendary Kolbus company.

Kolbus, a manufacturing pioneer in the late 19th Century, built durable devices to replace the wooden tools used to make everyday products of European life. Their bindery machines were especially well-regarded and often credited with accelerating the spread of new western ideas and political philosophies. My grandfather planted a seed in father's mind about this emerging future, one in which books could be mass produced and spread literacy and enhance the dignity of common people. So, printing and binding was not a vocation for father, but rather his contribution to a modern future.

His story of the machines began, he said, on a summer morning after the war, his injuries healing, mastery of the cane improved enough that he could walk on his own in the cool afternoons while mother cared for Ira, Leja and Mayor Evanko's son, Ivan. He was confident he could make the long, arduous trip, knowing that his friend Grygoriy would watch over his family, just as Clara was watching over Ivan. His departure happened without fanfare from the crude railway station the Polish government had built on the newly completed rail link between the southwest corner of the Ukraine and the city of Krakow. From there, he would travel to Berlin and finally, after two weeks, arrive in Rahden west of Hanover, and the Kolbus factory.

Mother packed him a loaf of black bread, a wedge of hard cheese and several apples inside a fabric sack that also held clothing, a small knife to cut the bread and scare off potential bandits, and a newly bound bible that was intended not for spiritual support, but rather as evidence in case my father needed to convince the Kolbus factory owners of his printing and bookbinding skill. Sewn into the waistband of his trousers were the crisp German currency notes, his fortune and his family's future, that would pay for the machines.

"I didn't sleep that first night," father said relating the

trip. "The train was crowded, mostly with men, their faces dirty, their eyes dull. They were from the war." He had seen many like them. More riders joined at other stops, and they sat on wooden benches, shoulder to shoulder. Everything smelled of the open piss pot in the back of the car and stale cabbage, he said. At night, the train car was black. No moon or stars outside. No lights.

"In Krakow the following morning, we all left the train, and it was a great relief to be in the open air again. The station was big and crowded, and people hurried here and there boarding or departing. Many ate a round roll with a hole in the center and sesame seeds and salt across the top. I bought two. The bread was warm and delicious, and I ate it with my cheese on a bench where I could watch the people and the trains.

"I was close enough to the tracks that I could see the curved lip of steel that lined the inside running surface of the train wheels and kept them on the rails. I had never seen this, and hadn't until that moment understood how the wheels stayed on the tracks. I marveled at the powerful steam engines, black smoke rising from the coal furnaces, the massive scale of it all.

"And the people, oh the people. So many, and all so different. The rich women were unlike any I'd ever seen. Not like the women here. They wore light-colored linen skirts, and some had long pieces of fabric that dragged on the dirty floor behind them. I didn't understand this, why they would allow their fine clothes to scrape the ground. But it was their waists that were most amazing. I couldn't take my eyes away. Those waists, small like a child's. I could have wrapped my fingers around them. The men with these women wore vests and coats. They walked like roosters with their heads high, their eyes straight ahead. They didn't even glance at me.

"As I watched and ate, a man approached me. He was not one of those fine men with fancy clothes. He wore heavy boots with nailed soles, his baggy wool pants sagged at his waist despite suspenders. A small boy, no bigger than Ira at the time, was holding his hand. The boy's face was dirty and his pants torn.

"The man asked if he and the boy could sit with me and pointed to my travel sack on the bench. I lifted it and cleared a space for them. He said his son, Leo, had not eaten since the prior afternoon and, pointing to the remaining piece of bread in my hand, asked for a morsel for the boy.

"I had never met this man before, but it seemed we knew each other. His long face and sharp nose were familiar, his uncombed blond hair looked like my own when I was a younger man. I thought he and I had been soldiers together, but he said he hadn't fought in the war. I reached into my travel sack, tore the second roll in half and handed one piece to the man and the other to his son.

"The boy's eyes went wide as he looked at the half roll and then at me, unsure if he should accept my offer. When he did, the roll went straight to his mouth, and it vanished as fast as a firefly's light."

Father would usually smile broadly at this memory, the boy's distress relieved by an act of generosity. This time, his face didn't change.

"I talked with the man while he and his son ate the rolls, and we shared the last of my cheese and apples. He told me he and his wife were teachers in Warsaw before the war. She died of typhus and left him with their son, a child, just like Grygoriy and Ivan, I thought. He lost his job, and they were forced from their home. They were traveling to his family in a town near Krakow, where his young sister lived with his mother. He was a wise man, an educated man, and despite being penniless and hungry he radiated a calm that eased my own worries. We talked about his journey and mine, why I was traveling so far for the machines in our buchbinderi. These machines, I told him, would insure my family's future. He laughed and said: 'Your kindness will insure your future.' When he and his son left me, he said: 'I hope I can someday repay what you gave us today. Have a safe journey to your destination and back home.'

"Even though he left me there in the Krakow station, I saw that man's face again and again as I traveled. It was as if he were beside me. His calmness stayed with me. We haven't seen each other again, but his name is Michel. His son is at the university in Krakow, where Michel now teaches. I send them a special book from our bindery each new year, and he sends books from the university. I am not so happy that he is a Marxist, but Leja is thrilled when his packages arrive with books that describe new ideas about transforming the world."

Michel later re-entered our lives and affected us profoundly. If I'd known that, I might have asked more questions as I listened to the story. Instead, I focused on father's face as his voice trailed off into silence. There was no exuberant description of the bustle and crowds of the Berlin Haupbahnhauf. No wonderment about the modern and comfortable German trains. Nothing to suggest fascination with the sophisticated and well-dressed travelers. Whereas he usually described each step he took to ensure the machines were properly secured for their long journey and the joy he felt when he finally pried open the wooden crates at home, today he let that all pass with a sweep of his arm, saying, "And I returned with all of this."

Ira and I watched as he shuffled across the room, now seemingly unaware of our presence, extinguishing the first of the three kerosene lamps, then the second and the last, plunging the room into a gray, near darkness. He opened the door to the workshop and walked out without looking back or closing the door behind him.

My parents talked often about money. Without the government printing and book-binding business, there was no longer enough of it. The small luxuries began to disappear. There was no honey for our toast. My mother's varenyky were filled with potato rather than meat, and the soups that gave her such pride became watery. Even though winter was past and the days were warmer, the house always felt cool and damp. The coal bin was rarely full, and my father sent me and Ira to the woods instead to gather wood for the family stove.

Everyone but me was working to earn money. My father and Ira kept the buchbinderi operating, completing small projects for the rabbi, the mayor and even the town's Orthodox priest. My mother was cleaning the homes of wealthy Jewish families, a task that humbled her, but one she approached with enthusiasm and energy. Leja stopped attending school and was tutoring the boys of those families, whose parents aspired to send their sons to a university when it was time to choose the direction of their lives. She was smarter than any of them, but no one ever suggested she might have such choices. I was too young to work for money, so I did what I could to assist each of their individual efforts, or at least not be a burden.

"Your job is to study hard in school," father said to me. "And maybe someday you will work with your head and not your hands."

The truth was, I didn't learn much in that one-room Polish school, except maybe how unjust and flawed the place was. Education wasn't the point of it. What mattered to the harsh, scowling school marm who sat in the front of the room was winning the favor of the sons and daughters of the town's powerful families. The Ukrainians were destined to work in the fields of the Polish-owned farms, she said, and so deserved little of her attention. The Jews she would have tossed out entirely if Mayor Evanko had not insisted that the classroom be open to all children.

"Nicholas, your paper about the resurrection of Jesus is excellent," the teacher said to the Goreki scion one afternoon. It was shortly before Easter Sunday and Passover, an especially risky time to be Jewish in our town. "Perhaps you can read it to the others. And children, write down what he says."

The teacher tapped a ruler onto her desk to cue Nicholas. Seated in the first row of the room, he stood and turned to his classmates in smug triumph. His smirk dissolved, though, into what every student in the room recognized as animal fear. He read slowly, crudely as if seeing the words for the first time. Sweat gathered on his upper lip as he haltingly read one word, looked at his classmates, read another, stopped and then reread the words. Stifled laughter rose from the Ukrainian boys sitting behind the Polish students. One whispered to another: "The priest wrote that for him." The response: "But the priest didn't teach him how to read." The laughter grew louder and spread through the room. Nicholas struggled with each word, until his lips just refused to continue. He sat down, his head lowered, rings of sweat circling his armpits and lining the center of his back. The teacher smacked her ruler on the desk several times to silence the room, before snatching the paper from him.

"That was excellent," the teacher said. "Let me continue."

As the teacher read, she walked around the perimeter of the room, striking the walls from time to time with the long ruler. She read quickly. I tried my best to write what she said, but the orientation of my desk, with the writing surface on the right, made it difficult for my left hand to reach the paper comfortably. I was left-handed and had been taunted by the teacher in the past to use my *correct* hand to write. There was no way I could keep up with her dictation using my awkward right hand, though. The teacher came directly behind me, and I could sense her eyes on my left hand, smell her stale breath as she read.

"If Christ has not been raised, then our preaching is in vain and our faith is in vain," she said.

I saw the blurred movement of the ruler before I felt the sharp pain across my left hand, it took a moment for me to connect what my eyes saw and my hand felt. As the ruler came down again, I thrust my arm backward and away, so the blow struck my desk, snapping the ruler into two pieces. My arm also made contact with the teacher's leg, which took a pointed, probably painful hit from my elbow.

Her surprised eyes caught my own. The fury in them was red and ugly like the bruise that was already forming across my left wrist. For a moment, she was speechless, and the room was silent. She grabbed me by the hair and yanked me from the desk.

"You dirty infected Jew," she said for the hundredth time, the thousandth time? "Get out."

She pulled me across the room and outside, holding my hair and my collar until she released me at the top of the schoolroom stairs. The door slammed behind her.

And that was my last day of school, ever.

I expected father to be angry, but this new injustice was greeted with resignation. He couldn't change what happened in the classroom, on the streets or in the rooms where powerful men exacted revenge for petty slights. He could only share with me something that guided his life, and he hoped would help me better understand my own.

"You need to pretend," he reminded me. "Go along with them. Keep yourself safe. That is the smart thing to do most of the time. But you're old enough now to know that a moment always comes when you can't do that any longer, when shame and frustration rise from your heart like the morning fog on the river. You can't stop it. It surrounds you, and you can no longer see clearly enough to make a *safe* choice. When that happens, you make *another* choice.

"So, enough with this school for you. Leja will teach you at home the way she teaches the others," he said as he turned to look at his daughter. "Yes?"

"He's already almost as smart as me, papa. So, maybe we can teach one another," she answered, grinning with pride. "But remember, Wolchi, I said *almost.*"

I felt great relief that I hadn't disappointed my father, and a surge of affection for my sister. She was my best friend, and she'd always been my best teacher, someone who never made me feel less than her. I could read, write and work with numbers better than boys much older than me because of her instruction since I was small. Yet, more than these skills, her lessons taught me to think about the world beyond our town.

"Wolchi, there is a city in France called Paris," she once told me, as she leafed through the pages of a book titled *Cities of the World*. "The streets are lit with gas lamps as far as anyone can see. People walk those streets at night as if it were the middle of the day. La Ville-Lumière they call it. Paris, the city of lights."

"Wolchi, there is a place in America called New York," she said another time, pointing to pictures in that same book. "The buildings are higher than the trees. They touch the clouds. Skyscrapers they call them."

Those images of the world's great cities provided a backdrop for what she really loved about the idea of Paris and New York. These places, she said, allowed people to live freely, to speak what was on their minds, read books and magazines of their choosing, where no one would realize or even care that she was a poor girl from a poor town in the middle of nowhere. She didn't know how anyone could get from our part of the world to these other places, but she never allowed herself, or me, to forget that these other places existed.

"These are the days before tomorrow," she would say. "We have to live them as if tomorrow will be the best day we've ever known."

As I lay in bed that night replaying the day, the growing unease I first felt after the fight in the street several months before returned. I couldn't give it name or form words to describe it, but I knew that, like the river in autumn, there was something to fear. I thought about mother's belief in powerful forces that could protect us. I thought about Leja's hopefulness and my father's practical encouragement. All of those things were enough for now. Go to sleep, Wolchi.

Chapter Five

The bells at either end of town tolled all morning, louder and more insistent than a typical Sunday. The urgency of bringing the faithful to church seemed more immediate than usual. It was the Catholic Easter, and outside our window the parade of mostly Polish worshippers from the town and the nearby large farms made their way to the church in the central square, while the Ukrainian Orthodox faithful, scheduled to celebrate their Easter Sunday a week later, filed past to their church on the hillside.

Everyone was dressed in clean, but ordinary clothes. The Ukrainian men wore rough jackets, some with crudely knotted ties, and the women had chosen floor-length peasant dresses, aprons and full, white scarves to cover their heads. The children wore ill-fitting attire, passed down from older siblings or parents. The Polish churchgoers were easy to spot in their more elaborate finery. Tailored jackets for the men, dresses made from cloth imported from elsewhere in Europe on the women.

The Goreki family rode past them, their clothing finer than any other, in their elaborate carriage decorated with brass and polished wood, pulled by two horses. Two women sat in the back, one young and one older, each peering disdainfully ahead as they rode past those walking on the road. Igor

Goreki, Nicholas at his side, held the reins. All they needed were crowns on their heads, I thought, to erase any doubt about their position, power and wealth.

Everyone in the town knew Igor Goreki, even though few could explain how he had assembled such outsized influence. The older men at the synagogue recalled him as a youthful, arrogant army officer from Poland who rode into town on a horse in the spring of 1910 with a small group of other soldiers, and quickly became a nuisance. They confiscated several homes near the central square and spent most of the day drinking at the tavern and harassing girls on the street. Then they became dangerous. Their intent was to implement a policy of the Austrian Empire to redistribute valuable real estate owned by Jews or people who were not Roman Catholic to Poles loyal to the Habsburg Monarchy in Vienna — men such as Goreki. No one was actually sure such a policy existed, but Goreki and his men insisted they had both papal and royal backing for their theft.

He maintained a hated police force of fellow Austrian soldiers, two dozen men who helped him exercise authority and keep the local government officials under control. They also led his enthusiastic anti-Semitic attacks by enflaming the passions of local Poles with diatribes and lies. Goreki himself was noted for the great delight he took in confiscating small Jewish farms in the productive fields south of the town and tormenting the rightful owners until they left the community. This was his way to insure none of them would reclaim what he had stolen. His pogroms, the old Jews said, were as unpredictable as they were brutal. The only way to stop the attacks was for the Jewish farmers to agree to his terms of sale, which offered a small fraction of true value. If a desired plot was owned by a non-Jewish Ukrainian, the Polish mobs overlooked the religious distinctions and became equal-opportunity brutalizers. Over the course of a decade, he and his cronies assembled vast agricultural lands across the region, creating great wealth for themselves and deep hostility among the region's Jewish and Ukrainian peasants.

Leja stood beside me as Goreki's carriage passed. She pointed at them, and although no one else could hear, she whispered: "Pigs."

The sun, brilliant and white, was already high in the spring sky, its light glowing as it passed through the leaves of the budding trees. This was a beautiful day for a holiday in which kindness, God and faith should be at the front of everyone's thoughts. At least that's what my schoolteacher would say was at the heart of the Easter celebration. I knew the truth of it, though, that Easter Sunday was also the day priests would tell the story of how Jesus rose from the dead, and the story of how Jesus got dead. For them, the idea that Jewish rabbis and moneylenders had killed Jesus was an historic fact, something they needed to share in their sermons. So, it was not surprising when their congregants took to the streets during the Easter season in a celebratory mood after the sermons and confronted Jewish people - men, women, children, the old and young - saying to them with the certainty of faith that, "You killed our lord."

This had been directed at me over the years. "I didn't kill anyone," I would say. "I never met your lord." Usually, the taunting was no more than that, but sometimes gangs of boys, some no older than eight or nine, threw rocks and harassed old observant Jewish men praying outside the synagogue, pulling the prayer shawls from their shoulders and the black leather tefillin boxes and straps from their heads and arms. Ira and I and our friends, a gang of us, would wander the streets ourselves on Easter. We'd yell at those boys and threaten them until they ran off. The old Jewish men, unappreciative, would scream out, "Heathens, you are all heathens," including us in their condemnation. The synagogue men didn't appreciate our good deeds, because strict observance of Torah and Talmud were the only qualities they considered when assessing the worth of others. We continued to protect them, though, because if not us, then who?

This was the push and push-back of the town and its Jewish residents that marked the Christian holiday spread over two Sundays, one for the Catholics and another for the Orthodox. The truth was, despite the skirmishes and occasional violence, there was also a festive atmosphere about the days that I anticipated with excitement. If the weather was fine, everyone would be out on both Sundays, no work to do, dressed up, greeting neighbors and friends as they walked the streets eating pastries topped with jam and decorated with tiny, frosted rabbits.

Teenage boys and girls gathered in the town square. The girls, away from the watchful eyes of their parents, left their heads uncovered, their hair, shining in the sunlight, tossed provocatively by the breeze. The boys tried awkwardly to win their attention with horseplay, jostling and conversations loud enough to be heard from across the square.

If you were Jewish, though, it was always a time to be part of a crowd made up of your own. It was fun to be out, but there was safety in numbers. No one would bother you if you were young, strong and with a group of similarly robust friends.

It was not a good time, though, for a Jewish boy to kiss a Polish girl in the street right in front of everyone.

I should have seen it coming, because I forgot to touch Golem's belly in the rush to leave the house that Catholic Easter Sunday and join Ira and some friends on a walk into the town square. If I'd seen it coming, I could have dragged Ira home before he spotted Katia, the siren of his daydreams, who was standing there among her girlfriends. When he saw her, Ira's eyes locked. Taller than her friends, she was not to be missed in a crowd. Her long blonde hair, almost white, was pulled back from her face in a ponytail; she was striking and uniquely beautiful, a light in a dark room, and Ira was the moth headed straight for her.

Katia seemed delighted when she saw him. She watched him break from our group and waved shyly as he walked quickly toward her. I saw the teenage boys across the street, almost in unison, stop their pushing and shoving when they noticed the intruder in their midst, this tall, handsome Jewish boy, with his head full of curly hair and his face animated by a broad smile, who was now standing beside the object of their own desires.

Katia laughed when Ira reached her and began talking. I couldn't hear them, but I had a pretty good idea what he was saying. I knew Ira could talk. He was a charmer, and I'd seen him in action, creating a quick bond with women and girls, young and old, by speaking to them softly and kindly while looking into their eyes. It was as if he could hear their thoughts and anticipate their expectations.

"I'm so happy you're here," Ira was probably saying to Katia. "I was hoping to see you."

A shy smile from Katia.

"What are you and your friends doing? Hello, girls," Ira would surely say.

Several of Katia's friends turned toward him with their own shy smiles, and I thought that would be the moment to grab him, do what I must to get him away. That light is too hot, and that moth might be consumed if it gets too close. But, I just watched.

I imagined he was saying: "It's really hard to talk here with all these people. Don't you think? You can't really say, or do, what you want when everyone's listening and watching. Like right now, if no one else were here, I would kiss you."

Katia's eyes opened wide. They were saying 'yes.' Her friends, listening more closely, looked on in anticipation. "Did he just say he would kiss her?" they thought. "Yes, do it!"

Well, maybe he said those things or maybe, without a word, he just placed his hand in hers, bent toward her face and gently kissed her. For a moment, he lingered, her lips pressing back. And just like that, it was too late to stop the trouble, because it was crossing the street toward Ira and the girls while my friends and I were moving, too, hoping to fill the space between them and the gang of boys. The girls backed away, but Katia stood with Ira, holding his hand, looking at his face in wonderment and something more instinctive. We all saw it, the girls, the other boys, my friends, and it was that look between the two of them, boy and girl, that froze us in place.

The altercation did not happen, at least not in the bloody manner that these things usually played out. There was shouting, threats, some jostling, really nothing more than what the Polish boys had been doing among themselves when we walked up. Ira and Katia stayed wrapped in their bubble, unaware for several moments of the tumult around them. Then she kissed him, quickly this time, and drifted back into the crowd of her friends who surrounded her with an excited banter.

"Ira, time to go," I said, without him apparently hearing a word. I said it louder and pushed him away from the others. He was not worried, though, and in no hurry to leave the square. What was he thinking?

"Did you see that, Wolchi. She kissed me back. It was wonderful."

———•••———

Mother disagreed. As Ira, unable to resist sharing his romantic euphoria with my family that evening, related the tale of his Easter Sunday kiss, I could see her displeasure. She was in the kitchen mashing a pot of potatoes, the sound of the iron spoon growing louder with each stroke as it struck the iron pot with increasing force. Clang! Bang!

Ira was animated, more so than usual. Father often teased that he could have been an entertainer had he not been such a talented bookbinder and had performing been a more respectful profession. Leja believed he was a hopeless romantic, whatever that meant, like the boys in some of her books, and was destined to break hearts and in turn have his own life tragically altered by love. He paced the room, gesturing with his arms, speaking to us as if we were an audience gathered for his soliloquy.

"Her eyes were on me the minute we walked into the square," he said. "It was as if she were waiting for me, you know, as if she knew I was coming."

Clang! Clang!

"It was like the first time I saw her, when she and her

mother were walking past the workshop pulling a cart with their milk to the market. I opened the door. I remember how the air felt on my face, cool and dry, the first days of autumn. I remember the smell of ripe fruit, the sound of her footsteps, the brushing of her skirt on her legs as she walked. We noticed each other at the same instant, startled by each other's gaze."

Clang! Bang! Bang!

"Her mother saw none of it. But Katia's eyes held mine as she passed," Ira said. "And then, she slowed, looked back over her shoulder and lifted her hand, waving for an instant, smiling, before quickening her pace to match her mother's. I knew from that moment . . ."

The clamor from the kitchen grew so cacophonous that it jolted Ira from his memories. Mother had thrown her spoon forcefully into the pot and was roughly wiping her hands on a towel.

"And what did you know, Ira? What could you know?" she asked. "Had you even spoken a word to this girl? Had you met her father, who will treat you like the cow droppings he cleans from his boots? What could you know, except that this would become trouble for you and us?"

"Her mother likes me," Ira said. "I walk with them some afternoons when they pass the workshop. I help them pull the milk wagon to the market. I make her mother laugh. She calls me 'curly boy,' and . . ." Mother stopped him before he could continue.

"Walking with someone. Talking to them. That's different than what you did today in front of the town people," mother scolded. "Do you think this girl's father and her brothers . . ."

"Katia. Her name is Katia," Ira interrupted.

"Don't you think they are speaking right now with

Katia about why the two of you are wrong, why you can't be together?" Mother continued. "Do you think they won't knock on our door and warn you to stay away from their daughter, to stick to your own kind? Don't we have enough trouble already with the Gorekis? And then you kiss this girl in front of the whole town."

"Mama, it was a wonderful kiss," Ira said. "But it was just a kiss."

"No kiss is 'just a kiss,' Ira. Every kiss is complicated," she said. "Don't see this girl again, son. Listen to me."

Leja and I sat motionless, enthralled by this performance that now had two players and so much drama. Father shifted awkwardly in his seat, silent, leaving something important unsaid.

Mother turned to the rest of us, ending the discussion and trying to make hers the last words. "Leja, help me with supper."

Ira, though, wasn't ready for this to end. His good mood evaporated, his joy and energy gone. The charming smile turned into something more determined. He was in a struggle with the unmovable force that was our mother.

"No," he said, letting the word hang over the room for several seconds before saying it again. "No, mama. I will see her again. I will kiss her again, too, if she lets me. I think we're in love."

"Ira, you can't do this now," mother said. "Our family is already suffering from this mess with Goreki and losing the government business. If you anger more people they will also try to hurt us. You know they will."

"You're being unfair," Ira interrupted and looked at his sister. "Why can Leja and Ivan be together, but you think something is wrong with me and Katia? Why don't you stop them, Mama? It's not fair."

My mother was surprised that the discussion had veered in this direction. She fumbled and muttered quietly to herself before responding.

"Leja and Ivan are friends," Mother says. "They were babies together, and they're friends now. Nothing more."

Leja's eyes went wide as she listened. She knew the falsity of what mother had said, as did I, as did Ira, as did father. Surely, mother knew that Ivan and Leja shared something much deeper than friendship, that, while they may or may not have been intimate, they shared a unique intellectual and emotional bond.

Mother stared at her oldest son, and then looked to her husband.

"And, Ivan and Grygoriy would never hurt us," mother continued. "It's different."

Chapter Six

A few days later Mayor Evanko visited us in the buchbinderi. He and father were in a close, quiet conversation in a far corner, trying not to be heard. Ira worked on the laminating machine, while I disassembled a series of gears on the sewing machine. The stitching panel was out of alignment, and I had assured my father I could correct the problem. I'd been studying the machines and the technical drawings that accompanied them in the months since I stopped attending school, and I understood how they operated. A bent retaining pin was the problem, and I had used a hammer and a wooden block in a failed attempt to straighten it.

I needed a new pin. There was a machine shop on the other side of town, the only place I knew that could make us a new part. It was run by old Mr. Koperski, who repaired plows and metal threshers for the farmers, but also fabricated the screws and bolts that were used to secure the wooden railroad ties to the tracks of the newly built rail line. I had sometimes stopped on my way from school to watch him from the street outside his shop. He always worked alone at a hulking drill press or a metal stamping machine, and what I later learned was a lathe that turned pieces of raw steel into fasteners and custom machine parts.

My father was still in quiet conversation with Evanko, so

I shared my plan with Ira before heading out carrying a technical drawing of the sewing machine, the damaged pin and an unfamiliar excitement at the prospect of stepping inside Koperski's shop.

"I know you," Mr. Koperski interrupted when I entered and began explaining my problem. "I used to see you watching me. While the other boys were playing in the street, you would be peaking around the door to see inside. I wondered where you'd gone. I haven't seen you for months."

He wiped his hands on a threadbare cloth dotted with dried grease stains, metal filings and sweat.

"I am Marcus Koperski," he said, extending his right hand. "And to whom do I have the pleasure of speaking?"

I awkwardly took his hand, which was calloused and strong. His short fingers were bands of muscle and bone that encircled my own with a grasp that was oddly gentle, even though I knew there was no escaping him until he decided to release me.

I blurted out a response while he held the handshake. "My name is Wolchick, but my family calls me Wolchi. My father's name is Marcus, too. He's a bookbinder, and so is my brother, and they have a broken stitching machine, and I tried to fix it, but it needs a new pin, and . . ."

"It's a pleasure to meet you, Wolchi. Is it OK if I call you that?" Mr. Koperski asked.

I nodded. He gently released my hand, took the papers and pin, and walked to a crowded wooden worktable, scarred by decades of nicks and gouges. He pushed aside a pile of mechanical drawings, blue ink on white waxy paper, and unfolded my papers.

"So, let me see, Wolchi. What do we have here?"

I described the workings of the sewing machine and the

stitching panel illustrated on the papers. He listened atten-tively, nodding when I explained the job of the retaining pin in attaching the panel to the gears that drove the machine. The pin, he explained while examining it closely, takes the full force of the machine's movement, and its failure was the inevitable result of a flawed design.

"But that is not a problem we can fix today, is it?" he asked. "Today, we need to make a new pin, so your father and brother can get back to work."

He reached into a wooden crate below the table and sorted through a collection of steel rods and plates. Finding one rod that met his expectations, he led me across the shop to the metal lathe. Beside it, he had a collection of tools that he said were needed to precisely measure or cut the metal of his projects. They were called calipers, taps and dies. He also had metal files of varying roughness to hone the finished result.

As he calculated the dimensions of the damaged pin, he described the history of the lathe and its function in a way that suggested he had not thought about these things in many years. The lathe, he said, was the most important tool in his shop. If he could only have one machine, it would be this one.

"It will take this piece of steel," he said, holding up the rod he had found beneath his worktable, "and shape it into the part you need. It will be exactly the same. Maybe better."

He allowed me to insert the steel rod into the belly of the lathe and clamp it in place, before he adjusted a series of dials to reflect the measurements he had made of the pin. He pointed to a heavy dual pedal below the table and then a stool beside it and said, "So, get to work."

The pedals spun the lathe. The faster I moved them, the faster the machine revolved. A high-pitched screech filled the room as filings dropped from the metal rod and transformed it into the needed pin. Mr. Koperski removed the finished object and carefully filed loose burrs and other imperfections.

"Here you are young man," he said as he presented the pin to me like a sacred object. "You are now a machinist."

"Thanks. Thank you, I mean," I said, once again blurting out my words with excitement. "Thank you."

I bolted from the shop, forgetting to ask about his payment. I clutched the pin tightly in my hand, waving back at Mr. Koperski who watched from his doorway as I ran, fast as the day I ran from the graveyard demon. Fear was not coursing through my body, but rather a sense of wonder and confidence that what I held in my hand could mean something new and better for me.

When I reached home and opened the door to the shop, Mayor Evanko was gone, but Ira and father sat beneath the window now, an ashen look on their faces.

"Papa, I made this new pin. I can fix the stitching machine," I said, triumphant despite the gloom in the room. I handed the pin to my father who examined it carefully, nodding, a thin smile crossing his lips. "Mr. Koperski at the machine shop helped me."

"Wolchi, this is excellent," my father said proudly. "You will be an engineer someday."

While I reassembled the stitching machine, father and my brother silently gazed out the window. The only sound in the shop was the turning gears and moving parts as I tested the results of my repair. Father broke the silence.

"So, Ira, let's finish early today," he said. "It's a beautiful spring afternoon, and I think I should take mama for a walk. Maybe all of us can go, the way we once did, see people, breathe in the day."

I was spinning the gears on the stitching machine, and it was running like new. No one noticed but me.

———◦◦◦———

We'd gotten out of the habit of taking family walks after the street fight with Nicholas Goreki and his gang, so father's urging to do so was surprising. In the past, if the sun was shining on a Saturday afternoon, the family would take to the streets and join the ebb and flow of town life. We'd visit markets, see family friends, drink a warm cider with sticks of cinnamon in the winter or share small baskets of local fruit in the spring and summer. Mother would hold father's arm, both as an expression of affection and to steady his gait as he walked with his cane. Leja and Ira walked behind them, a bit bored and embarrassed. I reveled in these moments of family tranquility, though. We were together, and I liked it.

Mother was hesitant at first, but relented to my father's persistent urging. "Mama, we need a walk," he said. "We need to be with people."

Leja was not yet home from her tutoring job, I assumed, so just four of us set out. Before I shut the door behind me, I made a quick swipe at Golem, touching his brown belly gently. The town square was busier than earlier in the day. Two crowds had gathered, the larger at the steps of the town government office and the smaller beside the tavern, where the melodious sound of a bandura was rising above the street. A small man with rounded shoulders and a cloth cap drawn close to his eyes plucked with the fingers of both hands at the twenty-one strings of the instrument, which looked like a harp with a short neck, but smaller.

My parents walked toward him and stopped to listen to this most exotic sound, the musical passages rising higher and higher, until the musician started singing with passion about a gypsy girl who had enchanted him and stolen his soul.

Ochi chornye, ochi strastnye
Ochi zhguchie, I preskrasnye
Black eyes, passionate eyes,
Burning and beautiful eyes!
How I love you, how I fear you,
It seems I met you in an unlucky hour!

Father turned to face my mother, his hands around her waist, and they began to dance, awkwardly at first but then with remarkable fluidity, three good legs and a cane moving in slow rhythm as one. He was softly singing the Russian words of the song to her.

Oh, not for nothing are you darker than the deep!
I see mourning for my soul in you,
I see a triumphant flame in you,
A poor heart immolated in it.

Mother looked at the people standing nearby, self-conscious, and then turned to stare at father. His eyes were closed, his lips singing.

But I am not sad, I am not sorrowful,
My fate is soothing to me.
All that is best in life that God gave us,
In sacrifice I returned to the fiery eyes!

He smiled faintly when the music stopped, the song complete. He held mother's hands as she stepped back from him.

"Almost like when we were young, mama," he said softly. "Almost like we were young."

I looked for Ira to discuss what had just happened, but he was headed across the square toward the group on the steps of the government building. With the music stopped, I could hear the voice of a man speaking to the crowd, shouting actually. The voice was Ivan's.

More of the people in the square moved to listen, as did mother, father and me. That morning, Ivan said, the Polish government at the direction of Igor Goreki withdrew financial support from any business that was not Polish owned. This was an attempt, Ivan said, "to steal our businesses the way they stole our farms." It meant that even the small projects my father was receiving from Mayor Evanko would now stop, and our family would be pushed even closer to ruin. This edict was not just a vengeful act aimed at my family, however. It was an assault on the livelihoods of a broad group of people and an escalation, Ivan said, of the war being waged by Poland against the Ukrainian people.

Leja stood beside him, handing him sheets of paper with the words he spoke. "The hand of the tyrant is at our throats," he read aloud. "He will choke us until we are gone from this land of ours, of our fathers and grandfathers. He will squeeze the breath from us until every farm, every shop, every business is a Polish farm, a Polish shop, a Polish business. We must rise up."

From the crowd, a chant began. "Rise up. Rise up." In the front of the crowd, on a step just below the one from which Ivan spoke, Ira, a head taller than the others, tugged Leja's arm, trying to move her away, as she pumped her right arm in the air, encouraging the crowd, "Rise up."

The crowd responded, as her entire body grabbed at the sky when she leapt up and chanted, "Rise up."

"We must unite, my friends, under our nationalist banner and resist the tyranny of men who would deny our history and steal our futures," Ivan read, and the crowd cheered. Two young men behind him on the highest stairs waved flags I had never seen, blue shields with yellow swords. Another handed leaflets to those in the crowd, with titles that said, "Principles of the Organization of Ukrainian Nationalists" or "Question Everything: Building a free Ukraine." Ira kept tugging at Leja as the crowd grew more animated and loud. My father took my hand and led me and mother away from the demonstration.

"This is not a place for us," he said.

As we moved quickly away, I saw the uniforms of the Polish police, an armed unit of ten men, headed toward the demonstrators from the opposite side of the square, some armed with carbines and infantry rifles. The musician resumed playing his bandura, creating a haunting soundtrack to the unfolding confrontation.

"Leja, Ira," mother said. "We need to get them."

"Mama, no," father answered. "Stay with us. Ira will get Leja. I see him."

I could see him, too, as he pulled my sister away more aggressively, pointing toward the approaching military unit. The crowd dispersed in every direction, like a dandelion in a gust of wind, and Ira and Leja ran away from us to the safety of the narrow road that followed the river along the hillside. Beyond that was deeper woods.

"Fast. Let's get away from here," father said. "Those soldiers will murder whomever they catch."

———————◆◆———————

After mother and father were safely at home, I slipped away to find Leja and Ira. I knew where to look. They would find safety at Big Rocks, a clearing hidden inside the deep, beech-tree forest that spread south from the banks of the Stryi River. It was a sacred place for many, where a peasant uprising against the Austrian monarchy two decades before was crushed and many of the town's young men had died.

Children, including me, gathered here to hunt lizards, pick berries, build night-time bonfires or recreate the battles their fathers and brothers had fought. We wielded tree branches as rifles. The collection of smooth, hulking boulders were hills to be captured, and the spaces between them were secure spots to hide treasures. The invisible enemy didn't return our mock fire, and the armies of children always won the day, raising their weapons in celebration from the tallest boulder, shouting unintelligible sounds, feral and familiar.

I heard them before I saw them, the voices of a small group of young people rising from the quiet of the dense trees and freshly sprouted spring leaves. The sun shone behind them, and they were partly hidden by the bright light filtering through the forest. I crested a hill that overlooked the rocks and recognized Ivan, Ira, Leja and a dozen young people, all young men but for Leja, familiar faces from the rally.

I squeezed beside my sister and brother listening as the group discussed ways to extend their influence and strike at the Polish authorities. One name kept being mentioned. "Goreki." He was the target of their anger for the punitive and unfair actions against Ukrainian, and Jewish, businesses in the community. He was the one squeezing them, hurting their families.

Before I understood what was happening, Ivan led us through the woods toward the Polish farms, the largest being the one assembled by Igor Goreki after the war. My father had warned us to stay away from the Polish farms and avoid the sons of the landholders who wandered those roads prepared to start a fistfight, or worse, when they spotted a vulnerable Jewish or Ukrainian kid. We weren't alone or vulnerable any-more, although as we emerged from the woods into the flat farm fields it was clear we were without a plan. Several young men, unprompted, ran into the newly planted fields, shouting "rise up." One by one, the rest of the group joined them. So did I.

We laughed and raised our arms in triumph, running along the lines of planted soil trampling the seedlings, leaving deep boot prints in the soft dirt. This liberated us, releasing the anger and anxiety always just below the surface in our town. The excitement I felt earlier in the day after repairing our binding machine was replaced by the infectious energy and power of the crowd as we ran through Goreki's fields, a youthful band of soldiers fighting an enemy that now had a face.

The petty vandalism of the Polish farms continued through the summer that year, although I didn't take part after that first night. Crops were uprooted, horses and sheep set free from corrals. My father attended loud meetings in the town hall at which angry Polish farmers blamed the Ukrainian and Jewish shopkeepers for stoking anger among the young people attacking their fields. In turn, those shop owners blamed Goreki's policy of restricting government spending for devastating the lives of their families, forcing many to sell their businesses to Poles arriving from the west to capitalize on the restrictive rules. This, in turn, sparked a boycott among Ukrainians and Jews against those Polish shops. Every member of the community took sides.

Mayor Evanko kept those meetings from breaking into brawls, father said, but it was clear to him that the tension in the town would grow worse unless Goreki reversed his edict.

Early that September, the last days of summer turned the town cool in the afternoons, and the breeze carried the sweet scent of apples being crushed into cider. Ira, without much work to do in the buchbinderi, got into the habit of meeting Katia and her mother on the road near our home to help them pull their milk wagon to market, their relationship now well established among those who knew them. Even mother greeted Katia when she saw her in the town.

Leja and I walked with Ira one afternoon as he headed to his regular meeting place when we saw Katia in the road ahead on her hands and knees, the wagon beside her overturned, milk running from scattered jugs. Her mother was not with her, but she was not alone. Nicholas Goreki lurked a few yards behind her.

Ira ran to her, calling out. "Are you all right?"

He took her elbow and helped her stand. Katia looked at her overturned cart and then at Goreki. This was the first time I'd seen him up close since our fight. His face had healed, but his nose had set at an odd angle, with a prominent lump near his close-set eyes.

"I was just trying to help you clean up this mess. Wasn't I?" he said. "Get it off the road before others need to pass."

Katia turned to Ira and shook her head. Ira rose to his full six feet, six inches and stepped between Goreki and Katia.

"Maybe I could also get some milk from your little milk maid as a reward for my help," Goreki said, looking past Ira and leering at Katia. Then to Ira: "She is yours, isn't she? Everyone knows she's a Jew lover. Such a waste."

Turning back to Katia, grabbing his crotch, he said: "Why don't you come with me. I am a good Christian boy, and my father has money. Lots of money."

Ira pushed Goreki's chest, making the shorter, but thicker man stumble backward. He quickly recovered and headed toward Ira, but stopped suddenly and stared at Leja. She had retrieved one of the fallen steel milk buckets and was standing beside Ira, her threat clear as she swung the bucket in a small arc toward him.

"Ok, then. I'll let you help the bitch gather her wagon and be on her way," Goreki said. "She's all yours if that's what she wants. But maybe I will see you again sometime when your crazy sister isn't around."

Leja took a small, threatening step toward him, and Goreki backed away. "Crazy," he muttered as he walked, keeping a wary eye on Leja and the bucket. "Crazy." When he was far enough away and at no risk, he put his finger to his lips, suddenly combative and courageous. He shouted to us: "I'll see you again. Until then, shh!"

We saw him again sooner than any of us expected. The town's annual Barley Moon meeting was scheduled for the town hall that evening on the night of the autumnal equinox. This was usually a sleepy affair at which a small number of men representing various groups made requests or directed complaints to the community's leaders, in effect the senior Polish landholders and business people who had direct influence on the actions and spending of the government. No one could recall for certain why the meeting was held when the full moon was in the September sky, but I heard my father once joke that the moon provided light for the drunken men stumbling home from the tavern, which provided free refreshments following the meeting. It was the promise of free cider and liquor that got the men to turn out (and only men were welcome), and induced Mayor Evanko, who presided over the gathering, to wrap up quickly and efficiently. Leja said the whole affair was a curious, homegrown version of the ancient harvest festivals once popular in our part of the world, when the bounty of the season was celebrated by everyone passing out drunk.

This year's event was not the usual affair, however, as anger about the political and personal divisions dividing the community neared an explosive point. Men from across town arrived early and filled the town hall, spilling onto the steps outside. Word of this unusual civic energy spread from home to home and brought out more citizens, even the women and younger people who had always been excluded and who rarely walked the streets after dark. Something was sure to happen that had never happened before, and no one wanted to miss it.

Even my father and mother joined the crowd, with Ira, Leja and me alongside. When we arrived, I could see Nicholas Goreki at the top of the stairs with a gang of his friends blocking access to the town hall's open door, shuffling furtively from side to side like a group of hogs trying to reach their trough, but whose exit from the barnyard was blocked. Ivan and other young men stood in the street, trying to get a look inside the open town hall door.

"Move so others can get inside," Ivan shouted to those blocking the door. "We need to be inside."

"My father said to keep you out," Nicholas Goreki said. "You cannot go in. Only the men."

Things went on like this for quite a while, the shouting outside interrupted by louder shouts from inside the town hall. I heard Igor Goreki's coarse, angry voice inside the room promising revenge on the "animals attacking our farms," and the equally angry voices of other men promising that "if our families are hungry, yours will starve." Ivan and his friends started chanting: "Rise up." They lifted banners adorned with blue shields and yellow swords, and slowly, like a fog fast approaching from the distance, others at the edge of the crowd took up the chant until the entire square was engulfed. Men from inside the meeting hall streamed out, pushing past Nicholas Goreki and his thugs to join the tumult outside.

"O.U.N. O.U.N.," the crowd began shouting.

Igor Goreki emerged from the meeting hall, with Mayor Evanko just behind him .Goreki was shouting at the demonstrators. "Stop. Stop this now." He couldn't be heard over the frenzied noise, or, if he was heard, he was being entirely ignored. Goreki grabbed his son's arm and pushed him toward Ivan, motioning for him to do something to stop the rebellion. He turned to Mayor Evanko, and I could see his lips move. "Your son," he was saying. "Your son."

Nicholas Goreki and his friends pushed toward Ivan and the men waving the O.U.N. banners. The crowd moved away from the town hall, forming a "V" with Ivan at the front, heading toward the river in the bright moonlight. Ira joined the marchers, but when Leja tried to join, as well, father gripped her hand firmly.

"Leja, please. Stay with us," he pleaded. "This is dangerous."

"Papa let me go," she answered.

"Stay away from all these angry people, my Leja. There's is nothing but misery in their slogans and flags," father said. "We need to stay to ourselves, stay low while everyone shouting at one another, follow the rules as we can and wait until this passes. Leja, I know, I've seen this before. They will kill each other, over money or at the behest of a corrupt king or to convince others that their religion is the best one. Now they fight over the political future of a place that will never have one. Please stay with us."

Leja listened carefully to father. She stopped trying to pull away and instead put her arms around his neck and pressed her cheek against his.

"I love you, papa. But I need to go," she said. "So do Ira and Wolchi. It's our future. We can't let others decide it."

Father let go of Leja's hand, and she took mine. We joined Ira in the crowd of hundreds marching out of town. "Everything will change today. You'll see," Leja said. "They can't stop us."

But they did.

As we marched through the darkening forest toward the taunting yellow face of the rising moon, enormous in front of us, I saw the silhouettes of armed policemen waiting in the distance, blocking the path to Big Rocks. The marchers didn't slow. They continued up the hill waving banners, fists clenched in the air, chanting: "O.U.N. O.U.N." I wondered, did anyone else see the armed men? Should I warn them?

"Leja, look," I said, pointing toward the rising moon and the dark stains of the policemen in the moonlight.

"They can't stop us," she said again. "There are too many of us now."

From behind, I heard the shouts of an angry mob, and then cries of pain. Nicholas Goreki and a gang of his thugs walked among the marchers now, striking randomly with sticks at men and women alike. Some fought back, but they couldn't prevent the attackers from knifing their way through the slower-moving crowd toward the three of us near the front. Leja and Ira chanted with their fists raised and didn't see the danger behind them. I pulled Leja's hand to edge her out of the crowd into the woods along the road and called out to Ira. I pointed behind us at the marchers falling to the ground under the assault, the erupting chaos. Ira took Leja's other hand, and the three of us broke free into the forest.

The brush and branches scratched my arms and face as we made our way deeper into the dark woods searching for a safe place where the moonlight couldn't find us. We stopped, breathing hard, and lay on the ground hidden from the road. I saw other marchers escaping into the woods, but most were caught between the police and Goreki's thugs in a random explosion of violence. Leja hugged me to her chest, covering my face with her hand, but I heard what was happening. The thud of fists and sticks hitting flesh and bone, the crack of rifles being fired, and the rapid, disingenuous trill of songbirds in the trees disturbed from their night's rest by the carnage.

"They're killing them," Ira whispered.

"We should do something," Leja replied. "Help them."

She made no move to do that, though. None of us did. We could have kept running, probably should have, but we were frozen, silently watching and listening as the cries of broken people became less shrill and a quiet exhaustion fell over the police and armed men. They shuffled among their victims, distracted and seemingly confused about what to do now that they'd beaten the unarmed marchers into submission. Some laughed, in a jovial mood, eager to head back to town and a night of celebration at the tavern.

The birds quieted, and we lay still watching as Nicholas Goreki walked among the victims, prodding them with his weapon, nudging them with his foot. He looked into the forest, where marchers noisily fled and shouted into the night, a deep, primal scream, reaching his arms above his head. His howl, like a wild animal, announced the defeat of his enemy. "Get the rest of them," he called to his men, pointing toward the woods.

We began running again, with Leja in the front, navigating past fallen trees and rocks, the moonlight casting yellow light and our shadows on the forest floor. A small group of the marchers trailed behind, following her. She knew these woods and guided us on paths she and Ivan had discovered or created during their walks and explorations. Every tree seemed mapped in her mind, every rock and stream anticipated. The soldiers and thugs couldn't keep up, didn't want to either, so we reached safety quickly.

A dozen of us huddled at the edge of town assessing what had happened, what we'd seen. The men in the group, including Ira, promised revenge, offering imaginary details about the next time. Leja encouraged them and kept repeating, "They can't stop us." I searched the dark faces in the group. "What happened to Ivan?" I asked.

The excited chatter stopped. Everyone anticipated the answer to my question, but no one said it.

CHAPTER SEVEN

Mayor Evanko brought Ivan to our house the following morning. His arm was wrapped in a bloodied cloth, his cheek bruised and dirty. He was not moving. His eyes were closed.

"His friends brought him to me. The police will come to look for him," Evanko said to mother, as she helped lay Ivan on the ground in a corner of the house hidden from the main room. "Please keep him here until I fix this with Igor Goreki. And please help him."

My father, sister and brother had gone to the central square to get news about the previous night's violence and about Ivan's fate.

"Wolchi, go find your father and bring him home," mother said.

I ran out, but got just a short way from home when I remembered Golem. I had not touched him when I left the house, and this wasn't a day to be out without his protection.

I opened the door and came back inside, where mother was hugging Evanko. He squeezed her hips with his hands, her arms wrapped around his shoulders, her face buried in his neck.

"We will take care of him, Grygoriy. As we always have," my mother said. "He will be safe."

A moment passed before they saw me. When they did,

they hastily broke off their embrace. Mother stepped away from Evanko and nervously smoothed her dress, glancing at him before turning to me.

"Go, Wolchi. Get your father," she said. "Tell him Ivan's here, and he's hurt."

I heard her words, but they sounded far off, an echo in the forest. I felt dizzy again, unsteady, and I held my breath. One hand still on the door, I was half in the house, half on the street, when I remembered. I watched mother, her face tight, her eyes narrow, her mouth moving, her unintelligible words ringing in my ears, images of her and Evanko flooding my mind, and I remembered. And I understood something I'd seen a long time ago.

"Wolchi, do you hear me? Go," mother said.

I reached around the door and touched Golem. He saw them, too, and his expression seemed changed, no longer aimless and vacant. Was it surprise on his face? Alarm? Was he seeing what I felt? I left without a word to find father.

Days passed. My house was crowded with people. Evanko was coming and going to check on Ivan. The rabbi visited. Even Katia came to see Ira to make sure he had not been hurt. Ivan recovered quickly, though. With Leja and mother doting over him, his energy returned, but his combative spirit remained muted. Mayor Evanko said Ivan was safe from the police. Being the son of the mayor had certain benefits, even for one of the leaders of a partisan rebellion. Others that marched that night were less fortunate. Three men died, young men, shot or beaten by the police or the vengeful mob. I knew them.

They were Leja's friends, my former classmates, and now they were dead. Many more, like Ivan, were injured, and everyone I knew seemed to be in a state of shock, unable to make sense of the violence unleashed on the town's sons and daughters. The Polish residents of the town, however, felt newly emboldened and began denigrating the Ukrainian peasants and Jews they encountered on the streets and in the shops.

"Remember, we are the wolves, not the sheep," Igor Goreki said to my father one afternoon when he passed us in front of the buchbinderi. Father turned his eyes away and didn't respond, as Leja had always done when confronted by our teacher in school. I could hear him in my mind saying, "This was a time to pretend you respect them. To keep safe." My father, thankful that his children had escaped harm during the bloody encounter, also made it clear we were fortunate our "bad decision" to join the marchers had not resulted in tragedy.

"We stay to ourselves now. Keep quiet. Do you understand?" he said more than once. "It's not time for something new. We just need to get to tomorrow. Each day, get to tomorrow."

For me, each moment seemed impossibly far from tomorrow. What I'd seen, not in the bloody forest but in my home, was a dusty cloud enveloping me. My body moved. I spoke. I ate with my family. I helped my father and brother in the workshop, but I was not among them. I was listening to a voice inside me trying to put words to the memory of my mother's face against Evanko's neck, his hands on her — and the first time when I was six years old and saw more than that. I wanted to tell this to someone, but I needed words I didn't yet have.

I'd forgotten about that first time, until I saw them again. Then, the memory rushed back and replayed over and over, each time more vivid and graphic. It was a summer afternoon, and my father sent me to fetch mother from Evanko's house. The house was up the hill from the center of town, a solid field-stone structure set behind a stand of mature linden and oak trees. It was built in a broad meadow, and the sun would bathe it in light all day, unlike the shadows that surrounded our house. Mother planted a large vegetable garden there each summer, a source of great pride. "From the garden," she would say when she cooked something she'd grown. I recall her eagerness to spend afternoons there tending the garden and how happy she was when she returned.

When I walked through the trees toward the house that afternoon, I expected to see mother hunched over her plants weeding and digging or hauling water from a stream behind the house. She wasn't there, though. Perhaps she'd already gone, left for the market on her way home, and I'd missed seeing her. I stopped to admire her garden. Even I could recognize it was something special. Small mounds of flowers adorned the squash plants, with tiny bursts of color at the center of the blooms that were the new fruit. Tomatoes hung pink, warm and ripening from wooden stakes. Beans clung to tangled branches.

I heard her voice cry out from somewhere in the house, so I went to a small window beside the door and looked in. The sun poured through larger windows on the other side of the room, illuminating the two of them, standing, mother's skirt bunched at her waist. Evanko held her, and he was thrusting at her, hitting her hips with his own. His face twisted, and his eyes stared up. Mother made animal sounds and looked toward the floor.

I remember walking home quickly on the road, coming through our door and being glad father wasn't there to ask about my errand. I was confused and tried to block what I'd seen from my mind. Pieces fell from the picture one by one as if from a wooden jigsaw puzzle. When my mother returned home, she was calm, happy. She looked at me as she always did, stroked my hair, just another day. And that's what it became, until I saw the two of them again, and the puzzle pieces reassembled into something I understood and that I needed to share.

I lacked the courage to speak to mother about this. How could I? What would I say? How would I describe what I'd seen? What would happen if she became angry? What would happen if she cried? So, I waited until Ivan was well and returned home, until Leja was away tutoring her students, until Ira and father were in the workshop and mother at the market. I waited until I was alone in our house, and I wrote mother a letter. I told her what I had seen, that I was confused and worried about what this meant, that I needed her to explain how this fit with the fragile idea of a family. I put everything down on a piece of paper, folded it and placed it under mother's pillow.

The next time I saw that letter, father, seated on mother's bed, held it in his hand.

Part Two, 1934

"There is always some madness in love.
But there is also some reason in madness."
– Fredrich Nietzsche

CHAPTER EIGHT

Mine was a place defined by love and the myriad ways it makes humans behave irrationally. Whether bathing in its warmth when we have it or hiding in the cool gloom of its absence, we are at its mercy. The love a parent feels for a child or a child for a parent. The love that drives two people, overwhelmed by desire for the other, to thrust themselves against the odds into an uncertain future. The affection, less hot, that grows from familiarity, experience and a shared commitment. The love that becomes overwhelmed, like an untended garden, by the vines of outside entanglements and grows dry and brittle.

All of these are part of my story.

Father was solemn in the months following my crude attempt to make sense of mother's infidelity. He was distant from me and absent entirely from mother's life. He spent his days in the buchbinderi, despite the lack of paid work, fashioning books and bibles from remnants of his past jobs.

Mother sent meals out to him with me, and we rarely spoke, until one afternoon late that autumn as he sat at a worktable quietly eating and I could no longer bare the silence.

"I'm sorry, Papa," I blurted out. He looked at me quizzically.

"What are you apologizing for, my son?"

"It's my fault. I shouldn't have told." Then he understood, and nodded his head before answering.

"You're young. You should never have had to know."

"What will happen?"

"To you, Wolchi? Everything will soon be better than before."

"No. To you, Papa?"

"That, I don't know."

He walked to the nearby stitching machine and showed me some paper and cloth sheets he had been binding.

"Do you see how well this machine works?" he asked me. "Look at the perfect binding on these. It was never this good until you fixed it."

Father left us a few weeks later. I stood with him at the railroad station as his westbound train slowed to a stop at the platform. He bent so that his face was near mine, and he held my shoulders.

"Listen to me, Wolchi. I am going to Krakow to see my friend Michel," father said. "You remember him? The man with the little boy from the train station when I went for the machines? He says he has a job for me there. We need the money, Wolchi, and I need to be away."

"I don't want you to leave, papa. I'm sorry for what I did," I answered.

"Wolchi, Wolchi. Stop this. You did nothing wrong. You are a fine boy, and I am very proud of you," he said.

I tried, but didn't control my tears. I couldn't recall the last time I'd cried. Had I ever cried in front of my father? He wrapped his arms around me in a strong hug and held me there, both of us motionless, the early December wind cold on our faces except for where our cheeks touched. He placed his hands on my face and wiped my tears with his thumbs.

"Listen to me, my son. Listen carefully. I have paid Mr. Koperski at the machine shop to train you. Go see him while I'm away and he will teach you. He's a good man, and he will give you a skill that no one can ever take from you. No matter where you go, when someone asks you who you are you will be able to tell them. 'I am a machinist.' Not a Jew, a Ukrainian or a Pole. Just a man with a gift for working with machines."

"When will you come home?" I asked.

"I don't know, but I promise I will come back. Remember to see Mr. Koperski."

He stood and tried to lift me off the ground, the way he always had, to bring my eyes level with his own.

"Oh. You have gained more than a few kilos. I can't even raise you up anymore." For the first time in weeks, I saw him smile. After he mounted the steps onto the train, he looked back, still smiling. I held that memory, his face joyful, his eyes squinted and crinkled at the corners, for the many months he was gone.

<hr>

As father had promised, Mr. Koperski welcomed me, and I became his student. Six days each week, from sunrise to dusk, I worked in his small, crowded shop. It didn't take me long to develop enough skill that he allowed me to start and complete routine projects on my own. I worked the lathe and filled countless wooden boxes day after day with the long, sharp metal screws that would secure wooden railroad ties on the expanding Polish rail network. When he worked on intricate projects, such as the wheels and connecting rods for train engines, he would let me watch.

He was kind and gentle, but also a demanding taskmaster. Once, just a few days after I began working, mother came to the shop with a hot lunch for me. When she appeared in the doorway and called my name, I stopped working. Koperski lifted his protective mask, turned brusquely from the project he was fabricating on a press and muttered something unintelligible under his breath. He glanced at me and then stared at mother.

"Hello, I am here to see my son," mother said.

"He's working," Mr. Koperski said without greeting her.

"I have lunch for him."

"He is working. Leave it by the door." He turned to me. "Back to work. You need to finish."

That was it. He repositioned the mask over his eyes and returned his attention to the drill press.

At first, I thought Mr. Koperski was angry at mother, the way I was, because of what I believed was her disloyalty to our family. I suspected incorrectly that he knew the circumstances of father's departure. Mother, not deterred by his abruptness, continued bringing a hot lunch from time to time, always quietly leaving it by the door. One day, though, she walked boldly into the shop and placed her cloth bag on a workbench beside him.

"Lunch for two," she said, and turned for the door without a further glance at either of us.

Mr. Koperski never looked up or acknowledged her, but he eagerly shared the soup and bread with me when we stopped for our midday meal.

"Your mother is a fine cook," he said. "But eat quickly, there's work to do."

Chapter Nine

Food was mother's connection to me during those months father was away, as winter became spring, and the spring another summer. Our house felt empty and unfamiliar. Mother worked in the homes of wealthy Jewish families. Ira spent time with Katia at her family's small dairy farm or working alone in the buchbinderi. Leja tutored what seemed like every Jewish child in the town or helped Ivan write political treatises at the Evanko home. I often saw her carrying packages in and out of the buchbinderi in the evenings, which seemed unusual, but so did everything else in our lives at the time.

She was the only one of us who had contact with Mayor Evanko. Even mother had sent him off when he knocked at our door one evening checking on our, and her, well-being. I turned my head when we passed on the street, more ashamed than angry, but that didn't stop him from acknowledging me the next time we saw each other.

Mother maintained a stubborn stoicism about how our lives had been upended, and built a sturdy facade that allowed her to work, make meals, shop at the market and clean our house as if time had frozen in the moment before father read the letter. I wasn't even sure if she had read it. She hadn't mentioned it to me, nor I to her, and she never acknowledged any role in the abrupt transformation of our lives.

"Your father is in Krakow for work," she said to me.

On the surface this was true enough, and I never challenged that narrative, nor did Leja or Ira. I was content to let the urgency of each day's routines push aside what I didn't understand. It was fine that the passage of time allowed more and more dirt to fill the hole that held the memory and the guilt I harbored. I was content to sit silently at our dinner table night after night, usually alone, and hurry through meals while mother delivered a monologue of family news along with plates of food. She tried to nudge me from my brooding with dishes I always craved, the doughy varenikas filled with meat or potatoes and fried in fat, or the thinly sliced chicken filets filled with butter, garlic and onions, but to no avail.

"Your brother is helping Katia's father build a small house on their farm," she said one night. "For the two of them, I think, to live when they get married. But the rabbi will not marry them, not unless Katia becomes a giyoret and promises to raise their children as Jews. Maybe Ira will allow the priest to marry them and become a Christian. I hope not. A kenahora on that. Are you hungry for more, Wolchi?"

She changed subjects without transition.

"Do you talk with your sister? It seems she only comes home to sleep. She spends her evenings with Ivan doing what I don't know. Maybe talking about politics or meeting with those O.U.N. people to plan what? A revolution? We saw what happened the last time they did more than talk. Goreki and those Polish police are watching everything, and she needs to be careful.

"Are you hungry for more, Wolchi? Eat some more."

Ira and Leja didn't typically join us for meals in those months after father went away. They left home early and returned in the evening with little to say. I missed them both, but mostly Leja, with her books and stories about esoteric ideas and faraway places. I dwelled during my work day in close tolerances calculated in microns. Imprecision was unacceptable. What I understood was what I could hold in my hand. Her world was bigger, messier, filled with possibilities and imaginings. Her appetite to understand and shape each thing she encountered was insatiable. I felt her absence in my life as profoundly as I missed my father.

On Friday nights, though, she and Ira would be home early enough to join for dinner. These Friday family meals were a stubborn habit none of us could shake. Although father was not with us, we were more complete with one another, than apart.

Mother typically was quiet on these Fridays, content to resume her familiar role orchestrating and delivering a meal and the opportunity for her family to be together. One Friday, though, early in December, a year after my father had left, she had an agenda and wasted little time pursuing it.

"I want to know what is going to happen with you and Katia," she said to Ira, as she set down the plates of food. "The people I work for ask me, and I don't know what to say. Will they marry? Will her father allow it? Is Katia pregnant. I don't know how to answer them."

"Stop it, mama, okay," Ira responded, his tone unusually sharp. "Why do you even care about the old ladies whose houses you clean and what they think? Our family isn't their concern."

When father left, the joking carefree version of my brother went with him, leaving behind a man more somber and anxious. That's who was with us at dinner that evening.

"We have plenty of other things to worry about, mama," Ira said.

He unpacked his burdens, then, and we all saw that his load was too heavy. He told us we needed more money, that the idle buchbinderi needed work. Mother, he said, should charge "those rich Jews" more to clean their houses, and Leja could tutor more students and earn extra for the family. Mr. Koperski, he said with a frown aimed at me, should be paying a fair wage, and father should be sending more money home from his job in Krakow. The cold weather, he continued, his voice barely audible, also affected Katia's family farm, and they were suffering, too.

"I don't know what to do about those things, mama," he finally said, frustration and defeat in his voice "So, I don't care what others want from me."

There wasn't much any of us could say after that, or so I thought, until mother repeated her question.

"What is going to happen with you and Katia," she said. "Do you plan to marry her?"

Ira's face tightened. His hands gripped the table edge.

"Ira, tell her. Tell her or I will," Leja said.

Ira's face softened, his right hand released its hold on the table and covered Leja's. He nodded to her.

"We want to get married, mama, but Katia's father will not let her convert and become a Jew. So, the rabbi cannot marry us," he said. "The priest says I must renounce my faith to be married by the church, and you know I can't do that."

"A kenahora," my mother interrupted.

Ira continued: "There is only one other person who can marry us."

My mother nodded her head, while my sister and brother

carefully watched her. Although I didn't understand where this was headed, clearly she did.

"And you want me to say this would be alright?" mother asked. "That we should ask Grygoriy, because he is mayor, to be the one who marries you?"

She turned her back to us and walked away, one hand over her mouth, the other smoothing the front of her dress.

Was this really happening, I wondered. Was Evanko about to be invited back into our lives with wounds from the past still raw and unhealed?

"I've already asked him," Leja said. "And he agreed, but only if you . . . " she paused. "Only if you and papa say it is okay. He will not marry them without your permission."

Mother turned back to us and walked close to Ira.

"This is a lot to ask, especially of your father. You understand that," she said.

Ira nodded. "We love each other, mama. If we can't be married here, we'll be forced to leave and find a place to be together. In the city, or in Russia."

Mother sat down, the first time I could ever recall her sitting at our table with the rest of us, rather than hovering behind. She had something to say.

"Your grandmother arranged for me to marry your papa, you know," she said. "No one asked if I wanted it, if I loved him. It was just decided, when I was your age, Leja. Just a girl. My own father was dead and we were so poor that the two of us, your grandmother and I, slept in the same bed above the oven in one room no bigger than this kitchen. Mother said a good man would keep me safe and give me a home to raise my own children.

"First, there was a man from America who came here and

wanted me to marry him. He had a lot of money and lived in three rooms with his own mother, but he was fat and short and his breath smelled like cheese. I hated him. Mother told me I would learn to like him after we were married and that he would take me to America where I could live the best life. He showed me a necklace that he said was gold with diamonds and promised he would give it to me on our wedding night. I thought, 'Who needs a necklace from a short, fat smelly man.' The rabbi had arranged for this man to meet me, and he was ready to marry us as soon as my mother said 'yes,' which she did, because the man offered her money.

"The night before the wedding, I cried the whole night. I couldn't sleep, and I begged mama not to force me to marry that man and go live far away. I hugged her while I cried, and I said I would not let go of her, and would not leave without her. Finally, she told me I didn't need to marry the fat man. I was so happy, but the rabbi was very angry. He spit on the ground when my mother told him and shook his finger at me. 'You'd better make a Golem to protect yourself,' he said to me, 'because I can't help you anymore.'

"Mama kept looking for a husband for me and found your father. He was the one, mama said. His heart was good, his body strong, and he had a skill and a desire to work. He was not a 'synagogue bum,' she told me, who would pray all the time and send me to work to support him. No one asked me, 'Do you love him?' I did like him right away, though. You know your father was very handsome. He looked like you, Ira. Not so tall, but the same face. He made me laugh, and he was very polite to mama and promised her he would be a good husband. So, we agreed to marry. The rabbi, though, said he wouldn't do it, he wouldn't marry us, that God had intended me for the short, fat smelly man, and now, well, there was no easy way to undo the harm I had done. He wanted money, even I knew that, but we had none and your father had none, so we couldn't have a Jewish wedding from the rabbi.

"Your father had an idea, though. He had joined the Austrian Army. All the young men were doing that in the years before the war. It was an easy way to make money. Who knew there would be such fighting and death once the war started. So, father had the Austrian district captain marry us right in the town square. My mama was crying with joy, and your grandfather, your father's father, was buying beer for the men in the square, and there was pumpkin cake with cream and there was music. Your father danced with me and sang to me, *Ochi chornye*, because of my dark eyes. I started to love him that night."

We watched mama when she turned to stare at the front door, the way she did while waiting for father to return home for supper in the evening. "And I never stopped," she continued.

Leja saw something in her gaze before I did, the gnawing remorse, like the memory of a wound that had scarred, but still ached.

"Then why?" Leja asked.

I could hear passersby on the street, my heartbeat, the sound of the coal burning in our stove, because none of us even breathed. How could a room be so still?

"Sometimes things happen with a man that a woman cannot stop," mother said very softly. "When he is powerful and she is not, when her husband, injured in the war, needs her to care for him, and their children are hungry because there's no money, and the man, that man who has money and power, offers to help, no, insists that he help, but expects something in return. Then it starts, and it can't stop because the woman knows the man can say the truth and she would be the one hurt, just her and her children and her husband. Not the man."

Mother rose from the table and cleared the dishes slowly, wearily, carrying the burden of what she had done, but doing so without guilt. She said to Leja, "Why? Because I believed I had to."

Mother looked to the front door again as she walked to stand beside Ira, placing her hand on his shoulder. "*Ochi chornye,* it was a most beautiful song," she said. "If you love this girl, Ira, you should marry her. Whatever you need to do, I will help."

Ira sprang from his chair and lifted her a foot off the ground with a suffocating hug. He kissed her cheek. "Thank you, mama. Thank you."

Leja clapped her hands twice before clasping them together, as if in prayer, astounded by mother's confession, but also filled with joy for her brother.

"Stop, Stop. Put me down. Right now," mother said curtly, the smile on her face betraying her true emotion. She smoothed her dress, looked at Ira and reminded him: "But you must ask your papa."

Chapter Ten

Ira left on the train to Krakow the following day to get father's permission to marry. Leja and I walked with him to the station, the three of us bundled beneath layers of sweaters and coats to protect against the cold, dry wind that foretold the harshness of the coming winter. We sent him off, waving and shouting. As his train left the station, Leja grabbed my hand and began walking in a direction away from home.

"It's freezing," she said. "Let's get out of here."

We walked quickly and silently across a meadow toward the hill where a familiar fieldstone house was visible through the barren trees. A trail of smoke rose from the chimney, and Leja broke into a run as we got close, energized by the promise of a warm room. She entered the house through a back door without hesitation, with the same familiarity she might come through our door at home. I followed more cautiously and paused outside letting go of Leja's hand.

"I don't really want to be here," I said.

She grabbed my hand again insistently. "I know. Just come with me. I need to show you something." She turned toward the figure in the room, Evanko seated at a table near the stove, a book in his hand and more of them piled beside him, but did not acknowledge him. He greeted us both without visible surprise, the way he would in the street, as if this were just another day from a time before. I didn't want to, but I nodded in response, relieved when Leja urged me to follow her down a flight of stairs. At least I didn't need to speak with him.

In the dim basement, Ivan, his back to us, was hunched over a table.

"Ivan, look who's here," Leja said, throwing her coat onto a chair and edging beside him at the table. "Let me see."

Ivan greeted me with a hug, his hands tapping my back. "My friend," he said. "It's been too long."

He had grown a beard, neatly trimmed, since we were last together. Our relationship had been victimized by the larger drama affecting our families, and our time had been limited and awkward for the past year.

"Wolchi, come here. I need to show you this," Leja said.

She was standing over a crude tabletop printing device, spinning a metal crank that turned a screw that lowered an inked metal plate onto a sheet of paper. She reversed the crank and lifted the printed page proudly, as if it were a work of art or a divine creation. Other printed sheets were stacked on the table, more piled on the floor. As my eyes adjusted to the dim light and I looked around the room, I saw we were surrounded by sheets of paper and thin, bound books, which I suspected was the work of my family's buchbinderi.

"What is all this?" I asked.

"It's a revolution," Ivan said, as he placed his arm around Leja's waist.

"We can't fight them with weapons, but we can fight them with words," Leja said.

I was taken aback, not by what they said, but by the casual closeness between them. They seemed like different people.

Ivan, a man I didn't know with that beard, stared intensely at Leja, her face smooth and angular, a woman's face, not quite familiar anymore, her lashes long, her eyes bright, her lips parted just slightly. He was enamored of her, and I felt I was interrupting an intimate moment between strangers. Leja saw my unease.

"I thought you would be excited," she said. "I wrote all this. When we have enough books we'll give them to O.U.N. leaders in surrounding villages."

I recovered and said: "No. No. This is great. Let me see one." I was thinking that in the past year I had missed more than my sister's intelligence and kindness in my life. I had also missed her transformation into a woman in love, not with the man beside her as I first thought, but rather with big ideas to shape our world.

Her treatise was titled: "*Question everything.*"

It began: "As Ukrainians, we are members of a community united by history and common suffering. Christian, Orthodox or Jew, we each have a responsibility to that community, not just to ourselves. As human beings, we also have the right to liberty. We are free people. As the French revolution defined it, though, liberty doesn't mean an individual can do as he pleases toward another. Liberty means freedom from oppression by the government. Isn't it time that each Ukrainian was liberated from oppressive Polish control?"

I remembered her chanting in the square, marching through the streets, the faces of others as they watched her. They looked to her for a vision of the future, and the courage to create it. Ivan and even Mayor Evanko were soldiers in her army, each being shaped by the political thinking of a seventeen-year-old girl.

"I need your help," Leja said. "These pages we're printing need to go to the buchbinderi for Ira, and the pamphlets he makes need to come back here. People already see me carrying bundles in and out every day. I'm afraid the police will stop me and discover what we're doing. Ivan and I can't be seen doing this together, and I can't do it alone. Maybe at night, after work, we can go out together, you and me?"

That's how I was recruited into the ranks of the Organization of Ukrainian Nationalists, and I soon began nightly treks with Leja carrying unbound papers and books between our buchbinderi and the Evanko basement. I was not a true advocate of the O.U.N. rhetoric. But just as I was persuaded by my mother's faith in Golem and my father's belief that people reached a point when dignity forced them to embrace an uncertainty, I was confident that my sister's dedication to her political vision was worthy of my own.

Chapter 11

When I walked into the room, he was waiting. His back was to the door, and he and Ira were sipping tea at the table. I didn't recognize the heavy sweater he wore or the way his hair was long on top and swept to one side, but I recognized his voice even before he turned to the door and looked at me. I'm not sure why I froze in place, staring as if at a ghost, or why I continued to stare even after he said my name.

"It's Papa," Ira said. "Papa."

Then I was at the table, my arms around his shoulders, my face pressed into his neck, the faint smell of mint and good sweat confirming that this was, indeed, my father, back in our house, back home, and I thought: "If I keep my arms tightly about his shoulders, he can't leave again."

When he left more than a year earlier, I assumed his return was imminent. I'd lay awake nights wondering if the next morning would be the one when I would open my eyes and see him at the table, waiting for me. Sometimes I was certain I'd found him when I saw a man on the street with a halting gait, a cane, or the familiar lines radiating from the corner of his eyes. Each time was a disappointment, and each made the memory of him harder to retrieve. So, on the evening when at last my father was with me, I could not convince my arms to let him go. I clung to him. He said my name over and over.

"Papa, are you staying?" was my response. He put his mouth to my ear and whispered. "I once promised I would come back. Now, I promise to stay."

He'd brought me a gift, he said, and was eager to share it. He searched his travel sack and handed me a heavy box wrapped in cloth. The box was a foot long and wide, and at least two inches thick. It was wooden, smoothly sanded with a fine oil finish. I ran my hands across the wooden surface, top and bottom. It was like touching a well-worn leather saddle. Two metal hooks held a cover to the base of the box. I fingered the hooks and hesitated.

"Go ahead," father said. "Open it."

Inside was a set of machinist tools, taps and dies used to cut precise threading patterns into metal or repair damaged fasteners. I had used Mr. Koperski's as needed at the machine shop, but owning these tools distinguished a journeyman machinist from others less skilled. I lifted the round dies and stick-like taps and ran my fingers across the sharp cutting surfaces made of steel forged and hardened with heat and pressure. Each was stamped with a very small, round symbol. A face? The head of a bullfrog?

"The Golem," father said. "So, you will always be able to recognize your tools when you are in a big workshop someday, in a big city. No one else will have the eyes of the Golem on him as he works."

Father laughed at his own words, a hearty, full laugh that made his face flush and the lines in the corner of his eyes extend almost to his hairline. When Ira and I started to laugh, too, it felt so good, like a time from before.

Father had returned with another gift, one that dramatically transformed our family's day-to-day life. The "Radetsky project," he called it. Almost overnight, the buchbinderi was abuzz with activity. Father and Ira worked late into the evenings. The small stacks of hand-printed sheets Leja and I carried to and from the workshop contrasted with the wooden crates being delivered or hauled away several times each week by horse-drawn carts. The crates coming in were filled with pages from a professional print shop in Krakow; those going out were stacked with finely bound books headed to shops in Stryi and L'viv. From time to time, father would print a special handmade edition using our own printing press, books he would carefully create from special papers and leathers. Those books were offered to collectors in cities as far as Moscow and Warsaw.

Some nights, after working all day at Mr. Koperski's shop, I would help Ira and father maintain and repair the printing and binding machines. Leja would organize the outgoing books in crates, marking the boxes with their destinations and a description of their contents. We no longer had time to assemble Leja's political treatises. They would have to wait. We worked late into the night before returning home and falling into a dreamless, exhausted sleep — all of us except father, who had the energy of a younger man, two younger men.

"Yes. I'll be finished soon," he'd say and send us away. "Go to sleep. There are one or two things I need to do."

If I'd awaken in the quiet of the night, I saw the yellow light of the kerosene lamps still glowing in the buchbinderi. Ira sometimes found him in the morning asleep on a small cot in the workshop. The work, rather than wearing him down, built him up. He moved about the workshop with great confidence, managing the multitude of details associated with cutting, stitching and binding what I later learned was a book of great interest across the Ukraine and much of Europe — *The Radetzky March*, by Joseph Roth.

Leja was the only one of us who knew that name at first, a great writer, she said, whose books captured the demise of the Austrian empire and who was a creative voice for Ukrainians longing for a unified home. His work was in great demand, and father's buchbinderi was making books for the cities of Western Ukraine and beyond. "Roth is a genius," Leja said.

My father had a more nuanced view. "He is a beautiful man with God's gift for words, a Jew, who grew up just one hundred kilometers from here. We were in the war together, you know. I saved his life," my father said matter-of-factly, and he told that story like this.

"We were stationed on the Eastern front near the river, and for months it was very quiet. We knew the Russians were in the woods across the water, and they knew where we were, but the only fighting was in the local tavern between bored, drunken soldiers. That's where I met Roth, after he was knocked to the ground by a big Prussian boy who took offense to having his mother compared to parts of a horse.

"He was laid out flat, his drunken eyes glassy and staring at nothing, his deeply clefted chin and thin lips wet with blood and spit. I recognized him as the journalist in my company, a lieutenant whose job was to write about the progress of the war for the citizens in Austrian cities far from the front. He wrote lies mostly, or at least nothing close to the truth. I dragged him away just as the Prussian boy, himself on the ground after falling in his own drunken stupor, rose to his knees and vowed further to avenge his mother's soiled name.

"Lieutenant, we need to leave before that farm boy finds his legs," I said to Roth.

" 'My dear friend,' Roth said. 'That boy couldn't find his legs with a compass and a map or his ass with both hands. But you're right just the same. We should go.'

"We hurried out of the place, and I thought I would help him back to his room and then go off to sleep myself. But he spotted a group of men singing on the roof of the tavern, bottles in each of their hands, having climbed up with a ladder, perhaps for a better view of the dark river and the Russian campfires on the other side, or perhaps just because it seemed a festive idea.

"'Will you look at that' Roth said. 'A party on the veranda.' He mounted the ladder quickly and climbed to the roof. That's where I saved him, on that rooftop. Not from enemy fire, but from his own drunken bluster.

"The men were playing a bravery game. With no enemy to battle, our soldiers had few ways to prove their bravado, so the consumption of massive amounts of drink became a favorite way to demonstrate manliness and stamina. The game on the roof required each man to sit on the parapet edge, lean backward off the roof and take a long drink from his bottle. This was foolish, but not likely to be fatal, because their legs could hold them in place and prevent a fall.

"'You're all cowards,' Roth bellowed. 'Let me show you how a real man plays your game.' He grabbed a bottle from the nearest hand and climbed to stand on the roof parapet. Even the other drunken men realized this was madness and asked Roth to sit down. Falling from this roof would be the end of him. Roth laughed, taunted them, hopping from one foot to the next demonstrating his balance and his recklessness.

"He yelled out 'budmo, cheers,' and the other men responded as he leaned back and took a drink. He yelled again, 'budmo, budmo,' and again the men responded with two loud cheers as he drank from the bottle. Then again, three times, 'budmo, budmo, budmo,' and as the men responded, Roth leaned back to empty his bottle, too far to hold his balance, and began to fall.

"I was the only man on that roof not soaked with drink, and good thing I was there, because I grabbed Roth's legs as his head and shoulders vanished over the edge. I heard his bottle crash to the ground and his head strike the side of the building with a firm thunk. The other men silently watched as I pulled him back up to the roof. Sitting dazed on the parapet, blood streaming down the side of his face, Roth broke into a deranged smile, lifted his hand as if it still held the bottle and shouted, 'budmo.' The men surrounded him, clapping his back in congratulation, and placed a new bottle in his hand."

My father paused from his storytelling, had a drink of tea, and continued.

"I saw him often in the following months, and we talked about Austria, the royalty, socialism, what we would do once we were home. He was transferred to Vienna before the fighting began, and I didn't see him again for all these years — until a man with a deeply clefted chin and thin lips walked past me in Krakow a few months ago, a man whose face was older, but familiar.

"He was teaching at Janghellion University, where I worked in the bookbinding shop at a job my friend Michel found for me. Roth and I met from time to time after that. He was already a famous writer and had written a book about the war, *The Radetzky March*. He liked to talk about our time by the river, what had happened there after he left, inventorying his dead and wounded drinking companions. He said I was the only friend still alive who knew him then. He offered me money, quite a lot, to make copies of his book for people in our part of Europe, for his lantzmen he called them, to read his words. He wanted to help me. This is the work we now do everyday."

Chapter 12

Grygoriy Evanko was missing from that war story. As quickly as he'd been banished from our everyday lives, my father had also erased him from the narrative of his war years. Evanko had always been portrayed as a constant companion through the initial boredom on the war's Eastern front and a vital comrade during the brief, but bloody, months of battle. "We were like brothers," my father had said. But now, their bond was broken.

Father gave his blessing to Ira's wedding plans, and he certainly knew the day was approaching when he and Evanko would stand beside one another and either mend their tear or leave it frayed forever. So much had gone unsaid, at least to me, since father's return home that there was no way for me to predict how that inevitable reunion would end.

I was much more concerned about a relationship closer to home. In most ways, father was his old self. He was open and loving to me and Leja. He treated Ira with new respect and pride. He worked tirelessly and enthusiastically in the buchbinderi. He seemed happy, except around my mother.

When they were in the same place there was a practiced lack of acknowledgement. They communicated by speaking aloud to the room, and fulfilled their minimum obligations to one another politely and without outward emotion. They each listened attentively to Ira's wedding plans, Leja's hopes for political change and my accounts of lathes and presses, but only when the other was not in the room. When we were all together, mother receded into the background, and father grew sullen and quiet.

Leja said she noticed that neither father nor mother had any remaining objections to her involvement with O.U.N., with father even helping to package her essays into the books that she and Ivan planned to distribute across the countryside. Ira said they no longer seemed concerned about his boundary-crossing relationship with Katia, with mother even helping Katia at the market select fabrics for a wedding dress. I noticed how they struggled to maintain their indifference to one another, like two magnets whose polarities were confused, repelling one another even though it would be so easy for one to just turn and reverse the force that was keeping them apart.

My parents orchestrated their comings and goings to avoid close encounters. All of us left the house early each day. At night, when father didn't sleep in the workshop, he slept near me and Ira on one side of the house, while mother slept in a bed with Leja on the other. On Friday evenings, though, our separate lives converged at a crowded supper table. After weeks of these meals feeling as if we were in one of mother's simmering pots, the whole mess boiled over.

Mother was uncharacteristically mechanical in her attention to the family that evening as she served supper. Plates clattered too loudly when she placed them on the table. Strands of her hair, normally pulled neatly back from her face, were loose about her eyes. She mumbled as she worked at the stove.

While father sat silently, Leja, Ira and I recounted our days and plans for the days to come. Mother, completely excluded from the conversation, became increasingly agitated and difficult to ignore. I ate quickly, hoping to escape the unsettled predator at our periphery before she attacked, but our meals ended only when one of our parents declared them finished. That was our rule. Leaving the table before father or mother gave the okay was discouraged.

Father, his back to the kitchen where mother stalked her pots and pans, was unaware of the crisis building behind him. He slid his chair away as if to leave the table. I saw this as an opportunity to escape and stood. Ira followed. Father reached down to retrieve a napkin, leaving Ira and I awkwardly standing when mother turned toward us in anger.

"Supper is not finished. Sit down," she commanded. "Everybody, sit down."

We obeyed. Even father stopped and sat upright, leaving his napkin on the floor.

"Eat without a word to me? Treat me as if I'm not here, like I'm your maid and cook to be ignored, treated as if I'm invisible," she continued, her face red with the temperature of her kitchen and the heat of her frustration. "Not in this house."

My father finally turned to look at his wife in confusion. My mother pointed at him with the wooden spoon in her hand. "Not even you," she said.

She threw the spoon to the ground with a feral scream and pushed past us, through the front door into the cold evening without a coat, a scarf or another word. She slammed the door shut, and I heard the rattle of Golem on the shelf, a whisper in the ringing silence she left behind.

We sat confused, frozen, until Leja pushed away from the table and went after her. "Mama, wait," she said running out. My father rose from the table, also. He retrieved his coat and calmly said: "Back to work." He walked through the door and closed it behind him gently, as if trying not to awaken something sleeping in the house.

Chapter 13

On Sunday, I went back to work, as well. Mr. Koperski was building more and more parts for the expanding national railway, and he expected me at the shop early until late six days each week. When I walked in, the sun had just edged over the horizon, but Mr. Koperski was already at a work bench grinding a railcar axle, metal shavings and sparks forming a cloud like flies around fallen fruit. His stooped posture and his heavily lined face gave no indication of the energy he had for work.

Koperski Mashyna was a business started by his father fifty years before as a blacksmith shop, later evolving to repair farm machinery and now focused on rail and engine parts for the PKP, Poland's railroad. I was a key component of the shop's recent success. Despite my age, not yet fifteen, I had become a journeyman machinist with the skills needed to match the pace and quality expectations of the older man. He nodded with approval when he reviewed my work and began paying me wages on the one-year anniversary of my apprenticeship. Each month when he accompanied our shipments to the railyard in Krakow, he left me to work on my own.

Late that Sunday afternoon, two men entered the shop, both dressed in expensive wool overcoats and fur hats. Their boots clicked noisily as they made their way across the shop to greet Mr. Koperski. "My friends, welcome," he said to them. "How was your trip from Krakow?"

The three spoke for several minutes before Mr. Koperski motioned for me to join them.

"My apprentice," he said, his hand on my shoulder. "He is already the town's best machinist. Wolchi, these men are from the railroad coming to check on us."

He gave my shoulder a conspiratorial squeeze. "I was just telling them that we could not get this job finished in time if not for your hard work, your good work."

One of the men extended his hand, and I shook it firmly, the way father had taught me. "Nice to meet you, young man. Thank you for helping my old friend Mr. Koperski," he said.

"He's been a good teacher," I responded. "He's taught me everything."

"Yes. He was my teacher, too, many years ago in Krakow," the man said. "Have you ever been to Krakow, young man?"

I had not, and said so, but also related the tale of my father's recent return. "I would like to go there sometime."

"When you do, make sure Mr. Koperski tells you how to find me at the main PKP machine shop and turnaround," the man said. "I'll have a job for you, if you want one."

I looked back to Mr. Koperski, and he smiled proudly. Clearly, this was his suggestion.

"Thank you," I mumbled.

"No, thank you, young man. It's a pleasure to have met," the man from Krakow said.

That evening, we closed the shop well after 9 p.m. The town was quiet, cold and dark. A few late revelers lined the bar at the tavern, but I otherwise had the streets to myself as I hurried home. I thought about my meeting with the railroad men and their offer to work in Krakow. Leja and I had spent so many evenings envisioning new places and our lives amid the crowds and energy of a city. She talked about the books she would read, the art she could see, the impassioned discussions she could have in the cafes at night if we lived in a city. I imagined the wonders of a modern world. Cars with engines that propelled them rather than horses, electric streetlights, machine shops ten times the size of Koperski Mashyna. These had always been daydreams, no more real than the malevolent ghosts of the graveyard, laundry hung in the yard that in the right light looked like something surreal. This was different, though.

I wanted to share this news with my family and tell them I could work in Krakow, speak the words aloud to make them real. As I came toward the house, I saw a lamp lit in the buchbinderi, my father still at work, I expected.

"Papa, papa," I called as I entered the workshop. There was no one there, at least I couldn't see anyone in the dim light of the room. "Papa?"

In the corner, on the small cot, I saw the faint outline of two people, asleep, breathing slowly. Father draped his arm over the back of a woman, her dark hair loose, her face close to his. Mother. The kerosene lamp flickered and the room went dark, so I left them alone, and together.

CHAPTER 14

Ira was insistent that his wedding be held on the steps of the town hall near the spot where he first touched his lips to Katia's two years before.

"I want everyone to see it when I kiss her again as my wife," Ira said.

He had been defiant from the start about their relationship, pushing back hard against the naysayers and haters who worked to drive them apart. Katia and Ira's love affair had been the talk of the town after their Easter kiss. The adults shared my mother's initial disapproval, seeing only hardship and ill fortune for a young couple that ignored religious and cultural conventions. Crossing the line that had separated generations of Christians and Jews in the name of love was not something to be condoned. Who knew where that could lead? Young people, though, thought the pair magical, a tonic for the looming hopelessness they felt about their own lives. Here was love, true love, love impeded by unreasonable obstacles, and what could be better.

Their relationship had an undeniable energy. When they walked together, people watched them pass, some scornful, some reverent. The Polish boys taunted them, envious of Ira's good fortune and intimidated by Katia's aloofness. They stole bits of time to be together on the evening streets or in the shadows of the forest. For two years they persisted in the face of an uncertain future and marched toward what they saw as their destiny.

Ira's defiance about the wedding location, however, was no match for the will of the mothers of the bride and groom, whose more practical heads prevailed when they selected a wedding spot in the relative privacy of Katia's family farm. The couple planned to live in a new house Katia's father, with help from Ira, had been building for more than a year on a plot cleared a hundred yards from the larger main house. The new home already had furniture, and the couple would be able to spend their first night together there as a married couple.

"When you kiss her in this place in the woods," my mother told Ira, "the birds will rejoice and their singing will let everyone know that you kissed your new wife. And, there will be no Polish thugs shouting at you from the road."

The wedding would be held beneath a canopy of beech trees near the new house. It was a beautiful place, with fresh leaves filling the branches above, the wet smell of last year's autumn decaying on the ground, the snowdrops and crocuses adding dabs of color to sunny spots in the forest floor.

The afternoon before the wedding, Ivan, Leja and I were preparing the spot where family and friends would gather, when Katia joined us, her arms filled with fresh cut daffodils and budding willow branches. We assembled rough wooden benches in a semicircle around a raised alter, ground covered in hay and bordered behind by a lattice of branches, and Katia scattered her flowers.

"I've always felt there was a force in these woods," she said as she worked. "That these trees are alive in ways we can't see.

These flowers are a tribute to them."

Katia was an uneducated woman. She couldn't read or write, and she had no spoken aspirations beyond the simple life of her family's dairy farm in this isolated corner of Europe. Leja expressed skepticism about Ira's relationship with Katia, assuming beauty was her only asset and the basis of her brother's attraction. Katia found Leja's political rhetoric and unfamiliar ideas foreign and even threatening. In the months leading to the wedding, though, the two became closer, sisters that neither had until they met one another.

Ivan still liked to mock Katia, though, and make her the target of jokes.

"I think your mother has been giving Katia some lessons about the ways of the spiritual world," Ivan said to Leja while they watched Katia spread her flowers. "I'm sure Katia will appreciate the Golem she will get as a wedding gift."

"Stop that, Ivan," Leja scolded quietly. "She's okay."

Katia laid the flowers and willow branches into patterns, weaving their ends together with string into a series of triangles, some with lines through their centers.

"Katia, what are you doing with those flowers?" Ivan said, ignoring Leja's warning.

"Air, fire, water, earth and spirit, of course" Katia said, pointing to each of the triangles in turn.

"Of course, spirit" Ivan said, struggling to conceal a smirk. Leja pulled at his arm and shook her head.

Katia did not see him, though. Instead, she was on her knees staring intently at the triangles she had laid across the ground, adjusting their position so that some were placed with the triangle's flat side pointing away, and some reversed.

"The spirit brings the other elements into balance and

creates safety," Katia said. "Without it, there is confusion, disorder and danger."

"Do you really believe those shapes will protect you?" Ivan asked, more curious than contemptuous.

Katia calmly rose to her feet, carefully brushing the dirt from her hands and dress before answering him.

"They represent something important to me. I believe they have kept my family at peace. I believe they brought Ira into my life. They have given me hope," she said, moving a hand to her belly, gently stroking it.

"Do you believe that the symbols on your O.U.N. flag or the words in your pamphlets will protect you?" she asked Ivan.

Ivan mumbled a response that I didn't hear because I couldn't stop staring at Katia's hand, still moving side to side and up and down over her middle. Leja was staring, too.

⸻◆⸻

On the wedding day, my family and Ira's friends made our way through the streets toward Katia's family farm. We had dressed in our fine clothes, the young men and father in western-style hats with flowers tucked into the brims and dark suit jackets, mother, Leja and the other women in embroidered muslin dresses, their heads covered with brocade scarves. All of us, men and women, wore black boots, well-worn but polished to the best shine we could coax from the aged leather. I walked beside Ira, tugging with one hand at the dress overcoat I'd outgrown in the past year and carrying a small gift box with the other.

Ukrainian tradition required the groom's family and

entourage to visit the bride's house on the wedding day and ceremonially buy the bride from her family and friends. The men held small gifts of chocolate or baked goods that they would share with the women in the bride's entourage. Ira's box was the largest, containing an Old Testament bible he'd bound in leather and engraved with an image of a sun rising above a mountain, heaven and earth. He intended to present this gift to Katia's father before we entered their home. My mother carefully carried a cloth bag she held in front of herself with both hands. We must have been a sight to behold for the town's people as we passed.

We turned off the main road onto a narrower rocky path that led to the surrounding farms. A small group of young men, with Nicholas Goreki at the front, headed in our direction. Both groups could not pass without one stepping into the weeds and dirt beside the road. There were many more of us than there were of them, but Goreki's group gave no indication they would let us pass. My father ambled to the front as we walked, his stride interrupted by his limp, but otherwise purposeful and strong. He didn't slow as he approached the young men, and like a ship's bow through turbid water he continued without a word into the midst of Goreki and the others, scattering them in his wake and clearing a path for the wedding entourage behind him. We passed the men without exchanging words or glances as father pulled away from us with an extra boldness in his stride.

We arrived at Katia's farmhouse past midday, but the weather was still cool for an April afternoon. Ira strode to the front door and knocked assertively, the rest of us crowding behind him. A muscular man with a weathered face and thinning hair greeted us. Katia's father I assumed. He was wearing a traditional long white coat and white pants tucked into high boots. An embroidered and fringed belt hung from his waist. His mustache, as white as the coat, drooped below his mouth and was animated with movement when he spoke.

"Welcome, Ira," he said, before also greeting father and mother by name.

"I have this gift for you and your family," Ira replied, handing the box he held to the older man. "I hope you will invite us into your home and allow me the honor of marrying your daughter."

Katia's father opened the lid of the box, nodded approvingly and stepped aside to allow all of us to enter. We moved past him and joined the group of women and family friends standing with Katia beside a stone fireplace. The room was decorated with symbols resembling the ones Katia had placed on the wedding alter. Triangles inside circles hung from the wall, and yellow daffodils filled clay pots on the fireplace mantle.

Ira did not hesitate, his excitement uncontainable as he hurried to Katia, grabbed her hands in his and squeezed. He whispered to her, and she laughed, a laugh so joyous and infectious that the rest of us began laughing, too.

The men made their way to the women and girls surrounding Katia and presented their gifts. They bowed and exchanged their boxes for corsages, while I was searching for someone who could receive my box. All the younger women and girls had been claimed by the others, and I found myself presenting my gift to an older woman. Fine lines marked her face; grey streaks were woven through the blonde hair below her scarf. At first, I didn't recognize her as the woman I'd seen countless times walking down our street with Katia, pulling a cart with jugs of milk. But looking at her so close to me, there was no mistaking her for anyone other than Katia's mother. I took a deep breath and felt an unfamiliar stirring in my chest. "Thank you, Wolchi," she said. "It is an honor to receive a gift from such a handsome young man."

"You're welcome. And you look very handsome, too," I mumbled. "I mean you look very nice."

I felt my cheeks redden. She smiled at me, a kind and open smile, and I could feel my neck flush with heat while I stared at her lips. What a fool I must seem to be, frozen there, a boy turned to stone by gazing at the face of a woman. I might have remained that way forever with my mouth agape and my arms hanging loosely at my sides if mother had not walked up and placed her hand on my arm. She extended the cloth bag she had carried from home. "A special gift for the couple's new home," my mother said.

I backed away from the two women, but Katia's mother touched my shoulder. "Wait," she said. "You have forgotten this." She held a blue flower, a corsage in return for my gift, and she carefully pinned it to the lapel of my overcoat. Her face was close to mine, and I could smell her skin, fresh strawberries and hydrangea. She bowed to me, once, twice, and, again I stared, confused. I wasn't sure what to do until my mother broke my reverie with a circular motion of her hands.

"Bow, Wolchi," she said. With my eyes turned away from them, I did. Once, twice, and I would have kept right on bowing had I not spotted father in a corner of the room with his face inches from Mayor Evanko's.

He faced me, his eyes locked on his former friend in the way I knew was reserved for times when he expected full attention. He connected your eyes to his, a bolt to a fastener, until he chose to release you. From the look of things, he didn't plan to let Evanko free anytime soon. He clearly had a lot to say. My father, a formidable man despite his infirmity or perhaps because of it, made it difficult for others to take advantage of him or feel pity toward him. His anger felt ominous if you were its target, but when that anger ceased you felt released from a dire fate and thankful he'd liberated you.

I politely thanked Katia's mother, backed away and wandered closer to the two men. Father's voice was low, and his face still very close to Evanko's.

"It was a betrayal, Grygoriy," father said. "A betrayal of the worst kind because I loved you both. You are my best friend, still, but what you did cannot be forgotten. Clara and I have a life we will live together. Our children. Our home. But you and I share nothing anymore."

A long silence ensued, the two men still eye-to-eye, nose-to-nose.

"I hope, Marcus, that sometime again there will be something," Evanko said.

From the open front door, Katia's father clapped his hands several times, and waved his arm above his head. "It's time," he said.

We lined up, Ira first with a bridesmaid to escort him on either arm and Katia's remaining friends and family behind them. The bride followed with a groomsman on each arm and Ira's family, including me, and friends in tow. Father and Mayor Evanko were last to leave the house. They didn't speak, but they walked together for a time until father joined his family and Evanko found his place at the front of the procession. Father did not watch him walk away, and Evanko did not look back.

The procession made its way on a dusty path alongside the fenced field of dairy cows and the milking barn. Dogs ran beside us, yelping and baying at this odd group of humans crossing their domain. The air was clean and free from summer flies and stinging bugs, the sun was shining, and our mood was bright.

From the front, Ira yelled, "I will marry you today, Katia. Will you marry me?"

Katia replied, "I *will* marry you, Ira. You are my man."

Ira stopped and tossed his hat into the air. The girls around him giggled. So did Katia. A wave of laughter then coursed through the procession, as another hat launched upward, and another and another.

"I will marry you today, Katia," Ira shouted. "You are my woman."

When we reached the altar in the woods, a groomsman and a bridesmaid spread a large white wedding towel, with lace fringe and embroidered with blue flowers, across the ground. Ira and Katia, holding one another's hands, stepped onto it together. Mayor Evanko began to speak, crowns were raised above the heads of the bride and groom in the Ukrainian tradition, and Ira smashed a glass with his foot in the Jewish tradition. When they kissed at the ceremony's end, all of us rose to our feet clapping.

When the kiss lingered, we shouted. When Ira lowered Katia into his arms, never letting his lips leave hers, we began a celebration so raucous that it wasn't just the birds whose rejoicing was heard throughout the town.

CHAPTER 15

I recall the two years following Ira's wedding as if I saw them through a gauzy filter. Our lives were ordered and mostly free from the threats that had whipsawed us in the years before. Days blended into weeks and months, and the routines of work and family allowed us all to imagine that a new reality had settled over our town and our lives. I was a fixture at Mr. Koperski's shop, working long days amid the comforting clatter and whining of machines. Father and Ira were binding scores of books each day, as the demand for Joseph Roth's *Radetzky March* showed no signs of ebbing in the western Ukraine and beyond. Mother was emotionally restored by our return to an unremarkable, familiar pattern that allowed her to tend to the home and basic needs of our family.

Leja experienced moments of drama after some close encounters with Polish police while she and Ivan transported their political treatises to communities outside of town. Being accompanied by the son of a respected mayor kept Leja from any harsh outcomes, but their printing and bookbinding enterprise grew increasingly risky, as anti-Polish sentiment grew in the region and the authorities stepped up efforts to root out insurgents.

When we gathered on a late spring evening in June 1937 at our Friday night table to celebrate Leja's twentieth birthday, no looming threat distracted us from the joyful custom of these celebrations. The retelling of a birth story by father, the festive family meal served by mother, and the banter among me and my siblings were familiar rituals that marked the passage of years for as long as I could remember. Golem still watched over us on the shelf, a bit faded in the spot where I touched him on the way out the door each morning, but his protective powers remained unchallenged because here we were all together — plus three.

Our table was never spacious, and even though father built an extension that slid out from beneath when we needed to accommodate extra diners, we were shoulder to shoulder as the birthday celebration ended with pieces of honey cake.

"I wish you a sweet year, Leja," Ivan said. "You are my partner and my best friend, and . . ." He was interrupted by a squeal from Naftali, born six months after Ira's wedding and now, at eighteen months old, already had his father's explosion of dark curls, Katia's long eyelashes, and red-dimpled cheeks uniquely his own. He was educating us about what happens to honey cake when it is chewed, mixed with milk and left on exhibit in a toddler's open mouth.

He sat on Katia's lap, and she coaxed him to stop the show, covering his mouth with her hand, a look of amused exasperation on her face. "He has a mind of his own," she said.

"His father's son. That's for sure," Leja said. "Already the clown, but quite charming at the same time. Let me take him, Katia."

Leja lifted Naftali from his mother's lap and carried him to the front window. "You come with me, mister. Let your mama have a minute of peace."

Ira moved closer to his wife, placing a hand on her shoulder, rubbing gently. "Mama, papa, we have news," Ira said. "Naftali will soon have a little brother."

"Or sister," Katia interrupted, dropping one hand to the waist of her white and burgundy dress.

Mother quickly wiped her hands and came to the table, grabbing her son and Katia in a hug of sorts, her face between theirs. "Oh my God," she said. "This is wonderful news."

"Mazel tov," my father added.

I gave Ira a thumbs up and a nod of my head, and Ivan applauded quietly. "Bravo," Ivan said. "The world needs another of your beautiful babies." He turned to my father. "But this house will also need a bigger table."

"Leja," my mother called. "Did you hear their news?"

Leja had not heard. Instead, she and Naftali stared out the window at something in the street. The baby waved his hand, "Bye bye," he babbled. "Bye bye."

"Papa, Ira, you need to see this. Quickly," Leja said.

Ira was first to the window. "What are they doing here?" he said. Father came beside them. "Leja, take the baby away from the window," he said.

Ira opened the door, and I could hear men, a lot of them, speaking loudly in Polish. Ira stepped into the street and shouted. "Stop. What do you think you're doing?" The sound of glass breaking, wood cracking and louder shouts brought Ivan and me to the door. Father let Ivan pass to the outside, but he blocked my way. "Stay in here," he said.

Ira and Ivan stood amid a crowd of a dozen men, some dressed in police uniforms, others in ordinary clothes. Nicholas Goreki was with them, his arm raised and a wooden club in his hand. The door to the buchbinderi was open, and one of his men entered the workshop. When he turned, I saw the fish-hook scar on his cheek just, as I had the night we fought in the street steps from where we both now stood. "Look for the books," he shouted. "Take the books."

Ira and Ivan in the workshop doorway tried to block the others, spreading their arms across the broken entry. "Stop this," Ivan said. "I am Mayor Evanko's son. You must stop." And they did, unsure if they had the authority to ignore Ivan, until Nicholas Goreki extended his club and pushed Ivan and Ira aside. "It was *my* father who sent us, and we'll go in," Goreki said as he entered the buchbinderi. He stopped, looked directly at Ivan and with pointed sarcasm said: "But it was *your* father who gave up the Jews and told us where to come. I followed you and your girlfriend once and saw you taking packages from your house. When we found the books and papers there, your father was happy to tell us these people were the real troublemakers."

I heard boxes being overturned. Papers and books were thrown from the smashed windows. Finished copies of *The Radetzky March* littered the street.

"There's nothing here," the scar-faced man said as he left the workshop. "No O.U.N. papers. Nothing."

Goreki grabbed Ira by the shirt collar. "Where do you hide them?" he said. "We know you make them here."

"We've done nothing wrong," Ira protested, breaking free. "Why are you doing this?"

Father still blocked the doorway to our house preventing me from leaving. Now, Katia was at the door, as well, trying to get past him.

"Leave him alone," Katia called out. "Get your filthy hands off him."

Goreki turned to her and smiled. Ira trying to push past the policemen into the workshop, never saw Goreki's club as it landed across his head. I pushed father aside and ran out, with Katia just behind me. Ira lay on the ground, and we held him, blood on our hands and clothes.

Goreki looked down at us, his club raised. Ivan grabbed his arm, pulling him away. The scar-faced man said: "There's nothing inside. We can't arrest them."

Goreki shook his head still staring down at the floor, while Ivan held him away from us. "Arrest them for something else, then," he said. "For being Jewish filth, for wasting our time."

"Just get out of here," Ivan said. "You've done enough."

Goreki stepped closer to Katia and nudged her with his foot. "Maybe she wants to come along with me?" he said. Then pointing at Ira, "I don't think that one will be of any use to her for a while."

He laughed, smug and arrogant as he poked Katia again with the toe of his boot. But when she grabbed his ankle and flipped him hard onto the ground, the self-important smile transformed into confusion and shock.

Ivan tried to keep him on the ground, but Goreki, now with the strength of a wounded animal, pushed him off and kicked Katia hard in her unprotected belly. I leapt up, and, before Goreki saw me coming, tackled him to the ground. He landed hard, again, this time face first into the dirt and stones of the roadway.

"I will hurt you, you bastard. I'm going to kill you," I shouted, flailing at him until the scar-faced man pulled me away, pinning my arms behind me.

"Just be still if you know what's good for you," he whispered in my ear, his face touching mine just like the night he attacked me and father in the snow. I wondered if he remembered that night, because I surely did.

Goreki brushed the dirt and debris from his arms and scanned the scene with contempt: Katia and Ira injured on the ground; the scar-faced man restraining me; Polish policemen and the other men gathering around him; books and papers strewn on the street.

"We'll be watching you, all of you," he said. "And when we find proof, you'll be gone."

As he walked away from us, his finger came to his lips in the maddening gesture he used to lord his power over others, power that I knew to be precarious and the cloak of a coward. I locked eyes with him as he left, until he looked away.

CHAPTER 16

Ivan and I carried Ira into the house. His eyes were shut, blood caked thick in his hair and across his face. He lay limp in our arms.

"Put him here," my mother said, clearing the pillows and blankets from my father's bed beyond the kitchen. We placed him down gently. "Ivan, go bring the doctor. Quickly."

Father held Katia around the waist and helped her through the door. She was bent in pain. "Ira," she called. "Is he alive?"

"He's being cared for. The doctor is coming," my father said. "You need to sit."

Naftali cried loudly, thrashing in Leja's arms. She was trying to comfort him, but she also had me cornered trying to understand what had happened.

"Who did this?" she asked.

"They came for the O.U.N. books and to arrest you," I replied, angry, lashing out because there was no one else in the room I could blame. "Mayor Evanko sent them here."

"What? Evanko? That isn't possible," she said.

"Nicholas Goreki said so," I replied. "Said they found your books at Evanko's house, and he sent them here to save himself and Ivan."

"Nicholas Goreki did this?" Leja's face flushed. I could sense her confusion. This didn't make sense. Why had they not arrested her, she said. How could Mayor Evanko, who had helped her and Ivan, suddenly turn against her? Why had they beaten Ira and Katia?

Naftali became quiet, whimpering softly. "Mama," he was saying, over and over. "Mama." Katia called from across the room. "Bring him to me."

"Katia, are you alright," Leja asked. "What happened to you?"

As Naftali climbed on his mother's lap, arms around her neck, Katia grimaced. "My belly. He kicked me in the belly. It will be okay. How is Ira? There is so much blood."

Father and mother huddled around Ira. "Ira, my baby, can you hear me," my mother said, her face close to his. Father was holding a wet towel to Ira's wound. Leja and I stood quietly behind them. Across the room, Naftali lay his head on Katia's shoulder, his thumb in his mouth, silent. Mother's voice, despite being just a whisper, filled the room. "Ira, my baby boy. Ira." He opened his eyes. They were glassy, unfocused. "Mama," he murmured.

———————•◦•———————

I had no sense of time before Ivan returned with the doctor. Was it hours? Minutes? All of us froze in place. Naftali asleep in Katia's arms. Father, mother, Leja and I beside Ira, his eyes open for a moment and then closed. My family shared a space so small we could easily touch one another. My hand on father's shoulder. Father, one hand holding Ira's the other on mother's back. Leja squeezed my hand firmly, the other joined father's on mother's back. We all felt an unspoken fear and anger drifting from each of us into a single cloud of confusion.

The doctor moved us away and examined Ira's wound. He washed it and poured alcohol on it. Ira did not move. I watched with my parents as the blood was cleaned away, and I saw white bone breaking the skin where the club had struck him. Nausea crept up my chest, and I ran out the door, without reaching up to touch the Golem, who seemed powerless this evening to protect us, breathing the warm evening air deeply, inhale and exhale, in and out.

Leja and Ivan were in the street collecting the books and papers strewn about during the attack on the buchbinderi.

Leja: "Why did your father tell them?"

Ivan: "Maybe he didn't? Maybe Goreki was lying? It wouldn't be the first time."

Leja: "How else would they know?"

Ivan: "Maybe they saw me carry packages from here."

Leja: "Oh my God. Did you know they were coming?"

Ivan: "No. No."

Leja: "Did your father tell you they were coming?"

Ivan: "No. If father said anything to the Polish police he didn't tell me."

Leja: "If you are lying to me now, Ivan, I could never forgive you."

Ivan: "I didn't know. I swear. I tried to stop them, to help your brothers and Katia."

Leja: "Your father. Why did he do this?"

Leja, her arms full of dirty and torn books, began to cry, softly at first and then without control. Unable to stop sobbing and gasping for air, her hands shaking, she dropped the books. Ivan froze beside her, just watching her cry and tremble. So, I took her in my arms, held her, told her she would be fine, that everything would be alright, just as she had told me countless times.

As the doctor prepared to leave later that evening, he was grim-faced. I recognized him and his bleak manner as Dr. Levy from the synagogue, where he was among the elders who expected strict adherence to the rules of Jewish Orthodoxy. Mostly, they were men who believed they could protect themselves and their community by embracing ancient traditions and rejecting modern science and ideas. Dr. Levy, while an enthusiastic man of prayer, was also a well-trained man of medicine, having studied in Kiev, the Ukrainian capital, and perfected his techniques as a surgeon in the bloody battles of the eastern front. My father said the doctor saved his leg and maybe his life during that war, and they had maintained a warm friendship in the years since.

Ira's head was wrapped in thick gauze bandages that already showed spots of blood. His eyes open, he watched father beside and the doctor. "Keep him still and quiet. No talking," the doctor said. "We'll know tomorrow how serious this is. But you need to be prepared. He is badly hurt."

As he spoke, he looked at Katia seated in the corner of the room, Naftali curled in her lap, her face ashen, not listening. Her eyes were slits, her face sweaty.

"Young lady," the doctor said to her. "Do you understand what I said about your husband?"

Katia did not hear him. Dr. Levy, anticipating what was

about to happen, rushed to her just as she and Naftali began sliding from the chair to the ground. The doctor eased her down and lifted Naftali, still sleeping, into Leja's arms. "Help me," the doctor said to me and Ivan. We carried Katia to a bed near Ira. She was limp, her skin hot. There was a spot of blood on her dress below the waist.

"Mrs. come help me," the doctor said to mother. "Everyone else, please, get away."

Chapter 17

Katia's baby died. That's what my mother said to my father the next day. It's what Leja told Ivan, and it's what Katia told me. I heard the others talking in whispers as if there was a need to keep this from the rest of us — Ira, who lay unconscious, Naftali too young to understand, and me. So, I told Katia what the others were saying and asked if it was true. She looked at me with a questioning gaze of her own as if considering this for the first time. Naftali slept, wrapped in the warm curve of her body. She stroked his curls and kissed his cheek. "This is my only baby now," she said. "And he is fine."

But Katia was not. Even when her health later improved and strength returned, part of her seemed missing. An edgy alertness replaced her peacefulness. Her confidence became a constant wariness. Naftali was never far from her watchful gaze. "Mama, no," Naftali argued when she'd pick him up if a sound outside startled her. She'd hold him tightly, not saying a word, while he thrashed in her arms trying to escape, kicking his legs. "No, mama. No."

Her pale skin, her greasy hair pushed away from her face with pins, and the plain grey dress she wore day after day stained with spots of food. This was not the woman who always took pride in her appearance, who brushed and carefully tied her hair behind her ears in a tight ponytail or left it to fall casually across her face.

While Ira slept during the day, she and Naftali gathered flowers from the surrounding fields and woods. They'd return with armfuls of trillium and Lenten roses, anemones and blue hyacinth, bundles of yellow and orange, blue and white. Katia prepared poultices with the flowers, placing them on Ira's wound, and made teas that she drank with him in the evening when he had enough energy to sit up in his bed with Naftali between them.

I saw her once in the woods near the cemetery digging in a bed of wildflowers at the edge of a fence, gathering blooms, I thought, for an herbal cure. Naftali waddled around her on unsteady legs, falling then standing, laughing then howling with delight at some miracle of life that he'd just seen or heard for the first time. A butterfly in flight. A ray of sunshine through the trees. A cloud. The call of a blackbird overhead, sad and wise. The smell of a spring afternoon in the wet forest.

Katia talked to him, a non-stop banter, at least that's what I thought at first. I stood behind her, close enough that I expected her to turn and acknowledge me, but it was Naftali who saw me first. "Woe woe," he called and ran to me holding a delicate sprig of bluebells he'd plucked from the ground. That was his name for me, which he said like the sound of a train whistle extending the second syllable until his breath faded. "Boudah, boudah," he called loudly, what I knew to be his word for flower. I lifted him, and snuggled my face into his neck.

"You will always be here nourishing the flowers in the spring, sending leaves to the trees," Katia said, still without acknowledging me. "This place will be yours, even though you will never walk on this ground."

She held a small piece of cloth cut from the patterned white and burgundy dress she wore the night she was injured. It had a blood stain. She tore it in two and placed one half in a small hole, covering it with dirt and flower petals. "This part of you will lie here in peace, and another will avenge your death." She clutched the other half in her hand, stood and greeted me with a gentle touch to my cheek.

Two weeks after the attack, Dr. Levy gave Ira a hopeful prognosis. He was healing well, the doctor said, fortunate that Nicholas' blow had struck the hardest part of his skull. Hard heads, he said with his hand on my father's shoulder, ran in the family. The fractured bone would heal, a scar would decorate the skin above his right ear, he might walk with a slight limp in his left leg, mirroring father's gait, but after a few more weeks of rest the worst lingering symptom would be a desire for revenge.

"That I can't treat," the doctor said. "To be a Jew in this place means to live with this affliction and keep it from becoming a tragedy for your family." The need for revenge, he said, is a contagious disease, and we can't allow our enemies, men like Nicholas Goreki and his father, to become infected with it.

I thought about his words, his prediction that a tragedy might befall our family. How much closer to tragedy could we come than the attack on Ira and Katia? Wasn't the loss of her child tragic? The damage to the buchbinderi? Who would stop the Gorekis and their men from committing worse crimes against us, crimes not inspired by vengeance, but by evil and a hatred passed from father to son for countless generations? I remembered my own father's advice, heard his voice in my head, "Go along with them. Keep yourself safe. That is the smart thing to do. But a moment always comes when you can't do that any longer, when the shame and frustration rise from your heart like the morning fog on the river. You can't stop it. It surrounds you and you can no longer see clearly enough to make a *safe* choice. When that happens, you must make *another* choice."

Was this one of those times?

Katia stalked the room as the doctor spoke, examining imagined threats and circling Ira's bed, Naftali in her arms. She stopped beside me and said, "You were right about what you said that night. We need to kill him."

CHAPTER 18

Katia and I were not the only ones unwilling to follow the doctor's advice. Mother and Leja each had a plan to avenge our family. Their unique efforts emerged slowly and separately over the coming weeks and culminated in a cataclysm of violence that, while I didn't understand it at the time, would be the inevitable explosion that would scatter my family into an uncertain future.

I threatened Nicholas in an emotional moment, and I was surprised that my anger, uncharacteristically, had not ebbed as the weeks passed. It remained a stubborn resident, a demon, that, while mostly inconspicuous, always lurked in a dark corner. After Ira, Katia and Naftali left our house to return home, mother would send me to them with bundles of bread, fruit and meat. When I walked the quiet evening streets through the narrow pathways to the surrounding farms, alone with my thoughts for the only time during the day, the demon emerged. My fists clenched as I walked. I mumbled threats and played out bloody confrontations, throwing my fists at an imaginary enemy in the shadows.

The route took me past the road to the Gorekis' sprawling farm. From where I walked, I could see their large house lit with kerosene lamps, and the barns, storage buildings, fenced pastures and the planted fields stretching into the fading orange dusk. Their possessions were vast. They had so much of everything, and seeing it all nourished my anger, but also restrained it. I wasn't sure I could ever resolve this conflict between bravado and reluctance. As it turned out, when I was forced to choose, bravado had its day.

One evening, I saw Katia and Naftali walking from the Goreki house, their backs toward the road, tossing flowers from a basket. Naftali saw me first, shouting my name with great enthusiasm. "Woe woe," he said, pointing toward me on the road. "Woe woe, boudah." Katia looked back without acknowledging me before resuming her task.

"Flowers?" I asked, when she met me at the road.

My question hung unanswered as she poured the remaining contents of the basket, hundreds of acorns crushed into small pieces, to form a triangle pointing back at the Goreki home.

"The flowers are dried hyacinth," she said. "They will bring pain to whomever walks on them. The broken acorns will bring fire and bad fortune."

She took the bundle of food from my arms, turned and walked away with Naftali. It seemed as if, to her, I had never been there.

A few days later, my mother revealed her plot for revenge, when she accompanied me on my evening delivery of food to Ira and Katia. She walked quickly and silently beside me, setting a pace that I struggled to match. She was a head shorter than me, but was walking as if downhill, fast, leaning into her steps. Her hair was tied uncharacteristically back in a tight bun, a colorful kerchief covering the side of her face and her ears, not a strand of hair loose or visible. She carried a box the size of her hand fashioned from small sticks, the bark carefully peeled from each to reveal the green of new wood. The sticks were bound with knotted strings, leaving the contents of the box visible between the slats of the lid. In the box was a small piece of Katia's blood-stained dress, the piece remaining after Katia's cemetery ritual.

"Mama, why are we rushing?" I asked.

"Before the sun sets I must leave them this gift," she answered, emphasizing her last word with sarcasm. "The dybbuk cannot be freed except in the day's fading light."

I knew mother's superstitions, her belief in things strange and useful that helped explain inexplicable turns of human existence. She usually kept details of these to herself, content to weave superstition subtly into daily life. The way she spit three times when she saw an injured or sick bird in the woods, pulled her ear when she sneezed, the salt she left in small packets in the corners of our house and sometimes in the pockets of our coats, and the quiet tap of her knuckles against our wooden table were all designed, according to father, to ward off evil in various forms that might slip past the watchful gaze of Golem.

I never made light of mother's beliefs the way Leja and Ira did, and the idea of a protective Golem and all of mother's rituals comforted me. Yet, whenever she talked about dybbuks, spirits of the dead that invaded living souls to torment them, it frightened me. The box my mother was carrying contained what she believed held the spirit of a dead soul. She walked down the path to Goreki's house alone, careful to avoid stepping on Katia's dried and crumbled flowers. She placed the box outside the front door and opened the lid. The door swung open, and Igor Goreki looked with puzzlement at mother, who stood straight, staring into the eyes of the taller man, but pointing down.

"That is the blood of the child your son killed. My son's child. My grandchild. It is the blood of an innocent soul," she said. "And that soul will infect the evil people in this house and drive them mad."

Goreki stood speechless for a moment, his gaze moving from the small, fierce woman on his doorstep and the gift she had placed at his feet.

"Get away from me you witch," he finally shouted. "And take that, that thing away with you."

Wordlessly, mother walked off, leaving Goreki awkwardly considering the box. When she reached me by the road, she smiled in triumph. He hadn't moved and still stared down trying to understand what had been placed at his feet.

CHAPTER 19

Leja was shouting again, at father this time. She had earlier changed from the simple dress she wore each day into a pair of rough men's trousers, a crude belt and one of my work shirts. With her hair pulled back and away from her face, in the dim light of our house she could easily have been mistaken for a younger version of me. Leja had just shared her plans with us, and father was imploring, "Don't do this."

A raid on Goreki's farm and the farms of other wealthy Poles was planned for that night, she said. Dozens of O.U.N. supporters would destroy crops, burn barns and storage buildings. The past acts of vandalism were mere warnings. "This time we will hurt them for what they did to us," she shouted at father. Ivan and the others were already in the woods, waiting, she said. I didn't need to ask her where.

Minutes before, mother told her about the dybbuk, that everything would be made right, that the spirits would exact revenge on the Gorekis, and she did not need to intercede. Leja shouted back: "They are guilty of more than hurting Ira and Katia, mama. They have the power and the money, and they will keep taking from us and doing as they please unless we fight back."

I walked to the door, opened it, touched Golem and turned back to Leja. "You coming?" I asked.

"What are you doing, Wolchi? You're staying here with mama and papa," she said.

"Not a chance," I answered. "And, don't start yelling at me, too."

For as long as I could remember, Leja had watched over me, and I was comfortable deferring to her judgment. Don't walk on the street close to the tavern alone, she'd warn. Or, don't be in the woods by the river after dark. Or, don't tell the men working on the railroad that you are Jewish, because you don't look Jewish. She knew what was best for me, I assumed. I never doubted that and never questioned her. Even more than my parents, I trusted her to understand when danger was hidden in the shadows. On the night of the O.U.N. raid, I saw that danger clearly, and would not be dissuaded from confronting it.

"I mean it," she said. "Stay home. I'm not taking you."

"I don't need you to take me. I'm going," I said.

She looked at me as if for the first time, half a head taller, muscled up from my work at the machine shop, not a younger brother that needed protection, but a young man whom she might rely on to protect her.

"When did you go and grow up on me?" she asked. "That doesn't mean I won't worry about you. You can't come along unless you're careful. Don't be a hero, alright? Promise me."

I didn't need to answer, because what could I say? Neither of us knew what we were walking into, whom we would encounter, how we would respond if we faced real danger. All I wanted to do was let loose that demon I had been hiding, to give in to the powerful anger and frustration I'd felt since I saw my brother in a pool of his own blood, his wife injured beside him. That anger had built inside me since I was younger, bit by bit, each time I turned away from a confrontation because I was outnumbered or didn't respond to belittling words from a teacher threatening me with a wooden ruler. I wasn't young anymore, though, and I understood that what was about to happen would be no minor skirmish, no street fight with bullies ending with a bloody nose and hollow taunts.

"Take care of your sister," father called as Leja and I walked away. His words were familiar, but the object of the sentence had always been *brother,* and he had been speaking to Leja. When I looked at him, he offered a barely visible smile, while mother gripped his arm. At least I thought he smiled. He seemed tired, and maybe that smile was just a fragile expression of the fear he surely felt as his daughter and son went into the dangerous night.

Leja and I walked in silence, entered the woods and traveled along the river toward Big Rocks. It was a moonless night, quiet but for the rush of the river and the hoot of a nearby Ural Owl hunting, as would we, for prey in the dark. When we saw light from torches and kerosene lamps in the deeper woods, Leja took my hand, stopped, then took the other.

"You don't have to do this," she said.

"I'm staying with you, Leja."

"You don't have to do this, Wolchi. I'll see you tomorrow at home."

"I'd rather stay here and help you make tomorrow the best day we've ever known," I answered.

She laughed, shook her head and, still holding one of my hands, ran toward the lights in the forest.

CHAPTER 20

I expected them all to be young, these partisan soldiers, but they weren't. I recognized some of them, old farmers from outside of town, their beards gone grey and their shoulders stooped. There was no mistaking them as the men mother had bought potatoes and carrots from in the market before the Polish government had seized their farms and transformed their lives. I would see them over the years on their way to church, but they had mostly vanished after their livelihoods were stolen, left with just enough land to feed their families and the need to work that land hard, because the threat of hunger and disease was always just one cold winter away. Here they were, dozens of them leaning against the tall rocks, smoking, talking quietly, greeting one another like old friends gathered finally for a long-delayed reunion. Their sons were with them, older boys I remembered from school as lumbering, but honest companions to Ira during impromptu soccer matches. They stood among their fathers and uncles, impatient, but festive, shuffling from foot to foot, scanning the dark forest. They held lamps, axes, hand scythes with carved wooden handles, and large metal containers filled with kerosene.

Ivan stood atop the tallest boulder, pointing a long gun to the sky, arms raised, like a wolf silently howling into the moonless night. Leja, a handgun tucked into her belt, distributed rifles and other weapons from their hiding place in a crevice beneath the boulder. She motioned to me and tossed down an axe handle. "In case you meet anyone you'd like to smack across the head," she said.

The crowd at Big Rocks grew through the night, and hundreds of armed men had gathered by the time groups began leaving in different directions. Ivan led some men south, back toward the river away from town. "You stay with me," Leja said as she started west, I was certain, to Goreki's farm. The mood was nothing like the one several years ago when I'd joined Leja and Ivan in that heady night of mock revolt and celebration when we vandalized farm fields and chanted partisan slogans. The men following Leja walked in a single line without speaking. Each of them, I thought, had his own demon ready to be released. I was between two men as old as my father. The last war had left them scarred, but hardened for what the evening might bring.

"What's your name, boy? one asked.

I told him, and he said: "Wolchick, you will tell your children about this night many years from now. And when you do, tell them about the old men like us who stood with you. Don't forget us."

The rifle shot echoed through the woods before I could answer. Then another and another. It was not clear from which direction they came, and the men fell to the ground, searching the trees. More shots, that clearly came from behind us in the direction Ivan had gone. From the front of our line, Leja called back for us to move. And we did, faster than before, running noisily toward the forest edge.

At the tree line, the farm fields opened ahead of us, acre after acre of late spring wheat, alfalfa and oats. The men went in every direction. Some poured kerosene on the crops near me, and I felt the rush of heat when the fuel ignited and the ground burst into orange flames. Goreki's house and barns were just half a kilometer ahead, maybe closer, and Leja headed toward them. I followed.

I thought this must be what war would feel like, that probably this was a war. Father had told me that nations resorted to guns and armies to settle disputes because their powerful leaders could remain safe, far from the battles, while the sons of powerless men were sent to die fighting other powerless men who were not truly their enemies. War, he said, was entertainment for cowards who wore crowns. If those men had to fight, there would be no more wars. His stories were always about those who fought, not about the battles. I was thinking as I ran toward Goreki's home that father had never told me how he'd been wounded, what it felt like to be injured and to bleed lying on the ground not knowing if that moment would be the end. When he told that story it was about the bravery of fellow soldiers who carried him to safety, the skill of the doctor who saved him and the kindness of a Red Cross nurse, dressed inexplicably in a spotless white dress amid the blood and dirt of the hospital, who wiped his face with a cool cloth during his nights of feverish dreams.

This moment felt different for me, more personal. I knew the enemy. I'd seen his face. He was not like me. He could never be my friend. When I smashed a window near the front door of Goreki's house, I saw that face in my mind, sharp and clear as if it were staring back at me. When one of our men poured kerosene through the broken window and another lit the fuel with a burning torch, the floor inside erupted, and I shouted at that face. "You bastard."

Then, there they were, Igor Goreki and Nicholas, inside the house beating on the flames with blankets. Through the window I saw Igor Goreki's wife and daughter, looks of terror on their faces. One shouted. "Jesus, dear Jesus, we're going to die." Were these also faces of the enemy? Should I help them?

Leja pulled me away toward the barn, where our men were releasing horses and livestock into the fields, where fences had been cut and broken. The animals ran from the flames toward the road and the forest. She led me to a carriage house behind the barn, swung open the tall door and handed me the axe in her hand and a lantern. "All yours," she said. Inside was the ostentatious carriage the Gorekis rode to church and anytime they needed to flaunt wealth and power. I recalled Igor and Nicholas Goreki like roosters perched in the front and the arrogance of the women riding in the back, never acknowledging the men and women stepping aside to let their carriage pass.

My first swing of the axe across the wooden spokes of a wheel dropped the carriage to the ground. This object so grand was also so fragile. The brass ornamentation on the doors rang against the axe blade and bent beneath its force. Blow after blow splintered the wooden floor, separating it from the iron frame and axle. The leather of the seats tore, and the bits of wool batting beneath floated like dandelion seeds through the room.

My arms grew heavy. Sweat ran down my face. I heard gunfire outside, three shots, pop-pop-pop, and when I dropped the axe to wipe my eyes I spotted a shadow at the door and the barrel of a rifle. Boots came through the door first, then the legs of a man and the face of my enemy.

Nicholas Goreki seemed as surprised as I was as he stood

framed by the arch of the open door, the light of the single kerosene lamp orange on the skin of his soot-marked face. I reached for the axe on the ground and leaped behind a pile of broken wood and steel from the carriage, knocking over the kerosene lamp. A bullet struck the ground behind me.

"Get out here or I'll shoot you," Nicholas Goreki shouted. "Out from there, or you're dead."

The straw on the dirt floor burned, a fast-spreading flame that danced from stalk to stalk toward my cover. Another shot, this one ringing against the iron carriage frame, startled me with its proximity. The amplified sound of it hitting the iron snapped my head up, and I saw Nicholas Goreki, motionless just inside the door, pointing a rifle at my head.

"Come on. Come on," he yelled. "Or I shoot you."

I remembered the shots I heard outside just a few moments before. Three of them. Had he shot Leja? Was she just outside the door needing help, dying? My father had told me that courage was something all of us had locked inside of us, something that would break free in a moment we wouldn't choose and in a way we couldn't control. This was my moment. I stood and ran toward Nicholas Goreki, a wild man emerging from the flames wielding an axe. Before I could reach him, there was a gunshot and then another, both close, but not from Nicholas' gun. His eyes went wide and he stumbled toward me, dropped the rifle and grabbed my shoulders to stay on his feet. The back of his head was covered with blood, so much blood that it was impossible to tell where it came from. It stained my shirt and arms. I pushed him away, and he fell to the ground hard, as if he'd been dropped from the sky. I kneeled over him, breathing hard, trying to slow the cacophony of the heartbeat pounding in my ears. I took his rifle and studied his face, turned to the side awkwardly, his eyes open, one hand near his mouth. Despite the smoke filling the carriage house, I sat for a long while to be sure there was no breath, no movement of an eyelid, nothing but his dead hand now unable to touch an index finger to silent lips.

Loud shouts outside caught my attention. "Stop. You are under arrest. Don't move," a man's voice demanded. I stepped out of the smoky carriage house and saw the Polish police, dozens of them, chasing O.U.N. members through the fields. Leja was on the ground just steps from me, a policeman's knee on her back, her handgun beside her. "Don't move," he shouted again. By the time he saw me approaching from the back, it was too late to stop or deflect the blow from Nicholas's rifle as I swung it like a club and knocked the officer off my sister, my father's words echoing in my ears. "Take care of your sister."

I pulled Leja to her feet, and we ran through the smoldering fields. When we reached a dense spot in the forest we stopped, out of breath, and she asked. "Is he dead?"

I was slow to answer. "Nicholas Goreki. He had a rifle, so . . . did I kill him?" she asked again. "I had to shoot or he would have shot you."

Since the attack on our family, Leja's anger had intensified toward the men she viewed as oppressors, and her rhetoric had grown more intense. Her true passion was words and ideas, and she would have been content to limit her revolutionary zeal to authoring books and speeches. That was not to be, though, because the violence of others unleashed a fierceness in her that was unapologetically deadly. Three years before, she ended a street fight with a coal bucket wielded as a weapon, and now she'd put two bullets into Nicholas Goreki's skull.

I nodded. "He's dead," I said. "I had imagined him that way so many times that I wasn't sure at first if what I saw was real. There he was, bleeding, lying in the dirt, and I didn't know what to feel. I wasn't happy. Not frightened. I didn't think to help him. I just stared at his face until I was sure he was gone. And then I thought, it was a good thing."

Our men ran into the forest to escape the police, who did not follow them, maybe because they feared an ambush in the darkness or because there was a limit to their courage and commitment to defend the status quo. As the fleeing figures became more distant, they shouted for the men to stop and surrender, before turning away from the forest to stand and watch flames engulf Goreki's farm.

"Thank you," Leja whispered after a long silence.

"For what," I asked.

"For not getting yourself killed. For getting me free from that policeman. For taking care of me and being here right now while I come to terms with what I've done," she said.

"You did what was right," I answered. "Don't think otherwise. You did what's right. You took care of me, you helped me, the way you always have."

"That's what we do now, it seems," she said. "We take care of each other."

After the forest became quiet, we made our way carefully toward home, listening for police on the road. They would surely come looking for us and the others, and when they did we needed to be at home where, when the knock on the door came, we could say, "Officer, we've been here all evening."

CHAPTER 21

When that knock did come the following morning and father opened the door, it wasn't a policeman on the other side. Instead, Mayor Evanko stood expectantly, looking haggard, beaten down, so much older than I'd remembered him from just a few months before. Father did not greet him.

"Can I come inside, Marcus? Please," Evanko asked.

When he entered and the door closed, he looked at me and Leja. "Thank God you are here," he said to us. "Thank God."

Leja's response was sharp. "You shouldn't be here. After what you did, you shouldn't be in our house."

Evanko had a questioning look on his face. Just a few weeks had passed since his information led the police to us, but he seemed unaware. "You sent the police here. They almost killed Ira and Katia." He nodded his head.

"I'm sorry. It was the only way I could protect Ivan," Evanko said. Then he paused. "And now look."

He started to cry. Deep sobs, erratic breaths. He dropped his hands to his knees as he struggled to remain standing. My father led him to a chair and sat beside him. "What is this?" father asked. "Why are you here?"

Evanko did not answer for a long moment, his emotions overwhelming him. "Last night," he began, "last night there was trouble." He looked at Leja, then me. "You know there was trouble."

"Are you alright, Grygoriy?" father asked, his tone softer, his hand on Evanko's shoulder soft like the touch of a friend. The animus of the past three years was gone, replaced by an unspoken intimacy between two men who shared war and now struggled with the fear of all fathers whose children had grown and left their protective embrace. Mother entered the room and stood beside the men.

Evanko shook his head, closed his eyes and covered them with his hand. It was shaking.

"Ivan," he said. "It's Ivan. He was killed, Marcus. Shot by police on the road to the Polish farms. They brought him to me this morning."

Leja gasped. So much death.

"Much of Goreki's farm was destroyed before the police got there," Evanko continued. "Someone shot Nicholas Goreki. He is dead, too. That's why I'm here."

Evanko pointed at me. "The police are coming for Wolchi. They heard him threaten Nicholas, and one saw him in the place where Nicholas was shot. They say he attacked a policeman to escape. They are coming for him, Marcus."

"Papa, no," Leja said. "I'm responsible. I saw Nicholas with a rifle. I followed and heard him threaten Wolchi. I saw him raise his rifle."

"Leja, stop," I shouted. "Papa, I killed Nicholas."

Father tried to make sense of all this. Ivan's death. Destruction at Goreki's farm. Nicholas' death. Police suspicions that I had killed him. Leja's near confession. My confession.

Mother ended an awkward quiet when she said to father, "They have to get away from here. They need to leave." Father nodded, newly energized, and pointed at us.

"Go pack clothes, your things," father said to me and Leja. "Quickly."

Father peered through the front window, looking down both ends of the street while Leja and I placed our clothes into two crude rucksacks. Mother added bundles of food.

"Leja and Wolchi, come with me," father said when we finished and stood beside him. "Grygoriy, stay here with Clara. When the police come, tell them you couldn't find me, that Wolchi and Leja may also be dead or wounded and that I went to the forest to look for them."

Father walked into the street searching left and right for police or others who might see us. The streets were empty, and he motioned for us to follow. I touched Golem as I left the house, and mother sobbed in the doorway, as father led us into the darkened buchbinderi, still in disarray from the attack several weeks before.

"You stay here. Quiet. I will come for you," he said.

Leja and I waited, seated on the ground farthest from the door. In the quiet, I held her hand, breathing in rhythm with her, the smell of paper and machine oil surrounding us. Dust floated in the light from a broken window, and that light was enough to see the outlines of her face watching the door.

"What do you think will happen to us? What should we do?" she asked with uncharacteristic uncertainty. I usually asked questions. She usually had answers.

"Papa will tell us what to do," I said. " Do you remember the story he likes to tell about the English man who owned a stable and would give his customers only one choice of a horse?"

"Yes, he called it a Hobson's choice, take the horse nearest the stable door or none," Leja said.

"I think Papa has made a choice for us," I said. "And it's our Hobson's choice."

Leja laughed softly. She knew as well as I that father was a man who planned for change. Jews, he often said, had better be ready to pack up and leave because there is usually no warning before the Cossacks come. An escape plan for his family was something he'd contemplated and now initiated.

The sound of men on horses outside abruptly ended our discussion. There was a loud knock at the door to our house, and we heard mother and Mayor Evanko speaking with the Polish police officers, following father's script. The buchbinderi door swung open, and a uniformed policeman looked into the room, bright afternoon light filling the darkness. The mounted police waited outside, their horses snorting, neighing, eager to move. I held my breath, and Leja squeezed my hand. The policeman took a tentative step into the room, but just one, before his commander shouted orders from outside, and he hurried away without closing the door. The police rode off, and a few moments later mother gently closed the buchbinderi door.

CHAPTER 22

Hours passed, and we marked them by watching shadows from the west-facing window move across the room. Mother had stuffed our sacks with cheese wrapped in cloth, chunks of salami, cake and hard pieces of black bread. We marveled that she was able to prepare this feast so quickly. We ate, talked and waited. Leja wondered about Ira, Katia and Naftali. What would become of them? And what about mama and papa, I asked? Would we all need to flee?

"None of them has done anything wrong," I said. "But they might be held to account because of what we did."

"Because of what I did," Leja said. "I killed a man. They won't let me escape from punishment. I know we're in this situation because of me. I shot him."

"No one but you and I will ever know that," I said. "The police believe I shot him, so let them believe what they want."

It seemed Leja was considering for the first time what she'd done and what I was asking her to do now. "Thou shall not kill. Thou shall not lie. I guess I can add those to my list of sins." She sounded glib, trying to appear light-hearted, but the weight of Nicholas Gorek's death was on her now.

"You're right," I said. "We wouldn't be in this mess if you hadn't shot him. Instead, I would be in a hole in the cemetery and you would be standing over my body, saying goodbye."

"But still," she said. "I'm sorry. You didn't need to be with us last night. I shouldn't have let you come."

"Wasn't your choice," I answered. "I decided to be with you. Now, we're hiding in a dark room together, and neither of us has many choices left."

The questions about what would happen next swirled through my mind. I asked Leja about Mayor Evanko. Would Ivan's death make him vengeful toward us, or would he help protect our family, the way he had in the past?

"I think he blames me for giving Ivan ideas about revolution and freedom," Leja said. "Poor, poor Ivan. Am I responsible for him, too?"

I didn't care about Ivan, and I said so to her. His relationship with Leja and the rest of us had always felt off to me, sometimes genuine and sometimes transactional. And now, Leja's teary doubts and her rush to take responsibility for what others brought upon themselves was self-indulgent, not useful. I said that to her, too.

"The Poles in the town, especially Goreki, will want a pogrom," I said. "There will be no preventing it this time. Every Jew will suffer. Mama and Papa. Ira, Katia and the baby. I am scared for them."

Leja shook her head. "Ukrainians will not join them," she said. "They were with us burning the farm fields. Mayor Evanko will not join them. They will all keep fighting. They may turn against Jews another time, but they won't help Goreki now."

It was close to dusk when we heard the clatter of horse hooves again and the wheels of a wagon. The buchbinderi door opened, and father called for us.

"Time to go, you two," he said.

"Where, Papa?" Leja asked, as he stopped us at the door and scanned the street to insure no one watched.

"Listen to me carefully," he said. "You are going to Krakow, just the two of you. It is close enough that you can travel there quickly before the police begin to search, but far enough and a city big enough that Goreki and his men cannot easily find you once you are there. Mr. Koperski will help get you to safety. My friend Michel will help you once you arrive. He and I made this plan long ago, because I've told you that a Jew needs to be ready to leave. Michel doesn't know you are coming, but he is always in some sense expecting us, so he will welcome you and care for you."

He pointed toward the wagon. Seated on the driver's bench, Mr. Koperski sat stiffly staring at the two horses on the other end of his reins, not turning to watch father help us into the rear cargo bed of the four-wheeled wagon. Crates of machine parts were stacked three-deep on the floor, and we sat between them, hidden. *Koperski Mashyna* was handwritten on the top of each crate, and *PKP Krakow* was stamped on the sides. The boxes, filled with the metal parts Mr. Koperski and I made in past days, were headed to the railroad yard in Krakow, as were we.

Father handed us each a small sack filled with Polish currency and coins. "Stay hidden until you are far from here. Tell no one but Michel what has happened." He looked directly at Leja. "Do you understand what I am saying?" She nodded. He looked to me. I nodded, as well.

"People will ask you where you're from and who you are. If it's a Jew who asks, shrug your shoulders and say you are a Jew who has no home; if you are asked by a Pole, proudly say you are a peasant from Eastern Poland in Krakow for work.

If anyone asks more than that, Wolchi, just say you are a machinist; Leja, you are a teacher. Nothing more."

He leaned into the cart and kissed us warmly on our foreheads. "We will be together again, my dearest Leja and Wolchi," he said. "But, now, it's time for you to go. Be safe."

He draped a canvas sheet over the top of the crates, securing its corners to the cart, and signaled Mr. Koperski with a tap on the wagon's wooden side that it was time to leave. For the next hour, we bumped slowly over the rough roads from our house to the rail station. Koperski would greet passersby on the street, never speaking to us directly.

Leja had hold of my hand again, her left and my right, as we sat facing one another in the faint light beneath the canvas cover. With her free hand, she tapped my knuckles. One, two, three, four, five, her lips mouthed the words silently. One, two, three, four, five. She was recalling a game we'd played as children. Maybe I was three years old, Leja six. She would touch each of my knuckles and have me count with her. "One, two, three, four, five little fingers," we'd say together. Then she would touch my ears and move her face close "One, two little ears," she'd whisper, before putting her finger gently on my nose, which would elicit a triumphant shout from us both "and one Wolchi nose." This was how she taught me to count.

Her fingers trembled as she touched each of my knuckles over and over again, as if my hand were a talisman that would protect her from the men pursuing us and the dark thoughts in her head. This was a tell for me, when her hands shook. Others saw her as all bravado and confidence, but I watched her hands to know the truth. When we learned of our mother's unfaithfulness, Leja was stoic. Her hands told a different story, one I chose to ignore because I needed her strength.

After Evanko's betrayal and the police raid that left Ira and Katia injured, she was the one in need, her hands clenched, shaking. And I held her. Now, I grabbed her hand again, our fingers interwoven. "I'm not letting go," I whispered, and she rested her head on my shoulder.

"I didn't mean to kill him," she said.

The wagon slowed, and I could hear the click-clack of train wheels and the pounding of a diesel engine, at first distant and then loud and close as a train arrived in the station. The wagon stopped near the tracks, and it took a few minutes for the horses to settle, snorting and stepping ahead, then back. Mr. Koperski left us briefly and returned with other men, who helped load the wagon, horses and all, up a ramp onto a railcar. One of the men shouted up to Mr. Koperski, "Ten hours today to Krakow." A door on the car rolled closed, the metal ramp dropped loudly onto the ground, and the train inched forward.

Once we were traveling fast, one corner of the canvas cover was lifted, and Mr. Koperski motioned for us to leave the wagon. The railcar, though closed on all sides, had no roof, and when I stepped out of the wagon the rush of evening air felt like I'd leapt into the cold water of an unfamiliar river. I'd never been on a train, and noticed that Leja was looking around, her hair loose and caught in the wind, with the same sense of wonder.

"It's okay. You won't blow away," Mr. Koperski said with a faint smile and a deadpan humor belying his usual serious manner. He pointed to a bucket in the corner past the horses. "For us when we need to," he said. "The horses will not use the bucket, so watch where you step."

He reached into the wagon, searching beneath the crates,

and retrieved a familiar wooden box. He handed me my tap and die set. "You will need these in Krakow at the PKP machine shop," he said.

I opened the box and ran my fingers over the tools, a habit I'd developed for checking whether any had been misplaced or come loose from the carved compartments that held them. At least that's what I said to Mr. Koperski when he asked about my routine. I knew, though, that the habitual touching of this gift from father was about more. These were the tools that defined me in a world where factories and machines had replaced the farm and the plow. Those small taps and dies were evidence of my skill and readiness for what was ahead. I fixed what was broken. I explored what was mysterious, and I tried to make sense of my life with my hands. Touching the Golem by our door at home as often as I had, thousands of times surely, was how I connected to the past and mother's beliefs. The wooden box of tools linked me to the future and what my father believed. I thought about him as I placed the box carefully into my rucksack and wondered whether this journey would show me the wisdom of his convictions or the simple truth of mother's faith.

"Come, you two. I have bread and cold soup for supper," he said. "We have a long trip."

The three of us sat in the far corner of the railcar, away from the horses and out of the wind, sharing food and the journey. Mr. Koperski was especially fond of mother's strawberry cake and was delighted to see Leja unwrap a large piece. He stared at it with unsubtle craving, and Leja noticed.

"This is my favorite, too," she said, handing him a piece.

She hadn't previously met Mr. Koperski, and I could tell she was eager to know more about him. As they shared the cake, she deluged him with questions designed to extract facts about his life. None of her inquiries required more than a brief nod or a single-word response, and Mr. Koperski seemed to enjoy the casual exchange, happy to oblige her curiosity. With no challenging questions, the mood was light and friendly, until she asked something I'd been wondering myself. "Why are you helping us?"

He leaned against the metal side of the railcar, the movement of the train shaking his upper body. He wiped crumbs from his lips and took a long drink from a bottle of tea before leaning forward again.

"This one," he said, placing a hand on my shoulder, "has been like my own son, or like the young man I would have hoped my son could be. But I don't have a son, young lady. I lost him many years ago, and the short answer to your question is that I didn't want to lose another."

"How did you lose your son?" Leja asked without hesitation. Mr. Koperski tensed. He squeezed my shoulder. Why had Leja challenged this private man with a question so personal and designed to share a memory he might not want to recall?

"You don't need to talk about it," I said. "My sister didn't mean to ask that."

"No, no, my boy. It's fine," he answered. "It's just that I haven't spoken of it in some time. Nor has anyone asked. So, let me think how I can tell this story in a way you'll understand."

He packed away the food and drink he had spread around him, stood and walked to the front of the rail car, where he spread hay across the ground so the horses could feed. He reached into a bag hanging from the wagon's seat and allowed each horse to nuzzle and eat a small apple he held in each hand.

"And now my story," he said, when he sat back down and faced us.

"My wife's name was Shayna. Shayna madela, her father would call her. That means beautiful girl in Yiddish. Her father owned a fabric and dress store in Krakow, Ta Kremowa Sukienka, The Crimson Dress. It's still there, in the Market Square in the center of the city. He was Jewish. Shayna's mother is Polish, Catholic, like me, but she would say shayna madela to her daughter anyway, because that was exactly what Shayna was.

"I met her when I was still young. Can you believe I was once young, Wolchi, just a few years older than you and an apprentice like you in a workshop where my father sent me to learn to be a machinist? I remember riding a horse with him all the way from our town to the city. There was no railroad then, just a muddy road and miles of forest. So, you are lucky to be able to make this trip in such luxury," he said and laughed aloud, enjoying his joke and the memories his story unearthed.

"On Saturdays, I would go to the Market Square with the other workers to visit the cafes and restaurants and see all the people. There is a leaning tower in the square, and I liked to climb stairs to the very top and look out over everything. It was the tallest place in the city and it made me feel like I could see my home, which I missed very much. I was lonely in Krakow.

"But one time, we were sent to the square to work, on a Thursday in June, a sunny warm afternoon, one of those days I will always remember. The way the air smelled, the warm breeze, a few white clouds in the bluest sky I had ever seen. It was probably the most beautiful day I have ever lived. There was a statue that needed to be fixed to a pedestal, a new statue of a Polish poet, Adam Mickiewicz."

"I know about him," Leja said. "He is very famous. They say he was like Goethe or Byron and that he inspired an uprising to win independence for Poland from the Russian empire."

"You are a very smart young woman," Mr. Koperski said. "That's all true. You and he would have had much to speak about, I think. But I didn't know any of this. I was a machinist, not a scholar, and I had been sent to the square to drive long iron screws through the base of the statue to fix it to the stone roadway.

"The work was hard. It was hot, and the square was crowded as we finished the job. A small stage was set up near us, covered in flowers. There was to be a ceremony of some kind, and I remember hurrying to get done so I could leave before the crowd, already close to me, grew any larger. My shirt was wet with sweat, my hands covered with dirt, and, as I said, I was hurrying and grew careless when my hand slipped and scraped against the sharp thread of an exposed screw," he said looking squarely at me. "And that's why I always say to you, Wolchi, that our work requires full attention, and that bad things happen when you become distracted."

He paused and drank more tea. I knew he was looking for the words to continue, and it took a moment for him to find them.

"But in this case, something good happened along with the bad. The bad? My hand was bleeding, covered in blood, and when I dropped my tool the loud sound made the people near me turn to look. I may have also loudly said a word I should not have spoken there in a public place. I don't know, but people were staring at me. I was reaching for a rag to wrap on my hand, when a person from the crowd offered me a kerchief, a lady's kerchief, as white and clean as any piece of cloth I had ever seen. I took it, raised my head to offer thanks, and I saw her."

He paused again, and Leja, eager for the story to continue, said, "Who? Your shayna madela?" Mr. Koperski did not answer, but acknowledged Leja with a nod of his head.

"Sweaty, bloody, on my knees in the dirt of the square, I looked up and saw the most wonderful face smiling back at me. 'Can I help you?' she said to me. I just stared back, like a fool. I couldn't find a single word to say to this kind and beautiful woman. I just stared at her as if I was that stone statue of the poet. Finally, I said something foolish. 'I have gotten blood on your kerchief,' something like that, which she thought was amusing. She said: 'I'm glad you're not badly hurt, and don't worry about that kerchief. I have plenty of them. My father sells them in his store just behind us in the square.' Then, as more people pressed toward the stage, she faded back into the crowd. That's how I met my wife."

The train slowed, and he stood to look into the passing darkness. "We are halfway now, going through the mountains for the next hour. We will be in Krakow by morning. So, maybe you should get some rest while you can."

"Your son?" Leja asked. "What about him?"

He remained standing, leaning against the railcar siding, the train moving slowly through the mountain pass. "I've told you the happy story," he said, "and now you still want to hear the sad one? Okay.

"I returned to the Market Square that Saturday, as always, with my fellow workers. This time, though, I was not interested in the cafes and the people. Instead, I searched for a shop that sold ladies kerchiefs. I'd tried to wash the blood and dirt from the one Shayna had given me, but it was no use. I planned to buy a new one for her, and see her again. Let me make this part of the story shorter by saying that, yes, I found her, and we spent each Saturday of that year together. She married me the following June on an afternoon almost as lovely as the day we met."

He turned away from us and looked out again over the edge of the railcar. The moon was rising behind the mountain peaks, a sliver of silver and white across the sky like a scar in the darkness. I stood and joined him. The train had slowed to a crawl as it rounded a bend and began descending into a concentric spiral of tracks, illuminated by the moonlight, that would deliver us to the flatter plains beyond. Mr. Koperski pointed down to them and poked my arm with his elbow. "Do you see that pattern of the tracks winding down the mountain at a constant angle?" he asked me. "A helix, just like the drill bits we use, and the screws and springs we make, and even the design you see on shells gathered from the sea. That pattern is one of the great discoveries of engineering, Wolchi, one of the true mysteries of life. It makes me believe there is a God, because how else could this have happened? Who else could have made this wonder?

"But I believe that this God, who created something so brilliant, is a God who doesn't understand something so basic as love and joy, things that even the simplest person, the smallest child feels in his heart without explanation. The same God who gave us the magic and power of the helix angle, took my Shayna and my child, leaving me alone."

The squeal of the train wheels on the winding tracks

and the grinding of the steam brakes controlling our descent through the curve were too loud for him to continue. He sat down, as did I. Leja and I leaned closer as he continued.

"Shayna came with me after my apprenticeship ended," he said. "She never complained that I had taken her from Krakow, a city with culture and learning and new ideas to my home in the middle of a Galician forest beside a river that flooded every spring and autumn, where the only books were bibles, and where any dress she wore was stained with dirt as soon as she stepped into the street."

He pointed at me and Leja. "You understand, because it's your home, too. She never complained, though. The mountains were beautiful, the sky crowded with stars and her heart, she said, was filled with love for me. I was a lucky man, a joyful man, especially when Shayna became pregnant. When you live in a small, quiet place, your life becomes that way. I worked all day in my father's workshop, but I lived for my time with Shayna. We were like one person. We cared for each other, planned our family, were close in every way. Even though we shared my father's house, it felt we were the only people in it, the only people for kilometers.

"One morning, close to her time, she woke me while it was still dark. She was in pain, something seemed wrong. I awoke my father and sent him for the midwife, while I sat with her trying to comfort her the best I could with a cool cloth on her forehead and reassuring words. 'The midwife is coming,' I said to her. 'Soon we will have our baby and everything will be fine.' But Shayna was not well. She was hot and sweating, our bed was wet and stained around her legs with a faintly red liquid.

"The midwife and her daughter arrived and said the baby

wanted to come, but it was not time, that Shayna was not ready. All we could do was wait. So, we waited for hours. Shayna was crying, screaming sometimes. I held her hand, tried to cool her forehead, and when the midwife said the baby was turned the wrong way inside Shayna, and that she needed the doctor right away, I ran to bring the doctor. The whole day had passed. It was night. The doctor wasn't at his house, but at the tavern, his wife said. So, I ran there and went through the door like a madman. The doctor was drunk, I could see that. He was singing Polish songs with the other men, but I pulled his arm and urged him toward the door, nonetheless. I told him it was my wife, my baby."

The breathless retelling of his story, his words fast as if he were again running through the streets, left Mr. Koperski winded and wistful. He stopped speaking and stared into the dark distance. The train, now off the mountain, picked up speed. The air was warmer in the valley and filled with the smell of freshly cut spring hay. He continued his story.

"The doctor pulled his arm away. 'I would like to help you Koperski, but your wife is a Jew,' he said. What difference would that make, I asked. She needs a doctor right now. 'Get the Jewish doctor,' he said. Igor Goreki has told me that I am a doctor for Polish people only, not the Jews, not the Ukrainians. Just Polish.'"

"Goreki? Who was this Goreki, I asked him. I had never heard of him. My wife might be dying, and the doctor turns his back because of Goreki? He was new in the town and put in charge by the Polish government. 'I'm sorry,' the doctor said. 'Go to the Jewish doctor, Levy. He can see her.'"

"Dr. Levy's house was far from mine, in the Jewish neighborhood, so a lot of time passed until I found him and he came back with me. It was too late. I knew it when I saw her. Shayna and the bedsheets were covered in blood. The midwife was sobbing. The doctor tried to help her, tried to get the baby out in time, but Shayna had stopped moving. Her eyes were closed. Her lips apart. 'If only I could have reached her sooner,' the doctor said. But he hadn't, and she was dead. When the doctor pulled the baby from her, he was dead, as well. My son."

Leja was crying. She slid beside Mr. Koperski and hugged his shoulders. "I am very sorry," she said. He patted her gently on her back. "My dear girl, thank you," he said. "It's the way of our world, isn't it? Cruel. But sometimes you have a chance to do something that's right and good. On the night my wife and son were taken from me, I walked away from whom I had been. I could no longer be part of a people who had taken everything from me, and I became part of something else.

"So, now, I am taking you on this journey away from that place because of what happened to me. I do it to honor my son and respect my wife's memory," he said, pausing and pointing a finger at me. "And I do it because I promised my friends at the PKP railroad that I would bring them the best young machinist in the Ukraine." He turned to Leja and, with great emphasis, said, "And I do it because I now see that you, Leja, have not yet fulfilled your destiny."

We sat quietly after that, the train wheels rumbled below us, the diesel pounded ahead. I drifted into a sleep of disturbing dreams, chasing my father through a shaking house, a place with stairs that went up and down without any pattern. I saw him stop as he reached the top of the stairs, a younger man, healthy and smiling. I ran toward him, but he ran away, a fading image like the lingering glow of an extinguished light.

I walked through room after room searching, and I saw my mother in a tiny bed. She waved at me, beckoning with a Golem statue in her hand. I called for my father, running from room to empty room, as the house shuddered more violently, and I reached with both hands to steady myself on the undulating walls.

"Wolchi," a man's voice said. I opened my eyes, and Mr. Koperski's hand was on my shoulder. "We are nearly there."

The rising sun glowed orange on the Vistula River, and the peaked belfries of a castle caught the faintest morning light. Our town, our friends, even our family seemed like part of my dream, and I awakened to a new place with no memories for me.

Part Three, December 1937, Krakow

*And said Poland: "Whoever comes to me will be free
and equal, because I am FREEDOM."*
– Adam Mickiewicz, The Books of the Polish Nation

CHAPTER 23

The turkey leg slipped into his lap when the quiet Polish guy tried to cut it with a knife. Who cuts a turkey leg, I wondered? Just bite it. I heard someone call him Karol, but we had not been introduced. He looked around to see if anyone was watching him lift the greasy leg back onto his plate. I caught his eye and poked Leja with my elbow to get her attention. Look at him.

At the head of the table, Michel raised his glass of wine, French, he said, and toasted us, his friends, students, houseguests, like me and Leja, everyone who had gathered around his impossibly large table set in one corner of his improbably large dining room to celebrate the Christmas season.

"Rich men have wealth," he said. "The rest of us have one another. Here's to the rest of us."

He drank the wine to a chorus of "na zdrowie," all of us with glasses raised except the quiet Polish guy sitting across from me and Leja. He was whispering to the man beside him, his father I guessed. The square blunt jaws and prominent noses tilted a bit right suggested their relation. The older man nodded, and only then did the quiet Polish guy take a swallow from the wine glass. He coughed. I could relate.

I'd only had my first taste of wine a few months before, shortly after we arrived here at Michel's home in the center of Krakow, near the city's revered Jagiellonian University, where he taught philosophy and religion. The city had been a revelation for Leja and me. Krakow wasn't Poland's largest city, but its scale overwhelmed me, as did its beauty. Michel said artists from across Europe lived and worked here, and that Krakow had always been one of the continent's centers of great thinking and creativity, which thrilled Leja. I was equally excited that Krakow was an historic rail center for Central Europe, once the connecting hub for trains that linked the Austrian, German and Russian Empires. It baffled me that I had lived just 300 kilometers from this place for so many years with no awareness that a world like this existed. When Leja told me as a child about the magic of Paris and New York, I assumed those places were unreachable, existing in another universe. Yet, here I was, allowed to walk the cobblestone streets shadowed by ancient stone buildings in a place that for me held all the magic of any city in the world.

Shortly after we'd arrived, Michel arranged a dinner, more intimate than this one, to welcome us to what he called our sanctuary. I became dizzy that night from drinking too fast and eating too little, and had been a careful wine drinker since. So, I thought I should warn the Polish guy, who I suspected might have just tasted alcohol for the first time, that one glass would be enough. He was a bit older than me, his skin and hair more fair, his arms and shoulders more slight, his manner more reserved. He hadn't spoken since he sat down more than an hour before to anyone but the man beside him.

"Do you like the wine?" Leja asked him. He didn't respond, his face reddening as he turned his head away, fingering the small St. Christopher medal around his neck. "I am Leja, and this is my brother Wolchi," she continued, undeterred. Nothing from the Polish guy. "I'm a student at the university, studying French," she continued. He raised his eyes back to her.

"Karol," he said after a moment, his face stern and serious. "My name is Karol Wojtila. And, to answer your question, I think the wine tastes like medicine."

That caught Leo's attention. Leo, Michel's son, sat beside Leja and had been in an animated discussion with a young woman to his left whom I recognized as one of my sister's classmates. Leo and Leja. I sometimes teased her with that. "Say both of your names fast ten times." She could never do it, and what did that portend for their relationship, I'd ask. They became close after we arrived in Krakow, and now were lovers trying to keep their affair private. She attended classes at the university studying French at Leo's suggestion. He was an advanced student planning to attend the Sorbonne in Paris beginning the coming summer who also helped teach one of her classes. It was better, he told her, to keep their relationship private and avoid "confusion" about his role among the other students. Better for her, he said. Better for him, I knew.

"It's French, the wine," Leo said to Karol. "My father says the French don't make the best wine, just the best wine we can afford. You don't like it? Perhaps you're accustomed to something better?"

Karol, a person who clearly avoided confrontation, crinkled his nose in surprise while considering a response. More than a moment passed before he answered Leo's assaultive question.

"Why do the French never have more than one egg for breakfast?" he asked, deadpan, directing his question to all of us. We waited. He waited. "Because one egg is un oeuf." Karol's timing was excellent.

So, the quiet Polish guy, I concluded, had both a distaste for alcohol and a sense of humor. Perhaps we could become friends. I laughed. Leja laughed more enthusiastically. Even the girl sitting beside Leo laughed. Leo, on the other hand, frowned, looking at the women on either side of him through glazed, intoxicated eyes.

There were thirty people in Michel's dining room. He loved a crowd, and loved to gather them in his spacious, spartan, but distinctive home on the edge of the city's old square, in a neighborhood once filled with Renaissance Era noblemen. Paintings by local artists hung on grey, worn walls. Sculptures and flower-filled vases crowded the rough, mismatched tables throughout the room. His Paris-themed December party, everyone had told us in the weeks leading up to the night's festivities, was the most anticipated event of the year for anyone in the University community fortunate enough to be invited. There was ample food, wine, a musical quartet and excited conversation intended to recreate, as best as anyone in Krakow knew, the energy and creativity of a Parisian party. The room was truly abuzz, as if swarms of bees had gathered near the tall ceiling in a hazy, alcohol-soaked frenzy.

Leo began tapping a fork against his wine glass. Two times, then three, then a continual series of clinks until the din in the room quieted and the band went silent.

"Your attention, please. Your attention, please," he said as he stood. "For your entertainment tonight I would like to introduce you to Karol Wojtila from . . . Where are you from?" he asked Karol.

With everyone silent and listening, Karol replied almost in a whisper, his face crimson and stern. "Wadowice."

"There you have it, Wad, oh, we, che," Leo said, with a dramatic pause between each syllable. "We have an expert in French humor from Wadowice."

Leja pulled on Leo's sleeve and whispered, "Stop it. Leave him alone." Leo brushed her hand aside.

"Tell me Karol from Wadowice, would you honor us with a few more food-inspired French witticisms?" Leo said.

The partygoers shifted uncomfortably in their seats and on the dance floor. Leja again tried unsuccessfully to pull Leo back into his chair.

"Perhaps something about a baguette or a cafe au lait or a steak frites?"

Karol turned to look at the staring faces. First right, then left, and then directly at Leo. "I'm sorry to say I know very little about French food, and what I know would not be very amusing."

"So what else can you share with us that's French," Leo persisted. "A phrase, a love poem, a song. This is a French celebration, after all."

"I have studied French philosophers," Karol answered. "They were important in my studies before the university."

Leo, more animated, moved behind Leja. "Surely this lovely lady who finds you so amusing would like to hear a quote from one of them," Leo said. "Is that too much to ask, Karol of Wadowice?"

This unlikely confrontation between the outgoing arrogant son of our host and the restrained humble young guest was more entertainment than any of us could have hoped for. The willingness of people in Krakow to engage in this sort of meaningless battle baffled me when I first encountered it. Everyone associated with the University seemed eager to argue about things that didn't matter at all. Some academic detail or imagined slight. Words were rarely just words, but instead were sharpened into weapons intended to demonstrate one man's intelligence and to bloody another. At home, when people argued, the disagreements were genuine and the outcomes sometimes violent. What was happening here, though, was theater, just the way people passed the time.

"Voltaire said we should judge a man by his questions rather than his answers," Karol said loudly. "My question for you, Leo, and I ask it hoping truly to understand your answer, is what have I done to anger you?"

Michel quickly moved from his place at the head of the table and stood beside his son. "Alright, that's enough, Leo. Please, everyone, that's enough. My apologies, Mr. Wojtila and Karol. Please, let's resume our dinner," Michel said. He motioned toward the musicians. "Play, play."

Leo sighed, obedient, but hesitant as he returned to his seat. "I would like to know," Karol continued more softly and directly at Leo. "Because if I did anything inappropriate, I will make it right."

Music again filled the room, louder than before. A Polish tango brought couples to their feet. And, as if awoken from a deep sleep, Leo jumped up with startling energy, pulled Leja toward the open dance floor and began to dance.

"Leo thinks you embarrassed him in front of the girls," I

said to Karol. "You made them laugh, and he felt it was at his expense."

"I was the one embarrassed by his question," Karol said, his face still grave, tight-lipped, and his fingers again stroking the medal around his neck. "I thought a joke would allow me to avoid further attention."

"Well, I'm sorry to say, Karol, that not only have you attracted Leo's attention, but it seems my sister has noticed you, as well," I said, motioning my head toward the dance floor where Leo was whirling Leja around in a stiff embrace, while she was looking back at Karol, apologetic that she had been torn from their nascent conversation.

A tango quartet was less interesting to my sister than a potential discussion about Voltaire. So, I knew what was going through her mind as Leo, nimble with his dance steps despite his wine consumption, guided her through a set of athletic moves that made other couples steer a wide course. As it turned out, Leo was right about Leja. She was happy to hear a quote from a French philosopher and now wanted to sit with the shy Polish guy and talk about free will, ethics and Voltaire's enlightenment.

Karol's fair skin was a truth detector, and his emotions lit up his face like a sunrise when he saw Leja's eyes on him. I could almost feel the heat from across the table as it rose off his neck. He looked away from her and down at his lap, his head bowed as if in prayer. "Turkey stain?" I asked. He looked up, nodded, and I detected, for the first time in the evening, the faintest smile on his lips.

Chapter 24

The guests had gone, when just after midnight there was a quiet knock at the door. Leo slept on a small sofa, Leja beside him reading a leather-bound volume of something with a French title. I helped Michel and his housekeeper clear the table of half-empty glasses and plates. Another knock, this one more urgent. Leja and I instinctively moved out of the room and stood in a spot where we could not easily be seen from the door. Mr. Koperski and Michel had warned us that we should assume Igor Goreki and the police had alerted their colleagues elsewhere in Poland to their interest in us. Even the bribes Mr. Koperski paid the soldiers at the train station to look away when we arrived did nothing to ensure that others would not ask questions about two newly arrived young people who'd moved into Michel's home. So, we were cautious.

"Yes, yes," Michel called when there was a third knock. "Just a moment." He piled the dishes he held onto a table beside the door and opened it. He shouted something, a sound that was neither pain nor pleasure, not surprise or resignation. Perhaps it was relief? "Lu, Ludmilla."

A woman stood in the doorway, and Michel hugged her. Her face was buried in his shoulder and hidden by strands of her hair. She seemed shapeless beneath a thick winter coat and sweater. "Lu, you are here. Come inside. I didn't know you were coming. You are alone? Leo, Leja, Wolchi. It's my sister. Here from Vienna."

Michel ushered his sister into the house and sent me to retrieve her luggage from a waiting carriage, a wooden trunk and a leather valise secured with a man's belt. They were heavy, and I struggled to carry them. This was not a short-term visit. Inside the house, Leo had stirred awake and, still seated, offered a half-hearted embrace to his aunt. The valise was heavy, and I didn't intend for it to hit the ground quite as loudly as it did when my fatigued arms let it slip and it hit the floor with a startling thud. Startled by the sound, everyone turned to me, including Ludmilla.

I wasn't the sort of person who held another's gaze once the interaction became awkward. I took no pride from being able to stare a person down the way my railroad supervisors at the PKP machine shop were taught to do as a demonstration of authority. I didn't avoid eye contact so much as engage in it sparingly, because people who stared into the eyes of another usually stared with anger or loss, and who needs to see that. But when Ludmilla's eyes locked on mine, I did not look away.

I brushed a bead of sweat from my temple and tried to understand what I saw in her. It wasn't the heat of anger or the dryness of loss, but something more dewy, and it reminded me of an afternoon several years before when this same awkward feeling washed warm over me while I held the gaze of an older woman.

She lowered her eyes, walked toward me and said, "Thank you for carrying in my bags." She extended her hand, anxiously I thought. "I am Ludmilla." I don't recall exactly what I said in response when I looked at the rest of her face. I just remember her laugh as I took her hand and said something about her bags being heavy. "Like my heart," she said, "before I had the pleasure of meeting you."

Aunt Lu, as Leo called her, moved into an empty bedroom in the rear of the house, unused servant's quarters adjacent to the kitchen, with a view to the small yard and the university buildings beyond the stone fence. I rarely saw her in the weeks after her arrival. The house was large and my work schedule demanding, so days would pass without my seeing anyone at home.

Two days before Christmas, I returned from work late, cold and tired after walking through the snowy streets, when I heard Ludmilla singing. I was in the kitchen, making tea and rooting about for leftovers when the soft notes of her voice drifted through her door. She sang a popular song I'd heard on the radio. *("Love will forgive you and transform sadness into smiles.")* I moved closer to her room, first to listen and then to watch her on the other side of the partly open door. She stood at the dark window, staring into the yard. Her voice was plaintive, her hands outstretched as if trying to touch an audience of snowflakes on the other side of the glass. I thought I should go back to my tea-making, that I was intruding, but I couldn't turn away. I stood looking through the partial opening of the door, teacup in hand, until she ended the song with a loud flourish. *("Love, my dear, forgives you everything.")* I felt a chill, but not from the cold, and I was so enthralled by her voice that I didn't move when she turned from the window and stared at the shadow interrupting the light from the kitchen.

"I didn't realize I had an audience," she said, opening the door. Her face, cautious at first, softened when she saw me sheepishly clutching my teacup. "Once again, you've turned sadness into a smile." Pointing to my cup, she said, "Maybe you can make me one of those?"

Chapter 25

Ludmilla needed no prompting to tell her story. She began singing in the Krakow opera as a teenager, she told me. That's where she met her husband, a cello player in the orchestra. The two of them sang and played together for a decade in Krakow before he joined the revered Vienna Philharmonic. Vienna was magical in the mid 1930s, a city steeped deeply in European culture and manners, a place where Jews, like her husband, lived freely and participated at the highest levels of society. Even though she was not Jewish, dozens of the Philharmonic musicians were, and the two of them enjoyed a life of music, art, nightlife and friendship that made no distinction between them.

Everything changed when the extremist Nazi party took power in Austria. Life became increasingly difficult, even dangerous. In the fall of 1938, armed gangs began marauding through Vienna's Jewish quarter, empowered by compliant Viennese authorities who refused to control the escalating criminal activity. The violence reached a crescendo on November 9, when the synagogue across from Ludmilla's flat was burned. She and her husband spent the night huddled in the darkness of their rooms listening to screams and the sound of glass shattering on the streets below, as Nazi paramilitary gangs broke windows and looted Jewish-owned businesses. Two weeks later, as the curtain was set to rise on the Vienna Philharmonic's first December holiday concert, the Nazis took away the Jewish musicians, including Ludmilla's husband, and silenced the music.

"Our friends tried to help him," she said, twisting the cold cup in her hands. "I waited for him in front of the dark window, listening for footsteps on the street crunching the broken glass. Again and again I'd ask myself: 'Is that him walking?' Sometimes I sang the song you heard, hoping in my mind that he could hear me."

She stood and extinguished the stovetop flame beneath the kettle. Her heavy robe had become loose, and her neck and the top of her breasts were lit by the yellow kerosene lamplight.

"Each day the streets became more frightening," she continued. "Jews and those the Nazis called 'Jew lovers' were beaten, shops and homes were destroyed, people disappeared. Every day was worse than the last. I was frightened, and I needed to come home, to Krakow, where things like that couldn't happen. I'm ashamed I didn't wait for him, but I knew in my heart he was gone. He *is* gone. All of them are gone."

She sat down, and her robe fell open. I wish now I hadn't stared so obviously, but being close to a woman, especially this woman, in the dim light, in the hours when dusk is long past and dawn is still far off, made her story fade to black and the closeness of her body become illuminated. She pulled her robe closed, leaned forward and, without speaking, kissed my cheek before returning to her room. I sat alone afterward in the kitchen, listening as she sang again, so softly that only I could hear.

CHAPTER 26

The front door was open and Leo and Leja stood outside the house when I returned from work the following day. It was Christmas Eve, and the railyard had sent its workers home early.

"Aunt Lu, hurry. It will be dark soon," Leo called into the house. "The *grzane wino* will be cold if we don't get moving."

"We're heading to the Christmas market," Leja told me. "Apparently, it's the thing to do on the night before Christmas in Krakow. All the students will be there. Plenty of hot wine and pierogis, Leo says. You should come. It will be fun."

The idea of drinking hot wine on the cold streets of Central Square, while eating amid a crowd of drunken Krakownians was not a compelling argument to get me to abandon my plans for an early supper and a good night's sleep. That's what I was explaining to Leja, when Ludmilla burst through the door. "Aunt Lu (my sister had adopted Leo's term of endearment), can you convince this guy to come out with us tonight?"

"Yes, come on Wolchi," Leo urged, slapping me hard, too hard I thought, on the back.

"I'm not sure how convincing I can be," Ludmilla said to Leja, as she took my arm and aimed her gaze directly at me. "But it won't be fun unless he is with us." The festive mood and the woman on my arm could not be denied, and we began walking before I could even respond. The Christmas market, I now thought, would be the perfect way to spend the evening, especially if Ludmilla kept pressing her breasts against me, holding my arm with both hands.

She wore the same lumpy coat as the night she arrived, and a brightly colored knit hat pulled low over her forehead. A light snow fell, and passersby didn't offer her a second glance the way they watched other women whose clothing choices were more provocative. I stared at her as she spoke and wasn't watching where I walked. As we entered the square, a drunken reveler stumbled into us, knocking me to the ground, and Ludmilla with me. Lying on my chest, she made no effort to move at first, and we lay there, her weight full on me, my arms wrapped tightly around her, as others walked past.

"I suppose we need to stand up," she whispered to me, as the drunken man offered us a drink from his bottle. I was snow covered, head to heel along my back, and Ludmilla, laughing, began to brush me clean when the man, too, began wiping snow from my back and shoulders.

"My apologies, kind sir. Let me help you," he said, teetering from side to side.

"Get away from them," Leo warned, as he pushed the man, who stumbled to the ground. The container of wine in his hand shattered on the ground loudly, and Ludmilla stiffened, pulling close to me.

"Let's just go. Please. Let's go," she said, her face ashen, frightened.

That was the night I glimpsed something about her that later became evident, like the clearing sky at the end of a storm, snow stopping, a few stars appearing, just bright enough that I could find them as the clouds thinned and drifted away.

Long after Leja and Leo departed for home, Ludmilla and I found reason to stay and wander through the outdoor shops in the market, to warm ourselves at the open bonfires where men roasted sausages, to drink mulled wine poured from aged wooden barrels that had warmed the citizens of Krakow for many Christmases past, and, late in the night, to toast the statue of the Polish poet Adam Mickiewicz, perhaps from the same spot Mr. Koperski first glimpsed his Shayna. I was drunk and leaning on the statue pedestal, when I pulled Ludmilla close and kissed her, a bit clumsily until she took hold of my face, pressed her lips hard against mine and draped her leg around my thigh. The noise from the crowd in the square faded, and the kiss lingered. I could smell and taste the sweetness of the wine and felt the cool air on my wet lips when she moved her mouth away. It was dark behind my closed eyelids, and when I opened them, Ludmilla was watching me.

In the dim light of the kerosene streetlamps, she touched my lips and began to cry.

CHAPTER 27

I had sex with a woman for the first time that night, and it was not what I'd imagined. I felt oddly alone in Ludmilla's room, like a player on a stage who's part of someone else's drama. I was there for her. She made that clear, as she guided me with each touch, moving my hands where she wanted them, my head and mouth to places on her body that made her moan when I kissed her. She said nothing when she turned me on my back and straddled me, until she whispered "yes" when we were finished.

We lay together afterward, buried in a thick feather quilt, quiet for a time before she began talking. She was breathing slowly and deeply. I could feel the patient rhythm of her heartbeat and the way the tension had left her shoulders and hips. She had found a new calmness, one that allowed her to construct memories from the scattered shards of the past month.

"I could have saved him," she said, as if our conversation from the previous night had never ended. "Our Jewish friends months before said there would be a pogrom, that things in the government had changed, that we were not safe. No, that *he* was not safe. He wanted us to leave, to return here, where we had friends and family and where there were no Nazis."

On her back, staring at the ceiling, she continued: "I

should have listened, but I loved Vienna, at least the way it had been. I told him I would not give up my life there, that nothing bad would happen. I would not be chased out of my beloved city by ignorant hooligans. The nights of dancing, the fine dinners, the beautiful people from across Europe who we were among. I believed the good citizens of Vienna would never become our enemies, that the Nazis were a distraction, a damaged fringe on an otherwise beautiful ballgown.

"Even as things began to worsen, I resisted believing what my eyes saw. Young men wandered the streets taunting the observant Jewish men, pulling their beards and tossing their hats into the mud, but they were just children. Harmless, I thought. The Nazi propaganda placards pasted over notices at the opera house announcing Aryan music as an alternative to the Vienna Philharmonic? Madness. Could you imagine anyone choosing a German street-band blowing tubas into a noisy square over our great orchestra? But people did, most did. I was credulous, but unmoved in my opinion that we were safe and that what was happening in our city would not last.

"I was naive, and selfish," she sighed, as she laid her face onto my chest. "The night of broken glass should have been the end of it. We should have boarded the next train to Krakow. But we were frozen in place. Shock and confusion replaced my confidence in the *good people of Vienna*. The damaged fringe had spread and unraveled the ballgown that was our city. There was nothing beautiful left."

She shifted nervously, her breathing shallow, her hands cool and clenched in mine. She felt broken. "You couldn't have known what would happen," I said.

"That's not true. He told me, but I didn't listen," she continued. "Everything after that was so quick, but maybe we could have run away. I don't understand why we stayed. What were we waiting for?

"I didn't even see when they took him. His friends said it was on the street, outside the opera house. He went there, even after the opera had been shut down, to practice with others for whom there was just a single thing to do in times like those — play their music. One day, he didn't come home. I wasn't sure they had him. I had hope. I couldn't find him. I tried. Some said the Jewish musicians went to a work camp. Others said men in uniforms loaded them into a rail car and shot them."

There was a long silence, and I didn't have the words to break it. "I know he is gone. I feel it. And not a day passes without me remembering that I never told him goodbye."

She sent me away after that, back to my room, where I watched the rising sun brighten my small window and Christmas morning arrive as I drifted into a deep, dreamless sleep that ended with Leja shaking my shoulder. "Get up," she said. "The guests are here for lunch."

Chapter 28

We gathered again around Michel's dining table, a smaller group of family, Leo and Ludmilla, and friends with no place else to be on Christmas morning, my sister and I, along with Karol Wojtila and his father, Karol Sr. Recent newspapers were scattered on the table amid the cakes and teacups. Michel had brought them out when our conversation shifted to the chaos enveloping Germany.

"Jews Ordered to Leave Munich. Fine Shops Wrecked."

"Four Synagogues Set on Fire in Frankfurt on the Main, Many Jews Arrested."

"Wave of Destruction of Jewish Synagogues, Homes, Shops Outside Berlin."

"Anti-Jewish Outrages in Germany; Gangs Unhampered by Police."

"They are killing Jews in Germany and Austria. They are rounding them up, burning their stores and homes, killing them, " Michel said. "And where is the outrage from the rest of us, from Christians in this holy season. I cannot believe

Europe is embracing these madmen, the Nazis."

"It is just the Germans," Karol Sr. answered. "We are not German. This is not a problem for Europe or for us."

Holding up one newspaper after another, Michel said: "Look at these pictures of burning stores and hospitals, of murdered men lying in the streets."

"Just German hooligans, nothing more," Karol Sr. said. "Hooligans angry because a Jew killed a German diplomat in Paris. I have heard this from people who know, people I trust. These are just hooligans blowing off steam, not a threat to us."

I watched Ludmilla as she followed the back-and-forth. Michel looked at her, too.

"I'm sorry to say Mr. Wojtila, you are wrong," she said forcefully. All of us held our communal breath. "You are a wise and good man, but you are wrong."

She told them her story. Karol Jr. listened most attentively as Ludmilla, a woman without his father's age and experience of being a soldier at war, challenged the older man. Karol would later tell Leja that this was a disruptive moment for him, because he had never done what Ludmilla was doing, to challenge authority so directly. After his mother died, Karol's father became the center of the young man's life, his rock and reliable shepherd, whose words he never questioned. And now, Ludmilla had silenced him with the chilling details of her last months in Vienna.

"But I hope this would never happen here, in Poland," she said.

Karol, interrupted, nodding agreement, watching his father and rising to his defense. "In Wadowice, Jews are our friends, we all live peacefully. Here at the university, there are many Jewish students, as Leja can attest."

Leo, still annoyed by his confrontation with Karol weeks before, said: "Didn't you hear what Aunt Lu just said? Vienna, one of Europe's great cities, became a different place overnight. Is provincial Krakow immune to that?"

"I believe we are better, yes," Karol answered. "Jews are free to live as they choose in Poland. Things here are normal. Leja, Wolchi, am I wrong about this?"

As hesitant as I could be to answer an abstract idea like this one, Leja was loathe to miss an opportunity to do so. "Yes," she answered, before sharing the indignities of Jewish life in our small town, the petty disrespect, the violence, the way Polish leaders stoked hatred to control the nationalism of the Ukrainian people. Anti-Semitism was embedded in Central Europe. The boundaries that separated Poland from the Ukraine, and every other nation from another, did nothing to change the core belief of many across those boundaries that Jews should be endured, but never truly accepted. For every tolerant, decent man like Mr. Koperski, there were dozens like Igor Goreki, whose animus toward his Jewish neighbors was as clear as the mustache on his face. And for every Goreki, there were thousands of others, everyday people whose deeply held hatreds and beliefs hid behind a thin veneer of self-interest. They were tolerant when it suited them, but when the time was safe or convenient, those true beliefs burst into small or murderous acts of aggression toward neighbors, friends and even lovers.

To be Jewish in Eastern Europe in the years after the first World War meant living with constant uncertainty about the non-Jews you knew. We hoped most were like Mr. Koperski, but often discovered that some, even the ones closest to you, would become Grygoriy Evanko and trade your safety to protect their own.

Even at that moment, on Christmas morning 1938, eating cakes and drinking tea in the home of our friend and protector, I knew Leja and I shared the same calculus as we assessed each of those around the table. Would Michel, who'd already risked his own safety to harbor us, turn his back if there was an unfriendly knock on the door? Is Leo, my sister's intimate companion, to be trusted if his drinking friends embrace some Polish, right-wing delusion that turns the streets of the Krakow Jewish quarter into a killing field? Will the honorable but naive Wojtilas, father and son, embrace and protect their Jewish neighbors and university students when they see that Polish Jews are not free to live as they choose? Even Ludmilla, with her anguished guilt for indulging her vanities when she had a chance to save her husband, even she might repeat that behavior if Leja and I needed her help.

I chose to trust these people, and I told them so in the hope that this conversation about hate and danger, would end. My head, already heavy and dull from my previous night of too much *grzane wino,* needed a break. I also hoped, as I glanced Ludmilla sitting beside me, that I could find a way back into her bed before the day ended.

Leja, though, was energized by the discussion. She would not let it end. Politics complicated her relationships. Even those she believed harbored no ill will toward her because of religion would be passed through a second filter. How could the Poles she knew believe so deeply in their own national independence, but be deaf to the voices of Ukrainians calling for the same? It was an argument she often had with Leo, and despite her fondness for Michel and her respect for his connection to our father, she maintained an emotional distance from him. Perhaps these men were not closeted anti-Semites, but could they really be trusted? While I rubbed my aching temples, she explored that question with enthusiasm.

"At home, Jews are singled out every day for mistreatment," she said.

"Those are the Ukrainians," Karol Sr. interrupted. "What do you expect of them. They are as bad as the Germans."

"No, it's the Poles we worry about," Leja said. "Not you and Karol, or Leo and Michel or our other friends, but the Poles who came like conquerors to our town after the war and stole what we had, land, livelihoods, our history. We can't speak of our Ukrainian past or fly our flag. They stole from everyone, and then tried to turn our Ukrainian neighbors against us with lies about who had made their lives a misery.

"If it rains too much or too little, they say the Jews did it. If your child becomes sick with typhus, it was an infected Jew who had it first. If your son loses a running race, the Jew must have cheated. Jews drink the blood of Christian children. They hide evil within their beards, so they should never be touched. They killed Jesus. These are lies that Polish leaders in my town say again and again to turn others against us and keep their control."

"But this is what the Austrians and Germans did to us," the young Karol said. "We were oppressed and only now are free and living in a united Poland. We are not oppressors. "

"In my home, in the Ukraine, you are," Leja said, as she stood and lifted one of the newspapers. "And I want you to understand the danger we all face. When some of us are denied freedom, none of us is free. We are all at risk, and you, my dearest Karol, will recognize what Voltaire said. We are at risk because those who can make you believe absurdities can make you commit atrocities. That is what Jews know.

They have lived it for generations. My fellow Ukrainians now understand they may soon be victimized in the same way as long as they live under an oppressive foreign hand."

She took a deep breath, a drink of water and allowed the silence to add emphasis to what she said next. "And I believe it may also become your future here in Poland, absurdities becoming atrocities. You are vulnerable as long as you tell yourselves you are not oppressors in my country."

Leja had been transformed during her time as a university student. In just six months, she acquired an almost magical ability to command the attention of others, even those older, better educated and more worldly. Her mind never lost a detail from her life or from the books she read, and she had the unfiltered courage to say what was on her mind to anyone.

"When we marched and demanded freedom," she continued. "Jews and Ukrainians side by side, they beat us. The Polish police beat us." She recounted the rallies on the steps of the town hall and the confrontation in the forest. "Some of us were killed."

We listened, engrossed. Even Leo, who often intruded when Leja was the center of attention, sat attentively. Karol, his face quizzical, watched her like a student in master class. Michel, Ludmilla and Mr. Wojtyla admired her, too, seeing what I saw in the power of her words and their delivery. She was no ordinary woman.

"When they attacked you, what did you do?" Ludmilla asked.

"What would you do? How far would you go?" Leja retorted without pause. "Would you fight back the best you could? Hit them with sticks if they killed your friends. Would you burn their fields and their houses, destroy the symbols of their arrogance and oppression? Would you shoot their sons if they threatened the people you loved?"

Leja tipped into an emotional and dangerous place, on the edge of revealing a secret that could toss our lives into chaos. Michel saw it. I saw it. She was wide-eyed, animated, ready to tell her story, all of it.

I'd seen her become passionate about her politics before, but usually in the practiced and controlled way she'd perfected through hours of rehearsal in front of the small mirror in our home. I remember her reading aloud when she was young from the books Michel sent as holiday gifts over the years or the news magazines from street peddlers, and the words of the politicians and philosophers of the day became her own.

"Keep people from their history, and they are easily controlled," was a favorite line she repeated over and over when she was just 12 years old, her finger pointed at the mirror while Ira and I, and even mother and father from time to time, watched in the evenings after supper. If we would clap and hoot encouragement, father would playfully ask that we quiet down to prevent our arrest for seditious behavior. "Shh. Do you know what happens to people who quote Karl Marx around here?" he'd say in a grave tone before breaking into a smile and hugging her. "They get hugs from their papa. But, maybe a little quieter would be better."

So, I knew what to do.

"Shh," I said forcefully, as the others turned in surprise at my interruption. " Do you know what happens to people who quote Voltaire around here?"

A moment of confusion crossed her face, and then recognition. Without missing a beat, she said:

"I will not quiet down, Wolchi, but I will take a hug."

I gave her one. I could feel her pounding heart begin to calm against my chest as I whispered. "This is our history, and no one else needs to know it."

Then, Ludmilla said:. "You asked me how far I would go? What would I do?" She paused, and we waited for her to continue. "When the question is that simple, the answer is also simple. Fight them with everything, or run away. But sometimes the question is not simple. Sometimes we don't know what to do, because we don't understand the question."

CHAPTER 29

I slept alone on Christmas night and for many nights afterward, wondering when I would see Ludmilla again. I left early for the railyard each day, even Saturdays and Sundays, and returned well after dusk. We saw one another in passing, and Ludmilla seemed to be away from the house even more often than me. When I came through the door one snowy evening in late January I discovered why. Leja and Leo at the dining table shared university gossip, and I listened. Ludmilla, Leo said, had rejoined the university chorus and was taking part in nightly winter concerts. And what a homecoming, he said.

"Those concerts have never been so popular," he laughed. "All the guys follow her like puppies. And I warn them, 'You may look, but do not touch.' "

Michel, seated on a wooden rocker beside the room's fireplace, lowered his newspaper as I walked toward the kitchen and welcomed me with enthusiasm. "Our hard worker has returned home," he said, with emphasis on home. "I hope your day was a good one."

"It was long," I answered. "But this is the best part of it, to return here, to home."

Michel's generosity to me and Leja was a great gift. From the moment he greeted us on the street outside his house when we climbed from hiding in the back of Mr. Koperski's wagon, he acted as if our surprise arrival and sudden addition to his household was something ordinary and wonderful. "I've always wanted to meet you both," were his first words, ushering us quickly off the street. "It is such an honor that you are here."

I recalled father's description of him as a man who seemed familiar, like a lost brother. Michel's prominent nose, the crinkles beside his eyes when he smiled, the hearty laugh when he enjoyed his own jokes all reminded me of father. Our transition to his house and our new life had been smoothed by the sense that we were with a man we knew. He introduced us to others as his niece and nephew from what he called "the country," an unspecified place that made people nod with recognition when they heard him say it. He was a familiar and trusted figure on the campus, and others accepted his words at face value.

He was quirky, too, and liked to run for exercise through the gothic quad, winter and summer, rain or sun. He was training, he said, "in case Poland needs a 50-year-old athlete in the next Olympics. The way we performed in Berlin in 1936 suggests I will have a chance." Students greeted him, some gently mocking his exaggerated gait, lifting their knees high as he did and pumping their arms with exuberance, calling *pan olimpijczyk,* Mr. Olympian, as he ran past.

There was something heroic about him, I thought, his infectious calm, the way he welcomed others into his life and helped them. "I can't heal the world, Wolchi," he once said. "But I can fix what's right in front of me, my corner of this world, make it better, the way your father does."

He told a different version than father of the story about their meeting twenty years before in the Krakow train station.

"Your father is very modest," Michel said, when I summarized his version — Michel and Leo sitting with him, sharing his food, helping him prepare for his remaining journey.

"Your father saved me," Michel said. "Let me tell you. I was a broken man after my wife died. I had lost my love, our home, my job. I had difficulty even caring for little Leo. Sadness was crushing me. I was alone and lost in Warsaw, a big place where no one cared about us.

"I decided to leave, and I was traveling to my mother's home near Krakow. I meant to give Leo to her. My plan, honestly, was to kill myself and stop the pain I felt. We were sitting on the ground in the Krakow station, awaiting a train, and I was thinking I could die in that spot. Why even go further? And your father, a stranger, he comes to me and asks if Leo and I were hungry and if we would honor him by being his guest for a meal. *Honor him* were the words he used. Me and Leo, dirty, sitting on the floor of the crowded station. Can you imagine. Everyone who passed walked around us as if we were diseased, and your father offers his hand to me, and then to Leo, lifts us to our feet, sits us down on a bench and hands us bread and cheese as if we were family traveling together. We ate and talked about Leo and about your family and, before long, we even laughed at silly things Leo said. It had been so long since I'd laughed.

"I still don't understand how his simple act of kindness changed things. It reset me, reconnected me to my boy and made me see a way forward. It took months to return to myself, but that was the day healing began, when your father touched us like a holy spirit. I think about it often and discuss it with my students. Human decency, I tell them, may be more powerful than the greatest armies of Europe, more sustaining than religious faith. These are great truths that your papa taught me."

He walked with me to the kitchen, while Leja and Leo continued their amused speculation about Ludmilla's impact on the young men of Jagiellonian University.

"You look a little morose tonight," Wolchi. Is something wrong?" Michel asked.

I could hear Leo's voice in my head, "they follow her like puppies," so I steered clear of the important truth and offered another.

"Work is very hard, Michel," I answered. "The army has taken over so many of the trains for soldiers and equipment, worried about Germany. Every repair we do must be done immediately. It's very busy."

Michel, his arm across my shoulder, said. "Come, then. Let me warm up some dinner for you while we discuss things."

By the time I'd finished the roasted chicken and potato dumplings he prepared and drank two cups of tea, Michel had laid it out for me. The conversation was exciting enough to distract my puppy-dog eyes from Ludmilla's closed door. She wasn't in the room, but the memory of us was.

"I will send word with Mr. Koperski to your parents about our idea to see what they think," Michel said. "Take a day off from the railyard sometime, and let your sister and Leo show you around."

The idea? Become a student. Study engineering. Learn to design and build structures that redefined, as Michel said, the way people lived. A bridge. A faster train. A better car. A ship so large it could cross any sea in any weather. Michel had thought this through, and he presented his vision in a compelling way, acting the showman as he described my future. My skills with tools and machines were evidence of my potential, he said. And, flattered, I agreed.

"Leja, Leo, come here. I have news," Michel called.

While he was detailing our discussion to them, Ludmilla returned and joined us in the kitchen. Her cheeks were bright red from the cold, and her hair dotted with melting snow-flakes. When she greeted us, she gifted me a lingering glance.

"Wolchi has some news," Michel said with great enthusiasm. "He will enroll at the university next fall to become an engineer. He will be a brilliant engineer don't you think?"

"I'd like to see more of the school," I corrected. "And then decide."

"I'm so happy for you, Wolchi," Ludmilla said. "You will love being at the university."

Especially if I get to see you more often, I thought.

Leo joined in. "Perhaps he will become the leader of your fan club, Aunt Lu." Leja and Leo laughed at this.

"What do you mean, Leo?" Ludmilla asked, and I could see a flash of anxiety on her face.

"We all know, Aunt Lu," he said. I tensed. Did they, I wondered? How could they?

"We all know how you have cast a spell on all the boys. They think you are grand and a rare beauty," he said. "The sound of your voice leaves them weak and filled with . . ." His voice tailed off.

"They all love you, Aunt Lu," Leja said. "It's remarkable the things they say."

Leo continued, as if he hadn't heard Leja. "Filled with ardor, consumed by it, really. You have a magical impact on them."

"Alright, Leo. I think Ludmilla has heard enough," Michel said. "Let's leave her to prepare for bed and do so ourselves."

I lingered as the rest left the kitchen. Ludmilla touched my arm and spoke. "It really is wonderful news." She took my hand and turned my palm, rubbing my fingertips gently. "These are not the soft hands of a schoolboy, though. A little rough."

I dreamt of her that night, or a woman like her, and was aroused in the darkness by a warm body beside me. "Quietly," Ludmilla said, as she stroked me and slipped my hand into her nightdress. She rubbed her nipple with my fingertip and exhaled softly. "A little rough," she said.

————◦•◦————

The sun woke me the following morning, a bad sign, and I jolted upright. It was a workday, and I was usually out in the pre-dawn before others in the house left their beds. I could hear Leo and Leja in the rooms outside my bedroom, very much awake and arguing. Beside me, Ludmilla curled deeper into the warmth of the feather comforter. Another bad sign, or a wonderfully good one. I touched her shoulder softly, her naked shoulder, which was connected to her naked body, whose heat I felt rising from beneath the comforter when I lifted the corner to see more of her. It worried me to be with her in the morning light, to run the risk of others knowing. But my eyes studied her patiently, and my hands searched for places I couldn't see.

"Come here," she said, her eyes barely open as she pulled me down to her. I began thinking of ways to spirit her from my room before Leja or someone else figured out I was not at the railyard. We'd be quite a picture if the door opened, the two of us, trying to hide beneath the covers of my small bed, or me sitting up ordering the intruder, probably Leja, to leave us with some privacy. What if it was Leo or Michel opening the door? What then? Leja might listen when I asked her to leave. She might even keep her discovery a secret, become our co-conspirator. But Michel and Leo? They would feel betrayed, wouldn't they, maybe angry enough to send me away? Would Leja be banished, too, though innocent of any dishonesty and disloyalty? All of this swirled through my head, as Ludmilla began to kiss me. What we were doing was something to be hidden, wasn't it? I heard Leo's words, "Do not touch."

"You need to leave," I said softly. "Before someone finds us."

She moved my head below the covers. "Just hide under there for awhile," she giggled. In the darkness and warmth, her smell intoxicated me. The room and my mind went quiet, and I wondered how long I could stay there, hidden from everything, everything that had ever been.

CHAPTER 30

Ludmilla and I went about our lives, friends sharing a big home. She sang in the university choir, and I built train parts at the PDK railyard. We cloaked our affair in the routines of every day. We made ourselves ordinary in the shadows of the big lives lived by Leja, Leo and Michel. We had tea in the evenings by the fire and listened to the others share their academic triumphs and slights, sat beside one another at weekend meals with people from the university who debated the risks of Nazism versus Marxism to Poland's independence, and I made visits in the dark to Ludmilla's bedroom when the house and streets outside were quiet.

Fear of discovery clung to me like snow on a coat collar, white and cold until it melted with the warmth of her touch. This was irrational, she told me. Why hide from people who loved us? Surely they would be happy we had one another? That confidence reflected her belief that the world actually was the way she wanted it to be. To me, though, the unquestioning loyalty of family and friends seemed unreliable, like the conscience of the good people of Vienna. So, I remained paranoid, alert and steadfast in my unwillingness to share our relationship with others, while at the same time oddly cavalier about the more dangerous threat of being discovered in Krakow by Igor Goreki.

I accompanied her on trips to the bakery, the green grocer and the butcher on weekends, routine errands that allowed us to pretend while out of the house that ours was a typical relationship. She sometimes wrapped her arm around my waist or clung to my hand on uneven sidewalks. No one knew me on the streets of the university district, so I felt anonymous among the other Saturday shoppers and let her touch linger for as long as she chose. People knew Ludmilla, though, and from time-to-time passersby would greet her by name, looking at me as they passed, searching their memories to place my face.

We successfully kept our relationship hidden for months, but by early spring, perhaps intoxicated by the warmer days and the promise of summer, a relaxed recklessness crept into our outings. I rubbed her knee when we sat at a cafe drinking tea. She chanced a brief kiss when we thought ourselves invisible in the crowd.

One afternoon, as we walked along the shopping street beside the town square, Ludmilla stopped at a store window and pulled me close. "That is beautiful," she said, staring at a flowing red dress. "Don't you think that's beautiful?" She pointed up at the sign above the shop door, "Ta Kremowa Sukienka," The Crimson Dress, the shop owned by the family of Mr. Koperski's wife, Shayna. We stood there, crowds passing behind us, while she admired the dress and I told her their story.

"That is very sad. I hope our love story doesn't have a tragic end." Ludmilla said and turned away from the window to look at me. "You saved me from despair, and I couldn't stand to lose you. I couldn't survive it again."

An elderly woman, her arms filled with packages wrapped

in brown paper, stood behind us, looking at us questioningly. She'd been listening. "Did you know my Shayna, my daughter Shayna?" she asked.

"I know someone who did," I answered.

She handed me the packages and unlocked the shop door. "Come you two," the woman said. "Come inside. Come see the dress, miss."

I told her what I knew about her daughter. She sat behind a small table cluttered with pins, bits of fabric and a sewing machine. She was still and quiet. Ludmilla delicately handled the red fabric of the dress. "Look at how the satin shines even in the shadows," Ludmilla said.

"I have a picture," the woman said to me. "Let me show you." She rummaged in a drawer beneath the table and recovered a black-and-white photograph in a gilded frame of a young woman in a flowing satin dress standing beside a tall, young mustachioed man, Mr. Koperski. They smiled broadly in the photo, holding one another's hand. "My Shayna," she said, handing the photo to me, "and her Marcus. He is a good man."

She walked to Ludmilla and touched her face. "Shayna was a beauty like this one."

The woman removed the crimson dress from the display and took Ludmilla's hand. "Come. Let me see this on you," she said. I sat for a long while studying the photo and listening to the activity behind the heavy curtain separating the store from the back dressing room. Ludmilla laughed. The woman barked orders. "Turn left. Stand straight. Don't move while I pin this."

Ludmilla pulled aside the curtain with a playful and triumphant flourish. "What do you think?" she asked. The dress, while beautiful as a display in the window, came to life on Ludmilla. The vibrant red of the satin where it touched her bare skin, her dark hair untied falling onto her shoulders, her arms graceful and lean as she turned one way and the other holding out the bell-shaped skirt flowing beneath the fitted bodice.

I had never seen anything like this and had no words to describe it. "Come on," she prodded. "How do I look?"

I hesitated. "Nice," was all I could manage to stammer.

She took my hand, and I stood. "You will need to take me dancing in this," she demanded, admiring the dress. Hand in hand, our bodies close, we began moving about the small shop, spinning slowly, just the two of us in our own sacred place. Ludmilla looked off into the half distance and sang softly. "*Love, my dear, forgives you everything.*" The old woman, a broad gap-tooth smile across her face, clapped silently as she watched us. And when I spun us and faced the front window, I saw a small crowd had gathered to watch from the street. They clapped, too, for the wonder of the moment, a beautiful woman on a warm spring day in a glorious dress, and, perhaps, for the man lucky enough to be holding her. It took a moment for me to recognize the figure at the center of the crowd, his face nearly pressed against the glass of the window, smiling most joyfully, waving and mouthing my name. I could faintly hear him saying, "Wolchi, it's me, Karol."

This was what I had feared for months and what I once had been diligent to avoid. I dropped Ludmilla's hands and stepped away, hoping Karol had not seen what was surely obvious to anyone with eyes and a brain. Outside the window, he kept waving and smiling broadly. "It's me Karol." The old woman opened the door for him. Ludmilla urged him inside, hugged him and asked as she displayed the dress, "What do you think?" Karol did not hesitate. "Wow," he said.

The remaining crowd outside lingered, most still pressed to the window hoping the dancing might resume, while others walked slowly behind them, gazing in curiously as they passed. A man slouched against the arched pillar between the walkway and the square, smoking and shuffling his feet. The brim of his cap pulled low hid the side of his face in shadow as he peered into the store over the heads of passersby. He and I made momentary eye contact, and it seemed he knew me. He stubbed out his cigarette on the stone archway and turned to walk away. Daylight touched his face, and I saw it, just the bottom of it, the fish-hook curved scar near his mouth. But it was enough.

I turned away abruptly from Karol, who touched my shoulder to keep me from walking off. He and I made awkward conversation for what seemed a lifetime while I waited for Ludmilla to change clothes. We talked about the military build-up on Poland's western borders, the lovely spring weather, the friendship he had developed with Leja at school. Just moments before, I might have blurted out, "Please don't tell others that you saw Ludmilla and me together." Instead, I worried about a more tangible threat, and as we three walked home I kept glancing over my shoulder, looking for a face following us, a face with a scar from home.

At dinner, I was agitated, unsettled by the encounter with the scar-faced man. Had Igor Goreki found us, or had I imagined more than was there outside the dress shop? Probably, worries about my love affair being exposed had frayed my nerves and left me paranoid. Because why had the man walked away if, as I feared, he was searching Krakow on behalf of our enemy from home? I picked at my food and decided to keep the encounter from Leja. No need to worry her with my uncertainties, at least not yet.

Alone with my thoughts, I listened as the others discussed Leo's summer travel plans to Paris. The train through Vienna would be fastest, Michel said, but Ludmilla urged travel via Berlin, because Vienna was where the darkness that haunted her still lived.

"There is no way to avoid the Nazis," Michel said. "Unless you sail through the North Sea. And if you do that, well, you might as well leave tomorrow to arrive in September."

"It will be fine," Leo said. "The Nazis will not bother me. I'm not a Jew. I'll be okay."

"Thank goodness you're not a Jew," Leja said, annoyed. "That would be terrible for you."

"I'm not being rude, just realistic about things in Germany," Leo responded. "A Jew is not safe there, or Austria, but I would be. Aunt Lu knows what I mean. They didn't bother her."

Ludmilla, watching Leo and the others, said, "There was a time, Leo, when I wanted them to take me, too, when the guilt of not 'being bothered,' as you say, made me wish I'd been taken away and shot beside my husband." She turned to me. "I don't feel that way anymore, but when you pass through those places you will not be alright, Leo. No one can be."

Michel said: "Maybe you should wait and not go. Wait until things are settled and safer. I think all of us would prefer if you did that."

"That's worth considering," Leja said. "You know the

Germans are not happy with the French for supporting Polish independence, for joining with England to oppose the invasion of Czechoslovakia. French armies are on the border with Germany. Waiting a year until things cool down seems a wise course." Her tone changed, becoming flirtatious. "And it would also make me very happy to keep you close to me."

"I wouldn't be happy," Leo responded roughly. "Who would want to stay in this place when they could be in Paris? Father, you know how long I've worked for this."

Leja, defeated, turned away from him, her eyes red, on the edge of tears.

"I for one think Krakow is a fine place to be while the rest of Europe is on the edge of war," Ludmilla said. "Don't you, Leja? Come, help me with dessert. Fresh strawberries with cream."

As they walked to the kitchen, the two women who meant so much to me, I tried to imagine a life where the three of us were together and safe. Where would we be? How would we get to a safe tomorrow from these days of turmoil? I watched them until Leo said, "What about you, Wolchi, my man. Do you think I should stay or go."

I knew Leo was not asking for an honest opinion. He was fishing for someone to back his ambition to be in Paris at the Sorbonne come hell or artillery fire.

"Paris," I said, "seems very far away. If I were you, I'd stay close to home where there are people who care about you."

This was not what he wanted to hear. "You didn't stay close to home, you and Leja, did you? You're here instead of whatever crappy little place has your people."

He was right, of course, but his presentation discouraged my acknowledgment and ended the discussion.

"I can't argue with that," I said. "So, I would support your leaving, or not. Whatever decision you make will be the right one for you."

Leja and Ludmilla returned to the dining room and the conversation ended. Ludmilla carried a bowl overflowing with strawberries, red and full with spring, Leja brought in the cream, whipped to an airy mound.

"Fresh from the market today," Ludmilla said. "When Wolchi and I saw them, we couldn't resist."

Leo cast a sidelong glance at me, and I wished Ludmilla had not called attention to us being together. My sense of dread returned. What was I worried about, I asked myself, and was I worried about the wrong thing? Relax. Have a strawberry.

"Aunt Lu has a great idea," Leja said as she laid scoops of whipped cream on each of our plates. While she served Leo, he rubbed his hand down her thigh. "She'd like us all to come see her show tomorrow. It's the last before the season ends, and some of us, Wolchi, have never heard her sing."

I had, of course, heard her — in her bedroom, an audience of one, not something I could say while everyone else at the table awaited my response.

"I'm probably working," I mumbled weakly, my eyes down, watching the table.

Ludmilla stood over me, a spoonful of fruit halfway to my plate. She placed the bowl and spoon on the table and took my hand. "Please sir," she said in her most charming, teasing voice. "It would make me so happy." Her eyes were on me, eyes that said to anyone who could see them that she was watching someone who was more than a friend. I nervously looked at the others. They stared at us with what I believed was discernment, or was it just amusement at me being dumb-struck because I was the focus of Ludmilla's attention.

"Okay, I'll go," I said too sharply, pulling my hand away too carelessly, too quickly, knocking over a glass and spraying water onto my lap.

"Wolchi, what are you doing?" Leja said, as she came over to blot the water dripping from the table. "You're acting very strangely." I stood, wiping the beaded water from my trouser legs.

Then, Leo said with a laugh: "You see? They all act this way around her. The boys at school fumble and stumble when she's nearby. If she talks to them, they stare like mutes. And if she were to touch someone's hand like she just did to Wolchi? Watch out. The poor boy would piss his pants."

"Leo, please stop," Michel scolded.

Leo pointed to me, my wet spot, laughing. "Like him. Look at that. Your secret's out, Wolchi, my man. Your secret's out. You have joined the long line of boys with a love crush on my aunt."

I considered wiping the grin from his face with the truth. More than a crush, Leo, my man. Instead, I smiled and blushed a bit, before sitting down and allowing the conversation to drift to other subjects. After a minute, Ludmilla slid her chair closer and let her hand drift to my lap. Leo and Michel, continuing their verbal battle over Leo's plans, did not see. Leja, though, watched, first with confusion and then slow comprehension. She took a breath and opened her eyes wide, taking in what was new in the room. Instead of pushing it away, I held Ludmilla's hand and squeezed.

<hr>

"How long," Leja asked me that night in my room. "Tell me everything."

Reluctant at first, I dripped out details. She extracted them one by one, exacting and determined in her search for every morsel of truth. Before long, her questions ended because I couldn't stop talking. I described the night I heard Ludmilla sing, the way she filled my thoughts, the drunken kiss in the town square, the nights since. So many important things had gone unsaid between me and Leja, and now I said them all.

"Wow," she said. "If Leo finds out he'll go insane, you know. He's jealous of anyone who even talks about Aunt Lu at school, like it's his job to scare others away. He makes jokes about it all the time, like tonight when you spilled the water."

This was not reassuring. "You can't tell him then," I pleaded. Despite having lived with Leo for nearly a year, we hadn't become friendly. He often greeted me with a sneer, eyeing my work clothes dismissively when I returned home from the railyard, sweaty and greasy, excluding me from conversations with Michel or Leja. "This isn't something you'd be interested in, Wolchi, my man," he'd say. He was older, his intellect intimidating, and his groomed good looks sent the clear message that he and I had little in common beside being together for this moment in time. I hadn't told Leja any of this, did not disclose that I was wary of the man she was with, the coldness with which he treated her, of his unpredictability and the way he used words as weapons. I was defenseless against that, and what would I say when he discovered his beloved aunt and I were lovers, had been lovers in his house, under his nose for months? "Promise that you won't tell him, or anyone," I said to Leja.

She lay down on my bed, staring at the ceiling. "No worries. Leo and I aren't speaking much these days, anyway, in case you didn't notice tonight," she said. I waited for her to continue, but she just stared.

"Do you plan to tell me why?" I asked after a few moments.

"It started when he told me that he loved me right before Christmas. Do you believe he said that? He was drunk, and I probably reacted the wrong way. I didn't know what to tell him, and he got embarrassed and tried to act like nothing happened. We haven't been the same since.

"Then we got into it pretty good the same night over that Martyna girl. Remember her, the one at the Christmas dinner?" I did. Leo had spent half the evening entertaining her, and the other half insulting Karol, leaving Leja mostly on her own.

"I asked why he spent more time with her than with me, if he loved me. It was stupid to be jealous, but I was. So, he said he loved me, but he shared intellectual interests with her. I mean, what does that even mean? In class, they speak in French to one another, they laugh at each other's jokes, as if I weren't there. When he's not at home, at the library or wherever, I imagine that they're together. I get into a dark place about it, and then remember the other things, Nicholas Goreki and Ivan, and can't make the thoughts stop," she said.

"I get very lonely when I think about Ivan, when I remember how he died, why he died. I feel responsible and that I deserve to be punished. Then I think about Nicholas Goreki, bleeding, dying on the ground, where I put him. It all scares me. I can't breathe with those things in my head, like I'm drowning. So, when Leo says he loves me, I think about all that. Crazy, huh?"

"Do you love him? Leo, I mean," I asked, happy to be the one asking, rather than answering.

"No," she said, and let that lonely word hang in the room like dust in the dim light. "I think I still love Ivan. At least I miss him very much."

This was the first time Leja and I had each said the word "love" in a way that suggested we actually understood what it might mean. I was unhelpful in sorting her emotions, though. I had never heard her say she loved Ivan, but if she did, that was fine with me. Being in love with a dead man was better, I thought, than being in love with Leo. A dead man couldn't hurt her, at least not as much.

"Did you tell Leo about Ivan? How you feel?" I asked.

"Leo doesn't know anything about who I was before we showed up in the back of Mr. Koperski's wagon," Leja said. "You'd think he'd ask questions, try to know me better, but he's content with the little I've told him. It leaves him more time to think about himself, I suspect.

"By the way, I'm happy for you and Aunt Lu, I mean Ludmilla. I don't think I can call her Aunt Lu any longer," she said. "I honestly would not have imagined the two of you, and never saw it before tonight. So, your secret should be safe. Like I said, Leo has a hard time seeing what's not about him."

Then I said something, without thinking, that Leja didn't seem ready to hear. "I hope he'll leave soon for Paris. It will be better for you, for both of us, when he's gone."

CHAPTER 31

Sometime in the 13th Century, Medieval-era craftsmen built the church used as a concert hall by Jagiellonian University. Despite the relatively small size of the church, it would have taken as many as two generations of masons to complete the structure, fathers and sons who devoted their lives to building the place even though there was little chance they would ever hear a soprano's voice or the lustrous sound of a violin echo from the stone they laid. The hardwood pews, worn smooth over decades by the touch of churchgoers, were hewn from trees older than the city itself, harvested from the forests that once surrounded the university.

In the third row from the performance stage, right of center, we gathered on the last night of spring in 1939, part of a dense crowd filling the chapel for the university choir's annual solstice concert. Goodbye to spring and the turmoil of the past year. Hello to summer and the promise of better, safer days. Leo sat closest to the center aisle, and I was farthest from it. Leja, Michel, Mr. Wojtyla and Karol sat between us.

"It was thoughtful of Leja to invite my father and I tonight," Karol said to me as the singers, more than twenty young men and women, including Ludmilla, entered the stage. "I have heard the choir practicing some afternoons when I walk across the quad. I don't think it's sacrilege to say they made me think of the voices of God's angels. I don't mean to say I have heard those angels, but when I do I will know them because of this choir."

Karol's slight awkwardness, deep intelligence and belief in spiritual ideas larger than the day-to-day churn of life were an endearing combination. He was a good friend to Leja, whose willingness to question authority from her own more contemporary view, kept Karol grounded in the reality of a turbulent Europe.

"Leja invited you because she really likes being with you," I said. "She says yours is a good match for her mind."

Karol laughed, too heartily as the auditorium quieted and the singers' voices began to rise from the stage. "She certainly has a way to bring me down to earth," he said, again too loudly. "And I believe I lift her up."

A tap on the shoulder from a grey-haired woman seated behind us quieted him, as music filled the room and muffled his apology. He leaned close to me and said, "She is very special, your sister."

The music and singing fueled a unique energy in him during the hour of song. It was difficult to watch the performers with so much action beside me. On the edge of his seat, he seemed to follow with his eyes the invisible musical notes as they played off the walls of the church. His applause was first and loudest at the conclusion of each song. He tapped my knee in excitement when Ludmilla began a solo and whispered "wonderful" when her song ended. When she and the lead male singer stepped to the front of the stage for the final song of the evening, Karol could hardly remain seated. The music had filled him with so much lightness I believed he might float into the air. I put my hand on his shoulder to calm him when Ludmilla began to sing, her rich, dark voice filling the Gothic church with a song I knew. He looked at me as if I'd awoken him from a dream, placed his hand on mine and squeezed. A calmness fell over him, and we listened to the song I'd first heard in the still of Ludmilla's bedroom months before. This time, I believed she was singing to me.

"Love forgives you everything, turns sadness into smiles," she sang. "Love is great at explaining, unfaithfulness, sins and lies."

The male singer beside her interrupted with his song.

"Ochi chyornye, ochi zhguchie

Black eyes, passionate eyes, burning and beautiful eyes!

How I love you, how I fear you. It seems I met you in an unlucky hour!"

Ludmilla continued. "Even when you curse in despair, saying it's cruel and vile."

They went back and forth this way, until the male singer, his voice loud and pleading, sang his final words. "I see mourning for my soul in you. I see a triumphant flame in you, a poor heart immolated in it."

And then, Ludmilla ended the medley. "Love forgives you everything, because love, my dear, is I."

The chapel fell silent as the ghost of her voice hovered and echoed. Karol leapt to his feet and broke the quiet with enthusiastic applause. Leja watched him, absorbing his joy, before rising to her feet. All of us stood with him then, shouting and clapping. Ludmilla scanned the enamored crowd, every man there in love with the idea of her, every woman wishing for a bit of her magic, before settling her gaze on me, her smile wide and warm. She held my eyes as she bowed to acknowledge the applause. Her hand touched her mouth and reached out, and I knew that if I were beside her that kiss would find my lips.

Karol remained manic while we waited outside at the bottom of the church steps for Ludmilla, and his enthusiasm for the music infected the rest of us.

"I enjoyed that so much," he said loudly to his father and Michel, as other patrons streamed past into the street. "It was beautiful in a way I find difficult to describe."

Michel nodded. "You aren't alone," he said. "As many times as I've heard Ludmilla sing over the years, even when she was a little girl practicing in front of the window in her bedroom, the sound of her voice intoxicated me."

Leja stood beside Karol, studying his face. "It was easy to see how much you enjoyed it," she said. "The whole room could see it."

"I hope I didn't embarrass you," Karol said, as he took Leja's hand. "Sometimes I'm too much, aren't I? After my mother died, father told me my emotions became like a tea kettle at full boil, and I know I still can be very," he hesitated, "very passionate."

Karol's young life had been marked by tragedy. His mother died of a heart attack when he was nine years old, and his older brother died when Karol was twelve. His father helped him through those trying times with a combination of religious faith and a ceaseless urging to live in the moment and feel all of life's pleasure and pain. "What you do today will matter to you tomorrow," I once heard him say to his son.

"Live with righteousness and no regrets, embrace today, and your future will be remarkable."

Leja dropped Karol's hand and wrapped him in a hug, holding him close and hard, burying her head into his shoulder. "You made the evening even more special," she said.

At the top of the stairs, Leo was waving his arm wildly. "Over here, Aunt Lu. Over here," he called. Ludmilla was making her way onto the steps, carrying a small bag, surrounded by her fellow singers, all of them buzzing about their queen with the excitement of a hive of honeybees. Leo went to her. "You were marvelous, Aunt Lu. Just marvelous," he said, almost shouting, looking as lovestruck as he often described the university boys. "Let me take that bag."

Ludmilla walked past him as he lifted her bag to his shoulder, came directly to me, and stopped very close. "Thank you for coming tonight," she said. "It made me happy when I saw you. Very happy." She reached for my face, placing a hand on each cheek, and gently pulled me toward her. The kiss was not brief or friendly. It lingered and moved through me like an electrical charge, a jolt that took my attention and held it until she released me.

"What was that?" Leo said.

Leja and Karol surrounded Ludmilla with congratulations and excitement. Michel and Karol's father joined them, so Leo never got an answer. But perhaps he hadn't noticed the kiss, because he was looking down the street where faint shouting and singing, a different type of song than had marked the evening, grew louder and closer. I recognized the tune, the Internationale, a song aging Russians in our town sang in the main square each May Day. It was the anthem of socialists across Europe, with stirring French lyrics calling for workers to rise up against tyrannical kings. The words of this song, however, were Polish, and it was not an anthem calling for the oppressed working class to be empowered, but rather one that promised a Europe free of Jews and other untermensch. Two dozen chanting and singing young men turned a corner and headed toward us and the others leaving the church. One of them waved the Reichskriegsflagge, the flag of the Imperial German armed forces until 1921, and others carried banners with hand-drawn swastikas.

"They are singing about Hitler," Michel said, rushing toward the men, waving his fist as he shouted. "Get away from here. Take your 'Hitlernationale' and go back to your caves."

The men sang louder. Some spat obscenities at Michel as they passed. We joined him in confronting the marchers, as did others leaving the concert. The crowd swelled around the men and blocked their way. Surrounded, they stopped and defiantly sang their song louder, waved their banners more violently.

"Nazi criminals," Karol's father shouted.

"Go back to Germany," Leo added.

"God is watching and sees your evil," Karol said.

"Jew-loving bastards," one of the marchers shouted back. "We will cleanse this nation of you."

Over the shouts and the singing, a woman's voice rose, low at first, and then louder and full-throated. Ludmilla was singing the refrain from the original Internationale, "Comrades, listen to the Signal! Onward, to the final battle!" Leja and I joined her, the three of us in song confronting the marchers. Slowly, other voices sang, until the street echoed with a triumphant answer to the Nazi hatred. The marchers scurried away, silently into the dark.

CHAPTER 32

We were shaken by what we saw and heard that night. The evening of celebration ended abruptly, and we walked home on the eerily quiet streets with a nagging awareness that we were no longer protected from the madness that was creeping across Europe, that, despite a naive faith, we had never been protected. There would be a time, soon, when those men and others like them would return, and a French song sung by a courageous young woman would not be enough to turn them away. I felt it coming, saw it as plainly as I saw the change in all of us in the weeks that followed. It was as if we were each tossed into the wind that night and had landed randomly into altered lives.

Ludmilla and I enjoyed a new boldness. Why should I worry about our relationship being discovered? Why had I ever worried? I noticed Leo's discomfort when I held Ludmilla's hand or she kissed me gently on the cheek, but he never objected or even acknowledged anything out of the ordinary. He became obsessed, instead, with news of the day, bringing accounts of military build ups in France and on the Polish western border to his every conversation, speculating how they might affect his plans, still unchanged, to live in Paris come September. Leja threw herself more energetically into her studies, but her nonstop writing and reading didn't slow the sadness and dread spreading over her like a shadow.

"The trains haven't stopped from Krakow to Berlin and then to Paris," Leo said to her one evening in August while the three of us sat at the kitchen table, open texts and notebooks spread in front of Leja and the day's newspaper in front of Leo beside a glass of wine, his third. "These troop movements by the Germans at our border are just for show, to make the Polish government align with Germany against France. They will never attack us." He said this more to the room than to either Leja or me. "Can you imagine what the British would do if German armies crossed the border? It would be suicide for Hitler."

Leja looked up from her books. "What will you do, if they attack Poland before you leave? You might have to join the army," she said.

"Never happen," he quickly replied. "I'll be at the Sorbonne, drinking wine at a cafe in a few weeks. But I could ask you the same question. I could ask both of you. What will you do? Being a Jew would be risky if the fascists rolled into Krakow."

I'd thought about that almost continually since the concert, father's admonition in my mind to be prepared, have a plan when danger loomed. But I didn't know yet what I would do. If I stayed with Ludmilla, where would we go, and what would happen to Leja? Ludmilla was also torn by indecision when I asked her the question Leo now asked. "Don't you think everything will be alright?" she said, and then "No. No. It won't be."

Leja, though, was certain.

"I will shoot at them from the rooftops," Leja said cavalierly to Leo. "Maybe I can get a few of them before they get me."

Leo laughed. "You could never kill anyone," he said.

"Maybe your brother would. Not you."

"Wolchi knows I'm the killer in the family," Leja continued. "He's the lover."

Leo grimaced.

"What Leja means is that she's the decisive one. She's not afraid to act, and would be a formidable enemy in any battle, political or otherwise," I said.

Leo stood, walked behind Leja and placed his palms against her cheeks. "Is this the face of a killer," he said, as he turned her toward him. She stared back. "I'm actually quite experienced," Leja said. "I've killed one man with a gun and another with love."

"She's joking," I quickly interjected.

"Well, I know what it feels like to be injured by your love, or, more correctly, by a lack of it," Leo said and dropped his hands away. Leja's face turned grim and reddened. Her right hand trembled. That occasional involuntary movement that worsened in the past few weeks as the arguments and confrontations with Leo became more frequent. I was sure she was about to cry, so I gripped her shaking hand.

"You're a hard man to love," I said to Leo. "You're mean."

"Little brother weighs in, the family expert in matters of the heart, or should I say matters of the chuj," Leo said, grabbing his crotch combatively. "I should have thrown you out when I found out how you'd been sneaking around with Aunt Lu. If father had let me, I would have done it."

"Don't bring them into this," Leja said. "Lu and Wolchi have something I envy, that you should envy, as well."

"The only thing I envy is that he gets more in my house than me," Leo said.

"Fuck off," Leja said, pulling her hand from mine and

pushing her chair back without warning, striking Leo. "Just fuck off and go to Paris."

Leo watched her leave the kitchen, unsure of his next move. He turned to me, shook his head and said, "I should have left weeks ago."

When Leja was small, she liked to argue with Ira. She was mama bear, and I was her cub, so I was never the target of her ire. Our brother was, though. They could disagree about anything: Who ate the last bit of food at dinner, who touched the other's book, who made fun of the other in front of friends, and even who started the conversation that had deteriorated into their argument. I realized later that, even then, she was fighting for her place in a world that had little room for a woman or a girl with the spirit and aspirations of my sister. Ira was a sparring partner who taught Leja never to let another person beat her down. The confrontation with Leo, though, had left her shaken.

"Remember how you and Ira would fight when we were kids," I said to her later that evening trying to distract her with memories as we sat in her room. "It made Mama and Papa so angry because they couldn't get the two of you to stop. Then, one day, the arguing did stop, just like that, and never again."

I thought Leja was listening, but I couldn't be sure. She had turned away in the dimly lit room. "Why? Do you remember why?" I asked. She didn't answer. "OK. Would you rather talk about what happened tonight?" No response. "Should I just leave you alone?"

She turned and took my arm. "Stay. I'm sorry. I didn't want you to see me crying." She wiped a tear from one eye, then the other. "He promised to bring me chocolate if I wouldn't start any more arguments with him. Ira, I mean.

The thing is that he never did. I never got any chocolate, but I stopped anyway. I just needed a reason to end the bickering. To make a change. It was wearing me down, but I couldn't back down from it, either."

She turned away from me again. "That's the way Leo and I have been for months. And what I said to him tonight was because I need to make a change. I feel crushed by everything that's happened, and he makes it all feel heavier."

She leaned closer, and I held her, not speaking, squeezing her tightly as her sobbing grew louder. "I miss Mama and Papa, and Ira, too," she smiled at the mention of his name. "I think we should go home."

I left the house early the following morning, so I could arrive for work at the railroad main station and the adjacent repair yard by six a.m. The August sun was rising when I began the thirty-minute walk across the city's central square. Michel joined me, the way he often did before jogging to his university office. We talked about family and the risks we faced because of the imminent threat of war. When we reached the park surrounding old Krakow, once the site of the stone walls that protected the city in the 1400s, the spot where he usually waved goodbye and took off running in the opposite direction, he stopped and lingered.

He pointed to the massive Gothic Barbican looming ahead of us, the fortification that once anchored the city's protective walls. "That is a monument to our past failures at war. We are a nervous country, worried about the next assault, knowing that we have a pitiful history and that nothing is going to stop the German armies, or the Russian armies, if they come. It's also a reminder that, if they do, none of us will be safe."

He clapped his hands onto my shoulders. "I will do what I can to protect you and your sister, you know that, but this is very serious business, a very dangerous time, and I can't predict what will be."

He ran slowly away from me, back through the park, and I considered his warning: If the unstoppable machine of war rolled through Krakow and the rest of Poland, I was on my own.

When I reached the railyard, the sun was still low, but already casting long summer shadows behind the steam engines lined up outside the central building. A dozen of them crowded the yard today, more than usual, awaiting refueling or repairs before resuming their journeys, either to the western border with train cars filled with machinery and weapons, or to the east, pulling mostly empty cars destined for the Central Industrial Region where they would be filled with new loads of weaponry. The yard was squeezed into a strip of land between the park and the tracks of the central station, so it was easy to see the trains and watch passengers arrive or board. Spare axles and steel brake pads, parts most commonly needing repair, were piled beside open pits, where workers labored beneath the hulking train engines. Though it was early, cacophonous noise already filled the outside work areas, the pounding of metal on metal, screeching train wheels, the shouts of men engaged together in heavy, hard work.

I arrived at the central building, and the relative quiet of the machine shop, and joined our group of ten machinists gathered in conversation.

"There are already double the number of trains," the oldest of them said. "Day and night. That can only mean one thing. War is coming."

I was the youngest, two decades the junior of most. All were married, with families, hard-working, capable machinists and decent men whose scarred and perpetually dirty hands fabricated and repaired the parts that built the Polish rail network after World War I.

"Who will we be fighting this time," another asked. "The Germans or the Russians?"

"We will be road kill, either way. Cows on a train crossing," the older man said. "Rolled over by their tanks and cut to pieces by their bullets."

"This railyard has survived other wars," another man said. "Won't we be safe here? They will always need this place."

"This place, maybe, but will they need us?" a third man said.

Gloom and dark humor hung over the group, and even the sunlight could barely penetrate the grease-smeared windows of our mood.

"It will be hard, if we run, to go west. The trains headed there are too crowded with machines and airplanes, and will have no room for us. So, I hope it's not the Russians who come for us," the third man said. "If it's the Germans from the west, though, there will plenty of room on those empty railcars to head the other way."

"We could join all of the Polish soldiers running for the mountains in the Ukraine," a fourth man suggested dismissively. "But what happens if the Germans come on trains from the west and the Russians from the east and they meet each other right here in this rail yard?"

That made everyone laugh, an acknowledgement of the national unease over the future that had afflicted Poland's people for generations. If someone could attack, everyone understood, they would.

The oldest man interrupted the laughter: "Like I said, road kill."

Maybe we were, I thought, as we all drifted to our work-tables to begin the day. Maybe there was also an idea hidden inside this workday banter. Empty trains were headed east toward an isolated town, home, where the danger of a vengeful Polish autocrat seemed quaint beside the threat of an advancing Nazi army. Yes, I thought, we should leave soon, very soon.

CHAPTER 33

On the morning of August 25, 1939, a Friday, England signed an aid agreement with Poland, promising to protect it in the event of a German invasion. The news raised spirits across the country and suggested to many that the long-anticipated invasion by Nazi forces would not happen. Late that same night and early the next day, however, German agents slipped into southern Poland from Czechoslovakia and attacked a remote, strategic section of rail line about 80 miles south of Krakow. The rail line was the shortest route between Vienna and Warsaw, and the German army hoped to secure a choke point on the line, called the Jablonkow pass, in the hours before a planned invasion. The attack failed, but as news of the incursion spread over the weekend, it muted Polish confidence that their borders were secure and reignited fears of imminent war.

Karol kept banging on the door even as I opened it. He was perplexed and rushed past me into the house. It was still early. Leja and Ludmilla, at the kitchen table with cups of tea and plates of toast, stared at him sleepily when he burst into the room, with me behind.

"Did you hear? Did you hear?" he asked excitedly. "The Germans attacked."

We had not heard, and instead had been speculating about the positive affect of the security agreement with Great Britain. Karol provided a dramatic and sobering recounting of the events just a few hours from Krakow. German saboteurs sneaking across the border in the darkness, attacking and capturing the train station at Mosty, being repelled by Polish forces when they tried to secure the vital pass at Jablonkow, and the brave Polish soldiers pursuing and capturing the terrorists when they fled toward the Czech border. The tale seemed contrived or exaggerated at least, but Karol assured us every word was true, shared with his father by a former fellow soldier who had taken part in the battle. The area of the attack was defended by soldiers who were once part of his father's former military unit.

"He's very patriotic, and he wants to rejoin the army," Karol said loudly. "It's crazy. He's packing to leave right now. I have to stop him. He's too sick. Leja, can you help convince him. He likes you and will listen to you."

The commotion attracted Leo and then Michel, and they crowded into the kitchen.

"I'll go with you," Leja said, and she tried to slip past Leo who blocked the doorway.

"Wait a minute, where are you going?" he asked, grabbing Leja's arm. "What's going on?"

Leo had arranged to spend the day with Leja, what would be their last before he departed for Paris. He told me he hoped a romantic afternoon and evening would repair their relationship enough to survive their separation. "I want her to love Leo," he said to me, referring to himself in the third-person and emphasizing "love." And here she was, rushing out without explanation, with Karol.

"I have to go," Leja said.

"When will you be back?" he asked sheepishly.

"I'll be back as soon as I can," she answered.

"But we have plans," he said.

:Let go of my arm," she answered.

"But I love you, and I'm leaving for Paris in the morning," he said, pulling her closer.

"Let go of me. This is not about love for you. It's about winning, getting what you want," she said angrily.

"But I'm leaving for Paris," he said.

"So, go to Paris," she said. "And leave me alone."

Then she was gone. When evening fell on the city and she returned, Leo was gone, too. Leja looked about the house for him until Ludmilla took her hand. "He's not here," she said, an affirmation of what Leja already knew. When she began to sob, there was more fatigue than sadness in her eyes.

Later that night, I lay beside Ludmilla, both of us naked under a thin sheet. The window was open, and sounds from the square drifted into the dark room, ghosts in search of the sleeping city. We had sex earlier in the day, but unenthusiastically, more a distraction than an expression of passion. After spending the day together alone in the house, we sat with Leja for most of the evening while she talked about her sadness, mourning the loss of what was familiar and contemplating what was to come. She wanted to say those things to Leo, but he was gone, likely nursing his own dark mood somewhere in the taverns and cafes of the old city.

Now, alone again, we just listened to the city outside and to our slowly beating hearts. I touched Ludmilla gently, and she sucked in her breath. I put my fingers on her belly, sliding them over her naval, back and forth, up and down. She giggled, ticklish, and grabbed my hand, taking it between her legs, holding it there as she moved her hips. She rolled her buttocks from side to side, a close circular motion, and slipped her finger through mine, touching herself. "Come here," she said and pulled me onto her.

We were quiet lovers, a habit honed by the nights in each others' rooms when the house slept around us. When I was with Ludmilla this way, there was always a moment when I lost awareness of anything that was not immediate and very close. I saw only my lover's face and body, only heard her soft sounds, smelled and tasted the mix of soap and sweat on her skin.

So, I didn't hear the bedroom door open, or see the shaft of light that knifed in from the kitchen. I only felt Ludmilla's hands pushing me away, and when I opened my eyes I saw her reaching to cover herself with the tangled sheet. I heard her gasp, and then his voice.

"Aunt Lu. Aunt Lu," Leo said softly. "Oh shit."

He studied Ludmilla's face and then mine with a confused look, not surprise so much as recognition of something he'd once known, but had forgotten.

"What are you doing here, Leo," Ludmilla said.

"I'm sorry," he said, sounding like a child. "I didn't see anything. I didn't see anything."

He backed out of the room and sat at the kitchen table without closing the bedroom door. I thought he'd fallen asleep, until he started to mumble, in a conversation with himself.

"All my lovelies," he said clearly enough. "All of them have left me."

Chapter 34

It was hard to miss Leo and Michel when they arrived at the rail station late the next morning. The horse-drawn wagon they'd hired clattered up to the platform too fast, and the two horses reared when the driver pulled them to a stop, scattering other travelers boarding the east-bound train. From my vantage point in the adjacent repair yard, I watched them hurriedly unload Leo's bags and carry them through the boarding door. The train was set to depart, and the conductor waved his arms above his head to signal the engineer to begin moving. The scene confused me, because Leo's intended train toward Prague and then Paris had left thirty minutes before, and he was now aboard one headed in the opposite direction, east to L'viv. As the train pulled away, I ran toward it in an urgent and ultimately hopeless effort to get Leo off the wrong train.

Michel waved as the train cleared the edge of the station. "It's very kind that you came to see Leo off, but you just missed him," Michel said. When I explained what had happened, he laughed. "This Paris trip has been jinxed. First it was delayed over and over again because of the border issues. Then Leo overslept this morning, and we needed to make a mad dash to the station. And then he boarded the wrong train?" he asked, bemused. "He should have stayed home."

Leo would soon realize he was traveling away from Paris

and be forced to leave the train and return to Krakow. His first opportunity to do so would be in Tarnow, seventy-five kilometers away, where he could, after a lengthy wait, be on a train west and arrive back in Krakow after midnight.

Leja, Ludmilla and I accompanied Michel when he returned to the Krakow station to await Leo that night, all of us uncomfortable because of our final hours with him but glad for a chance to say goodbye in a proper way. We were an odd group standing on the dimly lit platform looking into the darkness at the edge of town for the single beam of light announcing an approaching train. An empty freight was ready in the service yard to make the trip east once Leo's passenger train cleared the tracks. And we waited.

"Leo will be happy to see all of you," Michel said. "I know he sometimes acts badly, but he is a good boy and all of you are important to him. He has had a lonely life with me, so I might have spoiled him just a bit. You know his mother died. His grandparents, he didn't know them very long before they were gone, too. No siblings. Just me. And Lu, and then the two of you, who became like family to us the past year," indicating me and Leja.

"Your father, Marcus, told me a long time ago that a father must prepare for the day when he can no longer protect his child, when his child will leave him, that the best way to love your son or your daughter is to make sure, when that day comes, they can live without you and navigate an adult life in this heartless time and place where we live. Whom they love, whom they hurt, whether they fight or run. Whether they travel to Paris or stay at home. I can't decide those things for Leo, anymore, only he can."

The night was hot, but a steady wind blew. Leja shifted

uncomfortably as if chilled and pushed her hands deep into her jacket pockets.

"It's not easy," Leja said. "All of it, everything comes at you all at once, and you make mistakes that feel like the heaviest weight. Sometimes, it's hard to even move, much less know whom to love or hate or whether to fight or run. It's hard."

Michel nodded. "When I was younger, in the days after my wife died and Leo and I had nothing, I thought the obstacles we faced couldn't be moved, that we were trapped in a world where our desperation was invisible and insurmountable," he said. "I know what that feels like, and hope I never feel that again, Leja. But better times did come."

I turned when I heard the distant whistle. A faint light headed toward us. The conversation stopped, and we edged closer to the tracks to await the approaching train. But it didn't stop. Polish soldiers waved and shouted through open windows as the train continued through the station. Ludmilla returned the waves enthusiastically. It was a troop carrier heading to the Polish border to fight what we all believed was an inevitable battle with the Germans. When the last of the cars passed, Ludmilla dropped her arm and took my hand tightly. "God protect them," she said, although none of the passing soldiers could hear.

We waited for hours past the scheduled arrival time of Leo's train, until a worker from the railyard spotted me, waved and crossed the tracks. "The train from Tarnow has been cancelled," he said. "It's not coming tonight." I asked him why, but he just shrugged. The next morning when I arrived at work, I got my answer.

Shortly before midnight on August 29, 1939, bombs hidden in two suitcases by German terrorists exploded at the Tarnow central train station. It was an unusually hot and humid night, with temperatures outside near 100 Fahrenheit, and hotter in the waiting hall where the bombs were placed. A military transport departed a few minutes before with hundreds of soldiers, and a crowded passenger train would arrive a few minutes afterward. When the bombs exploded, the lucky ones who escaped only with injuries had been sitting outside the station to escape the worst of the heat, but those inside were torn apart or buried in rubble. Twenty people died, thirty-five were seriously hurt, but the terrorists did not succeed in severing the east-west rail link that connected central Poland with its western region and the Ukraine. Two days later, German forces invaded Poland from the west; two weeks later, Russian armies crossed the eastern border, effectively dividing Galicia at an agreed line one hundred fifty kilometers east of Krakow, and seventy-five kilometers from the Tarnow station. A short distance farther east, across the boundary, Russian soldiers occupied my Galician hometown, where the Jews and Ukrainians welcomed them as liberators from the oppressive Poles.

CHAPTER 35

The news struck like a punch from behind. Leo gone because of an act of fate. We all asked questions without answers, exploring scenarios that would have put Leo anywhere but the Tarnow central station that evening, imagining detours that would have altered the events that left him in the wrong place. Fate's unseen hand was too simple an explanation for why he died, so we scratched at the possibilities hoping something more meaningful would surface. Sometimes we found ways to blame ourselves for our indifference toward him, our anger, or our unwillingness to stand up to his stubbornness and vanity. Did fate do this to him, and to Michel, Leja and Ludmilla, who mourned their loss with heart-breaking tears and anger mixed with fear for their own safety? Or, was the explanation simply that Leo died at the hand of German saboteurs on the day war exploded in Europe?

He was just the first. In a short time, death was all around us. At the railyard, more trains and more military equipment headed west, but now wounded soldiers filled the previously empty cars that returned. Horse-drawn wagons ferried the injured and dying men away from the station to Krakow's overwhelmed hospitals. Poland was at war, and fate was armed with an endless array of killing machines.

The University, in odd contrast, went about its routines.

Faculty debated the ethics of teaching and learning at a time of war, isolated somehow from the fear elsewhere on the streets. Students filled nearby cafes, talking, flirting as if it were two weeks earlier and it was still a fine idea to enjoy the fading days of summer with a cool beer and a cigarette. Farmers sold fruit, vegetables, milk and meat from stalls at the foot of the statue of the Polish poet, Adam Mickiewicz, who had once written: "In the cup a little devil, of a bob-tailed German brand, greeted all the guests, most civil, bowing, prancing, hat in hand."

Then the killing, the German devil, came to Krakow. On a quiet morning as I crossed the park beyond the old city on my way to work, the orange and pink sky promised a serene day. My mind wandered in the quiet dawn until I heard the drone of propellers behind me and saw the airplanes, barely recognizable until they passed over the University buildings and the churches protecting the old city square. In a moment, they were above and all around me, so fast and loud and low that I felt the warm draft and the noisy vibrations of their engines as they passed. Ten of them spread in formation like a flower as they turned down toward the rail yard and began firing their guns. Bullets ripped into everything, the ping of metal in contrast to the soft thudding sound as bullets struck the ground or cut down my helpless coworkers frozen in place by the sudden assault. As quickly as they'd come, they were gone, sweeping across the sky in bold arcs, the orange and pink sunlight igniting their wings in a cool fire as they descended over the Market Square behind me and unleashed another hail of bullets.

I ran toward the yard. As the sounds of the airplanes and the gunfire faded, quiet returned briefly until screams and moans from the bloodied men rose like a morning mist from the chaos of the yard. If it was fate that took Leo, then it was fate that slowed my walk to work that morning and kept me out of the railyard when the planes came. Fate, I knew, would not always be so kind. The airplanes had been efficient and brutal. Men lay dead and dying all around me as I moved through the yard to the machinist shop. The building had collapsed on one side where bullets had cut through the wooden beams supporting the roof. The machinists inside had fared better than those outside and emerged frightened, but whole, from beneath the tables and beside the metal cabinets where they'd hidden. One by one, as their powerlessness became panic, they ran in every direction, hoping to escape before the airplanes returned.

Alone in the machine shop, I found my box of machinist tools and opened the lid. The taps and dies imprinted with the face of a Golem were undisturbed inside. Even though I used these tools everyday, I hadn't looked at the imprint for months. Now, I recalled father's words when he handed me this gift: The protective eyes of the Golem, of fate, would be on me wherever I worked. And, indeed, it seemed they had. I ran out of the shop with the wooden box under my arm. I needed to find Leja and Ludmilla, and we needed to get out of Krakow.

As I ran, I watched the sky, now blue and bright, for the airplanes. The Market Square was chaos. I made my way through overturned stalls, past bloodied men and women, and stopped outside Ta Kremowa Sukie, the small shop with the crimson dress. The old dressmaker was on the ground inside, shards from the shattered window strewn about and the torn crimson dress beside her. I kneeled and brushed aside strands of hair from her face.

"Grandma, are you hurt?" I asked. She recognized my voice, or perhaps my sweaty, dirty face. "You know my Shayna," she said. "Are you taking care of her? Make sure you take care of her."

She stood and walked about the shop, touching the small sewing machine and lifting each spool of thread carefully to examine it. "The broom," she said as she reached behind the counter. "I need the broom." She retrieved it, and began to sweep.

"Let me do that, grandma," I said. "Let me help you."

She pulled away and lifted the torn crimson dress from the ground. She shook it up and down, sending broken glass about the shop. "You give this to my Shayna," she said, thrusting the dress into my arms. "Take her dancing."

She set aside the broom and opened the drawer in the table, retrieving the framed photograph of the youthful Mr. Koperski and his wife. After studying it, she handed that to me, as well. That's when I saw the blood staining her own dress crimson. "You're hurt," I said. "Let me help you."

She was thin and frail, small enough that I could lift and carry her through the square to the University's hospital. She held the crimson dress, the photo and the box of tools, as I pushed through the crowded hospital entrance past the wounded gathered inside. I kept walking with her, the dress fabric flowing around us, a silk talisman that parted the surprised onlookers, until we reached a room with white-coated doctors and nurses huddled over patients on bloody beds. A young doctor, startled at first by our entrance, rushed to help. "Over here," he ordered, as he lifted the old woman from my arms placing her with unexpected gentleness onto a stretcher as I retrieved the tools, the photograph and the dress. "We will take care of her," he said.

The old woman watched me as they wheeled her into the treatment room. "Take her dancing," she called. "She loves to dance."

<hr>

Frenzied citizens on the street hurried past Michel's house when I unlocked the front door. They shouted: "The Germans. The Germans," as if others did not recognize the military force that had surged into the city like an angry summer thunderstorm. Church bells tolled urgent warnings. Once inside, I saw through the window a grey, open car with two small red and black swastika flags on the fenders. It parted the crowd and drove slowly past with three uniformed German officers inside. Foot soldiers trotted beside it. Then came truck after truck pulling artillery pieces or filled with more soldiers.

Ludmilla touched me from behind.

"They're everywhere," she said. "I heard on the radio that Warsaw is also under attack, but our soldiers have stopped them."

I placed the tools and the dress on the floor and held her closely. "There are no Polish soldiers anywhere here," I said.

She bent and lifted the dress, recognizing it, and looked at me confused. Smiling, she asked, "What is this?"

I told her the story. "She remembered you," I said. "You remind her of her daughter."

Gunfire echoed in the street, just outside, and we both instinctively kneeled to the ground. We lay there, just beneath the window and held each other, entangled in the smoothness of the dress.

"I'm frightened," Ludmilla said.

"I am, too," I answered.

"No. I mean I'm frightened for you. You can't stay in the city. You and Leja need to leave," she said.

"None of us can stay. You and Michel also," I argued.

She didn't move or even breathe for a moment before straightening herself high enough to peer through the bottom of the window. "Where are all those soldiers going?"

The rail station, I said. The town hall, and the University. She stood quickly and took my hand. "Leja and Michel," she said. "We need to find them."

Outside, soldiers in the trucks stared blankly at us as they passed. Ludmilla smiled and waved in a way others might describe as enthusiastic, waving as she had when she saw the Polish troops at the rail station weeks before. Still smiling at the soldiers, she led me down the street and into a pedestrian alley, part of a network that snaked through the old city. Once hidden from the street, I asked, "What was that?" Looking behind us, she whispered to me robotically and without conviction, "Pigs. German swine."

We walked toward the University through the narrow, cobblestone pathways. Shuttered windows, empty cafes, a child's high-pitched laughter somewhere close, men hurrying past on bicycles, a woman crying, and the two of us rushing to find Leja and Michel before the Germans took control of the University and started isolating and removing anyone who looked like trouble. The Nazis knew that artists and other thinkers who rejected their propaganda posed a threat to their control, perhaps even more than the hapless Polish army. Just as they had taken away the musicians, teachers and writers in Vienna, they would eliminate them in Krakow, Poland's intellectual heart.

The German trucks and troops had taken up positions on the grass outside the University commons when we arrived. We walked close to the buildings to avoid them and entered the interior tiled courtyard, which linked the hallways of the various academic communities. Students stood in the brick archways, as the group of three German officers walked across the courtyard. "What do you want here?" shouted a student, wearing a cotton flat cap pulled low near his eyes. "This is a free Poland." The senior Nazi officer, his long leather coat an odd sight in the late summer heat, stopped abruptly, and the others halted behind him.

"Is there a patriot in the crowd?" he shouted, as he scanned the students. "Come, let me see you. I would like to discuss freedom with someone at this fine university."

He walked to a nearby young man, a random choice, and tapped his chest. "Did you know your government has oppressed scores of ethnic Germans for years in the west of your country and kept them separated from their motherland? Have they enjoyed a free Poland? Tell me."

The officer moved close, his lips nearly touching the terrified student's eyelids. The officer then turned to a young woman beside them. "And what about you, young lady? Ah, I see you are Slavic, no?" he asked. She said nothing, and he placed his hand below her jaw turning her head from side to side. "You don't need to answer. That nose, that chin, which will become ever more prominent on your face as you grow old and fat, could only adorn the face of a Slav." He released his grip on her. "But let me ask, do you feel free in this country?" he asked calmly. "I believe your people in the Ukraine, like my German brothers, feel enslaved by their Polish masters."

He scanned the group again before walking across the

courtyard, stopping beside the student with the flat cap who had shouted at the soldiers. "So, make no mistake, young man. I am here as a liberator."

When he drew his small, black handgun and used it to flick the student's cap from his head, the others nearby gasped. He began shouting. "And the next time you see a German officer, do not speak to him. Do not shout a question. Do not even breathe. Do you understand?" The young man stared without speaking. "I asked you if you understand," the officer shouted louder, spit flying from his lips, the gun barrel now pressed against the student's cheek.

I saw the flash from the gun before I heard the blast echo against the courtyard bricks. The student fell backward, like a tree felled by a storm. The German holstered his gun, wiped spattered blood from his face with a white handkerchief and walked slowly with the other officers into the University building. Others in the courtyard chaotically rushed away, leaving the student lying dead and alone on the ground.

"Oh, god," Ludmilla said, her hand over her mouth.

This was a moment I would replay in my memory for years and imagine myself in a more heroic role. I could rush at the German officer and knock away his gun. Or, I might take his gun and have him begging for his life. Or, I could raise a rallying cry that led the students to attack and beat those German officers until they were on the ground as bloody as the dead man. I didn't do any of those things. Instead, I stood and watched, like everyone else, frozen by the inexplicable horror. But I'd had enough, too. Courage is often difficult to distinguish from carelessness, just as cowardice and caution can be confused. So, perhaps, in the fog of fear, I had grown careless.

"We have to find them, now," I said, as I took Ludmilla's hand, pushing into the building past the fleeing students. We searched the hallways and classrooms. Michel's office door was ajar, but he was not inside. We ran toward raised voices down the tiled hallway, where a group of faculty and students blocked the entrance to the Collegium Novum, a vast hall that functioned as the heart of the University, a place for lectures, faculty debates and important meetings of the academic community. They faced down the three German officers in an argument over the soldiers' presence. "You do not belong here," an elderly professor in the front said, pointing his finger in an animated debate with the senior German officer. Michel, Leja and Karol stood at the back of the group. Karol saw us first and waved, motioning us to join. But I didn't move. One of the Germans followed Karol's eyes and looked back toward us. I began motioning enthusiastically back to Karol and shouted, "Let's go. We'll be late for class." The entire group turned to me. All three German officers moved their hands to their hip and the guns in their holsters.

"Karol, Leja we need to go. Now," I shouted again. "Remember what professor said. We can't be late again."

They stood staring back, confused, so I walked into the crowd, past the German officers, took my sister's hand, tugged at Karol's arm, motioned with my head to Michel and began to back away. I pushed the three of them gently, urging them to hurry. They kept turning to the crowd, but I kept pushing, until a hand, blood smeared on the fingers, grabbed my shirt collar.

"You see," the senior officer said to the crowd. "You need more dedicated students like this one. He doesn't care for politics, just his studies. Am I right?" he asked me.

"Go," I said to Leja. Karol nodded to me and tugged at

her sleeve and Michel's, leading the three of them out of the crowd.

"Did you hear me, boy? I asked a question," the German said.

"Yes. I'm sorry. You startled me. I am late for my class," I replied, as Ludmilla took my hand.

"And what are you studying. Tell me." He spoke to me, but his eyes were on Ludmilla. She returned his gaze, then looked away flirtatiously.

"I would like to be an engineer."

"I am happy to hear that you are not a philosopher, or an artist, or, god forbid, a politician like these others. Good for you, studying to become useful to us," he said derisively, releasing my collar and sweeping his hand over the crowd. "They are telling me my presence at their university is not welcome, and I am trying my best to persuade them otherwise." He paused. "Hurry," he said to me. "I think you are late for your class."

He was watching Ludmilla, while we walked away. I could feel his eyes on her as we hurried toward the door. When we reached the others outside in the courtyard, a single shot echoed down the tiled hall, following us into the midday sun.

CHAPTER 36

The streets grew quiet after dusk. No people. No wagons. No soldiers. The city held its communal breath, and everyone hid, waiting. We sat together at Michel's table for dinner. Karol and his father were with us. Leo's chair remained empty, and this meal felt like a memorial for him, the first time we'd gathered since his death and, maybe I thought, the last time we would ever be together.

I told them my plan, to ride the empty railcars east to relative safety in the Russian zone, to change trains in Tarnow or begin walking if the rails beyond had been destroyed. There would be room for all of us when we reached the isolation of our small town. We would be safe, surrounded by family and friends — and at least one formidable enemy named Igor Goreki, Leja noted. We didn't yet know how to manage that.

For everyone but me and Leja, though, these details didn't matter. For everyone but us, the question was why. Why leave at all?

"You need to go as soon as possible, before the Germans block the roads and railways," Michel said. "No Jew will be safe here."

"No one is safe, Michel," I answered.

"I won't leave Krakow," he said. "Not so long as those barbarians are threatening the University and my students.

My colleagues have all vowed to stand together, and I will stay to protect what matters." He paused, in thought. "With Leo gone, it's all I have left."

"You do understand they shot one of your colleagues and a student today. What's to stop them the next time," I said.

"They can be reasoned with," Michel said. "They are intelligent men, and they'll need our support eventually."

"Michel, let us help you the way you helped us," Leja pleaded. "We owe you that, and Papa would want it. He would insist you come with us."

"You two owe me nothing except a promise to go where you'll be safe. That's all Marcus would ask," Michel said.

Karol's father banged once loudly on table to get our attention. "We must fight them," he shouted. "We can't run away." He was ashen, his breathing shallow, his posture bowed. He wore a Polish officer's uniform jacket, three decades old, which hung on him limply. "We are not cowards. We are men. We must fight back."

Karol placed an arm over his father's shrunken shoulders and straightened the older man's uniform epaulets.

"Papa, there is no more Polish army," he said softly. "They've already lost. This is a different war than the one you fought."

"Karol, you'll come with us, won't you?" I asked. "My family will welcome you."

"Michel is right. You and Leja must leave, but father is too weak," Karol said. "I need to stay with him."

Leja put her hand over his. "We can help you with him. It will be okay. Come with us?"

"I would like to go with you, be with you, but no," Karol answered. An awkward silence followed. He gripped her hand in his and looked at her as if they were the only two in the room. "But let me ask you. If I did, what would that mean for us?"

Leja, surprised, paused before responding, "Voltaire said we should judge a man by his questions rather than his answers. Remember telling us that," she asked. "So, should I judge your answer, or your question?"

Karol's face flushed. He was in unfamiliar water with her. "You must go, my dearest Leja," he said. "But I will be here when you come back." He removed the small St. Christopher medal from his neck and clasped it around Leja's. He leaned close and placed a gentle, single, sad kiss on her cheek. "This was my mother's," he said. "It will keep you safe until we meet again."

Ludmilla had been quiet most of the evening, keeping busy serving and clearing dishes, refilling glasses, distracted and oddly apart from the rest.

"This is not Vienna, you know," she said suddenly, speaking to all of us. "Austria and Germany are the same place, all of the people are German, so they could do as they pleased. Everyone went along. This is Poland,. The things they did in Vienna, people would never do here. It will be different."

"You plan to stay here?" I asked. Although we had never spoken of it, whenever I thought of the future I assumed ours would be a common one. Now this.

Her optimism was a delusion, I knew, and Michel looked troubled. "It was difficult what happened to you in Vienna," he said. "It was terrible. So, I understand your hope that what you experienced there cannot happen to you again. But we need to be realistic about what we will encounter."

"I understand these people. What happened to others

there, will not happen to us here. We just need to get along, not argue and fight with them, and we'll all be fine," she argued too loudly. She looked at me, and before walking from the room she said: "I will be fine, Wolchi. Just fine."

Dinner ended awkwardly and quickly after that. Michel urged Karol and his father to stay the night. The streets, he said, would not be safe. Before she left the room, Leja shyly returned Karol's earlier kiss. "I will miss you, Karol," she whispered to him. "I am proud to know you."

When Michel and I were alone, he took my hand, shook it firmly for a long while. "This world is not good enough for you and your sister," he said. "Tell your father that I did what I could, for as long as I could. All we can hope now is that he was correct, and that human decency is more powerful than the great armies of Europe." He released my hand. I didn't know what to say other than "goodbye."

<hr>

Ludmilla carefully sewed the torn sleeve on the red dress. I lay on her bed, watching her methodical stitching, loop after loop. I felt cold under the sheet. It was still September, but it was cold. I wondered why she was wearing just that thin nightgown. Her nipples got hard when the temperature dropped, and I could see them, even from across the room. She was cold, too.

"Why don't you come to bed and get warm," I asked.

"I need to get this dress mended," she said. "There may be parties. The Germans like to have parties, you know, and I'll need to look my best."

I thought of her in that dress, remembering the time

we danced in Ta Kremowa Sukie, the tiny shop where any passerby could watch. There was something in that memory nagging at me, a piece that didn't fit with the picture I'd constructed of this woman who'd seduced me and then absorbed me without resistance into her damaged reality. When she danced, who was she dancing with? The look in her eyes that afternoon in the shop was the look she often had, distant and unfocused, the same one she had right now as she sewed a dress she'd wear at parties in an occupied city to dance with other men, with that Nazi officer perhaps, who'd taken an interest in her at the University. One thing was certain, she would never again wear that red dress to dance with me.

"You know that I'm leaving in the morning, don't you?" I asked.

"One minute," she said. "I'm nearly finished."

She ran her needle through the back of the stitch before biting down and cutting the thread with her teeth. A red piece of it hung from her lip like a feather in the mouth of a cat who'd just killed a bird.

"I want you to come with me," I said. "We would be safe in my town until all of this ended, and then we could come back."

She sat beside me and ran her fingers through my hair.

"Oh dear boy," she said. "My poor boy. You should know Ludmilla better by now. I couldn't live in a place like that. There would be nothing for me there."

———◦•◦———

Light trickled into my room early. I'd left the curtains open. Was it already morning? The honey-colored strands crawled across my face and woke me, piercing my eyes in a way that was shocking at first, but should not have been. I thought I'd know what to do when this moment came, but I was twisted in the sheets and confused about what was ahead. Where was she? From the moment we met, I now realized, she had been misunderstood, by me and everyone else. Now, alone in my room, the unexpected light on my face had, in just five minutes, shattered my belief that we could have a life together.

I wanted to say goodbye, so before Leja and I left the house I went to her room. The door was open, her back to me, as she sat on the bed, her arms crossed over her chest, staring out the window at the ancient stone buildings aglow in the early morning. The red of her dress and the light of the rising sun tinted her shoulders and neck a shade of ginger, like the fading paint of a museum portrait. Her voice was low, almost a whisper, but in the quiet of the house I heard her singing.

"Love forgives you everything," she sang, "because love, my dear, is I." Then I understood, because love was never us.

Part Four, October 1939, Galicia in Eastern Poland,
a small town south of L'viv

If you want a happy ending, that depends,
of course, on where you stop your story.
— Orson Welles
The Big Brass Ring

CHAPTER 37

We returned home the way we'd left nearly two years before, facing backward on the rear of a horse-drawn cart, this one filled with baled wheat and rye from a small farm ten kilometers from our town, just across the border that now separated Russian and German troops. Leja knew the farmer driving and others in the rural countryside because she had spent months traveling with Ivan to spread the principle of Ukrainian independence and enlist support for the O.U.N. When we arrived at his farm, tired and hungry and asked for help traveling the final distance to home, the farmer readily agreed. Leja, he said, was someone important. "She knows the right way," he explained. "And people listen to her."

The farmer made this trip often enough, so wouldn't attract attention, and even the presence of a young man and woman in the back of his cart, disheveled and dirty, wouldn't draw suspicion from the Russian soldiers manning check points along the road. Just three peasants scrapping by under the oppressive hand of Polish control.

"The Russians are happy to be here," the farmer said as our cart passed a group of soldiers resting beside the road. "They came and not a shot was fired. Everyone welcomed them and had a big party. The women handed out bread and salt to soldiers on the streets. Men were drinking. Well, almost everyone was happy. The rich Polish people over there stayed away." He pointed in the direction of the large farms, including Igor Goreki's, outside the town. "They know what's coming for them, because to the Russians, Poles and Nazis are the same."

The cart turned at the corner and stopped as a group of soldiers crossed from a large encampment by the river and walked toward the town square. As if on cue, a carriage drawn by two horses pulled to a stop behind us. The driver, wearing a suit and a Homburg hat stiffened and shiny with shellac, impatiently stood and strained to see what blocked his way. I recognized the carriage before I looked at the man. The brass on the side boards was scratched and uneven where it had been damaged and then straightened. Broken and charred pieces of wood, once polished and smooth, had been reassembled with rough nails. I marveled that the carriage could still operate, considering the beating I'd given it with the blade of an axe.

Igor Goreki's impatience with the delay on the road blinded him to what was right in his view. He scanned the street, looked at our cart, at us and back at the street before recognition exploded on his face. If his eyes had been flames, we would have been incinerated. He dropped the reins of the carriage, jumped down from the seat and was beside us in an instant.

"You. Get out of there. Come down here," he shouted, a bit of froth oozing from the corner of his mouth.

His shouts caught the attention of others nearby, including several of the Russian soldiers. He grabbed my leg and began pulling me from the cart.

"Get your hands off him," Leja said.

I pushed him away with my free leg, and he fell to the ground, his hat tumbling into the dirt. When he stood, he growled like a wild animal. "I will kill you myself," he said.

Before he could take a step toward me, though, two Russian soldiers, their rifles drawn, intercepted him.

"No one is killing anyone today," one soldier said, his weapon pointed at Goreki, as he studied all of us. The farmer's humble cart. The once-elegant carriage. The farmer. Leja and me in our dirty clothing sitting amid piles of grain. Goreki in his expensive suit, his well-trimmed hair and mustache. The soldier eyed the dirty Homburg on the ground and pointed at Goreki.

"Yours?" he asked.

When Goreki nodded, the soldier thrust his bayonet through the crease in the Homburg's center crown and offered the skewered hat to its startled owner. He waved his hand at the farmer urging him to drive away. Goreki stood still in the middle of the street holding his ruined hat, and never took his eyes from us as we rode away.

Some things had changed in our town, but some had stayed just the same. That was also true for me. I felt older, wiser and more wary in a way that I could not have explained at the time. But when the farmer's cart stopped in front of my childhood home and Leja reached across and hugged me, the best, strong hug she knew to give, my exhaustion overwhelmed me, and I was a child again in the comfort of her arms.

"Welcome home," she said.

Mother was inside absent-mindedly wiping the table, her head down, and, for a moment, I thought she'd not heard the door open. When she saw us, she stared without breathing, all of it out-of-context for her, until I said: "Mama." She dropped the cleaning cloth and rushed to us, wobbling from side to side the way she did when she was in a hurry and didn't care who was watching.

She said: "Oh my god. You are here." She hugged us both and began shouting.

"Papa. Papa. Come now. They are here. Leja and Wolchi are here."

I thought it might not be the best idea to announce that fact to the town just yet, given the crimes some believed we'd committed. And Mother's voice was surely carrying through the open windows. Yet, since our return had been noted in such a dramatic way by the street confrontation with Goreki, I thought it better to let her shout the news to father and everyone else on the street, than quiet her. She did not release her grip as she called for him, yelling at an ear-splitting volume with her face between ours and her arms locked across our shoulders. When she wasn't calling for father, she was kissing our cheeks, and I felt her tears warm on my face.

"Let me see you," she said, releasing her fierce hold but keeping us at arm's length. "You are thin and so dirty." She laughed, placing her hand to her mouth. "But you are home. That's what matters. Where is your father. Papa. Papa." She shouted again and went to the back of the house, shouting through the open window facing the buchbinderi. "Papa. Come. They are home."

When father limped through the front door, I didn't wait for him to reach us. I grabbed him in my arms and, rather than wait for him to lift me, I lifted him. I felt strong. He felt smaller. I held him aloft, his cane dropping to the ground, the front door open, with no regard for the passersby watching. Our planned, quiet return had become the opposite, noisy and eventful, and the sight of him, the feel of his rough shirt on my face, his smell like fresh bread, his warm chest, made my remaining caution vanish. Oh, how I'd missed him.

We spent that afternoon and evening close to one another — mother, father, Leja and me. Mother had sent for Ira and Katia, who came from their farm, with Naftali, nearly four years old. No one said very much, and there were long moments of quiet. We sat at the table near the kitchen, eating, drinking tea, sharing inconsequential news from the town. The presence of one another in this familiar place seemed enough at first. Father asked about Krakow. He'd received letters from Leja and me via Mr. Koperski while we were gone, but he wondered, now, about the past month since the Nazis invaded. News from there, he said, had been scarce and what had come was unnerving.

"We assumed bad things," father said. "And feared the same for ourselves until the Russian army arrived. Many of us, especially Jews, thought that was a miracle." He paused for emphasis and added, "But many of the townspeople wish it had been the Nazi armies that came."

Leja told them about Leo, and father grew grim. "Such heartbreak for his father," he said. I told them about the random shootings in the Krakow railyard and the University, and about Michel and Ludmilla, and their decision to stay in the city. "The Germans will torment or destroy anyone who doesn't help them," father said. "Michel will be their enemy. I hope God can protect him."

A gloominess fell over the rest of us. We grew quiet again, and I became aware, without speaking it, of the dangerous future we faced. Those armies slaughtering innocent people in Krakow were just a day's journey from where we sat, celebrating our reunion, thankful we had so far avoided the worst.

Naftali fell asleep on Ira's lap and began snoring softly. The sound of it interrupted our somber mood. "You should hear his father snore," Katia said. "Oh, we've heard. We've heard," Leja retorted. This was funny. We laughed. What an odd thing that a sleeping child, so small, had the power to lift us all back into a moment of joy.

"He's grown so much," Leja said to Ira.

"He is happy despite the chaos," Ira said. "The ignorance of innocence, I think. He's fascinated by the soldiers, and already aspires to join the Russian army when he grows up."

"Well, let's hope the Russian army is back in Russia by that time," Leja said. "Perhaps he could join a Ukrainian army?"

I saw father scowl at Leja's comment. Always with the politics, he would be thinking. Leja is always with the politics. He would typically try to shut that down to avoid yet another argument about the country's political future, but tonight was different.

"A number of us from the Jewish community are meeting with the Russian military leadership tomorrow evening to discuss their governance," he said to her. "You and Wolchi should come with Ira and me. They are looking for Jews to join their Marxist youth movements."

Leja, her arms over her chest, defiance on her face, didn't need to say a word to communicate how little she thought of father's suggestion. His embrace of the Russians, we all knew, did not reflect any deeply held belief. This was a man who fought against the Tzar's armies in the first World War and was now extolling the worth of Marx and Engels to his sons and daughter. It made no sense any place other than in Galicia, the embattled, ever-morphing place he had always called home. He made a practical calculation that the Russians, with their socialist ideas about equality for all oppressed people, even Jews, provided room to maneuver his children toward a better life. He never imagined something better for himself. But for his children it was possible, and he'd identified an opportunity with the Russians.

"You know I always told you, in the world as it is, we must choose," he said to Leja. "Now we must choose which army will be our army, which ideology will provide us shelter?"

"And which," Ira interjected, "will get us a bit of payback for the abuse and indignities of the past twenty years."

Ira's face bore evidence of those. The scar on his right temple and the dented bone above it, left by Nicholas Goreki's club, reminded us of the cruelty of Polish rule.

"It is not enough that Nicholas is dead," he continued, touching his scar gently. "It's all of them that did this to me. I am in favor of the Russians, because they will take care of things. I won't need to worry whether some Polish thug or Goreki himself will attack me or harm my wife or son as long as the Russians are here."

Naftali stirred, and Ira wrapped his arms around him, cradling him in the safety of strong shoulders and deep love.

"We should go with Papa and listen to the Russians," Ira said, turning to me and then Leja. "They won't protect you if you choose something else, and things might become unpleasant."

I was thinking about what "unpleasant" might mean for people like Goreki, whose presence still loomed over our family even though his public influence had waned in the wake of the Russian occupation. If he came for me or Leja, would the Russians protect us? Could anyone?

Chapter 38

The knocking at the door the following morning was urgent. Leja had left early to visit Ira's farm, and I was alone with mother and father.

"Marcus, Marcus," a voice called from the street. "Open up. Marcus, Clara."

Mother wiped her hands on her apron as she walked from the kitchen. She recognized the voice of the man pounding on the door, because she unlocked it without hesitation. Even before the door had swung fully open, Rabbi Breslov pushed his way inside, red hair unkempt beneath his hat, his prayer shawl billowing behind. He chewed on strands of his grey beard in the corners of his mouth like the bit of a horse's bridle, before brushing them aside to speak.

"Clara, where is Marcus? The Russian commander has asked for him. Asked for him by name," the rabbi said, breathless. "He needs to come with me right now."

Father, unhurried, joined them. Placing his hand on mother's back, he kissed her cheek before acknowledging their guest.

"Rabbi Breslov, to what do we owe this honor?" he asked. That's how he always greeted the rabbi, and I had never been certain whether this was a sign of respect or a gentle mocking of the rabbi's self-importance.

"The commander," the rabbi continued. "The Russian commander spoke your name and asked me to bring you to him."

Father seemed puzzled. "I planned to join the others this afternoon."

"No. No. He wants you now, without the others. We met a few moments ago with the priests, and he asked me to bring him the bookmaker, the man who does printing. Marcus, that's you."

The rabbi's intensity amused me as I watched from a corner. He seemed more like an amateur actor portraying a rabbi, than the real thing. To what do we owe this honor, I thought, and snickered softly. The rabbi heard and scolded me. "There is nothing funny about the Russian commander asking for your father. He is a serious man, an impatient man. He may be a Jew, his name is Girshman, Commander Girshman, but he will have no tolerance for disrespect from us." Then he softened, and a kind smile broke his lips. "Wolchi, I also must say that I'm happy you are safe and at home. We all worried."

The mood in the room shifted, and the rabbi's anxiety spread like a spill. Father was quiet. Mother, beside him, looked concerned.

"Why does he want you, papa?" mother asked.

"Who could know?" father said. "I think if he meant me harm, though, he would have sent soldiers to collect me, rather than the rabbi."

"Papa," I interrupted. "I should go with you? You asked me yesterday. I should go, too." It wasn't that I could offer protection if the commander intended harm, but having been away from father for so long gave me the need to stay close if this was to be a time of trouble. It's what he'd always done for me.

"Wolchi, no, you stay here," mother said. "Maybe this commander wants papa because he has heard things from Igor Goreki." When she said his name, she pursed her lips and made a feigned spitting motion.

Father thought otherwise. "I would like his company, mama," he said. "And the commander may want to hear from Wolchi about Krakow. No one else has seen the German army there." He nodded toward me. "Maybe wash your face and wear a clean shirt, though. Out of respect."

The Russian army had bivouacked along the western bank of the Stryi River. Their encampment filled the dry, flat ground on a plateau beyond the road, avoiding the flooded, muddy banks and turbulent currents farther downstream. The commander's tent was at the highest point, at the end of an uneven path beaten into the brush and grass. Soldiers spread beneath him, hundreds of men, lounging beside fire pits and under canvas awnings, their horses tied to trees nearer the river. They seemed unprepared for war, almost casual, as if they were spending a leisure day beside the river, enjoying the clear morning with friends and family.

The rabbi entered the commander's tent first, holding my father and I back with his hand. Several uniformed officers stood around a worn table examining maps and other documents, speaking softly among themselves.

"Commander, I've brought the bookmaker," the rabbi said.

An older man, the sleeves of his uniform shirt pushed up to his elbows, pointed with his hand without looking at us. "Sit. I'll be with you in a moment."

The crude wooden chairs along the wall of the tent matched the table, weather-beaten and water-stained. I recognized them from the town hall meeting room. As father limped toward them, the commander turned and watched him. His fellow officers did so, as well. Father, his eyes averted, his cane leaving a trail of round indentations in the dirt behind him, made his way to the chairs and sat gracefully down. I sat to one side of him, and the rabbi the other.

"You are the bookmaker and printer, the man named Marcus?" the commander asked. Father nodded. "I am Commander Girshman, Samuel Girshman. Your leg," he pointed at father. "Where?"

Father understood the question, and described the battle in the forest and hills of the eastern front in the final days of the "last war" in which a shell exploded near his trench and shattered the bones and muscle of his right foot and calf.

"You wore the uniform of the Austrian army, I suspect, and fought for the emperor," Girshman said, running his fingers through thinning hair, his face lined and serious. "I fought there as a younger man, myself, but obviously for the Tzar."

The rabbi interjected, "There was no choice then for a young man here. He had no choice. The Austrians . . ." Girshman raised his hand. "Quiet," he said. "Please don't interrupt."

This meeting with the commander had not gotten off to a good start. The rabbi, chastened, slumped in his chair. Father, silent, looked directly at the commander, each taking a measure of the other. After a moment, Girshman continued.

"We fought against each other then, but now we seem to have an enemy in common." He bent and tapped his right leg below the knee. Father straightened when he heard the hollow wooden sound from beneath the commander's pant leg. "And a few other things."

He walked slowly to father, extended his hand and received father's in return. Both men stood facing one another, and their handshake lingered. "Now, let's talk about how you can help me."

Girshman sent his officers and the rabbi away, but my father urged him to include me in the discussion.

"He's just back from Krakow and saw the Nazi invasion there," father said. "Perhaps he can help you, too."

Girshman nodded and walked to the table, urging us to join him. He picked up a book, a familiar one, a special edition of Joseph Roth's "The Radetzky March," handmade by father and Ira. "An excellent book," the commander said. "I have read it twice. It tells a story we both know quite well, Marcus. Don't you agree?"

He opened it to an inside page, and pointed to a small agate notation that recorded the date and place of publication, 1937, at father's buchbinderi. "And the quality of the printing and binding, look at it, worthy of the words inside." He held the book in the air between us and turned it from side to side as if admiring a fine art object.

"How fortunate for me that the man who made this book is right here in this town, right here in my tent," he continued. "So, Marcus, I'm sure you are quite busy, but I would like to engage your services to help me educate your fellow citizens about the virtues of Soviet ideology."

From among several piles of documents, he retrieved a stack of eleven-by-fourteen lithographs and spread them across the table. Drawn in a minimalist style with red and black ink, they praised or eulogized Soviet leaders, Karl Marx, Vladimir

Lenin and Joseph Stalin, and described a workers' paradise that was transforming agriculture and industry while building a modern European nation. One sheet highlighted the Soviet military, with a squadron of aircraft flying over Moscow and Stalin presiding from a raised platform to the delight of waving crowds. Another featured farmers and peasants crowded into an endless field of grain admiring a larger-than-life Stalin hovering above an industrialized farm. They were not subtle.

"You see, my army has captured your town, your country," he said. "But the hearts of your people? Their deeply held beliefs? Those are separate battles, and I know not everyone is happy we are here."

"What do you want me to do?" father asked, cautiously.

"You are a printer, correct? I want you to print. You are a bookmaker, so make me books," Girshman said. He pointed to the table. "As many of these as you can. We will hang them in the town, bind them into books and take them to every village from here to L'viv."

His eyes caught the light in a way that made them flash. There was madness in them, like the look the Nazi officer had in Krakow before he shot the student.

"Agreed?" he asked. Father nodded. What else could he do. "Excellent. We should begin immediately." Girshman then placed his hand on my shoulder. "Now, young man. Tell me about Krakow."

It was clear he wasn't expecting much when he pulled a chair under him, draping his legs across the seat with the back facing father and me. He studied me, interested in something other than my recounting of the aerial attack and the executions at the university. I spoke without his seeming to hear, until he interrupted.

"Your name? Tell me your name," he said. I did. "Wolchi?" he asked a bit scornfully. "What is your proper name?" I told him.

"Wolchik? In Russia that is Vladimir A man's name, a good Russian name. The name of a leader, Chairman Lenin's name. If you tell Russian people your name is Wolchi, they will see a soft heart and someone to be ignored. Tell them you are Vladimir, and they will respect you."

I felt flattered by his attention and enthusiasm, but he was a powerful man in the uniform of a conqueror, and he also frightened me. I didn't know how to reply, but didn't need to because another Russian officer entered the tent just then and took Girshman aside. They watched me as they spoke. The officer pointed toward me with certainty, nodding his head. When he left, Girshman sat back down and moved his chair closer.

"I have just heard some news, Wolchi," he paused and emphasized my name. "My officer tells me you had a skirmish in the square yesterday with one of the town's fine Polish gentlemen."

"Igor Goreki is not a gentleman, and nothing about him or his family is fine," father interrupted angrily. Girshman nodded to my father in seeming agreement.

"But we can't have fights in the street," Girshman continued. "This needs to be a peaceful place, one free of disorder and criminal behavior. Don't you agree, Marcus?"

"Igor Goreki has been a plague on this community from the day he and the others arrived," father answered. "He has attacked my business, my home, my family, and those of every Jew and Ukrainian. He is detested."

"So, he is the guilty one in this situation?" Girshman

asked. "Is that what you're saying, because the fine Polish gentleman told my officers that Wolchi murdered his son. Shot him, unprovoked, in the back just steps from the sanctity of his own home, and then ran away. Now, he wants justice, for your son to be punished."

The tent was silent, and I struggled to find my voice. "He would have killed me," I said. "He tried to kill my brother, his wife, too, and he would have killed me."

"This is a serious matter, one I can't ignore," he said. "You've been accused of a serious crime by a fine Polish gentleman."

"If I need to be accountable, do what you have to do. But just to me. No one else. Don't hurt my family," I said defiantly.

"Who said a word about hurting anyone? Marcus, you should be proud of your son. He has courage, a sense of honor," Girshman said, standing and returning his chair to its place beside mine along the tent wall. "And because you offered so graciously to help me, I will return the favor by helping your son."

He gathered the lithographs from his table into a single stack and handed them to me. That was it. We were dismissed. The commander called to his officers, who re-entered and took places around the table. I helped father walk as quickly as he could toward the door, to get out before the commander changed his mind, but we were not quick enough.

"Wolchi, or should I say Vladimir? One more thing," the commander said. "What would you like me to do with the fine Polish gentleman?"

CHAPTER 39

What happened the next day was extraordinary. The bells of both churches tolled, as they would on any Sunday, but this wasn't any Sunday. The bells didn't stop after ten minutes, nor after sixty. They continued to peal until they had drawn citizens to the streets surrounding the town hall. People were everywhere, including crowded in front of our house, asking bewildered questions of one another. What is this? No one was sure if we were awaiting a joyous parade or a horse-drawn wagon carrying a corpse. Russian soldiers cleared a path down the middle of the street and stood as sentries minding the open space.

Father, mother, Leja and I stood in the crowd a few feet from our door when I saw Mayor Evanko pushing toward us. He was wearing his ceremonial military uniform again and had even thought the occasion worthy of his olive-colored, brimmed fez. I had not seen him in more than two years, since Leja and I fled and when the sting of Ivan's death was still fresh. He didn't appear older or worn by time and bitter memories. He looked surprisingly fit as he deftly maneuvered toward us and waved from a few feet away.

"Leja, Wolchi. It's like a miracle to see you again," he said, placing a hand on each of our shoulders. Leja stepped away, but I allowed him to hold on, without stiffening this time, because instead of a threat in his touch I felt his fear. Mother and father watched without greeting him.

"You look well," Evanko said, tapping my shoulder now as if in congratulations. "You are taller and stronger. A man." He again tried to place his hand on Leja's shoulder, but she stepped away again to avoid him.

"Grygoriy," father said. "What brings you to us, today? We haven't seen you in months."

Evanko came closer to father. I saw him watching mother, but she didn't acknowledge his gaze. "The soldiers have arrested them, all of them. Even Igor Goreki and his police," Evanko said. "They will all go to Russian prisons or worse."

When he got no reaction from father, he continued: "They say you and Wolchi saw the commander. That he asked you about these men, about Goreki. What did you tell him?"

Father sighed softly. "We told the truth."

I turned in the direction of rising shouts and the sound of approaching horse hooves on the hard dirt road. A line of wagons rolled toward us, and as they passed people hurled stones and epithets. This was neither a parade, nor a funeral, but a bit of both. In the back of the first wagon, five men, including Igor Goreki, were tied to the sideboards, their hands behind them, trying to avoid the debris showering the cart. As it passed us, Goreki, his face and head bloodied either by a soldier's beating or by rocks that had hit their mark, didn't look up. I called his name. He didn't look up. I lifted a stone from the ground and flipped it in a soft arc like a rainbow and watched it strike the side of his face, not hard enough to hurt him, but hard enough for him to see me.

"What did you say about me?" Evanko asked father, as a second cart and then a third filled with Polish prisoners passed us. I recognized some of the men, thugs who had joined Nicholas Goreki when he attacked father on the night of my thirteenth birthday, vigilantes who ransacked the buchbinderi and watched when Nicholas struck Ira and kicked Katia's pregnant belly, police officers who'd mercilessly beaten O.U.N. marchers in the woods. And there, in the last wagon, sat the scar-faced man who'd been there at all those times and who'd haunted me even in Krakow. I felt strangely powerful while I watched. I saw the same in Leja's face, and when I looked at Mayor Evanko I knew he saw it, too.

While father stared at the passing prisoners, Evanko turned to me. "Wolchi, what did you say about me?"

I was unsure how to answer. This was a man who'd escaped uninjured from a war that crippled or killed most men of his generation, including father, a man whose wife had died and left him a widower with a young son and then lost that son at the hands of Goreki's police, a man who'd selfishly betrayed his best friend and nearly destroyed the friend's family, and now, here he was looking fit and well in his military uniform with badges and ribbons, his high stiff collar and that foolish fez, asking if Russian soldiers would be coming for him next.

"No one asked about you," I said. "At least not yet."

CHAPTER 40

Two soldiers came for me late one afternoon that week, and Mother urged me, again, not to go with them.

"Your Commander Girshman, he did not send the rabbi this time. I will tell them you're not here," mother said when she came into the buchbinderi where I was working with Ira and father, the way we were meant to be. I was bent over the disassembled printing press, which had lain unused since the Polish police ransacked the buchbinderi two years before, and its parts were scattered on the floor around me.

Mother navigated the obstacles to stand directly over me. "Did you hear me," she said loudly. "There are soldiers outside looking for you." If I didn't seem concerned, it was because that morning I had walked through the town square, past groups of soldiers near their encampment. Most ignored me. None acted a threat. I saw the soldier who intervened when Goreki attacked me on the street. He thrust his rifle bayonet toward the ground in greeting and laughed. No, I felt like one of them, rather than one of their victims.

When mother came in, I had just returned from a visit with Mr. Koperski, where I'd gone carrying a sack of damaged parts from the printing press, which I meant to repair at his shop, and another more valuable item. When I opened the door to Koperski Mashyna, it was as if for the first time. The room seemed bare. One of the lathes and a drill press had been removed. Dark oil stains marked the places the machines had once stood. Mr. Koperski sat with his back to me at his cluttered worktable filing a metal horseshoe. Dozens more were stacked beside the table in the place once filled with more intricate parts destined for the Polish railroad. I called his name, and he turned. I thought I saw a faint smile before he barked out: "Sit down already and help me. These Russians have made me a blacksmith, like my grandfather."

The soldiers had confiscated half his machinery, he told me, and shipped it east to Donbas, "the Soviet industrial heartland," he said with cynicism. "They asked my permission to 'share the modes of production' with the people of the Soviet Union. If I'd refused, of course, I would have become a mode of production at one of their work camps." He was angry, more bitter than I'd ever known him. It had taken Goreki and his men years to begin looting from the people of the town, Koperski said. It took the Russians mere weeks.

"At least they bring me their horseshoe business," he continued. "But maybe you have something more interesting for me in that sack you carried in?"

What I retrieved was not what he expected. I handed him the framed photograph from the Krakow dress shop. He studied it, wiping clean the dusty glass with his sleeve. "She gave this to you, the old woman, Shayna's mother?" he asked. I nodded and described my final hours with her after the German air attack. "She is a fine old woman. I pray she makes it through," he said, fingering the gilded frame, trying to remember.

"Shayna and I were very young in this picture. See the dress? You can't tell, but it was satin and red, and the night she wore it, when this photo was made, we danced and danced to celebrate the new year. It was a happy day."

The two of us worked, not on the Russian horseshoes, but rather the damaged printing press parts, and talked when we could about the others he knew in Krakow. What about Michel, he asked. Why had he stayed?

"Why did you stay here?" I said to him. He laughed and nodded, his mood lighter.

"You're right. Maybe you noticed the Russians and Germans are very different in some ways, but they are the same in ways that matter most," he said. "So, perhaps Michel and I both know there's nowhere for any of us to go."

I returned home that afternoon eager to reassemble the repaired parts of the printing press, and had just begun when mother burst in. While she stood over me, father looked through the window at the waiting soldiers.

"What did they say?" father asked.

"They want him to go with them," mother answered. "And they called him Vladimir."

⸺ ⸱⸱ ⸺

Commander Girshman sat behind the table in his tent, with his officers on either side. He wore a pair of gold-framed pince-nez on a cord that he removed and let drop to his chest when I entered.

"Sit, young man," Girshman said. "Can I offer tea. Something stronger?"

"No, commander," I said. "Nothing for me."

"There's no need to be so formal. I thought we were friends. Please, call me Samuel," he said. "That fine Polish gentleman who was causing you such worry is headed to a place where he won't be a bother again. I took care of that for my friend."

He continued, "But now, what should I do with you? That Goreki fellow was a bad one, and it seems most are happy to be rid of him. Yet, there are people who still say you killed his son and should be punished."

I stayed silent, but was thinking of mother's words. "He did not send the rabbi this time."

"You look worried. Don't. I can't punish a friend," Girshman said. "But I need to show people here that I am fair. So, Wolchi, no Vladimir, you are going on a journey."

He pointed to a map open on the table between us. "We are here," he said, tapping his finger on the name of our town. "But soon, you will be here." He slid his hand to the other end of the map, spread his fingers and waved them over the eastern end of the Ukraine. "We need men with your skills, engineers, men who can build what we need to fight a war with the Germans. You are going to Donbas, the beating heart of the Soviet industrial heartland."

One of the officers, a thin bookish man, showed me other maps, more detailed, that displayed the locations of coal mines and steel foundries. The Soviet economy depends, he said, on the reliable extraction and transport of Donbas coal and its conversion into the steel used to build the war machines aimed at the Germans and the plows needed to feed hungry citizens. The vast, deep mines near the city of Donetsk needed men to repair the heavy excavating equipment and maintain the busy rail links north toward Moscow into central Russia.

"I've told them about your skills," Girshman interjected. "Said that you are a leader. Someone they can count on to embrace this moment in history."

There was too much new information for me to process and understand, and as I looked at the Russian maps and listened to the bookish officer drone on about the economic output of the region, I was confused about everything except one thing. The power and control I'd felt over my future just days before had been an illusion. I was back at the mercy of another.

What about my family, I asked. Are there people who want them punished, too? "Will you send them away?" I asked. "Will they be safe?"

"Of course, they will stay here. Your father and brother have important work to do, and they need your mother." He thought for moment and leaned back in his chair. "If your sister would like to join you, she would be welcome. Donbas is a place where many young citizens have gone from across the Soviet Union to work. It is a young workers' paradise."

He returned his pince-nez to the bridge of his nose and leaned closer to me. "You don't need to worry about them."

He walked around the table and extended his palm. When I stood, he waited for me to respond. He wanted me to shake his hand, and I wanted to run from him, go home and tell my family that they needed to run, too, away from this place. But, Mr. Koperski's words filled my head: "There is no where for any of us to go."

"We will take good care of your family," Girshman said. "The Soviet army is here and will protect our loyal citizens."

He took my hand, shook it enthusiastically and smiled. The two officers at the table nodded their heads in apparent agreement and smiled, as well. This was, I later learned, the "Russian nod," a gesture that seemed to say "yes," but meant something else, something you could never discern and something those who nodded and smiled would never reveal.

"You will bring great pride to your family," he said. "Everyone here will know the name of Comrade Vladimir."

CHAPTER 41

I was hopeful that Leja would come along. As much as I resented Girshman's order, I also felt the looming threat of the Nazi army and understood that Donbas, or wherever I was headed, would put some kilometers between me and them. I understood why father and mother could not go with me. I understood why Ira would not want to travel to a place far from Katia's family. I didn't understand Leja's refusal, though, and, as we waited for my train in the bitter cold of a January morning, I tried once again to change her mind.,

"Someone needs to look after them," Leja said of our parents. "You have no choice but to go. And that leaves me."

This was the point she'd been making since I first told her and my family about my banishment. "One of us needs to stay, and you can't," she said. "If we had told the truth about how Ivan Goreki died, I'd be the one packing my bags, not you." I couldn't convincingly argue, but tried, nonetheless. When I went away, it would be the first time ever that we would not be near one another, and I already selfishly felt the loss of her. I would miss my parents, Ira, Katia and Naftali, but I couldn't yet imagine being apart from my sister. I'd already said goodbye to everyone else, so, I persisted until my very last moments at home and pressed to have her join me.

"I can arrange for a horse-drawn cart filled with oily

machine parts to take us," I said. "I know how you enjoy that mode of travel."

"Very funny," she said.

"So, I suspect if I also offered a train ride in an open freight car, especially today in the middle of January, you would still say no?" She shook her head, but she smiled. Progress?

"You promised someday to show me Paris and New York," I said. "Perhaps, I can show you Donbas instead."

"The Paris of the Soviet industrial heartland? Very tempting," she said, her voice thick with sarcasm. "But I must say no."

I was out of clever things to say, as my train pulled into the station, so I asked her what was really on my mind.

"When I'm gone, who will notice when you get sad? Will anyone be there when you get really dark the way you do? When your hands shake and you need a brotherly hug, what will you do?" I asked.

She waited and thought about this for a long time, so long I assumed she would not answer as my train stopped at the platform.

"I'll write you letters," she said, and that was it, but for a brief kiss on the cheek and a briefer goodbye as I boarded the train and watched her wave one time before turning for home.

———————◦•◦———————

The train car wasn't much warmer than the platform, and the only empty seats were far from the crude stove that provided heat. A spot by a window, though, gave me a view of the river we were about to cross and the valley to the south where the spires of my town's two churches broke above the barren trees. I hugged my burlap travel bag to my chest to ward off the cold and a creeping loneliness.

The celebration of my twentieth birthday the night before had been muted. Everyone avoided the obvious subject of my departure, everyone except mother, who found a way to ask the detailed, obvious questions that had gone unanswered in the weeks before. None was more pressing to her than those that began with when. She wanted to know *when* my train would depart, *when* it would arrive, *when* I would begin work, *when* I would eat and *when* I would sleep. It was a litany that reminded me of a Jewish prayer. "These words I am commanding you today are to be upon your hearts, and you shall teach them diligently to your children, and shall talk of them when you sit in your house, and when you walk by the way, and when you lie down, and when you rise up." All of it, though, was really about a single question she finally asked as she placed pieces of honey cake on the table at the meal's end.

Once we each had a slice of the symbolic dessert that promised sweetness in the coming year, she sat down with us for the first time during the meal, signaling the significance of what she was about to ask. We waited for her to speak. "When," she finally began. "When will you come home?"

As the train slowly climbed the wooden trestle on the bank of the river and rolled out over the water, I could picture her face, hopeful and worried, as she asked that question. I realized she had never crossed this river. It was the icy line in winter and the flooded barrier in spring and autumn that separated her life from the mysteries and dangers she feared in the Russian east.

She loved the river itself and shared that with her children. She took us in the summer to the swimming hole that formed when the river flow became gentle and taught me,

Leja and Ivan how to skip stones across the calm water. The secret, she told us, was to bend down close to the water and throw the rock as if there were a low roof over your head. And remember, she would say, throw the rock hard. In the spring, she would take me to a bend in the river, where men from the town fished for pike and catfish. Once, we saw a man pull a mammoth carp from the river, a fish bigger than me, and I started to cry, frightened by this monster from the deep. She held me and showed me the fish's eyes. Evil men, she said, had the same menacing look as the carp, and, if you meet a man with those eyes, it is always best to look away. Igor Goreki, she would often say, had the eye of a carp.

She would not take us in the fall. The river, filled with the autumn rain, was treacherous then. Currents swirled into powerful eddies and could plunge a man to the bottom and hold him there until his body grew limp and he was cast dead back into the flowing river. So, she came to the river alone in those months to retrieve buckets of clay, softened by the flooding waters and enriched by rotted leaves, that she shaped into earthen pots and plates that she baked until dry and hard or, when the need arose, she fashioned into the figure of a golem to protect the people she loved. The river had mystery and power for her, and the crossing of it, more than the journey itself, made mother worry for me. It was a strange land, a Russian land, that stretched east beyond the other bank, and she needed to know when I'd cross back.

"Maybe in the summer," I told her. "When we can all walk to the river edge, bend our knees and skip stones all the way across to the places I'd been."

The train sped east through the cold night. The car was crowded with men and women, all noticeably young, and was noisy with the babel of more languages than any one person could know. Despite the darkness, few slept. The cold left me alert also, but dreamy, my mind replaying the past in a random, disconnected, tired narrative. Songs played in my head, then images, then words all in a jumble.

Was this journey like my father's when he set out to the west toward the other edge of Europe, to Germany, in search of his holy grail? I thought of him anxious as he rode the train, generous when he encountered a beleaguered man and his son, determined as he made his way back to his place, the place he was meant to be, with the precious machines he hoped would transform his family's life. Now, in much less than a lifetime, that hope was gone, and he could not ensure his family's future. He could not even repeat his journey today, because the political winds had shifted again and armies had formed, again. When he said goodbye, he told me never to stop looking for the place I was meant to be.

No, my journeys were uniquely my own, because what was I in search of, after all? I had run away to Krakow and found Ludmilla there. I ran from her and the Nazi invader into the arms of a Russian invader who sent me away on this train. In the haze of half-sleep, I heard Ludmilla singing, and for a moment saw her reflection in the dark train window, felt my body stir and heard a song others sang about a woman like her. "Ochi chornye, ochi strastnye, black eyes, passionate eyes."

I rummaged through my pack for a drink of water and a bite of bread. At the bottom, I felt the wooden case of my machinist tools and beside it an unfamiliar hard object, like a stone wrapped in cloth. I lifted it and saw the clay face of our Golem. Mother had hidden him in my bag, to protect me as I ventured across the river, I guessed, and holding it was oddly comforting. But what about Leja? What about Ira? Even in the dim light, I could see the bits of paper with my name and their names at the bottom of the hollow statue. Here in my hand, Golem could not watch over them. I felt panic, the need to return home and restore Golem to his proper place beside our door. As I turned the statue in my hand, I saw the aleph, mem and tav, spelling the word truth, on its chest, reflected in the train window. As I spread the cloth back over the carvings, the first letter became hidden. Mem and tav remained, spelling the word death. I covered the statue quickly, not wanting to see it any longer, and pushed it deep into my pack.

Chapter 42

Morning. I knew it had arrived not because the sun had risen. If it had, there was no way to see it behind the ashen pale of low clouds and coal smoke that left the sky the color of dirty snow and the dirty snow the color of the smoky sky. I awoke alone in the train car. Young men wearing red armbands herded crowds on the platform toward a low-slung series of buildings. Everyone on the train had been headed to the same place, and we had arrived. The wooden sign in the station announced Donbas, and a hand-lettered banner beneath it proclaimed in Ukrainian and Russian that this was the "beating heart of the Soviet industrial heartland." The Russians were nothing if not consistent. The slogans they repeated by rote had no relationship to reality, but, when repeated often enough, they began to sound familiar and something near the truth.

I was eager to leave the train to find a bathroom and some food, so I joined the queue of travelers being directed by the men in armbands. The men were friendly and faceless, happily shouting, "Food in a warm room," and waving their arms enthusiastically toward the nearby buildings. Everyone in the lines around me was young, reminding me of the Jagiellonian campus, but their drab grimness made clear they were not headed to a morning philosophy class. "Food in a warm room," the men shouted, and I was surprised when I reached the entrance to one of the buildings that those men were not guilty of Soviet hyperbole, and that, indeed, the room was warm and crowded with others gathering around tables filled with pots of soup, loaves of bread and stacks of soft cheese.

Everyone was eating and talking loudly, some in Polish, others in Ukrainian or Russian, and even some in Yiddish. Where had all of these people come from? More men in red armbands stood inside and recorded names, hometowns and occupations on clipboards as we entered. The efficiency of everything impressed me. As I ate, I watched the red arm-bands as they went about their tasks like shepherds counting their flock. An older woman near the front of the room stood on a small platform watching over them, and us, shouting an order from time to time. She was a big woman. She held her thick arms, each with a red armband, tightly crossed over her ample chest, her hair tied back so tightly it pulled the skin of her face taut against her head. When she unclasped her arms and clapped twice to get our attention, nothing above her neck moved, but everything below jiggled and wiggled with her moving arms.

"Comrades. Comrades," she said loudly. "Welcome, comrades."

We then paid the price for the warm room and the hot food, as Comrade Masha spoke for an uninterrupted hour about the inevitable triumph of Stalinism, Marxism and the Soviet world view.

"You will make our destiny a reality. Each of you holds a piece of the puzzle that will be Russian greatness," she finally concluded. When she stopped talking the room fell into awk-ward silence. The newcomers looked at one another. What were they to do now? Could they resume eating? Maybe it was fatigue or gratitude for the speech's conclusion, but I began to applaud.

No one joined me. It was too late to stop, though, so I stood and applauded louder and more forcefully. Everyone in the room stared, while I watched Comrade Masha eying me with defiance from her perch on the raised platform. Then, one of the red armbands standing beside me smiled, nodded his head and, doing his best to express approval, joined in. All the other arm bands began clapping, too, and the room exploded in raucous appreciation for Comrade Masha's oration.

I felt some pride as I surveyed the happy men and women who, given a reason to celebrate, had let loose the tension and fear that accompanied them from whatever village or town they'd fled. This seemed a good thing to us all. Comrade Masha, upstaged perhaps, thought otherwise. She pointed and motioned for me to join her at the front. I retrieved my pack and made my way warily toward her. I was in no hurry, hoping she'd become distracted by the din in the room and would let me melt back into the crowd. Comrade Masha focused on my every step as I came closer, however, scrutinizing me as I approached as if I were a stray dog that had wandered into her yard. Was I rabid and dangerous or just a hungry pup eager for a pat on the head and a piece of meat.

"What's your name?" she barked when I stopped a few feet from the platform. I told her it was Vladimir, thinking a good Russian name would assuage her pique. Instead, she stepped closer, hovering above me like a statue, and folded her arms back across her chest. "What is your occupation?" I told her. "Where are you from?" A Ukrainian town near L'viv, I said. She scrunched up her face in disapproval. "There is no Ukraine," she said. "There is only the Soviet Union."

She stood still, examining me up and down. Good dog or bad, I could almost hear her thinking. "Do you support the goals of the Soviet Union or were you mocking me with your applause?" she asked. This question, like the one the Russian soldiers had asked Mr. Koperski, had just one answer.

"I was inspired, comrade," I answered without hesitation. She uncoiled, her face relaxed, and her arms came away from her chest. "Good," she said. "Because we need men like you to help lead these others. They need to learn what you seem already to know."

I hoped she was done with me, and I turned to slip back into the anonymity of the crowd. "No," she barked as she came down a set of stairs from the platform. She was as tall as I, standing eye-to-eye when she grabbed my elbow, her grip firm. "You come with me," she said.

Chapter 43

The bureaucrats in the next building greeted me with boredom when Comrade Masha released her grip on my arm and deposited me with instructions to put my enthusiasm and skills to good use.

"This one is a leader," she said to the others, a compliment, I thought, until I understood that leaders in the Soviet Union, like tall flowers, have their blossoms snipped to blend better into the Russian landscape.

Thus began my four-year immersion into the virtues and failings of the Russian state, which would during the course of the coming world war be responsible for the deaths of twenty million people. Some died from bullets and bombs, some from starvation, and some because of the whims of Soviet functionaries eager to exercise power.

The bureaucrats did their best to trim me into conformity by dispatching me to Carbonite, a smaller, bleaker, colder version of Donbas named for the explosive used to extract coal from the deep mines dotting the countryside. My task, they told me, was to transform the Carbonite mine, currently a relic of another century, by helping others build rail tracks to carry coal more efficiently from the mine's bottom. I was to fix things. A mekhanik, they called me. If the machines setting the rails broke, I was to fix them. If the electricity failed, fix it.

And, the best news, they said, is that Comrade Masha would oversee all of that as the apparatchik in charge of Carbonite and its surrounding region.

Two days later, I climbed down from an ore carrier that had deposited me and a dozen other men on a crude wooden platform, stopping for just a moment before rolling forward to the mine shaft excavated into the hillside.

"Ants," the man standing beside me said as we watched workers walk from the mine entrance with sacks of coal and others descend back in after emptying their sacks into the rail cars. "They are ants relocating the riches of their underground colony."

"From the beating heart of the Soviet industrial heartland," I added, with a balance of sincerity and cynicism so he could appreciate either, depending on his point of view.

"For the benefit of all the Soviet people," he concluded, grinning broadly as he thrust out his hand. "My name is Levuska. My friends call me Lev. I hope we will be friends, so please, Lev."

I would learn over the following months, as we truly did become friends, that Lev wanted to be liked by everyone in a sincere way. With an explosion of blond curls on his head and a toothy, exuberant smile, he was a magnet for others, especially the dirty-faced, peasant girls who worked side-by-side with the men extracting and hauling coal from beneath Carbonite.

He and I shared a dormitory room with two others in a cluster of buildings with communal toilets and showers, and a vast dining hall used by all the men and women at the mine. We also shared a fascination with the coal girls, as we called them, young and demure but beginning to explore their power over men at the mine. At night, we would trade tales of the ones who had caught our attention, attempting to describe the hair of one, the face of another, the shape of a third, having only glanced their faces and not much else, because their heads were hidden behind crude wraps and their bodies masked beneath rough woolen dresses.

This was our distraction from the monotony of the work. Although I was fortunate, as was Lev, that ours were among the least grinding of the mine tasks, they were soul-smothering, nonetheless. He monitored gauges that measured the amount of methane released by the mining process and watched over the ventilation system that was the lungs of the mine. If methane levels got too high in the shaft, blasting elsewhere could create an explosion, killing or trapping miners. Often, he and I were side by side in the mine while I checked the functionality of the ventilation. For ten hours each day except Sunday, from dawn until after dark, we labored far below the surface of Carbonite, and the only joy was a glimpse of the bright eyes of the girls with coal-black faces and, if we were lucky, the white line of a smile.

Especially hers.

I didn't know her name, but I first saw her after I'd been working for two months. She was new in Carbonite, I knew, because her work clothes were still free of the tears and stains that quickly accumulated underground. She looked Middle Eastern, not Slavic like most of the other girls. She was dark skinned, dark hair, dark black eyes. Ochi chornye. It was her job to bring fresh drinking water to the workers, and I'd see her two or three times each day when she walked past me with water sacks slung over her shoulder headed down to the miners extracting the deep coal, and later returning up with empty sacks. Short and, as best I could tell, thin, I marveled at her strength, making her way deftly through the mine despite the weight of the water. When she walked past me, she raised the water sack and asked: "Mekhanik?" She'd stop, refill my canteen quickly, without speaking another word. I assumed she didn't know Russian, Ukrainian, Polish or any of the languages I tried. So, our interactions were mostly silent. I would motion for her as she approached and hand her my canteen. She'd fill it and hand it back, but, before she walked away, she always looked me in the eyes and smiled.

Lev joked about her after I confessed my infatuation. "I've never seen that one," he said to me, his face grinning broadly. "I believe she's a dream, you know, a sprite of the mine who is only visible to lonely boys who spend their days in darkness below ground." He called her my Carbonite Coal Nymph.

Lev had his own fantasy girl, a tall, blonde kitchen worker who cleared dishes and wiped tables after meals. The first time he saw her she was serving bowls of potato soup to the women across the room. He had never been close to her, but when he spotted her at a distance, across the dining hall or disappearing behind doors to the kitchen, he would call out, "potato soup girl," and wave. When I'd look up, she'd be gone, vanished or imagined, I never knew. I called her Lev's Potato Angel.

He was a handsome guy, though, more at ease with the attention of women, so he got more of it than I. The girls would brush past me in the dim mine with hardly a look, but their gazes lingered on him in hopes he would notice and reward them with his magnetic smile. He always took the time to offer them at least a flirtatious raised eyebrow or a kind nod. I understood why women clustered near him, but what puzzled me was the way men jockeyed to sit beside him at meals or cheerfully helped him with his work, as eager for his attention as the young girls. They seemed fearful, but also enamored. One evening, on the eve of our much-anticipated May Day celebration, I discovered the reason why.

We were all excited about May Day, a holiday from the mine and an occasion for a lively party to celebrate workers, the coming summer season, and a host of things the Soviet leaders thought we should be grateful for. The dinner offerings that night would include more meat, fruit and even cakes the likes of which, everyone said, we'd not see again until next May. So, we were all in a fine mood, especially Lev, who held court in our corner of the dining hall, regaling us with a story from his childhood about accompanying his mother from their home in Kursk on a trip to Moscow. "Why," I asked, "did she go to Moscow?" The other men at our table looked at me, as if I was ignorant and had insulted Lev with my question. They knew something about Levuska Petrov that I did not.

"She was seeing some commissars, the bosses, you know," he answered. "She left me alone at a fancy hotel near Red Square. I was just ten, and the lady who watched me wasn't paying much attention, because she was too busy flirting with a waiter who kept bringing us pastries on a silver cart, so he could hang around. I ate as many as I wanted, so many that I felt sort if ill and left to look for the vannaya to do my business."

The men at our table listened intently, and no one interrupted when Lev paused to fork some meat from his plate and chew it before resuming his tale. He swept his gaze across the men around us to regain their attention. "I didn't go back to the person watching me. She was too busy joking with that waiter to notice when I walked past to a group of women in the bar. This was interesting to me, because I had never seen women so fancy. Their hair was decorated with bows and lace. Their dresses showed a lot of their skin, a lot of skin, and their faces were made up as if they were on their way to a party.

"Vladimir," he said to me, resting his hand on my shoulder as if the story were just for me. "I wish you could have seen them. I couldn't help but stare. So, I stood nearby and watched as they talked and checked their reflections in small mirrors, until one of them motioned to me. 'Come over here, handsome boy, and let us have a closer look at you,' she said. I wasn't shy, so I walked up to them and said hello in my most adult voice, the way my mother had taught me.

"There were four of them. Two with blonde hair, two with black. Two were thin and two were not so thin and one had very big, you know." He made circular motions with his hands near his chest. "I figured out when I was older that they were there for the men, the ranking comrades and important visitors. Prostitutes, you know.

" 'What a polite young man,' one of the women said to me, one of the thin ones, as she ran her hand through my hair. 'I wish I had these curls,' she said, and laughed. 'He will be irresistible to the ladies when he's older. That's for sure,' the other thin one said. One of the women took my hands and very gently led me closer to her. She had the big ones, and I stared at them as I stood there. I noticed a small mole on her chest just above the line of her dress. I couldn't look away. I took a small step closer and could smell her perfume. And they were right there," he said as he again motioned with his hands near his chest. "I could have touched them. They were so close. 'What's your name?' she asked me. And that's when I heard my mother, shouting from the hotel entrance.

"'Levuska,' mother called. 'Levuska, what are you doing?'" I saw her marching toward me, fast, like a soldier heading to battle. She pulled me away, frowning at the four women. 'There's nothing for you here,' she said."

Lev stopped and took a deep breath before continuing. "But she was wrong. I turned to the woman with the big ones and smiled at her. She smiled back. Then, she winked at me, pulled down her dress just a bit and showed me one of them."

The boys at our table roared, congratulating him for, even at age ten, being the sort of person who could get a woman to expose herself. Lev laughed, too, not with them, but at them.

"No, no, you fools," he said. "I'm just telling you a story to make things more interesting. I didn't see anything. What really happened was my mother dragged me by my arm back to the lady who was supposed to be watching me, smacked her across the face and made me spend the next two days inside our room doing school lessons with some old man who smelled like socks."

The men around us at the table slumped, until Lev said: "But don't worry boys, I've seen a few since." And the men laughed again, happy their hero had ended his story in a way that also ended their disappointment.

I was still puzzled by the new information about Lev. "So, if your mother is an important comrade, what are you doing in this place? Shouldn't you be hanging around Moscow bringing Stalin his tea or doing whatever the sons of Party people get to do?" I asked.

Lev shrugged. "I think she wants to keep me away from the fancy ladies in Moscow bars," he said. "But maybe she will get me out of here when she discovers the mines are just as dangerous for a young man, what with the Potato Angel and her assorted dirty-faced sprites all about the place," he said, playfully poking me with his elbow.

He turned to the front of the room, where workers pushed tables together to form a small stage. The speeches were about to begin. We heard them nightly at the conclusion of the evening meal. Carbonite comrades, men and women of different ranks in the local Communist Party, talked about production goals missed and scolded us to work harder. Sometimes, we sang patriotic songs celebrating the proletariat, the Soviet regime and, of course, the greatness of Joseph Stalin. Tonight, we were told, there would be a special speech by our leader visiting from Donbas.

Comrade Masha had come to inspect and inspire us as we began our May Day celebrations, and as she climbed steps to stand on the low tables in front of our dining hall, applause, unlike the last time I saw her, spread through the room, greeting her as if she were a Bolshoi prima ballerina about to begin her Swan Lake dance.

As Comrade Masha spoke, Lev turned to me and said: "Mother is looking well. Don't you think?"

———•◦•———

Letter from Leja, April 15, 1940

Dear Wolchi.

More than three months have passed since you left, and I have thought to write you often since we received a message about your location. Today I wish you were here, not because this day is different than yesterday or the days before. But, rather, because it's not. A dulling monotony has settled over the town. It makes me feel alone, and what better person to cure that than my brother.

Time has stopped for me. We all stay at home, perhaps because the weather is cold, or because the Russian soldiers have taken to patrolling the streets each morning and evening. They are grim-faced and grey and walk as if they are lost and wandering. They don't speak, even when they pass close by. I am troubled by them, their plodding sameness, so I stay inside most of the time. Sometimes I wonder if I should have gone with you on your journey, but then realize this is the place I should be just now. Maybe that will change sometime, though.

I help father and Ira with the printing and binding work in the buchbinderi. I have mixed feelings about this work, because the posters and flyers we make are everywhere in town telling lies to people. At least father says your friend (ha!) the Russian commander has been generous with payments. Mama cooks meat for dinner several times each week, and she bought new clothes for Naftali, who is growing very tall, with the money.

For most of the others in town, though, things are much harder. The Russians feed their soldiers with vegetables and cheese from our farmers, without paying them. Many people here are hungry because of that, and they are angry at the Russians. Some, openly talk about a better time if the Germans come. That is crazy.

Mayor Evanko has been given a new job by the commander, and he is responsible for identifying people who have criticized the Russians. Some of them are made to attend rallies in the town hall and listen to the garbage propaganda about a worker's paradise being built in the Soviet Union. Others get sent away. Some are my friends from the O.U.N. I guess I shouldn't write things like that in case someone other than you read this, but I don't care any longer if others know how I feel. The Russians are no better than the Poles, maybe worse. Our town has become a shapeshifter like one of mother's dybbuks. Different uniforms march on our streets, but the same evil is here. The Russians offer us a different form of servitude, but leave us with the same sense of dread. Papa says they are just Cossacks with an ideology, no better than the warriors who marauded through the villages here for centuries, but they are able to use words as weapons as well as guns and bombs.

The good news is that Igor Goreki is still gone. People say he has been imprisoned with other Polish and German "undesirables." Good riddance, and this is something to be thankful to the Russians for.

Ira, Katia, Mama and Papa want me to send you their love. They hope you visit us soon.

With love,

Your sister, Leja

CHAPTER 44

She walked right up to Lev when her speech concluded, applause still scattered about the room, and offered him a hearty hug, running her hand through his hair. He returned her embrace with a strong squeeze of his own, lifting her slightly from the ground.

"Levuska, my boy. You have the strength of two men. Put me down," Comrade Masha said to her son with an oddly girlish laugh.

"We have to be strong here, Mother. Otherwise, this place will kill us," he said, releasing her.

"But you are not carrying a rifle and freezing in a bunker somewhere in the west, are you?" she responded, still smiling. "Be grateful for that."

Comrade Masha saw me watching them and wrinkled her nose into a scowl. Lev placed an arm around my shoulder.

"Mother, this is my friend Vladimir," Lev said. "He is the man who fixes the machines in the mine when they break. And they always break, right Vlad?"

Before I could respond, Comrade Masha cut me off. "I know this one. A troublemaker," she said, still scowling, or perhaps hiding a faint smile. "He's your friend?"

Before Lev could respond, she cut him off, too, and

pointed to me. "Tell me, is your work progressing properly? I understand there may be delays. If you cannot keep up with the schedules, there will be consequences."

I assured my comrade leader that all was well. "I was happy to hear the applause tonight for your speech, Comrade, unlike when we last met. It seems everyone now recognizes and is inspired by your leadership."

She shrugged and grunted. "You have a gift, Vladimir, that's for certain. A gift for words," she said. "Everyone loves a man who can make us feel so important that we look past the pile of manure and see only his flattery."

That's when I knew she liked me, and thank God she did, because a year later she saved my life, after I saved Lev's.

Letter to Leja, April 30, 1940

Dear Leja.

I was so happy to receive your letter. The days here are also routine and the same all the time, so to get a letter from my dear sister was like seeing the sun after a long day in the mine.

That is the story of this place, darkness. Long days, darkness in the morning when I enter the mine, darkness in the evening when I depart, and the haze of coal smoke in the air all the time.

I don't intend to sound gloomy. But I need some of your famous words of encouragement these days, as it seems do you. I can hear you saying: 'Remember, these are the days before tomorrow. So, let's make a plan for tomorrow.'

I have friends here, one good one named Lev, whose mother, I just discovered, is the senior comrade overseeing all of the coal mines in the region. Can you believe that? She placed him in this place to keep him away from the German armies and the potential front if there is a war. I worry if she is concerned about that, because you and the family will be in the middle of things if those armies invade. Commander Girshman promised he would protect all of you, but I wouldn't count on that. If he is like the Russian bosses here, he tells us what we want to hear and then does what is best for himself. So, I hope Lev's mother is wrong and everything stays safe where you are.

Also, tomorrow is a holiday for us, May Day, and the workers will celebrate. People say there will be a big party at night, and we'll all be together for food, music and dancing. At least we won't be in the mine, and maybe, just maybe, your letter is an omen that the sun will be shining, too.

Write again soon.

Best love,

Your brother, Wolchi (They call me Vladimir here, but you know that's not who I am.)

CHAPTER 45

At ten p.m., the May Day party was still in full swing, but I'd stopped. Stopped eating. Stopped drinking. Stopped dancing. I sat and just stared. Others partied with great energy, but I'd lost enthusiasm for the celebration after the band played Ludmilla's song. When the stout female singer bellowed, "Love forgives you everything," it was as if an ill wind from the past extinguished my candle. There was a wisp of smoke, then nothing but the clock on the wall, big hand straight up, little hand on the ten.

I hadn't thought much about Ludmilla since arriving in Carbonite, and only Lev had heard me speak of her on the occasions when loneliness brought her, like tonight, suddenly back to mind. Just hours before, all I could think about was the party that would break the monotony of work. It had me excited. It had us all excited. I could feel it everywhere. There would be no speeches, no need to feign attention to anything but the food, beer and vodka, and maybe something more. The men, showered, shaved and dressed in the best they could find, lined up early waiting for the doors of the dining hall to open and the celebration to begin. The women crowded outside their dormitories, their faces scrubbed, heads uncovered, equally eager to begin the evening, but restrained by the steady gaze of the older Soviet watchwomen. Like starters in a race, they held back their signal until the men were inside, and then, bang, the young women rushed toward the doors.

Lev and I, stragglers who'd not queued with the other men, found ourselves surrounded by these women, all laughing and jostling past us, like a flock of low-flying colorful birds riding the wind.

"What's your hurry, girls," Lev called to no one in particular, but to all of them at once. "Lev and Vladimir are right here." But his mating call was not strong enough to slow the flight toward the big party, and they hurried past.

"We should be on the lookout for your dark-haired mine nymph," Lev said to me. "I suspect she enjoys a good party, and perhaps she will take pity and speak to the poor machinist she has enchanted."

"I will watch for her, Lev, along with any sign that your blonde potato angel is anything more than a ghost of your imagination," I said.

I threw my arm around him and gave him a brotherly squeeze as we approached the dining hall.

"We are truly a sorry pair, my friend," he said. "Hopeless and romantic, but mostly hopeless."

I heard the music before I opened the door, and the sound of the band and the loudness of the crowd lifted us, like a wave, toward the center of the room. Tables near the walls were lined with food and wooden barrels of beer. Men and women crowded in front of the band, danced and sang along with a Russian folk song, something about the promise of spring and the fullness of summer. This was going to be fun, I thought.

A girl with a white bow in her hair took my hands as I passed, and we danced as Lev wandered farther into the crowd.

Her hair was loose around her shoulders. As she moved, it swirled about her face, and she laughed, happy to be with me, I thought, until she dropped my hands and grabbed those of another man walking past. I stood awkwardly at the center of a moving mass of dancers. Were these the grim, lethargic miners I labored with each day a hundred meters below this room? Transformed by the music and the occasion, the men and women around me radiated new glamour and excitement.

I was glad to be with them. It was easy to grab the hands of a girl and move her about the room to the beat of the music. If I was lucky, she would look at me and smile, perhaps blush, and allow me to dance closer, her head near my shoulder, her hair clean and minty near my face. So, I ate and drank, and drank some more. I danced with the girls, many different ones. One told me her name. "I am Angelina," she said. "An angel?" I asked. "No, Angelina, Angelina." The music was loud, but I saw her lips. "Angelina," they were saying. To me, she was an angel, perhaps Lev's angel, and I told her so, but my words evaporated in the din of the music and the crowd. I wanted to hold onto her until I saw Lev, because this could be the girl. So, we danced and laughed until the band played that sad song. With Ludmilla on my mind, I released Angelina, and she drifted away.

I'm not sure how long I sat alone on the hard wooden chair in a corner of the room. There was no sign on my chest saying, "Danger, stay back," but everyone kept their distance. By the time Lev spotted me, the party had begun to settle. The lights in the room dimmed, and the band played more quietly. I was a little bit drunk.

"I lost you," he said, bringing a chair to sit beside me. "Are you okay?"

"I met her," I said. "Your angel."

"You look like you've seen a ghost, not an angel," Lev said. "I know that face, my friend. This droopy portrait of misery is the face of a man who has slipped into bittersweet memories."

He pointed at me, his finger close enough that it couldn't be ignored. "Oh, it feels so good to think about her," he mocked me. "Oh, it hurts me so to think about her." I swatted his hand away, and he laughed. "That's more like it. Now, stand up, so we can get a beer and you can help me find my angel before someone steals her."

The beer barrels had a crowd around them, but we pushed our way through. The men and women talking, flirting, reminded me of evenings in the cafes of Krakow's old city. For a moment, I imagined what it might be like there this evening. German soldiers crowding the bar, hovering around female university students. Ludmilla laughing at a table with that senior Nazi officer in his long leather coat, smoking a cigarette as he stroked her upper arm.

What was I doing? Stop, I thought. Just stop.

I must have said it aloud, because Angelina, who had come up beside me and was holding my arm, quickly took her hands away. "Hello, again," she said, tentatively. "It's me, Angelina. I wondered where you had gone."

Lev interrupted, his timing excellent, as he squeezed in front of me, extending his hand toward her. "He went searching for his friend. His friend Lev. That's me. Nice to meet you, Angel. . . ?"

"Angelina," she replied as she shook his hand and fell under the spell of Levuska Petrov's famous smile. They laughed and were already holding hands heading to the dance floor, where couples moved slowly to the music, edging their bodies close to one another. I was alone again, this time standing in the middle of the crowd plotting an escape back to my corner or someplace farther. The clock, its hands straight up, said midnight, and the party was over for me, or so I thought.

"Beer, mekhanik?" I heard a woman's soft voice ask from behind. I turned carelessly and jostled her hand, which was extending a beer-filled cup toward me. The beer splashed on us both.

"Sorry," I offered meekly and began wiping the spilled liquid from her arm while she did the same to me. It was an odd dance, each of us rubbing our sleeves along the arm of the other, while more beer sloshed onto the ground. This girl seemed familiar. I looked at her face, perhaps too intently, because she smiled and turned her eyes away shyly. Had we danced earlier? There was something about her. Then she smiled again, and the light caught her dark eyes, a flash from a black center.

"I should stick to bringing you water," she said quietly, again extended the mug of beer. "There's some left if you want it."

My mine nymph, I thought, the words twisting in my head as I kept repeating them. There was no doubt. She was shorter than me, and the slight upward tilt of her face was exactly the same as when she handed me jugs of water. Without the dust of the mine, I saw she was not Middle Eastern at all, just dark-haired, dark-eyed and lovely. Her clean face looked soft, and I wanted to touch it, just to be sure she was real.

"Can I touch your face?" I asked, as if in a dream.

She laughed. "Take the beer," she said. "My name is Mischka."

Mischka, I thought. God's closest angel, my angel, and here she was handing me a beer. This *was* going to be fun.

———◆———

Letter from Leja, June 15, 1940

Dearest Wolchi.

How are you, dear brother? I thought of you this morning when Mr. Koperski came to the buchbinderi to help Papa repair the printing press. He asked about you. The press has been running eighteen hours every day, churning out the posters and propaganda booklets for the Russians. When it broke, Papa said he wished you were still home and he could see you make the repairs. He and Ira are both very nostalgic for past times when the three of you worked together. They talk about it often.

Mama misses you, too. She won't let anyone sit in your spot at the table, which is quite silly. "We can't let him think he has lost his place in our home," she says, as if you could see what's happening in our kitchen. If for some reason you do see us, don't be angry at me for eating your piece of the strawberry cake mother served tonight. It was delicious. Speaking of Mama, did you know she made us a new Golem for the shelf by the door? It was bigger and uglier, if that's possible, than the old one, the one she gave you. I hope you haven't lost it, but if you have don't tell her. It would make her worry. She made the new one last autumn when the river flooded and there was "special mud." You know how excited she gets about the "special mud." Anyway, a few days later, it fell from the shelf and shattered. She left the shards on the floor for days before sweeping them up. "Golem is gone," she said afterward, but I'm not sure what she meant.

The Russians have continued to arrest many of my O.U.N. friends. No one believes anymore that the Russians will support a free Ukraine. They have been quite brutal in making sure no one speaks against them. I sometimes wonder why they haven't come for me, because I've met with many of the men arrested and have put words to their frustrations and anger. It might be that Mayor Evanko, who is still an informer for Girshman, protects me because of Ivan or because of his past friendship with Papa. Or maybe Girshman just likes our family because of the work we do for him. I don't know.

I believe things will get worse, though, because many of O.U.N. friends believe the Nazis would be preferable to the Russians, that they would allow us to form an independent nation while the Russians, bound up in their dreams of a Soviet empire, will always block us. They have hidden guns and other weapons at Big Rocks in case the Germans invade, not to repel them, but to help them drive out the Russians. You and I have seen what the Nazis are capable of, so you understand why I am fighting this idea. Increasingly, though, I am a lone voice. Maybe that's why I haven't been arrested.

I apologize for all the talk about politics. I know it bores you. But you're the one who calls me Karl Marx in a babushka, so, I know you understand.

All my love from home,

Leja

CHAPTER 46

We would meet on the hillside behind the dormitories. In the evenings after dinner when the light, fading from the evening sky, colored the grey tableau that was Carbonite with faint threads of orange and red, we'd walk hand in hand or sit on a blanket placed over the small squares of grass that had pushed through the rocky rubble. Mischka invented a game, a talking game she called it, and each night she identified a topic to discuss. Families. Friends. Hometowns. Food. Religion. Fears. Dreams for the future. It made us feel close, talking this way about things we'd rarely shared with another, and the conversations often ended in a kiss. Many kisses, actually. Good long, slow ones that were not prelude to anything but more of the same.

Mischka lay in my arms one warm evening on the last day of June, fireflies lighting the hillside below us, the moon a crescent low in the sky, when she sat up abruptly.

"What should we talk about tonight?" she asked.

"The moon?" I answered. "Look at the moon. It's the same moon we saw on the night we met. Let's talk about why that moon is always watching us. Come back down here."

"I'm serious," she scolded. "If you don't have a topic, I will choose one." I had the distinct feeling that I was being set up, but for what?

"Tell me about the women, the women you've loved," she continued.

"That would be a short conversation. You," I said.

"Before me. Tell me about any women, you know, who were with you."

"It would be better if you first told me about your men, since this is your idea," I said, trying my best to back away from this discussion.

"No. No. I gave you the chance to identify the topic for tonight's talking game, and you passed. You know the rules. I now get to listen to you talk about my topic."

Mischka was a stickler for rules. Order and process made her happy. Her father was an alcoholic and absent when she was small. Her mother, impoverished and struggling, left her and her older sister mostly on their own at a young age. She was saved, she said, by the Soviet system of predictable routines and the anonymity of mind-numbing work. She'd worked on a collective farm in the Crimea, near her home. She'd operated machinery in a steel mill outside Lugansk. And now, she didn't object to the long days in the mine, the scheduled meals and activities, the control the Soviet bosses had over each day and night. Our evening outings and these discussions had also become part of her predictable rhythms. It was what we did to end each day and reaffirm that I was now part of her life, so there was no way to slip out of the lariat that she'd placed around my neck.

"So, tell me about them," she insisted. "I know I'm not the only one."

At first, it seemed to be going well. She listened attentively, as I described meeting Ludmilla, the song she sang while I secretly watched, the Christmas Market, even our first kiss. Maybe I should have skipped from that to the morning we said goodbye. But in much the same way that Mischka loved order and process, I cherished detail. They were the jig-saw puzzle pieces I assembled to understand and remember. I kept talking and talking, oblivious to her growing unease, until she interrupted.

"How could you have ever left her," Mischka said, putting on a show of indifference. "She seems perfect for you."

Then I blurted it out, the words that for months would be a wall between us.

"You're right. I was very much in love with her," I said. "But."

"But?" Mischka asked.

"But then I wasn't," I said.

Mischka stood and brushed bits of grass from her dress. She turned her back on me and looked down the hill toward the lights of the dormitories. "I'm tired," she said, and walked away toward the lights.

"Wait," I called after her, but she didn't stop walking.

It was difficult to explain. I was in love with Ludmilla, then I was merely troubled by her memory, and I fell in love with Mischka, all in the span of months. Mischka took these facts and concluded it was just a matter of time before my feel-ings for her would fade, too. This made her sullen. I reassured her, but admitted that I didn't understand either how quickly I could forget one woman and replace her with another.

"What's going on with you and Mischka?" Lev asked one night at dinner after it became apparent to everyone in Carbo-nite that the chill surrounding her and me had nothing to do with the weather. I explained, and he pointed at me, the way he did when he wanted to get my attention, and said: "Let me tell you something."

He said it loudly enough that the others at our table stopped their own conversations and awaited his advice.

"A man needs to be in love at least once, for the fun of it," he said, "before falling in love for the joy of it."

The men roared with approval, banging on the table and repeating "for the joy of it." Lev lowered his voice and leaned close so only I could hear what he said next.

"If you want Mischka to believe this, you need to make her laugh, do something fun and stop moping around apologizing for what you did before you met her," he said. As the men around the table leaned in to eavesdrop, he turned back to them, his audience, and offered some final advice.

"And if you want the girl to love you back, forget the word 'you,' and forget the word 'me.' To make sure he was understood, he clarified: "It's like friends. The two of us. Just 'we.' Always say 'we.' "

The men rewarded him again with a round of table-banging and laughter. A new crop of Romeos was born, and love would surely soon flourish in the Carbonite summer.

I found Mischka later that evening outside her dormitory talking with a group of other women. Twilight was about to ease into night and the air, heated during the fifteen hours of summer sunlight, had cooled. I walked directly to them and asked Mischka: "Can we dance?" She was puzzled. "Dance?" she said. "Here?"

"Why not?" I said and extended my hand. "There's no music," she said eyeing me suspiciously, as if I was luring her into a hidden trap. "I can hear it," I said. The other women giggled, watching us. She glanced back at them, shrugged and touched her fingers to mine.

"OK. Let's dance," she said. I took her in my arms, close,

and we moved in silence, just the sound of wind in the hill-side trees.

"Where's the music? I can't hear it," she said loudly to her friends, whose laughter grew. One of them called out: "Sing, mekhanik. Sing." I did, quietly at first, close to Mischka's ear. The women began clapping. "Sing, mekhanik. Sing. Sing, mekhanik. Sing." So, louder and off-key, I repeated to Mischka the song father sang to mother when they danced in our town square.

Ochi chornye, ochi strastnye
Black eyes, passionate eyes

Mischka looked at the people standing nearby, self-conscious, and then she turned to me. I closed my eyes and in the loudest voice I could find sang out.

Ochi zhguchie, I preskrasnye
Burning and beautiful eyes.

I kept singing, and the women kept rhythmically clapping. Mischka laughed, pressed her cheek to mine and said: "This is fun."

Letter to Leja, January 15, 1941

Dear Leja.
I have news. Big, important news. I am married, since the end of the last year. I should have written sooner, but so much is happening here. Where to start?

First, her name is Mischka. You would like her. She has olive skin, dark hair and eyes. I thought she was an Arab when we met, but she's not. She is from Crimea. She is independent, strong and brave, and she has brought consistency into my life and made me happy. My friend, Lev, I told you about him in my other letters, got married on the same day. What an afternoon. We gathered in the dining hall with our friends, and Lev's mother, the mine boss, married the four of us. His wife's name is Angelina. Because we got married before the new year, we were given a bonus, enough money that we might take a holiday to Crimea this summer, where I will be able to touch the sea for the first time. Tell Mama that the water there is safe, and she need not worry if I swim. If we can, we will come home to see everyone afterward.

Now that we are married, we moved to a new dormitory with more privacy, just me and Mischka in one room, and we share a kitchen and sitting room with three other couples, including Lev and Angelina. I am a bit ashamed to tell you that I placed Golem in a corner where he can watch over us. As I often said, it can't hurt.

Everything suddenly makes sense here. I feel there may be a future in the Soviet Union. I already am responsible for finishing a rail project in the mine, and I'm happy to tell you that it is going well. The work is easy for me. You know I can fix any machine, and the devices being used here are simple compared to Papa's printing and binding equipment and the railroad components I've worked with in the past. So, they treat me with respect and say I will be given more people and more projects if I continue on this path.

Who knows if that is true, though. One of the things that doesn't make sense to me about the Russians is how often they lie. They lie even when there is no cost for telling the truth or when the truth is so obvious as to make the lie comical. The Russians are great storytellers, Lev says, and everyone has a bit of Fyodor Dostoyevsky, Leo Tolstoy or Nikolai Gogol in their hearts. I simply believe they are liars, and this trait is contagious. I told everyone here my name is Vladimir, so everyone calls me that. "Good day, Comrade Vladimir," they say, and in the style of a lying Russian I respond as if that is my name. I remember Commander Girshman saying Russians respect a man whose name is Vladimir, because that was Lenin's name, and maybe that's why I do it. What a dumb reason to be respectful, though, but it seems at least in this case Girshman told the truth.

I worry about you, given the changing political situation at home. I wish you could just forgo your involvement in those matters until the world around us becomes more calm.

Please give everyone love from me and tell them all my news. It's been a year since I left, and there have been many days, maybe most days, when I wanted to leave and return home. I feel differently now because of Mischka, but I still miss my family and wonder when, and hope, we will be together again soon.

Your brother,

Wolchi (I would never lie to you.)

CHAPTER 47

The snow started falling heavily at midday, and the sky darkened early. At 3 p.m. I could barely see my hands while I worked outside at the mouth of the shaft. Knee-deep drifts had frozen over the ventilation pipes, and pumps that cleared dangerous methane from below had choked to a stop. I was outside with Lev to uncover the pipes and restart the ventilation system, but the work was pointless, the snow and wind relentless. As fast as we pushed away the drifts and chipped away ice to get the pumps running, the pipes clogged again, and everything stopped.

"I am thinking about our holiday in Crimea," Lev said, as he dug with a small shovel to clear the narrow pipes. "Close your eyes. Imagine the sand and the tepid sea. You and Mischka. Me and Angelina."

He turned his head to the sky and opened his mouth to catch the falling snow. "Ah! The snow is melting before it reaches me because of these warm thoughts. It feels like a summer rain on my face."

I smacked his arm. "Your imaginary rain is freezing your face into a mask of ice," I answered. "And it's doing the same to all of this." I indicated the machinery and pipes.

The snow halted the rail cars from deep in the mine, so no coal was coming to the surface. Most of the workers, including

Mischka, had been sent back to their dormitories for the day. Just a handful of miners were underground, continuing the painstaking process of breaking the coal free from the rock and chipping it into pieces small enough to leave the mine once full activities resumed.

Lev and I had been working on the ventilation system for hours and knew methane would be building inside the mine, creating the dangerous possibility of an uncontrolled explosion. The small, targeted blasts miners use to loosen coal from the rock strata would amplify into an inferno if the air was dense with methane. The gas was odorless and invisible, so miners weren't permitted to ignite a blast unless the methane gauges in the mine showed safe levels. It was Lev's job to monitor those levels and provide permission to use explosives.

"Are we clear on the gauges," a series of miners would call, one after the other, to relay the question up the mine shaft slope to Lev.

"Clear to blast," was the expected response that would then echo back down, one miner calling after another. But Lev was often distracted by the routines of his job or a pretty face and wandered from his post. The miners knew it and impatiently set off blasts if he was slow to answer them.

"I need to go down and warn them," Lev shouted at me, straining to be heard over the wind.

"Be careful," I said. "I'll keep trying to get the pumps running."

I turned to watch him hurry into the mine opening, and the hood of my coat filled with the wind and pulled off my head. The snow blinded me. I touched my face with ice-covered gloves. It was numb. So were my legs and hands. I chipped at the new thickness of ice on the pipes and pumps with little effect. This was hopeless, and I needed to get out of the storm. I scrambled toward the mine, clutching my tool bag and holding my hood against my head. I felt warmth at the mine entrance ahead and hurried toward it when a rush of super-heated air knocked me backward, and the sound of an explosion deafened me. The ground beneath me shuttered. Rock and dust rained down from the roof of the mine like black snow.

I hesitated, waiting for another blast or more rock to fall from the mine roof. Then, I cautiously made my way to where the elevator to the mine floor should have been. It was gone. Ropes hung from above, but only an empty hole was below me. Where was Lev? Where would he have been when the blast occurred? The sloping, winding shaft beside the elevator, where the new rail line was installed, was intact, and I was able to begin down toward the mine floor. Smoke stung my eyes and limited what I could see. The candles that usually lit the tunnel lay broken on the ground. The deeper I went, the darker it became, until there was no light at all. I could feel the hazy cloud of dust and smoke on my face as I went lower, walking cautiously, until I reached the mine floor. Shattered bits of wood and steel from the elevator and broken roof supports slowed me further. I called for Lev, saying his name again and again, shouting it. The mine was deadly silent, so quiet that when I stopped I could hear drops of water dripping from the roof into puddles on the ground.

I continued through the darkness saying his name until I reached a pile of fallen rock blocking my way. There was no going farther into the mine. I was ready to give up, resigned to what seemed to be Lev's fate, and the fate of the other miners behind the wall of rubble. I dropped to the floor, exhausted, confused and already feeling guilty that I was on this side and not the deadly other. In times like that, when certainty replaces hope, a magic moment can sometimes occur. Something so out of context and unbelievable can take place that for a moment it feels like a dream. And so it was. There, beside my feet was an intact candle complete with the tin of matches miners often slipped for convenience into a space between the arms of the tin frame. When I lit the candle, the walls of the mine floor came into view, the brightest light I could imagine after my journey through the darkness.

The fallen rock blocked nearly all of the shaft ahead. But in a corner, I saw a man's fingers jutting from chunks of broken earth piled on the black floor. They didn't move, but this was surely a man's hand. I began tossing aside the coal that hid the arm, and hid the shoulder and the face of my friend, who lay covered in the debris. I said his name again, this time with my own face close to his so I could feel his breath, faint, but warm on my skin. I wiped dirt from his eyes, and he opened them. He looked around in the faint light trying to understand where he was, what had happened. "The others?" he asked. When I shook my head, he closed his eyes again.

Twenty men died that day, but Lev was not among them. I dug him free with my hands, one rock at a time, and carried him over my shoulders up the winding rail line shaft to the mine entrance, one small step at a time. When the rescuers outside took him from me, I dropped to one knee, exhausted, and Lev, his eyes open again, touched my shoulder. "We made it, didn't we?" he asked, and there it was, that smile like a lighthouse in a storm. "But why is Crimea so cold?"

———— •⊷• ————

Letter from Leja, February 15, 1941

Dearest Wolchi.

I've just read your January 15 letter and had to write back immediately. I shared your news with Mama and Papa, and they are very happy, especially Mama, who put her hands on her cheeks and cried when I told her. In fact, she is still sobbing a bit as she cleans up in the kitchen while Papa drinks his tea at the table with me, and I write this letter to you.

Your news was very welcome today because we needed something to break the sad mood we've had since the new year when we learned Ira must serve in the Russian army. The Russians want the young men of the town to help defend it from the Germans, who they believe may attack. Ira is still not physically well since his head was injured in the fight with Goreki, but the Russian officers who came to his house said he was well enough. Other young men have left town to take up arms in the rural areas and resist the Russians. But Ira said he would do what is expected of him to keep his family safe and will wear the Soviet uniform. He left for the border two days ago and will be stationed just a few kilometers from where Papa served in the first war, near the San River. Papa joked that Ira will be able to hear German voices at night coming from the other side of the river, just as he had heard Russian ones while serving in the Austrian army. More than twenty years have passed, but so little has changed.

We worry about him. Papa says the Russians didn't train any of the men from the town before sending them to fight. War, he said, is not for the inexperienced. It's not for anyone, if you ask me. Katia sent Ira away with a bag of dried flowers and grasses that she hopes will keep him safe, and Mama is upset that she could not make him a Golem, because the river mud is frozen. I promised him that I would look after Katia and Naftali as best I could, and would work with Papa in the buchbinderi printing posters and leaflets.

There is no end to that work, and I'm now traveling into the rural countryside distributing the propaganda leaflets and sheets of Soviet news from Moscow. I see many of the farmers and other friends I know from years ago when I was bringing them leaflets and books about Ukrainian independence. They ask why I'm now talking about the U.S.S.R., and not the O.U.N.. These are simple people, and they care about independence. I don't know how to answer them and wonder if that is something I will ever again champion, or has that dream died with the arrival of two power-ful armies that get to decide our fates. I know, too much politics, so I'll stop.

On the brighter side, the Russians remain generous in paying us for the printing and bookbinding. There is nowhere to spend all that money, though, so Papa has us hide it at Katia's family farm. For the future, he says. For the future? I wonder what that means anymore. You are gone. Ira is gone. Most of the men of the town are gone. Danger seems to lurk in every corner here, and I go to sleep most nights more afraid than fatigued.

I'm sorry I allowed sadness to creep back into my mood. I'll try to stop that. I am truly excited about your news, and your optimism gives me hope, as well.

Mama and Papa send you love, as do I.

Leja

CHAPTER 48

That was the last of Leja's letters I read for many years. She kept writing, but there was no way to post anything, so she placed each letter inside the pages of a book she'd shared with me as a child, *Cities of the World*. That's where I found them when I finally returned home.

Before that, though, there was the war.

On June 22, 1941, the German Seventeenth Army crossed the San River from Poland into the Russian-controlled territories of Galicia, and the world that briefly had made sense to me exploded. We heard the news about the attack several days later, when the sharp wail of sirens woke us before dawn. We were ushered sleepy and confused into the dining hall, where Comrade Masha stood atop a table at the front and shouted for our attention.

German tanks and planes had blitzed the border, part of a massive invasion force, she said, stretching from the Arctic to the Black Sea, whose goal was to destroy the Soviet Union. The Germans expected quick victory, and on their march to Moscow they intended to claim the coal fields and factories of the Donbas as their first prize, "the very ground on which we stand," Comrade Masha said. "But they will not have it."

The plan, she explained, was to destroy what we could not carry when we retreated from the advancing armies. "Burn these barracks, our machines and the crops in the fields out-side," she shouted. "Flood the mines. Shoot the farm animals. Level every bridge we cross. This will be our victory."

There it was again, I thought, as I listened and eased Mischka closer to me. Leveling this place didn't feel like vic-tory, but Russian leaders always found a way with their words to turn retreat into heroism, black into white.

"Is this really happening," Mischka asked, her face pressed against my shoulder. "Is this the end of us?"

We had money, the rubles we received as a wedding gift from the state, I said. "We can run away." But we didn't need to run, because Comrade Masha had planned a more man-aged departure for her son, his wife and his best friends. Even before the destruction of Carbonite was complete, the four of us boarded a train crowded with refugees from the west and began a long trip to safety.

For fourteen days, we rode through vast stretches of southern Russia and Kazakhstan before crossing the moun-tains that separated Europe from Central Asia. As we traveled, I searched the faces of others on the trains. Was that crip-pled man seated by the window my father, the worried older woman beside him my mother? Every soldier reminded me of Ira. Each young family reminded me of him again, and Katia and Naftali. When I first glimpsed a young woman who'd walked into the far end of my train car after days of travel, her defiant look so reminded me of Leja that I stood and began making my way through the crowd to reach her. Mischka pulled me back without a word. At each station stop, I had new hope as I studied the refugees leaving the train or board-ing. At each departure, hope was lost.

———————•◦•———————

Letter from Leja, June 30, 1941, unmailed
Dear Wolchi,

*The Germans have come. Their tanks arrived yesterday eve-
ning, then truck after truck filled with soldiers and the officers in
open cars. It was like Krakow, except the armies didn't stop here.
They drove through the town and even ignored the foolish women
and men, who greeted them in the streets with bread, salt and
beer. "Welcome, liberators," they shouted. "Ukraine will now be
free." What fools. The Russians were brutal, but I fear the killing
hand of the Germans will be far worse.*

*I don't know if you will ever read this, because there is no
mail, no way for me to send anything. But I will write, nonetheless, hoping that someday you might hold this in your hand and
understand.*

*They killed Ira. I am crying as I write those words. He's dead.
I know what you are thinking, but the Germans didn't kill him.
Two weeks ago, he surprised us and arrived unexpectedly as we sat
down, all of us, to celebrate my birthday. We were at the table,
the door opened, and there he was. It was wonderful. You should
have seen Katia and Naftali, the looks of joy on their faces. He told
us his commander had given him permission to visit. It was quiet
where they were on the front, and the commander allowed his men
a short break. He was with us for a wonderful week. To see him
with his son, who is growing tall and handsome like Ira, was a gift
to us all. He and Papa showed Naftali how to work the printing
press in the buchbinderi, and the little guy was so happy to help.
The two of them went back to the farm in the evenings, where it
was quiet, Ira said, and he didn't need to think about Russians.*

We knew the Germans were coming when the Russian soldiers began hastily breaking their camp and preparing to fight, or flee. I couldn't tell at the time, but it turned out to be the latter. They rounded up the young men they saw on the streets, calling them traitors for not wearing the uniform of the Soviet Army. The men who volunteered to fight were spared, but the others, the others were murdered. Some were hung in the town square from light posts, others shot in the street. It was horrible. I didn't see what happened to Ira, no one did, but Katia said he was trying to rejoin his unit and left them, running into the woods wearing his ordinary clothes, not a uniform, toward the east where he hoped to find a friendly farmer or a Russian truck that could take him back. Katia heard shooting. She found Ira shot dead, a unit of Russian soldiers nearby, and on the hill in the distance several men, O.U.N. she said, looking down on her. Someone yelled, "traitor." Katia doesn't know who. It doesn't matter who pulled the trigger, whether it was O.U.N. or Russian soldiers, because in truth it was this place that killed him. Hatred and death have soaked into the soil for centuries, and sometimes they rise up to take the innocent.

Papa buried him on the farm, in a quiet place beneath an old crabapple tree, a place that we hope Ira will always know peace.

I am numb from writing this. It brings pictures into my mind that I don't want to see.

We love you.

Leja

CHAPTER 49

July 1941, Swerdlovsk, Central Soviet Union

It was the largest city I'd ever seen. We caught sight of it long before we arrived, its buildings and industrial smoke visible after we'd crossed the Ural Mountains, but were still miles away. This was to be our sanctuary, Comrade Masha said, two thousand miles from the fighting, the place where war was unlikely to reach, but where we could help win that war. Long lines of rail cars filled with machinery and industrial equipment crowded the tracks on both sides when we arrived at the central station. Ours was the only train that carried people, it seemed. Even the platforms were mostly empty, but for a small group of Russian soldiers standing casually at the entrance to a building across the tracks.

One of them waved his arm, motioning for those leaving our train to approach that building. The four of us, bags over hunched shoulders, joined an orderly queue outside the closed doors.

"We are a long way from Crimea, my friend," Lev said to me as we stood waiting with the others. He had largely recovered from the injuries he received in the mine accident. The only visible evidence of his trauma was his right hand, which was still locked in a half-clenched claw-like, position.

It made handshaking and back-slapping awkward for a man who thrived on both, but he had healed and was his old, talkative self.

"What are we waiting for exactly?" he asked, more of himself than of us. "Everywhere we arrive is like this. We line up without being asked, stand in the midday sun without any idea as to why. No panic, just patience. No complaining, just compliance. Like good Russians. Like ants awaiting commands from our queen."

His familiar diatribe made me smile. Lev, the child of a woman permeated with Soviet dogma, was a keen and persistent critic of everything she stood for, and I was his willing straight man.

Motioning to the machines and heavy cargo crowding the station. "I believe we have found our place," I said. "Once again, we are close to the beating heart of the Soviet industrial heartland. Everywhere we go, it seems to follow us."

"For the Motherland, for honor, for freedom," Lev deadpanned.

We'd played this game before: "Our cause is just, our enemy will be crushed," I added without hesitation.

Lev surveyed the line of people behind us, stretching back across the tracks and growing longer as more people departed our train. "Long live the endless lines of workers and peasants, the true guardians of our Soviet borders," he said, pausing for a moment. "All of them, good Russians — and ants."

Mischka and Angelina sat on the ground, tired and bored with the conversation.

"Sit down," Mischka said, pulling my wrist as she announced that "it's time for the talking game."

Angelina laughed and clapped her hands quietly. She

loved the talking game. Lev rolled his eyes. He would resist briefly and then surrender. I knew better than to complain, because Mischka would not be deterred. The game helped us through the painful boredom and uncertainty that dominated our journey, so why stop now, she argued.

"Let's talk about previous journeys," Mischka said. "Before this one, where did you leave? Why did you leave? Whom did you leave?"

No one was talking, until Angelina touched Mischka's arm and said: "You should start. You never go first."

Mischka was ready for this invitation. In fact, I knew the topics she proposed for our talking games were usually ones she'd already pondered. I'd learned the hard way, that the game was often a set up. Playing it opened the door for her to share what she wanted us to know, or learn what she wanted to know about us.

"I'm glad you asked," Mischka teased. "I would like to talk about leaving my home, two years ago in Crimea, a place called Alushta on the Black Sea."

Lev and I sat beside the women. "We are not in Crimea, but we will hear about it just the same," he said to me, thumping his curved fingers awkwardly onto my back.

Mischka cast a disapproving glance and hushed him. "You have nowhere else to go and nothing else to do, so just listen."

She continued: "It was difficult to leave Alushta, because I had never been anywhere else. I was just fifteen, and my whole life had been there.

"My mother worked for a rich family, caring for their house, a mansion really, near the beach. We lived in a small room in the town, and mother left early in the morning and came back after dark. I remember going to school and my sister looking after me when I was older. I don't know about when I was a baby. I don't remember that, and mother didn't like to speak of it. I didn't know my father. He was never with me, and mother never talked about him, either. She was an unhappy woman, you see, quiet, brooding.

"My sister left before me. She was five years older. A recruiter came to our town one summer looking for people to work on farms in the far east of the Soviet Union.. My sister signed up right away, even though she had no idea where she would be going. Maybe she's near where we are now? I hope she's safe, wherever she may be,

"After she left, I wanted to go, too, but the recruiters who came back the following year said I couldn't sign a contract and leave home until I has sixteen. I lied about my age and agreed to work in a steel factory in Lugansk. When I told my mother, she cried. I had never seen her cry, and it scared me. I almost changed my mind and stayed with her. But she wouldn't let me. 'There's a life for you somewhere else,' she told me. 'I promise there is. Just go find it.'

"I went to the beach the morning I was to leave, and saw the sun rising over the sea. The sky was grey overhead, but an orange and pink band of light stretched across the horizon at the water's edge. When the sun finally came up, the color spilled over the clouds and turned the sky to the east and the water below into a patchwork of crazy colors. I shivered, because I felt worried about beginning my journey alone. The sunrise also made me think that there was a god somewhere who could help me find the life my mother promised."

Mischka paused, as two men approached us with water jugs, allowing us each to take long drinks from wooden ladles. The day was hot, and there was no indication the line we'd joined was going to pass through the doors guarded by the soldiers anytime soon. So, she continued.

"Those steel mills in Lugansk were harsh, and for two years I searched the sky in the morning and at night for that same sign, something that would give me hope. There was nothing there for me, so I took another journey alone to Carbonite, looking for something, someone."

Mischka turned to me and took my hand. "Then I found him. He was no sunrise over the sea, but I knew he was special," she laughed. "Even in the darkness of the mine when I first saw his eyes and his happy, happy smile, I knew.

"The next time I saw the sun paint the sky the way it did that morning in Alushta, I was with him on a hillside, and I understood that I was no longer alone, that my next journey would begin with someone else beside me."

Mischka looked at each of us when she stopped speaking. Lev nodded his head in appreciation. Angelina sobbed quietly and said, "That makes me so happy." I locked my eyes on Mischka and touched her cheek. God's closest angel, I thought. My angel.

"My turn," Angelina interrupted excitedly. "Mischka, you made me think about when I left home. Isn't it odd that none of us is home right now? And look around us. No one is home."

"We're not on the beach in Crimea, either," Lev interrupted with a laugh.

"Where was home, Angelina?" I asked. She was rarely this animated. Angelina, quiet, calm, confident and a good listener, found it a challenge to compete when she was with Lev, who had a bad habit of high-jacking conversations. Her glance toward me was knowing. It thanked me for giving her back our attention.

"I was born in Minsk, a big city in Belarus. My mother is still there, and she sends me letters. At least she did before we left and before the Germans attacked there. She was a nurse during the first war, and she met an American soldier who was there to help the Belarussians. He was injured and in her hospital. He was my father. We lived together after the war, the three of us, in a flat near a park, and I recall walking with them as a little girl on summer evenings, chasing birds that gathered near a fountain. I would run toward the birds, and they would rise up in a rush of moving wings, the flapping so loud that I couldn't hear my mother shouting for me to stop, to come back to her. The birds frightened my mother, but my father, laughing, held her hand, and she would laugh, too. She was very happy then, and so was I.

"The Russians made my father leave the country. At least that's what my mother told me. They thought he was an American spy. I was still young, so I don't remember him going, but I do recall our walks in the park were never the same after he left. My mother held my hand tightly when we were out, like she was afraid she might lose me, too. And when I tried to work free to chase those birds, she would pull me back."

Lev placed his arm around Angelina's shoulders while she spoke, and he kissed her gently in a gesture of tenderness and love, a new man, a different man than the one who just months before told bawdy tales over dinner and flirted carelessly when he saw a pretty girl. Angelina put her hand on his and continued.

"We had a good life there, and I imagined someday that I would become a nurse like my mother. I never expected I would leave, but the Russians had other ideas. When I turned eighteen they told me I had to work, and there was no work for me in Minsk. I remember the exact words when the official told me I would serve the Soviet Union 'in the best way by doing what I was best suited to do.' That turned out to be working in a kitchen at a coal mine in the middle of Eastern Ukraine. Not what I expected.

"On the day I left home, my mother came with me to the train. I don't know which one of us cried more. I said through my tears, 'I will be back, mommy.' That made her stop crying. She wiped her tears and then mine, holding me on the railway platform, and said: 'Maybe you will come home, my girl. I would like that.' "

Angelina stopped speaking and dug through the canvas bag she carried. She retrieved a small brass object, circular, the size of a small coin. She held it so we could see the image of an eagle on the face of it, holding a pair of branches in its claws.

"She gave me this. It's a button, a memory she'd kept since she found it beside my father in the hospital, torn from his bloody army coat. When she handed it to me on that train, she said: 'And maybe you will go somewhere else. I would also like that.'

This was her talisman, like my Golem, a connection to the past and protection while she searched for her future.

"Where is your father," I asked. "Do you know?"

"My mother said he was from New York, but he could be anywhere, or he could be dead," she answered.

"New York? Maybe he lives in a skyscraper," I said, eager to share what I knew from the book Leja had read to me as a child about a city far away where the buildings were taller than the trees and touched the clouds, and where everything was possible.

"Perhaps," Lev said. "We should go there after we see Crimea." That made all of us laugh, but it also got me thinking. Why not?

Letter from Leja, November 1941, unmailed

Dear Wolchi,

I don't know what day it is, but I know it's November because the trees are bare, the sky is grey and the daylight ends before dinnertime. I am living with Katia and Naftali at the farm. I came here after German soldiers came looking for me. They said I helped the Russians and wanted to arrest me. Mama and Papa told them I had run away with you, which was a good answer and made me think, again, that I should have done just that. Mama and Papa made me go to the farm, but refused to come along even though it is safer here than in town. You know how stubborn they can be.

The Germans hate Jews, and they encourage the town's people to be disrespectful and often violent to the old ones, pulling on beards or hair and spitting on people, that sort of thing. I fear it will soon be worse. They freed the Russian prisoners, including Igor Goreki, that bastard. I believe he sent the Germans to me, for revenge, and not because I worked with the Russians. Almost everyone worked with them, Mayor Evanko, the whole bunch of them. Even Goreki would have done so, if given the chance. Now, the town's people act as if they fought from the start to drive out the Russian army. Such liars, but Papa says they are merely trying to survive, just like us.

There is a group, still just a few, organizing to fight back if we need to. We have guns, you know where, and believe we can stay hidden at friendly farms to the west of here. I have friends on those farms. They will protect us, and I promised myself I will have a gun in my hand the next time Germans come looking for me.

Naftali and Katia are safe here. She is masterful at keeping the realities of war from her son, even though I know she's frightened for him and deeply sad about Ira's death. She taught Naftali to gather eggs from the chicken coop in the back, and he proudly does so each morning, counting the eggs and comparing the number to the previous day. It's such a normal thing, and I like to be with him and hold his hand while he goes about his work. I forget everything that's happening when I'm with him. I'm just in the moment. Today, I remembered when you were his age. I was nine. It was your first day to go to school. Mama made you promise to hold my hand while we walked together. I thought you would be embarrassed to do that, so I dropped your hand once we left the house and Mama couldn't see. Do you remember what you did then? You put my hand back in yours and held it very tightly. You said you didn't want me to be scared. Me. What a big man you were, even then, worrying about your sister.

I know you can't write, so I'm left to imagine your life now that Russia has been invaded. I hear that German troops advanced past Donbas last month and are headed to Moscow. I assume you ran from there before the armies came, but I can't be sure where you are. I wish I could speak to you for just a moment, so I could know if you and your new wife are safe. It's troubling not knowing where you are, but when I close my eyes and see you in my mind, I imagine your small hand in mine, and it gives me hope.

Your sister,

Leja

CHAPTER 50

The calendar page hanging from the door read February 1943. Each day that had passed was marked with a single black line, twenty in all. When I anxiously knocked, the page tore off the nail and fell to the ground. A grumbling voice inside asked, no ordered, me to enter while I fumbled to retrieve February. When the door swung open, the hulking figure of Big Boss stared down at me, the ripped calendar still at my feet.

I'd worked for eighteen months in his factory, a place more sprawling than my hometown. We manufactured tanks, big guns and other necessities of war. The Russians called it Uralmash. We were all there, the four of us, the tavarishy, or comrades, as we were now known disparagingly around the place, because when we arrived we amused ourselves by greeting one another on the factory floor with stiff shouts of "comrade." Everyone thought we were true believers, rather than jokesters, especially after word got out about Lev's mother. Once that happened, the nickname stuck.

"Comrade," I said shyly to Big Boss, extending my hand in greeting. "I am Vladimir."

He was more than one of the top apparatchiks at the factory, he was also a massive man, big in every way. He left my hand unshaken, my arm oddly stretched into the dead space between us. He wasn't looking at me. Instead, he stared at the calendar page under my boot. His three chins undulated in waves above his chest when he motioned to the floor with his hand, and raised his eyes to consider me. Head to toe, he looked me over, taking the measure of the young man who had torn his calendar from the door and now stood there rather than picking the thing up.

"If you broke something here, who would fix it?" he asked.

"I would, sir," I answered. Was this a trick question?

"If a man who works for you breaks something here, who should fix it?" he asked again.

"Of course, he would be expected to do that," I said, and the anxious fog surrounding me cleared and I saw the very obvious point he was trying to make. I kneeled, retrieved the calendar page and tried my best to return it to the nail that once secured it to the door. It was not to be.

Big Boss shook his head impatiently, like a parent disappointed in his simple son. "I hope you are better at fixing our machines," he said, as he turned his back and returned to his desk. When he sat and saw me still frozen outside his door, holding the torn calendar page, he laughed, the hearty, full laugh of a fat man enjoying this unscripted show.

"Come in, already," he said. "You're letting out the heat."

I sat on the hard, spartan chair across from him, still holding the calendar page, my hand trembling a bit. A coal-burning stove in the corner kept the room warmer than other parts of the massive factory, but I still felt the cold through my coat.

Big Boss pushed a tray of cakes across the desk toward me. "Eat," he said. "You look thin."

Everyone in the place was thin, I thought, with the exception of the man across from me chewing a mouthful of dough and sugar. I took one, then a second of the small pastries. For most of the past six months, I'd eaten nothing but the pasty cereal and watery milk served each morning, or variations of the thin potato soup and hard, dark bread served each evening in the drafty dining hall attached to our dormitories. I wanted nothing more than to devour those cakes on the spot, but instead I placed them carefully in my coat pocket, a treasure to be bartered later for a few pieces of meat or chunks of cheese that could be shared with Mischka, Lev and Angelina. I kept eyeing the tray and the single remaining pastry, while Big Boss watched me. "Eat that one," he said. When I retrieved the last cake, he gently slid the tray back toward him, brushed crumbs from the platter and slipped it into a desk drawer.

"I know things are hard for you and the other workers," Big Boss said as I savored the sweet dessert. "We all suffer because of this war. But our job is also a noble one and must be done. We are, as Comrade Stalin says, a worker's paradise on earth, and our enemies cannot be allowed to destroy this dream. Don't you agree, Vladimir?"

Everyone knew that the lofty rhetoric of Marx and Lenin that had birthed the Soviet Union had long ago given way to a unique form of tyranny crafted by Joseph Stalin. There was no poetry in the day-to-day lives of factory workers. There was hunger, plenty of disease and endless displays of cruelty by the bosses. The workers of the Soviet Union were certainly at war, but to me the enemy was closer than the German army to the west. I couldn't say that to Big Boss for the obvious reasons, and because the cake held my full attention.

My hesitation encouraged Big Boss to continue. "And everyday I am thankful that I am here, rather than starving in a frozen, bombed out hovel in Leningrad with the Germans laying siege. I hope you are, too."

This time, I nodded. What else could I do, because I understood the implied threat. We all did. The fate of each one of us rested in the hands of this man, and the other bosses at the factory. They could keep us or send us away to where bullets and bombs were the most likely cause of death, rather than malnutrition and disease.

Big Boss told me I had distinguished myself among the new workers. Where, he asked, had I learned my machinist skills? I took my last swallow of cake and nervously told him the story of my father, my apprenticeship with Mr. Koperski, and my time in the Krakow rail yards.

"It's a good thing we got you before the Germans did," he said, smiling. "We both need men like you to win this war."

Big Boss picked up a sharpened pencil from among a dozen set beside a schematic drawing of the factory he now studied. He tapped the pencil on a corner of the diagram.

"And that's why you're here today," he said. "I need you to do more, to train other men to fix machines the way you can. Do you understand?" There was just one correct response, so I nodded again.

"We need to keep this factory moving twenty-four hours each day. Everything must be working properly, making weapons for our soldiers. And you will be responsible for the machines right here."

He slid the schematic drawing toward me, and pointed with his pencil to the area I had been assigned since July. We manufactured assault guns and tank destroyers that Big Boss told me had proved effective in the battlefield.

"Our production target is now double," he said to me. "And you must make sure our machines can handle this. Understand?"

I would be given ten men who would learn to repair and maintain the drills, lathes and milling machines that turned raw steel into armament.

I hesitated. It was impossible to say "no," but what could I get in return for a "yes."

"First, I would say that I am honored to be chosen for this task, and I welcome the opportunity to assist the Soviet people in their struggle against oppression," I began. "Let me also say that I am honored to work for a man like you, who is so clearly the best of our great nation. I believe your face should be on posters across the Soviet industrial heartland, a reminder that workers are the true guardians of our nation."

Big Boss smiled, the flattery penetrating his gruffness. When he stood to end our discussion and send me away, I continued. "But I need some things from you."

His smile went slack, and he sat back down awkwardly. Impatiently, he pointed his pencil toward me. "Well, what is it?"

Big Boss, in addition to supervising a large section of the Uralmash, had also placed himself at the center of a lucrative black-market trade in the plant and the surrounding community. Ten eggs were a dozen in our factory kitchen, because two went to the Big Boss. Chicken backs were the only meat that made it into the soup, because Big Boss got the rest of the bird. Soap, medicines, clothing and even heating coal flowed through his cadre of crooks. He was accustomed to being the one making demands and was surprised that I sat there, someone he could cast off to the army as tank fodder with a scribble of his pencil, asking for something in return for following his orders.

Thinking about Lev, I quietly said, "I need to choose my

own workers for the training." He nodded, relieved I wanted so little.

"Some will be women," I continued, thinking of Mischka and Angelina. He nodded, again. Still, nothing to lose by agreeing.

"And food. We need more proper food. We all will." His eyes grew wide, this man who looked to never miss a meal, at the mention of food, that scarce and valuable commodity.

He shook his head again, the way he did when we'd met a short while before, but now there was appreciation in his eyes, respect for the evolution of his simple son into a crafty bargainer.

"One additional ration at the end of every day of work," he replied gruffly. "If no work, no extra food. In fact, if no work, no food at all. So, stay healthy and keep working."

He stood again, stretching his hand toward me to seal our agreement. When I reached to take his hand, the torn calendar page drifted back to the ground.

"Do you know why that calendar hangs on my door, young man?" he asked, gripping my hand and gently pulling me toward him. "To remind everyone that each day in this place is another day alive, that each day here is not a day when an enemy will try to shoot you or blow you apart, and that the person who decides whether you get another day on this calendar sits behind the door.

"So pick that up, and hang it back," he continued. "You've earned another day."

———•◦•———

Letter from Leja, March 1943, unmailed

Dear Wolchi,

I returned to Katia's house just minutes ago, and I thought you were here. It's very late, almost morning, and I saw you standing by the window looking toward the road. The moon was shining past you and your shadow was the only dark spot in the room. Katia and Naftali are asleep, so I walked quietly toward the window and whispered your name. I heard the wind blowing, and you moved as if you were being blown about, like the tree outside the window whose swaying branches reached for me in an embrace.

Of course you're not here, and thank God for that. The Germans have ripped the soul out of this place, and it feels nothing like home. I like to sit by candlelight late at night when I am alone and the house is quiet. Sometimes I browse through my book about the world's great cities. You remember that one? Yesterday I was looking at pictures of Paris, the City of Light, and wondering if it has been darkened by the Nazis, because surely it has. I wonder if Jews there were forced to stand in the town center while German soldiers urged Christian children to throw stones at them, pull their beards and kick them. Did the men and women of Paris watch without intervening while their Jewish friends and neighbors were stripped of their clothes and marched naked through the cold streets to the forest near the old cemetery, where a muddy ditch became their graves? This all happened here, so why not Paris? Why not Krakow and Warsaw? Why not in every European city where German armies now walk the streets? That must be what is happening.

The true evil of the Germans is that they have found others, local men, whose hatreds and petty grievances could be unleashed to do the murder. They freed Igor Goreki after the Russians left. He is back among us, the eager leader of a pogrom that has destroyed the Jews of our town.

I know this is a confusing way for me to tell you that Mama and Papa are dead, but even weeks later I need to hide their deaths in my mind amid other thoughts and other images. If all I see is them, I become cold, breathless and unable to move. But if I can hide their deaths amid my imaginings of Paris, well, I can breathe and go on. Papa and Mama fought back, or at least tried to fight back. They were shot in the buchbinderi when they refused to join the march of death. That's what I was told by our friend Mr. Koperski, after he found them and brought their bodies to Katia's family farm. He helped me bury them beside Ira's grave. Katia and Naftali surrounded the spot with small stones, hundreds of them in a circle, and I said prayers for them. Or, maybe I said prayers for myself. I was surprised by how well I recalled the things we learned in synagogue as children. It's been years since I said those Hebrew words, but they found my voice when my mind was dull with loss and I couldn't otherwise speak.

I am in hiding. The Germans or their henchmen would arrest me, or worse, if they could find me. A small group of us, some you would know, is fighting these enemies, the perpetrators of this madness. We stay hidden in the woods or on rural farms, and I sleep in Katia's barn during the day. After dark, we fight. We hope to kill one Nazi each night. No more than that, so they consider us a nuisance rather than a threat and don't hunt us. Tonight, before I returned to Katia's and wrote this letter, I shot a German soldier walking in a patrol past the mass graves near the old Jewish cemetery. He was young and looked like a student. In another time, I might have been his friend. But tonight, I was the dybbuk in the dark who shot him in the face and watched the others with him drop to the ground in terror. I'm glad the German soldiers and their henchmen fear the darkness. That seems right to me, because they created it.

The sun is almost up now, and the shadow in the room is gone. I need to get to the barn and sleep, but I will kiss Naftali and Katia for you, because I know that is what you would do if you were here with us.

Leja

CHAPTER 51

Lev spooned the rice into a second bowl, eyeing each portion. "Even?" he asked as he handed the bowl to me. Last night he brought soup with a remarkable amount of chicken, noodles and carrots. "This is the bottom of the pot," he explained. "They give us the water on the top and keep the bottom for themselves." And the night before, he had those potatoes, fried in fat with crispy onions and a bit of bacon.

"Where do you get this stuff," I asked, as we headed toward the hospital with the rice bowls, each covered with a cloth and carried close to keep them hidden from jealous eyes. Food was scarce and meagerly provided by the factory. None of us was starved, but we were hungry, all the time.

"Cigarettes," Lev answered. "Better than rubles. I can trade them for anything."

We walked slowly, both exhausted, covered in oil and grease because the factory had no soap, working sixteen hours each day and spending nights at the hospital, bringing food to Angelina and Mischka. Big Boss had made good on his promise of "no work, no food," and the two of them received nothing but hospital rations for the past two weeks. Angelina was sick with typhus fever, as were most others on my work team, each gravely ill or dying. Mischka, while not infected, had been ordered to bed by the doctor, her belly round and heavy with our child, and her heart working dangerously hard to keep them both alive. Hospital workers, assuming that patients were likely to die, skimmed food from their meager plates or sometimes just failed to feed them, keeping those meals for themselves. Lev made sure our wives did not go hungry.

Disease had left our corner of the Uralmash factory limping and close to a halt, as machines broke down and I ran out of workers who could repair them or hours in the day to do the work myself. Lev helped, trying to do more than his usual assistant activities, but his crippled hand limited his usefulness as a machinist. It didn't hinder his bartering skill, though, and he even used "the hook," as he called it, as a prop to win sympathy from the old women in the kitchen who traded extra food for a few harsh-smoking Russian cigarettes, gifts from Comrade Masha when she visited her son at the plant the prior month.

The outside doors to the hospital were open when we arrived, even though it was January. The thinking was that the fresh air would blow away the typhus infections spreading among factory workers, leaving so many sick that dormitories were being converted to hospital wards seemingly overnight as residents fell ill. Just open the doors and hope for the best was the treatment plan.

Angelina had a room with two others near the building entrance, and Lev waved his crooked hand in farewell as he went inside, greeting her loudly. "My angel," I heard him say. "How are you feeling today." Mischka was isolated in a large room with other women and babies in what passed for a maternity ward at the far end of the corridor. When I opened the door to her room, though, another woman was in her bed.

"Where is she?" I asked. "Where's my wife?"

The woman, moaned softly, her hands folded across her enormous belly, and stared back in confusion.

"The girl who was here," I said. "Where is she?"

A young nurse came from across the room and took my arm. "The baby," she said. "The baby." She led me into the corridor, through door after door, into a small room, dark and unsettlingly quiet. When Naftali was born, Ira told me that Katia had screamed the most frightening screams he had ever heard in what could have been pain or something more primal. He didn't know what to do, but didn't need to do anything, he said, because Katia's mother was there with other women who kept him outside, where he stood beside the door until Katia's shouts suddenly stopped, and he heard the faint squeak of Naftali's first call to the world.

The nurse pointed to Mischka, her eyes closed, a single dim table lamp illuminating her face. "Why is she so quiet," I asked. The nurse held my arm and pointed to the bowl of rice in my other hand. "She can't eat," the nurse said. "Sleeping." She took the bowl from me, lifted the cloth cover, smiled, and walked away. I approached the bed cautiously, unsure what to do. If our baby was coming, as the nurse had said, why was the room so hushed? Where was everyone? I stood beside Mischka and touched her cheek gently until she opened her eyes.

"I was worried when I couldn't find you," I said. "Are you alright?"

She said nothing and looked at me dreamily as if trying to recall my name, who I might be, why I was standing over her and touching her face.

"What happened?" I asked.

The tear blossomed like a flower from the corner of her eye. It hung for a moment on her lower lid before rolling across her cheek to my hand. It felt warm in the cool room when I wiped it aside, softly, barely touching her face with a single finger. Then more tears came. I put my arms around her shoulders, squeezing my cheek against hers, and whispered, "I'm sorry." Tragedy had been a familiar companion for everyone at the factory, so I assumed the worst. "We can try again for a baby when you are better."

She pushed my arms away, oddly playfully, and gently pulled me over her toward the bed-side light. "A girl," she said. There, hidden by the height of the bed, was a tiny cradle. I saw the wrinkled face topped by a shock of black hair. My daughter stared at me in wonderment, and I could see my reflection in her dark eyes. Her gaze would not let me go, and I surrendered to it, holding my breath so not to disturb the perfect silence in the room. It was so quiet, as we took the measure of one another, my baby and me (Who was this little person? Who was this man?), until she grimaced, her eyes growing wider, and howled a deep, long cry that ended when Mischka reached down and placed our baby on her chest.

———⚫———

When they fell asleep, I hurried down the hall to share the news with Lev, but he was curled in the corner of the room near Angelina's bed, asleep on the cold, hard floor, his coat collar pulled high over his face. Angelina also slept, the empty rice bowl on the covers above her lap, her hair combed, her face peaceful. She looked better. In the quiet of the hours between midnight and morning, only I was awake, my brain electrified by the new life, warm and safe on Mischka's breast. I needed to do something, but didn't know what, until I heard my father's voice, the memory from my childhood. *The very first words your mother says to me after you were born, 'The Golem.' The Golem.'*

I know that Leja and Ira would have mocked me, their eyes rolling, had they been there as I rushed back to my room and retrieved the aging statue hidden along with our stash of rubles beneath a loose floorboard under the bed. My mother's faith in Golem's power had found a permanent place in me, an irrational place for sure, but also one that gave comfort and anchored me to a belief that there would be a future for my family in the tumult that surrounded us. I wished in that moment, as I held Golem and remembered the thousands of times I'd habitually touched his belly before leaving the safety of our home, that Leja's hand, Ira's hands and the hands of my parents could also have touched him in the years since I went away. Every one of us needed this Golem, but Mother had given him to me, because maybe she knew his power didn't come from the dried river mud she'd shaped into its body, the Hebrew letters spelling "truth" on its chest, or the torn bible pages with the names of her children inside, but rather from the gift of her faith in it, a gift she gave to me. *Golem has always protected Jewish people, my people, and it now protects us.*

There was no paper in our room, so I tore apart a five-ruble note, carefully separating a small section from the image of a Soviet aviator and the patriotic slogans that covered most of it. The scrap of paper was white, unprinted and just large enough for me to write my daughter's name with a bit of charcoal from the small stove we used to heat the room. Before I folded the paper and slipped it into the hollow statue, I read the name aloud, Anya, over and over, hearing the magic of it, like a prayer. Anya, child of grace.

———— ••• ————

The Golem was still in my hands when an urgent knock-ing on the door woke me from a deep, dreamless sleep. It was late morning. The room was bright, and I hurried before opening the door to return Golem to its place beneath the floorboards.

A man I recognized as one of Big Boss' errand boys, without a word, handed me a sheet of neatly folded paper and hurried away. How perfect this sheet would have been to inscribe my daughter's name for protection with Golem, When I unfolded it, though, my mood changed. In Big Boss' choppy hand, the note read: "Where are you?" Translation? Get here right now because I want to yell at you about things you cannot control.

I hurried to Big Boss' office, and noticed on his door that sixteen days had been struck through with black pencil marks on the calendar page for January 1944. Sixteen more days I'd been alive thanks to the grace of the man inside the office. I stood ready to knock, and through the fog of my fatigue I realized my daughter had been born the day before, and that I'd also been born, twenty-four years ago, on the same day. I whispered, to no one, "Happy birthday to us."

I stood outside thinking about the three years since I last celebrated the day, the one with my family around our table in the warmth of home. Had it really been three years? Where were they now? What was happening to them? The news from the war suggested we were winning, that the Germans had stalled. We received reports that Russian tanks, the tanks we built at Uralmash, had pushed the enemy back over the Carpathian

Mountains, which would mean my town had been liberated. That news gave me hope, but it was a blind hope.

I knocked, careful to avoid striking the calendar page hanging on a single nail, and stepped inside. Big Boss looked grim. His shirt collar was dark with sweat, even though the room was cool. Red splotches covered his cheeks, and I could hear the rattle in his lungs when he drew a breath. Typhus. I knew the signs. He offered no cakes, no cups of tea, not even a seat. He pounded on the table with his forefinger, pointing to handwritten logs of factory output. The numbers circled in red indicated each day production had fallen short of unattainable goals, and red circles dominated the sheet he waved at me, as he coughed and sputtered with the exertion of these small movements.

"Our boys are dying while they wait for our guns and tanks," Big Boss managed to say between labored breaths. "This war would be over if you could just keep up, if your area could just keep up. Someone needs to be accountable. Moscow will not accept this. This is your responsibility."

Coughing overtook him, and he could no longer speak. He kept waving the paper with the red circles at me as if he were anointing me, or threatening me, the paper infused with powers beyond those of men. This was the production report, an official Soviet accounting of the factory's efforts, an accounting, I knew, that would usually never be seen outside this office. Instead, Big Boss would prepare a new report, a fiction with numbers adjusted to eliminate the red for some and shift blame for failure onto whomever Big Boss decided could be sacrificed. This was his job, to lie, allowing his superiors in Moscow to be pleased with their own accomplishments and giving them no reason to punish him, or any of his chosen men, with a trip to the battlefront. So, despite his tirades and irrational demands, I considered him an ally in our common effort to stay alive, until this moment.

"You, you are responsible. I can't keep you here any longer," he pointed an accusing finger.

"My workers are all sick or dead from the typhus," I replied calmly to Big Boss. "I am doing the work of ten men, even though my wife, my Mischka, gave me a baby daughter last night."

Big Boss was not listening. Long bouts of coughing spilled from deep in his lungs and filled the room. His face flushed as red as the Soviet flag hanging limply behind his desk, his eyes the color of the flag's yellow hammer and sickle. Truly, he had become one with Mother Russia, when his coughing stopped, his lids went wide, his face and body stiffened, and he slipped sideways from his chair with a thud that rumbled across the wooden floor. I rushed to him, slapped his cheek gently, and thought to call his name. But what was his name? No one had ever said it to me. He was just Big Boss. And then he wasn't, because he was dead.

A few days later, a written message reached us, and the new Big Boss had a name I knew: Comrade Masha. The message posted throughout the factory (so much good paper wasted) described her as a patriot, someone who had kept the supply of steel and coal moving to our factories, and tanks and guns flowing to our brave soldiers (and cigarettes to her son).

I thought this was excellent news, and another reason to celebrate. Mischka and I had a new baby, Angelina was on the mend, Lev's mother was now our Big Boss, and I was not headed to the front because Comrade Masha was someone who could be trusted to make the numbers work in our favor, who we could count on to secure her own ambitions, while keeping us all alive.

That night, we walked from the hospital, the five of us, the tavarishy plus one tiny baby girl wrapped in a blanket in my arms. We shared a pot of red borscht and a loaf of fresh black bread when we reached our rooms, the bounty from Lev's latest deal with the smokers in the kitchen. We shared another thing, too, something that felt new: A sense that maybe the end of the worst was near.

———————◆◆———————

Letter from Leja, January 15, 1944, unmailed

Dear Wolchi,

I am not sure of today's date, but I am pretending it's your birthday, because I know the day should arrive sometime soon, or maybe has just passed. I heard German soldiers celebrating the new year at the tavern some days ago, so I am confident I am not far off and can still wish you the happiest of birthdays, my dear brother.

Our celebration would be quite different if you were here. Our table would be less crowded. Just you and me, Katia and Naftali. Who would tell the story of your birth? Who would bake the honey cake? Maybe we would invite Mr. Koperski, who is a very kind man and always asks about you when he visits the farm. He is alone, without much to do these days. They destroyed his workshop. Destroy, destroy. That's all they seem to know, those animals. That's what Papa always called them. Remember? The men in the town who were always ready to drink and fight. Wild animals.

But they're worse now than even the most rabid dog. The Germans have allowed them to run amok, to cleanse the town, they say, to leave nothing for the Russians when they arrive and to leave every Jew dead. Igor Goreki is their leader. They came looking for me and Naftali yesterday. Katia's father scared them off while I hid. Katia told me what happened, that her father said Naftali was not a Jew, that he would be raised as a Christian boy. And, as for me, I was not welcome at his home, which of course was not the truth. Katia said the men wanted to search the house and barn, but her father pointed his rifle at Goreki's head and promised he would be the first to die if he and his men did not leave.

At night, I hunt the Germans. But they hide, because they know we control the forests and the dark roads. The big battle has gotten closer to us, too. The town hall is now a hospital for the wounded, and there are hundreds of men in there. Each day, more are carried over the bridge on trucks from the east, and we can see the smoke and fire from the battlefield in the distance across the river. The Russian army will be here soon. I can feel it. We plan to protect the bridge if the Germans try to sabotage it in retreat. We'll be outnumbered, a hundred to one, but it's a battle we need to fight. It might be where we all die, on the banks of that river. But if we save the bridge, the Germans will be overrun and they will die, too, on the same streets where the good people of our town were murdered, where Mama and Papa died.

This might be my last letter to you. In a way, I hope it is, and that sometime soon, before your next birthday or mine, we'll be together, that you will come home or we will be somewhere else, together. When we are, we can decide what might be next for us all. For you and your wife. For me. For Katia and Naftali, too. (If I am killed, this letter will be with the others inside our book,

"Cities of the World." You can read each one and know what happened here while you were away. I think I won't die, though. Because if I do, who will bury me?) When we're together, we will look through this book at pictures of those cities and find our place. Paris? London? New York? We can't stay here, but there is surely somewhere we can go, even in a world broken apart.

Happy birthday, Wolchi, and goodbye, for now.

Your sister,

Leja.

CHAPTER 52

Letter to Leja. June 1945

Dear Leja.

The war is nearly over. I finally believe it, and I'm coming home. I saw a picture last month of a Soviet flag flying over the Reichstag in Berlin, with Russian soldiers around the building. I think you will be getting mail again soon, too, because there are trains and trucks going west everyday to supply Russian soldiers. I hope you receive this letter, so you and the family will know I'm on my way home.

We are leaving next week, the four of us. No, the five of us — me, Mischka, my friends Lev and Angelina, and my baby girl, Anya. Yes, a baby girl. She has dark hair and dark eyes, but I see your face in hers, especially her smile. She is more than beautiful. She is my beating heart. I can't wait for everyone to meet her. Lev and Angelina are going to Minsk, where she will look for her mother. We are coming to you, Mama and Papa, Ira, Katia and Naftali — home.

Most of the workers here are being forced to stay until the government decides where they will be needed after the war. But Comrade Masha, the Big Boss and Lev's mother, is letting us leave because we are refugees, people from outside the Soviet Union who were displaced by the war. Since Angelina and I both fit that description, our families can come with us. Comrade Masha wanted us to stay, especially Lev, but she kindly approved our requests to travel away and even found us space on the special trains that have been organized to move refugees from the far east back to their home countries. She has come to like me over the years, and I will always be grateful that she helped me avoid the fighting and is now helping us get home.

I can't imagine what I will find when I get to you. The war has been very hard here, especially to get food. Many people I know died of starvation, tuberculosis and typhus, but we made it through. I was sick for weeks, but Lev and Mischka brought me extra rice and potato bread, sometimes bits of chicken, and that helped me get better, while others around me at the hospital died. I expect you faced the same at home, and that Mama and Papa had a hard time. I hear stories from returning soldiers who say that people in small towns and villages did better than those in cities, that the Nazis didn't have enough soldiers to occupy every place and they left towns like ours alone. I assume all of you stayed at the farm with Ira and Katia. That is what I would do, and why I'm sending this letter there. More food at the farm, more places to hide if the Germans did come. That is where I will go when I arrive.

I had a dream this morning, and maybe it was the reason I decided to write. I had a dream that I was in the buchbinderi with Ira and Papa. Papa was calling to me, but disappeared whenever I walked toward him. I told him to stop moving, but he couldn't hear me. He was skinny like a skeleton and a little unfamiliar, but I recognized him each time he appeared in another part of the workshop, partially hidden behind a machine or stacks of books. He kept calling me, but it was loud in the room because Ira was running the printing press. I told him to stop so I could hear Papa, but Ira couldn't hear me either. Then suddenly everything was quiet in there, and I saw Papa laying in that bed he had for when he worked late. Mama was beside him with her arm over his waist. She was crying, like a baby. When she turned to look at me, the crying stopped, and she was smiling. I asked her, 'Are you happy?' And that was it. I awoke to the sound of Anya. Mischka held her, and they smiled at each other. I squeezed my eyes shut to bring back the dream, because I wanted to hear Mama's answer. That will have to wait until I see her, though, and I can ask the question again.

I must get to work. Even though we're leaving soon, we're all working until then. First, I will arrange for my letter to be on a train today headed west. Please look for us after you read this, because we will be close.

Our love to you, Papa, Mama, Ira, Katia and Naftali, my precious family.

Wolchi

We were put on a train that was a series of cattle cars, each with double bunks on either side and an oven at the center, crudely fashioned from a fifty-five-gallon drum with a chimney through the roof. The cars near the engine were crowded with refugees from farther east, so we were given a spot near the rear. Lev was appointed the boss of our car thanks to Comrade Masha, a role that gave him control of food rations and other necessities. One of the perverse ironies of Soviet proletariat society was its passion for complex hierarchies. Each railcar had a boss; the train had two bosses who oversaw the others, and those two bosses reported to a station leader, who greeted our train at each stop.

It took us three months to cross central Russia into Ukraine, the train moving at a pace not much faster than a horse-drawn cart and at times coming to a complete halt for hours without warning or explanation. Lev and I left the train during those prolonged stops and searched for nearby farmers willing to exchange fresh milk, butter and vegetables for a few of Lev's cigarettes or the rubles we'd accumulated. When the farmers noticed Lev's damaged hand, he'd nod ruefully and say, "The war." They would nod in return and put an extra egg into our basket or an additional handful of carrots and potatoes. I carried a smelly bag of Anya's diapers from the train, and offered a ruble or two to the farmers' wives for some boiled water and a bit of soap. I usually did the washing, but at times, in small acts of human decency, the women washed those diapers for me. At night, Mischka and I wrapped the wet cloths around our bodies to dry them while we slept.

Lev and I knew the day was approaching when we would board different trains and the tavarishy would be no more. He and Angelina would travel to Minsk, while I would continue west with Mischka and Anya. He didn't speak of it, and neither did I for the months we trekked across Russia. We were content to be with one another and allow the future to unfold, as we'd always done, across the thousands of miles we'd traveled. So, we were unprepared to say goodbye on that morning in September when we pulled into the crowded and noisy central station in Kiev and the bosses came through the cars urging those of us continuing to L'viv and the west to leave promptly before the train turned north.

Mischka hurried to assemble our belongings and secure Anya to her chest with the makeshift carrier she'd fashioned from an old sheet, the baby's long legs hanging to her mother's waist. I searched the station through the window for Lev and Angelina, who had left the train to barter what they could for their onward journey. One of the bosses pushed luggage and bags off the train. "Let's go. There are others waiting to board," he said. "You must leave if you're not destined for Minsk or Warsaw. L'viv train is across the tracks."

He hurried us off. Anya cried loudly in the confusion, dust and noise of the rail platform. Crowds surrounded us, while we stood like stones in a river, people streaming past in every direction.

"We can't leave until we see them," I said to Mischka, whose efforts to calm our daughter were failing.

When I'd first met Lev, we were on a train platform not unlike this one. Four years had past, a lifetime in this war. We had become brothers, not of blood, but of necessity and need, and I selfishly didn't want us to be apart. If I urged him, would he change plans and come with me to the west? I knew he wouldn't, just as I knew Leja would stay behind when I implored her to travel with me when we stood on another platform in yet another place. These rail lines were crossroads, the places where we were forced to pick a path and move on from the life that was. And always, it seemed, we left something important behind.

"Comrade," a voice behind me called. Lev was coming through the crowd holding Angelina's hand and bundles of food. "Or should I give up on that comrade business now that we are no longer in Russia?"

I saw that Lev was confused by the sight of us standing amid the crowd with our bags and baby.

"We have a different train," I said. "We have to leave you."

Angelina didn't hesitate. She hugged Mischka, wrapping

arms around her and gently placing her face against Anya's. "My precious ones. We will miss you so," she said. Mischka began to cry and lowered her head onto Angelina's upraised cheek, two women and a small child face-to-face in solitude amid the confusion of the crowded platform.

"You are my brother," I said to Lev. He dropped the packages and held me in a hug, his unfamiliar strength lifting me from the ground.

"And you will always be mine," he replied, releasing me and clapping my shoulder. "We made it, you know. We made it through. And look at all we have. My angel. Your angels."

"I'll find you again someday," I said. "I promise that."

"In someplace better than this, I hope," Lev said, as he handed me two of the food bundles from the ground. "Who knows where. Maybe in your New York City? I would like to see those buildings that scrape the sky."

Chapter 53

A familiar autumn had arrived in my town. From the opposite bank of the river, the trees were still showy with full crowns of red and gold clinging to grey branches. The church steeples and town hall tower poked above the tree line, proof that my childhood place, at least some of it, was still there. We had ridden in an army truck from L'viv, because the trains no longer came this way. The tracks were destroyed in the fighting years before, and no one cared enough to rebuild them.

The truck left us at the foot of the bridge that crossed the river. The bridge still stood, but the damage was plain to see, and no vehicles would cross it. A makeshift pile of lumber was under one end of the structure where the steel of the abutment and pier had separated, and the bridge deck now rested on the wood supports.

It was clear no one cared to rebuild the bridge either. "A good welder could repair that in a day," I said to Mischka pointing to the damaged steel as we stood and considered whether to walk the bridge or cross the river on the barge that shuttled horse-drawn carts along a tethered line tied to each bank.

A bored Russian soldier guarding the roadway took our identity cards, examined them closely and acknowledged our journey with a nod. "You've come a long way," he said, and then pointed toward the bridge. "It's okay," he said. "It's okay for you."

Anya was strapped to my chest facing out, her eyes wide and enthralled by the colors and movement. This was her first autumn outside the factory, and what a wonder it was for her, having just spent months in the grey and drab olive of the train to now be outside on a brilliantly clear October afternoon with the blue and white of the river and nature's display in the trees. She waved her arms and babbled, embracing it all. When I held her this way, I saw the world as she did. It was a tonic for the anxiety that weighed on me, like dialing the radio away from static to soothing music.

"Then we'll walk," Mischka said to the Russian soldier. She felt the upbeat energy from our daughter, and it raised her spirits, too. "But if we fall in, will you rescue us?"

The soldier handed back our identity cards and replied soberly: "I wouldn't worry about the bridge, Miss. But when you reach the other side, watch yourself. The people in that town, they're evil."

We lifted our bags and walked onto the damaged bridge. Shells and other explosives had left the surface pockmarked with holes and cracks, so we stepped carefully. What had the soldier meant? "They're evil," he said. And as hard as I tried to keep the radio in my head tuned to my daughter's joy, the static rushed back.

———◆◆———

We walked the town's main street, the three of us, Mischka and I stepping past rubble that was once homes and businesses while Anya laughed and shouted at the ravens that flocked on the trees beside the river. I stopped outside Koperski Mashyna, its door broken and lying on the ground, and climbed over broken bricks and lumber to go inside. It was empty, but for scattered oily rags, bits of metal and a stray cat that patrolled the debris. No one had been in the workshop for a long while.

Three older women stopped outside and stood beside Mischka, watching me and Anya as I stepped back into the street.

"Koperski?" I said to them, pointing back at the abandoned workshop. "Where is Koperski?"

One of them shook her head, but the other two stared at Anya, with vacant, troubling eyes, seemingly surprised to see anyone young and alive. One reached up and touched Anya's face, before Mischka stepped between us and pushed the hand aside. The old woman cackled, and the three of them walked on. One turned back to us and said, loudly enough that I knew we were intended to hear, "They didn't get them all." At the time, I wondered what she meant.

Nothing around us seemed like my town. Perhaps too much time had passed for me to recall it clearly, but as we walked through the central square everything felt foreign. The tavern, usually alive with music and camaraderie this time of day, was dark and empty. The local farmers, who would crowd the square in the fall selling their goods, were absent. Not a single one was there. The only other people we saw were soldiers standing beneath the Russian hammer and sickle hanging above the town hall doorway. They eyed us, prudently watchful, as we passed, believing us to be strangers to these streets.

The Russians had papered the walls of the town hall with familiar propaganda posters. Red soldiers and airmen promised glorious victory. Joseph Stalin urged workers to build the tools of victory. They covered posters hung by the Nazis, some of which were still visible, a war of words still being fought on the streets. Among them was a series of small sheets hung in a block, dozens of them all the same, printed in deep red with a six-pointed Star of David covered by a large rat. "The crimes of the Jew," the posters read in block Ukrainian letters. We hurried past, staring straight ahead and away from the soldiers. Even Anya, so animated just moments before, was silent and wary.

We turned the corner toward my house and the buch-binderi. I pointed Mischka toward them, now excited to see something familiar that seemed intact and unaffected by war. When I got closer, I saw the six-pointed star painted in yellow on the front door. I handed Anya to my wife and stepped inside my childhood home. Like Mr. Koperski's workshop, everything was gone. Nothing was there. They had moved away, I thought, all of them, to the farm, perhaps, or some-where else safe.

I stood in the corner of the room and remembered Leja's reading spot and her secret library. Was it still there? I pushed on the loose wallboard, and it popped open. Periodicals and books still crowded the space inside. She would never leave this all behind. I searched for our special book, the *Cities of the World,* as dread fell over me. I pulled everything from the hiding place rifled through what was now scattered on the floor. Where was our book? Where were they? Mischka put her hand on my shoulder.

"Look," she said.

A group of men and women on the street watched us through the open door, and I ran to them.

"Where are they," I said.

The crowd stepped away from the house almost as one when I approached, all of them with that vacant stare.

"Where are they? " I asked, as I scanned the group for someone I knew. They looked familiar, but unrecognizable because their faces were worn and hard.

"They're gone," one man said.

"Gone where?" I asked.

"Gone," the man answered. "Just gone."

Like a swarm of flies caught in the wind, the group drifted down the street, as I glimpsed a man walking toward me from the buchbinderi waving his arms. The midday shadow hid his face, but I recognized his self-assured gait as he moved quickly toward us.

"Wolchi. Is that you?" the man called. He came closer, and I saw his unnerving blue eyes and flat broad brow, aged and marred by creases, but undeniably the face of Grygoriy Evanko. He wrapped his arms around me in a theatrical gesture, improvising a scene in which the other actors had departed from the script. I kept my arms at my side until he released his awkward embrace.

"It's a miracle that you are here, a great miracle," he said.

He acknowledged Mischka and Anya, studying them briefly but without real interest, before taking my arm and leading me toward the buchbinderi. He opened the door, encouraging me to step inside.

"After Marcus and Clara died," Evanko stopped as he saw my expression go dark. "Yes, they died. You didn't know? The Germans."

"What happened?" I asked.

"The Germans. That's all I know," he answered. "But let me show you what I've done here — since then."

He hurried us inside. Mischka found a chair near the window, Anya in the carrier over her shoulders, asleep.

"The Russians have me printing these," he said and held up copies of the posters I saw on the town hall walls. "And they pay, they pay just fine."

The buchbinderi was dirty. A dusty film of disuse covered the cutting and binding machines. A kerosene lamp had been hung from the ceiling over the printing press, presumably so it could be used more easily during the night. Evanko positioned a large sheet of paper on the press, lowered the pressure plate and then raised it, proudly displaying four images of a Russian propaganda poster shiny with wet ink as if he believed I'd never seen the miracle of print.

"I print them, and give them to the Russians," Evanko continued. "They hang them everywhere. And they pay."

I walked around the buchbinderi, gently touching the machines, the rags Papa used to meticulously clean them, the bed he slept in, the one in my dreams.

"What did the Germans do to my parents?" I asked.

Evanko sighed and shrugged his shoulders. "No one knows what happened," he said.

"Could they be alive somewhere?" I asked more urgently. "How do you know they're dead?"

He sighed again, shrugged again. "It's what people say. That's all I can tell you."

I stood beside a small pile of boxes in the corner. The flap to one was open, so I reached in and retrieved a sheet printed with a large rat in front of a yellow Jewish star. The box was full of them. Evanko rushed to me, grabbed the poster from my hand and thrust it back into the box, which he closed and secured by interlacing the flaps.

"It was a different time when the Germans were here," Evanko said softly. "None of us had a choice but to go along."

"Did you kill them before you stole the buchbinderi from them?" I asked.

"Marcus and Clara? Oh no. God no. They were my friends. Despite everything that happened, we were friends. They died right outside, I'm told, not like the others."

He paused, his face turned to the floor. "They killed all the Jews, Goreki and his men. Most of them were marched to the cemetery, forced into a ditch and shot. Some jumped into the river to escape and were shot while they struggled to swim. But I didn't see this, it's just what people say."

In my mind, I heard the voice of the soldier at the bridge. "The people in this town, they're evil." It was something I always knew, but now truly understood.

"And after they were gone," Evanko said. "I thought someone, someone close to the family, should take the buchbinderi and keep it running. So, here I am."

CHAPTER 54

We walked up our road, then past the Jewish cemetery and along the river, listening to the sound of the water and the raven calls from the aspen trees. When had all these black birds taken nest in the town? There were hundreds of them, perched on high branches in groups of two or four, looking down as we walked the path along the river that would take us to Katia and Ira's farm. I held out hope that, when we arrived, we would be greeted by my brother, my sister and maybe my parents. Evanko said they were dead, that they must be, but no one had seen them after Goreki, with the blessing of the Nazi occupiers, started the pogrom that erased Jewish life from my town. So, I had hope.

We rested by the river, eating the last of our bread and cheese, Anya drinking what was left of her milk. I recalled for Mischka the lore of the river and its power, a force our family trusted more than we ever trusted the police or the army or the rabbi at our synagogue. Anya toddled near us, digging a stick into the soft earth and then pointing it at the black birds above us. The ground beyond her banked gently toward the river, but I watched her carefully as she played, my mother's warnings engrained in memory. I took her hand and walked nearer to the water's edge, but not too close. I found several small, smooth stones and shared my secrets for skipping them across the water, making them soar high up sometimes and then landing them with a splash. Anya watched and tossed the rocks with each hand, making some progress after a while, reaching the water and laughing. Someday, she would be good at this, I thought, and Mama would be proud.

We resumed our journey. The road turned away from the river and emerged from the forest into hilly fields still covered by unharvested grain and sunflowers. Smoke trailed from the chimney above a farmhouse. I could see someone in the front of the house, maybe two people, and my spirits lifted, my stride quickened. Soon, they saw us, too, and walked toward us. I knew it was Katia when I saw her hair loose behind her flowing off her shoulders. Was that lean and long boy beside her Naftali? As their pace quickened, so did ours, Anya bouncing joyfully at my chest in her carrier. We reached each other just fifty yards from the house and stopped abruptly, not sure what to do, how to greet one another after so long, and so much. Anya extended her arms, as if anticipating an embrace, and Katia took the tiny hands in her own, smiling a joyous smile. Anya giggled, delighted.

"We are so happy to meet you, my darling girl," she said, and turned to look at me and Mischka. "I felt your spirits here for months, the three of you, and I knew we would be together."

We stood in the road marveling at this moment, the long stillness of it, how familiar but surprising at the same time. I stared at Naftali, his face already a preview of the man he would become and a reminder of the father and grandfather who preceded him. I didn't know how to ask the question at first, but we all felt it lingering unspoken in the cool afternoon air.

"You look so much like your Papa," I said to Naftali. "He must be proud of you."

Naftali looked at his mother, puzzled, unsure what to say, and then I knew.

"Ira? I asked Katia. "The others?"

She looked down and shook her head, tears welling onto her face.

Perhaps I should have been better prepared for this news, but it hit like a sudden kick from a horse, my ears exploded with a loud ringing only I could hear, my breathing stopped, and I could feel the heat rising from my neck and face. Anya felt it, too, and turned her head back to look at me. She opened her mouth, and her loud, doleful cry overpowered the ringing. I took a breath and spoke.

"How," was all I could say. So, she told me the story of Ira's death, alone in the dark woods, not knowing which enemy killed him.

"Mama and Papa?" I asked.

"They are buried there, beside Ira, in the clearing," Katia said, pointing to the open field beyond the barn. The sun blinded me, but I followed her hand and looked at that spot, where I saw what I thought must be a ghost running from the barn toward us, just a dark shape with an aura from the sun around it. The black spot grew larger as it drew close enough to have a face, and that face had a smile, and the smile belonged to my sister, who stopped running just a few feet from me and simply said: "Thank God."

We told stories for days. Mine were about the unexpected

journeys that took me to places unimagined, and then brought me back to another unimagined place that once was home. They were about my friends and my wife and child. They were about a daily fight for survival, and how that inspired a dream in me about other places. Leja and Katia had not journeyed, and their stories told of hardship and loss, the slow erosion of the emotional ground that supported them, as the people they loved were brutally taken. Their dreams weren't of another place, but of the place and people that were now gone. When we sat together talking at night, each one of us might, without warning, turn away, overwhelmed not by a memory but by a glimpse of the future without the people we loved.

Those first few days, I often sat outside beside the graves in the early morning, while Anya and Mischka slept. I imagined how Papa might have lifted my child as he'd lifted me, seemingly astounded by how she'd grown overnight, and making her laugh with him. I saw Mama in the kitchen, teaching her granddaughter to bake the celebratory honey cake, the way she'd showed Leja. There was no recipe for it, just the understanding that was passed from one generation to the next without a word of it spoken. I knew if I had then been able to ask Mama that question, "Are you happy," she would answer, "yes." And Ira, oh Ira, I wished I could see him make his son smile, the way he would cheer me when I was gloomy, with a silly face or a teasing joke. "Smile," he'd say. "It's the second-best thing you can do with your lips." I didn't know exactly what he was talking about then, but the frown always left my face nonetheless when he said it. I mourned everything that could have been.

On the afternoon that I read Leja's unsent letters, I sat for a long time trying to count the hundreds of stones Katia and

Naftali had placed around the graves. Wildflowers had sprung up around them, hiding the smaller stones. I carefully brushed aside the flowers to make the stones more visible as I went, but I kept losing count. Again and again I failed, and I became furious. I yanked clumps of goldenrod and ironweed from the ground without purpose, in a rage, cutting my hands on the sharp stems until all the flowers lay in yellow and violet piles atop exposed mounds of dirt, and I sat on the ground sweaty and breathless.

That's where Mischka found me later, I don't know how much later, sitting amid the flowers with Leja's letters in my hand and the "Cities of the World" book open in my lap.

"Anya is with your sister," Mischka said, and sat beside me. "They are becoming best friends, Auntie Lala and your daughter. The two of them are counting together, on Anya's knuckles and ears."

"She did that with me when I was small," I said. "I remember that. We also liked to look through this together."

We began leafing through the book, the way Leja and I had done so often. Sharing this ritual with my wife calmed me, and I embarked on an absentminded journey through the pages, hoping the book's pictures could replace the ugly images that were looping through my brain. The Palace of Westminster and St. Paul's Cathedral in London, and not the town's people greeting the Nazi invaders. The Trevvi Fountain in Rome where I might toss a coin and make a wish, and not Ira, Mama and Papa alone and dying. New York City, always New York City, where there was a statue that would welcome me if I ever sailed into the harbor. "Give me your tired, your poor, your huddled masses yearning to breathe free, the wretched refuse of your teeming shore." Yes, that was me, that was us. I kissed Mischka and closed my eyes to imagine the moment when we would see the sun set behind New York City, our backs turned on what had been lost.

CHAPTER 55

We had been at Katia's for a week when Mr. Koperski came riding up the road in his battered cart.

"The old grandmas told me a young man with a Russian wife and a baby came around looking for me," Mr. Koperski said before climbing from the cart and extending his hand. His grip was strong as ever, but his hands had become more smooth and soft. He no longer worked the way he once did. "And I guessed, no, I hoped, it was you."

It was a joy to see him, and I told him so.

"You always were easy to please," he said with a broad smile. "Now, help me with these."

When he turned and walked to the back of the cart where he'd piled vegetables, buckets of milk and three loaves of bread, I saw an angry red gash that spread up from beneath his shirt to his neck. He moved carefully and stiffly, his balance uneven.

"Let me do that," I told him, and stepped in front to begin unloading the cart.

"A few things for your family," he said. "Being out here, it can be hard to find everything a baby might need."

We had a dinner together that night with Katia's parents and Mr. Koperski, sharing the bread and food he had brought and the chicken Katia harvested from her backyard flock. The older men drank beer and were in a lively mood, which raised everyone's spirits. Celebration, so unlikely a short time before, now seemed overdue.

Mr. Koperski, especially ebullient, held court during the meal, a man so often alone that a group of warm friends around him unleashed a torrent of emotion and memories. He said Mischka and Anya reminded him of his lost wife and child. He noted that my face might look older, but he still saw the shy teenage boy who'd walked into his shop a decade before asking to learn. He recalled meeting Leja on our journey to Krakow in the back of his cart and in the open railroad car, and his mood became quieter, more thoughtful.

"I knew from the moment she and I spoke that this woman was extraordinary, that she was destined to do something exceptional," he said, placing his hand gently on her arm. "But how could I have known that she would become a soldier, the leader of our partisans fighting the Germans. She was the one, and she convinced me to join her and do what I could, what an old man could do."

He turned his head and pulled down his shirt collar to reveal the long red wound down his back. "Nearly had my head blown off, along with a few other parts, but it was worth it to help her and the others drive out the Germans," he said, tapping Leja's arm.

"I remember after you two had gone to Krakow, Igor Goreki came to me with a few of his goons because he thought I had helped you. He was smart enough to figure that out, but not smart enough to know I would never help him. He said it was my patriotic duty, and that I had a responsibility to my race, to help him find you. The Jews, he said, had caused too much trouble already. He offered me money just in case patriotism and hatred weren't enough.

"He had men watch the shop and my home, and even follow me when I traveled to Krakow with deliveries. I would see you from time to time on those trips, Wolchi, working in the railyard. I wanted very much to say hello and see how you were, but I couldn't. You understand? You looked fine, though, and that's what I told your father and mother when I saw them."

He stopped and touched Leja's arm again, looked at me nodding and then at Katia.

"The world is worse for the absence of your mother and father, and for Ira," he said. "And the world is also worse because Igor Goreki still walks among us, as if he were an innocent and good man. This troubles me. I've demanded that the Russians arrest him for his crimes, but they say there haven't been any accusations but mine. What crimes, they say, and dismiss me as an old man with a vivid imagination. Others are frightened of him, or need his money, and won't say the truth.

"So, everyday when I see him, I'm angry. With the Germans gone, he does business proudly with the Russians, openly stealing the land and possessions of the Jewish people his men slaughtered in the streets just months before."

Everything Koperski said was correct and right. This was the story of our town. Goreki, acting without fear of consequence, took what he wanted, spread hatred, enjoyed protection from other powerful men and survived like an insect through upheaval and war. Only Leja and the band of angry patriots she had once organized had ever held him to account and extracted a bit of vengeance for his crimes.

Now, she was ready to finish what was undone.

"We killed his son. Now, we'll kill him," Leja announced to a stunned silence at the table.

Mr. Koperski cautioned that the Russians would not allow it, that they had restored a semblance of order to the town and would punish anyone who threatened that.

"You can't just kill a man like Igor Goreki and walk away free," he told her. "Our desire for revenge needs to be tempered by that reality."

Leja thought otherwise.

"That doesn't matter to me anymore," she said. "He's the disease that sickened this town, and it's time we are cured of it. I keep asking myself why I didn't kill him before. I had so many opportunities. When we burned his fields, we could have thrown him into the flames. Or, when I shot his son, I could have walked to his house and finished him and the rest of them. So, I'm making myself a promise right now, in front of the family I have left and with the memory of Mama, Papa and Ira in my heart, that I won't make that mistake again. The next chance I get, he will die."

Leja's passion burned hot and with certainty, and perhaps that was why the fire could spread so unexpectedly in new directions. She was a patriotic nationalist, until she became a Nazi hunter. She once dreamed big, about places faraway, and now her world had narrowed to just a single goal. In all that time, one thing was constant. She remained fearless.

She turned to me and then to Mr. Koperski. "Help me," she said.

"I won't let Goreki take you away from me, too," I said with more edge in my voice than necessary. "If you kill him, it will be the end of you, too."

The Russians were unnuanced people when enforcing

their rules of order. There was a process, a right way to do things, and those who deviated from the process were punished, I told her. As Lev had taught me, tall flowers in the Soviet Union have their blossoms snipped, and a young woman who kills a town elder will end up dead herself. We were all Soviet citizens now, for better or worse, and had to behave as such.

She placed her hand on mine, her grip firm and steady. "I have no choice, Wolchi," she said, looking down at Anya asleep in Mischka's arms. "I understand why you can't help, but don't try to stop me."

CHAPTER 56

Russians loved political posters. They admired the vivid images of righteous workers and soldiers pasted on the walls of their factories, train stations and town squares. Stalin used them to communicate his world view and solidify power across a disparate Russian empire and then again to maintain morale during the worst days of the war. He knew the posters connected everyday Russians to common experience and history, things they knew in their hearts to be true, but rarely spoke about. So, I figured if they worked for Stalin, they might work for me.

As we traveled home across the Soviet Union after the war ended, we often saw groups of people gathered in front of a newly displayed poster in animated discussion about what they saw. These were cultural moments, a shared entertainment, and that was true in our town, as well. It wasn't patriotism that made the poster walls such a popular gathering spot, because our town was a place where some thought themselves Russian, some Polish and some still imagined themselves something they called Ukrainian. No, the town's people stood in the central square day after day admiring proclamations about triumphs of the proletariat and the Soviet army because they were bored and hungry to know more about the postwar world beyond our streets. They wanted entertainment and information, and the posters provided both.

The opportunistic Grygoriy Evanko had figured that out and was producing dozens of posters each week for the Russians after he stole my dead father's business, and I expected he wouldn't object when I used my father's printing press to put an end to Igor Goreki in a way that would preclude my sister from carrying out her promise of vengeance.

"Let's kill him the Russian way," I said to Leja while we walked along the river toward Big Rocks, where she hoped to retrieve a hidden rifle.

I told her Katia had used paints made from flowers and herbs to draw a frightening image of a man with a rat's head wearing Goreki's signature Homburg hat. He wields a thick club, slashing at a throng of men, women and children at his feet, who are reaching up to him in fear and desperation. In their hands, they hold a list of crimes stretching back a dozen years, written in both Russian and Ukrainian. Red letters across the top of the image read: "The crimes of Igor Goreki."

"Come with me to the buchbinderi. You can help me print the posters," I urged. "Mr. Koperski and I plan to put them up tonight. The entire town will see them by day's end, and then the Russians will take care of him, rather than you."

"The idea is brilliant," Leja said. "But let's see who gets him first."

She returned with me to the buchbinderi carrying a German Mauser sniper rifle with a hardwood stock and a 4X scope, rather than any intention to help me. The rifle and a cache of ammunition were hidden inside a cloth bag over her shoulder. This was the way she carried her rifle when the Germans controlled the town, she said, and no one ever stopped her, a young innocent-appearing woman, to ask what was in the bag. She was certain no Russian soldier would bother her either, while she stalked Igor Goreki.

Evanko and Mr. Koperski were inside the buchbinderi when we arrived. Not only did Evanko allow us to use the printing press, he enthusiastically took on the task of printing the posters himself, excited by the idea of exposing Goreki. Even Evanko, who had carefully avoided confrontations over the years and had prospered in the shadow of his evil, hated him.

"He will shit his trousers when he sees these," Evanko said. "And his first stop will be here to punish me."

"Let him come," Mr. Koperski interjected. "His time is done, and I will stand with you if he shows his face here."

Mr. Koperski held up a finished poster from a stack on a table and brought it to Leja.

"These will surely expose the crimes of our dirty rat," he said.

Leja took the poster and turned it to the light, admiring it closely. She pointed to the rat's mustachioed face.

"When I see him, I will shoot him right here, in his ridiculous mustache. If I am able to fire twice, the second bullet will go here," she said and pointed to the center of the figure's skinny chest, where the rat head ended and a man's body began. "I'll make sure both the man and the rat are dead."

Leja was not easily deterred, even when she was a young girl with a soft face, long braided hair and passionate political ideas. Papa had a way of calming her when her outrage over political and personal slights exploded. "Your time will come, my dear Leja," he would say. "Until then, you can't fight every fight." That young girl was gone. She'd been fighting for years and was hardened, her hair cut to her shoulders, a small scar on her right cheek from some forgotten battle. There would be nothing in Leja's life, until she accomplished the next thing, and all her mind's energy was focused there. There would be no stopping her. She planned to lie in wait at the edge of the woods near the river until Goreki came riding up the road to church in his ornate carriage. She would call his name until he turned to look at her, confusion turning to recognition in his eyes. And then, pop, pop. He'd drop the reigns of his carriage, the horses would slow, and Goreki would slump before falling into the road.

"I can leave town after that," she said. "I know every farmer between here and Krakow, and they'll help me. Maybe Michel and Ludmilla are well and would have me back, just as if the war had not happened and I was young and running away after I shot the other Goreki?"

"Why don't you help me mount these posters before you start hunting and escaping?" I asked.

Leja slung the gun bag over her shoulder, and I thought she'd be gone in a moment, not just from the buchbinderi, but maybe from my life. Instead of walking out the door, though, she grabbed a handful of posters and pointed to a bucket of paste.

"You bring the bucket," she said.

She hugged Mr. Koperski, and even acknowledged Evanko when he nodded at her. She had warmed, and for a moment, when she paused and looked around the workshop, I wondered whether she saw them in the shadows the way I had in my dream. Maybe Papa was saying, "This is not your fight."

"Wolchi, are you coming," she shouted from the open door.

Maybe, he had convinced her after all. Or, maybe, she was just saying goodbye.

CHAPTER 57

It took several hours to hang the posters. The streets were quiet, and Leja and I barely spoke as we worked. A low mist from the river made the night air cool, and the streetlights cast a brown glow like muddy water on the walls of the town square and along the road that paralleled the river. Anyone walking or riding through would be sure to see the posters when the sun rose and burned away the mist.

We were alone on the streets, nearly finished, when a patrol of Russian soldiers turned the corner by the town hall and spotted us in the shadows. They drew rifles, yelling commands in Russian. "Identify yourselves," one shouted.

"I am Comrade Vladimir, from the workers' factories in Sverdlovsk," I replied.

"What are you doing? Step away from that wall," the officer in charge of the group replied, tensely walking toward us. "Drop what you are carrying."

We placed our posters, the bucket and Leja's weapon bag on the ground and stepped closer to the streetlight so we could be seen more clearly.

"We are hanging posters, nothing more," I said, reaching down and lifting one for the soldiers to see. They all walked a few steps closer, their faces ghostly in the mist as they approached.

"Give me that," the officer said, taking the poster from me. All three soldiers studied it, no longer watching us because the poster had captured their attention.

"Who is this Goreki fellow, and why are you out here at night hanging these?" the officer asked sternly, his rifle still raised in our direction. The other two continued to study the poster, and one nodded his head. "Tak khorosho," he said. So good. The officer persisted. "Answer me, now."

"I am Comrade Vladimir. I work with Commander Girshman," I said.

"Girshman? He's dead. Who are you, and what are you doing here?" the officer demanded more sternly.

The other soldiers, hearing alarm in the officer's voice, dropped the poster and pointed their own rifles. Leja kneeled and took hold of her bag, lifting it to her hip as if to fire the weapon inside. "Don't," I whispered to her.

"What is that? Drop that," the officer shouted at her.

"We print these posters and are paid to hang them in the town," I said loudly in reply, stepping between Leja and the soldiers. "We are from the printing shop."

"You, drop that bag," the officer commanded again taking a step toward me.

Leja touched my neck softly. "I love you, brother," she said, and began running into the darkness beyond the streetlamp. She was practiced at fast escapes, and vanished before the soldiers had a chance to pursue her. I watched her melt safely into the misty night, until a soldier's rifle stock struck me from behind and everything went dark.

———— ·•· ————

In the years since that night, I've heard the stories many times about what happened, but who knows if they're true. No one told it the same way. Mr. Koperski, Leja, Evanko. They all said they saw it themselves, but how could that be. Not one of them told it the way the others did.

The soldiers arrested me and held me in a small room inside the town hall until morning. It was a Sunday, and when I opened my eyes I was greeted by the head Russian shaking me awake, and church bells summoning the faithful. My head throbbed where the soldier's rifle had landed and the pain was made worse by the ringing bells and the persistent questioning of the Russian. He didn't know what to make of me, how to make sense of my explanation for being on the streets the previous night. "Who authorized you," he asked me again and again. "Under whose authority." A higher authority, I thought, and urged him to contact Comrade Masha in Sverdlovsk who I hoped would vouch for my loyal-Soviet credentials and get me out of whatever trouble I was in. And what about the other one, the dark figure who vanished into the night, he asked. I shrugged at that question each time he asked. The head Russian finally shrugged himself and left to investigate the growing commotion outside the town hall.

To hear Mr. Koperski and Evanko tell it, the Catholic and Orthodox faithful passing in the street never made it to church that morning. They stood slack-jawed reading aloud from the list of crimes on the poster and laughing at the mustachioed rat wearing a homburg hat. They grew quiet after a time when their amusement faded into awareness that perhaps they, too, were guilty. The churchgoers, at first entertained by the clever artistic posters, became concerned that their own names might be recorded on a placard somewhere else in town. Instead of continuing to church, people stood, cautiously looking at one another. Mr. Koperski said the onlookers saw themselves on those posters staring down from the walls and trees that lined the streets, and believed Goreki was a symbol for all they had done, fearing they would be held to account along with him. Evanko believed the posters inspired remembrance and shame, as they did in him, and perhaps encouraged silent prayers for those who died at their hand or because of their indifference.

The crowd grew larger, clogging the streets below the steps, even while the steps themselves remained empty, no one eager to get too close to the accusing posters. The mix of laughter and quiet homage creating a disturbing rumble. Mr. Koperski and Evanko both recalled the moment when that rumble stopped. It was as if a switch had been thrown and silence spread through the square. The only sound was that of horse hooves and the wheels of a once-fine carriage growing louder as it neared the town hall and the nearby Catholic Church. The driver of the carriage shouted at the people blocking his way, who moved aside briefly before surging behind him, like water rushing around a drowning swimmer.

"Clear the road. Step aside," Igor Goreki shouted, standing up as the carriage inched through the crowd. "What is happening here?"

The men, women and children, all dressed for church, or a funeral, in their cleanest and best clothes stared at him and his wife with knowing eyes. The carriage inched toward the church until a man's voice from somewhere in the crowd called out: "The rat has arrived."

Most of the others stirred uncomfortably, unwilling to join in heckling Goreki, a pastime that had been a common entertainment for Ukrainian men before the war. They searched the crowd for the lone voice, which shouted again: "There goes the rat in a hat." At this, laughter rippled through the square. Goreki, confused by the attention and the swarm of people so close, urged his horses to move faster, but the crowd pressed closer, blocking the carriage.

The horses reared up, as the carriage slid awkwardly to the side. Goreki, alarmed, climbed down with his wife into the crowd, which parted for him as he fled toward the safety of the unoccupied town hall steps. He reached the top and surveyed the people in the square below. His gaze fell on Mr. Koperski, who had pushed to the front and was pointing at the postered wall.

"Acknowledge your crimes, you rat. Look," Mr. Koperski shouted, repeating it again and again.

The head Russian and a group of soldiers came outside, confused by the commotion and the angry chanting man at the foot of the stairs. Evanko tried to pull Mr. Koperski back into the crowd as one of the soldiers descended the stairs toward them. He stood his ground and repeated, "Turn around and look." The soldier did so, thinking the old machinist was shouting at him.

Goreki pointed down at the crowd. "Arrest that madman," he said to the soldier, who stood staring up, perhaps noticing the homburg tilted awkwardly and the mustache, exactly the same as the rat's. The enraged, red-faced man at the top of the stairs stared back, until his wife pulled his arm and spun him to look at the wall behind them.

It started to rain. Goreki stood, his back to the crowd, scanning the images of accountability, "The Crimes of Igor Goreki," repeated over and over on the walls and along the streets, as far as he could see.

"Who did this?" he demanded of no one. "This is insane."

The head Russian, as was his habit, shrugged, even though he knew I was locked in a room just inside and could've been outed as the culprit. I like to believe that having met Goreki, even briefly, the Russian had a moment of insight and understood that every word on the posters was true. Thus, he became our accomplice.

Goreki pulled posters from the wall, first carefully but then in a mad frenzy, clutching the torn sheets under his arm like treasures. "It was like watching a rabid animal tear at its own fur," Mr. Kopersky later told me. "He had lost all reason, all control."

The crowd parted for Goreki again when he ran down the stairs toward his carriage, still clutching the posters, shouting incomprehensible threats. Leaving his wife behind, he climbed up and harshly struck the horses with his crop, turning them away from the square. He drove them hard through the bystanders, knocking some aside and forcing others under his wheels. The soldiers and some of the men in the square gave chase as the carriage turned along the river and sped dangerously over the uneven dirt road, already slick with the rain.

From my room in the town hall, all I heard was shouting and, oddly I thought, the church bells tolling again, as if this Sunday was beginning anew. If I'd been outside, I would have urged the Russian soldiers to pursue him faster, to arrest him before he reached the woods rising above the Stryi River's muddy banks, where Leja lay in wait.

Instead, Goreki drove his carriage blindly through the rain, bouncing along the muddy track beside the swiftly running river. Mr. Koperski and Evanko joined the men and soldiers in pursuit. The carriage pulled ahead, and they lost sight of it as it turned and made its way up a steep section of the road with a treacherous drop from the edge down to the water. They both recall hearing the splintering of wood, the wheels shattering. By the time they climbed the hill and saw the carriage, Goreki was gone. His horses were perched at the road's edge, the harnesses broken from their collars, and the carriage overturned on the slope below. A shallow divot ran the few feet from the carriage to the river, where a man may have slid inadvertently or at his own choosing into the swirling river. Torn posters littered the ground, and dozens of the smiling, mustachioed rats gazed up at those gathering on the riverbank.

The Russians made fast work of their assessment. Goreki, gone mad, had lost control of his horses and was thrown onto the slippery banks and into the inescapable currents of the river. Others, believing that evil is more likely to survive than not, assumed, that without a body ever found, it was likely Goreki lived and escaped to a place where he could plot his return and revenge, a cockroach that couldn't be killed.

Leja told her version of the story more times than I can count. It was the cornerstone that allowed her to build a life from the rubble left after the war. She waited all night, she said, watching for Goreki's carriage in the morning on the way to church. When she heard the commotion in the town square and realized she'd slept as he passed, she fell into despair and decided to hunt him, find him amid the crowd and shoot him on the street with the entire town as witness. She was walking down the road to fulfill her mission when Goreki's carriage turned the corner, fleeing the town square, and bounced toward her. Recognition flashed on his face, and he struck the horses with his crop, urging them straight on toward Leja, who dove aside for safety. Goreki turned as he passed, watching her with a scowl that morphed into surprise when his carriage slipped from the roadway, struck some rocks and broke apart. He was launched onto the muddy bank, posters flying about like falling leaves. When he stood, a bit stunned, and tried to climb the slippery bank to the road, one shot sent him tumbling backward into the swells and whitewater of the river. Leja escaped back into the woods and watched as the soldiers and others arrived and began speculating loudly about Goreki's fate. She imagined him tumbling deep in the water, his life fading and his eyes, his evil eyes, face-to-face with a curious carp that wondered whether this drowning man was suitable for a meal. She thought she should reveal herself to the soldiers and tell her story right then, erase any doubt about Goreki's fate and cement her legacy as the one who finally ended him. Then she thought, what good would that do? Instead, she remembered the one person she needed to tell, and headed back through the woods to find me.

The first time I heard the story was late that night, when I arrived back at Katia's farmhouse after being released by the Russians who, while still bewildered by the events of the day, saw no reason to confine me. "It's not a crime for a reliable comrade to hang a poster," the head Russian told me. " Clearly, Comrade Masha had weighed in. "What that madman did to himself, is not on you."

I was dispirited during my walk from the town hall. This didn't seem to be a moment for celebration. The air was thick, almost liquid, and the hard rain soaked my clothes and shoes. I chose a path through the town, so I could pass my family's home. The street was silent, shrouded in the calm of abandonment. I touched the door, intending to push it open so I could see one last time what remained beside memories. I stood outside letting those memories fill me, some dark as the night and others bright like the morning. I wished I could see Mama, Papa and Ira one last time, feel their warmth when I held them, hear their voices, inhale the unique, subtle traces from the air they exhaled. Just one last time.

The wind blew stronger and louder. The rain fell in sheets. I shivered, as cold as I'd been for months, perhaps ever. So, I opened the door, more to find shelter than solace, and took a step inside. The room was almost black. There was nothing to see. Some of Leja's books lay ruined in a corner. My doing. A few items of clothing were scattered about. Broken glass and pottery littered the floor in what was once our kitchen. I couldn't go farther, and I turned to leave when an old habit lifted my arm to the shelf beside the door, expecting to find the squat statue whose job had been to keep us safe. The shelf was empty. Golem was gone, of course, packed inside my belongings by Mama many years before, and now, having traveled across Russia and Eastern Europe with me and my young family, it had returned to the place of its creation. I wondered what would have been if Mama had kept him here, on that shelf. Would we all be together now, them saved from the horror of their unpredictable and unimaginable deaths? Or would my family be mourning me?

I ran the rest of the way to Katia's farm, trying to escape the ghosts that suddenly seemed to rise everywhere from the soft earth beside the road. As a child, I believed unsettled spirits lurked near the old Jewish graveyard and the nearby river, and I was careful to avoid that place after dark. Now, I felt them all around me, everywhere, so many souls wandering.

Mine was indeed a place defined by war, but also by the ugly secrets buried with its Jewish men, women and children in the old cemetery and in the mud of the river. I ran hard, my lungs on fire and my heart pounding like the wheels of a train on a scarred and crooked track. There was no escaping those ghosts, at least not yet.

I opened the farmhouse door and they were all sitting beside the fire — Leja, Mischka, Katia, the children. Anya cried out when she saw me and lifted her arms into the air. I went right to her, not saying a word to the others, and cradled her, pressing her onto my wet coat and face. This made her laugh, a funny full laugh that scrunched up her face and opened her eyes wide, the kind of laugh that is without caution or reserve, a happy child's laugh. She held me with her stare, her eyes so wide and dark that I could see tomorrow.

Epilogue

January 2000, Phoenix, Arizona

I never walked the streets of London. Never saw the lights of Paris. There was New York, though, for more than fifty years, and now this place, somewhere I never imagined existed. Arizona. I am here with my daughter Anya and her family. They have a big house, and they let me stay for the winter in a separate building in the backyard that they call a casita. It's very nice.

She is an aviation engineer, married to a doctor. My grandson is thirteen and wants to be a basketball player, but, maybe, if that doesn't work out he will become an engineer, too, because he's good at math. I gave him the set of taps and dies that had been a gift from my father, not expecting him to use them so much as preserve them, which he does on a shelf in his room beside his sports trophies. My ten-year-old granddaughter loves to read and is a student government president. She wants to change the world, and I encourage her to do that, despite protests from her parents who would like their little girl to be less opinionated.

Anya is having a little party, just family, this evening to celebrate my eightieth birthday and her fifty-sixth. "It's a new century, Papa, with so much to be grateful for," she said. "Especially that we're together on our birthdays." I tried to talk her out of it. No one alive at eighty wants a party that inevitably becomes a reminder of all that's been lost. And don't try to put one of those foolish hats on my head, I told her. They are for children. Anya is stubborn like her mother, though, and will surely figure out a way to get a picture of us all with those plastic party hats on our heads.

It will be our first family photo without Mischka, my wife, who was always the one leaning her head onto my shoulder in those birthday pictures, without a hat. She did things her way, right up to the day she died. She never wore silly hats in our pictures, and she said no to the medicine her doctor prescribed to keep her alive, because it made her miserable, she said. If the lung cancer was to kill her anyway, well, she wanted to die with her hair. She got her way, she always got her way, and when she left us on the first day of Rosh Hashanah, the Jewish New Year, just four months ago, her hair was full and thick, black streaked with grey, and tied back in a braid. It was probably the coal that caused the cancer, the doctors said, all the dust that lay hidden in her lungs from her work in that deep mine where we met. We survived so much. We built such happiness in the new place, and to have specks of black rock from across the world come back and end her life, well, it seemed unfair. The rabbi said the gates of heaven were open for her because she died during the Jewish holy days, which was good, I thought. I didn't believe any of it, but chose to take comfort in his words.

We buried her on a cold, grey afternoon in a crowded cemetery off the Brooklyn-Queens Expressway in New York City, the sound of slow-moving traffic and the squeal of truck brakes mixing with the words of prayer from the rabbi. Anya stood to one side of me; Leja held my hand on the other.

My sister arrived in New York the evening prior to the funeral from Tel Aviv, the first time she'd left Israel to visit me in all the years since the war ended and our lives took separate paths. Leja became a soldier and a Zionist organizer, who finally had the chance to create a nation that deserved her, where she was wanted and respected. She even enjoyed a moment of notoriety when she was photographed in Jerusalem shaking the hand of Karol Wojtyla, whom the world called Pope John Paul II. She told me the two spent a lovely hour together, talking about their days at the Jagiellonian University before Europe was torn apart. The history books did not record those discussions, but Leja recalled that, when she returned the small St. Christopher medal Karol placed around her neck as we left Krakow, tears welled in his eyes and he said, "We are together again, and now will always be." Six months later, the State of Israel and the Roman Holy See established formal diplomatic relations, a coincidence perhaps, but Leja always hinted otherwise. Either way, this was a big deal for Israel.

I last saw her years before the funeral on her sixty-fifth birthday. Leja had no children. So, Anya insisted her aunt not be alone for this milestone occasion and arranged a trip for me. I didn't want to go, fearful that somehow I might not be allowed to return home, that a flaw in my past would be discovered and the American citizenship I'd earned would be revoked. I relented, though, and was happy I had. Leja and I spent a week of afternoons sitting by the beach not saying much, but just content again to be close. We ate dinner in the evenings at her Herzliya apartment overlooking a bus garage.

She even made us a honey cake one night. It was all very nice.

The funeral was different, not a celebration. In honor of Mischka, though, Leja and I played the talking game all night after she arrived from the airport, jet-lagged, sleepless and manic. "Tell me everything," she demanded, her vitality and energy belying her age. "Just tell me everything." I did, and we talked in the kitchen of my Brooklyn flat until the gloomy morning interrupted and a black Lincoln arrived out front, sent by Anya, to drive us to the cemetery. When they lowered Mischka into the ground, I cried and dropped to my knees at the edge of her grave, not in prayer, but to have one last moment close to her. When I felt the damp ground through the fabric of my slacks, I reached up and took my sister's hand. She helped me, both of us unsteady, to my feet. While we rode home in the backseat of the Lincoln, Leja tried to brush the dirt from my stained knees, but I stopped her. "Not just yet," I told her.

Lev called me the next morning, apologetic that he had not been able to travel from Minsk to attend the funeral. He was too old now to make that trip, anyway, I told him. "Your angel is gone, my dear friend. But her memory is a blessing to us all," he said.

After we parted in the crowded L'viv train station in 1945, I had no expectation we'd ever talk or see one another again. Who knew where he had gone after he and Angelina boarded that train to Belarus? How could he know where Mischka and I might be? Then one Sunday in September 1960, I saw him.

I was reading the Daily News, New York's Picture Newspaper, on my front steps, which I liked to do when the weather was warm and I could watch the neighborhood children play slap-ball in the street and young mothers wheel their carriages across Lafayette Avenue to the park. I read the News all the time, even in the evenings after my long shifts at the machine shop near the Navy Yard where I worked. Anya and I read it together when she was still in grade school, with her helping me pronounce the challenging phrases. She learned the language and the culture of our new nation much faster than Mischka and I, insisting we only speak English at home. "Mama," she'd say when her mother spoke Russian or Polish. "Teacher says we'll always be greenhorns unless we stop talking like that." So, the newspaper became our English language textbook, and I especially savored the fat Sunday edition, which had so much to read and there was enough time to do so.

On that morning in September, the front page had a picture of the Soviet Union's leader Nikita Khrushchev amid a crowd of Russian diplomats shortly after he had disrupted a session of the United Nations General Assembly with a fiery speech. The News called it a political circus, and published a photo mocking the Russians, with dozens of men and women gesticulating and laughing as they crowded around Khrushchev. That's when I saw him. Not him exactly, but rather a raised arm with a wilted hand, claw-like and half-clenched, pointing at the camera and, it seemed, at me. I almost didn't recognize him. He'd grown a bit fat, and his hair had thinned, his face, once lean and handsome, had become round. But that right hand, the hook, was the same. Sitting beside him was an elderly woman, her hair pulled back severely from her jowly face, and that removed all doubt. Time had changed them, but Lev and Comrade Masha were surely in New York.

I went to the United Nations building the next day and made my way through layers of security to the Russian offices, wielding my wartime identity papers. Comrade Vladimir to see Comrade Levuska Petrov, please. I walked into his office, and he was behind the desk, looking like a big boss, which of course he now was. He spilled his tea when he recognized me, and every year when he was in New York for the United Nations General Assembly meeting, until he was too old to travel, we ate a shared lunch from a paper bag sitting on a bench facing the steel, stone and glass office towers touching the western sky in Midtown Manhattan. Angelina came with him once, and she and Mischka sat on a nearby bench imagining where her father might be, not because she wanted to find him, but because she wanted to talk and talk with her old friend.

Our birthday party, as expected, left me morose. Having the kids sing to me and happily recount school activities, their sports and newly learned jokes couldn't overcome a powerful surge of memory and nostalgia. After the cake and the pictures, Anya and I sat at the outside patio table. I gazed at the tree-less desert landscape that passed for a backyard in this part of the world, while she stared at me, kindly but a bit puzzled as I spoke.

I missed Lev and Leja, I said. They were both so far away. None of us would ever cross the ocean again to sit together on a beach or a park bench. We might speak on the telephone from time to time, or send one of those thin blue sheets that fold into an envelope for mailing overseas. These were modern marvels, for sure, and better than eternal silence. I tried to recall whether I'd told them where I was, that a letter or a call to New York would not reach me. I didn't want them to think I'd vanished like so many others in our lives. Anya assured me she could alert them.

I told her about her cousin, Naftali, who phoned me sometimes from one of the pay telephones installed near the town hall in the years after the Soviet Union collapsed and what was now the Ukraine began to modernize. We don't really speak the same language well enough any longer to do more than exchange pleasantries, but he loyally maintained our connection with his periodic calls over the creaky Ukrainian phone lines. He lived his life on the family farm, raising grain for his cows and selling milk and cheese in the town square. His three sons now ran the place, and he liked to sit in the shade beside the graves of his father, grandparents and his mother up on the hill behind the barn and watch the birds soar over the farm fields. He was the one who called to tell me Mr. Koperski died several years after we'd arrived in Brooklyn. In his final years, he was a regular guest for Sunday dinners with Katia and her family, and that made me happy.

I never learned the fates of Michel and Ludmilla, but I assumed the worst after reading reports of the Nazi terror that emptied Krakow of intellectuals and Jews. The Nazis arrested all one- hundred-and-eighty-one members of the Jagiellonian University faculty shortly after Leja and I escaped the city and sent them to a concentration camp. As Anya said, no one lived through six years of that. I wrote to them after the war, hopeful, but the letters were to ghosts.

And now, here I was in the cool afternoon of the Arizona winter. With Mischka gone, Anya was urging me to leave New York and live permanently with her.

"We have plenty of room," she argued, as she cleared the paper plates covered with the remnants of a white birthday cake and icing the colors of the shiny paper hats we had all discarded onto the table. "And the kids would be so happy to see their Tata Wolchi everyday. They miss you when you're not here."

It was clever for her to talk about my grandchildren. Ever since I arrived here for Thanksgiving, they had been a tonic for my sad and tired spirit. My thoughts felt barren and windswept after Mischka died, but when I departed the airplane in Phoenix and those two children wrapped their arms around me, smelling of candy and good sweat, my thoughts blossomed with color and life. I was in the desert, now, but my family was an oasis.

"Just think about it, OK?" Anya said, as she walked toward the house, her arms filled with the remnants of our birthday celebration. "We can take care of everything. Move your stuff for you. You wouldn't even need to go back to the city."

My daughter the engineer had probably already worked out the details. I pictured muscular moving men carrying boxes from my apartment to a truck double-parked and blocking the crosswalk near the corner, forcing mothers with strollers to detour onto the busier street facing the park. I loved that park, and I would miss it if I moved away. It was where I taught Anya to ride a bicycle and where she climbed trees with the other immigrant kids when we were just off the boat from Europe. It was where I walked or sat for half a century watching the majestic elm trees blossom in spring, lose their foliage in autumn and catch falling white flakes on snowy winter mornings — and finally die one after the other of Dutch Elm Disease, which had journeyed from Europe on a ship, hidden in a stack of wooden siding, like coal dust deep in a woman's lungs.

Why shouldn't I move? The old neighborhood wasn't mine any longer, and hadn't been for decades. I'd watched multiple generations of immigrants come and go, the sounds on the streets shift from Eastern European voices, to Spanish and now French. Mischka and I were a neighborhood oddity, the old white man and woman who had curiously clung to a community that no longer existed. When it was the two of us, it made sense. It was our place, which we had sacrificed greatly to reach, the only place we could be. We had no desire to be uprooted again. Now, Mischka was gone and nothing seemed left for me there but a chunk of ground lying empty, waiting, beside her.

So, why not? Anya and the kids were delighted when I told them the news. "I'll take care of everything," Anya said. "Don't you worry."

I accepted her hug and kiss on the cheek and assured her that I had no worries, just secrets. I smiled. She looked at me quizzically and nodded her head at what she assumed was a joke. I did have a secret, though, and I wondered when I should tell her. She was sure to discover him at some point, and it would be important that she understand why he was there, and why she needed to respect and preserve my decision.

I walked slowly toward the back of the yard, where the grandchildren didn't play and the hard-working, friendly land-scaper never ventured. He was from Guatemala and reminded me of myself in our early days in New York, and I liked him. I navigated past the solemn Saguaro cactus with arms stretching up toward the endless sun, the bursts of Bougainvillea and Yellow Bells, the holes carved into the hard ground by the gecko and spiny lizards, and stopped at the stone wall separating my family's home from the wild desert.

I reached my hand into one of the ornamental openings and retrieved the dusty, weathered statue I'd hidden shortly after I arrived. I chose this spot for Golem because it offered a good view into the valley and toward the city skyline, where he could diligently scan the horizon for signs of misfortune. There was nothing to watch over back in that apartment in Brooklyn, and almost everything I cared for now was right here. I'd slipped the names of my grandchildren when they were born into Golem's body, now overstuffed with almost a century of yellowed bits of paper.

When I tell Anya what I've done, I will explain Golem to her. She's surely seen him on the shelf near our apartment door while growing up, another bit of bric-a-brac that Mischka and I displayed, items that to Anya had no connection to our new lives. I will tell her about her grandmother, the mud, the river, the safe passage we made through the European war to America with Golem packed in our meager belongings. Her engineer's mind will reject my belief the way Ira and Leja teased my mother about hers. Just an ugly lump of mud, she might say. I will hear my father's voice and repeat his words when I tell her that I believe it's more than that. She will listen finally, stare at me and understand something important, as if for the first time.

"You put my name in there when I was born?" she will ask." And the kids?"

I will nod, and she will say: "I guess it can't hurt."

Dream for a Second

JES SMYTH

WELLIUM
publishing

Wellium Publishing, LLC

Published 2024
Printed in the United States of America
ISBN (hardcover): 979-8-9863946-9-5
ISBN (softcover): 979-8-9863946-5-7
ISBN (ebook): 979-8-9863946-0-2

www.jessmyth.com
www.welliumpublishing.com

Cover Design by Kari Brownlie

It is precisely the possibility of realizing a dream that makes life
interesting.
– Paulo Coelho, The Alchemist

1

Lena

L ena would dwell on whatever she wanted. She had every right. Others, however, seemed to disagree.

"I'm afraid I don't follow," she said, even though she did. Surely, this customer wasn't going there with her.

The old woman leaned into the counter, silver hair balanced on top of her head like a bird's nest, and peered at Lena with beady eyes.

"Don't dwell on it for too long," she said, as clearly as the first time. She readjusted the bag on her hunched shoulder, yarn and knitting needles poking out of the opening.

"I'm afraid I still don't follow," Lena said. The old woman, whose name had slipped Lena's mind, came into the coffee shop twice a week and ordered the same thing—Earl Grey tea, two lemon slices, and one cube of sugar—and sat where the sun was brightest. A towering traveler's palm tree occupied the same corner, soaking up the scarce Oregon sunshine, the tips of its waxy green leaves grazing the ceiling. It was a necessary burst of color in the stark white space and Lena's favorite spot to sit during her breaks.

"You need to move on, my dear, and get yourself out there." The woman gestured with her arm to the entrance of the shop.

Lena's shoulders began to rise. Coffee Rocks had been her home away from home for the last eight years. The name of the shop was a tongue-in-cheek homage to Oregon's favorite pastime, sport climbing, a type of outdoor rock climbing. Lena never understood the attraction of scrambling over rocks, even fake ones, but enjoyed a good play on words and relied heavily on coffee. She was also desperate for money then, so it had seemed like a good fit.

Last year, the owner had mentioned franchising the business with Lena as her partner, but those talks eased up after the accident.

"Will that be all?" Lena forced a smile. She did not have the energy to be polite to a regular who was notorious for poking around where she shouldn't. Not today. Honestly, not for a long time. Thirteen months, to be exact.

"How old are you, Lena?"

Lena felt her eye twitch as she held the smile. She knew exactly where this was headed. The you're-too-old to-be-single conversation had already taken place with her mother. If you asked her mother, however, she would say twenty-three hours of natural labor entitled her to her opinions.

"I just had a birthday in March," Lena said, pushing at her hair. The color was dark and unnatural, a result of little sleep and a midnight run to her local grocery store for a box of hair color.

"Oh, my dear Lena. The same month as, well, you know..." The old woman lowered her voice even though she and Lena were the only two people in the airy coffee shop. "As the accident." Lena placed two lemon slices onto the white porcelain plate and grimaced as the acidic juice crept into a hidden cut. An entire year—well thirteen months now that it was April—without Seth. The familiar threat of tears pricked at her eyes.

Lena nodded to the woman, hoping her brain would retrieve the name of this someone who clearly knew too much about her situation. Then again, Lena's memory had walked out the door the moment she received that phone call.

He just stopped breathing.

Lena had shouted profanities at the woman who'd witnessed her fiancé's last breath, one that should have been hers to keep, then threw the phone across the bedroom. Her and Seth's bedroom. It smashed against the wall and shattered like confetti. Her heart, in a state of shock, had witnessed the uncharacteristic outburst and then crumbled to the floor too. It had been there ever since.

Lena could ask the customer for her name but what did it matter when it would just be forgotten again?

"You look to be about thirty-three. Not much time left for babies. You need to find someone soon. Your baby-making years are coming to a close."

Lena watched slack-jawed while the woman moved the plate and oversized mug into her sun-spotted arthritic hands. This customer was known to offer tidbits of outdated advice, either to Lena or one of her coworkers: *Why would he buy a cow when he's getting the milk for free!* A harmless regurgitation of outdated one-liners.

Until now.

"All right, Joyce," Clair's voice shot out from behind Lena. *Joyce?* Lena felt her face scrunch at the unfamiliar name and wondered what else her mind had failed to absorb in the last thirteen months.

"There's a new policy. We no longer accept unsolicited tips or advice. Cash only," Clair said.

Lena felt her body go rigid. Clair was the owner and had the right to speak to her customers as she saw fit. But Lena's urge to apologize—for what exactly, she wasn't sure—bounced on the tip of her tongue.

Clair turned and looked up. Lena had seven inches on her boss's five feet. If Clair were a dog, she'd be a smart and stubborn French bulldog. Lena wasn't sure if smart French bulldogs existed, having only known one in her life. Seth's parents' dog, Marty Cruz, was notorious for running into the glass patio door more often than through it. Regardless, Clair's short stature and strong will mimicked that of one.

"Lena, someone's on the phone for you. Apparently your voicemail box is full. Again." Clair gave her the side-eye. Lena offered a half-hearted shrug. Those close to her knew to send a text, not call. "He said it was time-sensitive and mentioned someone named Douglas," Clair said. Dread rushed into Lena's bloodstream.

Speaking of Seth's parents. Lena hadn't spoken to Mr. and Mrs. Cruz for six months and felt terrible about it.

"See, Clair," Joyce said, the wrinkles on her face deepening as her smile grew. "The girl doesn't need my *valuable* tip. She has a man waiting for her in the wings already. Good for you, Lena. I knew you were a smart one. And not just 'cause your face is always buried in those heavy-looking books."

Lena grimaced. She hadn't opened a textbook for her business management program since Seth's death. Hence her failing out of business school.

"Honey," Clair said, her hands moving to her hips. "This man sounds much too old, even for the likes of me. Besides, isn't it a bit fast to be dating again? It's only been a year."

"Thirteen months, actually." Lena could barely get the words out through her clenched jaw.

Joyce shot Clair a withering look. "It's time for Lena to move forward. She needs to make babies! She's wasting her eggs with each passing minute. Don't you get it?"

"With all due respect, Joyce, a woman's uterus does not obligate her to have children," Clair said. "Besides, Lena is still working through her grief and she's nowhere near the last stage." Clair patted Lena's hand as if she were a helpless puppy.

Lena's temples began to pulse. This was ridiculous. The two women were arguing like Lena wasn't standing right there and like she hadn't fought against the same thought since Seth's death. *She wasn't doing grief right.* But how could she? She kept picking at the scabs of past regrets, which only aggravated her grief.

She gripped the counter and tempered the urge to scream at the top of her lungs. As the words *geriatric pregnancy* came out of Joyce's mouth, Lena felt certain her insides were going to explode.

"Okay, that's enough," Lena said, like she was holding them at gunpoint. She'd never owned a gun in her life. A pocket knife and pepper spray were her go-to safety measures, but apparently, she had the voice of a gun owner. "You two have no idea what you're talking about."

The two women snapped their mouths shut. The hum from the steamer filled the silence. They didn't deserve an explanation. It hurt like crazy, still, and she wasn't okay. But all she wanted was to be left alone. It was easier to feel okay that way.

"Douglas is an old family friend of Seth's and is completely harmless," *and made out of metal*, she wanted to add, but didn't. Let the two women busy themselves spinning their own stories.

"Excuse me," Lena said and pushed open the back door, the sound of disapproving voices fading as the door swung shut.

Lena walked toward the phone lying on a steel counter, the spiral cord snaking up to the base anchored on the wall. For a moment, she considered taking the receiver and returning it to its cradle. The phone was prehistoric enough to warrant a poor connection, even if it was a slightly assisted one. As Lena's hand touched the cool plastic, an image of Douglas flashed behind her eyes. Her hand jolted away as if burnt. She'd meant to visit Douglas after Seth's accident, but the thought of going alone was too much to bear. Seth would be heartbroken to know how long Douglas had been left alone.

It seemed cold hard reality had become unavoidable. With a trembling hand, she placed the phone to her ear and hurtled into the first of many unknowns to come.

The smell of gasoline greeted Lena as she walked through the back door of the garage. Seth had only wanted the best for Douglas and had kept him in a neighboring town where well-off residents owned one too many garages. This particular garage was like a time-share vacation property, with heated marble floors, cathedral ceilings, and triple the square footage of her current apartment.

Two vehicles wrapped in canvas were parked side-by-side in front of Lena, with four additional vehicles, some covered and not from this decade, lined up behind. Hazy light streamed through the tiny square windows from the front garage doors up ahead. The light switch was to the right but Lena wasn't ready for the abuse of fluorescent lighting, not yet. Somewhere the hum of a heater kicked on and filled the silence.

Lena had once felt at ease among these cherished items, each protected from the harsh realities of mother nature. But as she walked alongside one of the cars, her arms plastered to her sides so as not to risk a scratch, all she could see was beauty wrapped up in suffocating darkness.

Except for Douglas. His white pop-top camper roof seemed to wink at her from the left. As she got closer, his evergreen paint sparkled, like it had been recently waxed.

Lena hadn't immediately warmed to the 1983 Westfalia VW van when Seth bought it, the day before he proposed to her. She'd been in shock—at both surprises. Seth had bought something that looked straight from the junkyard—smelled like it too—and the very next day proposed marriage after five years together. But Seth's excitement for both their engagement and the rusted bucket of bolts had been infectious. He'd talked her through the plans for the old VW camper van, mapping out the work required to turn Douglas into something great. It was a lot of work. But that was Seth, seeing the potential in imperfection. Which, she supposed, had worked in her favor.

On their first date, Lena had spilled her cup of coffee into his lap. With her nerves tangled in regret, she vigorously patted his thighs with a fistful of paper napkins, convinced he'd never call her back after this. Seth sucked in a breath and froze. Then the feeling of something much too hard to be his thigh grazed her hand.

She pulled her hands away. "I am *so* sorry."

Seth's gaze fixated on her while the edge of the table dripped coffee onto his gray chino pants. A large wet spot, impossible to miss, had spread over the crotch of his pants. But he didn't seem to care. His deep blue eyes remained on her and only her.

"So let me get this straight," he said and rubbed his tanned cheek, a stark contrast to her constant pale skin. She would later learn he kept a year-round tan since he was part-Hispanic as his father was born and raised in Mexico. "You're a barista, who serves coffee and other hot beverages daily, and you do so with unsteady hands. There's a story in there somewhere."

Lena wasn't sure if he was a writer looking for his next book idea or if he was actually flirting with her. She hadn't gone on a date for months, so she didn't know any better, but her mouth twitched and her insides warmed. *She liked him.*

"What can I say," she said, twirling a long strand of fiery red hair around her finger—her attempt at flirting back. "I like to lean into my weaknesses."

Seth's face broke into a wide smile and her heart tripped over itself. He stood up, seemingly oblivious to his *peed-your-pants* look. His high cheekbones were somehow more prominent now that he was standing tall, his thick chestnut hair swooped to one side. The man was handsome. Lena's liquid knees confirmed the fact.

"You are imperfectly unexpected, Lena. And I can tell I'm in big trouble."

Lena wasn't able to respond to the first half of Seth's sentence. Her feelings were jammed somewhere between her heart and tongue. She gestured at the bottom half of his body instead. "Well, yes. I ruined your pants."

Seth shook his head, smiling. "I can replace my pants. You see, the trouble is I'm pretty sure you're about to ruin my heart, and I have no intention of stopping you. I'm actually hoping that you kind of maybe do."

That wasn't the last time Lena felt convinced Seth was meant to be a writer. He had an innate talent for speaking as naturally as a flower blooms, beautiful and inevitable. But instead of telling of beauty, he worked to capture it in photos and had been on the fast track to becoming the next big outdoor photographer. A profession that kept him away for months at a time, and one he would eventually never return from. Not that either of them could have predicted it.

Which was why he bought Douglas. Seth wanted to travel cross-country every summer until the day they were too old to manage it. The inaugural trip was planned for May of last year. Seth died in March.

Lena focused on the flat front end of Douglas and waited for the tears to come as they always did. Douglas's large rectangular windshield was crystal clear, not a speck of dust or a fingerprint to be seen on his surface. Seth's father had told her yesterday about the mechanic he'd hired shortly after *"it became evident you weren't going to take care of Douglas."*

She'd bristled at the judgmental tone. Didn't Seth's father understand she had struggled to take care of herself until recently? Then again, understanding and caring were two totally different things.

But Douglas had never looked better. His round moon steel hubcaps and chrome bumper seemed to illuminate in the dark. The slatted exterior plastics looked pristine, as if never used. Which she supposed was accurate. According to Seth's father, Douglas was road-ready and belonged in Florida since the title was in Seth Senior's name now. Not hers.

She gripped the van's keys in her hand, the one and only set to exist. Seth's father requested she be available for the handover whenever he figured out who would be driving Douglas home.

Home.

The longer Lena stared at Douglas, the quicker her breath went in and out. This vehicle was built to be driven and was meant to carry out Seth's dream in the process. His home was on the road.

Lena gripped the cool silver handle on the driver-side door, smooth and sturdy, then pushed the button. With his signature creak, Douglas opened up and exhaled straight into Lena's face. The smell of sun-warmed leather with a hint of vanilla wrapped itself around her. She closed her eyes and inhaled. Memories of Seth settled into the bottom of her lungs, warming her chest and calming her beating heart. She counted down from five and closed the door without getting in. Her eyes fluttered open, prickling but dry. She wasn't crying.

She wasn't crying! There were no tears and no indication that she was going to end up sobbing on the ground next to Douglas, and was that—*no it couldn't be*. She reached up and touched her mouth.

"Oh my god," she said to nothing and everything. Opening his door again, she flung herself into the bucket seat.

"I'm not sure what's happening, Douglas," she said, wrapping her hands around the large steering wheel, "but I'm smiling, and it's all because of you."

A certainty settled into Lena's stomach once she returned to her apartment an hour later. She opened the contact list on her phone, tapped the name *Mr. Cruz* and waited for the trilling to stop. In two weeks' time, the first weekend in May, and fourteen months following Seth's death, she would finally leave for their road trip.

2

Palmer

Palmer refused to dwell on it. He had every right to his decision, even if it was rash. Others, however, seemed to disagree.

He pushed a bank check across the knotted-wood kitchen table. "This should keep the business from going completely under," he said. He rubbed his thumb over a tiny scratch. Palmer had crafted the table as a wedding gift for his friend, using only reclaimed Douglas fir wood. It was a piece he hoped to replicate and sell, eventually. Once his family's business affairs were straightened out first. "My parents, well, Drew specifically, have no idea, which means I'll need backup." He knew Mark wouldn't understand or even agree with his plan. Palmer was after his friend's legal advice more than empathy.

Mark scratched the tip of his long nose then scrubbed the same hand over his smooth jawline. Palmer was definitely the hairier of the two, although that wasn't saying much. Mark barely managed a five-o'clock shadow. "You're telling me you secretly sold your house and plan to invest the money back into Husky's?"

"And keep my parents from having to sell their house," Palmer said.

Mark looked at the check and whistled. "You don't even like the name," he said. "Why not just let it go?"

Mark did have a point. The name—"Husky's Fine Furniture"—had become a sticking point the day Palmer refused to attend college at his father's-father's-father's alma mater, the mascot of which was a husky.

"We've been selling furniture in the original location for almost seventy-five years," Palmer said. "And my father wants to *let it go*, as you say, with no regard to the family's legacy. He's lost his damn mind." The sound of a ringing cell phone echoed from the living room. Palmer took a sip of his spicy bourbon. "I'd like to avoid the legalities, but it's inevitable. You know how my father feels about lawyers, but you're like a third son."

Mark tucked a chunk of black hair behind his ears, his expression measured. "Are you loaning this money to your father or buying the store from him?"

"That's a good question," Palmer said, his voice cracking slightly. When his father shut down nineteen of the twenty Husky's Fine Furniture locations, Palmer had been alarmed. As VP of supply chain, Palmer focused on materials and warehouse staff. Rarely was he involved in higher-level financials. *"Why bother with numbers when you're a better leader?"* his father had always said. But Palmer was beyond bothered. They were going out of business.

"Say I buy the business," Palmer said, leaning forward. "The original location remains in the family. But instead of the same tired warehouse furniture easily found online, I sell my reclaimed pieces, open an attached coffee shop or something, and bring in the younger homeowners." He sat back and took another sip. His plan sounded even better out loud. "It's not totally off the wall, is it? I'm not a young kid figuring shit out, I'm thirty-eight years old and more than capable of running my own business—" Palmer stopped short when a pregnant belly rushed into the kitchen.

"Sorry to interrupt," Shay said, apple-red hair falling out of her ponytail, cell phone clutched in hand. "Is it okay if I steal Mark for a second?"

"Of course. I can head out if you need me to," Palmer said.

"No!" Shay said, holding up her hand. "Sorry. I didn't mean

to shout. This pregnancy has my emotions all over the place." She motioned for Mark to follow her. "We won't be long," she said. Mark shrugged as he passed by Palmer.

His friend had certainly entered a new realm of life with which Palmer had no experience. In the span of two years, Mark had gone from dating an adventurous girl he'd met during a kayaking class, to marriage, then a new home, and, soon now, fatherhood. All Palmer had was a new beard.

Palmer pushed the wood chair back as his hair fell into his eyes. He had let himself go since the business closed its doors. *Kind of.* After his run-in last month with "the woman who got away," he'd quit shaving his face. And it itched like hell. Which, he reasoned, was a good distraction from the memory of running into Jolie. *Kind of.*

As Mark and Shay spoke in low tones in the next room, Palmer tapped the side of his empty glass, remembering the night vividly.

Carrie, his cousin and Jolie's best friend, had shrugged helplessly when he approached the table at their usual Friday night bar. Jolie offered a small wave with a shy, "*Hi Palmer*," and pushed her glasses up the bridge of her nose. Eight years had passed since she walked out of his life. Yet, in a matter of seconds, he was right back in it, enduring a gut punch of forgotten mannerisms. He didn't ask if she was married or happy or why she was in town, he just soaked her in, like the napkin underneath her bourbon.

He'd been dating other women, he wasn't a monk. But after his last failed relationship, he started unpacking the truth behind his poor track record. *He was the problem.*

His plan to offer someone a place in his world, with the hope she would be the perfect fit, wasn't realistic, was it? It was ridiculous. And he was not a ridiculous man. His pride revolted against the epiphany but he'd kept his hands busy. The dating apps remained unopened but his heart was far from closed. It had been split apart and put back together. When the time was right, Palmer would test out the updates.

On the upside, he had created enough pieces to eventually fill the small showroom in Husky's original location. Which he still planned to do, with or without his father's blessing. The thought had him up and reaching for the bottle on the kitchen island. As he poured, a photo on the fridge caught his gaze.

Underneath a pineapple magnet was a picture of Shay and another woman standing in front of a sunflower field, their arms looped around each other. The striking red hair, pale skin, and splattering of freckles across the nose made the two women appear near identical. This had to be Shay's sister, although Palmer couldn't recall her name. He did, however, remember the drama she had caused at Mark and Shay's wedding last year when she never showed up. Perhaps that broken bridge was mended now. He peered at the photo. Her eyes were more almond-shaped than Shay's.

"It'll be fine, Shay." Mark's voice grew louder. Palmer jumped away from the photo and turned as the couple walked into the kitchen. Both of their faces were drawn.

"I can't believe she decided to drive to Florida," Shay said, lowering herself onto a seat at the kitchen table. "Clearly, that van isn't reliable. And neither is she."

"Everything okay?" Palmer said, ducking around one of the crystal lights hanging over the island. His height had conditioned him to avoid low ceilings, doorframes, and lights, but he still hit his head more often than not.

"It's fine," Mark said, his tone pinched as he opened a drawer. He pulled out a phone book and began flipping through the pages.

"You know, Mark," Palmer began. Mark looked up from the phone book. "There's this crazy thing called Google now. You should give it a try."

Mark glared at him. "There's a twenty-four-hour towing company I can't remember the name of. But this will."

Palmer opened his mouth to state a more obvious solution,

but Mark raised his hand and shook his head.

"Who needs a tow?" Palmer asked.

"My sister," Shay said.

"That sister?" Palmer pointed to the photo. His face warmed like he'd been caught snooping around.

"The one and only," Shay said. "Apparently, this is a surprise visit and she's stuck an hour away at a forest preserve with a broken-down van. She said she didn't want to stress me out, but Lena has a knack for it." Shay grimaced and rubbed her protruding stomach. The pregnancy had been a surprise, according to Mark, but a happy one, Shay had added, when they told Palmer three months after the wedding. She was due next month. Palmer wouldn't admit how terrified he was of newborns, having never held one before. He'd recently started watching YouTube videos in preparation.

"Why not try my brother's auto shop?" Palmer said, wondering why Mark hadn't come to the same conclusion.

"You don't need to involve your family with Lena," Mark said under his breath, quiet enough for only Palmer to hear.

"I knew you'd have a solution, Palmer. Mark insisted we try this other towing company first." Shay shot Mark a look.

"It's probably too far for your brother," Mark said.

Palmer glanced at Mark who still had his nose buried in the phone book. "I can call him and see," Palmer said.

"This could be a waste of time for everyone involved," Mark said. "Your sister is stubborn as hell, Shay. She also sounded a little...unhinged."

"That's how she is now, Mark," Shay said.

Palmer looked at Shay then Mark, the hint of an argument in the air. He could fix this. "You said she's at a forest preserve. The only one I know an hour away is the Great Western trailhead. Is that where she's stranded?"

Mark reluctantly nodded.

"Okay. Great." Palmer clapped his hands together. "There's a lumberyard I need to go to in that area. They have these incredibly rare used railroad ties from the 1920s that I think I could work into a shelf of some sort, maybe a cabinet." Palmer looked at Shay, her expression glazing over. He cleared his throat. "If my brother can't do it, I will."

"I'm not sure she'll agree to it," Shay said as Mark mumbled, "She won't like it."

Palmer pulled out a chair and sat down. "Your sister called for help. That's what you're doing, right?"

Shay shifted in her seat and sighed. "Lena's only fifteen months older than me but you'd think we were born years apart. I mean, the girl has wanted to run her own show since high school. Back then it was owning a record store, until she moved to Oregon. Regardless, she's a coffee-hound who doesn't like attention, or asking for help, and unfortunately that's all Lena has managed to attract in the last year. And for the worst of reasons too—"

Shay's phone started to ring. "But I guess it's worth a try," she said before answering the call.

Mark sat down and placed his elbows on the table. He gave Palmer a slight eye roll. "This is going to take some convincing," he said. Palmer didn't know why the problem was such a big deal. That's what families did, helped each other out.

"Mark's friend has a tow truck and is headed out that way for...something. I can't remember what, stupid pregnancy brain." Shay went quiet while her mouth progressively turned downward.

"This is no different than if you found a local towing company. It's a legitimate business." Shay looked at Palmer and mouthed, *Right?* He nodded. "No, I don't know the name of it. It's local. Yeah, I mean, he would have to drive an hour, but—" Shay pulled the phone away from her ear and tapped the screen. "He's right here, he can give you all the details."

Shay held the phone out to Palmer, leaving him no choice but to jump into another family drama.

"Hey, this is Palmer, Mark's friend. Nice to meet you." Palmer heard Mark snort and glared in his direction. Yes, he was using his professional voice. He didn't know how to approach a problem any other way. "I heard you're in need of a tow truck and I happen to know one sitting around, waiting to be put to use."

The line was silent for long enough that Palmer worried the call had dropped. "Are you there?"

3

Lena

She was there all right. Smack in the middle of it. "Thank you for offering to help, but it's not necessary," Lena said. Having spent a month on the road alone, she relied on herself and trusted only Douglas. Well, *had* trusted Douglas, until he refused to shift out of reverse. Earlier, when the brake pedal had seized, Lena drifted backward into a trailhead parking lot surrounded by large oak trees. Moments later, a scratching noise sounded from the rear, followed by a burnt electrical smell, and then the engine died. Douglas wasn't going anywhere. And neither was she, but the sun was about to leave the sky.

"I can ask Shay if she has the time, or Mark—"

"We can't. We're having dinner with a friend!" Shay shouted in the background.

Lena should have known her sister was busy and that the phone was on speaker. "Or I spend the night with Douglas, although I'm not sure that's the best option."

"Oh, good, you're not alone," Mark's friend said. "I'll call my brother and let him know you're Mark's sister-in-law. I'm sure he could get out there first thing tomorrow."

"Sorry, I've forgotten. What is your name?" Lena felt like a jerk for asking but his quick reply suggested he didn't take her poor memory personally. *I used to be better at this.* "Palmer, I appreciate the offer. I'm afraid if your brother isn't able to come out today, I'll have to find someone else. I don't want to leave Douglas," Lena said, hoping to convince Palmer she could fix her own problems. *Some* of her problems. Okay, maybe just this one. The chatter of squirrels in a nearby tree felt like a well-timed mockery.

"I'm sure there's a hotel you two can find easy enough," Palmer said, sounding confused. "Listen, I'll call my brother, let him know the situation, and have him get in touch with you. What's your number?"

Palmer was not taking the hint. He wanted to help, daylight was fading, and Lena was running out of options. The last thing she wanted to do was cause more drama. The surprise visit to her family was meant to show she could take care of herself, but the universe had other plans in mind. Namely, to show her she wasn't capable at all.

With a sigh, Lena rattled off her number and then, for some reason, said, "Douglas is my van."

There was a pause. "Douglas is your van," he echoed. His voice sounded higher as if he found the comment funny.

"He was my fiancé's," she said, swallowing down the lump that always formed when she spoke about Seth in the past tense. "His paint is an evergreen color, like a Douglas fir. Which is why he's named Douglas. He's a 1983 VW Westfalia van."

"You're driving cross-country in a vintage van named Douglas," Palmer said. "I can see why you're stranded."

Lena straightened her back. "Douglas is fully restored with a Subaru engine and he's a split-year model, 1983 *and a half*," she said, stopping herself from saying more. From an outsider's perspective, the old van had simply broken down in reverse. Lena, on the other hand, was all too familiar with the inability to move forward. "He's just having an off day."

"Aren't we all?" Palmer said in a distracted way. "Let me call my brother and see if he can drive out. If not tonight, then tomorrow."

"Yeah, Lena." Shay's voice came in again. "Don't be so bull-headed!"

Lena's head began to ache. She had called her sister for

help, not Mark's friend with Shay shouting in the background. Regardless, she refused to leave Douglas alone. "I'm sure I can find someone here to tow us tonight."

The line muffled and then Palmer came back on. "Listen, I'll come and get you myself. I just need to get his tow truck."

A squirrel scampered across the gravel as she fought against the urge to ask why. "I don't even know you," she said.

"I'm a long-time friend of your brother-in-law and you're my buddy's wife's sister who needs help. What else is there to know?"

It sounded too simple and uncomplicated for Lena to trust him. There was always a catch. "I appreciate the offer, Palmer, but I can find a towing company in town, save you the trouble."

Palmer cleared his throat. "You're giving my brother's shop business and I can pick up my lumber a day early. It's a double win. But if you trust your van being chained and towed by an unknown local mechanic, and not by someone that can be vouched for, then by all means."

Lena glanced over at Douglas from her spot at the picnic table, her eyes moving from his friendly round headlights to his bug-splattered windshield. Traveling through life was messy, wasn't it? Like hitting insects at seventy miles per hour for days on end.

Keeping Douglas safe was Lena's biggest concern. Her discomfort with accepting a stranger's help would just have to take the back seat.

"Since you know Shay and Mark, I guess using your brother's company is the best option," Lena said.

"Great. Stay put and I'll get back to you," Palmer said, then clicked off.

Lena wasn't surprised by Palmer's impatient goodbye. She knew her stubbornness walled off many who tried to get in, but what other choice did she have after ten days in a van, dusty with Seth's memories. She was navigating a world of unknowns. Some of which left her to wonder, most of which left her in wonder. Like the morning after that snowstorm in Wyoming, when she awoke inside the van with a cold nose and an unparalleled view.

In the distance, yet impossibly close had been the Teton Range, glittering with a fresh blanket of snow. The tallest peak looked as if it was dancing with the brilliant blue sky while its siblings reached up in envy. It appeared fake, which made Lena feel indescribably real. She had dug into her pocket for her phone, aware a photo would never live up to the scene in front of her. Unless her finger could somehow transfer emotion onto a digital file.

The ache of Seth's absence had lifted ever so slightly that morning, and a mixture of relief and guilt had settled into Lena's consciousness ever since.

She shook her head free of the memory and focused on Douglas. If they could survive a snowstorm in Wyoming, they could certainly manage a breakdown in Illinois. "Help is on the way, buddy," she said. Then she waited.

The temperature outside had dropped enough for Lena to seek warmth in the back of Douglas. The twisted oak branches in the foreground turned ink black as the sky changed from blue to orange to a water-color purple. Palmer had called within five minutes of hanging up and informed Lena he would be there in an hour. He asked for the name of the forest preserve, provided his brother's shop number, and said *see you soon*. Within thirty seconds of hanging up, her phone had buzzed again, this time her sister.

"I'm not about to get kidnapped, am I?" Lena joked. Shay assured her Palmer was doing what he did best: being nice and helping out. Lena wanted to tell Shay she hadn't been alone with a man since Seth, but instead said, "I'll text you when I'm headed your way."

"Lena?" Shay said before hanging up. "Everything's going to be okay."

No. Everything wasn't okay. This was all her fault and now she had to accept the help of a stranger and pretend she didn't blame herself daily. For everything.

But everyone had their breaking point in a relationship, right? Seth was gone more than he was home near the end. It was an unbearable loneliness. If only she had known what true loss felt like.

Leave me at home, she sobbed into his pillow the night of his funeral, *just don't leave me forever.*

She spent those early days dressed in Seth's faded hoodie, pouring over photos on her phone and listening to saved voice messages. Somehow, she thought she could finish her course-work for the business management degree and move forward with the plans Clair had for her. But what was the point—when the ping of her phone were reminders to eat and not the daily text Seth sent of his face in a silly position. A year later, Lena's life had become circular and dizzying and utterly pointless.

Two beams of light in the distance sliced through the darkness, elongating the trees' shadows. Untucking her legs from the fold-down bed, Lena reached for the sliding door. Her stomach tightened. If this was a park ranger, she'd have a lot of explaining to do.

The sound of tires on gravel grew louder as a tow truck came into view. Lena took her first full breath in what felt like hours and watched a man exit the driver's door. Her hand stilled on the door handle as he stepped in front of the headlights. Palmer was tall. Unbelievably tall, like the traveler's palm in Coffee Rocks, except with broad shoulders and a beard-covered face. With his hands on his hips, Palmer looked like someone who knew how to solve a problem. Lena's heart thumped as she stepped into the chilly night air.

"You must be Lena," Palmer said, his hand extended out in front of him.

Relieved by the formality, Lena's shoulders dropped a half inch. This was a script she read daily. There was nothing to get worked up about.

"Thank you for doing this," she said, grasping his hand, the skin noticeably rough. Heat shot up her arm. She released his hand and said, "This is Douglas."

Palmer's gaze remained on her face, his expression unreadable, then he looked behind her. "The infamous Douglas, we meet at last," he said, moving around Lena to get a closer look. "I've always wanted to drive one of these. What's it like?"

Lena stood next to Palmer and stared at the massive windshield. The engine was in the back which meant the driver and passenger sat right over the front wheels. "It was overwhelming at first," she said. "Like the entire world is in your face. And I swear, the lack of nose on the front end adds twenty miles per hour to his speed, going forty feels like sixty. But the views are unparalleled."

"I can only imagine," Palmer said, sounding distracted. "Shay told me you're driving to Florida. Are you moving there?"

"No. I mean, yes, I'm driving to Florida to deliver Douglas to his owners," Lena said, a distinct prickle forming behind her eyes. *No.* There was no need for tears. She was delivering Douglas from point A to point B, simple and easy. "I don't have much back in Oregon. My parents are moving here to be closer when Shay gives birth," she said. "So, I'm not sure what will happen after Florida. If I get there. Douglas seems to have other plans."

Palmer scratched his beard. It felt like he was looking at her, but Lena couldn't tell in the dark. And she didn't trust herself enough to check, or allow herself to question why she cared. A cool breeze danced across her cheeks as the musk of damp soil lifted off the forest floor beyond the gravel parking lot. The crickets paused their chirping. Palmer finished seeing whatever it was he saw, and strode to the tow truck, calling over his shoulder, "This shouldn't take long!"

Palmer was careful while he hooked the chain to the axle and inched Douglas onto the truck bed. Lena hovered with a flashlight, doing her best to focus the light on Douglas. She shivered as the whir of the tow truck's crank continued. There was something about Palmer, an energy she found hard to ignore. Although, anyone in the presence of Palmer surely felt the same draw. His height alone stopped you in your tracks.

Twenty minutes later, the three were on their way. Shadowed cornfields and black sky morphed into one outside her window. It was dark outside, *country dark*, and the entire world had shrunk itself into just the truck's cabin. Lena lowered the zipper on her jacket as the heater filled the cab of the truck, intensifying the smell of gasoline and pine around her. Cracking the window, Lena breathed deeply, hoping the cool air would cut through more than just the oppressive warmth.

"Are you too warm?" Palmer said, reaching for the knob on the center console.

"A little. I think the day is catching up with me." Lena struggled to remove her arms from her jacket.

"I bet," Palmer said. She felt a pull on her left sleeve. "The lumberyard won't take long and my brother's shop is close to Shay's house. You're on the homestretch." Palmer's fingers grazed her exposed skin as he helped her out of the jacket. The truck's cab seemed to shrink. The gesture wasn't meant to be intimate, Palmer was just helping. *Being nice.* Like everyone else since Seth's accident.

Lena pressed at the skin Palmer had just touched, and asked, "What is it you do for a living? Something with your hands, I mean your wood. Not your wood, but lumber. You build...stuff." Lena choked on the last words. Clearly, she was out of practice talking to actual humans.

"Sorry," she said. "The last year has really done a number on me, and I seem to have lost the ability to have a normal conversation with a cute guy."

Oh my god.

Lena pinched her lips together with her fingers.

"Do you want to talk about it?" Palmer asked, surprising her.

"I know that's a weird thing to say, we don't know each other, but there's a safety in that, right? When we confide in a stranger."

"I've run into a lot of strangers lately," Lena said.

Palmer glanced at her, then back to the two-lane road. "Were they companionable strangers? Like the people you find in an airport?" Palmer said. "You gotta steer clear of the *strange* strangers, though. Or worse, stranger dangers. Although, I'm probably coming off as the middle of the three right now, eh?"

A laugh escaped her. Yet another surprise. "I appreciate the offer, but my life is way too messy to take you up on it."

"Lena." The sound of her name felt like a hug. "You're talking to an unemployed homeless man with a questionable beard. I'm the last person to judge how disorganized a person feels."

"That's a first," she said, unable to stop herself. She didn't trust Palmer's quick understanding and was too worn down by other people's judgments to even try. Then, for no good reason at all, she blurted out, "I broke off my engagement two days before my fiancé died in a freak accident."

The tow truck hit a pothole with a tremendous thud. Lena jerked her head around to check on Douglas. He was still there, smiling and enjoying his free ride. Palmer's eyes locked on Lena's as she turned forward. Her stomach jolted.

Palmer focused on the road again. "I'm sorry about your fiancé. I can't imagine how hard it must be for you."

"It happened last March, over a year ago. I guess that's supposed to mean something—*one year.*" She paused, thinking about the winding drive into Park City, Utah, when she'd spilled her guts. To Douglas. It was as if Palmer's presence elevated her into the same thin air. Lena stared out the passenger window, seeing nothing. "I used to be calm and focused and driven. Now I'm just angry and tired and on the road, in motion, but... lost."

The whistling wind coming from the cracked passenger window filled the silence. She waited for the usual foolish feeling to take over and aggravate her regret, but it didn't. Instead, something else happened—something unexpected, something she didn't realize she needed until she was right in the middle of it. Palmer's hand covered hers and, in a gentle movement, squeezed it.

She turned to look at him. His brown hair was moderate in length like his beard—which was far from questionable—and faint wrinkles appeared around his eyes as his mouth curved upward. He was really...not supposed to be this attractive. Lena's resistance to seeing any man clearly since Seth's passing was melting away, and it didn't feel right.

"What about you?" Lena said, reclaiming her hand. Palmer was acting like he understood, better than most, which was confusing. "Sounds like you're in the middle of something, too."

The blinker sounded as the truck slowed. The headlights illuminated a lumberyard. "Later, I promise," he said, opening the door to exit. Lena sat back in her seat as Palmer's figure disappeared into the shadows. *I promise.* She'd heard those words before, like a warm blanket over chilly doubts. But there was nothing at stake here.

"Douglas," she said out loud. "What are we going to do?" But, as expected, all that followed was silence.

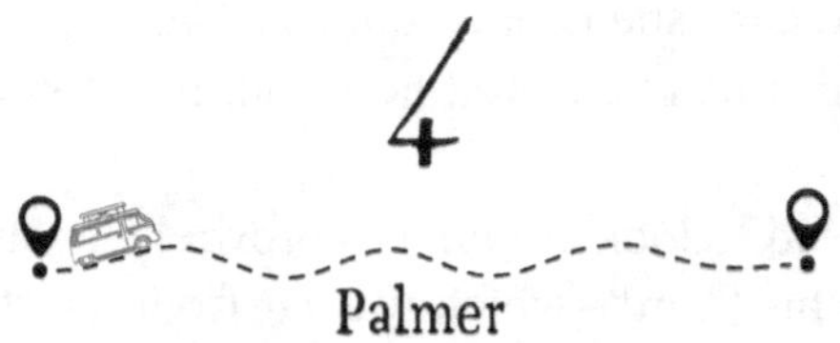

4

Palmer

I t was seven o'clock on Saturday morning, and Palmer needed coffee. Normally, he would still be in bed, snoring no doubt, unconscious to life. Instead, he was up early and in town with a truckload of his stuff. Today was moving day.

Carrie had offered her basement couch as a temporary fix to Palmer's homelessness, but his father insisted he move back home. Palmer wasn't a fool. He saw right through his father's apparent generosity. According to his father, "no son of the Eriksson lineage would ever be homeless." Yet, the same man of supposed family values had turned down Palmer's proposal to buy the *family* business, without a second thought.

"It's a failed business, son. You don't want it, trust me," his father had said while politely returning the legal papers with Palmer's offer. "The original location is the bank's problem anyway, and has been for some time."

"A mortgage shouldn't prevent me from buying the business." Palmer gripped the papers in his hand.

"It's complicated, son. You best stay out of it." His father's attention began to drift. He didn't care, that much was obvious. Palmer wasn't about to go easy on him.

"Dad, this company has been my entire life. You owe me an explanation. What the hell is going on?" His father stared at him—the lines on his face deep, the stubble on his chin gray—then started to talk.

Palmer pulled into the coffee shop parking lot and gripped the wheel. His chest still felt tight from everything his father had revealed.

The property had been in foreclosure for years, but his father had somehow delayed a public auction on the property. Indefinitely. And no one knew because it wasn't legal—how could it be? Then his father declared bankruptcy. Secretly. Until he announced they were going out of business. For good. He'd given up and let go, like a fart in the wind, not caring who was around when he did it. And now, his father's shady business dealings had thrown Palmer's future in reverse.

The abundance of patience Palmer would need to live at home would require more discipline than he had at the moment, but he had a plan. He always did. Living under the same roof as his father wouldn't change that. And caffeine made everything seem less impossible.

Pulling the door open to Riverside Roasters, Palmer came to a halt. No one was there. The back area was dark, the tables and couches empty. The far windows overlooking the river were covered by sheer curtains blurring the view. A clank sounded from the kitchen as his eyes caught sight of the brick fireplace, absent of its usual glow. In his storage unit, where all of his furniture lived, was a half-finished coffee table made out of crates that belonged right there, in front of a crackling fire. He planned to donate it to Patti, the owner, once he found a proper woodworking space and showroom of his own. He would also need more reclaimed wood. Two of his go-to suppliers had been cleaned out, most likely by him. But where there's money, there's a way, and he had plenty of money. Even if he no longer had a home to call his own.

"Hello?" Palmer called out. A voice from the kitchen shouted, "Coming!" Palmer froze as the door swung open. Materializing from behind the counter and staring up at him with large almond-shaped eyes, was the girl with the van. Lena. He hadn't seen her since that night two weeks ago.

"Hi, Palmer," she said like she was expecting him. A clip-clopping sound accompanied her limping gait toward the register.

"What happened to you?" he said. *Nice opener, dude.* In his defense, he was capped on surprises for the week, and this one was a triple whammy: the mysterious girl from out-of-state was somehow in his hometown coffee shop with what appeared to be a broken leg. His immediate concern for her well-being was, well, concerning.

"Oh, you mean my ankle?" Lena swiped a piece of hair away from her forehead. The black color from two weeks ago was fading into a deep auburn. Palmer hadn't meant to notice her hair, or how much more she resembled her sister now. But he couldn't help it. He was curious about Lena.

"I broke, like Douglas," she said. "Did you know that the half year in *1983 and a half* makes all of his parts super expensive and hard to find?"

"Any car part before the year 2000 is expensive and hard to find," Palmer said.

Lena nodded. "I recently learned this automotive common knowledge. I also learned I have very little money to my name, and I'm not allowed to drive for the next six to eight weeks. But, lucky for me, Patti was willing to hire me temporarily. And I no longer need crutches. So, there's that. At least there's that."

"I would think being on your feet all day with that cast-boot-thing goes against doctor's orders," Palmer said. "Please tell me you sit when you can."

Her hands fisted before she flattened them on the counter. "I'm doing the best I can given the circumstances," she said flatly.

Right, not his place to ask if she was taking care of herself. But who could blame him? Two weeks had passed since she'd arrived with a broken van, and now she had a broken ankle.

"Well, you've got a great mechanic working on your van," Palmer said. "Gregor will find the parts quicker than any chain shop and for the right price. That I'm sure of."

Lena's face softened. "I like him. He's determined and hard-working, and possibly nocturnal," Lena said. Palmer shifted on his feet. He was those things, too. "It must run in your blood."

He smiled. "On my mother's side, yeah." Not his father's, though. His old man had given up on everything. Palmer pointed to her right leg. "When did you hurt yourself? Better yet, *how?*"

"The morning after Douglas was towed. It's stupid. You don't really care, do you?" Lena looked at him and then sighed when he didn't respond. "I was holding a mug of coffee walking into my sister's family room when I missed the step down, rolled my ankle, and cracked the bone landing on it. And all I could think as I was falling was, *I'm going to spill coffee on Shay's pristine cream carpet right before she has a baby because my dumb butt can't walk!* Which is bonkers. Why wasn't I thinking, I'm seriously going to hurt myself. Anyway, I didn't spill my coffee." Lena gave him a sad smile. "It took a lot of self-control to break myself."

The tone in her voice suggested there was more on her mind than a broken ankle. He would listen. Of course he would. But did she want to talk about it? "I've never broken a bone," he said. "I always look out for myself, though."

"Ah, I see. You're one of the careful ones."

"When I'm prepared, and there's a plan, I've found there are fewer opportunities for surprises."

"Maybe. I'm starting to notice the more I hold on to things, like that stupid coffee mug, the more I end up hurting myself in the end." She straightened as the front door opened. An older woman with a cane stood next to Palmer. "I'll be right with you," Lena said to the woman, then turned to Palmer. "All right, so. What would you like, Palmer?"

He would like more of her thoughts spoken out loud. "Can you pour a large cup of coffee, dump two espresso shots into it, and stir?"

Lena's eyebrows raised. "I can, but watch your heart. That much caffeine can't be good for it." She plucked a paper cup from the stack near the cash register and moved behind the espresso machine.

"This isn't an everyday ritual, trust me. My heart will survive," he said. *It always did.*

"That makes one of us." She looked at him briefly while the machine whirred before grabbing a pot of coffee from behind her. "There you go. Stirred, not shaken."

After paying, he stood at the cart in the corner, and poured sugar into his coffee. As the crystals dissolved into the dark liquid, and the smell of the beans started to seep into his mushy morning brain, an odd sense of purpose soaked into his plan. Lena was stuck in an unfamiliar town and knew only her sister. He would soon be stuck in a house he didn't want to be in. She would need a friend other than Shay. He would need a friend other than Mark. It was a logical plan, like waking up to a morning cup of coffee.

Palmer watched Lena limp toward the covered windows. "Here, let me help you with those," he said.

She jumped, her hand slapping the front of her chest. "I thought you left." She looked annoyed as she straightened the collar of her gray blouse.

Setting his cup on one of the tables, he walked toward the windows, sensing her hesitation. "It'll go quicker if I help," he said, clearing his throat. "So, are you staying with Shay and Mark for your, er, extended visit?"

Her crystal blue eyes were guarded as she considered him. "For now. Shay's so stressed and so pregnant. And my parents will be staying in the guest room after the baby comes. I feel like a pest, hovering around uninvited. Hey! That's a thought." She tapped an index finger to her lips and turned toward him distractedly. Palmer fought against the instinct to look at her mouth. "I could park Douglas in their driveway and sleep out there." Her face dropped. "Once he's fixed, that is." Lena nearly tripped over her booted foot as she reversed her stance to face the windows again. He rushed and caught her arm; a vanilla musk surrounded him.

"Thanks." She smoothed her hair, her cheeks pink. "This clod-hopper foot is impossibly heavy, and I haven't been good about taking the doctor-ordered, thirty-minute daily walks." She lowered her tone with a cough, "to help with your healing." A sharp laugh escaped from her mouth. "Like I have a choice in the matter. I have to heal."

Palmer pushed open a curtain as he soaked in Lena's candidness. She seemed unaware of her vulnerability and talked as if no one was listening. An observation he had pointed out years ago to another outspoken woman.

People really don't listen, have you noticed?

"Sure, it makes sense," he said, tying the curtains together. "You help yourself when you heal yourself." She nodded as she clutched a swath of fabric. "What else did your doctor recommend?"

"Painkillers," Lena said, releasing her hand from the curtain. "Which I refuse to take."

Palmer stood back to look at the unobstructed view. The river rolled fast, the water high and white-capped from a week of heavy rain. A roar of natural power was muted by the thick glass windows. "Are you in a lot of pain?"

"Oh, not really. It's a good distraction if I'm being honest." She shut her mouth as if she hadn't meant to say what she did. He wanted to urge her to continue. She *was* the perfect distraction from his small world of infinite stress.

"I'd like to be friends while you're in town," he said before he lost his nerve. *Real smooth, dude.* Not that he needed to be, he was going for platonic. Yes. A sincere proposal of friendship between a man and a woman.

"Well, I, um...maybe? I mean, yeah, sure. Why not?" Lena laughed awkwardly. "Sorry, I wasn't expecting you to say that. But you know my family and my current state of...life, and I know you're homeless. So I guess that's a pretty solid start for friends, yeah?"

Palmer smiled, feeling lighter. "I should tell you I'm no longer homeless—"

"Hey, good for you!"

"Because I'm moving in with my parents."

Lena covered a laugh with her hand. "Look at us, living with our families again." She shook her head and held his gaze. "Ever since my fiancé left this planet, those who have crossed my path have served a purpose. I never could tell if I returned the favor or if it was a one-sided deal. I won't wonder that with you, though, Palmer." Lena stepped closer and held out her hand. He grasped it, her skin warm and soft. The jolt of electricity shooting up his arm had reappeared, just like before. "To friendship," she said, releasing his hand with a smile.

"Friendship," he repeated.

The smell of fresh-cut grass greeted Palmer as he lowered to sit on the steps of his parents' deck. It was his first opportunity to sit since seeing Lena that morning. Taking a swig from his beer bottle, he closed his eyes as reality soaked into his aching muscles. Most of his personal belongings, mainly boxes and two dressers, were in the detached garage, while his handmade furniture remained in the windowless storage unit. His king-size mattress barely fit inside his shoebox of a bedroom. But that's all he planned to do here: sleep.

Right before coming outside, Palmer's father had called him into the sun room. Palmer had stood just outside the double doors, the smell of turpentine drifting toward him. A wood table dotted with paint sat in the middle of the room, cluttered with paint brushes, paint tubes, and mason jars of dirty water. Two large easels with paint-splattered canvases stood in the corners of the room, both offering a different angle of what appeared to be underwater scenes of something big and gray. Palmer squinted. "Looks like a potato," he said under his breath.

"It's a manatee," his father said, startling Palmer. His old man wasn't known for listening well.

"Has mom started painting?" Palmer leaned against the doorframe.

"Your mother? No. She's a planner, not a painter." His father scrubbed a hand over his gray stubbled chin.

"Then who's gone all Jackson Pollock?"

His father smoothed his hands over his crumpled khakis, also dotted with paint, and scanned the room. Palmer tensed. "I was going for Monet meets van Gogh while scuba diving in Florida, which I guess makes a Pollock. You've got a good eye, son."

"You're the painter?" Palmer choked on the words.

"It's been a passion of mine since I was a child."

"Right," Palmer said stone-faced. His father had ended generations of work to become what? A deadbeat artist? Excusing himself, Palmer went straight for the refrigerator to find something to wash down the anger, then came outside.

He leaned his elbows on his knees and stared at his parents' covered inground pool. His mom had recruited him to help open it up this weekend, just like in high school. He didn't mind. A carefree day by the pool was long overdue. Maybe Carrie could wrangle up the usual suspects for an opening day get-together. He might as well take full advantage while he was back home. Maybe piss his father off a little bit, too. And get to see some friends, old and...new. That was, if his striking new friend with a broken ankle attended pool parties.

"You really don't have that much stuff, man, and I want to thank you for that." Mark sat down and clinked the neck of his beer bottle to Palmer's.

"A lot is already in storage. Thanks for helping with the last of it." Palmer took a swig. "I was thinking of inviting a few people to the pool this weekend. I haven't seen much of you or anyone the last two weeks."

"We haven't had a Palmer pool party in ages," Mark said. "Those were wild times. I imagine it'll be much different now that we're in our thirties."

"All the more reason. We're not getting any younger," Palmer said, cracking his back. "I could smoke some chicken, maybe ask Chef Carrie to provide the sides." Palmer readjusted the waistband of his jeans. He had grown something of a gut over the last year eating Carrie's food.

His cousin had taken a shitty situation—losing her dream job—and turned it into chasing another dream instead: culinary school. Carrie was working with an investor to open her own restaurant, which she planned to do in the next few months. Palmer would craft a dining table for the banquet room. Once he found more wood. He rolled his shoulders back. Why was he thinking of pool parties and girls with broken legs when he should be scouring the state for reclaimed wood?

"We'll be there," Mark said. "Maybe not for the long haul, but at least until the food runs out. Shay wouldn't say no to an afternoon of eating."

"Cool, great." Palmer picked at the sticky label on his bottle. "Her sister is invited too, of course. How's it going at the house, by the way?"

Mark took a drink and shrugged. "Better than anticipated. I was convinced it was going to be nonstop drama, especially after Lena broke her ankle. You heard about that, right?" Mark glanced at Palmer. He nodded and motioned for Mark to keep talking. "Shay keeps telling me how Lena is a blessing in disguise. I'm not gonna lie, having her sister around during the final stretch of the pregnancy is kind of—I don't know. Shay's more grounded with Lena here."

Palmer raised an eyebrow. Hadn't Lena said the exact opposite this morning? That she was imposing? "I saw Lena earlier. If Shay hasn't told her that directly, she should. Also, we're going to be friends." He said the last part fast.

"Friends," Mark repeated. "You and Lena are going to be friends."

"Yeah. No harm, no foul, just friends," Palmer said, squinting at Mark. "What's with the face?"

Mark tapped his bottle against his leg. "You know she's driving her fiancé's van—the guy who passed away last year—to his parents in Florida, right?"

"I've been made aware," Palmer said. "Lena talks like she needs someone who listens."

"And you think that's you?"

Palmer stood up, stretching. "Yes. I do. We will be friends until she leaves. That's the plan."

"Well, I know there's no talking you out of a plan once you've made one." Mark stood up, a smirk on his face. "Just remember, things can and do change, like your dad randomly painting now."

Palmer groaned. "My participation in this alternate universe will not last very long. In fact, I have an appointment tomorrow to see a commercial space a block from Gregor's shop that just went up for sale. Can you come along, be my second set of eyes?"

Mark pulled out his phone and tapped on the screen. "To-morrow, I'm..." Mark scrunched his nose. "Damn, I totally for-got. Shay's parents are flying in, and I'm picking them up. But you could ask your new *friend.*"

Palmer rolled his eyes. "That's the only time you get to use that line. And thanks for the suggestion. I think I will ask my new friend."

Later that evening, and after a tense dinner with his parents, Palmer sat on the edge of his bed, flipping his phone in his hand as he waited for the sound of a text. He hoped to god the building tomorrow wasn't a complete flop. He needed a shop to work out of, and a place to keep his hands busy. The atmosphere in the house was borderline toxic. That, or his father's makeshift studio needed better ventilation. His phone vibrated with a message.

See you then!

Lena was quick to respond, which he appreciated. No games.

No excuses flooding his inbox. No, *maybes* or *let me check and sees*, only to receive an eventual *no* hours later. He asked a question, and she answered. What a refreshing change of pace compared to previous women he'd dated. Not that he and Lena were dating. Maybe that was the secret. Regardless, Palmer couldn't help it; despite everything else, he smiled.

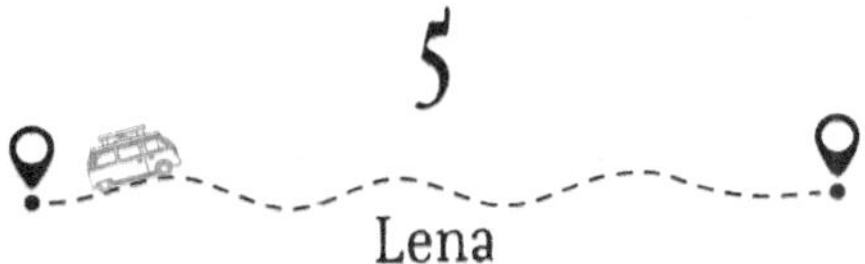

5

Lena

S he was flying. Not very well, but her toes weren't touching the ground. She floated, free and directionless, surrounded by nothing. It was a meaningless dimension. Until it wasn't.

There was a box she needed to find. It was for Seth, or from Seth—she wasn't sure—and was nestled somewhere on an unreachable shelf. Seth was outside, and leaving, always leaving. She had to open the box before he left. Why? She wasn't sure. The small turquoise-colored box came into view. She stretched her arms out further, lifted a little bit higher, and—was that a potato etched on the lid?

She bobbed up and down in the air, adrift among waves, unable to keep steady. Why was it so difficult to hold herself up? And what was that noise? It was loud, and repetitive, tugging at the very fabric of her being, calling her name.

"Lena?"

At the sound of her name, she descended into light as the shelf melted away. *No!* She kicked at the air. *Not yet!* Seth was waiting for her to find the box, waiting for her to say goodbye.

"Lena? Can I come in?"

Lena blinked. The vaulted ceiling of her sister's guest bedroom shifted in and out of focus. The door cracked open, and Shay's face poked out from around the corner.

"Hi, sleepy head," Shay said.

Lena propped herself up on her elbows. Sunlight peeked through the drawn curtains. An oil painting of her father's hung on the wall across the bed, his brush strokes winking at her. A crocheted blanket her mom had made lay crumpled in the middle of the room.

"I must've dozed off." Lena rubbed her eyes.

"Someone's here to see you," Shay said, lowering onto the end of the bed.

Lena covered a yawn, her ears popping. "Sorry, I missed what you said."

The look on her sister's face made Lena grow tense. Ever since her fall, Lena had been on her best behavior, clearing the dishes from the sink every night, keeping her personal items out of sight. Was Lena's broken ankle—never mind her grief—too much for Shay to handle so close to her pregnancy?

"Palmer is here to see you," Shay said.

Wait. *What?* "Why would he want to see—" Lena sat up fast. "Oh, crap." She watched Shay's eyes narrow. "No. *No.* It's nothing like that," Lena said. Shay gave her a disapproving "mmh-mm."

"I just woke up from a dream about Seth, all right?" It felt wrong to use Seth as an excuse, even if it was the truth.

Shay's eyes softened. "I heard you shout before I came in. Are you okay?"

"I'm awake." Lena twisted her hands together. She didn't want to talk about the dream. The ache in her leg pulsed and heat poked at the back of her eyes. It had been two weeks since she last cried—a reflex when she broke her bone. The tears trying to escape now were different. These were Seth tears: hotter, thicker, and meant to be shed in the safety of Douglas. "Palmer texted me last night and asked if I could look at a possible location for his woodshop today." She reached for her phone on the nightstand. Two missed calls and one text, all from Palmer. "And I stood him up."

"I'm sure he understands you need rest," Shay said.

The disapproving look on Palmer's face yesterday at River-side Roasters flashed through her mind. "I'm sure he prefers me in bed for the next six weeks."

Shay giggled. "What man wouldn't prefer a woman in bed—"

"Oh my god, Shay! I didn't mean it like that!" Her mind conjured an image of Palmer's bed. It was probably massive. *Stop it!* "We're friends, and I'll keep telling you that until you hear me."

"You're right, sorry. I don't know what I was thinking. Blame the baby!"

"You can't blame everything on pregnancy hormones, but I'll let this one slide." Lena stood up and offered a hand to Shay. With a loud grunt from both, Lena pulled her sister upright.

"Remind me not to sit down anymore." Shay tugged at the bottom of her maternity blouse.

"How about I remind you to stop getting up instead."

"You always were the smarter sister."

"And don't you forget it." Lena threw a smile in Shay's direction before disappearing into the bathroom. Palmer may be a friend, but the state of Lena's hair was not meant for public viewing. After a quick brush through her tangles and a swish of mouthwash, she returned to anxiously watch Shay side-step down the staircase.

"You're making me nervous," Lena said.

Shay gripped the banister. "This baby needs to come out. I can't live like this!"

A voice echoed up to them. "Shay, do you need help?"

"I'm fine, Palmer—"

"She'll need a banana split sundae with extra whipped cream once she's landed," Lena shouted over Shay's head.

"Coming right up," Palmer said, followed by the sound of the front door opening and closing.

"You're too much, Lena." Shay laughed as she continued her slow descent.

"The man asked. Might as well see how good he is at helping," Lena said. Shay's tongue poked out as she concentrated on the steps, oblivious to Lena's pinched tone.

Why did it seem like Palmer's help was a form of control?

Lena shook her head. She was seeking out wrongs in Palmer for no reason. Her dream was still gripping the edge of her consciousness, frustrating her. If only she had seen what was inside the box and rushed out to say goodbye to Seth, or, better yet, stopped him from leaving.

"Earth to Lena," Shay said from the bottom of the stairs.

"I'm coming, sorry." Lena's walking boot thumped on the hardwood steps as pain shot up her heel, grounding her into the present moment. That couldn't be good.

"You're as white as a ghost," Shay said once Lena reached the bottom. Her entire right leg was on fire.

"I landed on my heel funny." Lena forced a smile. "It's my fault. I've done next to no walking since I broke it. I need a walking buddy or something."

Shay waddled to the kitchen entrance, making it clear she wasn't the candidate for the job.

"It's a shame you don't have a friend in town who values your opinion and well-being." Shay pretended to look confused. "Oh wait, you do. Silly me."

Shay meant Palmer, obviously. Lena couldn't have made that strong of an impression on him. Not a positive one anyway, with her broken van and broken ankle. She sure hoped Palmer wasn't projecting some kind of image onto her. Whether he was or not, she could guarantee he would be disappointed by her. And she was done disappointing people. Well, other than herself.

"I could ask Mom to walk with me since she'll be around now," Lena said, following Shay into the kitchen.

"I'm pretty sure wherever I am, Mom will be," Shay said. Lena placed a glass of water in front of Shay. "And Dad is hell-bent on painting a mural in the nursery."

"Good point." Lena sat and took a sip of water. Her throat was impossibly dry. "I can walk the river path after work, make it part of my routine while I'm here."

"You're going to hobble alone in the dark? I don't like it. What if something happens? You should have someone with you. Like

Palmer."

Lena blew out a frustrated breath. "I'll be fine." She didn't expect Shay to understand how much Seth's death had changed her. Lena had found protection in the loneliness she carried around with her. And pepper spray. She didn't need anyone. "Besides, Palmer is probably too busy for—"

"Too busy for what?" Palmer placed a white paper bag down on the table.

"Lena thinks you're too busy to walk with her," Shay said. Lena gave her the death stare.

"I'm never too busy for my friends," Palmer said as he took out two boat-shaped plastic bowls from the bag.

"I can't believe you actually got us ice cream," Lena said. She leaned in and spied bananas underneath the plastic lids. Two pints of cookies-'n'-cream ice cream were also placed on the table.

"Bonus ice cream for later," he said.

"You're currently my favorite friend, Palmer," Shay said. She ripped the lid off one of the sundaes with the grace of a gorilla and moaned.

Lena was less zealous as she removed the lid of her sundae, but internally she was moaning too. Because, ice cream. Exactly what her dream hangover needed.

"This is delicious. Thank you," Lena said around a spoonful. Palmer moved the additional two pints of ice cream into the freezer. "Aren't you going to have some?"

"I'm more of a pie guy." Palmer towered over the refrigerator. Lena had always been drawn to taller men. She imagined kissing someone like Palmer would cause her neck to ache. She dropped her spoon in shock. Her stomach churned. Too much sugar. That's where the thought had come from.

"Lena said you were looking at a building today for your woodshop," Shay said. Lena fumbled to retrieve her spoon, her stomach in knots now. She owed him an apology!

"Yes! How did it go? I'm sorry I missed it. I fell asleep and got caught up trying to fly again." Lena reached for her water glass. Gulping down her embarrassment too quickly, she sputtered and coughed.

Shay squeezed Lena's shoulder. "Lena's always been a vivid dreamer," she said to Palmer, then turned to Lena. "You're flying now."

"Trying to. It's not easy." Her face began to warm. Shay was familiar with Lena's tendency to speak as if dreams were real. Palmer, not so much.

"I don't dream," Palmer said. He sat across from Lena. "Or I should say, I can never remember my dreams. Same difference. You, though—" His eyes were bright as he peered at her. "You remember your dreams and control them too. How wild it must be to wake up from something so vivid."

"It's different." Lena's voice cracked. Shay's head ping-ponged between her and Palmer.

"I had the time written down incorrectly for the showing," Palmer said after a long pause. "I'm walking over there now. I'd love all the opinions I can get on it." He smiled at both sisters.

Shay shook her head. "I don't think I can walk after all this ice cream," she said, scraping the bottom of her empty bowl. "Mark's due soon with our parents anyway."

"Oh, right, your parents are in town. All right, no biggie. Maybe you can see the space another time, Lena." Palmer stood up.

"I don't have to be here the moment they arrive," Lena said, a tightness forming in her chest. She disliked assumptions. They took away a person's curiosity. And freedom. "I saw them last month. Shay can have some one-on-one time with them before they start babying the grieving daughter."

Shay sighed. "They mean well."

"Everyone does." Lena shook her head. "I'll grab my jacket, and we can go." She stood with an audible gasp, her calf muscle squeezing. Palmer shot up and rushed to her side. Those stupid tears of hers threatened to spill out again. *Why was today such a roller coaster?* Because she couldn't reach that stupid box, that's why. "I'm okay, Palmer. I just need to get the blood flowing again. A walk will do me good."

Twenty minutes later, Lena sat on a foldout chair while Palmer stood in the middle of a gaping room, his knuckles rubbing his beard. She had insisted she could stand, but Palmer had persisted with the damn chair and refused to hear her excuses. Lena wanted to pout. But she was here as a favor, not to be a burden, so, she wouldn't. Not too much, anyway.

The realtor, a short woman with blonde, chin-length hair and over-the-top perfume, rattled off adjective-heavy details. The ceiling was at least two stories high, with an exposed red brick wall to their right. Edison lights hung off the many floating wood beams located a few feet below the ceiling, warming the space with their soft hue. A row of windows faced the main street, the ambient noise of passing cars muffled. Palmer's gaze caught hers once the realtor finished her memorized summary of specs and comps. He smiled. Her toes tingled.

"I'll give you and your wife some time to chat alone," the realtor said.

Lena's head jerked. "We're not—"

"Thank you, Nancy," Palmer said. Nancy turned her back and walked out the front door.

"You didn't correct her," Lena said.

"It's just auto-pilot realtor talk." Palmer cupped the back of his neck. "So, tell me what you think."

Lena felt her stomach kick her. Palmer was excited and looking at her like...like her opinion mattered to him. She stood slowly, pain rolling through her body. A musty scent drifted around her as she spun to take in the whole room.

"It's one hundred percent showroom-worthy. But not wood-shop-appropriate," Lena said. Usually, she tiptoed around the truth to please those around her, sacrificing honesty in the name of love. It was an easy excuse, love. Like brushing crumbs underneath a rug and calling the place clean. Seth's sad eyes flashed through her mind. She blinked. *Not right now*.

Palmer's smile dropped. "A voice inside my head told me the same thing. I was going to ignore it. Now I can't."

"I don't know if that's a compliment or a complaint," Lena said with a small laugh.

"A compliment for you, a complaint for me," Palmer said. "I'm glad you speak your mind."

Her body buzzed. Why did she suddenly want to bolt out the front door? Looking up at the ceiling, Lena regained focus. They were standing on a blank canvas inside a beautiful frame. Surely Palmer saw the potential. In the building. Not her.

"What if you wall off the back area for your woodshop and office? The front could be the showroom and"—Lena limped over to the entrance, spreading her arms out—"a small coffee shop with a standing counter under the window." She turned, startled by Palmer's closeness, the color of his eyes a mix of brown and evergreen. "Because caffeinated customers buy things," she said, her throat sandpaper.

The look on Palmer's face had Lena convinced there was food in her teeth. "I said too much," Lena said, pressing her tongue to the roof of her mouth.

"Did I mention the coffee shop idea when we towed Douglas?"

The corners of Lena's mouth lifted. He'd used Douglas's name as if the van was an actual person. "No. Actually, you made it sound like you had a space already. By the way, did you get the wood you couldn't find when we were there?"

Palmer blew out a breath. "That's a whole can of worms not worth getting into at the moment." He walked to the front door, peering out the window. "Any news on your van?"

"Gregor found two of the four needed parts, which is great. We'll discuss pricing tomorrow when I stop by the shop." Lena owed Seth's father an update, too, but was putting it off. He'd offered to pay for Douglas when they spoke two weeks ago, which she'd refused. She would rather be in debt financially. Emotional debt never went away.

"Thank you, again, for suggesting your brother's shop."

"You bet," Palmer said, his face in shadow. What look was he giving her, she wondered. "Incoming," he said, right as the front door swung open.

"All right," said Nancy, rubbing her hands together. "What has the happy couple decided?"

Palmer mouthed to Lena, *Just go with it.* He placed his arm around her shoulder, the scent of man and pine swarming her.

"We'd like to move forward and discuss next steps," Palmer said.

"Oh, fantastic! I'll pop out to my car and grab some paperwork." Fresh air blew into the building as Nancy exited. Lena angled into the cool air, her injured leg weakening by the moment.

The weight of Palmer's arm lifted off her shoulders. "You saved us from another unnecessary conversation with chatty Nancy," he said.

"Happy to help." Her head started to ache. "If you don't mind, I think I'll walk back so you can handle the fun details." She tried to keep her voice light. Palmer scanned her body, his mouth tight.

"You're in pain," he said, a statement of fact.

Lena nodded. "It's part of my M.O. now."

"I know you're going to do what you want, Lena. I'm learning this about you." Palmer scrubbed a hand down his face. "But if you could sit down over there again, I'll run to the house, grab my truck, and drive you home."

Why wasn't Palmer's face in the shadows like before? The wariness in his eyes cemented her to the floor. She hated being stuck in a fragile state.

"What about Nancy and the paperwork?"

"Tell her your brother-in-law is going to look over everything since he's a lawyer," Palmer said. "Sit, please. I won't be long."

After a moment, Lena gave in. "I'll repay you for all the favors."

Palmer smiled. "Not putting up a fight is payment enough for me, Lena." Before she could respond, he shot out the door. She stood there for a moment, the silence of the empty room amplifying the noise in her mind. "Not putting up a fight" was the least acceptable form of repayment. Her guilt raged against the relief she felt at being cared for by a man other than Seth.

"Did I just see your husband rush out the door?" Nancy said the second Lena's butt hit the chair.

Husband. The word squeezed underneath her ribs.

"Palmer and I aren't married. I'm his friend's sister-in-law," she said. Nancy's face was frozen, not a twitch to be seen. Lena squinted an eye. Was she even listening? "He went to get his truck. I can give him the paperwork. He wanted to look it over before moving forward and signing...stuff."

Nancy perked up at the mention of signing. "You're a doll. He knows how to reach me if he has questions." Nancy handed Lena the papers. "Lena, was it?"

"Yeah." Lena gripped the papers, recognizing the change in tone. Nancy was going to say something she didn't want to hear.

"The inside may be empty, but the outside is filled with surprises." Nancy winked, then turned and walked out. Lena stared at the closed door. Were all realtors this strange?

Shivering, Lena remembered the city bench she'd spotted earlier and hobbled out of the building. Sunlight would warm her sudden chill. She turned toward the bench but stopped midpivot. There was something etched on the glass door of Palmer's maybe new space. It was small and covered in dirt, but she had seen it somewhere before. Somewhere recently. Peering closer, Lena's eyes grew wide. It was the image on the box lid, the potato from her dream, except it wasn't a potato at all. It was a manatee.

6

Palmer

P almer stared out the windshield of his truck at his parents' detached garage, his stomach twisting into knots. All of his woodworking equipment was in there, unorganized and jammed into a dusty corner. The garage was large enough for a temporary shop. But his father had refused to clear an area for him. And for no reason other than that he didn't want to, it seemed. Why had he thought his father was too old for such childlike stubbornness?

Stretching his hands to relieve their sudden ache, he grabbed the seller's contract off the passenger seat. He had reviewed the terms and conditions with Mark a week ago. It felt like a new beginning then. Now all he saw as he thumbed through the pages was another obligation shackling him to this town—a place he'd lived his entire life, when, in reality, he could build furniture anywhere in the world, couldn't he?

Palmer scratched his beard and looked out the driver's window. The two-story house stood before him, the front-facing windows glowing against the descending blue hour. He was stalling. Inside, his mother was waiting to serve yet another home-cooked meal at the round kitchen table he'd sat at as a child. He would listen to his father wax poetic about being an artist while his mother asked if he had any dirty laundry, and Palmer would go through the motions of a life in reverse. But not today. He threw the truck's gear into reverse instead.

"Mom called me asking if I'd seen you," Gregor said once Palmer stepped inside his brother's apartment. The murmur of an announcer's excited voice echoed from the kitchen. Gregor lived above his auto shop, rarely wore clothing without oil stains on them, and cut his hair once a year. He was a true-blue bachelor with the shortest commute in town. He also hated silence.

"I sent her a text right before leaving," Palmer said, digging into his jeans. A notice on his phone's screen informed him that his message had failed to send. Palmer forgot his parents' house—no, his house—the place he currently slept at—was shit for cell service.

"Do you have a curfew now too, bro?" Gregor let out a huge belly laugh. Palmer didn't think it was that funny. Although if the tables were turned, he would have given his brother a hard time too.

"Here. Booze." Palmer held a bottle of bourbon out in front of him.

Gregor examined it. "Nice find," he said.

Palmer followed Gregor through the main area and toward the galley kitchen. The space was modest in size, with light gray walls, a well-worn couch, and a flatscreen television. Gregor had lived in the two-bedroom apartment for five years. The lack of furniture and bare walls told a different story.

"I'll never turn away gifts of bourbon, but why are you giving me a bottle?" Gregor removed the plastic from the top and pulled the cork out with a satisfying *pop!* Palmer found two glasses in the cabinets he'd refinished for Gregor, surprised they were clean and put away. Actually, Gregor's entire kitchen appeared near spotless, not a dirty dish or crumb in sight.

"It's a thank-you for lending me your tow truck the other night," Palmer said.

"Cheers, brother." Gregor clicked his cup to Palmer's.

They both sniffed, then sipped. Dark fruit, tobacco, and leather. The liquid heat coated Palmer's insides. A nice warm blanket to relieve his stone-cold stress.

"How about we get dinner somewhere?" Palmer asked. "Between the bankruptcy, me moving, and you being busy at the shop here, it's been a while since we've hung out."

"I've got plans in an hour," Gregor said, a smile creeping across his face. "Otherwise, I'd say yes to a bite."

Palmer raised an eyebrow. Gregor was a workaholic homebody, not a plans-in-one-hour type of dude. "Is it a date or something?"

"Uh, not really. Lena is coming by for something she left inside her van. I'm gonna ask her to grab a drink." Gregor's cheeks were turning red. Palmer's grip tightened around his glass. "We need to go over all the repairs so far," Gregor continued. "Talk about a payment plan."

Palmer wasn't sure if Gregor had a habit of asking clients out. It wasn't something Palmer would ever consider himself. Then again, Husky's Fine Furniture clients were married couples looking to fill their new homes. Single people probably ordered cheap pieces of furniture from IKEA. Or drove vans across the country.

"And you normally do that over drinks?" Palmer took a healthy gulp.

Gregor shrugged. "Sometimes. There's no harm in getting to know someone a little better, right? Her van alone makes her interesting."

It felt like Palmer's entire body had slammed into a wall. *Get to know her better.*

"It's actually not hers—" Palmer stopped himself. He had no right to tell his brother what he knew about Lena. Just like he had no right to tell Gregor how to run his business.

Gregor's eyes narrowed. "I know you helped her out, and she's Mark's sister-in-law. But I'm kinda getting the impression I'm stepping on your toes."

"She doesn't know many people in town," Palmer said. "So we're hanging out as friends." Although his new friend had yet to ask him to join her for walks or confirm if she was going to the pool party tomorrow.

"Well, then, now she'll have two while she's here," Gregor said, splashing more bourbon into his glass.

Palmer knew his brother well enough to see he was nervous and fibbing. He also didn't want to think about Lena with Gregor. He couldn't envision those two having much in common. Although, come to think of it, he didn't know much about Lena, either. But there was an undeniable connection between her and Palmer, wasn't there? A connection he wanted to ignore and cultivate at the same time.

"Tomorrow's pool party is turning into quite the event," Palmer said, changing topic. "Carrie invited way too many people and made way too much food, as is her style. You think you'll stop by?"

Gregor made a face. "If I do, it won't be till later. Kind of been avoiding the house lately. Dad's freaking me out. Don't get me wrong, I'm glad he's not drinking all day with nothing to do, but it's such a one-eighty, you know? Hell, 'course you do. You're living under the same roof as the man."

At least Palmer wasn't the only one having a strong reaction to his father recently. "Trust me, as soon as possible, I'm out of there," Palmer said.

"Any chance your new woodshop has a second-level apartment?" Gregor spread his arms wide. "If so, welcome to the best bachelor life, brother."

"It doesn't. I don't think. I'm undecided whether that's the space for me." *Or if I plan to stay.* Palmer finished the rest of his drink. The burn in his belly would help dull the impulse to share more than facts. "Plus, locating wood around here has become a pain in the ass."

"Might be time to look outside this little town of ours," Gregor said as his phone vibrated next to him. He tapped on it, then looked at Palmer. "What time does your pool thing start tomorrow?"

"Why? I thought you couldn't make it till later."

Gregor's fingers tapped on his phone again. "Lena texted. She said she's stopping by the shop tomorrow instead, before heading to the pool." Gregor's face looked like someone was walking on *his* toes now.

Palmer tried to stop his smile from taking over. She was coming tomorrow. "Everything starts around two o'clock. If she's coming with Mark and Shay, then I imagine they will be the first to arrive."

The whoosh of a sent message sounded. "I'm out of the shop all day tomorrow," Gregor said, frowning. "So, looks like I'll miss her."

"Any chance you can stop by the party sooner? Maybe catch her then?" said Palmer. His offer completely contradicted his relief. It shouldn't matter whether Gregor did or didn't see Lena. But, damnit, it did.

Gregor straightened his shoulders. "Maybe. Let's go eat, eh?"

"Carrie told me she invited a couple of single friends tomorrow," Palmer said as they walked out of the auto shop and into the evening light. A cool breeze relieved his whiskey-warmed face and brought the faint smell of roses, as sweet as opportunity. "You never know what the night could bring."

"She's not matchmaking with me in mind, *Palm Tree*." Gregor shoved Palmer's shoulder. Both the Eriksson brothers were above average in height, thanks to their Swedish great-grandfather, who had measured in at six foot seven inches.

"Been there, done that," Palmer said with a return shove. "Carrie's well aware I have no interest in dating her friends."

"Right, right. Carrie's friend, what was her name again?" Gregor stood in front of the restaurant, a shit-eating grin on his face. "I guess a friend's sister-in-law is the logical next step."

The smell of ground beef and spices reached Palmer's nose as he walked to the entrance, calling over his shoulder, "You're a dumbass."

Slices of blue sky peeked through the disappearing clouds the following day. Palmer had been grateful for the earlier cloud cover. Hauling cinder blocks from one end of the yard to the other had left him a sweaty mess. Carrie arrived thirty minutes early to help him assemble the last parts of the homemade smoker.

"I'm less convinced of your plan than when you told me yesterday, Palm Tree." Carrie stood back and surveyed their work. The concrete rectangle wasn't the prettiest of sights, but Palmer was confident it could smoke chicken. If not, Carrie had brought enough food to feed the entire neighborhood.

"It's all in the spirit of trying new things, cousin." Palmer wrapped a sweaty arm around her shoulder and squeezed.

"I'd rather not experience salmonella poisoning, thank you," Carrie said, nudging him.

"You're skilled enough to spot an undercooked chicken." Palmer patted her head, then dodged her playful slap. "Or have your husband be the taste-tester. Where is he, by the way?"

Carrie smoothed the front of her sundress. "He's not coming."

Palmer squinted as the sunlight hit his eyes. "Talon never misses a party."

"Don't I know it," Carrie said under her breath. With a sigh, she looked at Palmer, her blonde hair curling around her heart-shaped face, her expression guarded. "I have some sorting out to do with him."

Palmer scratched his cheek. His beard annoyed him daily. It was too long. A meaningless problem compared to whatever Carrie was implying. "I don't know the first thing about being married, Carrie. But if you need someone to listen, I'm here."

Carrie touched Palmer's forearm. Her fingernails were painted a bright neon pink, and the diamond on her ring finger glittered. Talon was a fool if he thought he could do better than Carrie.

"We've been married for five years in July. He keeps pointing out it's only been five years! The engagement I thought would last a lifetime should count for something, right? He won't admit it, and please don't repeat this to anyone— He doesn't do well with change."

"Does anyone?" Palmer said with a laugh before he could stop himself. Carrie frowned. He didn't want to make things worse for Carrie. He could help. "Is there anything I can do?"

"No. It's a season in my marriage with him. It'll pass." Carrie's gaze flickered to a point over his shoulder. "Mark's coming down the hill, and holy cow, his wife is ready to pop!" Carrie sounded envious as she pointed her chin upward. "Who's that with them?"

Palmer turned. Lena was in the lead, her eyes on the ground as if to ensure their path was clear of any obstacles. Shay clutched onto Mark a few steps behind as they navigated the grassy downhill slope.

"That's Shay's sister," Palmer said, diverting his eyes from Lena's walking boot and exposed legs. *Those shorts are short.* "Gregor's working on her van."

"Right. He mentioned her when I was on the phone with him yesterday. *The nomad.*"

"He called her a nomad?" The label didn't fit Lena. He supposed, though, she did come off as a wanderer, even if temporarily— She'd traveled much farther than he ever had. Did Lena intend to live like one, though? He couldn't imagine living day-to-day in a tiny van. Or had she revealed something personal with Gregor and not him? The thought bugged Palmer more than it should. He needed to find his swimming trunks and jump in the pool.

"That's what nomads do, right?" Carrie said. "Live in vans. Well, some of them. I've actually never met one." Carrie squinted. "Why would someone come to a pool party with a broken leg?"

Palmer patted Carrie on the head again, this time to annoy her. "Because someone told her you're an amazing chef providing all the food today." He dodged another slap from Carrie and called up to the group. "You made it!" Carrie's grumbles faded as he trotted toward the fence's gate.

"Did I get the time wrong?" Lena said once she reached the cement patio. She glanced behind her, then turned her face up at Palmer. Freckles dotted her nose. Why did he suddenly want to know every single freckle she had? "Add it to the list of all the other crap I can't keep straight," she continued. Her smile didn't reach her eyes.

"This is an open-ended, come-whenever-and-as-you-are type of shindig," Palmer said. Lena nodded and jutted her chin toward Shay and Mark. They were stopped on the grass with Shay rubbing her stomach.

"I told her not to come," Lena said. "She's been having random pains all morning. But she insisted. Your cousin's cooking must be out of this world or something."

Palmer patted his midsection. "This gut is proof of her talents."

Lena's gaze flickered down briefly. "I'm looking forward to seeing it. The food that is." Lena sucked in a breath, turning again to look at her sister.

Palmer touched Lena's forearm. Her eyes jumped to his.

"Maybe it's better Shay is here enjoying herself," he said. "She's not overthinking whatever may or may not be happening."

"Yes, you're right. But that will not stop me from checking how long it'll take to get to the nearest hospital."

"Ten minutes if I'm driving."

"Which you won't be." She spoke sharply as if she didn't trust him. Then again, why would she? They barely knew one another.

"I only meant it's not far," he said, taking a step toward the pool. "Anyway. I should set up a table for all this food, so—" Palmer hitched a thumb over his shoulder as Lena's fingertips touched his arm, freezing him in place.

"Sorry." She swallowed, her throat bobbing. "The anticipation of a new life in the midst of loss has thrown me for a loop."

"I can't imagine the roller coaster it must be, Lena." He wanted to comfort her and reassure her that she was stronger than she thought. Was it his hopeful imagination playing tricks on him, or did she move an inch closer?

Mark's booming "Hello!" sliced the moment in half. Palmer did his best to act nonchalant as Lena shuffled to the side.

"Shay needs a table and food stat, Palm-o," Mark said, sweat marks dotting the middle of his shirt. Mark hadn't used that nickname since their college days, when sleep was scarce and stress was abundant. Which meant Mark was ready to let loose. Lena was right; perhaps Shay should have stayed home, if only to keep Mark there with her.

"This way," Palmer said, guiding them to a table farthest from the keg. Lena tugged on his arm once Shay and Mark were situated.

"I'll keep an eye on him," she said, her whole body radiating unease. "And I don't plan on drinking."

"Carrie's food will distract them, trust me." Palmer heard Lena sigh. "I could use some assistance if you don't mind." Palmer never asked for help. And would argue that this request was another means of distraction. For Lena.

"Of course," Lena said and followed him to the pool house.

They stood side-by-side, organizing the trays of food—grilled vegetables, baked beans, and corn on the cob—her shoulders grazing his chest as she stepped in front with serving spoons, her vanilla scent reaching up to him. The word *friends* began to lose meaning the longer he repeated it silently in his head. Off to the side, the glistening pool winked at him. Yes, he planned to jump in. He would sorely need to, eventually.

7

Lena

Once the trays of food were arranged, Lena retreated to where Shay was sitting. Her skin burned from Palmer's earlier hand graze, which was ridiculous. She knew it was her dopamine-seeking traitor of a brain trying to convince her the gesture meant something more. When in reality, it didn't. Most likely. No, it didn't. It couldn't.

She slumped into a chair across from Shay and rolled her shoulders back with a sigh. Her body hurt. Everywhere. The exhaustion from working on her feet for eight hours a day was taking a toll.

Over the last two weeks, she had followed the same routine: come home from work, fall asleep on the basement couch with the television on, and wake at midnight to a growling stomach. Usually, she forced herself upstairs to eat a snack—two slices of toasted bread with butter and cinnamon—then returned down the dreaded hallway of photos from Shay and Mark's wedding, a nightly reminder that she had missed a huge moment in her sister's life.

Lena hadn't been able to pull herself out of her apartment and stand next to Shay as her sister said "I do." She'd been too lost in the desperate thought: This wasn't how life was supposed to be.

Her regret continued to surface, questioning a past she couldn't change, but at least she was with her sister who would soon give birth to a beautiful baby. That was the thing about life—it carried on.

Lena rubbed her eyes and focused on the vibrant green pasture in the distance. It amazed her that red barns and polka-dotted cows could be found five minutes from industrial parks and shop-lined streets.

"I'm glad you came today," Shay said. "I've barely seen you all week." Shay sipped from a sweating cup of lemonade. The flush on her face was pronounced. Even with the shade from the long branches of an old oak tree overhead, the humidity was thick and stagnant.

"I've been working double shifts this week. The parts for Douglas aren't cheap, and I refuse to lean on Seth's parents financially." Lena readjusted herself in the plastic chair. Her leg felt like a sausage inside the sleeve of her walking cast. She had passed on the waterproof option, a no-brainer considering her aversion to swimming. But the pool was taunting her with its sparkling water.

"I see the point you're trying to make, Lena. And I think it's honorable, the commitment you made to this journey for Seth." Shay leaned her elbows on the table, steepling her fingers. "But you're sinking money into something that doesn't belong to you. Weren't you going to open a coffee shop in Oregon with your boss? Why not think about *your* dream for a second?"

Lena grimaced. Her sister was known to cut straight to the point. Lena could argue that she *was* thinking of her dream—the one with the unreachable box. Shay was being literal, though, and Lena had no intention of entertaining future aspirations at the moment. This was about the inaugural cross-country road trip in a van she was now responsible for, one that had broken down on her watch. She couldn't change the past, but she could spend her hard-earned money getting Douglas sorted out.

"What I want doesn't matter right now, Shay. Anyway, there might be a payment plan. I haven't talked to Gregor yet. I can't even find time to check in on Douglas."

Lena had woken in a cold sweat the other night and realized she'd never looked in the glove compartment. There was something in there—she was certain of it—and for no reason at all, she feared what she might find.

Shay drained the remains of her lemonade, yet somehow her flush had gotten deeper. "Sorry you weren't able to make it there before we got here. Mark and I can drive you to the shop later today," Shay said.

"It's okay. I think it's closed for the rest of the day now," Lena said, as Palmer came into view. "Do you know where the bathroom is?" The urge to move had taken over.

Palmer approached. "The pool house has a bathroom, but I think Mark's in it," Palmer said. He held a plate filled with two huge baked potatoes overflowing with melted butter, shredded cheese, sour cream, and green onions. It smelled divine.

"You must have really good hearing," Lena said, wondering how much he had actually heard.

"I'm good at a lot of things." Palmer smiled and set the plate in front of Shay. "Mark asked me to deliver this to you. Extra butter. Light on the salt." He scratched his beard and turned. "I'm headed to the main house for tortilla chips— You could use the guest bathroom, Lena."

"Are those tortilla chips for guacamole?" Shay said, an eagerness in her tone. Lena cracked a smile. Where most women were grumpy in their last trimester, Shay was simply hungry.

"Carrie's making a fresh batch as we speak," Palmer said, offering a hand to Lena. Her heart skipped a beat as he helped her up.

"Well, don't keep a pregnant lady waiting!" Shay shooed them away. Lena stuck her tongue out at Shay and followed Palmer up the deck steps.

The smell of sauteed onions greeted her once they stepped inside the air-conditioned house. Palmer walked through the arched entryway and past two cream-colored armchairs, his stride purposeful. Lena hobbled behind, trying to keep up. Did he forget she was broken?

"The bathroom is down the hall, to the right." Palmer pointed toward a shadowed hallway. "I'll be in the kitchen."

Lena thanked Palmer, even though she wanted to ask why he seemed so agitated. She began her slow walk toward the white door up ahead. A distinct smell reminiscent of her childhood stopped her. *Turpentine.* On instinct, she veered to an open set of double doors on her left.

The view before her brought an unexpected lump to her throat. The airy sunroom looked to be someone's art studio. A large canvas in the far corner brought her further into the room. It was an abstract outline of a rounded head, two fins on an oval body, and a large flattened tail in the back. She knew what this was. Her heart was racing It was a coincidence. It had to be.

"Hey, you." Palmer's voice made her jump. He stood in the middle of the double doors, arms crossed.

"You have a painter in your family," Lena said, focusing on the canvas again. Her nerves had crawled into her hands. They were shaking. First the box in her dream, then the etching on the glass door, and now a painting in Palmer's house. *Why?* "Someone who's painting a manatee.'

She heard Palmer's footsteps approach as his arm grazed hers. The hum of the ceiling fan rotated the room's air. Dishes clattered in the kitchen. Palmer sighed and Lena fought against a wave of shivers.

"It's a recent development, I assure you." He shifted away as if he just noticed his closeness to her. "I'm surprised you got a manatee out of"—he waved his hands over it—"that."

Lena rubbed her elbow, unsure why Palmer was acting like the room was off-limits. "I'm a trained art-looker," Lena said. Palmer gave her a funny look. "I grew up watching my father paint." It was a talent she hadn't been born with—crafting blobs of paint, or slabs of wood, into something beautiful. But she carried high regard for the vulnerability of the process.

"I don't think I'd call my father a painter. He's more of a

headache, to be honest," Palmer said.

"The same father who recently shut down the furniture business," Lena said. Palmer's mood swing made sense now. His rigid posture made it clear he didn't want to be in this room. He wanted her to follow him back to the kitchen, she wasn't stupid. "Does your father make furniture like you?"

Palmer laughed sharply, taking her off guard. "No." He kept laughing and wiped under his eyes. "He inherited the business when his father died. I had to fight tooth and nail to get a piece of my furniture on the showroom floor. Out of twenty locations. A measly armchair in a corner, mistaken for a waiting area more often than product." Palmer's hands were fisted by his sides. This wasn't an angry man. This was a hurt one. "It doesn't matter," he said.

"Why is he painting manatees? Do you know?"

"It started with a documentary I watched years ago." A hoarse voice similar to Palmer's came from the double doors. Palmer groaned and, for whatever reason, pulled her closer to his side.

"You had to linger, didn't you?" he whispered, his breath warming her neck.

"I like artwork," she whispered back.

"Are you going to introduce me to your friend, son?" A shorter and grayer version of Palmer entered the room.

Palmer tensed. "Dad, this is Lena. Lena, this is my father, Drew."

"Nice to meet you, Lena." Palmer's father smiled, his cheeks dimpling. "We took a family trip when the kids were younger, do you remember, son?"

Palmer grunted some sort of response.

"I wanted to swim with them," his father continued, "but it wasn't allowed back then. Did you know manatees have no natural predators? It's pollution, a depleting food source, and humans that injure and kill manatees."

It seemed the air in the room was getting thinner. "I learned a little bit about manatees last year," Lena said. "My fiancé was on-location in Florida taking photos of the wildlife."

"Did he get the opportunity to swim with them?" Palmer's father said, his tone hopeful.

Lena's injured leg began to tremble. "Maybe. I mean, I—I don't know." Palmer's arm tightened around her. "He's actually... He's no longer—" Lena couldn't put into words the reality she had tried so hard to find peace in. Her escape to the bathroom for a moment to herself had backfired epically.

"Let's find a place to sit," Palmer said. She could barely nod. "We'll revisit memory lane another time, Dad. This way."

Her feet barely touched the ground as Palmer walked her toward a living room. They sat on a couch underneath a row of windows overlooking the front yard.

"Talk to me," Palmer said. His voice was so gentle it could have been butterfly wings kissing her cheeks.

She took a deep breath. "Seth hit his head on a cement pier while snorkeling," she said, looking at nothing and feeling everything. "One of the swimmers helped him out of the water. The back of his head was tender but nothing else. It wasn't until hours later, and in the company of the same group of swimmers, that he complained of a bad headache and passed out. He stopped breathing not long after he was admitted into the hospital."

"Jesus," Palmer said under his breath.

She swallowed hard. "A woman from the group called and told me he died of a brain hemorrhage." The woman had been Seth's guide while he was in Florida and had traveled to Oregon for his funeral. The tears in Eliana's eyes as she introduced herself made Lena wonder if Eliana had developed feelings for Seth or vice versa. The thought had stung, like sitting on a million wasps. She was still sore from it.

"I need to go," she said, struggling to get to her feet.

"Wait, whoa, hold up." Palmer's hand landed on her arm. She pulled away. The fire on her skin was too much to handle. "Is your leg okay? Where are you going?"

She stood, wavering. "My leg constantly hurts, Palmer. What do you think?" she snapped. "I need to go to your brother's shop. There's something in the glove compartment that I'm meant to—never mind. I sound nuts."

"I don't think you're nuts, Lena."

"You don't need to sugarcoat the truth. I know how off-balance I am." She looked down at her broken ankle, stalling. "Seth's accident isn't why I froze earlier, and opening up to you about it now isn't why I have to go. I've become less vigilant. It's like—" She looked around the unfamiliar room, willing herself to keep talking. "I'm a lifeguard overlooking the many bobbing heads of grief, waiting until they're done swimming up there. In my head."

"You're watching over your grief to keep it safe," Palmer said, his voice free of judgment.

She eyed him. Did he really understand something that felt this unnatural or was he putting on an act to help her feel better? "Until it's pruney and ready to get out, yeah. See, I'm totally nuts." A loud rumble from Lena's stomach sounded.

"How about we eat something and then figure out how to get you to my brother's shop?" Palmer motioned to the kitchen entrance. "I know Carrie would be disappointed if you didn't try her famous...everything, really."

She crossed her arms, aware that her expanding aggravation was a classic response to her growing hunger. Palmer's suggestion would distract him from her emotional mess. "This is an agreeable plan," she said.

Palmer looked amused. "It's that easy, huh? All right."

Lena offered him a smile. "Insider tip: I'm easily persuaded by anything food-related."

"Anything," Palmer repeated, scratching his cheek. "So, rocky mountain oysters aren't a problem for you?"

Lena laughed. "I have yet to try that delicacy. And, yes, I know what those are, in case you're wondering."

He grinned. "Noted."

"Do you have dimples like your father?" The question was out before she could stop it. "I mean, it's hard to tell because of your beard, you know, I was just curious." *Ugh, stop!* It didn't matter if Palmer had dimples. It made no difference whatsoever. Shaking her head, she tried to deflect. "Another side-effect of hunger—random and unnecessary questions."

"I've never been asked this question before," Palmer said. He positioned himself in front of her and jutted out his chin. "What do you think?"

This was what she got for asking. Now she had to look at his face, like really *look* at it and imagine him without a beard. She transferred her gaze to the floor and mumbled, "Dimples are an unavoidable genetic thing, right?"

"Who said Drew is my biological father?"

Lena jerked her head upright. "But you have the same eyes and hairline and broad shoulders, come to think of it—"

Palmer poked her arm. "Lena, I'm teasing you."

She glared and poked him back. "You should pick on someone your own size."

"A person's strength does not depend on their size."

"Yes, it does."

"No, it doesn't."

"Yes. It does." Lena put her hands on her hips, staring him down. He mirrored her stance.

"Okay, sure," Palmer said, releasing his arms. "The larger you are, the more you can throw your weight around."

"So, size does matter," she said.

"Well, that's a different conversation entirely." His smile grew. Lena's face was impossibly hot.

"I was talking about mental strength," he continued, "and from what you've shared with me and how you've carried on each day since..." A beat passed. He stared out the window, preoccupied. Was she supposed to say something? "I hope you realize how strong you are. You should never doubt your strength."

Lena shifted her weight to her good leg. She didn't need his validation, and she definitely couldn't handle the inevitable guilt she'd experience for feeling good about it. "My struggles aren't strengths. It's survival, Palmer." Her tone was razor-sharp.

Palmer took a step back.

"Hey! There you two are!" Carrie appeared, wiping her hands on a towel. "You must be Lena," she said, walking further into the room, her arm extended.

"Hi, you're Carrie, right? It's nice to meet you," Lena said, grateful for the interruption. Carrie's handshake was surprisingly firm. This woman meant business or knew business. Either way, this was strength, someone who had their shit together. Surely Palmer recognized the difference.

Carrie beamed at Lena before focusing on Palmer. "Gregor's looking for you," Carrie said to her cousin. "He's poking around your smoker thing. You might want to get out there."

Palmer's face dropped. "Why does he insist on being a pain in the ass?"

"Because he's the youngest and craves attention." Carrie batted her eyes. "Lena, would you mind helping me with a few things in the kitchen?"

"She needs food, too," Palmer said.

Carrie raised a well-manicured eyebrow, then turned to Lena. "How old are you, Lena?"

"I, er—" Lena looked between Palmer and Carrie.

"I imagine you're in the double digits, right?" Carrie said. "Perfectly capable of feeding yourself when hunger strikes."

Lena pushed down an involuntary giggle. "Yes, that's correct."

"Palmer, you heard her. She's capable of taking care of herself. Your brother, on the other hand, is not."

Palmer grunted. He seemed to do that a lot with his family. "I'll meet you outside," he said and stalked out of the room.

"He means well," Carrie said once they were inside the kitchen. She handed Lena a serving bowl of guacamole. "If it ever gets to be too much, don't hesitate to keep him in check. He's a recovering white knight." Carrie picked up a tray of tacos and two bags of tortilla chips and headed to the back of the house.

"I kind of figured. It doesn't bother me," Lena said, even though it did. She had zero tolerance for men covered in armor. Regardless of the intent.

Carrie held the door open with her foot. "Why's that?"

"Good question," Lena said as she walked out into the bright sunshine.

"Lena!" Mark shouted from below. Shay was clinging on to him, the bottom half of her sundress wet.

"Lena!" Palmer said at the same time, dashing around a table and up the deck steps. He removed the bowl from her hands. Gregor hovered at the base of the steps, waving and mouthing, *Oh boy.*

"Lena!" Shay's voice was strained. Lena tried to run down the steps, not thinking, and almost fell. Palmer caught her by the arm. How many times was this man going to be there, saving her from herself.

Shay was red-faced and panting. Mark explained the situation as they walked past the deck steps. "Her water broke, and the contractions are coming fast."

"What can I do?" Lena asked.

Shay stopped and placed both hands on her knees. Once she caught her breath, she locked up. Lena felt tears spring into her eyes. Her sister was clearly in pain, but was nonetheless glowing.

"Call Mom and Dad," Shay said. "Keep them at the house. Mark will message everyone once the baby arrives."

"Whatever you need," Lena said.

Shay smiled bravely. "See you soon, Aunty Lena."

Lena blinked, her eyelashes damp as she gave Shay a brief hug goodbye.

"You okay?" Palmer said after they watched Mark and Shay drive away from the house.

She nodded. Palmer brought out an easy trust in her, but right now, she needed her walls. The cascade of thoughts in her head felt like wet cement, shapeless and impossibly heavy.

She was going to be an aunt to a baby boy or girl. A new life was about to enter this world. A life Seth would never know.

8

Palmer

The tension in Palmer's forehead tightened as he glanced out the windows of Riverside Roasters. It was five o'clock on a Friday, and he was way too caffeinated for the hour. He had spent the last four days sitting at this very table, ignoring his realtor's six unopened voice messages, while he waited for Lena's eight-hour shift to end. Soon they would go on their daily thirty minute walk, while Palmer also figured out his next step. With his business. Numbers, why did it always come down to numbers?

"I refuse to make one more iced coffee today." Lena slumped into the chair across from Palmer. They were at the tail end of a late-June heatwave. "Do you ever drink your coffee cold?"

"I drink caffeine in all forms," Palmer said.

"Spoken like a true American." Her eyes darted to his open notebook, filled with names and addresses. A list of twelve out-of-state reclaimed-lumber dealers stared up at him from the page. Kentucky. Tennessee. The one in Alabama was by far the most enticing.

"You have neat handwriting," she said, stretching her neck to get a closer look. "Precise and blocky. Which is fitting for someone who has to be precise with blocky things."

"Well, thank you," he said, boasting false confidence. Lena's comment made him feel naked. He flipped to a fresh page and handed her the pen. "Show me yours." Warmth spread through his belly. *No.* He would not think of her naked...for very long,

67

anyway.

She hesitated. "My handwriting looks like a third grader struggling to write cursive. It's not pretty."

"Beauty is in the eye of the beholder," he said to a set of rolling eyes. She grabbed the pen and wrote "*Imperfection is perfection*" with sweeping letters and uneven spaces.

"You're right," he said. "It's atrocious."

Lena swept her fiery red hair over one shoulder—he much preferred this natural color—and pursed her lips. "Cold coffee is atrocious." She winked.

He laughed. "You're in a good mood, aside from under-caffeinated patrons."

"Oh, I can't complain. It's part of the job description, and a paycheck. My medical bills haven't come in yet, but that's a worry for another day—" Lena's eyes sparkled. "Douglas is fixed!"

Palmer sat back in his chair. "That's great," he managed to say. "Gregor must have sped up the timeline on those repairs." His arms felt like lead. Lena's ride out of town was ready to go. The only thing keeping her here was her broken ankle.

"He figured out how to fix one of the most expensive parts without having to replace it," she said, bouncing in her seat. "Douglas is back and I have extra change in my pocket and I am no longer an imposition in the house of my adorable and screaming baby nephew." Lena had transformed into a beam of light. "In three weeks, this stupid boot on my leg will be gone, and I'll be back on the road. You've been a huge help, Palmer. I can't thank you enough." She popped up from her seat with surprising agility and wrapped her arms around his shoulders. Palmer held his breath. If he were to inhale her scent, the inevitable reaction in his body would be impossible to control.

She stepped away from him and it was like the Grand Canyon had opened up. Beautiful yet gaping. What the hell was wrong with him?

"Oh! I almost forgot," she said. "Gregor offered to drive Douglas and me to my sister's house. I was going to head over to his shop after my shift."

He sucked in a breath. Her scent lingered, kicking him in the gut. Her name was called from the front.

"I should get back to work," she said.

"I'll be here. We can walk to my brother's shop when you're done."

"You don't have to—"

"I know," he said. "I want to."

She lifted her chin, her eyes a cloudless blue sky. "Okay," she said firmly and hobbled away.

Okay. The word that had broken into a million pieces when said by another woman, had held itself together when spoken by Lena. It was raw and genuine and somehow served as a reminder: Like Jolie, Lena would soon be swept away, this time by the open road.

Palmer picked up his pen. Lena's handwriting stared up at him. *Perfectly imperfect.* Lena was a perfect balance to an imperfect life. An idea began to take root inside his head—one that was so unorthodox, he wondered if it was meant to grow there at all. Surely, he couldn't ask to join her on the remainder of her trip so he could scout lumber suppliers. The question would sound as absurd as it felt in his head. He flipped to a fresh page in his notebook. Lena had her plan in place, and he would, too. Once he shifted his focus away from Lena's troubles and called these suppliers.

They walked up the hill in silence as the outline of Gregor's shop loomed in the distance. Lena's earlier excitement had been replaced with intermittent sighing.

"Did you get a chance to look in the glove compartment yet?" Palmer asked, remembering their conversation from a week ago.

"No," she said. Car horns honked up ahead, and the exhaust of a motorcycle roared.

"Why not? It's pretty important to you, right?"

"It is." They stopped at an intersection. The fading sunlight enhanced the headlights of oncoming cars. Palmer squinted while Lena adjusted the backpack on her shoulders. He had offered to carry it for her earlier and was shot down immediately.

"So, why the delay?" he asked. He might as well be pulling teeth. What had happened between their handwriting hug and the end of Lena's shift to cause such a change? Unless—had she picked up on what he was thinking earlier? He wasn't *that* transparent with his feelings. Right?

"I'm a good listener." He sounded clumsy. Without realizing it, Lena had put into question the strength of his own intuition.

The stoplight changed and they walked into the street. Palmer's hand hovered at the small of her back before he pulled it away.

"I was reminded today that good news doesn't exist anymore," she said once they reached the sidewalk. "Ever since Seth's death, any forward progress has come with a catch, and I'm left to deal with yet another problem. Douglas is fixed? Great. Here's another problem for you, Lena." She heaved out a long sigh. "God. I could use a break. You know? A break from having to deal with everything all the time on my own. I'm just really fucking over it." Lena's voice echoed off the brick buildings lining the street. A man and woman up ahead turned to look at them. Lena's mouth pinched into a straight line.

"What's the catch today?" Palmer asked. He wasn't concerned with her outburst. Lena seemed like someone who needed to uncage her emotions more often.

"I don't want to talk about it." Lena huffed as her cast thumped against the concrete. They reached the top of the hill. Gregor's shop was to the left. A small park surrounded by a chain-link fence was on the right.

"Let's go over here for a second." Palmer motioned toward the park. Her gaze locked on the metal slide jutting out of the playground rocket ship. Palmer had gotten stuck at the top of the rocket ship when he was six years old and his grandma had climbed up to rescue him. He had avoided heights ever since but learned an easy lesson that day; helping those you love sometimes meant squeezing into spaces not built for you.

"There's no way I'm sliding down that ancient-looking contraption," Lena said.

"What if I did, and you got to watch?" He would face his childhood fears and do it for her.

A car zoomed by. "All right." Lena pivoted toward the playground. "If you're serious, then prove it."

"Wait, hold up," Palmer said. "Before I embarrass myself in front of you, because I will get stuck in that thing, tell me, please, what happened?"

Lena's shoulders slumped. "How long have we known each other?"

He wasn't used to answers being questions. That was his own tactic. "A month, maybe a little less. I haven't really thought about it." That was a lie. He had thought about it and wondered if she felt the same pull to him—natural yet uncontrollable.

"We can both agree it hasn't been very long," she said. "I know you're a helper, someone who cares and goes out of his way to be there for others. I would hate for you to waste your time on this random mess of a woman who's leaving town soon." She pointed a finger to her chest— "Me. I'm the woman."

"Lena." He wanted to shake her. *You deserve the care!*

"Sorry," she said. "My leg is throbbing."

Palmer swallowed back all the questions hot on his tongue: *Is it normal for your leg to throb? Are you taking care of yourself? Why are you so upset? Don't you trust me enough to tell me?* Instead he said, "You don't need to apologize. I'll make a fool of myself another day. Let's get you to Douglas."

Palmer helped Mark clear the remaining dishes from the dining room table while Shay, Lena, and their parents sat in the other room, cooing over the baby in Lena's arms. It was the least he could do after crashing their family dinner.

Gregor had been up to his elbows in car grease when they'd arrived at the shop earlier. Lena insisted she could come back another day, but Palmer offered a more logical solution, and, with a bit of persuasion, Gregor agreed Palmer should drive the van to Mark and Shay's house. Because logical plans weren't worth arguing over. A fact his father seemed incapable of accepting. Like the very reasonable plan Palmer had suggested last night over another home cooked meal with his parents.

"You all right, man? You look like you want to punch something," Mark said as he wiped his hands on a towel.

"I might need to visit the gym's punching bag soon," Palmer said, unclenching his jaw.

"Sure, that could help. Or you could tell me what's bugging you."

As a general rule, Palmer avoided complaining. He would rather focus his energy on solutions. These issues, however, were lingering. "I have nowhere to build furniture, my parents' garage is not an option, which makes no sense to me, but whatever. The local reclaimed-wood suppliers are cleaned out, and I'm stalling on moving forward with the downtown space because I...I don't want to be in this town anymore." Palmer shut his mouth. He didn't need to shove his problems onto a new father who had bigger concerns than a shortage of space and barn wood.

"Then go," Mark said, like all Palmer had to do was open a door.

"You really think I can pick up and leave just like that? What about my family and their debt? What about Husky's and the possibility of keeping the family business alive? What about—"

"What about what you want?" Mark said. "Your father declared bankruptcy and is shutting down the business. With that comes relief from the crippling debt he may or may not have. You don't know. The man hasn't been totally forthcoming with his finances, why would he start now?"

"Exactly. There might be something I can do to keep Husky's—"

"I've never known you separately from your family or the business," Mark said, his lawyer voice turned on now. "You're steadfast in your loyalty and committed to the plan your family put in place. That was commendable then, but it's no longer your reality. You have endless possibilities, Palmer. If you just dream for a second."

Mark's name was called from the other room. He looked at Palmer, his expression heavy, then walked out of the kitchen. Mark's truth bombs had left a high-pitched ringing in Palmer's ears.

"It's your turn," Lena said from the arched entryway. She walked up to him with the sleeping baby in her arms. His earlier conversation with Mark evaporated. "I've never done this before."

"It's okay." She moved the baby closer to him. He reached out instinctively and took the new human into his arms. Hugo's skin felt like a piece of wood Palmer would have spent hours sanding.

Lena leaned into him. "It's not so bad, is it?"

Palmer was about to agree when the baby's eyes popped open and a sound much too loud for such a small body shot out of his lungs. Shay materialized from the other room.

"I got him," she said, as she took her son from Palmer. "That's his *I'm awake and fucking hungry*, cry." She cringed. "I just said fuck, didn't I? Oh fuck. I said it again."

"He won't remember," Lena said with gentle reassurance. "Do you need anything?"

Shay laughed hysterically while Hugo continued to wail. Lena shot Palmer a worried look.

Shay sobered, then pointed between the two of them. "You two would make cute babies." She nodded once and walked out of the kitchen.

Lena opened and closed her mouth. "Did that just happen?"

"Uh, yeah. I think so," he said, his forehead beading with

sweat. Babies in general made him nervous but the thought of making a baby with Lena was downright disastrous to his nerves.

A pinkish hue colored Lena's cheeks. "Shay is clearly very sleep-deprived," she said and shook her head as if to clear away the comment. "I have something to tell you. Not here, though. Will you come with me?" Her voice was tentative, as if she worried he might say no.

"Lead the way," he said with a sweep of his arms.

Palmer opened the passenger door to the scent of sun-kissed leather and sunk into the cushioned bucket seat. Earlier, when he sat behind the steering wheel, he'd been surprised at how well he fit, considering his height. The two-minute drive had been fun, and Lena was right: Sitting over the front axle brought the road straight into his face. Lena sat in the driver's seat now with her hands gripping the steering wheel.

"Seth's father hired a driver to take Douglas the rest of the way to Florida. He'll be here the day after tomorrow," she said.

It took Palmer a second to catch up. "Why would he do that?" He had no idea if Lena had a good relationship with her fiancé's parents. She rarely talked about them.

"Because," she said, sounding like she hadn't slept in days. "It's his van, and it's fixed, and I'm not, and he probably thinks he's doing me a favor, relieving me of the obligation. But, he's not. It's actually breaking my—" Her voice cracked, her eyelids red-rimmed. "It hurts."

"He can't wait three weeks until it's safe for you to drive long distances again?" Palmer said, a burn in his lungs. He didn't like seeing her upset. Sure, it could be an altruistic decision, like Lena suggested. Sitting in a car for hours on end after breaking a bone couldn't be enjoyable. But it seemed like a decision made by someone who didn't really understand Lena.

"I guess not," she said. A tin-can plinking sounded from over-head. Over and over.

"Raindrops on the rooftop," he said, smiling.

She inhaled and closed her eyes. "Just stop and listen."

The sound intensified. Sheets of rain blurred the outside view.

"I'll drive Douglas," Palmer said before he could think it through any further. His heartbeat sped up.

Lena's eyes snapped open. Her hands dropped to the bottom of the steering wheel. "Why?"

Because the idea had been tumbling around in his brain all day. If he didn't say something, the thought would turn into a nuisance. He picked at the hem of his shirt. "That notebook I had earlier? There's a list I put together of a bunch of re-claimed-wood suppliers. Twelve in total."

"Twelve? Wow! I thought you said the locals were cleaned out." Lena turned in the seat, her expression soft and hopeful. "This solves a big problem for you, right?"

It was a big problem solved. Except another one had taken its place and he had no idea what to do with it. "Most of them are located south, in states you'd have to drive through to get to Florida. I was thinking of visiting a few."

She nodded. "So you drive Douglas and hit up some of these locations on the way, got it." Her expression hardened. "What happens when you find a supplier you want to buy from?"

"I rent a box truck once Douglas is returned and load it up on the way back," he said, resisting the urge to touch her as a way of reassurance.

It wasn't a complicated plan, logistically. The risk of developing feelings for Lena during their time together did complicate things. But who was he kidding? That risk was inevitable; wasn't it happening already? He would just have to remind himself of his distaste for heights. Maybe that would stop him from climbing up those growing emotions. There was no space for him to squeeze into anyway, except inside her van as a friend. Her situation alone made that a glaring reality.

"So, what do you think?" he asked.

"I think"—she pointed to the glove compartment in front of

him—"I'd like you to press that button for me. Please."

The rain overhead drowned out most of Lena's voice, but Palmer heard her loud and clear. She had mentioned the glove compartment at his pool party while opening up to him in a disarming way. Now was no different. She was asking him to release an unknown. To reveal what she was so eager to know. He leaned forward and pushed the button. The caramel leather door fell open. It was dark inside and appeared empty, except there was something in there, slender and folded.

Palmer reached in and pulled out a brochure. *SWIM WITH US at Tampatee* was typed in bold across the top. Underneath the lettering was a picture of a plump manatee and her calf. A name—Eliana—and a phone number were handwritten at the very bottom.

He handed the brochure to Lena. Her fingers grasped around it slowly, her arm suspended in the air as if she'd forgotten how to move. She opened her mouth before turning away. Her hair blanketed the side of her face. A tear splashed onto the word *US*. Then her voice rang out.

"Is this real, or is this a dream?"

Palmer twisted in his seat to get a better view of her. He couldn't be sure if what she said was a joke. "You're not dreaming, Lena. This is real."

He watched her work the pad of her index finger over the side of the brochure as if she wanted the paper to cut her. Up and down, her finger worked the edge. He didn't know what to do or say. This woman, whom he barely knew, needed to be whomever she chose in this moment. He allowed the helplessness to rush through him and waited as she processed her thoughts.

L ena traced the delicate handwriting with her index finger. *Eliana.* It was the name of the person who had attended Seth's funeral, the swimmer who called after the accident, the woman who last saw Seth before he left this earth.

A shiver coursed through her as her vision blurred. Palmer touched her arm. Startled, Lena looked up.

"Are you all right?" His eyes were dark and filled with concern. The pouring rain made it difficult to hear him. That, or her heart pounding in her eardrums.

"I don't know." She wiped her tears off the brochure with her shirt, the scent of stale coffee lifting from the scratchy fabric. She had cried in front of all sorts of people since Seth's death. It shouldn't matter if Palmer witnessed a rogue tear. Still, one was too many to let get away.

Two manatees stared up at her from a vibrant floor of green seagrass. The color contrast on the brochure seemed to enhance their potato-like shape. The longer she stared at the smiling manatees, the more her throat tightened. Why had Seth kept this brochure in Douglas and not in his suitcase? It didn't make sense.

"Is it a coincidence if something keeps happening?" she said, turning the brochure over and over in her hands. The box in her dream, the etching on the window at the downtown shop, the painting at Palmer's house, and now this. There was no logical reason why this was happening.

"That sounds more like a pattern," he said.

Lena bit her bottom lip. "Even if it seems random?"

"Is it random if it keeps happening, though?" Palmer said. "Patterns help us organize thoughts and establish order in our lives. Especially when life's chaotic."

"Chaotic," she laughed. "The only signal I can tune into lately." She jiggled her uninjured leg as her body buzzed. It was as if she were at the starting line of a race, waiting for a gun to shoot off. She wanted to run hard and fast. Run away from the pressure of grief, the memories of Seth, the smell of Palmer, and a pungent reality of a life stuck in reverse.

"Maybe this is a sign to do something about it," Palmer said.

Lena felt his gaze on her. The sky outside grew darker as the wind rocked the van on its wheels.

"You're not supposed to make sense of the nonsensical, Palmer." She leaned over and shoved the brochure into the glove compartment. How could she possibly say *I think I'm supposed to find the place with the manatees because I keep seeing them, even in my dreams* without raising concern? Palmer would certainly retract his offer.

"Were you serious before?" she asked. "About driving Douglas to Florida?"

Palmer looked out the passenger window, then turned and aligned his eyes with hers. She felt a flash in her stomach as lightning streaked across the sky. Palmer had a face meant to be looked at.

"Are you saying no or yes?" he said.

Lena wrapped her arms around the electricity in her stomach. Palmer, confident as he was, had volleyed the topic back into her court like a seasoned pro.

"This van isn't the most spacious," she said, "and we'll be on the road for hours driving and sitting. Think about it, Palmer." Lena caught the fire in his eyes. His name burned the tip of her tongue, too. "We spend our time together walking along the river, avoiding goose poop and ducking away from those damn red-winged blackbirds." She trailed off, unable to voice her most significant concern. That she would have to share the second half of Seth's cross-country dream with another man.

"Honestly, Lena, the hours in my day go by slower while I wait to walk a measly thirty minutes with someone who—" Palmer leaned back in his seat. She saw his Adam's apple bob. "Who refuses to accept help in any form."

The hair on her arms stood up as a bolt of lightning lit up the sky again. Their time together *was* too short, and the hours leading up to seeing him *were* too long. But she didn't have the luxury to daydream about Palmer's handsome face and broad shoulders. Her obligation was to Douglas and to Seth's dream. She couldn't allow herself to feel anything else.

"I don't refuse help," she said. "I make sure all options are considered before bringing someone else into my chaos." A crack of thunder sounded directly overhead. She flinched. Lena had learned that the less she relied on other people, the more she controlled her mess. But control and acceptance were two totally different things, and she had yet to accept the clutter in her mind.

She glanced at Palmer with his hands folded in his lap. He was a patient man. At least, she hoped that was the reason for his silence and not a manipulative tactic to keep her talking.

"I was supposed to take this trip with Seth." Lena placed her hands on the steering wheel to steady their tremor. Palmer shifted in his seat but remained quiet.

"I spent weeks researching destinations: national parks, quirky pit stops, motels, and restaurants. Not to mention the museums and zoos and landmarks and...I went a little crazy." Lena's grip tightened. She had been convinced that planning a perfect trip together was the way out of her loneliness. "I printed everything I could find and put it all in a binder. Seth found a sticker that looked like Douglas with a mountain backdrop and put it on the cover." Lena swallowed. "We were supposed to leave in May, a few days after Seth returned from a four-month work trip in Arizona. But then he got a call for a job in Florida. He couldn't turn it down. So we delayed the trip for another month. I wanted to support him. What was another month alone, right? I just...couldn't." Lena released her grip on the steering wheel and rolled back her shoulders. The last part Palmer had already heard, the first night they met. *I broke off my engagement two days before my fiancé died in a freak accident.*

"I was lost in my loneliness, which pushed Seth away, and now he's gone forever." She took a deep breath before turning to look at Palmer. His expression was soft. "So, driving with me to Florida comes with a lot of baggage. I may cry. I may scream. I may need a random hug. I may not talk for miles on end. I may be a lot, is what I'm saying."

"I'm sorry, Lena."

"It is what it is," Lena said, even though she hated that saying. It was an oversimplified statement, like someone saying "I am who I am." There was so much more to it, but people, being who they were, didn't tend to listen very well. Except, maybe, the man sitting in the passenger seat of Douglas.

Palmer tilted his head slightly. The rain had returned to a light plinking on the roof. "You be who you need to be, Lena. I'm simply a second pair of feet helping you on your journey."

"You're more than feet, I would think—"

Palmer waved his hand. "You know what I mean. And I'll try not to have a heart attack from witnessing the miracle of you accepting my help." Palmer grinned.

"Well, I cannot be responsible for an attack on your heart," Lena said to Palmer's growing smile. It was difficult for her to not respond with a smile of her own. "So, you're witnessing the allowance of help rather than the acceptance of it."

"You say to-may-toh, I say to-mah-toh," Palmer said and glanced out the windshield. The storm had passed. He reached for the door handle. "We'll leave tomorrow then?"

Lena sat up straight. *Tomorrow?* Was her time on the road supposed to begin again? It seemed too soon, even though she hadn't planned on staying this long. So, what other choice did she have? It was a pace she would have to be okay with. "Let me make a call," she said.

Lena stood outside the van the next day. A warm breeze lifted the scent of river fish while she stared up at the brilliant blue sky. July's persistent heat was right around the corner.

The day before, after Palmer left, Lena had sent a text message to Seth's dad, informing him she would drive Douglas with the help of a friend. After a few minutes, during which she was certain Mr. Cruz would call her to discuss the matter in more detail, he responded with an "okay, kiddo" and a thumbs-up emoji. No follow-up questions whatsoever. He trusted her, it seemed. Which had left her with a mix of relief and anxiety.

"Earth to Lena," Palmer said. She snapped her gaze to his face. He held out another paper grocery bag. Seth's parents had no idea the friend helping her drive Douglas was a tall man named Palmer. It shouldn't matter. At least, that's what she kept telling herself every time Palmer's fingers grazed hers as he handed her supplies.

Lena peered inside the paper bag before setting it down on the van's floor. Somehow Shay had found time to rush out and purchase microwave popcorn for a van that didn't have a microwave.

Palmer placed another bag on the vinyl floor. This one had Twizzlers in it.

"I sent Mark out last night to get diapers," Shay said as she approached the van. "I asked him to get you a few things, too."

Lena looked at the baby resting in Shay's arms, his tiny fists flexing as he slept. Hugo sure was adorable when he wasn't awake and crying.

"Oh, good, it wasn't you who went shopping," Lena said. Shay gave her a blank stare, like she was sleeping with her eyes open. "Tell Mark thank you. It's very much appreciated, it's just"—Lena pulled out a family-size bag of Twizzlers—"he shopped like he was drunk."

"Mark's not drunk. He's sleep-deprived," Shay said. She gazed down at Hugo with glazed-over happy eyes. Her sister and Mark were drunk, all right, on new baby love.

Palmer snatched the bag from Lena's hands and tore it open. He pulled three ropes out with the agility of a man who regularly ate processed sugar.

"Twizzlers are the greatest of all time. Hands down the best food to keep you focused," Palmer said, offering one to Lena. She accepted the candy and pulled a bite off with her teeth, then chewed. And chewed.

"I forgot how much they make you work for them," Lena said.

Palmer gave her a chewy grin. "See? It takes focus." He reached into his shorts pocket and pulled out his phone. His smile faltered.

"I gotta take this," he said and placed the phone to his ear. Lena watched his shoulders slump as he walked down the driveway toward the street.

"Sweetheart!" Her mom stood on the wrap around porch a few feet away. She was holding a stack of white cotton towels. "Do you have enough towels?"

Lena swallowed the rest of her candy to respond but caught Shay mouthing something in her direction. Shay jerked her head toward the van's sliding door.

"Uh, let me check, Mom. Hold on," Lena said. She ducked inside the van behind Shay.

"Mom's on four cups of coffee and is in rare form," Shay said in a low voice. "She won't say this to you, Lena, but she's worried about you leaving." The baby grunted as if to agree.

"Please don't tell me it's because Palmer is helping me," Lena whispered back. Palmer's laughter shot out in the distance.

"No. Mark vouched for Palmer last night when Dad brought up his concerns. They were valid, Lena. Don't give me that look." Shay shifted the baby in her arms and blew away a strand of hair from her eyes. "Mom is worried about you seeing Seth's parents.

She isn't sure how they will receive you since you called off the engagement."

Lena took a deep breath. "Yeah. I know. I barely spoke to them at the funeral, too. From what I remember." Her memory was splintered from the emotional weight of that day.

"Do they know you're showing up with another man in Douglas's driver's seat?"

"Yes. Kind of." Lena swallowed hard. A chunk of Twizzler must have lodged somewhere inside her throat. "I sent a text yesterday and said I found someone to help me drive Douglas."

Shay pressed her lips together. Palmer's voice drifted into the van. It sounded like his call was wrapping up. Lena maneuvered around the bags on the van's floor and reached over the passenger seat. The glove compartment opened with a startling squeak. She took out the brochure.

"For all I know"—Lena lifted the brochure for Shay to see—"Seth had already moved on."

Shay squinted. "Who's Eliana?"

Lena placed the brochure back in the glove compartment and closed the door. "That's what I plan on asking Seth's parents when I see them."

The baby began to fuss. Shay bounced him lightly in her arms. "It's probably nothing, Lena. Why stir up something they might not know anything about?"

"She was at his funeral, Shay. Remember?" The one detail Lena would never forget. "Seth's parents talked to a woman with a deep tan and nose ring."

Shay's eyes widened with recognition. "Yes, I remember now," Shay said. "I didn't think much of it then. I thought she was a cousin or something. They did seem to know each other pretty well."

Lena nodded. "She was the one who called me when Seth went to the hospital. And, for whatever reason, that damn brochure with her name written on it, with those manatees on the cover, was left in Douglas for me to find. So, no, I don't care if his parents might get upset that a friend of mine, who happens to be male, is helping me drive Douglas. I want answers." Lena slumped against the opening of the sliding door.

After a few moments of quiet, Shay said, "Can I give you one piece of unsolicited advice?" Lena opened her mouth to say something but couldn't. By simply talking to her sister, Lena revealed things inside herself she didn't realize existed. But that's what sisters were for, right? To hold up a mirror with an entirely different reflection.

"I think I would like that," Lena said.

"It might be two pieces of advice," Shay amended. Lena smiled. Sisters were also known to take an inch and then take a little more. "Try to know the questions you want the answers to, like really know them, inside and out, before you ask."

Lena's gut clenched. She wasn't certain the one question she had avoided since Seth's passing would ever find an answer.

Would you have fought harder if I hadn't broken your heart? How will you ever forgive me?

Lena shook her head. Two unanswered questions.

Maybe she wouldn't ask anything at all. Maybe she would drop Douglas off at Seth's parents' house, tuck the keys under the driver's side floor mat, and disappear to a small beach town for an undisclosed amount of time. Or travel up the Atlantic coastline while purposely forgetting to charge her phone. Or hike part of the Appalachian Trail where cell service was nonexistent. Wait. Maybe not that; she still had a broken ankle.

"And second," Shay said. "You do need more towels."

"Oh, shoot!" Lena crawled out of the van as a gust of wind blew her hair every which way. Gray clouds covered the once clear sky.

Lena spotted her mom still on the porch. She was hugging the towels to her chest as she looked up at Palmer. Her mom smiled at him, and was that...a giggle?

Lena clambered up the porch stairs. Palmer offered his hand on the second to last step up.

"Thanks," Lena said. Palmer squeezed her hand before letting go. Heat crept up her arm and bloomed across her chest. It *was* warmer on the porch.

"Palmer was just telling me about his furniture-making business and the shortage of local lumber," Lena's mom said. "But you found a distributor in Tennessee, was it?"

"Yeah, and a few more along the way to Florida. It actually works out really well. I'm just glad Lena agreed to me helping her with Douglas." Palmer's left eye squinted in her direction. Or perhaps that was a wink. Based on the look Lena's mom just gave her, it was most likely a wink from Palmer.

"She was stubborn even before she was born. And refused to do things the normal way, isn't that right, dear?"

"Mom," Lena groaned. "You promised we would only relive my birth story once a year. On my birthday. Which has already happened."

Lena heard Palmer start to say something.

"Anyway, Mom! We do need those towels. Thank you so much!" Lena grabbed the stack from her mom and turned to face the stairs. She hadn't meant to be rude. It was just that... If Palmer asked to hear more about her childhood, Lena wouldn't be able to stop herself from sharing everything, and she really did not need her mother to be witness to that fact. She heard Palmer and her mom exchange polite goodbyes as she made her way down the steps.

Once Lena's boot hit the driveway with its trademark thump, her mom asked from above, "Will you be staying for lunch?"

"I'm not sure," Lena said.

"Thank you for offering, Mrs. Sullivan," Palmer said once he reached the bottom of the steps. Lena stared at him. Why was he answering her mom? She wasn't someone who allowed a man to speak for her when she was perfectly capable of speaking for herself. Was this the cost for accepting his help?

"But my brother just called and wants to check Douglas one last time before we leave. Is it too much to ask if we have it to go?" Palmer said to her mom. He looked at Lena with a serious expression. Something was wrong. His smile looked forced, and his voice sounded strange. Once her mom disappeared into the house, Palmer guided Lena toward Douglas.

"Gregor's on high alert. My parents are pissed I'm leaving. My father, in particular, wants all of my equipment out of his garage today. Gregor said he's on a rampage." Palmer stopped talking as Shay passed by, Hugo wailing in her arms. Shay gave them a helpless smile and kept on pace toward the house. Another gust of wind swirled around them and billowed up Lena's shirt, the humidity sticky on her skin.

Once Shay was out of earshot, Lena asked why. Palmer ran a hand through his hair. "It makes absolutely no sense. But that's my father for you. And I'm sure my mom is over at the house trying to keep the peace which means she's searching for ways to keep me here too. That's where I've always been for them, right?" Palmer's face had turned redder with every word he whisper-shouted to her. He placed his hands on the top of the van's roof and took a steadying breath.

Lena's head was spinning. Had he offered her too much of his time without realizing it? Would his family's disapproval change his mind? Was he backing out? A stickiness began to ooze inside her and she didn't like it. Against her better judgment, she had accepted Palmer's help, and now it might not even happen.

She gathered herself. Now was as good a time as any to practice being curious instead of anxious.

"They know it's a trip you need to take for your business, right?"

"It doesn't matter." Palmer's fingers drummed the top of the roof. "My parents assume I won't ever fucking go anywhere. Well, they're in for a big surprise. 'Cause I'm leaving with you." He pushed away from the van and looked at her.

Lena searched his face for signs of doubt. "Are you sure?"

"I've never been more sure of anything in my life." Palmer fixed her with a look she had seen before. The same look Seth had given her when he proposed.

10

Palmer

L ena's face clouded over like the sky overhead. Palmer suddenly wanted to take back what he said, which wasn't like him. Sure, he was heightened from his conversation with Gregor. And sure, his emotions spoke a truth he didn't quite understand, but he meant what he said. He had never been more sure of anything in his life.

"Maybe I just let this guy drive Douglas," Lena said. "Save you the trouble. I mean, your parents are freaking out and Gregor is smuggling your equipment out of their garage." Lena's gaze darted around as if she was looking for an emergency exit. "This is too much."

How quickly the solid ground underneath his feet began to sink. He was used to being too much in the height department, but not in other aspects of his life.

"Gregor owes me a lifetime of favors. And he would rather you and I drive Douglas to Florida than someone who was hired." Palmer hadn't meant to blurt out the last part. He was still trying to wrap his brain around...everything.

Earlier, while on the phone with Gregor, his brother had expressed the same frustration boiling inside Palmer.

"I didn't spend all that time fixing Lena's van so some other jackal could drive it," Gregor had said. "And I don't care whose name is on the title. As far as I'm concerned, that's her van. She just hasn't realized it yet. You can help her drive the damn thing, sure, but help her realize that van is meant to be hers."

Palmer had laughed. "What are you, a car-connection psychic or something?"

"I've been around a lot of vehicles and their owners. I know things," Gregor said in a flat tone. Palmer thanked Gregor for storing his equipment temporarily at the auto shop and hung up the phone. Now all that was left was to get on the road before his parents tracked him down and tried to physically stop him. At this point, he wouldn't put it past them.

"Why should it matter to your brother who drives Douglas?" Lena said suspiciously, as if she had picked up on his memory.

Her question seemed obtuse to him. Was Lena purposely overlooking her attachment to the old van? "You're telling me you came all this way just to hand over the second half of your journey to some stranger?"

"Why do you always answer questions with questions?" She had a point and, oddly enough, he was encouraged by being called out. Lena wasn't the sole reason he wanted to leave town and her face suggested he needed to diffuse the situation. He could fix this.

"Gregor repaired your van so you could bring it to Florida. You. Not some random hired hand. That's why it matters to him. Besides, me leaving town to help you is helping me, too. You know I need the lumber." He nodded once. If Lena felt he was leaving solely because of her, surely his plans would crush any implied pressure.

"I don't know, Palmer. I've encountered my fair share of upset family members. It takes a lot of time to repair the bridges you damage by leaving." The front door of the house banged open.

"Here we are. Two bags to-go, as requested." Lena's mom trotted down the porch steps and handed Palmer the bags. They were heavy and smelled like melted cheese and pickles.

"Now, promise me, Lena," her mom said, "don't you disappear on us. You're an aunt now." Lena's mom glanced at Palmer, her smile resembling Lena's, then lowered her voice. "Shay and Mark won't say this to you two, so I will. They've relied on both of you heavily since the baby was born. Just check in often, is all I'm saying."

"Of course, we'll set alarms if needed," Palmer said without thinking again. What was wrong with him today? Oh, right. He was essentially running away from home for the first time.

Lena gave him an odd look. He didn't blame her.

"Well, that's a relief," Lena's mom said. "I'm glad Lena has someone to remind her and to keep her safe."

Lena groaned. "I did get myself here, Mom, in one piece, as you like to say."

"Yes, dear. But it eases a mother's mind to know a respectable man is traveling with you now. And maybe Palmer can play mediator when you see Mr. and Mrs. Cruz, too."

"I'm perfectly capable of keeping myself *safe* and talking to Seth's parents." Lena's face had turned into stone. The wind rushed in, bending the tree branches overhead. A few green leaves fell onto the driveway. If there was a storm incoming, they would have to leave as soon as possible.

"We better get going, Lena," Palmer said. "Gregor is waiting to check on Douglas, remember?" He could prevent any unnecessary drama from cropping up between these two strong-willed women. The apple didn't fall from the tree, as they say. God, he hoped that comparison wasn't made about him and his own father. All the more reason to put space between him and his family right now.

After a series of goodbyes, which left Lena on the brink of tears, they were on their way to Gregor's shop. Palmer adjusted the rearview mirror as he backed out of the driveway. Lena dug into the to-go bag and groaned as she took a bite of the grilled cheese sandwich. He couldn't blame her eagerness, the smell alone was mouth-watering. Palmer glanced over from the driver's seat. The sandwich was nearly gone already.

"When was the last time you ate?" he asked. He should have reminded her to sit down and have one of the donuts he brought this morning. Not that she would have listened to him.

"I'm not telling you because I know you won't like the answer," she said around her sandwich. He wanted to voice his disapproval but kept his mouth shut. Lena didn't need a lecture.

Gregor was standing outside his shop when Palmer pulled in. There was a flatbed trailer off to the side of the double garage doors with what appeared to be Palmer's table saw. And nothing else.

"I tried to move fast, but the old man is quick. Or clever. Or has years of shady business behind him." Gregor scuffed his boot against the cracked pavement. "I don't know where the rest of your stuff is, man. I'm sorry."

"I appreciate you trying, bro," Palmer said evenly. If he allowed his gut to speak for him, it would result in an unpleasant outburst.

"Are you saying Palmer's equipment is being held hostage?" Lena said. "Why would your father do that!" Her voice echoed off the steel siding of the auto shop.

Palmer tried to keep his face neutral, but deep down, he wanted to grin wickedly. Any grievance he had with his father usually went unacknowledged. To hear someone voice what he'd buried for so many years was...nothing short of cathartic.

"I don't waste my time trying to understand my bloodline anymore," Gregor said. "But it's not right."

Lena crossed her arms. Fat raindrops began to fall from the sky. "Gregor, please, be the logical one and tell Palmer to stay here. He's not listening to me." Lena's face was heavy with concern.

His brother shook his head. "No can do, pretty lady. I'm afraid the secret rule us mechanics abide by has taken effect."

Lena's eyes narrowed at Gregor. "That makes absolutely no sense."

"That's the point." His brother placed a hand on Lena's shoulder. Palmer likewise squinted at his brother. "You're in good hands, Lena. I'll do a quick once-over on Douglas and you two will be on your way."

Palmer held up the keys and jingled them. His brother removed his hand from Lena's shoulder.

"You guys can chill upstairs. Probably best to get out of this incoming rain," Gregor said. Lena huffed in the background as he hopped into the van and started the engine. He popped his head out the window, his smile wide and unfazed by Lena's obvious discomfort. "Love that sound."

Once in Gregor's apartment, Palmer offered Lena a drink, which she refused immediately. He was going to suggest something to calm her nerves, like whiskey, but realized he didn't know if she drank alcohol.

Lena settled onto the edge of Gregor's slate gray couch and looked around. The couch was one of those modern contraptions, with a low back and stiff cushions. It had been on the showroom floor for two years before it was handed off to Gregor. Palmer had pleaded with his father to fill the empty space with one of his reclaimed pieces, but to no avail. He should have stopped asking after that first rejection. But hope certainly had a way of clouding observation, didn't it?

Palmer released his fisted hands and sat down next to Lena. The floor was more comfortable than this couch.

"Do you like whiskey?" he asked after a long stretch of silence.

She shifted her hair over her shoulder. "That's a random question," she said. He didn't think so, but her mind was probably somewhere else, based on her rigid posture and pinched mouth. "I used to be a wine drinker but switched to whiskey a few years ago. Seth and I visited a women-owned distillery in Portland. Which was cool to see, females taking up space in a male-dominated industry. The whiskey wasn't bad either, and, well, I became an appreciator of it."

"Gregor has a bottle from a Chicago distillery if you want to try something local—" Palmer stopped talking.

Lena placed her forehead into her hands as her hair fell forward. A wavy sheet of auburn covered her face. He stilled as a flash of heated embarrassment spread through him. His suggestion wasn't that out of line, was it?

Oh, shit.

Lena could have stopped drinking whiskey if it was linked to Seth. Which meant he had just inserted his foot into his mouth.

"Sorry, I didn't mean to bring up feelings or, you know, st-stuff unwanted," he said with a rare stutter. What was wrong with him? He was usually more confident when talking to mysterious women with self-proclaimed baggage.

"I'm not that fragile." Lena shrugged. "This is being human, right? People grieve, people break bones, and people heal. Eventually." She took in a breath and turned to Palmer. "I'm not sure you should be the one driving Douglas." Her voice held a gentle tone. It was beyond unusual for someone to continue to fight against his help.

"Bringing Douglas to Seth's parents was complicated enough when it was just me involved. Then you offered to drive, and I don't know. It feels like you're looking down on me as if I'm on the floor, unable to get up. And, I mean, you're likely always looking down on others, given your height, but—" Lena glanced at the ceiling and then back to him. Even in the dimly lit room, her eyes were an incredible crystal blue color. "I wanted you to walk alongside me, like you have been quite literally, and support me with my problems, not take them on as your own. But that's our conditioning, I guess. You're the fixer, and I'm the refuser." She sat back with a long exhale.

Palmer's entire body prickled as if a million fire ants had climbed onto him, and Lena's words were the burning itch of awareness. All this time, he thought he was the intuitive one that everyone relied on. Had it all been an act of conditioned behavior? When someone was struggling—his family, or friends, an old lady crossing the street, a cat stuck up in a tree, you name it—he took on their problems as his own. And where had that left him? He rarely veered off a straight and narrow path or even dared to dream of one that had yet to exist. He was surrounded by walls of obligation.

With a sinking feeling, he gripped the back of his neck. "Now I'm wondering how many toes I've stepped on by being helpful."

"I doubt it's that many. Remember, this is coming from me, someone who doesn't like help," she said. "And we just so happen to be meeting from opposite ends of the spectrum on this god-awful couch." Lena stood up like he imagined the Tin Man would, jerky with audible creaks. He fought the urge to reach for her arm and offer her something, anything, to help ease her pain. Instead, he pushed off the couch and switched the corner lamp on. A golden hue illuminated the dark room.

Lena looked everywhere but at him. "I could use a whiskey," she said and moved into the kitchen.

It took him a second to catch up. "You got it," he said and trotted after her, relieved to see her pull a stool out from underneath the breakfast bar and sit down. He reached into the cabinet above Gregor's refrigerator and pulled out the bottle he had brought over a few weeks ago.

Palmer placed one glass on the counter and poured generously. "You cool if we share? Since I'm driving and all."

"That works." Lena's expression was unreadable.

He pushed the glass toward her. She offered a small smile as she swirled the amber liquid.

"It's been a few months since I've had any kind of bourbon. This smells great." She took a sip, and her eyes fluttered closed.

He tried not to stare and caught himself wondering— Did her face look just as stunning when she slept, too? Lena swallowed and opened her eyes. "Tastes great, too."

A loud boom from outside startled Palmer out of his stupor. Lena yelped and gripped the counter. On instinct, Palmer moved toward her but veered to the bay windows behind her. She had made her point earlier— She wasn't his problem to solve.

Plump dark clouds filled the sky, releasing rain at a deter-mined speed. Thunder rolled, long and low. "Well, this wasn't in our plans for leaving town," Palmer said. Why hadn't he checked the weather this morning? They could have left earlier. Lena moved toward the windows.

"I forgot how often it storms in the Midwest." Lena peered out the window, then turned and looked up at him. The crease between her eyebrows from earlier had disappeared. "I kinda miss these summer storms. We don't get a lot of thunder or lightning in Oregon. Just, you know, rain. Tons of it."

"Did you drive through any storms coming here with Dou-glas?"

Lena shook her head. "If there was bad weather, I pulled off the highway and waited it out."

"Smart," Palmer said. But not ideal for making a quick getaway before his parents showed up. "So, we'll wait it out." He glanced at the clock above Gregor's kitchen sink. How was it three o'clock already?

Lena nodded, her mouth forming into a smirk. "Palmer, it's okay. We're in no rush."

"I'd like to avoid a run-in with my folks, as you know," he said.

"Here." Lena held out the whiskey glass. Her fingertips grazed the insides of his palm as the glass transferred into his hand.

"This will help," she whispered. Her hand lingered.

He was certain Lena's touch could make any man forget his problems, better than the strongest whiskey. A sudden warmth crept up his neck. Lena offered another smile and sat back on the stool.

"I'm glad your mood is improving but do you have to look so smug?" he said around the rim of the glass before sipping. The burn wasn't going to help his face cool off, but it sure felt great going down his throat.

"You may disagree with me. Actually, I'd be shocked if you didn't," Lena said as she sat back on the stool. "But you and your father should talk before you leave. And I think this delay is one big stormy sign."

"Not going to happen," Palmer said.

"Has this always been the dynamic between you and your father? It seems like you avoid speaking your mind to him." She placed her chin in her hand with an innocent look on her face, like she hadn't just asked the most loaded question of all time.

"It's complicated," he said, hedging. He pulled out a stool and sat next to Lena. There weren't many people who asked about his relationship with his father. Then again, those in his life had known him for most of it, so why would they ask?

"I was born into the family business, just as my father was, and his father before him, and my father's father's father before him." Palmer trailed off as a boom of thunder sounded overhead. Lena had lobbed a question he wasn't used to hearing, and he was struggling to answer it.

"I understand when implied obligation takes over personal goals and dreams," Lena said. "But Gregor isn't linked to the family business, right? He runs his own shop, and is still on speaking terms with your father."

Palmer twisted the glass on the counter. "Not until recently, and only after my mother insisted they end their cold war since we all live in the same town." His chest was tight.

"I've been the peacekeeper, the mediator, the reasonable and logical one, and frankly, Lena, it's all just a bunch of bullshit." The rain outside clinked against the windows like a tally counter keeping track of the many roles Palmer had filled over the years. He took a generous sip from the glass and pushed it in front of her. Usually, he was in better control of what came out of his mouth. "You finish that. I have to drive." Another boom sounded from outside. "Whenever this storm passes."

Lena tapped her finger against the glass with her long fingernails. Hers weren't painted like Carrie's, and he couldn't imagine Lena any other way. He felt her staring at him, but he kept his eyes fixated on her slender fingers and their rhythmic movements.

"If I can find enough courage to talk to Seth's parents about their son's death and potentially ask about a woman Seth may have been involved with after I broke off our engagement," she took a breath, "then you, Palmer, can talk to your father about whatever it is you need to get off your chest."

His thoughts picked up speed like a dreidel, spinning around Lena's confession and subsequent wisdom. She was seeking closure through courage, and he was—what? Stumbling around the way things had always been. But for what reason?

"You can do this," she said and placed her hand over his. The lights flickered twice and then went out completely. She didn't move, and neither did he. Her silhouette was outlined by the darkened bay windows. He could hear her shallow breathing as the smell of her surrounded him—vanilla and whiskey and something else. Something different. Just as he opened his mouth to speak, so as not to bend down and kiss her in the dark, the front door opened.

"Palmer." A voice just like his but deeper rang out in the darkened apartment. "We need to talk."

"You can do this," she repeated in a whisper. She squeezed his hand before releasing.

"All right," Palmer said, rooting in his pocket for his phone. He turned on the flashlight, then stood to greet his father in the other room. He could pretend, for however long that he was in the same room as his father, to indeed try and do this, just as Lena had said.

11

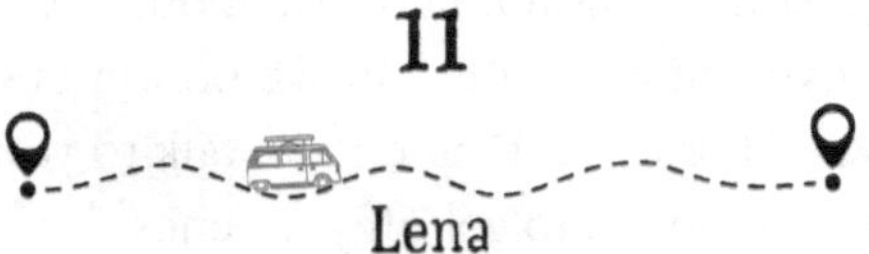

Lena

I nching toward the front door, Lena claimed she needed to check on Douglas. Which was mostly true. The energy in the room had dipped for obvious reasons, and her clumsy attempt at *Hello, sir, how are you?* had only made it worse. She needed out. Palmer shot her a pleading look, but she kept walking. He and his father had to hash out whatever this was without an audience. Especially one as awkward as her.

The stairwell was pitch black when Lena stepped out of the apartment. Turning on her phone's flashlight, she gripped the banister and took the stairs one at a time, like a toddler. She made her way down a second hallway and toward the shop's steel garage door. The air was stuffy and smelled of rubber tires, making her feel lightheaded. With a grunt, she pushed it open. Her dizziness grew tenfold as the smell of gasoline and oil swarmed her. The clang of tools on concrete rang out.

"Who's there?" a voice shouted from the opposite end of the garage. A beam of light flashed in her face. Gregor's head popped up from behind the back of the van. "I was just about to come up and get you guys. Took me a second to find a flashlight." Gregor approached her. He was always smiling, it seemed, which she appreciated. Grumpy customers had become her daily norm. It was nice to see a genuine dimpled smile. Just like his father's. How had she not noticed those until now? And why was she back to wondering if Palmer had them too? He never answered her question at his house, did he? Her face warmed at

98

the memory.

Thunder cracked overhead, a strange hollowness to the sound. "How's Douglas looking?"

"I dare say, better than ever. He's purring like a cat who knows they have it good if you catch my drift." Gregor winked. "I even got those string lights inside working for you." He winked again.

Lena pulled at the collar of her top, purposely ignoring his mention of the twinkle lights and his flirting. It was harmless, but she was in no mood to dodge around it. If she could fix Douglas on her own, she would. The implications of accepting help were why she avoided involving others with her problems. And yet, somehow, Palmer had found his way in, hadn't he? She shifted her weight away from the ache of her broken ankle.

"Your dad is upstairs," she said, which was followed immediately by a groan from Gregor. Well, that put an end to a possible third wink.

Gregor handed the flashlight to Lena. "I should go up there. Will you be okay by yourself?"

Lena blinked in the shadowed light. Gregor's concerned eyes mirrored Palmer's more than she cared to admit. "I'm not alone. Douglas is here."

Gregor smiled. "He looks pretty cool, all lit up."

Lena nodded and fought down the rising lump in her throat. "Good luck up there."

"Should be interesting." Gregor gave two thumbs-up and retreated. Once the door slammed closed, Lena moved past another car on risers and toward Douglas. The storm sounded further away now, although it was hard to tell without a window to look through. She squeezed around a massive red tool chest, her heartbeat heavy from nearly falling as she reached Douglas. Opening the side door, Douglas exhaled his trademark scent, making her feel more at ease. She climbed inside.

To the left of the small gas range was a switch for the van's interior lights. She hadn't touched it since Seth's death. Not because she had forgotten about it, but because Douglas had looked too alive when lit up from the inside. She had needed the false protection of darkness. It had kept the uncontrollable unilluminated. But that was no longer the case, was it? Something was emerging from the dark, and she couldn't stop it. Whatever it was, it was rising up to the surface. So, with a slight tremble in her hand, she reached forward and flipped the switch.

Seth wasn't supposed to propose when he did.

"I have to show you something outside," he said after bounding through the front door with the energy of a Golden Retriever puppy. He had spent the entire afternoon outside working on the old van.

"It can't wait till morning? I'm already in my pajamas," Lena said. Seth planted a fierce kiss on her lips and mumbled a stern "no."

She assumed his excitement was for the van and not a ring burning a hole in his pocket. Seth wasn't the marrying type—a fact he had shared on their second date. That was Seth for you, though, steadfast in communicating his opinions and wants.

"Trust me. You're going to love it." He bounced on his toes as she slipped on her shoes. His hand grasped hers as they walked outside.

The dark sky was dotted with stars and showcased a crescent moon as big as Seth's smile. His palm was damp and warm in her hand as they approached the vintage VW van. Lena peered through the foggy side windows and spotted a bottle of champagne on a torn vinyl seat. The inside was cast in a soft glow from what appeared to be white string lights. She felt a twinge of something she wasn't ready for but pushed it away.

"Douglas is looking festive this evening," she said, feeling silly. Seth had announced the van needed a name after purchasing the vehicle the day before. Lena had jokingly suggested *Douglas*, after the Douglas fir—the most common tree in Oregon—due to the evergreen paint.

"It's perfect," Seth had said in response to her idea, his cheeks flushed. Her heart had squeezed behind her ribs. She was all too familiar with that look and knew, from experience, that this enthusiasm was only temporary.

After eight years, Lena could fill in what Seth often left out in conversations. Especially when it came to new things and his one-track mind.

When they first met, his excitement for new things—*her*—had been flattering. Then, as they grew more comfortable together, his attention turned to taking photos and the new camera he later bought to take even better photos. When his photography account on social media skyrocketed, so did the job offers. And then, his hobby turned into a passionate profession. Soon enough, he was traveling and shooting on-location, and yet, he still craved the thrill of change.

Seth was an incorrigible nomad at heart, despite his homebody roots. It only made sense that his newest obsession was renovating a van in which to travel across the country. Lena was well aware Seth's focus would be on the van for the next six to twelve months.

So, when Seth bent down on one knee inside the van and asked her to marry him, she was startled. Stunned. And a little bit confused. Why now? Wasn't the van his latest conquest?

"I have never been more certain of anything in my life." His voice was warm like the gleaming lights above her.

Lena stared at the opened velvet box. A blue teardrop gemstone surrounded by tiny white diamonds and a white gold band winked up at her.

"I've spent the last six months traveling and taking photos and actually getting paid for it. A dream I never thought possible. But knowing you're here when I return from whatever adventures I've been tasked to capture, that's the real dream. You're my grounding, Lena. You're my home."

Lena should have paid attention to the voice in her head. *Why now?* But the light reflecting off her ring and Seth's glowing promises had stopped her. Seth looked so happy. He wanted to spend the rest of his life with her. Surely, that could serve as a Band-Aid over his absence. Surely, she could find a way out of her loneliness and into a new sense of contentment.

The two years following Seth's proposal consisted of him being away on-location while Lena remained in Oregon. Lena's boss at Coffee Rocks had promoted her to manager, and her business degree was nearly complete. She felt confident the dream of owning a coffee shop was within reach. Except one big piece was missing: her partner. So, she dove headfirst into planning their inaugural cross-country trip with Douglas and ignored everything else, including herself. She wasn't content; she was dissatisfied and alone. So alone. And their wedding date wasn't even set. But Douglas was road-ready, and Lena would have Seth to herself for two whole months. At least, that had been the plan, until everything changed. Again.

"You're home early," she'd said as Seth walked through their front door. She stood up from the table cluttered with textbooks and notebook paper and reached her arms to the ceiling to stretch. Usually, Seth would rush in and wrap his arms around her waist. Instead, he toed the doorframe with his shoe.

"I'm flying to Florida tomorrow," he said.

Her arms fell to her side. "I'm confused. We're leaving for our trip in two days. That was the plan."

"Lena," he said in a thick, saturated tone.

Her engagement ring suddenly felt too tight on her finger. "You took another job."

"I had to," Seth said as he took a step forward. She stepped back.

"You had to," she repeated as her body turned numb. Seth had chosen another month away from her. Maybe longer. What was the point if they only spent five days out of sixty together? Why would he propose a life together when he perpetually chose to be away from her? Was she only tolerable in temporary doses?

"It's a spread in *Travel+*, Lena. This is big. Too big to turn down. The exposure alone will be career-changing."

She should be jumping up and down in excitement for Seth. But all she could do was slump into her chair. Seth's recent travels had dimmed his desire to drive cross-country. Or maybe his love for her had dimmed. Or maybe she wasn't meant to be his home. But if she wasn't here for him, who would be?

"I guess we can postpone the trip. If that's what you really want," she said. She was a traitor to no one but herself.

Seth finally rushed into her, pulling her up from the chair, and wrapping his arms around her waist. Her breath caught as disappointment clashed with his joy.

"I promise," he said. His breath warmed her neck. "Once this job is over, it's just you and me and Douglas on the road, windows open and happy."

She should have told him their time apart was hurting her. She should have voiced her feelings and told him she needed him home in order to save their relationship— *To save his life*. If only she had been more honest with herself, maybe she wouldn't have given up and said goodbye. Maybe Seth would still be alive.

The slam of the shop door closing jolted Lena back to reality. The urge to rip down the white lights overhead spilled over her. She wanted to believe Seth had done a poor job of balancing his dream job and their relationship. Tearing off the inconsequential things hanging above her head would be cathartic, sure, but wouldn't give her what she really needed.

"Christmas in July!"

Lena jumped again at the sound of Palmer's voice.

Palmer crouched inside and surveyed her with imploring eyes. "I startled you," he said.

She moved to the bench seat, belatedly regretting not flipping the *off* switch on her way to the front. "I needed a good shove out of my head, so thank you."

He sat next to her. His long legs bumped up against her knee. "Do you want to talk about it?"

"Nope." She peered up at his profile. Somehow he looked

older. "How did it go?"

Palmer wiped a hand down his face. "I'm officially homeless." He looked at her and nodded. "Yeah, I should be surprised, too, right? My father has finally untethered me from his house, expectations, and business. I'm free."

"Where will you go? What about your equipment?"

"Gregor told my father to stop being a child and give me my equipment back. And I don't need to know where I'll go, do I? We're hitting the road!"

"Right, right," Lena said as she studied Palmer's wide smile. She couldn't tell if he was genuinely thrilled that his life had just blown up in his face. In fact, she had the sinking feeling Palmer was still playing the part of someone else's expectations, only it was hers he was fulfilling now.

"Would any of this be happening if you weren't helping me?" She hated loaded questions. This one, however, seemed necessary.

"Yes, Lena. You know I'm short on lumber." His tone took her by surprise, and not in a way that encouraged a long road trip alone together. "I would've left the state with or without you. You know this, and yet you continue to make me second-guess and almost feel guilty for offering to help you. And I get it. You're uncomfortable accepting anyone's help, but that doesn't mean you're allowed to project that discomfort onto the person helping you in the first place. That's not what we're doing here." His knee bounced as he stared straight ahead. "So, if you could, please let go of all the reasons that got us here and focus on where we have to go."

She was cemented to the seat, unable to move. She couldn't remember the last time anyone had treated her as anything other than a lost and grieving soul. Only while navigating herself through unknown roads had she felt a sense of resiliency.

Yet, Palmer was being upfront with her. He spoke in a way that implied she wouldn't break, when so many others had skirted around the truth, assuming she was too weak to handle it.

A warmth spread through her, as if she were in the driver's seat speeding down an open highway with the sun streaming through the driver's window. She had found strength in solitude. But strength could be found in honesty, too.

"I know I'm horrible at accepting help. You're right. But that's not what this is about. I'm second-guessing your decision because of the drama it's caused within your family. And if that has caused you to become impatient with me, or if my reaction wasn't part of your plan, then I think that's something you should let go of, too. I want to make sure you're not doing this to prove a point or to stay true to a promise you made to me, but that you're doing it for the right reasons." She sat back. She wasn't used to voicing her thoughts to anyone other than Douglas, where her words bounced around the empty space and disappeared out an open window. But there was no disappearing here. Palmer had just listened and absorbed her vulnerability like a sponge.

Palmer's eyes shined, igniting the tiniest spark from somewhere deep within her. It was a feeling so far away from the surface of what really mattered that she blinked, and it was gone.

"Then we agree," Palmer said as he leaned into her. "We both have to let go in order to go." He reached for her crossed arms and gently loosened them open.

The spark she had felt moments before returned and exploded into glitter and—"Lights!" Lena pointed out the window. "The lights are back on," she said, relieved Palmer had moved away to look out the window.

He turned to look at her. "I'm ready to go. Are you?"

Lena nodded. "Let's go."

He slapped his hands on his thighs and crawled out the side door. As Palmer walked further into the light, she looked up at the twinkle lights one last time. Her promise to Seth had served as a beacon, guiding her through the darkness, to here. Seth's light was meant to remain inside this van now. Trusting herself and her choices would require inner illumination from here on out. She swiped away a rogue tear, then flipped the switch off inside of Douglas.

"**W**hat's that you got there?" Lena asked as she rummaged through a plastic bag from the gas station store. Palmer had his notebook opened to the page titled "*Day One*" and ran his index finger down to five o'clock. They were supposed to be in Indianapolis by now, not fueling up at a gas station in his hometown. He groaned and closed the cover.

"It's kind of like a daily schedule," he said. He'd drafted the itinerary last night when he couldn't sleep and had meant to show Lena this morning, before other things happened. "That storm and my father stole three hours from our day."

"Here." She handed him a king-sized candy bar. "Take a break, and let me see." The notebook on his lap was replaced with oversized candy. He opened the wrapper while his nerves flip-flopped with each page Lena turned.

"Wow. I wasn't expecting the schedule to be so detailed." She returned to the first page. "I guess you need one, though, if you're going to hit all these lumber suppliers." She closed the notebook and tapped her fingers on the cover.

Palmer bit into the chocolate-covered wafer and paused midchew. He hadn't left any room for Lena's destinations. *Shit.*

"It's not written in stone," he said and handed the candy to her in exchange for his notebook. "Did you have any destinations in mind?" He eyed her somewhat warily. She didn't appear upset. In fact, she looked delighted as she chewed, but still. He wanted to fix this.

"Oh, me?" she mumbled while buckling her seat belt. "Maybe. I guess. It's all up in my head, though, not written down or anything."

"Well, here." He offered the notebook again. "You should write some of those places down, don't you think?"

She readjusted her seat belt. "I'd rather just get to Florida."

Palmer's hand hovered between the two bucket seats before retreating back to his side. He didn't know what to do. Her expression appeared calm and neutral, but her response had been sharp.

"I'll put this away then, if you're sure," Palmer said, stalling.

"I'm sure. You had to plan this trip for your business. It's different for me. Let's leave it at that, all right?" Lena lifted her hair off her shoulders, kicking up her vanilla scent. He gazed at her exposed neck for longer than he meant to.

"Come on," he said, unable to stop himself. "You must have some place in mind." Maybe it was the sight of her neck that had him pushing for her answer. Or maybe it was because needs mattered, especially buried ones. And he needed her to under-stand that hers mattered to him, too.

"Fine." She released her hair to open the glove compartment. "Consider this one big Sharpie marker on the fine print of your schedule."

"You want to swim with manatees?" he said, squinting at the brochure.

Lena shrugged while tracing the handwritten name with her finger. Just like yesterday. He hadn't spent much time consid-ering the significance of what she'd found. Come to think of it, Lena had distracted him with vague philosophical questions, diverting his attention from her reaction to the discovery. The rise in her shoulders and the frown on her face made it clear the brochure was more than a bucket list dream.

"Do you know her?" Palmer said. Was this the other woman Lena had mentioned earlier, the one connected to her fiancé before his death?

"I met her once. At Seth's funeral." She tossed the brochure into the compartment with surprising accuracy and slammed it closed. "I think we can make up for our lost hours if we sacrifice some sleep. What do you think?"

He thought the walls she had up would only cause more problems. But voicing his concern would only upset her. "I'm cool with it, if that's what you want."

Lena huffed. "You're the one with the plan, who needs to be in Indianapolis by now."

Palmer mirrored her forced exhale. "And you're the one who refuses to tell me why you need to swim with manatees. How are you going to do that with your ankle still in a walking cast?"

Lena glared at him. "That's my problem to figure out. Not yours." She tossed the candy back into his lap. "I can't eat any more sugar."

Palmer could take the hint. He took the last chocolate wafer and inspected it for imperfections, an exaggerated act to help break the tension, before putting the entire thing into his mouth. Lena sighed. He swallowed hard. She hadn't even cracked a smile.

"I don't understand why you treat me like a permanent person when it's clear I'm only temporary." Her voice was clear and strong.

Palmer took a gulp of water, stalling. "I'm convinced anyone who has met you, for whatever length of time, has never considered you temporary in their minds."

He stared straight ahead, expecting silence to flood the van.

"You say that like it's a good thing," she said within a matter of seconds, proving his instincts wrong, yet again.

"Why wouldn't it be?"

"Let's hope you don't find out."

Lena reached for her pillow and shoved it under her right leg.

"I have an idea I'd like to suggest," he said once they merged onto the expressway.

"Sure, go ahead. But stay in the right lane. Douglas isn't used to Chicago drivers." Lena's head snapped to the left, then the right. "I forgot how bad traffic is around here." She peered out the windshield as vehicles moved in all directions. Her hands braced the dashboard. "This van does not do well behind semis. Try to get ahead of this truck. Easy on him, though. Wait, right there. There's a spot!"

A flashback of Palmer's father shouting to *turn here*, or *get ahead of that car*, rang in his ears. What a terrible idea that had been, to drive together to each showroom for inventory reasons last year. He would never drive with his father again.

Palmer gripped the wheel and eased up on the gas, moving into the right lane ahead of the semi.

"Much better," Lena said with a hint of relief. Palmer glanced at her raised shoulders. Clearly, she was far from *much better*. "You were going to tell me something, right?" she said, looking at him.

He tried to relax his face. He'd forgotten how much control his father had over him while he worked for the family business. The realization had taken him off guard.

"Sorry. That was annoying of me," Lena muttered after a beat of silence.

"You're telling me how to drive your van. It's allowed," Palmer said. "Douglas doesn't do well behind semi-trucks. He likes the right lane best. He slips when it rains and is better off waiting out a downpour."

"You remembered."

"Of course. Douglas also wants you to know his current driver is doing great. In fact, he's impressed that he doesn't slam on his brakes."

Lena reclined in her seat, and although he couldn't confirm her smile, he sensed she was calming down. "So, tell me, what's your idea?" she asked.

Palmer flexed his hands on the wheel. His idea was bold, but so was their situation. "It's kind of a wild thought, but I'm willing to go there if you are."

Lena shifted in her seat. "Well, you have my attention now. What is this wild thought?"

Palmer smiled, encouraged by her playful tone. "I wonder if it's possible for us to remove who we think we should be in this situation, and just be who we are when no one is around." A police siren sounded in the distance as traffic came to a near standstill. "I just thought," he continued, "instead of polite conversations, we could be open and honest with each other." He held his breath and waited for Lena's reply. Either she thought he was completely off his rocker, or she was actually considering it.

"Is revealing all of your ugly truths truly freeing, though?" she asked.

"Who said the truth was inherently ugly? Truth is honesty. It's about being free of formalities or fakeness or, I don't know—"

"Fraud?" Lena cut in. "You were on a roll with those F words, I thought I could keep it going."

"Fantastic," Palmer smirked.

Lena laughed. "Funny." She turned into him. "I may fail at it."

"Maybe being your truest self removes the risk of failure," Palmer said. The traffic inched forward as the city skyline came into view. They were almost past the bottleneck portion of the Eisenhower Expressway and would soon head south toward Indiana.

Lena adjusted the vents on the dashboard and held her hand over the blowing air. "I hope he doesn't overheat."

"If he does, he does," Palmer said. He glanced at the rearview mirror, surprised by his response. The sun was low and would soon set, allowing the day's burn to cool off. He could have explained away her unnecessary concern. But he hadn't. Why? "We'll figure it out," he added.

Lena poked him in the shoulder. "We won't have to because Gregor confirmed Douglas is in tip-top shape."

"Then we're good," Palmer said.

Lena peered at him. "Why are you smiling like that?"

"It's just me being me, I guess. No mask, just me." He tempered the urge to reach over and squeeze her with childlike glee. This *was* freeing! Lena's gaze remained on him. He wished he could take a longer glance at her face. The look he caught before returning his attention to the road had jolted his insides, like hitting a pothole. He felt alert with adrenaline.

"You being you," she said, like she was reading the instructions off a box of macaroni and cheese. "With a smile that brings out dimples I've never seen." Lena turned away.

"Never say never." Palmer reached for the air vent to his left. He felt warm. He also felt certain Lena hadn't meant to say what she did. Perhaps the veil of social expectations between them would have fallen away regardless of his impromptu suggestion.

"In the spirit of complete honesty, I honestly don't know why I said that," she said with a bubble of laughter. "But let it be known: What lies underneath your beard is fascinating to me." She covered her face with her hands. "Oh my, this is definitely way too candid."

"Keep it coming. Seriously. However you want to show up during our time together, I'm here for it." Palmer steered onto the exit ramp toward I-65. It wouldn't be long before the thick traffic morphed into open roads and dark fields of corn. They were far from their destination, but he felt determined to get to his first lumber stop in Louisville. And with Lena's company and candid chatter, as she put it, he felt certain the hours would fly by.

"I'll try to keep the dimple comments to a minimum," she said, sounding tired. "I know it's just a distraction from the indents already in my mind. Kind of like those on your face. You know, like, a valley yet to be explored. Now I'm totally not making sense." Lena adjusted the pillow underneath her leg. "I might close my eyes for a second, if that's okay?"

"Yes, absolutely. Don't ever feel like you have to ask," Palmer said.

"You're right." Lena reclined her seat. "I'm going to close my eyes. I'll be back soon."

"I'll be here," Palmer said. It was a ridiculous sentiment with a strange sense of comfort in it. He wasn't going anywhere, and neither was she.

113

13

Lena

Lena gripped her overnight bag while Palmer unlocked the door to their motel room. One room. Two beds. A scenario impossible not to overthink. But they would be on the road again in less than six hours, so one room made sense. Lena only wished this logical decision didn't come with a side of insecurity.

Palmer pushed the door open with a grunt. A dimly lit floor lamp, two full-sized beds separated by a cheap-looking night-stand, and a blocky brown television on an equally cheap table, populated the modest room. It smelled of musty bleach but appeared clean.

"Not bad, all things considered," Palmer said as he shut the door, latching the chain to the wall. Her eyes darted around the room. It seemed to have shrunk in size with the door closed.

"I've stayed in worse." Lena placed her bag on the bed far-thest from the door and sat down. At least the mattress was soft and inviting. It took everything in her not to fall back in relief. Palmer walked by and flipped the light switch on in the bathroom. An air vent rattled.

"Well, that's loud enough to drown out any sort of noise, if you catch my drift," Palmer said, turning the light off.

Lena offered a tired laugh as Palmer smiled and sat down with a sigh. Something felt off. And maybe that was her fault. She hadn't considered how he'd feel about sharing a room with her. Palmer, the planner, was in yet another unplanned situation.

Was he uncomfortable with their arrangements?

Lena thought back to earlier when she'd spoken without a filter. It had felt like a spark when two rocks collided. Now shouldn't be any different. In fact, voicing her concerns was what Palmer wanted, right?

"I don't know about you," she said, "but I'm choosing to not overthink the fact that we're sharing a room for the night."

Palmer toed off his shoes and nodded heavily. "I'm too tired to actually form coherent thoughts, let alone overthink them."

Lena followed his lead and began to unlatch the fastens on her walking cast. "It's nice, though," she said as she pulled off the boot. Cool air hit the bottom half of her right leg. "You know, not sleeping in a strange room alone. It feels...safe." Lena touched her heel gingerly while tempering the urge to explain herself further. She was fine alone, too. *And don't you forget it*, she wanted to add. But Palmer wasn't questioning her strength, only she was. So, the shouting would remain in her head, directed at the one person who doubted her: herself.

"I learned a long time ago when I was a Boy Scout there is always safety in numbers," said Palmer. The creases around his eyes appeared deeper than before. "I would rather we stay together at night than separate."

Lena's heartbeat stuttered. Palmer's expression was foreign to her; he was a street sign in a different language. She was lost in the tenderness of his eyes and confused by the tension in every other visible part of his body.

Palmer cared about her in a way she couldn't understand. There was no room for that kind of relationship in her reality. And maybe that was the crux. Whatever could happen between her and Palmer wasn't allowed or realistic, not now and possibly not ever. Still, the thought of spending multiple nights in the same room as Palmer had her climbing underneath the comforter.

"One room will save us some money," she said, laying back. Stating facts also covered up unwanted truths.

"Lena," Palmer said. "It's not about money."

"I knew you were going to say that." She turned toward him and tucked an arm underneath the pillow. "I understand money better than...feelings." Squeezing her eyes closed, she breathed in deeply. The desperate need to feel a body around hers was overwhelmingly wrong, yet needed. How long had it been? *Too long.* How wrong was she willing to go? She pushed her arm out of the covers, stretching it toward Palmer. There was no hesitation, no furrowed brow on his face, no question about what she was hinting. He took her hand and moved around her like a magnet connecting to its polar opposite.

Palmer remained on top of the covers as his arm lay across her waist. He might as well be a weighted blanket. She melted further into the mattress.

"I should turn the lights off," he mumbled, his breath warm against the back of her neck. He smelled of pine and musk and something else. She didn't want him to go. If they fell asleep together, it had to be spontaneous, not premeditated. Turning the lights off would only shine a spotlight on what she was trying to avoid.

"Maybe in a few minutes." She trailed her fingertips over the skin of his arm and pulled it in closer to her chest.

"No overthinking," Palmer whispered into her hair.

You smell like my pillow, she wanted to whisper back. But her tongue was heavy, and her eyelids were cement.

"I'm glad we agree," she murmured and drifted to sleep.

A familiar wake-up call brought Lena out of sleep the next morning. Again, her ankle ached, and the dread of imminent pain kept her from moving. It was a pattern similar to the early days of Seth's passing when she couldn't get out of bed. Some of those early morning stings had disappeared since breaking her ankle. Part of her wanted to believe her grief had found a resting place in her mind. But she wasn't an idiot. She knew her physical pain had only temporarily replaced the other kind.

She remained still and took in her surroundings. For a moment, she thought she was at her sister's house. She shifted to her left and focused on Palmer's large frame in the bed across from hers. His body was partially covered by scrunched-up bedsheets.

Right.

She was in a motel room with Palmer's handsome face smashed into his pillow. His foot twitched as it hung off the end of the bed. At some point during the night, he'd left her.

She turned to stare at the popcorn ceiling, pulling the covers to her chin. Why had she initiated the random spooning last night? As if Palmer would have denied her. He was obligated. She should know by now, if saying no might hurt Lena, Palmer would always choose yes. She felt so stupid!

She turned to her other side and stared at the bare wall. He must have gotten up to switch off the lights after she'd fallen asleep. Then returned to his own bed to sleep. It was clear the man required one of his own. Why, then, was she hurt that he'd snuck away? Was she that terrible to wake up to?

Lena sat up and repositioned her right leg over the edge of the mattress. Sharp pain shot up from her ankle and engulfed her entire leg in flames. This wasn't good. The skin on her ankle was swollen and hot to the touch.

"You okay over there?"

She jolted, not ready to assess her pain. "My ankle is swollen."

"That's normal, right?" Palmer asked, his voice at least two octaves lower and doing things to her that she didn't want at the moment. Or maybe she did. She licked her lips, thankful her back was to him. "Maybe sitting in the van has something to do with it?" he added.

The heat from her leg had crept up to her pelvic region. If she flexed her foot, the pain might make her forget about Palmer leaving her last night, if she wanted it to.

"Maybe, yeah. I guess healing is meant to hurt." She turned toward Palmer. His hair pointed in all directions. The shadows on his face conveyed concern, and damn how she wished it was because he'd realized leaving her in the middle of the night was a mistake.

"Is there anything I can do?" he said.

Yes, she wanted to respond calmly. *Don't add to my pain*. "No. Morning stiffness is normal." Lena stilled. Had she really just said that? "What I mean is the rigid feeling of a broken bone is to be expected. I think." Why was she still talking? Palmer smirked, looking very much amused.

"You left me last night," she snapped, then stood up. The pain was so intense, her breath caught.

"Lena, hold up," Palmer started, but his voice was drowned by the noise of the bathroom fan and the closing of the door.

Lena caught a glimpse of her face in the mirror. The sight of her pale skin did not surprise her. Fatigue had planted itself in her bones the moment Seth died. This was how she looked now.

Palmer's commitment to fixing the unfixable was making things worse. This cross-country drive was not supposed to be with another man who exposed her insecurities, never mind her buried desires. Her focus had to remain on uncovering Seth's time in Florida before he died.

Lena rubbed at the dark circles under her eyes before turning away from her reflection. She straightened her back and reached to turn on the shower. Palmer and his charm would not distract her from the difficulties that lay ahead.

Twenty minutes later, Lena emerged from the bathroom with damp hair and fresh clothes. A Styrofoam cup sat next to the ancient television, steam dancing upward. The curtains were drawn aside, revealing a cloudy sky. Palmer's bed was partially made, because of course, the man with a plan would tidy up. Before Lena had a chance to sip her coffee and go in search of him, he walked through the door, notebook pressed to his chest.

"Good news," Palmer said. "The Louisville supplier can see

me this morning, as planned. Well, not exactly as planned since it's two hours after the original time, but he can still see me."

"That's good." Lena would need more than this tiny cup of caffeine to keep up with Palmer's fast-talking.

"So, Louisville is an hour away. Spend thirty minutes there, maybe. It'll be a rush. Then a three-hour drive to Nashville. This supplier may be the most unique one on this trip. His warehouse is jammed with rare finds."

Lena murmured around her cup, wondering what a rare find meant in the lumber world. It didn't matter, though, did it? Palmer would find his supply and move on. What did matter was her growing annoyance with the man who kept talking.

"Usually, saved pieces found in old homes before they were demolished. Window frames, doors, archways, floorboards, that sort of thing," Palmer clarified. She hadn't asked the question out loud, had she? "Your face looked confused," he added, then went on. "After Nashville, it's another two hours to Chattanooga. There are three suppliers there, all off-the-grid on dirt roads, I would imagine, so it'll be a drop-in-and-see type of situation. I was thinking we could get a room, and you rest while I run around. What do you think?"

She finished her coffee and set the cup down. Her stomach gurgled. So many stops. So much time waiting for Palmer to do his business. So many opportunities for her to become impatient. But this was part of their deal. So, she would just have to deal. After she ate something. "I think I'm hungry."

"Oh, I got us donuts. They're in the van," he said. "Are you all packed and ready to go? I'll check the bathroom, just in case."

Palmer darted into the bathroom before she could answer. Lena walked toward her bag as his voice rang out. "I'll grab your stuff, just head out to Douglas!"

"Are my arms broken, too?" she grumbled and left her bag on the bed. The ground wavered as she walked out into the muggy air. Water, then food, and then her mind could calibrate to Palmer's energy.

The smell of coffee drifted around her as she opened the passenger door. Two large coffees rested in the cup-holders. On the floor between the two seats was a flimsy-looking box and two bottles of water. Lena grabbed a bottle and took a long drink of water. She hated how prepared Palmer was at eight in the morning. In the span of twenty minutes, Palmer had located donuts and coffee. Waking life was not executed this perfectly so close to sunrise. Although chances were, the name of a local donut shop was scribbled in that damn notebook of his, next to all the wood suppliers. How quickly her reflective, solo cross-country trip had turned into dictated destinations, and they were only two days in.

Donuts.

This mood had to go, and donuts would guide the way. Lena opened the box and looked down at a dozen chocolate-frosted and glazed donuts. Not a sprinkle to be seen. About as utilitarian as sugar could get.

"I see you found the reason any human wakes up in the morning." Palmer hopped into the driver's seat. "I did a quick search last night after you fell asleep and found this place. It's called Minimadough. Like minimalist presentation but with surprise flavors."

"Oh, so that's why you left last night," Lena said before she could stop herself. Palmer had that effect on her. She took a large bite from a chocolate-frosted donut. Acidic marmalade hit her tongue. She frowned. Surprise flavors didn't mean good ones.

"You thought I left the room?" Palmer said. She forced herself to swallow and offered the donut to him. The utter bewilderment on his face was almost comical.

"I didn't think you left the room. Here. Take this."

He took the donut, and for a moment, she imagined pulling him in and kissing those full lips. The tension surrounding them was as sticky as the frosting on her fingertips. Clearly, her body was seeking relief.

Deal with it, she scolded herself.

"What's wrong with this one?" Palmer said, inspecting what she'd given him.

"You'll find out," Lena said before choosing another unknown donut from the box. Soft vanilla pudding coated her tongue. "Better," she mumbled.

Palmer took a bite from the donut she'd rejected and immediately opened the door to toss it out. "What was that?"

"Jelly-filled carnage."

Shaking his head, he smiled at her while turning the key in the ignition. "Should I try again?"

"That's up to you," she said. Why were they still talking about donuts? She thought for sure Palmer would have dived into what she meant by *So that's why you left*. But it seemed her vague comment had evaporated as quickly as the exhaust from Douglas.

"Off we go," he said.

"Yes," she agreed. Something was definitely off.

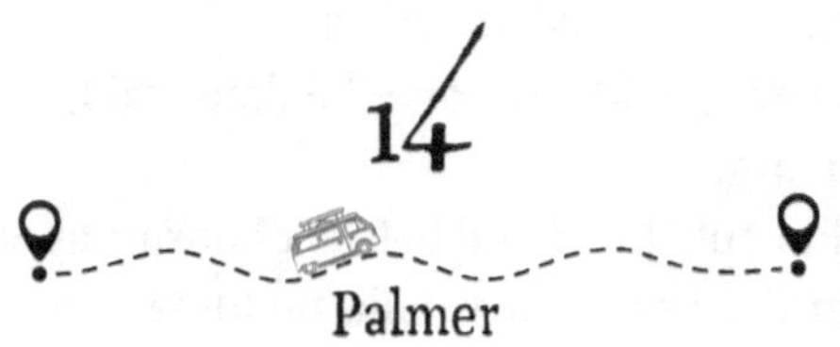

14

Palmer

Palmer had been drawn to aged wood long before the market turned trendy. He was fascinated by all the unknowns, his imagination ignited by the endless possibilities. What stories could the old pieces of wood tell from their time here? What history transformed them from smooth and gleaming centerpieces to rough and worn oddments? And how much of those remains could he make new again? Humans were no different than wood. Both were susceptible to the wear and tear of life. They were also both capable of remarkable transformation—but only with purposeful attention.

He glanced over at Lena, her red hair tumbled to one side as she slept with her pillow pressed against the passenger window. Lena was the opposite of what he knew so well. She was lighter fluid to the embers inside him—embers that could destroy everything unless he deprived them of the oxygen they craved.

Readjusting himself, he turned to focus on the open road. Earlier, when he'd walked among rows of commercial cedar, oak, and maple in the Louisville warehouse, he'd felt at home. The smell alone cemented him to his plan and would hold him steady as the search for reclaimed wood continued. But why did finding the supplies to start his dream have to be so complicated?

The biggest problem was finding unique pieces of wood. Although, saying goodbye to Lena at the end of this trip was a growing concern, too. He could get tangled up in his feelings if he wasn't careful. Tightening his hands on the wheel, he stole another glance at Lena. They were an hour into their three-hour drive to Nashville. Hopefully the supplier there would have something, *anything*, for Palmer to be excited about. Watching a beautiful woman sleep in the seat next to him could not be the highlight of his day.

The front end of Douglas dipped forward with a massive thud. Lena's pillow hit the windshield as he rolled over what looked to be a gaping pothole.

"Jesus, Palmer! Did you hit something?"

His eyes darted to check the van's mirrors. "I think I hit a pothole."

"Pull over," Lena demanded.

Palmer eased Douglas onto the shoulder, then darted out of the van. With the passenger door ajar, Lena stood motionless as she looked up. Palmer did the same. A wind farm, as far as the eye could see, surrounded them. The massive white turbines sliced through the air with an almost alien-like sound. There had to be at least fifty in the field, if not more, and for good reason. The wind was howling.

"You check the front end, I'll check his tires," Lena shouted against the relentless gusts.

Palmer nodded and walked to the front end. It felt out of place for Lena to take charge so quickly; he was usually the one shouting orders. But who was he to instruct Lena on how to deal with her van? He was just two feet, like he said. It was unfortunate his feet were attached to a body with a heart and brain. Lena was right, emotions confused everything.

Palmer bent down and ran his hand over the chrome bumper. It was dented, with an enormous scratch across most of it. "Shit," he said under his breath. The last thing Lena needed was another bill to worry about. He would offer to pay for the damages.

"Find anything?" Lena rounded the other side. Concern rippled across her face. He stood up, his knees cracking like a campfire log. Yes, the age of forty was upon him. In two weeks, he would be 365 days shy of it.

"The bumper has some damage," Palmer said. Lena walked around him.

"Oh." Her voice was swept away by the whipping wind. She covered her mouth.

"It shouldn't affect us driving," Palmer said. "And I'll pay for the repair."

Lena turned away. Her shoulders began to shake.

"Lena?" Palmer stepped forward. "What is it?"

A sob released from her, so raw and real, it drowned out the unnatural noise surrounding them. The back of her head shook. "It's just...this is..." She kept shaking her head. "This is what I was afraid of."

"It's nothing that can't be fixed," Palmer said, even though he knew she meant something else entirely.

"You're not supposed to be here!" She spun around, the wind tangling her hair.

"I know," he said gently.

"You're not supposed to see me like this!" Her fingers pressed against the tears on her face. "It took Seth months to find. It was all he talked about. That goddamn bumper. Then he finally found one and worked so long into so many nights that should have been spent with me, but instead, he was with Douglas, removing the rust and dents, and you fucked up!"

Lena stared at him, her breathing labored. She had warned him her moods would be unpredictable, and he had nodded in understanding. What he'd failed to consider was how he was meant to handle them. He wanted to pull her into him and hold on tight. It was a move he wasn't sure she would accept, but he tried anyway. His arms circled around her. The wind pushed her further into his chest.

"I'm sorry I didn't see the pothole," he said, hoping the rigidness in her body would loosen. He wouldn't dare tell her he'd been sneaking glances as she slept and trying to ignore his growing feelings for her with thoughts of wood instead.

She slumped into his chest. "It's my fault," she said as she grasped at her blowing hair. "I fell asleep."

"Lena, it is not your fault."

"Just like it's my fault Seth left for Florida. I should have told him to stay. Why didn't I tell him to stay?" Another sob escaped. "I thought I was past this part!" she yelled into her hands.

Palmer didn't know what to do. He wasn't about to offer empty words of comfort or encouragement. He had lost his grandparents a few years ago, but that was a different kind of grief. Losing a significant other at an age when family and friends gathered for weddings, not funerals, must have been unimaginable.

"Is there anything I can do?"

Lena looked at him straight on. Her eyes were bloodshot and determined. "Don't let me fall asleep."

The sound of a ringing cell phone saved Palmer from a response. Which was for the best. It was clear Lena was grasping at anything to gain control. An impossible scenario for both of them. His ego, however, was taking a hit.

"You should probably see who that is, right?"

"I know who it is," Palmer muttered. His father had been calling repeatedly since their departure. Each time, Palmer sent the call to voicemail. His father would never leave a message. He was too important to speak to no one.

The ringing stopped. Lena appeared calmer while the wind continued to whip around them.

"Are the tires okay?" he asked.

"Yeah, they're good."

Palmer's phone started to ring again. Lena frowned at him.

"I kept the ringer on in case a supplier needed to reach out," he explained.

"And you're not rushing to pick it up because...?"

"Because that's the ringtone I set for my father, and I've been avoiding his calls since we left." He wished he hadn't said that last part out loud. With Lena's current mood, her response could very well be *Go home, Palmer*.

"I thought you said Gregor mediated the disagreement and all was fine." Lena kept trying to catch her unruly hair in an almost reflexive way. There was a hairband in one of the cup-holders inside the van. He could fetch it for her and avoid talking about his father altogether. Except not really. The hairband would only delay the inevitable, and Lena would only be annoyed by his unsolicited help.

"My father has a hard time letting a bruised ego fade. He'd rather show off the damage, like fucking artwork."

The weight of her stare grew heavier with each passing second. "Oh, Palmer, your father cares for you. Maybe he's calling to make sure you're okay."

Palmer squinted up at the windmills. The blades turned in an effortless dance with the wind while that same force worked so hard to push him and Lena to the ground. It was mesmerizing to watch. The power of it all. *Bend so you don't break.*

"He's not calling because he cares. I'd rather make sure you're okay. And then Douglas. Sound good?"

"Right. We have a schedule to keep," Lena said, as she swung her door open.

That wasn't what he meant even though their window of time was narrowing. "Hey, seriously," he said after getting into the driver's seat. "I want to make sure you're okay."

"Stop." Lena's voice was so hollow he might have mistaken it for the wind whistling through a crack in the old van. "You don't need to pretend to care for the sake of occupying the in-between."

"I'm not sure I understand what you mean," Palmer said.

She sighed. "The in-between is someone who fills space until happily-ever-after shows up. This person keeps loneliness at bay during someone's in-between time. Kind of like a rebound. Although, honestly, I think you're too pragmatic for that fairytale BS."

"Oh, I mean, yeah?" Palmer said. Why did his ability to speak continue to falter in Lena's presence?

"So maybe when you find someone you can fall asleep with and not leave in the middle of the night, you'll no longer need an in-between."

Palmer couldn't keep up. Was she upset he had slept in his own bed as planned? "Maybe I don't have a space to fill—"

"Everyone has a space to fill, Palmer." She buckled her seat belt with a determined click. "All I'm saying is, being aware of what's temporary saves everyone a lot of heartache."

"And you're temporary," he said, repeating her comment from yesterday.

She pointed a finger at him. "You're finally catching on."

He clicked his seat belt with the same amount of determination. "I hate to break it to you, oh space-obsessed one, but technically everything in life is temporary."

"Of course you would use sweeping philosophical statements to cloak the hard truth of what this actually is."

"Do you ever think you're speaking from a place of defensiveness in order to protect yourself from hurt?" he shot back.

"I have hurt for well over a year! If anything, I am speaking from the depths of incredible discomfort. This isn't defense, Palmer, this is survival!"

How many times had he heard her say some variation of the same thing? This rhetoric she used for anyone that came close wasn't protection. It was preventing her from any possible change.

"You don't need to be in that place by yourself anymore, Lena. Don't you see? That's why I'm here. To help you. Whether you like it or not." Palmer forced his mouth closed. This wasn't how he had planned their morning to go. Gut-wrenching realizations were best shared over multiple glasses of whiskey, not lukewarm gas-station coffee. There was no turning back now, though. So, fuck it. "You have influenced the last month of my life more than you realize. So, call it philosophical, or woo-woo magic, or whatever you want, but I honestly believe our paths crossed for a reason."

She blinked rapidly before closing her eyes. Her head leaned against the headrest as she whispered, "Me too."

Palmer's chest deflated. A beat of silence passed. He took a breath and spoke. "Whatever this is," he said, "it's not an in-between. This is you and me together figuring out life for as long as we're on the go."

"And when we hit our destinations, what then?"

He wished he knew the answer. "It's not the destination, it's the journey."

Lena groaned. "All right. If you're going to veto the in-between, I am *so* vetoing the clichéd one-liners. Deal?"

"Deal," he said and started the engine. "Onward, ho?"

"Palmer!" Lena slapped his arm playfully. He turned the blinker on and checked for vehicles. Every part of him wanted more of Lena's touch. *My god*, he thought. She was so far from an in-between it should be concerning.

The tin-like clicking from the blinker focused him back on the task at hand. Which was driving to Nashville without hitting another pothole. An easy one to check off the list. Douglas glided onto the highway. Lena readjusted the pillow under her leg. Palmer shimmied down into his seat as a wave of contentment washed over him.

The potholes of unvoiced worries and bumps of unnecessary assumptions were in the rearview mirror now. Smooth roads ahead were his hopes from here on out. All he had to do was withhold his growing adoration for Lena as best he could.

15

Lena

A curtain of humidity greeted Lena as she pushed the screen door open. The tiny log cabin, one of nine in the Racoon Mountain campgrounds, was tucked in the shadow of the prominent mountain, and surrounded by tall pines with wiry branches and toothpick-thin needles. Anytime the wind picked up, the air whispered through the trees with a faint whistle. It was a last-minute change to their lodging, graciously offered by one of Palmer's contacts, Stu.

Stu had been standing on the rickety porch when they arrived earlier, wearing a wide smile, jeans with holes at the knees, and a torn Metallica T-shirt. He unlocked the creaky wood door and opened it to reveal a partially finished interior.

"I'm renovating all the cabins on the campground. This one is almost done." Stu puffed out his chest and ushered them inside.

The floors were rough and unfinished, but the air smelled of fresh paint, and the half-sized appliances sparkled in the corner of the main room. Lena made sure the plumbing was working. It was. This would have to make up for a second night of awkward sleeping arrangements. Only one of the two bedrooms had a bed. Well, two beds. Bunk beds, to be exact.

"I've never stayed in a log cabin before," Lena said, her inner child jumping up and down. It was an adult version of the tree house she never had growing up.

"I'll take the top bunk," Palmer said with a straight face.

"Just don't hit your head on the way up," she said while Stu laughed.

Palmer inspected the cabin for safety concerns before he left in Stu's pickup truck. Lena had fought the urge to shove him out the screen door while he poked and sniffed at each nook and cranny. *Free accommodations trumped safety!* Thankfully, five hundred square feet didn't take long to walk through.

And at long last, she was alone. Well, kind of. Douglas was parked at a slight incline on the gravel driveway, looking road-worn and dusty. The long scratch across his bumper seemed to wink at her. She would need to fix that mark, eventually. Right now, though, Douglas needed a good scrub and wax.

"I need that, too, bud," she said as she lowered herself onto a wooden rocking chair. The porch was surrounded by piles of knotted logs, each stack in the shape of a pyramid. She rocked back and forth, her gaze trained on Douglas. The flat canvas roof and rectangular opening for his pop-up tent were beckoning her.

Downtown Chattanooga was a ten-minute drive from the campground and a measly five minutes from a popular distillery that allowed overnight parking. Had she not broken herself, she would be there right now. Alone, with Douglas's tent raised high.

With a growing sense of dread, she realized popping the tent might never happen again. Her phone rang before she could spiral into her guilt.

"How are you holding up?" Shay asked in the same breath as her hello. Lena hadn't spoken to Shay since leaving. Oddly, it felt longer than two days. Hearing her sister's voice formed a lump in her throat.

She swallowed and glanced around. The area was lush with tall pines and swaying birches. A mosquito buzzed around her head. She swatted and replied, "It's hot as hell, Shay."

"Well, yesterday was the Fourth of July," Shay said with a laugh. "Summer in the South is not for the faint of heart. Good thing you're built for this, right?"

She grimaced. Was Shay implying Lena's heart was cold and made of steel now? Her stomach grumbled, reminding her she hadn't eaten since morning.

"How's Hugo doing?" Lena said, deciding to ignore Shay's comment. A hungry stomach meant her mind was ready to ravage negativity like an all-you-can-eat Chinese buffet—best to change the subject quickly.

"He's been waking up every three hours for five days now, and I am one hundred percent exhausted." A tiny coo echoed through the speaker. Lena felt the corners of her mouth lift. She wasn't a baby person. But she was definitely a proud aunt.

"Mom and Dad are still here," Shay said, lowering her voice. "They haven't found a house here yet and they refuse to return to Oregon. I know they want to be close to us and the baby and all that, but—" Hugo began to fuss, and Shay stopped talking.

"But what?" Lena's voice was much louder than she intended. Somewhere in the distance, an owl hooted in response.

"They're going to be with us for longer than expected, that's all. We'll figure it out. Nothing you need to concern yourself with." There was a loud burp. "He's been gassy lately," Shay said. "How's it going with Palmer and everything? Carrie stopped by to meet the baby and was dying to know if I had heard from you two. She has all these theories about what's happening on the road."

"I'm afraid to ask what her theories involve," Lena said, although she had a good guess.

"Two attractive single people alone together in a van driving night and day until they reach their destination. So much can happen on the road!" Shay spoke as if she were describing a book on her to-be-read list.

"So, she thinks we're like, what? Falling in love?" Lena choked on the last word. It sounded foreign coming out of her mouth. Sweat trickled down her temple.

"I think Carrie is trying to distract herself from her own problems. You should have seen her face while she held Hugo.

It's clear she's ready to have one. She also made it clear her husband isn't ready."

A mosquito landed on Lena's neck. "Damnit," she said, slapping it away.

"Sorry," Shay said, regret in her voice. "I know baby talk isn't your thing. And just so you know, I hold no theories. I know the backstory with Douglas and how difficult this must be for you. Carrie, on the other hand, might not know."

Lena flicked the smashed mosquito off her palm. "I'm sure Carrie means well. I'm just not the magical woman her cousin has been waiting for all these years." A sharp pain darted through her temples. The topic of Palmer's future partner wasn't hers to discuss in the first place. Come to think of it, Palmer's dating life was a complete mystery to her. Why was that? He knew so much about her. It was only fair she knew about his biggest heartbreak, right?

"Palmer isn't waiting around for a woman to complete his life. I can tell you that much," said Shay.

Lena's curiosity cracked its eye open and gave her a side-long glance. She knew that look. It wanted her to ask more. Even the simplest of nudges could reveal a Google search of results.

"He seems pretty determined to get his own business going," Lena said. "It's probably best for him to focus on what's important." Lena's curiosity crossed its arms. But gossip was not how she wanted Palmer's past revealed. She wanted to hear it from his mouth, voluntarily. If he ever did share it.

A beeping noise signaled another call was coming in. Lena glanced at the screen.

Crap.

"Shay, I gotta take this call. It's Mr. Cruz."

"Oh crap. Okay. Call me back!"

Of course, Shay understood why *crap* was an appropriate response. It was a sister closeness Lena hadn't meant to shut away when Seth died, but one she now realized would always be there, no matter the distance or months of disappearance.

"Okay. Or I'll text. Talk soon." Lena accepted the incoming call and hesitated before saying hello.

"Lena, is this a good time?" The greeting wasn't unusual for Seth's father. He used words with purpose, which made him a successful wildlife activist. *Hook, line, and sinker*, that was his motto. Lena knew this. Still, something was off. His tone. The timing. The question.

"I'm at the base of a mountain, so my cell reception might be a bit spotty," she said, over-explaining as she normally did whenever she spoke to Seth's dad. There was no reason for him to be calling. He knew she was on the way and the day she was scheduled to arrive. So, naturally, she expected the worst.

"This won't take long," he said.

Lena waited for him to continue, but he remained quiet. What was going on? She didn't like this. "Great. So, what's up?"

"I wanted to see if you and your friend would be interested in staying on for a few extra days. Lisa and I would cover your accommodations. There's a condo on the beach near us you can use."

"Oh, I'm not sure if Palmer will be able to." Lena cringed. She hadn't shared Palmer's name before. Or his gender. She forced herself to keep talking. "I can stay on, though. I'm going to visit a local tourist attraction not far from your house, actually. I believe the woman who was with Seth when everything happened works there. I was hoping to stop by and meet her, officially."

"Eliana, you mean. Tampatee is where she works." His voice was normal, not a speck of concern when he said that name out loud, but he might as well have punched her straight in the gut.

"Right. Yes," she said, the words stuck to the roof of her mouth.

"Perhaps I can invite her over for a cookout while you're here, save you the trouble of tourists and lines and all that."

"Oh, sure," Lena said, the air around her growing dense. Eliana was not a stranger to Seth's parents. She was the opposite. She was someone who shared meals with them. What in the ever-living *fuck* was going on?

"Great. I'll plan on it then," he said. "Either before or after we go through a few legalities from Seth's will and trust. It shouldn't take more than a day, but just in case, you'll have some time to rest up."

Her head began to spin. "I'm sorry, did you say will *and* trust?"

Seth's father had fallen quiet. "There's much to discuss," he eventually said.

Her ankle throbbed in rhythm with her heavy heartbeat. Lena pulled the phone away to look at her screen. Everything was fuzzy. Beads of sweat trickled down her back.

"I think my reception is going," she said, despite her four bars of service. "I will see you in a few days."

Seth's father agreed and the call ended. Standing up, Lena shoved the phone into the pocket of her jean shorts. She inched her way down the uneven steps of the porch and toward the front end of Douglas, her leg shouting in protest.

Seth has a secret trust!

She laid both hands on the front of Douglas, the metal cool and reassuring.

"Did you know about his trust, Douglas? Is that how he bought you? Why wouldn't he tell me? What else did he keep from me?" Lena took her hands away, tears pricking hot behind her eyes. "No. I am not going to cry about this," she said as if he'd asked. "I need to eat. That's all."

Sliding the side door open, she ducked inside and rummaged around for the microwave popcorn Mark had bought. She rooted in the overhead cupboard, her arms aching from the effort, and found the box far in the back. Hobbling past the passenger door, she paused. With anger seeping into her bloodstream, she opened the door, pressed the button on the glove compartment, and removed the brochure. The manatees smiled up at her. "I bet she knows," Lena said as she slammed the van's door shut.

Once inside the cabin, Lena placed her items on the small granite counter. The window air conditioner hummed peacefully in the corner. She glanced between the popcorn and the brochure, feeling anything but calm.

Manatees love to swim with you at Tampatee!

Her head pounded. She was hungry. Starving really, but knew she would have to digest the phone call with Seth's dad first. And the best way to process those types of conversations was through sleep.

Limping to the bedroom, Lena eased onto the bottom bunk. Her body buzzed with exhaustion as she worked the boot off, the cool air incredible against her flaming skin. Her fatigue barely registered the stiff mattress, and she drifted off quickly, dreaming of manatees, and water, and...pizza.

Lena's grumbling stomach woke her a few hours later. The room was dark, and the air smelled of melted cheese and garlic. Music trickled in through the cracks of the closed door. It was a familiar song with easy guitar strums and mellow vocals. In a heartbeat, she was back in high school, working part-time in a music shop and dreaming of opening her own store one day. That was before her love of coffee came into play. Since Seth's death, music morphed into background noise. It was an insignificant part of her daily life now. A space filler for the in-between. The sad reminder—another to add to an already long list—had her up and moving toward the door.

"Hey, sleepy head," Palmer said. His tall frame was bent low as he removed a pizza from the miniature oven.

"When did you get back?" She took a step in his direction but stopped short. A sharp pain radiated up her leg. "Shit, god-damnit."

"I'll get it." Palmer darted around her and returned with her walking cast before she could even blink. She would have marveled at his ability to be so in tune with those around him if she didn't feel weak with pain. Okay. She marveled a little.

"Here. Sit, please." He pulled out a chair from the table.

"I have no other choice but to sit." She limped over to the

chair. Why were Palmer's good intentions making her feel like an incompetent child?

He handed her the boot as she took a deep breath. "I forgot to put it on, I guess."

"That's good, though, right? That means you're forgetting about it, which means it isn't as painful." Palmer looked hopeful before turning to cut the pizza.

"I'm not sure that's the best determination for a healed bone," she said, fastening the boot around her leg.

"What is, then?" Palmer handed her a slice of pizza that filled the entire paper plate.

"When the doctor bends my ankle and tells me it's no longer broken," Lena said.

"I bet you can push yourself through this last phase without that thing on. Maybe that would help you toward your goal once we're in Florida."

She had no idea what goal he was talking about. "I'm delivering a van to its rightful owner. What difference does it make if my leg is still in my boot or not?" She took a tentative bite of pizza. The roof of her mouth shouted in protest, but the melted cheese and crispy crust were exactly what she needed. "This is way better than popcorn," she mumbled as she took another bite.

Palmer placed the brochure for Tampatee on the table. She set her pizza down.

"This is your goal, right?" Palmer tapped on the brochure.

"It's complicated." She picked at her pizza crust. "Especially after the call I had with Mr. Cruz and the trust I just found out about."

"Seth's parents want to discuss their trust with you?" Palmer said.

"Not theirs. Seth's." She didn't want to talk about it. "I don't want to talk about it." All she wanted to do was eat and go back to sleep.

"Okay. Well, it sounds like you could use something to look

forward to. Like swimming with manatees," Palmer said as he folded his pizza New York–style. He took a large bite and looked at her expectantly.

She set her pizza down—otherwise she risked tossing the crust at his forehead. She studied him chewing while two thoughts crossed her mind. One, no one from the Midwest ate pizza like that. Deep-dish reigned supreme, often with a fork and knife on hand, and thin crust was never folded. And two, she needed him to stop acting concerned whenever she brought up Florida. He would be long gone by then, anyway.

She snatched the brochure and tucked it under her thigh. "I'm going to see how I feel once I get there."

"If you commit to doing it, then you'd have more motivation to strengthen that ankle now. Hell, I can help you. This seems really important to you."

Lena's stomach began to ache as if she were performing abdominal exercises, and Palmer was yelling *One more!* With the news from Seth's father and all the unknowns she would soon step into, she wanted to shout, over and over, *Why do you care in the first place?!* She knew his answer. It would be the same one as a few days ago. *He's a helper.*

"You know what's important to me?" She placed her elbows on the table and situated her chin into her palm. Fluttering her eyelashes, she said, "You telling me why in the world you eat pizza like you're from New York."

Palmer's brows furrowed for a moment before he settled into an amused expression. "It's a long story," he said.

Lena sat back and smiled. Enough about her already. It was Palmer's turn to reveal some of himself for a change. Her curiosity perked up and nodded vigorously. *Yes*, it shouted, *he may even reveal something personal.* Lena shook her head free of the thought.

"I have nowhere to be tonight. Do you?" she said.

A tiny speck of something flashed in Palmer's eyes. "Just here with you."

Lena felt her cheeks heat. The room was warmer with the oven on. Reaching for her pizza, she took a massive bite and mumbled, "I'm all ears, then."

16

Palmer

The following morning, Palmer was greeted with a tight neck, sore shoulders, and a slightly bruised ego. But the sun was shining, and the roads were clear, even if his mind was a mess from the previous night. Lena had asked yet another question he wasn't used to answering.

The reason why he ate his pizza slices folded was the shortest story in the history of storytelling. He had meant to stir up a sense of mystery with his response to Lena the night before. What a huge miscalculation on his part. Lena had poked and prodded the *It's a long story* comment enough to reveal a weakness he didn't often share— His general impatience for eating. Which was why he folded pizza. Less surface to cover.

The look on Lena's face had validated his instincts to keep this strangeness about him hidden.

"Never rush pizza," she said, then chewed in slow motion. He fixated on the movement of her mouth, and caught himself wondering what else she didn't rush. If it looked anything like her appreciation for chewing, then he had to know.

"The best parts reveal themselves once they realize you're not going anywhere," she added with a sad smile. "At least when it comes to food."

"I'll slow down from now on," he said, meaning every word. She offered a noncommittal shrug and retired to the bedroom shortly after to "sleep off the pizza coma."

Fresh air and a sky cluttered with stars had drawn Palmer out to the porch. Ten minutes later, and with just as many mosquito bites, Palmer climbed the ladder to the top bunk and whispered good night to a gently snoring Lena.

The growl of a truck's engine yanked him out of his reverie. He checked the rearview mirror and groaned. Traffic in Atlanta was no different than in Chicago. Glancing at Lena, he felt his neck muscles tighten. Bunk beds were not built for grown men—especially not men like him.

"How about some music?" he suggested. The noise would help fend off his drowsiness. Lena, however, seemed content to sit in silence for the entirety of this trip. Which was weird to him. Who honestly enjoyed silence more than music?

"You're allowed to turn on the radio without permission, you know," she said, her tone a mix of playful and annoyed. She pressed the button and turned to a local radio station. Nirvana's "Come as You Are" crackled through the old speakers. Lena turned to look out her window.

Her mood was as pungent as the coffee smell wafting off her clothing. He had apologized earlier, the very moment he saw her waiting for him outside the coffee shop. His words had fallen short, it seemed.

Palmer turned the volume down once Kurt Cobain's melodic voice faded into a commercial. "I just want to say again— I'm sorry my meeting ran over. I'll make sure to text next time."

"It happens. You don't need to keep apologizing," Lena said. He waited for her to ask why the meeting ran late or how it went, but nothing came.

"I got distracted by this one piece of wood. The guy was pretty adamant about keeping it, but I may have wiggled my way into buying it. Who knows, though— He could very well make a beautiful table before I come back through with a truck." He was rambling in the hopes his words would cover up her bad mood.

"I'm sorry you couldn't take the piece with you today," she said with a sigh. "The sooner we get to Tampa, the sooner you can get on with your life."

Palmer's stomach dropped. How had his rambling implied any sort of impatience? His neck tightened. He was tired and sore and wanted to shake Lena free of her defiance. There was no need for it here.

"I don't have much of a life to get back to. Sure, there are bits and pieces, but hell if I know how to fit them together at the moment. So yeah, no rush over here." He turned the volume up on the radio. Lena's negativity was rubbing off on him, and he didn't like it.

"Right. You're in no rush. You're here to scout and buy as much wood as possible." Lena switched the radio off. "I don't want to listen to music right now."

"Well, I'm falling asleep and you're so—you don't—never mind." Palmer turned the radio back on.

"I don't want to listen to music," she said. The music turned off. "My van, remember?"

Palmer's knuckles grew white around the steering wheel. Why was she acting like this? He had tried to understand what was going on with her—the brochure, Seth's parents, the surprise trust—but to no avail. And now she was projecting her issues onto him. "Are you all right?"

She pulled at her shirt's collar and shook her head. "Like it's all my fault," she muttered.

"I mean, you put yourself in whatever mood this is. I'm just trying to—"

"Help me? What a crock of shit, Palmer."

"I was going to say I'm trying to figure out what's going on," he said, his tone measured. He flexed his hands. Remaining calm was a must with the idling bulldozer sitting next to him. She was ready to destroy.

"How many extra stops have you added to the schedule? Five? But you're in no rush, so why not? And you get to help me, too! Wins all around for you."

"These are lesser-known warehouses, gold mines if I had to guess, and they're on the way. It won't take too much time away from driving," he said.

Lena heaved a sigh. He could feel her glare on him. "It seems you've forgotten this is my van, my trip, my destination."

"I haven't forgotten, Lena." A burning sensation clawed at his rapidly beating heart. He knew what he wanted to say. It was her reaction he wanted to avoid. And at this point, she would say whatever she wanted anyway, so, *fuck it.* "Just remember this is my business, my time, my goodwill driving a van I barely fit in. You shut down anytime I mention the brochure or manatees or Seth's parents. I've taken the hint, you don't want to talk about it."

"No, I don't want to talk about it. I would rather deal with whatever is in store for me once I get there and move on. So, excuse me for feeling impatient while you add stops to an already long trip." Her voice trembled.

Palmer tapped on the brake as a sports car swerved in front of him. He couldn't argue with Lena right now, especially not in stop-and-go traffic. He had to fix this. "We'll arrive in Tampa on the day you told Seth's parents. Maybe a bit later in the day, but still the same day," he said. It wasn't much to ease her concern, but the delay in their arrival wasn't as bad as she was making it out to be.

A few beats of silence passed. The hum of the van's engine vibrated between them. A digital sign up ahead warned of congestion. Palmer reached for his phone, which was currently navigating them out of the city.

"Could you check—" An immediate *yes* cut him off.

Lena took the phone from him. "I've managed the road alone. I know what to do." His expression must have conveyed shock or surprise. "Usually, I pull over to find an alternate route," she continued. "Lucky for you, my hands are still in working order." After a few taps on his phone and a buzzer noise he wasn't familiar with, a voice that wasn't Lena's instructed him to exit the highway in a quarter of a mile.

"Back roads, here we come," Lena said.

Palmer felt a flicker of uncertainty. He didn't like straying from the highway in an unfamiliar suburb of Atlanta. Nor did he like sitting in unresolved tension.

"It's not for very long. We're going around what I assume is an accident," Lena assured him. He hadn't expressed his concern out loud. How did she know? She leaned over and lightly touched his shoulder. "They're touching your ears."

He rolled out his tight shoulders. It didn't help. His entire body was a rigid inferno. How could a simple touch heat him from the inside so thoroughly? "I don't like when you're upset," he said.

"I can see that. We have bigger things to deal with now." Lena pointed to an off-ramp. "This is our exit."

Palmer flipped on the signal and mentally crossed his fingers they weren't entering dangerous territory. The voice from his phone guided him to a street lined with fast-food restaurants, bars, and strip malls. It looked similar to the neighborhoods surrounding Chicago with all the concrete and foot traffic. Lena rolled down her window. A warm breeze spilled inside the van, laced with the smell of fried food.

He started to relax. They would be fine. His earlier paranoia must have been a result of too much caffeine and too little sleep. Right on cue, his stomach rumbled.

"You know what would be a great use of this detour?" Lena asked.

"Food."

"Chicken nuggets"

"And fries."

Lena pointed to a fast-food restaurant. "Dipped in a Frosty."

"The truest beacon of anyone's Midwest descent." Palmer gave a thumbs-up.

Once the food was ordered through a muffled drive-through speaker and french fries were distributed to his very eager hands, they were back on the road. The navigational voice informed them the highway was five miles ahead.

Lena polished off her chicken nuggets at a speed fit for a person twice her size.

"You were hungry," he said.

"You have no idea, or well, you probably do." She turned to him and cleared her throat. "So, a few days ago, you asked for honesty even if it was ugly," she said, her eyes cast down at her folded hands. "I don't like falling short of someone's expectations. One of the many reasons I wanted to drive Douglas to Florida myself. But I don't know how to talk about what is waiting for me there."

"I wasn't expecting it to come naturally, or for you to want to try it out in the first place," he said. "Besides, your truth is what you choose to reveal. There's really no failing if you're at least trying."

"I'm not used to premeditated reveals, you know? I'm more in line with those spontaneous moments when I say too much and then ruminate all night about it." She popped a fry in her mouth.

"I would much rather sit in our awkwardness than in our anger." He approached a stoplight and glanced at Lena. Her mouth was in a single line, her brows pulled together. She shook her hair away from her face and looked at him, her eyes steel.

"I was angry because you left me alone without my van in a strange city wondering where you were. On top of you telling me about the additional stops you added to the schedule." She took a spoonful of Frosty from her cup and gestured to it. "The sugar is talking."

He turned his attention back to the road. He had an idea. One that would distract her from her worries and keep him from losing too much time scouting wood.

"In the spirit of sugar talking for us, why not join me for the rest of these appointments? It's no different from when we looked at the space downtown. I could use your perspective, honestly. You point out details I no longer see."

"I don't know. I take most things at face value," she said,

holding out an open paper bag. He tossed his empty french fry container inside. "You see a plank of wood and envision all the ways you can make it into something else. I see wood and think of splinters."

"There aren't as many splinters as most assume. Although my hands are in a constant state of dehydration." The navigational voice interrupted him. He maneuvered Douglas into the right lane and onto a circular ramp to the highway. The line of cars was still substantial but moving. The voice informed them they would remain on Route 85 for 100 miles. Lena tapped his phone and closed the map. He appreciated the decision; it was one he would have made, too.

"So"—he snuck another glance at Lena—"what do you think?"

Lena fiddled with the air vents and kept twisting in her seat. "I think if you're going to use this trip to research a dream of yours, then maybe I could do the same."

"I think that's a great idea," he said.

"Thanks. I have more than you probably care to know," she said, her tone tight and impatient.

Lena never spoke about her plans after Florida. He'd assumed she would take it one day at a time like she was doing now and had left it at that. Which, he recognized, was a short-sighted view of her. Lena was nothing but expansive.

His body felt heavy with realization. This journey was the last thing Lena had to do before moving on with her life. Yet, here he sat, driving her van and putting himself first. How easily self-centeredness morphed into arrogance. There had to be a way to pursue the heart of one's dreams and not lose that same heart in the process.

"Lena, trust me, I do care. I want to know anything and everything you share with me."

She took a sip from her water bottle. "I do trust you—to not crash Douglas. Everything else is fair game."

He tried to take a breath but found his chest was too tight. *No more sugar revelations*, he wanted to declare, even though his heart desperately wanted to hear every word Lena offered.

"It's okay if you care more about your career than some stranger in the seat next to you. In fact, you should. I can handle being knocked down the list of priorities. I did for many years, regrettably. You owe me nothing."

"Lena—"

She held up her hand. "I will not join you in your search. I'll spend my time in coffee shops, taking notes. And if you're past the designated pickup time, I will call you."

"Right. Straightforward enough," he said. It wasn't though; her words felt like tiny bug bites on his skin. "As long as you're comfortable being alone, I thought that was part of the problem."

"I didn't know where you were with my van. Being alone wasn't the issue."

"Right. Got it." The traffic started to thin out. He accelerated to a speed Douglas preferred and hit the cruise option, thankful the van ran off a Subaru engine from the '90s and not its original. Cruise control wasn't a standard option in the '80s. "What notes do you plan to take in these coffee shops?"

She shrugged. "Whatever catches my eye."

"So, research for ideas to maybe one day...run your own shop?

She sighed. "I appreciate the effort with your questions. They kind of— It feels forced or something. How about some music?"

He nodded. Was she always this changeable? Listening to music was okay now, as was being alone, when just minutes ago she had been trembling with anger. He hoped it was her mind under stress and not a personality trait. But what did he know, he was there to drive, so he'd just keep driving.

17

Lena

Lena glanced around as she lowered onto a sunken antique chair. She took in the red brick walls and crystal chandelier, the sizable window in the corner—not original to the building, or so she assumed—and the red velvet love seat pressed against the farthest wall. A man and a woman spoke quietly, their heads bent toward one another, their hands intertwined. Lena moved her gaze to the most unique part of the coffee shop: the large black steel door opening out into the main area. It was unlike any door she had encountered in person. This room was an old bank vault, and the door epitomized old-time security, with clunky hinges and ancient-looking lynchpins.

She took a photo, then set her phone down and sipped her latte. Creamy and warm, with just the right amount of espresso to milk. She wiped the foam from her upper lip. Lattes were a barista's worst and best dream. More milk, less foam, triple espresso shots— Everyone had their opinions. An equal balance of espresso to milk was her preference but she had yet to perfect it.

Soon enough she would be behind the counter, whizzing about effortlessly, instead of fumbling over her own two feet. But one huge question remained: What would happen after this road trip? Part of her wanted to be close to her sister for the first time in their adult lives and watch her nephew grow. The other part of her was too confused to know up from down at the moment.

Tapping on her contact list, she scrolled to Palmer's name. Lena hadn't texted Palmer since his invitation to view the downtown warehouse. It was crazy to think that was only a month ago. Being on the road would do that though, distance you from your memories. The uniqueness of her surroundings called for a text, though, right? Okay, and maybe she wanted to extend a peace offering after giving him so much attitude in the van earlier.

I'm sitting in a Confederate bank vault.

She attached the photo, hitting send before she changed her mind. A chill slithered down her spine as the crystal chandelier flickered. What stories did these cracked walls hold? Certainly a building this old—most likely from the Civil War era—had witnessed grueling realities in its time. The air moved, like someone had opened a window. She shivered as a distinct damp basement smell took over.

Ghosts weren't a concern of hers, she was haunted enough by her memories. But something was off—the light, the air—like she was moving through an invisible sheet of molasses. If ghosts got stuck here on their way to the afterlife, she was sure it was because of the atmosphere. Her phone pinged before her mind could catastrophize the situation further.

A photo of dirt floors and black-stained wooden walls filled her screen. Beams of sunlight streamed through the panels of wood, the light hazy and dust-ridden.

I'm standing in an abandoned rickhouse.

Lena raised a hand to her chest, stunned. Gathering herself, she typed a response. The whoosh of a sent message sounded.

Only you could turn dust into beauty.

She quickly set her phone face down, surprised by her response and the fact that she had sent it. The lights flickered when she placed the mug against her lips. She gulped and reached for her phone the moment it pinged.

Only you would see beauty in dust.

She sat back and read the text again, tempering the urge to full-on grin. She wanted to revel in Palmer's wit and gossip to her heart that he was flirting. With her! It was her mind who wouldn't allow it, at least not for longer than a few seconds. Her phone pinged as if to signal that her time was up.

This visit was a bust. I'll be by soon.

Her stomach somersaulted. Sure, the caffeine was flowing and the room was giving off serious paranormal vibes, but she couldn't deny how great it felt to flirt with a man...*who is my friend!*

Shaking her head, as if that would center her—*what a joke*—she typed *okay*, then looked out the opening of the vault to an empty coffee shop. It was near closing time, she realized. The lights flickered and blinked, on then off, then on again. The musty basement smell intensified. She shot out of her seat, her ankle screaming at the sudden movement. A building this old was bound to have electrical issues, but she wasn't sticking around to have her assumption confirmed.

In her rush, which was a limping disaster at best, her good foot caught on the sill of the vault door and jerked her body forward. The mug in her hand shot out in slow motion and hit the ground with a terrible crash. Mortified, she bent down to clean up her mess. Sweat dampened her lower back as pain engulfed her every sense. She was stuck between a kneel and a squat. Struggling to find the will to right herself, her vision faded in and out. Distant footsteps echoed in the hollows of her mind.

"Here, I got you," a voice said from above, as clear as looking out a spotless windshield. Strong hands brought her upright. A pair of deep blue eyes met hers, too familiar to be a stranger's. Lena took a step backward. "Are you okay?" the man asked. He pushed away a chunk of brown hair from his forehead and smiled. Thin lips. High cheekbones. Shaggy hair. He even had a camera bag slung over his shoulder.

Lena squeezed her eyes shut and shook her head. This couldn't be real. There was no way this was real. She opened them again. The man was still there, staring at her with a puzzled expression.

"You're a photographer," she said, her voice foreign.

He looked down at the bag by his hip and then back to her. "Yeah, for a travel magazine. I'm on my way to Florida."

Lena's balance wavered. The air was thick with the same musty basement smell from earlier. The man caught her arm and guided her to a wrought iron chair.

"Let me get you a glass of water," he said. His voice sounded worn, as if he'd just gotten over a cold.

"No. Thank you." She refused to look at him for fear of confirming what was unthinkable anyway.

He sat across the table from her. She couldn't move. Why was he sitting down? Better yet, why wasn't she leaving?

"I had the best first date in a coffee shop before I left for this job." He drummed his fingers on the table.

Stunned beyond rational thought, the only word Lena could produce was, "Oh?"

"It was nowhere as cool as this place. Although to be fair, I didn't really take in my surroundings. This woman, with her fiery red hair, spilled her drink on me." He sighed. This couldn't be happening. How was this happening? Lena's legs had gone numb, and she feared her entire body would soon follow.

"Why are you telling me this?" she blurted, adding yet another regret to the memory.

"I was trying to distract you," he said with a shrug.

A petite woman with puffy hair and an apron tied around

her narrow waist walked over with a broom and dustpan. The scratching of broken porcelain against the tiled floor grounded Lena back into her body. She stood up and apologized to the employee for her clumsiness.

"Darlin', you're not the first," the employee said, her Southern accent thick. "People been tripping outta that vault for months now."

"You should be able to remove the sill from the floor," the man said. He stood up and walked to the vault door, placing his hands on his hips. The muscles on his arms poked out from under his short-sleeved collar shirt. Lena spied a large mole just above his left elbow. Her stomach cropped. He straightened his neck and looked at Lena with a shrug.

Lena's head jerked away as the same chill from earlier spread into her veins. Her body was shaking beyond control. Somehow, inexplicably, this man was her dead fiancé, and she needed to get out. Right now.

"I'd remove that damn sill myself," the employee said to Lena. The man hovered by the vault door. "But this here is a historical building. Which means we need permits. And if you haven't toured our little downtown area, every building is historic, so there's a waitlist." She dumped the broken mug into a trash can. "Would you like a refill, darlin'?"

"Sure." It was an automatic response— Rarely did she turn down coffee, but at this moment, she had meant to.

"But, uh, in a to-go cup," Lena added.

The man walked in her direction. Lena inched closer to the front door, willing the employee to get a move on. The smell of sandalwood and lemon drifted around her. What remained of Lena's sensibility gasped and sputtered for air.

"Seems kind of silly to require a permit when it's a modification for safety purposes," he said, readjusting the strap on his shoulder. "Why risk an accident, right?"

The hair on Lena's arms stood up. Seth had risked everything by going to Florida.

"I didn't know I was in danger," he said in a low tone. She froze. Had he read her mind? "I always planned on coming back to you, even if you didn't want me."

Lena's stomach plummeted to the molten core of the Earth. Had he really just said that out loud?

The woman turned to Lena. "It was a latte, right?"

"Oh." Lena's voice cracked. "Whatever is quickest is fine." She fumbled for the wallet in her bag, desperate to leave whatever Twilight Zone this was.

"Americano it is." The employee twisted the knob on the steamer. The loud noise made Lena's skin jump as her vision faded again. She rooted for something to hold on to, her finger-tips clawing onto something hard and smooth. The bell above the door echoed.

A voice from way up high kept saying her name. "Lena? Lena."

Lena blinked. A bearded face came into focus.

"Hey." Palmer said, his face flushed. "I wasn't sure if you heard me talking...right in front of you."

"Oh, good. You're here," she said, relieved to see him. Which she would *not* overthink later tonight. She needed the presence of someone undeniably real, and Palmer was as real as it got.

Palmer stared at Lena. "Are you okay? You look like you've seen a ghost."

She burst out laughing. It was a manic kind of cackle that made Palmer scrunch his face in concern. She sobered. Why was she sitting on the wrought iron chair? The one the man had brought her after her fall.

"What the hell," she said, standing up trance-like. She glanced over to where the man had stood, then spun around in a circle, doing her best not to fall over. The man was nowhere in sight. He was gone.

"Did you lose something? Your purse or something?" Palmer scanned her from head to toe.

"No. Nothing like that." She walked to the counter where the woman was pouring a drink. She leaned into the counter and asked the woman, "Where did he go? Do you know where he went?"

The woman gave her a funny look. "Where who went?"

"The man with the camera bag who was asking questions about the doorsill I tripped on. He was right here." She pointed to the empty spot next to her.

"You tripped? Are you okay? Where?" Palmer said. Lena gestured to the vault, annoyed with Palmer's stream of questions.

The woman clicked her tongue. "Darlin', it's been you and me here. Well, until this tall man of yours arrived."

"He's not my—"

"Oh, this is an easy fix." Palmer was standing at the vault. "Do you have a hammer?"

"It's an easy fix, honey," the woman said. She slid the cup across the counter. "But this here is a historical building. Which means permits."

"Permits," Palmer echoed.

Lena felt dangerously close to passing out. Again.

Palmer walked up to the counter. "Safety modifications shouldn't require a permit. Your city should allow it with an additional form, and whoa—" Palmer's warm hands brushed her shoulder. "You're not looking well, Lena."

"Gee, thanks, Palmer. Just what every woman wants to hear." Lena ground her back teeth in an effort to stop herself from further spouting off angry statements. She shrugged off his touch.

"Ah, she'll be fine," the woman said and pointed to a shelf filled with merchandise. "Our signature *Return from the Dead* coffee is darn powerful. We roast our own beans on-site." Several bags of coffee lined the wall. The label had a picture of wildflowers growing out of a skull. "Here darlin'. On the house."

Lena reached for the cup of coffee with a trembling hand, thanking the woman. Whatever just happened was too paranormal, too Hitchcock, and too damn real for it to be imagined. She offered her coffee to Palmer.

"I don't need any more caffeine."

Once inside the van, Lena found it impossible to sit still. Her legs buzzed and her ponytail felt too tight. They were on the highway to Tallahassee, where they would find accommodations for the night. Their final drive together would be to Tampa tomorrow.

She let out a sigh and ran her hands down her thighs. Palmer kept glancing at her. He probably thought she had to pee. Which would make more sense than what had just happened in the coffee shop. Releasing her hair, she ran her fingers through the ends. The man's face flashed through her mind. She squeezed her eyes shut. She had to tell someone. Otherwise she would end up going crazy.

"Something happened in that coffee shop earlier," she said. "Someone appeared...out of thin air." She took a steadying breath.

Palmer kept his gaze on the road. "As in, like...a ghost?"

"I think it was Seth." Lena covered her face with her hands and forced herself to keep talking. "He said he was on his way to Florida for work and randomly mentioned our first date when I spilled coffee on him. He even sounded like Seth, except more worn or something." She peeked through her fingers to see what Palmer was doing. He was driving.

"I thought you looked pale when I walked in," he said. "Now it makes sense."

"Well, I mean, most redheads are pale by default." She spied a smile as he scratched his beard. A nanosecond was all it took for her to wonder about his dimples again. *Talk about bad timing.* She shook her head and stared at Douglas's windshield. The view was dotted with various smashed bugs, messy and all over the place, just like her emotions. She leaned her head back against the seat. "It was like a scene plucked straight from a dream, and felt far too real."

Palmer tapped his fingers on the steering wheel. Why wasn't he saying anything? Oh god. Why had she opened her mouth? She sounded totally insane.

"It's okay. I know how crazy I sound," she said.

"You're not crazy, Lena. That entire town is haunted, I couldn't wait to leave," he said.

"Don't try to make me feel better," she said. Even though he had, in fact, made her feel the slightest bit better.

"No, I'm serious. The guy storing his wood in the rickhouse said it had been on the market for years. No one wants to buy it 'cause it's haunted. At first, I thought he was pulling my leg, but then we stepped inside, and it was like—" He blew out a breath and scratched at his beard again. "It was like the air held more than I could see. I'm not surprised you picked up on something, too."

"The air in that town was weird. I won't argue with you there. But what happened to me was a full-on hallucination." The muscles across her forehead tightened. Why was she still talking? Admitting this out loud wasn't helping anything or anyone.

"I think you saw what you saw for a reason." Palmer's face was free of judgment or concern. In fact, he appeared curious. "Did he do or say anything else that caught you off guard?"

Lena laughed. "All of it took me off guard. His face, that mole on his arm, his smell, each and every word he uttered—" She stopped talking. Her vision blurred.

Seth had planned on coming back to her.

Even if you didn't want me.

She rolled her window down and placed her face into the hot wind. Seth would have fought for them—fought for her—if things had gone differently. Was this the reason behind her otherworldly experience? For one of her unanswered questions to find a resting place in her mind?

She rolled up the window and blinked away the tired feeling

in her eyes. "At some point, once you leave and I'm alone, I'm sure I will unpack whatever I just imagined with many, many tears. But I do appreciate you entertaining this insane conversation, and I will now look for hotels in Tallahassee on my phone."

Palmer was quiet and doing what he did best: holding space for her while driving a tiny van he barely fit in. One more day and then their time together would be over. Maybe that's why Palmer was so patient with her; there was an end in sight for him.

"Lena," Palmer said in a tone so gentle it made her stomach clench. "No one is meant to bear all of their burdens alone one hundred percent of the time."

"Whether that's true or not, I prefer to be alone with my problems." Since she could remember, this was how she handled her emotions.

As a child, Lena's mom would offer hugs, and her dad took her for ice cream, but those big feelings always stayed tucked inside. As an adult, she still accepted hugs and had a tub of ice cream in the freezer at all times, but continued to carry her troubles alone.

"I'm used to it. Even when Seth was alive, I dealt with my problems solo. Most of the time." She focused on her phone, leaving out how much she feared letting anyone get close to her again. It took Seth years to crack a tiny section in her thick defenses. "Oh! Hey. This hotel is fifty percent off. It's a four-star hotel, too. Although I'm not sure what that means in the state of Florida, but what do you think?" Now she was doing what she did best: changing the topic and pretending what she'd just said hadn't been heard.

"What I think..." Palmer trailed off. Lena lowered her phone. Palmer's shoulders were raised and his knuckles were white. He appeared distracted. Lena poked his shoulder.

"You drifted off. Where'd you go?"

Palmer sighed. "My father has decided to sell the company to me after all and booked me a nonstop flight out of Tampa tomorrow night."

"He what?" Lena's phone fell from her hand. She scrambled to retrieve it before it slid to the floor. Palmer was such an expert at acting like everything was okay. If the table had been turned, she would have flipped it over.

"You're joking."

Palmer shook his head. "It wasn't a conversation, either. The man actually left a voice message, which is unheard of, literally. He has to know this latest demand is completely out of line."

Lena fiddled with her phone as she considered her next words. Palmer had been a constant ear to her worries and drama. She wanted to return the favor. And selfishly, his father's antics would answer questions about Palmer's future plans. Which meant she wouldn't have to ask. Which removed the possibility of uncovering deeper feelings in the process. Saying goodbye to Palmer wasn't going to be easy. Not anymore.

"The timing of it seems like a power play," she said. He nodded in agreement. "What's your gut telling you?"

He opened and closed his mouth. "My gut isn't telling me anything, it's too busy fighting with my brain."

She offered a soft laugh. "I'm familiar with the struggle." Her mind was in a fight too, but with her heart.

"So, yesterday when I spoke to Mr. Cruz, he suggested I stay at a beachside condo tomorrow night. It has two bedrooms," she said, stalling. The invitation would complicate an already migraine-worthy situation but Palmer needed time to think, and she wanted to help. Stretching her arms out in front of her, her fingertips grazed upon the space between fear and desire. "If you need an extra day to process or somewhere to go until you figure out your next steps, you're welcome to stay." She sounded more confident than she felt. Seth's parents would just have to deal with her travel mate staying on after all. Just like she would have to deal with Seth's secret trust.

"You're not sick of me yet?" Palmer said with a sheepish grin. *Far from it*, she wanted to say but shoved the words aside. It wouldn't be fair if she voiced her knee-jerk thoughts. Especially after hallucinating Seth into existence only a few hours ago.

"You don't have to decide until tomorrow—"

Palmer stole her hand from her lap and pressed a kiss onto her palm. The gesture was so quick, so unexpected, and so toe-tingling it could have been the wisp of a dream.

"I accept your invitation. Thank you."

Their hands separated. She pressed her palm against her flushed face. So much had happened today. And yet, somehow she wanted more of...this. Unbuckling her seat belt, she pressed her lips against the skin above his scratchy beard and mumbled, "It's my turn to help you, now."

18

Palmer

"I see you have a king suite booked for one night," the receptionist said. Her eye makeup was as thick as her perfume. The lobby desk she stood behind reminded Palmer of a disco ball. Neon rope lights outlined the perimeter of the lobby ceiling, the colors morphing from green to blue as techno music pumped through invisible speakers.

"I booked two queen beds," Lena said, reaching into her bag. She pulled out her phone. "Here's the reservation confirmation."

The receptionist squinted at the phone and then looked down at her computer screen. A frown pulled at the corners of her mouth. "There must have been an error when you booked. Our system has your reservation for one king bed, and unfortunately, the hotel is fully booked for the night."

Lena sighed and leaned heavily against the desk. He understood that sigh all too well. Their accommodations on the road had consistently come with hiccups, it seemed.

"This is the last night on our road trip, so we're a little drained," Palmer said. He took a quick glance at her name tag. "Two beds would be ideal if that's possible, Vanessa."

"It's fine, Palmer. It is what it is."

The receptionist—Vanessa—looked between them, her brows pulled together. "Personally, I'd say the king suites are way better. This room is on the top floor, which means you'll have a panoramic view of Tallahassee's rolling hills." Vanessa

159

clicked the computer mouse, and a drawer next to her popped open. She slid two vouchers toward Palmer, then went back to the drawer and handed him two more. "Congratulations on your last night. The bar is open till midnight," she said in a low voice.

"Well, now you're talking," Lena said brightly.

Palmer shoved the four free drink vouchers into his pocket and thanked the receptionist. Lena went to locate the elevators while he waited for the key cards.

"Does the bar have food, too?" Palmer asked the receptionist once Lena was out of earshot. They hadn't eaten properly all day. If Lena knew he was worried about her drinking on an empty stomach, her mood would surely sour.

"It doesn't, but I'm here all night. If you order food for delivery, I'll talk the bartender into letting you eat at the bar." Vanessa winked.

Palmer nodded. It was a flirtatious favor, and he was dumbfounded as to why. He looked homeless, smelled of old fast food and likely sweaty gym socks.

He'd certainly been sweating more than usual since his call earlier. His father's reaction to Palmer refusing to rush back home wasn't surprising. In fact, the news had only amplified his father's wild behavior.

"This is the family business, like you said, son! Get your brain back in your head and out of your pants—"

Palmer had hung up on him mid-sentence. He definitely wasn't returning home tomorrow night, not after that episode. Hell, maybe he wouldn't at all. At this point, he would need an apology from his father in order to go back. Or something just as unrealistic to happen.

Scooping up the key cards, he thanked the receptionist and met up with Lena at the elevators. She smiled at him while her upper body rocked gently from side to side. She often did this while standing in line, or waiting in general; an endearing trait, Palmer felt. He was going to miss her. Terribly. How could he not? His confidence in the unknown had only gotten stronger in Lena's presence. He was grateful their time together wasn't over yet. A drink or two was definitely in order tonight.

Once inside the room, Lena walked toward the windows and pushed the curtains open. Palmer stood beside her and took in the spectacular array of oranges, pinks, and purples drenching the sky. The soft *in and out* of their breathing was the only sound in the room. A pair of cotton-candy clouds floated lazily in front of the darkened hills.

"This is pretty great," Lena said, her tone a mix of awe and defeat. She turned to look at the bed. "It looks big enough for two."

On the opposite side of the room, a wooden headboard reached from floor to ceiling with two sconces in the middle, illuminating the king-sized bed below. Two large pillows sat on top of the white comforter, with two additional tube-like pillows striped in rainbow colors.

Palmer bumped his shoulder with hers. "I've slept across from you and on top of you." He choked on his own tongue. "On top because of the bunk beds. But, uh, you know, next to you seems like the next logical step." He cringed. "I completely botched that joke."

"It wouldn't be right if you and I didn't make this more awkward," she said and planted her hands on her hips. "We're grown-ass adults. We can share a bed. And after a few libations, all will be just fine."

Palmer understood what *fine* meant, but damn, he wished she meant what she didn't mean. He glanced at the square clock on the nightstand. It was eight o'clock. The hotel bar was open until midnight, which left plenty of time to shower and order food.

As if Lena had read his mind, she announced she was going to rinse off and disappeared into the bathroom. Once he heard the shower start, he called down to the front desk and asked for food delivery recommendations. Tuesday night in Tallahassee did not yield many options, not that he had any reason to impress Lena with food. So, why did he want to? And why did it feel like he was prepping for a date? He was hungrier than he realized. For food. *Damnit.* The thought of kissing Lena sounded way more satisfying than a slice of pizza right now.

Up until now, Palmer had done a damn fine job at keeping his brain in his head. Removing his arms from Lena on their first night in the motel was a testament to his control. But he was a single man who hadn't been with a woman for…longer than he would like to admit. His thoughts were allowed to wander in place of his hands. He hated that his father's voice was in his head, proving that Palmer was thinking with his—

"Next!" Lena's voice made him jump. She walked around the corner wearing a loose-fitting tank top and a pair of dark linen shorts. Her wet hair curled around her face, leaving drops of water on her bare shoulders. He tried not to stare, but good god, she was a sight with her glowing skin.

"Right. Okay. I won't be long," he said and quickly walked past her.

"So shaving your beard won't happen tonight. Got it," she said.

He was halfway into the bathroom, his hand hovering over the door knob. "You really don't like this thing, huh?"

"I want to know if I'll like your bare face more." Lena snatched her walking cast off the bed and began fastening the clasps. "Pretend I didn't say that."

Palmer's heart jumped into his throat. Like hell he would. He would shave it off right now if his razor and shaving cream weren't inside Douglas at the moment.

"How about this," he said, leaning his shoulder against the doorframe. "If you go without that thing on your leg tonight, I'll shave my beard tomorrow morning."

Lena looked up, her eyebrows raised high. "Tempting." She considered him. "Honestly, though, sitting in a van for three days straight hasn't done me any favors. It's been swollen a lot lately."

"Maybe what your leg needs is a little space to stretch out and feel normal," he said. It wasn't his business to boss her around like a doctor, but a little push out of her comfort zone couldn't hurt. "Would it be so bad to test out your healing so far?"

"Well, yeah, I could end up hurting myself again." She twisted her hands in her lap.

"If anything should happen, I'm here, and the room is a quick elevator ride." Palmer waited while Lena tapped her finger on the last unfastened clasp.

"Okay. I'll try it out."

"Really?"

Lena removed the walking cast and tossed it onto the nearby desk chair. It landed with a determined thump. "I swear, if you end up carrying me like a damsel in distress tonight—" She shook her head. "Go shower before I change my mind."

He did a faux soldier's salute and retreated into the bathroom, feeling as if he'd just won the lottery and his prize was Lena's trust.

The bar was packed for a Tuesday night. A group of young men dressed in wrinkled suits and loosened neckties occupied the blocky couches and stainless steel tables scattered about the space. They shouted and slapped each other's backs as the smack of pool balls sounded. Calypso music rang through the house speakers, loudly asking those who were listening, *Why don't we get drunk?*

Palmer spotted two metal stools tucked under the middle of the bar at the same time that Lena pointed eagerly, saying, "Grab those!"

Palmer hid his smile. Lena was moving at the speed of a turtle and Palmer was happy he could be of use. A few curious stares watched Lena limp along, but her gaze remained on him. The sparks in his stomach were hard to ignore.

Pulling out a stool, he offered his hand to Lena. She grasped it and an eruption of tingles traveled up his arm. Her smile was tense while she maneuvered herself up.

"I did it!" She raised her arms into the air. A round of cheers erupted from behind them. She glanced over her shoulder and waved sheepishly to the group. "Note to self, no more shouting."

"Ah, celebrate your wins. They're harmless," he said. He sat down and gave her a side hug. She leaned into him, laughing and gesturing to the bartender. He shifted his nose toward her hair, her vanilla smell too enticing to pass up. Straightening his back, he stole a glance before focusing on the back bar. Her cheeks were stained pink, and her mouth pursed as she looked at the drink menu. The sparks in his stomach shot into his throat.

Maybe he wouldn't ignore the jolts Lena gave him tonight. Maybe, instead, he could lean into the gentle arm-touches, playful knee-grabs, and arm-wraps around her shoulders. At least for tonight, the final night of their road trip bubble. He turned his knees toward her. He wanted her in his sight. Too many hours had been spent looking at a road with her seated next to him.

"The whiskey list is impressive for a hotel bar," Lena said and offered the menu to him. Her eyes darted down to his mouth, then back up.

He cracked a smile. "This bar is impressive for a hotel bar," he said, closing the menu down. He already knew what he wanted.

She smoothed her hands over the distressed stainless steel bar. "First, a haunted coffee shop, now a random bar with way too many neon signs. Today has been one for the books," she said. Shouts erupted from the group of men behind them. Lena shifted in her seat, a look of unease crossing her face.

He looked past her shoulder to a framed painting of Tina Turner, reminiscent of a comic book character. Next to the painting were double doors leading out to a patio. Empty lounge chairs with puffy cushions surrounded a circular fire table. The flames beckoned him to take Lena out into the firelight.

"I think we should try our luck outside," Palmer said. He tilted his chin toward the patio.

Lena turned her head, already nodding. "Those seats look way more comfortable and not as...loud," she said. She moved off the stool, and another jolt vibrated through his body as she limped away. Her drink remained on the bar. It was possible she had forgotten to take it due to her ankle. Still, her forgetting made Palmer feel closer to Lena. Perhaps she relied on him and knew he would take care of it...take care of her without having to ask. They were more familiar than strangers now.

A salt-scented breeze laced through the patio, the cool damp air sticking to his arms. The disappearance of the sun had lowered the hot temperatures, but it was still Florida in July. Lena was nestled into the corner of a convertible couch, her face lit by the fire.

Palmer set the drinks on the outer rim of the fire table. "Mind if I join you?" He tried for an ironic chuckle, but it came out sounding like a malfunctioning robot.

"You may join me," Lena said. She smiled as she patted the cushion next to her.

Palmer sat down, his leg pressing into Lena's. "Hi."

She shivered, her goosebumps visible. "Hi," she said.

The urge to lean closer and kiss the small freckle on the side of her cheek was overwhelming. He reached for his drink and took a healthy sip. Liquid stone fruit with hints of peaty smoke slid down his throat and warmed his grumbling stomach.

"We should order a pizza," he said as he rooted in his shorts pocket.

Lena sipped her bourbon with a contented smile. "I ordered a pizza while you were in the shower." She peered around him. "The driver knows to come to the bar."

"Well, you read my mind," Palmer said, wrapping an arm around her shoulders for their second side hug of the night. Just like before, she melted into him. This time she sighed and lingered before pulling away.

"Did I read your mind or your stomach?" She moved away with a nervous giggle. Her cheeks were pink as she took a small sip. "I'm a lightweight with poor jokes. Now you know."

"I want to know everything about you, Lena," Palmer said. The longer he sat with his leg pressed against hers, listening to the trickling water and sipping on whiskey meant to loosen tongues, the more certain he felt that he was going to kiss her.

"Palmer," Lena said, fiddling with the cushion's raised seam. "I told you I saw a ghost earlier today. You know more about me than anyone else in my life at the moment."

"I'm honored you shared that with me, you know," he said. She nodded. They had shared many vulnerable and unexplainable moments in the last three days. And he agreed, she knew more about him than anyone else, too. But he wanted more of what he didn't know, like the feel of her lips against his, the curve of her hips under his palms, the sound she made when she—

"Oh! Pizza's here!" Lena pointed, wincing when she tried to stand. "Crap, I forgot."

"I'll flag him down," Palmer said, standing with the caution of a man who very obviously wanted to devour the woman next to him. "You okay?"

"Are *you* okay there, old-timer?" Lena said.

"Oh, yeah, just, you know, my foot's asleep," Palmer said while walking toward the patio doors. It was a half truth. His body tingled—a departure from the numbness he had been living in for so many years. This trip had woken him up. And Lena was the fresh morning air.

19

Lena

Lena scarfed down the food with zero regard for ladylike behavior. She was relieved her appetite had returned after months of barely eating. Although, her diet had been more hearty than healthy since being on the road—the waistband of her shorts were a testament to that fact—but nothing a few runs on the beach couldn't fix. If she could run. Which she couldn't. No matter, Palmer was eating just as fast, and he seemed pleased with their progress.

Once the pizza was gone and their second drink vouchers were cashed in, Palmer announced he was going to shave his beard. Tonight.

"Tonight? I thought you said tomorrow," Lena said. She crossed her legs and jiggled her good ankle. Somewhere between the hotel room and her first drink, her grief had ducked out without saying goodbye. She hadn't meant for it to happen. But with the gurgling fountain in the background and the fire warming her bare legs, she was enjoying the company of a man who made her feel...things. She wasn't ready to return to herself yet.

She tapped her phone and squinted at the time. "How technical does *tonight* mean to you?"

"Well, there's a catch." Palmer removed his arm from the cushion behind her. Before she could pout, he placed his hand on her knee. As his hand slid down her shin, a warmth radiated up toward her inner thigh. His skin was rough and warm, making her forget herself even more. Palmer gently cupped her ankle. "You walk back to our room without spilling a single drop from your glass, and I'll shave this scratchy thing off." Palmer's hand lingered on her ankle. Lena's tongue stuck to the roof of her mouth.

The request was meant to challenge her, as Palmer had been adamant in doing the last few days. But there was something else to his request, another angle he was hinting at. Was his eagerness to shave his beard more than a silly bet?

His hand left her ankle. He patted her knee like a brother would and reached for his glass.

Right.

She was off creating fantasies in an alcohol-buzzed mind. Nothing more.

He peered at her over the rim of his glass, a glint in his eye.

Right?

"Do you think you can do it?" he asked.

That depends on how smooth your face will feel against my inner thighs.

She sputtered into her drink and shook the words out of her mind. Her inner voice could be so inappropriate at the worst of times.

"Is that a no?" He laughed.

"What? Oh! No. There was a bug." She swatted at the imaginary nuisance. "I'll do it if you're prepared to shave your beard. Which it seems like you are." She rose to her feet gingerly. Her ankle felt almost normal with the dulling effects of whiskey at work. Which also meant less than reliable reflexes.

Palmer stood up and handed her the drink—the singular most important object that would determine the fate of his face. Her walk would be even more nerve-wracking since she had a top-heavy nosing glass.

"I'll be right behind you in case you slip or lean or trip or whatever," Palmer said in reassuring tones. Lena swallowed down a burst of nervous giggles. He was taking her walk to the room so seriously. How could she not feel weak in the knees for that alone?

"Let's do this, then," she said with forced bravado. Palmer's hand touched the small of her back. They stopped in front of the patio doors. He turned into her, the pressure on her lower back increasing. She looked up at him, her chest dangerously close to his. He pushed a strand of hair away from her eyes. She took a steadying breath as a million white dandelion seeds danced in her stomach, begging her to make a wish. All she had to do was close her eyes, rise up onto her tiptoes, and forget about tomorrow.

"Palmer," she said, tapping the arm circled around her. He broke from his trance and took a step back.

He nodded but appeared disappointed. "You're right. No assistance! Onward, young lady. I have a bet to lose."

She pressed her lips together and moved into the air-conditioned bar. Had Palmer initiated a kiss, she wouldn't have stopped it. Was it meant to happen right now? Did she want it to happen? If Palmer did, she would. Maybe. Regardless, the thought was sobering enough to aid in her walk to win the bet. So, at least, there was that.

Once they successfully entered the hotel room, Palmer rushed back out to retrieve his shaver from Douglas, a huge smile on his face. He was the least sore loser she had ever encountered, seemingly thrilled to have lost. He returned in record time and went straight to the bathroom. Lena waited on the bed, her hands under her thighs, while the buzz of Palmer's shaver filled the room.

Any moment, Palmer would enter the room looking drastically different. God, she hoped he still had a chin. So many men lost theirs once their beards came off. She released her hands and ran them through her frizzy hair. It needed a cut, and she needed to stop worrying about Palmer's face. Swooping her tangled mop over her shoulder, she reached for her drink on the nightstand. The buzzing sound stopped. A burst of sparks shot through her stomach at the sound of the bathroom door opening.

She straightened her back as her eyes landed on Palmer's bare face. Two dimples. *Knew it!* And a slightly cleft but clearly there chin. She sucked in a breath. Palmer was ridiculously handsome. Why he chose to cover up half his face with hair was beyond her understanding.

He sat next to her. The smell of pine and musky aftershave hugged and enticed her. Lena was staring, she knew she was. The heat creeping up her neck and into her face confirmed it was out of her control, too.

"I've rendered you speechless. Is that a good or bad thing?" Palmer said with a smirk, clearly knowing the effect he was having on her.

Lena nodded and said, "Good." Her tongue was tied, otherwise she'd tell him to never grow a beard again.

"Right-o." Palmer grinned, his cheeks indenting. The distance between her and Palmer had shrunk in size. Palmer's smooth face was close enough for her to touch, if she didn't have a glass of bourbon in her hand. Which she did. Thank god.

Her mind was operating under the influence of whiskey and pheromones, raising the likelihood of questionable decisions. Like kissing a man, *this man*, for the first time. She wanted to believe she was strong enough to deal with the aftermath. Surely, her guilt would understand this wasn't just any man in front of her. This was Palmer. *Palmer.* Her intoxicated confidence gestured eagerly.

Palmer rubbed underneath his bottom lip, his dimples teasing his cheeks, then turned to the nightstand for his glass.

"Thanks for your help at the elevator," she said, forcing herself to look at the wall in front of her. She fiddled with her glass.

"Whoa. Did you just thank me for helping you?" He leaned in and inspected her face. "Who are you, and what have you done with Lena?" He tapped her nose playfully but his expression was pure fire. His finger trailed slowly down her cheek.

She swallowed, her throat impossibly dry, and whispered, "It's still me."

Palmer's fingers slid under her chin and tilted it upward. She gazed into his darkened eyes and wondered what he saw looking back. Did he see the broken woman from a sad past, or a woman who was far away from herself right now?

"I enjoyed our time tonight," he said, his breath warm with whiskey. "And I really enjoyed watching you with your little smiles and cute mannerisms. It's something I can't do much of when I'm driving." He stroked her cheek. "You're...you're beautiful."

All her nerve endings lit up. She felt exposed, yet reveled in the attention, like a work of art waiting to be framed by this moment.

Palmer took her glass and set it down on the nightstand. His hand returned to her face. She closed her eyes, waiting for her guilt to take over and yell *Stop this right now*. Palmer reached for her hands. Her eyes popped open. Palmer's face came into focus. Her heart sped up as he placed her hands on either side of his face.

"So, do you like it?" he said.

Her mind splintered in a thousand different directions. She liked everything about this moment, but was she supposed to? "I think so." Her thumb stroked his smooth skin.

He moved her hands to his chest. His heart drummed a strong and steady rhythm. Her fingers flexed into his cotton shirt. This was real. This was happening.

Their noses touched. His lips were a shadow passing over hers. "I think I would like to kiss you," he murmured.

Her mind didn't shout, or yell. It sighed, aching for his touch. She wanted to say yes. She should just say yes. Why wasn't she saying yes?

"And before you give me all the reasons why we shouldn't," Palmer continued, "I want you to consider the biggest reason why we should."

"Which is?" she asked, her voice hoarse.

His dimples winked at her. "Because we can. Because we want to. Because the law of attraction told us to."

"That's more than one reason," she said with a smile.

He cupped her face. "You have no idea how many reasons I have to kiss you, Lena."

His words lifted her into a state of weightlessness. She was floating, and he was there with her, waiting for her to say..."Yes."

His mouth met hers. She froze, unable to close her eyes. A tiny freckle underneath his left eyebrow looked back at her. *Holy crap.* They were kissing. Her lips were touching his. It was finally happening. She had allowed it, and she was going to enjoy it. She was enjoying it! Of course she was.

The feel of his lips on hers pushed aside her growing disbelief. Her eyes fluttered closed. Their kiss deepened as he pulled her against his chest. She wrapped her arms around his shoulders, his tongue teasing hers before trailing a line of kisses down her neck. She moaned and tilted her head back, surprised by the immediate need to feel his touch everywhere. She wasn't herself. She was someone else. Someone who could let go and transcend the gravity of her reality.

His mouth found hers again, his tongue dancing with hers in a passionate embrace. Stars appeared behind her eyelids. Her hands fisted in his hair. She was floating and falling at the same time. With a series of soft pecks, Palmer brought her down from the sky above.

He pressed his forehead against hers. "Wow."

She nodded, not trusting herself enough to speak out loud.

"We should have done that sooner," he said. He moved back and looked at her.

She nodded again. Her fingertips grazed her lips. They were swollen, but the corners were curved upward. She touched his wrist, his pulse racing under her palm.

"We kissed," she said.

"We sure did." Palmer swooped in for another kiss, then sprang to his feet. "If I don't stop now, I'll spend all night kissing you." He lobbed a thumb toward the bathroom. "I'll clean up in there, then we will sleep."

"Yeah, good idea," she said in a daze. Palmer gave a thumbs-up and disappeared into the bathroom.

Lena's palms raced down her thighs as she let out a breath. The sound of running water filled the quiet room. She touched her mouth again. Her next first kiss was an inevitability she hadn't considered since Seth's death. Waking up each day for the last year and a half had been challenging enough. The thought of dating never came up, because she didn't want it to. It was that simple. Plus, there were too many loose ends surrounding Seth's departure, too many questions yet to be uncovered.

Then Douglas broke down, and Palmer had come to the rescue. Tall, attractive, and intuitive, he could be pushy at times, but for reasons she'd been avoiding. She hadn't thought it possible to find anyone impossible to resist right now in her life. Palmer had proved her wrong. He was good at that. Damnit, though, she had tried!

She lifted her face to the ceiling, the lump in her throat growing. "I tried."

"You deserve this. It's okay."

She spun around. A picture of a French bulldog wearing an imperial crown stared back at her.

"I'm losing my damn mind," she said to the dog. The day had caught up with her, and she was hearing things. That was all.

A booming crack of thunder shook the room right as lightning flashed through the windows. She yelped and rushed toward the bathroom, colliding with Palmer's hard chest.

His long arms circled around her like a shield. "You're shaking," he said.

"The thunder startled me." Her voice was muffled against his shirt. She breathed in evergreen. "I also heard a voice tell me I deserve this, but it was probably the people in the next room, and maybe they deserve to be happy without a side of guilt, too." The levee had broken. Lena was crashing into Palmer with a flood of emotions. "Sorry. I'm tired."

Palmer released her. "You and I have followed a bullet-point list of others' expectations for long enough, don't you think? That voice is right. I think we both deserve this."

"You don't think it's too soon?" She twisted her hands together.

"Do you?"

She looked up at him. "No."

"Then why ask?"

A wave of exhaustion vibrated through her bones, but she knew the words would come. Palmer had that effect on her. She sat down on the bed and dug her bare toes into the stiff carpet. "My parents, Shay, my boss, even a few regulars back in Oregon, have all related to my grief through those damn stages. And sure, there's value in knowing what to expect but I was shoved into those expectations. And the only way out is when all of the stages are complete. As if humans are capable of metamorphosis." She covered a massive yawn and then whispered, "We're not."

Palmer sat next to her. "We're all just finding ways to feel okay with the skin we're stuck in," he said.

"Aren't we, though? Yes, my skin is damaged, and my emotions are ugly, but shutting me away until I'm better steals whatever light I have left. I know they mean well, I know it comes from a place of love, but... I don't know." She let out a sigh. She wasn't making sense.

"Which makes it impossible for you to find your own way." Palmer wrapped his arm around her shoulder.

"That's exactly it," she said with a quiet laugh and leaned into his embrace. Palmer's understanding sent sparks up and down her body. Or maybe it was the smell of his aftershave and the memory of his lips on hers causing the electrical reaction.

"Are you like this with everyone?" She tilted her head back so she could see his face. "You know, like, patient and curious and understanding and stuff?"

"I try to be. Some make it more difficult than others." He removed his arm from her shoulders.

"Oh, sorry if I've been a pain in the—"

"You opened up to me in the face of what probably felt terrifying. Because of you, my patience and curiosity comes naturally." His gaze dipped to her mouth. "Just like kissing you."

"Oh," she mumbled. Whoever he saw wasn't her. She was an imposter. This person before him might not show up tomorrow, no matter how much she wanted her to. Palmer deserved an explanation and a warning. Except she didn't want to do it. She wanted the impossible to happen again. So, she asked, "Can I kiss you...again?"

Palmer's dimples deepened. "You can kiss me again and again"—his hand circled around her neck—"and again." And their lips met.

You deserve this.

<h1 align="center">20</h1>

Palmer

F ive missed calls waited for Palmer the following morning. Three from Gregor and two from his father. He knew why both had called at the crack of dawn: His defiance meant Gregor was stuck in the middle once again. Which meant his father had most likely dragged Gregor to the "guilt diner" this morning—a mom-and-pop restaurant that had become known in their family for the stern conversations that often took place there. They made a killer omelet, though, even if seasoned with his father's unpleasant bullshit. Palmer hoped Gregor had ordered one, because he was not returning their calls. Not today, at least.

Palmer glanced at Lena. She was on her side with the covers tucked under her chin, her eyes closed, and her red hair knotted at the top of her head. They had fallen asleep with his arm draped over her waist last night. He had slipped effortlessly into slumber, a content smile on his face. A face that looked like his again. At some point in the night, Lena had scooted away, taking the covers with her. He awoke to a vibrating phone and ice-cold toes, but felt at ease nonetheless.

He had kissed Lena. Lena had kissed him. And if he played his cards right, there would be more kissing. Maybe even the making of plans that involved seeing each other after Florida.

His phone vibrated, making Lena shift. A text message from Gregor popped up.

Call me now. 911.

Palmer inched out of the bed and walked to the bathroom. He shut the door and leaned against the bathroom counter, tapping a return message to Gregor.

Unable to call at the moment. What's up?

Palmer set his phone down and looked in the mirror. He rubbed his chin, his thoughts wandering back to last night. He wouldn't dare admit this to Lena, but he had planned to shave whether or not she'd won the bet. Beards and humidity did not go well together. Lena's expression upon seeing him, however, was one he wouldn't soon forget. Nothing could have prepared him for the look in her eyes, her breath as she moaned, or the taste of her lips. His lack of preparation was now a source of unexpected satisfaction. Whatever today would bring, he was ready.

His phone buzzed right as he splashed cold water onto his face. Water dripped off his chin and onto the screen.

Parents. Divorce. Call me.

His vision blurred from the water on his eyelashes. Gregor didn't like texting, but Palmer understood his message. He scrambled for a towel and, in his haste, bumped his phone off the counter. With a disbelieving *thunk*, his phone dropped into the open toilet.

"Shit!" His hand plunged into the water. The screen blinked several times as if sputtering for air. Palmer shook it like a madman. "No. No, no, no, no." The screen went black. "SHIT." A faint knock sounded at the door.

"Are you okay, Palmer?"

He swung the door open. "I dropped my phone in the toilet." He continued to shake his phone. "Gregor sent a cryptic text about my parents and divorce, and I accidentally pushed it off the counter, and the screen went black."

"Is that an older version? Not waterproof?" Lena asked. He held it up for her to inspect. "Yeah, that looks old."

"I don't keep up with technology trends."

"Wrap it in a towel." Lena grabbed the van's keys off the desk and slipped on her sandals. "Douglas to the rescue!" She rushed out the door without a limp to be seen. For a moment, Palmer marveled at the change in her, seemingly overnight. Then he remembered his broken phone, the towel it required, and the drama he continued to endure from thousands of miles away.

Leave it to his family to implode in his absence, the exact reason why he never took vacations. It was apparent he was the family's glue. But stepping away from their dynamic had given him an eye-opening perspective. Fear loved to disguise itself as comfort.

Lena returned with a box of rice and a ziplock bag, her breathing labored.

"I tried to run but then remembered why I don't right now." She placed her items on the desk.

"You have rice," Palmer said, dumbfounded.

She poured rice into the bag. "Go ahead and put your phone on top of the rice."

Palmer unwrapped the towel and situated his phone in the bag like he was playing a game of *Operation*. "How long does it need to hang out in there?"

"No clue. I'm not entirely sure if it even works."

"And yet here you are with a box of rice..." Palmer poked her ribs gently.

Lena's cheeks grew pink. "One of my biggest fears, other than blowing a tire on an expressway, is dropping my phone in water. I packed rice for this very reason." Her smile was wide. It was bad luck that brought out Lena's goofy grin, but his disaster seemed more manageable as a result.

"Here." Lena held out her phone. "You can use my phone to

send Gregor a text."

A series of messages from Gregor looked up at him. The most recent was from a few days ago. Apparently, his brother *was* a texter. "I didn't realize you and Gregor were chatting."

"I reached out when Douglas had that weird thumping noise the other day. 'Cause, ya know, he's my mechanic." Lena gave him an expectant look as if she wanted him to nod and agree.

"He was going to ask you out, you know," Palmer said instead. He squeezed his eyes shut. This was so typical of him. Kiss a beautiful woman and his filter disintegrated.

Lena's mouth opened and closed several times.

Palmer gripped the back of his neck. So much for acting nonchalant and cool and, hell, not jealous. He wasn't jealous. He was—

"You have no reason to be insecure, Palmer."

He scoffed. "I'm not..."

Lena slid into his arms. "You're the first man I've kissed since—" Her eyelids fluttered. "You are good. No, you are great. You are a relief," she said and softly brushed her lips to his.

He was speechless, but his mind yearned for more, begging him to deepen their kiss.

Lena pressed her phone to his chest. "I'm going to shower." She gave him a shy smile before disappearing into the bathroom.

Palmer tapped the phone. He would much rather stay in bed with Lena than deal with his family. Or better yet, join her in the shower. His body heated at the thought. He shook his head. No, he had to focus.

He wasn't ready to enter reality, but his family's problems were happening with or without him, and he knew better than to delay. Punctuality was a standard in the Eriksson lineage. Although, it seemed divorce was too.

"Lena, hey! I wasn't expecting to hear from you." Gregor picked up on the first ring, his voice deeper than normal. "How's Douglas doing?"

"It's Palmer. Why is your voice so low?"

Gregor cleared his throat. "Palmer. Right. Er, I've been fighting a cold. Why are you calling on Lena's phone?"

It was Palmer's turn to clear his throat. "Mine got wet. What the hell is going on up there?"

"I'm doing well, too, brother. Thanks for asking." Gregor laughed lightly. Palmer had expected the sarcastic poke; this was how they communicated. Gregor continued, "From what Dad told me this morning, he wants to sell the house, and Mom doesn't."

Palmer looked out the window to a cloudless blue sky. It looked hot out already. "Wait, Dad wants to sell the house? Why? And why would Mom ask for a divorce over something like that?"

"There's more. Dad found a yurt in Colorado on a bunch of land. He wants to move his art studio"—Gregor said the next words like they were made up—"and live off the land."

Palmer barked a laugh. "The suburbanite man painting manatees wants to move to the mountains and *live off the land*?"

Gregor let out a sigh. "There's more."

"How could there possibly be more?"

"If you buy the business, he'll stay."

Palmer pinched the bridge of his nose. "That makes absolutely no sense. The business is bankrupt. Dad said there's nothing to buy."

"I guess Dad had a court-approved debt repayment plan to keep the business from officially closing its doors. I don't know, I'm the middle man. And I'm looking out for Mom now. Plus, Dad said you weren't willing to speak to him about it. So, I was left with no choice. Again."

"I mean, do you blame me for avoiding the man?" Palmer began to pace the room. "Why is the fate of our parents' marriage on my shoulders? This is our father's existential crisis, not mine."

"I get it." The line went silent. "When are you coming back home?"

"I don't know."

"Will you at least call Dad and talk to him?"

Palmer stopped in front of the window again. This was more than business now. It was emotional. It was his parents' marriage on the rocks. A call with his father would only be exhausting, like treading water for hours on end. "I'll have Mark call him. Maybe a lawyer can knock some sense into him."

"Oh, boy," Gregor said. "The old man will not appreciate your representation reaching out instead of you. Just sayin', bro. Could cause more of a fight than needed."

"Well, he isn't making any sense to me, or you, or even Mom at this point. Let's see if Mark has better luck."

"For what it's worth, I think Dad is handling things like a drama queen—" Gregor went quiet.

"But?" Palmer said.

"But I thought you wanted the business. What changed?"

Palmer's gaze darted toward the bathroom door. "I never said I didn't want it. But I gotta be honest with you bro, I think I can be more than the family business. No, I know I can be more. There is so much I want to do that I never allowed myself to even dream of before. Until now."

Gregor let out a low whistle. "I never thought I'd see the day when perfect Palmer realizes his own potential."

Palmer grunted. "I'm far from perfect."

Gregor laughed. "Oh, I know. Listen, I know it's rare I offer advice, being the younger sibling and all, but you have more control here than you think. Buying the business makes it *yours*. You could do whatever you want with it. A new take on a generational tradition. Or whatever."

Palmer toed his overnight bag on the floor. His shaver poked out from the opening. "You think Dad would agree to Husky's becoming a millennial reclaimed furniture store with a coffee shop attached?"

"If he's serious about selling it to you, then throw in all your off-the-wall terms and conditions. It's your money buying the business," Gregor said.

"I highly doubt Drew Eriksson has the self-control to stay out of my business, especially one that was once his." Palmer glanced up and saw Lena standing by the desk. "I gotta go, Gregor. But tell Dad Mark will be in touch."

"Should I call you on Lena's phone if anything comes up?"

"Yeah, for now. Good luck with Dad." Palmer clicked off. Lena's back was to him as she rummaged through her overnight bag. She had changed into a pair of white linen shorts with a short-sleeved shirt.

"A coffee shop would work perfectly in the space Nancy showed us." Lena peeked over her shoulder at him. The outline of a tattoo peeked through the translucent light-pink fabric.

Palmer placed the phone on the desk next to her. "You mentioned that while we were there. I remember."

She turned and leaned against the desk. "If you bought the family business, you wouldn't have to start from the ground up, right? That would allow you to focus on what you've wanted all along: selling your reclaimed pieces."

"Sure, maybe. But, it would come with many, many headaches. I don't like how my father has handled any of this, though. And I'm allowed to have a change of heart after all is said and done." He shoved a hand through his hair. "There would be a lot of strings attached if I did buy the business."

"Strings can be cut. It's the bridges you gotta watch out for," she said.

Palmer appreciated what Lena was doing. She was speaking her mind, unprompted and with little hesitation. A quality he hoped would filter through her other defenses, like the brochure and the manatees, and what her plans were after this.

"What is it you've wanted all along?" he asked. He needed a topic change from the mess and headache of his family.

"Answers. Closure." She shrugged. "New beginnings."

"And those can be found in Tampa?"

"We have to get there first," she said with a wink.

Oh, how he wished Lena would reveal more than vague

single-sentence answers. There was so much underneath her surface, if she would only let him dive in. Maybe that was the answer. Diving in. She did want to swim with manatees, right?

He scooped up the bag of rice from the desk. "Are you ready then? We have a long drive ahead."

Lena glanced around the room and sighed. "Let's get on with it, then."

Not long after they got on the road, Lena offered to join him at the lumberyard. Rather than question her sudden change of heart, he took her hand and kissed the back of it.

"I'd love to have you there," he said. "Thank you."

Lena mumbled, "You're welcome," then turned her face toward the passenger window.

The instinct to apologize—*for what, the kiss?*—grew more intense the longer Lena remained silent. They stopped at a coffee hut to order lattes before getting on the expressway. Lena seemed to perk up after that. He did, too.

Two hours later, Palmer pulled into a gravel driveway and parked in front of a two-story warehouse. They were halfway to Tampa and at the final wood-scouting stop. He turned off the engine and reached for his phone, tapping the screen out of habit. Nothing. Lena remained optimistic that the phone would dry out and power up later on today. Palmer wasn't so sure, but that was a problem for later on. Right now, he had to focus on wood.

"Wow, that's a lot of...stuff," Lena said as she unbuckled her seat belt. Palmer nodded. Off to the side of the warehouse was wood. Tons of it. Piled high and surrounded by a chain-link fence.

"I need to send Gregor a quick message," Palmer said. "Can I use your phone?"

Lena nodded. "I'll wait outside. I need to stretch."

Palmer kept his eyes trained on her back as he reached over to open the glove compartment. He pulled out the brochure and spotted an address underneath *SWIM WITH US at Tampatee!*

He fumbled with Lena's phone, typing the address into the navigation system. It wasn't like him to go behind anyone's back, especially Lena's. But, if Tampatee was on their way, it would be easy to suggest they stop. Lena would never know he had planned to take her there all along. A highlighted route appeared on the map, making his stomach jolt. It wasn't the most direct way into Tampa, but it could work.

Palmer exited Douglas and stretched his arms above his head. His back cracked in gratitude. He missed being able to sit up straight without the top of his head grazing the roof. However, he certainly didn't miss driving alone in his truck all the time.

Lena walked ahead, her right leg bootless and a sway in her hips as if she knew she was owning the gravel catwalk.

Palmer let out a low whistle. "Look at you walking on your own."

She glanced over her shoulder with a hair flip. He liked this Lena, the playful, happy one. "Some things happen overnight, I guess." She stopped at a pile of Victorian doors. It didn't take long for him to catch up with her.

"These are seriously cool. Look at that stained glass." She bent down and lightly traced the outline of a manatee with her finger. His brain kicked him in the ass, urging him to reveal his plans to Lena *now*.

"I could make you a nightstand out of that door," Palmer said.

"I love that idea," she said, rising from her crouched position. "I just wish I knew where I would put it."

"Well, usually it's found in a bedroom since people are in bed at night using their nightstand for various...bedroom thingies."

Lena gave him a gentle shove. "Make sure you hire someone else to do your marketing whenever you open your shop."

Palmer pulled her into him and lightly kissed the top of her head. He wondered if she noticed her, too. The woman who was climbing out from underneath the grief she'd been buried in. The woman he was falling in love with.

Palmer swallowed. Hard. "The great thing about building

furniture is it speaks for itself."

Lena scooted away from his hold and inspected another pile of antique wood. "So, the term *thingy* will not be used in your online catalog?"

Palmer considered her. He hadn't thought about the necessity of an online presence, he'd been too focused on finding wood. "I don't have a website. Yet."

"You would if you bought your father's business."

He walked right into that one, didn't he? "All right, miss smarty pants, I see your point. Let's go talk to this guy and see if I can scrounge up enough wood to fill a showroom first, yeah?"

Lena clapped her hands together. "I'm ready to find all the thingies!"

He smiled as a distinct feeling of ease came over him.

"After you," he said with a swoop of his arms. Even in the face of total unknowns, he was leaning into his growing feelings for Lena and was grateful to have her help for as long as time allowed.

21

Lena

Palmer had talked nonstop since their visit to the Gainesville lumberyard. Lena couldn't blame him for his giddiness. There had been an abundance of wood, and Mateo, the owner, had shared his dream of expanding into the Midwest since he had family roots there. And those roots happened to be planted in the town right next to Palmer's.

"A forward-thinking wood supplier asking a small-town woodworker to join forces." Palmer shook his head. "If Mateo is serious about partnering, it would be a huge edge in the industry," he said while changing lanes. They passed a minivan with a roof stacked with various-sized suitcases.

"It sounds really promising," Lena said. Lena was thrilled for him, but after two hours of listening, she was running out of ways to say the same thing. Although Palmer didn't seem to notice—he was in a different dimension entirely.

"It's more than promising, this is leverage." His dimples danced underneath the glow of his cheeks. She murmured in agreement and touched her lips, thinking back to the previous night.

Their kiss had been toe-curling and mind-altering for the most atypical of reasons: It had actually happened! And as she sat in the safety of Douglas, with the sunlight warming her face, she felt light with relief.

Kissing Palmer had been a necessary step, one she wouldn't have taken with anyone else. But it couldn't be anything more.

Their kiss had been a transaction. A check mark on the list of instructions for life after death. Whatever normally happened after a first kiss wasn't accessible to her. Not yet, anyway. How could it be? The hum of Seth's memory, so very near to her heart, was still there. Besides, Palmer was distracted by another chase.

They passed a sign informing them Tampa was thirty miles away. Lena's stomach jumped into her throat. In less than an hour, everything would change. Well, to be more accurate, as her emotions did tend to exaggerate: Everything would change tomorrow when she went to Seth's parents' house for an afternoon barbecue. For now, they would head to the condominium in Madeira Beach, forty minutes west of Tampa, and relax for the evening. Whatever that meant with a man she wasn't supposed to kiss again.

"We should probably check my phone again," Palmer said.

"Good idea." Lena reached for Palmer's phone in the cup-holder. She held down the necessary buttons and waited.

Three, two, one... the screen illuminated.

"The rice worked," Lena said.

Palmer glanced at her. "Seriously?"

Lena tapped the phone's screen. The background image was of magnified wood grain dotted with translucent and perfectly shaped raindrops. She held it up to show Palmer. "I like your wallpaper."

"Oh, thanks. Sometimes I use the camera on that thing."

"You took this photo? It looks professional."

Palmer nodded. "It's not. But thanks. You can put it back. I'll check messages later."

Lena noticed his hands gripping the wheel as she placed his phone into the cup-holder.

"Is everything okay?"

Palmer swallowed and nodded. "We're getting close. I'm ready to stretch out."

"Me too," Lena agreed. Her ankle was making its presence

known with its familiar burning ache. Although, she was encouraged by how long it took for her to notice. An electronic billboard came into view, another indication they were entering city limits. Lena swallowed as an animated manatee swam across the length of the billboard. She squinted at the banner floating behind its tail.

Visit me at Tampatee in 10 miles! Exit 145.

"Palmer," she choked out, her heartbeat instantly wild. "Look at that billboard!"

Palmer tilted his head. "Oh, shit."

"We're going right past it. In ten miles! I could have sworn the location was further east than our route. But maybe I was wrong. Or, wait! Maybe they have more than one location."

Palmer wiped at his hairline. "They don't. It's not a coincidence. I took an alternate route."

"You— What?" A tripping-down-the-stairs sensation coursed through her body.

"It wasn't that far off our original route, and I thought, I mean, I noticed— Let me start again." His hands were strangling the steering wheel. "You have a Band-Aid over whatever that brochure means to you. I see how irritating it's been for you." Palmer glanced at her.

She moved her hair to cover her face. She wasn't one to wear her emotions on her sleeve, not even close. It was her face that gave her away. If she faked a smile right now, Palmer would notice it didn't reach her eyes.

"I don't mean to sound rude," she said, wringing her hands in her lap, "but can you get on with it?"

"All right. Well, I thought you could rip the Band-Aid off and get it over with."

"I'm not ready," she said automatically. She clenched her jaw and blinked rapidly. She would not cry. This is what Palmer did—tried to help. Even though he wasn't asked. Although, she wasn't one to ask for help, and he knew that all too well, didn't he?

"What do you need to be ready for?"

"You wouldn't understand." Lena rolled down her window. She wanted to toss Palmer's betrayal into the thick humid air. "You're forcing me to make a decision I'm not ready to make."

"There's no way to prepare on speculation alone. Those thoughts are not rooted in reality. The only way to feel ready is to let go."

Palmer's gaze was heavy on her face. His words made more sense than she wanted to admit. She pushed the button on the glove compartment and slapped the brochure onto her lap.

"You're not wrong about me speculating. But you have to understand that's all I've got." She opened and closed the brochure flap. He was forcing her hand, making her speak about something she didn't want to honor with words or oxygen.

"Eliana was with Seth when he died. She was at his wake. She knows his parents. And yet, somehow, I only know her from this." She held up the brochure. "Whoever she is, I have to know who she was to Seth."

"Eliana swims with manatees," Palmer said as if to confirm the obvious. He let out a soft laugh. "Your reaction to seeing my father's painting, and then seeing that manatee at the downtown space, and your intense interest in this brochure—I honestly thought you just really liked manatees. Now I understand why you got so flustered."

"Flustered is one way to put it. Certifiably crazy is probably more accurate, but I thank you for your...gentleness."

"My father is crazy, Lena. You are not."

Lena shook her head with a smile. "We're all a little crazy in our own right."

"I'm perfectly fine," Palmer said deadpan.

Lena laughed. She couldn't help it. Palmer's humor was impossible to resist. "That's your crazy talking, you know."

Palmer smiled and winked. Up ahead was the off-ramp for Exit 142. In three exits she would either face her fears or wave from the window as she passed them by.

Lena twirled the brochure in her hand. Tomorrow wouldn't provide the same clarity as today—her mind would be too occupied with other details and surprises. She was sure of it. Maybe Palmer had realized this. If he had suggested visiting Tampatee earlier, she would have shut it down. She was sure of it. And maybe he had realized this, too. She was still annoyed with him, but going now did make sense.

"All right," she said.

Palmer sneaked a glance at her. She held up the brochure and nodded.

He squared his shoulders and flipped on the turn signal. "I will get into the right lane and say nothing more."

"I appreciate that," she said and leaned her head back. Closing her eyes, she focused on her breathing and hoped to god her mind would find the will to ask whatever questions it needed to find closure.

The parking lot was empty, aside from two passenger vans up front. Lena stepped out of Douglas and gasped. The air felt like she was poking at the beginning stages of Jell-O: not quite solid and totally unnatural. The sound of mechanical whirring filled the air.

"What's with the noise?" Lena asked once Palmer rounded the front end of Douglas.

He pointed over a line of palm trees. "There's some kind of factory across the street."

Lena spotted three smoke stacks poking up from behind the trees. "Why would a habitat for manatees be situated next to a factory?"

Palmer shrugged. "I'm sure you're not the first person to wonder the same thing."

"You're right. I am unoriginal in my thinking." Lena pushed his arm, his skin hot from the scorching sun.

"Lena, that's not what I meant." He went to grab her hand, but she stepped away.

"My nerves are talking. And please don't tell me I have nothing to be nervous about. I hate when people say that."

Palmer nodded. "Consider me your emotional boot, then. Someone who is here to support and stabilize you."

Lena shook her head. "I don't need a boot. Not on my ankle or on my emotions."

Palmer's face fell.

Damnit.

She was speaking too sharply to him, a reflex when people got too close and her emotions got too real. Squeezing her eyes shut, she tried again. "What I need is"—her eyes landed on the line of palm trees—"shade. When the sun gets too intense, I'll need shade."

"I'm good at being a tree," Palmer said. The tone of his voice forced Lena to look up. He appeared younger and older all at once. "Shall we?"

Lena nodded and moved toward the ramp with Palmer in tow. A sculpture of a manatee made out of blue metal circles stood at the entrance. Lush plants with waxy green leaves and soft auburn flowers surrounded the art. They walked up the ramp side by side and stopped at the screened-in double doors. A wooden sign on chains hung in the middle.

"Closed for the season." Lena read out loud then turned on her heel. There was nothing here. The sign told her as much. "That solves that."

Palmer caught her arm. Her body seized up. "It says the visitor center is open," he said.

"Great. Can I have my arm back?" Sweat trickled down her temple.

He released her arm. "We're here. It might be worth a look."

Lena looked around. Palmer's encouragement to do the exact opposite of what she wanted was infuriating.

Palmer pointed to a sign with multiple arrows. "What do you say?" He moved to the right and toward a small flight of stairs.

She pulled at the front of her shirt. It was stupidly hot out here. "Fine. A quick peek inside."

They stepped onto a smaller deck and through another set of double doors. Lena sighed in unison with Palmer. Air conditioning was magical.

"Welcome in, folks." A male voice boomed from somewhere inside. A surprising number of patrons roamed around the many glass display cases and interactive displays.

"Whoa," Palmer said quietly next to her. "Are you seeing what I'm seeing?"

A real-life skeleton of a manatee hung from the ceiling in the middle of the room. Lena moved forward to get a closer look. The bones in the manatee's front fins looked like human hands.

"The fins," Lena confirmed. "How incredible."

A man appeared wearing a khaki button-down shirt with the Tampatee logo embroidered on the pocket, khaki shorts, and Birkenstock sandals. It was a startling amount of brown.

"You're a little early in the season for manatee viewing but there's still plenty to see here! And, if you stick around for another, oh"—he glanced at his watch—"ten minutes or so, there's a presentation in our attached restaurant about our newest non-profit program launching this winter. Complimentary refreshments!"

"What kind of refreshments?" Palmer asked. Lena wanted to rib him with her elbow. They were not going to stay for a presentation.

"Manaritas," the man said. "Seapuffs, too." The man looked between Palmer and Lena with a knowing smile. "Tequila and spinach puff pastry."

Lena's stomach growled. Or maybe it groaned. Palmer was nodding enthusiastically.

"I'm not supposed to share this with anyone yet, but"—the man glanced around then said in a low voice—"you'll receive one free entry to our manatee swim tour at Crystal River if you become a donor today. And the presenter would be your guide, too. Seriously, it's an amazing opportunity." He pointed toward a wall of windows in the back. "The restaurant entrance is to the left."

"I see no reason why we can't check it out," Palmer said. "Right, Lena?"

"Uh, sure. Right. Manarita. Clever name." Lena's mind was racing, making it impossible to say much of anything.

"You can thank your presenter for that bit of wit. Eliana is her name. I'm Frank." The man tipped an imaginary hat and made his exit.

Palmer turned to Lena, his eyebrows raised high enough to touch his hairline.

Yeah. She too had heard the name.

"Do you need some shade?" he asked.

She smiled despite herself. "More than anything."

Palmer took her hand and guided them outside. He walked into a bright patch of sunlight and positioned her so she was facing him. His arms rose up like he was going to dive, blocking the sun from Lena's forehead.

"How's this?" The hem of his shirt lifted, exposing a patch of skin just below his belly button. Palmer's literal interpretation from their metaphorical conversation earlier in the parking lot had her moving closer to him.

I'm good at being a tree.

Her fingers grazed across his warm skin. She felt his stomach tense and heard his quick intake of air. To Palmer's credit, he kept his arms raised while hers wrapped around his waist, her hands underneath his shirt. His skin was warm and damp and seemed to absorb the intensity of what was about to happen. She had no idea what the hell she was doing. But she had to do it.

Lena lifted her face to his, her eyes trained on his lips. Palmer's arms lowered and pulled her into his chest, his eyes darkening. She was sweaty and doing exactly what she shouldn't be doing right now—craning her neck and pressing her lips to his. He cupped her cheek gently and kissed her like the shade would the ground.

Lena reveled in the momentary amnesia, then broke away and mumbled, "That'll do."

Palmer's lips twitched before kissing hers again.

"Hi, sorry, I don't mean to interrupt."

Lena jumped away from Palmer. A woman stood a few paces away with a clipboard pressed into her chest. A tie-dye headband held back her shoulder-length hair, the ends a lilac color.

Eliana.

"I have a sign-up sheet for the presentation. Frank mentioned you two were going to join." She held out the clipboard, her eyes cast downward.

"Thanks," Palmer said, taking the clipboard from her. Lena couldn't move. All she could do was stare. "You're our presenter, right?" Palmer asked as he wrote on the sheet.

Eliana looked up, her eyes bright and clear. Her gaze locked onto Lena.

"Here you go." Palmer held out the clipboard. Eliana made no move to take it. He looked at Lena and then to Eliana, then back to Lena, before Eliana finally spoke.

"I can't believe it's you, and you're here," Eliana said to her.

"I don't know why I am," Lena said. She had imagined this scenario for so long, and that's what she came up with?! *I don't know why I am.* What a stupid thing to say!

And she had been caught kissing Palmer, too. What a stupid thing to do! What judgments and conclusions was Eliana forming with each passing second?

Eliana stepped forward as if to hug her. Lena jolted away, her knee giving out with the sudden movement. Palmer was there, though, as he always was, catching her under her armpits.

"I got you," he whispered into her ear.

Lena righted herself quickly. "I broke my ankle, and it's still healing," she said as if someone had asked. No one had. Her anxiety required her to explain, and now she felt even more stupid.

"I'm so sorry, I didn't mean to startle you." Eliana's hand planted onto her chest.

Lena tried to brush her words away, but the movement caused stars to appear instead. She needed to sit down.

Eliana pointed in the opposite direction of the visitor-center doors. "I think an air-conditioned room and a Manarita are what we all need right now. Come with me. I'll take you to the super special entrance."

Palmer squeezed Lena's waist. Lena scooted away from his hold. She couldn't handle his nonverbal support right now.

"Sounds good," she said in a voice that didn't sound like hers.

Palmer offered his hand as they followed Eliana. Lena almost didn't take it, but she did briefly before letting go. She would have to endure the light without Palmer's shade from here on out and for as long as she could.

22

Palmer

An hour later, they were back in the van. It was rush hour in Tampa, and traffic was bumper-to-bumper. The temperature gauge in Douglas was higher than normal, which concerned Palmer, as did Lena's behavior in the seat next to him. She had been randomly giggling, on and off, since they left. No words, just spurts of light laughter. Maybe a second Manarita was the cause. Either way, Lena had invited Eliana over for dinner tonight, which also concerned him. Those two were a ticking time bomb. But he wouldn't dare voice his unsolicited thoughts. This was Lena's path to walk, and he would no longer interfere.

And now that his phone was working again, Palmer would spend the night ahead answering questions from Mark, while avoiding calls from his father. Hopefully, he could draft an operational plan to send to Mateo, too. Going into business with Mateo could be the biggest game-changer for Palmer's future. One that would eliminate, for good, the possibility of buying the family business. But first, he had to sort out his finances and deal with his father, which meant flying home sooner than he wanted to.

Palmer would have to tell Lena his plans. Another giggle sounded from his right. Not now, though, definitely not now.

"Okay, you gotta tell me." Palmer tried to sound as jovial as possible. "What's got you snickering over there?"

"Oh, nothing," Lena responded with a giggle. "It's just funny"—more giggling—"how poorly our minds paint the future for us. It's like asking a toddler to fingerpaint a recognizable self-portrait." She was laughing now, an infectious sound that made it hard for Palmer to keep a straight face. Oddly enough, even in the midst of whatever this was—a nervous breakdown?—she was making total sense.

"So, you're saying our minds are self-portrait-painting toddlers?"

Her head whipped around, as she pointed a finger at him. "I would bet a pretty penny yours is more advanced, but yes, everyone else is making a mess of their minds. Take me, for example, convinced Eliana was going to be the worst thing to happen since Seth's death. And maybe it'll turn out that way, who knows, but based on what I saw today, she seems like a good person." Lena took a deep breath in. "Of course Seth would fall for her."

"You don't know that for sure," Palmer said, although he couldn't blame her for thinking it. Eliana had captivated every person in that room from the very start of her presentation. She was both charismatic and humble.

"Which is why I invited her over tonight," Lena said with a series of head nods. "I want to know her. I didn't think I would, but I have to want to. I mean, she lives in the same apartment complex as where we're staying! It's clearly a sign."

Silence filled the van. He rarely took coincidences as a *sign*, but he understood what Lena meant and nodded his head. He went to turn on the radio and was startled when Lena swatted his hand away.

"Why aren't you saying anything?" She swatted at him a second time. "Something huge is happening, and you go quiet on me! Where's the bold and opinionated man who has been in this van with me since Illinois? Talk to me, Palmer. I need—" She cleared her throat. "Just— Talk to me."

"I guess I deserve those swats," Palmer said. Lena was speaking from a place of courage and hope, and he could, too. "You're so damn brave, don't ever doubt your strength, okay? Self-portraits are usually shit, anyway."

"Except for van Gogh," she said.

"True, although someone should have hidden the knives." Palmer made a slicing motion near his ear.

Lena covered her mouth to stifle her laughter. "Also, true," she said, sucking in a few breaths. "I'm glad we did this. I mean, yeah, I was upset earlier. You took a risk and pushed me to face a huge unknown. Had you not done what you did, maybe I would have never gone by myself." She reached over and squeezed his forearm. "I'll miss you when you go."

"I'm still here," he said, wishing his words could freeze time.

"Not for much longer." She leaned back. "Your phone has been buzzing nonstop since we got into Douglas. I know you need to get back to Illinois, as soon as possible I imagine."

His tongue itched inside his mouth. There had to be something he could offer her that would make up for their inevitable goodbye. But what?

Lena dug into her wallet and pulled out two manatee swim-tour vouchers. "She had everyone in that room signed up as donors by the end, didn't she?"

"Oh, without a doubt. No way I was walking away without becoming a donor."

"I had no idea manatees were back on the endangered species list, because of starvation of all things. It's sad." Lena held the vouchers out in front of her. "We'll get to swim with them at Crystal River. January, she said, right? That's when they come in for the warm waters."

"Which is also why the Tampatee viewing center is next to that electric factory. It warms the water." Palmer had read this bit of information while Lena was using the bathrooms.

"I totally forgot about the factory! Good to know." She placed the vouchers in the glove compartment. "Will you come back and swim with—"

The navigational voice interrupted Lena and warned of heavy

traffic ahead. Palmer groaned. They had thirty minutes to go, and the engine's temperature kept rising. Sunset was an hour away, but already the sky was showing off. Tampa Bay stretched before them, the water glistening as descending rays of sun covered the world in a pink and orange glow. He supposed the relentless heat should go out with such beauty, a reward for having muscled through the day.

"If sunsets weren't so stunning, do you think people would put up with this heat?" Lena said in a far-off tone. A long beam bridge with central cables came into view.

"I think the water has something to do with it. Do you think sharing a small space with someone for an extended amount of time connects their brain waves somehow?"

"I think mannerisms can be mirrored, sure," Lena said without hesitation. "But for brain waves to sync? I don't know. It's an interesting thought."

Palmer smiled. "The fact that you knew what I meant has answered my question."

"So, the answer is, maybe? No? Yes?"

"The answer is it's possible."

Lena shook her head. "I don't understand."

Palmer maneuvered onto the six-lane bridge. "Right before you said something about the sunset, I was basically thinking the same thing. That's all."

"Oh, okay," Lena said. He could feel her staring. She lowered her voice and wiggled her fingers like she was casting a spell. "We're cosmically connected."

"No more sharing with you," Palmer said with a laugh.

"I knew you were going to say that, you know." Lena poked his shoulder, then turned to look out the passenger window. "It sure is beautiful, though."

Palmer wished he could pull over and watch her watch the sunset. He hoped the beachfront condominium would provide another opportunity for that.

The traffic let up once they crossed the bridge. Twenty short minutes later, and much to his relief, they pulled into the con-dominium parking lot. Douglas didn't overheat, thankfully, but Lena would need to know about the temperature gauge. He glanced at her smiling face as she unbuckled her seat belt. He would tell her later. Definitely before the van went to Seth's parents tomorrow. Palmer ran his finger along the jagged edges of the keys before pocketing them. The thought of Lena without Douglas was wild to imagine.

"Oh, wow," Lena said once they stepped outside. A five-story white-plastered building stood in the foreground with an end-less horizon beyond. The sky was drenched in watercolors.

Palmer spied a boardwalk surrounded by palm trees leading out to the white sand beach. "I can't think of a better way to end our road trip than watching this sunset with you." He held out his hand. "What do you think?"

Lena looked at him as if she had just found a long-lost keep-sake. She placed her hand into his. "I think we need to contact someone about this mind-reading theory you have." Her eyes sparkled.

Palmer kissed the back of her hand while his gaze drifted to her lips. He wanted more of her, constantly, it seemed. Their kiss at Tampatee had been unexpected and entirely too quick. Eliana's interruption was the very definition of bad timing, and Lena had been jumpy ever since. He doubted she would relax enough to sink into his arms as she had last night. But Lena had a way of surprising him. Perhaps his dream of a good-night kiss would come true. For now, the closeness of her was more than enough.

He guided them onto the weathered wooden planks and down the narrow boardwalk. Green leaves and skinny palms surrounded them initially before thinning out into all sand. With Lena's soft hand in his and the salty breeze dancing off the waves, he felt both grounded and weightless. At the end of the boardwalk stood an empty bench. Lena released his hand and took a seat. Palmer followed her lead and placed his arm around her shoulder. She sunk into his side without hesitation. While Lena watched the sky's colorful performance, he watched her. The only sound came from the rolling waves, ambient and soothing, while the sea-soaked air skirted across his arms and shifted Lena's hair, stirring her vanilla scent.

A pang cropped up in the pit of his stomach. What lay before him was nothing but inspiration: the smells, the sounds, the colors, and the woman nuzzled into his side. He could see why someone would fill a thousand blank canvases with just this one scene, knowing they may never capture the moment just right but dedicating their life to trying anyway. Was this how his father felt when he decided to pursue his dream of being an artist? Palmer could relate, in a sense, to the creative pull he experienced with his woodworking. To harness the beauty he saw and create something tangible out of it was nothing short of remarkable. He took a sharp breath in.

Lena looked up at him. "What's happening?"

Palmer swallowed, and just as he opened his mouth to tell Lena the van was overheating and that he had to fly home tomorrow night, a voice drifted in from the beach.

"Hey, you guys!" Eliana ran up, kicking a wake of sand behind her. Lena jolted away from him. "Isn't this amazing?" Eliana said, her arms spread wide. She wore a black tank top with the khaki shirt from earlier tied around her waist. The upper half of her left arm was tattooed with tropical flowers. "The commute is a bitch, but this view is so worth it. I always come out here for the sunsets. Oh! Actually, I'm glad I caught you." Her eyes were trained on Lena. "I was thinking of bringing a bottle of whiskey for our dinner if that—"

"You're a whiskey drinker?" Lena asked.

Eliana fiddled with the knot around her waist. "It's a new hobby. Actually, Seth introduced a bunch of us to some of the whiskies he picked up while he was here."

Palmer felt Lena go stiff. The crashing waves filtered in through the silence.

"I think a bottle of whatever would be great," Palmer said as he stood up. "How about you come by in about thirty minutes? We haven't settled in yet, but it shouldn't take long."

Eliana looked between Lena and Palmer. "Great. I'll see you soon." She offered a small wave and retreated to the boardwalk.

"See you soon!" Palmer called out. Someone had to acknowledge Eliana's exit, and Lena was, well, she wasn't moving. "We should probably head in."

Lena's shoulders slumped inward. "I'm so damn tired," she said.

Palmer had to bend down in order to hear her. "It's been a long day, and you're probably hungry."

She hugged her knees into her chest. "I've been chipping away at this emotional concrete for too long." Lena looked up at him. "Almost every part of my body has lost feeling because of it. I'm tired of being numb."

Palmer sat down next to her and began to untie his shoelaces. He tilted his head and said, "Go on, take off your sandals."

Lena released her knees. "We don't have much time before—"

Palmer waved his shoe at her. "You want to feel things, right?"

Lena sighed and toed off her sandals, raising her eyebrows expectantly. He stood and offered his hand to help her up. The bench was positioned over the boardwalk, but after a few short steps, sand slipped between his toes, warm and cool all at once. He turned to Lena with a smile. She was looking down at her feet, her big toes wiggling in the grains of sand.

"The last time I was on a beach was the week before Seth left. The sand was cold and rough. This sand is like silk." She straightened her neck and looked out at the water. "The waves here are different, too, more graceful in how they meet the shoreline. The waves on the Oregon coast barge in with no regard to their surroundings."

"The last beach I was at was in Michigan. The sand off the lake is even softer."

"The lake?"

"Lake Michigan. I should take you sometime. Northern Michigan has turquoise waters like the Caribbean. You would love it." The words were out before he realized what he'd said. The last thing Lena needed to hear was imaginary plans for their imaginary future. His mind scrambled to bring them back to reality. "But the Gulf of Mexico is warmer, that's for sure." He sounded as uncomfortable as Lena appeared to be.

"Let's test your theory, shall we?" Lena smiled and walked ahead, leaving his previous comment about taking her to another beach in another state in the divots of her footprints.

Lena stood at the edge of where the water stopped its ascent. The waves chased away the sand as quickly as the sand made its reappearance. Palmer felt the instinct to pick her up and run into the water with her over his shoulder, anything to lighten the mood and live in the beauty of this moment. He felt her hand slide into his, and then, much to his surprise, she rushed into an oncoming wave, pulling him with her. They bounded into the water until her knees disappeared. She turned to him with a wide smile, one he hoped was free of worry and meant for this moment alone. Here. Together. In the salty warm waters off the Florida coast. His feelings for Lena were no different than the water surrounding him. Her presence was all-encompassing, in a natural and powerful way.

Lena yelped and grasped onto Palmer as a wave rushed toward them. He quickly wrapped his arms around her waist and lifted her into his chest. The water soaked the bottom half of his shorts, but he didn't care. Lena clung to him, her arms circled around his neck, her breath warm.

"Thank you," Lena whispered. "I think we're safe."

He hesitated, and she seemed to as well. But her hold on him was no less fierce.

"I can't stop thinking about kissing you," he said.

She let out a deep breath. "I don't think I could say no if you asked."

His arms lost some of their strength. Shocked by her words,

he turned into her as another wave pushed them together.

"Please don't ask," she said, her eyes round, pleading for understanding. "There's just too much, and...I need to stay focused."

His arms fell away from her. "I get it," he said, even though he was hurt by it.

"Thank you for insisting I take my sandals off." Lena looked back toward the beach. The sun was gone, leaving the sky in a mellow, purplish hue. "We should head in."

"Probably a good idea," Palmer said as he forced a smile. He had to remember she was not rejecting him. She was simply choosing herself right now. "Are you thinking of pizza for dinner?"

"You read my mind, again." Lena gave him a flirty smile. "I'm always thinking of pizza."

Palmer watched as she waded in to shore, and wished, like a damn fool, that his name was Pizza.

23

Lena

Palmer offered to pick up their dinner since the pizza shop was within walking distance. It was a logical suggestion; why pay for delivery when you could walk there? Lena suspected his exit had more to do with Eliana—Eli. She went by Eli. Palmer had guided the conversation from awkward hellos to easy chit-chat. Now, Lena appreciated his intuitiveness more than ever. He recognized that the buffer needed to go, and so he went.

"I'm glad we're doing this," Eliana said. She sat on a turquoise love seat surrounded by overstuffed pillows embroidered with sea stars. Lena perched on a kitchen chair she had pulled in from the breakfast area. The condominium was small and quaint with its beach-themed decorations. A little square kitchen was nestled off to the side of the main room, with an adjacent narrow hallway leading to the two bedrooms and shared bathroom.

"I am, too." Lena sat on her hands.

Eliana reached for a paper bag from the floor and rummaged inside. "What do you say?"

Lena eyed the bottle of whiskey, squinting at the unknown label. "Seth's recommendation," Lena said. This was the first time she had said his name to Eliana.

"A Florida whiskey from St. Augustine." Eliana handed the bottle to Lena. The glass was cool and smooth in her hands.

"It's a port finish," Lena said. She had tried whiskey finished in cabernet barrels not long before Seth left for his Florida trip.

They had both been impressed by the unique flavor profile. The backs of her eyes prickled at the memory as she stuttered, "Were you two, did you two—" Lena popped to her feet. "I'll find us some glasses."

"I guess you could say I fell for Seth a long time ago," Eliana said. Her smile was the same one Lena had been wearing since Seth's death. *Empty.* "Let me help with those glasses," she said.

Lena's mind scrambled, unable to keep up with Eliana's easy delivery of life-changing news.

She fell for him a long time ago?

"I'm going to use the bathroom," Lena said and managed her way down the hall. Her ankle shouted in pain like it was broken all over again. She closed the door and placed her hands on the counter. The sweet scent of coconut reminded her where she was: in a condominium meant for vacationing families and happy memories.

She wiped under her eyes and blinked several times. She could do this.

The woman looking back at her in the mirror was strong and ready to take on the unthinkable task of facing her ghosts. She had, after all, spoken to the energy of Seth, and had received empathy and understanding in return. The ghosts she had to face today were nothing in comparison. She would sit down with Eliana and accept, as best she could, whatever was revealed. After all, that was why she'd invited Eli over in the first place.

Lena walked into the main room with more ease, her ankle no longer in fiery pain. Eliana sat at the table with two glasses of amber liquid in front of her. Lena sat across from her and accepted the glass Eliana offered.

"To connecting with those we should have met sooner in life," Eliana said and held up her glass. Lena faltered, awestruck by her poetic toast, then raised her glass and tapped it to Eliana's. The taste of the velvety liquid and its wonderful deep port flavor took her out of the moment for the briefest of seconds. What had Seth thought of his first sip? What had he said? And how did the stranger sitting across from her come to know his lasts: his last drink, his last breath, his last kiss?

"Seth never got to try this bottle. He talked about it a lot, though. I bought it for us to try the day of his accident." Eliana's voice wavered. She twisted her glass on the table and looked at Lena with red-rimmed eyes. "I met Seth's parents when I first started working with manatees about eight years ago. His father was being recognized at our gala for his activism work, and I was in charge of writing a piece on him for the brochure. It was at the gala that I met Seth."

Lena's mind automatically did the math. Eight years ago was around the time she had her first date with Seth.

"I've worked closely with his family ever since," Eliana continued. "Their passion for endangered species is a huge reason why I formed a nonprofit inside Tampatee."

"I had no idea. Seth rarely spoke of his time in Florida, even when he went back to visit." Lena had never questioned Seth's decision to keep those parts of his life to himself. His father's disappointment in his career path had been the main reason Seth kept away. "You and Seth must have stayed in touch after the gala."

Eliana nodded. "I'm not going to lie, Lena, we hit it off so easily, which is so rare, you know? I was dating another man at the time, casually." Eliana paused and rolled her shoulders. "But I was also interested in dating Seth. He didn't live here, obviously, and he was more interested in you. We remained friends, mostly through social media. When my boss informed me Seth's magazine was doing a feature on Tampatee, I volunteered to be their guide. I wanted it to be a surprise, so Seth had no idea until the first day he showed up." Eliana took a sip of her drink. Lena noticed a slight tremble in her hand as she set her glass down.

"You two got together outside of his time taking photos," Lena said. It wasn't a question as much as an encouragement for Eliana to keep talking.

Eliana nodded. "Once I learned he was staying in the same building as me, I offered to drive us home. The day before his accident, he invited me in for a drink. We were deliriously tired and on a high from all the manatees we saw." Eliana took a generous sip from her glass. She pressed the back of her hand against her lips, her expression drawn. "The longer we sat replaying the day, the more I remembered how much I enjoyed his company, and started to wonder...what it would be like...to kiss him. I guess liquid courage is a real thing." Eliana searched Lena's face; for what, Lena wasn't sure. A hint of recognition that she understood Eliana and Seth had most likely kissed, perhaps?

Lena's emotions swirled around her like the whiskey in her glass, thick and potent, yet confined to a fragile vessel. Lena could become consumed by the image of Seth kissing another woman. It would be the easy thing to do: to blindly react to the pain she was feeling, to cut this woman down with her tongue. Yet, somehow, those expected sharp edges were too dull now to inflict pain.

Eliana's admission had been graceful and oddly humbling for Lena to hear. She understood more than was possible, given the situation, the draw and charisma of Seth. How could she fault Eliana for acting on what Seth had brought out in her? Lena hadn't been able to resist him either. She had been totally consumed by her first kiss with Seth. Yet, the memory was fading, dusty from neglect. She sat back as realization softened into her bones.

"I know I'm supposed to be angry or righteous or something," Lena shook her head. "But you've made me realize how much my guilt has worn down my memories of Seth. Like the sand I walked on earlier, those memories are not supposed to slip through my mind. They're supposed to be looked at in awe, like stars or something." Lena deflated into her confession. Why was she still talking? Why wasn't she shouting at the woman who had been Seth's last kiss? None of this made sense. "Did he tell you I broke off our engagement? He probably did." Lena took a sip of whiskey. "And then a couple of days after that, he—" She stopped herself. Repeating the timing of events was a pain reflex. Eliana knew when Seth had died.

"I knew," Eliana said gently. Lena half expected Eliana to follow up with some reassurance as to what Seth had told her, or how he had been feeling about the situation, but she remained quiet.

"I have every reason to hate you, but I don't think I want to." Lena sat upright, stunned by the honesty coming out of her. "I also tend to ramble when I'm taken off guard."

"I've found that the most unlikely of situations can reveal coping mechanisms that no longer serve us." Eliana reached across the table and gently placed her hand over Lena's. "I clam up when I'm taken off guard." She squeezed Lena's hand before letting go.

A lump formed in Lena's throat. She hadn't felt this kind of tenderness since leaving her mother and sister in Illinois. It was an unspoken bond filled by the women in her life which Eliana had effortlessly contributed to. Lena dipped her chin to her chest as her vision blurred. There was no room for anger or resentment for this woman. Those feelings could not exist for someone who had grieved the loss of love, too. It was beyond reason. But Lena felt certain; Eliana was meant to become a good friend. Lifting her head, Lena wiped at her eyes as relief spread through her body.

She raised her glass with a smile. "Another toast, if I may."

Eliana returned her smile with a chin-raise. "By all means."

"To restoring cherished memories and creating new friendships."

"Whoa, girl, look at you with your heartfelt toasts." Eliana clinked Lena's glass.

Lena laughed. "You're not the only one who can pull off one-liners over a glass of exceptional whiskey."

"I think we need to start writing down our toasts and make a book titled *Pour*-etry." Eliana popped up and twirled around until she spotted whatever it was she was looking for. "I have a journal!"

"You do? I do, too! In Douglas somewhere." Lena couldn't stop laughing, her face flushed from the whiskey. It was one of those necessary releases, and it felt wonderful to ache from genuine laughter again.

Eliana spun around and pointed her notebook at Lena. "I dare say it's a dying art, those of us who carry our words around like money in a wallet." Eliana placed a leather-bound journal on the table.

"I figured my scribbled thoughts deserve a fancy home," Eliana said. She must have noticed Lena's obvious stare. "They go through enough to get here."

It was as if Eliana's words had come out of Lena's thoughts. There was no doubt in Lena's mind Seth had fallen for Eliana while he was here. Had it not been for Palmer, and the natural connection formed during their time together, Lena probably wouldn't be sitting with these hard truths now. Maybe whatever had happened between Seth and Eliana had been the same. A knock on the door prevented Lena from overthinking it any further.

"That must be Palmer," Lena said.

Eliana walked to the door. "I'm seriously hungry and a wee bit tipsy," she said in an exaggerated whisper before turning the door knob. Lena was belly-laughing all over again as Palmer stepped inside.

"Hello, sir, we've had libations." Eliana danced away with the pizza box while ushering Palmer toward Lena. The sound of cabinets opening rang out from the kitchen.

"Is everything okay?" Palmer said as he lowered into a chair next to her.

"You have to try this." Lena pushed a glass toward him. He gave her a skeptical look. She fought the urge to roll her eyes and said, "It's going better than expected."

His shoulders descended. "I was worried." He lifted the glass and sniffed. "That's different."

"There could be no other drink to mark the day than this one," Lena said.

Eliana approached the table, her arms filled with plates and paper napkins. Palmer stood up. "I'll get the pizza," he said and disappeared into the kitchen.

Eliana watched him, then turned to Lena. "I like a man who takes initiative."

"Palmer likes to help whenever he can. That's actually how we met. Douglas broke down an hour away from my sister's house, and he drove out with his brother's tow truck." Lena thought back to the moment Palmer had stepped in front of Douglas. The significance of his presence had been felt almost immediately, hadn't it?

Eliana set a plate in front of Lena and said quietly, "He's way out of my league. But you..." She shrugged as she sat down. "I bet you give him a run for his money."

Lena's cheeks heated. "We're just friends."

Eliana poured whiskey into an empty glass, presumably for Palmer, then freshened hers and Lena's glasses. "Is that by choice or by obligation?"

Lena's stomach sank to the floor. Eliana saw right through her half-truth. *Shit.* What would Seth's parents see tomorrow? A woman in healing or a woman healed? "It's necessary," she said.

"What's necessary?" Palmer said.

Eliana eyed Lena knowingly, then held up a glass. "Whiskey with new friends."

"And pizza," Lena added.

It didn't take long for the large pizza to disappear. Eliana excused herself to use the bathroom while Lena and Palmer cleared the plates.

"How are you feeling?" Palmer said as he followed her into the kitchen.

Lena set the dishes into the sink and patted her stomach.

"Full."

"I mean with—"

"I know." Lena smiled and took the plates out of his hands. "I'm probably in shock, but I don't think it will matter tomorrow. I don't want to hate anyone who loved Seth regardless of the circumstances." Lena wiped her hands on a towel. "So, it's true, I do feel full, but in my heart. You know?"

Palmer closed the space between them. Her palms pressed against his chest. She was simultaneously relieved and annoyed that they weren't alone right now. The need to be held by someone was overriding her better judgment.

"Let's revisit this thought once Eliana has left," she said.

Palmer took a step back. "You bet."

"Great." Lena smiled and walked around him to exit the kitchen. Eliana had returned from the bathroom and was inspecting her nearly empty glass on the table. She looked up with a grin.

"I must meet Douglas," Eliana announced. "Tonight."

"Oh, he's a mess right now," Lena said. The back of Douglas had turned into Lena's closet, with clothes and shoes scattered everywhere. She'd planned to do a deep clean before returning him to Seth's parents tomorrow.

She sobered at the thought. Douglas would be gone by tomorrow.

"Well, yeah, you've been on the road traveling, not attending car shows." Eliana glanced at Palmer as he sat down. "Second opinion?"

"He's a mess," Palmer said.

Lena nudged him with her foot. "You're not supposed to agree!"

Eliana placed her elbows on the table and steepled her hands. "Douglas the van has pronouns." She pinned Lena with an intense gaze. "I need to meet him."

Lena saw Palmer's mouth go ajar. She couldn't help but feel the same way, too. Anyone who acknowledged Douglas without snark or jokes was more than worthy of viewing the mess inside.

"You know what, Eli?" Lena stood up, feeling lighter on her feet than she could remember. "I think Douglas needs to meet you, too."

24

Palmer

"**I** can't believe she had the audacity to suggest such a thing!" Lena stormed through the condominium door and almost slammed it in Palmer's face. His shoe stopped a full-on collision. He should have known that Lena's sudden silence after saying good night to Eliana had everything to do with the truth bomb that had been dropped on Lena moments before.

Lena spun around, her fists clenched at her sides. "And you—" She tossed an accusatory glare at him.

Palmer pointed to his chest. "Me? What did I do?"

Lena threw her hands in the air. "You agreed with her!"

"I said it wouldn't hurt to consider the possibility of asking to keep Douglas." The van belonged with Lena. She was just too stubborn to admit it.

"The whole reason I'm here, and *you're here*, is because we're returning Douglas to his rightful owners." She rubbed her forehead vigorously. "I am not his owner. I cannot request to be his owner. I do not have *the money* to even consider being his owner." She spun around and stomped down the hallway. A few seconds later, he heard a door slam. Before he could consider what to do next, Lena stormed out of the bedroom again. She pointed a finger at herself, her face, to be exact, while a single tear slid down her cheek.

"I promised myself I wouldn't cry over a stupid piece of metal. And look what you two did to me! LOOK!" She stomped her foot then slumped onto the hardwood floor. Hugging her knees

214

into her chest, she dipped her head. Palmer lowered next to her and attempted to crisscross his legs, knowing full well he was as flexible as Frankenstein's monster.

Lena lifted her head. He leaned to the left, then the right, struggling to remain upright, but remained vigilant in his position. "I read recently that sitting on the floor is a good indicator of how healthy you are," Lena said.

"I'm as healthy as a horse and as graceful as one, too," Palmer said, his voice strained. This was far too painful for a grown man's groin.

"Have you ever seen a horse get up off the ground? It's the least graceful thing ever." Lena stretched her legs out in front of her and pointed her toes.

"Exactly." He extended his legs and jiggled them. His bare calf muscles smacked against the cold hardwood. "I'm more of a bull in a china shop."

"Giraffe, maybe." Lena tucked her knees in toward her again. "It does hurt to consider the possibility of keeping Douglas," she said. "You said it wouldn't, but it does because it's not possible."

"How do you know?"

Lena shrugged. "I know it's not worth the risk. Besides, Douglas belongs on a beach."

"He belongs with you. It didn't take long for Eliana to notice it, too."

"Well, it's too late now. Speaking of"—Lena pressed her hands onto the floor—"we should get some sleep. Tomorrow's another long day."

Tomorrow.

Palmer's jaw clenched. Tomorrow was when everything changed. He would search for flights once Lena went to sleep and tell her in the morning. There was no need to add additional stress to an already tense situation.

"Well, hey, your own bed and bedroom awaits!" Palmer rose to his feet and helped her up.

Her smile was tired. "Sleep well," she said, hesitating before turning away.

He reached for her, not ready to let her go. "Wait." He touched her shoulder and then she was there, in his arms, hers wrapped around his waist. He dug his nose into her hair, breathing in her vanilla and leather scent. Her arms remained secure around him as they stood pressed into one another.

"I don't..." She peered up at him then pressed her face into his chest. "I don't know if I can be alone tonight," she mumbled.

His hold on her tightened. "I'm here."

She looked at him, her eyes dark. "For tonight."

"Tonight, tomorrow—" He swallowed his next words. "I'm here." His focus dipped to her mouth as his thoughts slipped into R-rated territory.

Lena removed her arms and laced her fingers into his. "Let's get some sleep," she said. They walked hand in hand to the master bedroom, his heart racing as his mind fought to keep up. He shut the door behind him. Lena flipped on a small bedside lamp. She looked at him, and the air crackled.

He took a step forward, his breath catching in his throat. Then suddenly, Lena's lips were on his, hungry and urgent, her hands fierce in his hair. On instinct, he gripped her waist, matching her pace as best he could. What was she doing? This was not the woman who had shared the ocean with him earlier, the same one who insisted she remain focused and out of his arms. How was this happening? Better yet, why was he even wondering?

Deep down he knew—aside from the primal need to feel every part of her—he knew exactly what Lena was doing. She was kissing him like it was their last night together. His fingers clawed at her shirt, searching for the skin underneath it. She broke away from his mouth and, with a wild glint in her eye, lifted her shirt over her head. He swallowed as his gaze devoured her delicate lace bra and exposed skin. Her mouth was back on his, their tongues dancing. She pushed him toward the bed with gentle nudges. The back of his knees hit the edge, and he fell onto his back. Lena didn't hesitate to straddle him, giving him the opportunity to take her in completely.

He knew this woman, with her icy blue eyes and fiery red hair. She was an extraordinary woman stitching together a life she hadn't planned on living. He admired her strength and, at the moment, her seductiveness. Would sleeping with her tonight tear apart what she had worked so hard to put together? Lena deserved more than just one night of lovemaking. She deserved a lifetime of adoration.

Lena transferred her weight directly onto his groin and swiveled her hips from side to side. It took everything in him not to flip her over and devour her from head to toe. Instead, he placed his hand behind her neck. Guiding her into his chest, he kissed her deeply, like a man falling in love.

"You're gorgeous," he mumbled against her lips.

She smiled and began to kiss his neck. Icy-hot bumps rippled on his skin. She was making this hard. Very hard.

"You're delicious," she breathed into his ear.

"God, Lena, is this what it's like to be with you?" His hands dug into her backside and squeezed.

She let out a gasp. Her mouth found his again, and her whole body melted onto him. The weight of her felt incredible. And damn, could this woman kiss. He wasn't sure how much time had passed before he noticed her hands undoing the button of his shorts.

His eyes flung open as he grasped her wrist. Her head jerked back as her brows pulled together.

"I want to," he groaned. "But morning will come soon enough, and with it, all the unknowns we have to face. I can't believe I'm saying this." He scrubbed a hand down his face. The cuddling and touching and kissing were a balm to their upcoming stressors. Was he wrong to want every inch of Lena without hovering complications? The longer it took for her to respond, the longer he held his breath with regret.

"You're right. One of us should be the voice of reason—" She cupped his face and kissed him fiercely. "You're lucky those dimples soften the blow." She choked on the last word. "Proba-bly not the best turn of phrase at the moment."

He groaned out a laugh and pulled her down onto him. "You're okay?" He felt her head nod against his chest.

"I'm here, and I'm okay. For tonight," she said.

"For tonight," he repeated.

"Pajama time," she said and rolled off the bed. With a sly smile, she removed her bra and walked out the bedroom door. He sat up as the room tilted on its side. What had just happened? He swung his legs off the bed and stood up slowly. Determination grounded him to the floor. He would find a way to prevent their final goodbye in order to keep her in his life.

Palmer walked with a spring in his step the following day. He had found an answer to keeping Lena in his life. It was so obvious he was amazed he hadn't thought of it sooner.

Wait a second.

He bounded up the stairs, careful with the two coffees in hand, and laughed. *Wait a damn second!* He *had* thought of it! While standing next to Lena at the downtown space back home, or no— *Wait. Wait!*

It was Lena. She was the one to suggest he wall off the back area to make it his woodshop and turn the front entrance space into a—

"Thanks for going to the coffee shop," Lena said as he opened the front door. She was riffling through a stack of papers on the table. "I didn't know there was required reading before attending this barbecue with Seth's parents."

Palmer placed their coffees on the table. "Are those contracts?"

"When Seth's father sent a message yesterday about a delivery today, I assumed it would be cleaning supplies or something, since they own the condo and all that. I didn't think it would be this." Lena held out what she had been glaring at. "It's Seth's trust."

"Oh, I don't think I should—"

"You're right." Lena threw the papers on the table. Puffs of steam might as well be shooting out of her ears. He knew he should have bought her a chocolate scone.

"It's so damn ironic. Seth had a trust and never told me, never *trusted* me enough to tell me. I am so furious with him!" Lena lifted her head to the ceiling and shook her fist. "I hope you can hear me up there!"

Palmer opened the lid to his coffee. He had no right to an opinion but *what the hell?* Why would Seth's parents send the trust before meeting with Lena first? Lena watched him with a blank stare, then pulled her cup toward her.

"Did Seth have a history of keeping secrets?" he asked.

Lena took a small sip. She closed her eyes as her face relaxed. "He was selective with what he shared."

Palmer nodded. He strived to be open with those closest to him, but he, too, was mindful of what he shared. Certain thoughts were better left a burden in his own head. "But you didn't doubt his honesty, right?"

"I never checked his phone like a paranoid girlfriend, no."

"Oh—" Palmer coughed on his hot coffee. "Yeah. Not so great being on the receiving end of those actions, by the way."

Lena scrunched her nose. "Someone checked your phone behind your back? Who?"

Palmer scratched his neck. His skin was rough and in need of another shave. He had meant to distract Lena with his comment but hadn't considered at what cost. "My father."

Her mouth pulled downward. "What reason did he have to check your phone?"

"It happened right after he refused to sell my furniture at one of our locations. He wanted to make sure I wasn't pitching my idea to our competition." Palmer remembered the betrayal, a furious kind of hurt he didn't know could exist. Eventually, he realized he was worse off holding on to the pain. For weeks, his creativity had deteriorated until he let go and picked up his tools instead. "Who knows where the business was financially. People go off script when their stress is unmanageable."

Or when their star child goes off the grid.

Taking a slow sip from his coffee, Palmer tried to shake the feeling that his father was manipulating yet another situation for his own benefit. Except, that's exactly what his father was doing, wasn't it? Palmer had fallen prey to the same old antics.

"Well, you're more understanding than most, but that's old news for me," Lena said with a smile. "I hope you at least have your phone password-protected now."

Palmer shifted in his seat. "Now that you mention it. It's on my to-do list."

Lena slapped a hand to her forehead. "Maybe you're too understanding."

"I wouldn't call it too much of anything, really. It's an acceptance of what life throws our way." He pointed to the papers. "I'm sure you can relate on some level."

"Obviously." She held out her palm and flicked her fingers. "Come on. Let me see it."

"See what?" Palmer emptied his pockets and placed a crinkled receipt from the coffee shop, a rubber band he found in Douglas, a bottle of ChapStick, and his phone on the table. Lena picked through the items and slid the phone toward herself. With a few quick taps and swipes, she returned the phone to him. "Enter a password you won't forget, then hit save."

He took his phone and squinted at her. "Your birthday is in March, right?"

"The seventh, why? Wait!" Lena reached across the table. "Don't use my birthday!"

Palmer held the phone above his head. "My birthday is on the seventh, too. So, technically, I'm not."

"The seventh of what?"

"Uh..." Palmer lowered his arms, caught in yet another consequential moment. "This month."

Lena's eyes widened. "This month?"

Palmer nodded and focused on typing the numbers for his password. He hit save and placed his phone on the table.

"Palmer," Lena said. "Why didn't you tell—"

"It's today. My birthday is today. I'm thirty-eight, and I don't want to talk about it. What I do want to talk about is something you might not want to talk about. So, can we talk? It could be your birthday gift to me."

"You just said you didn't want to talk about it."

"I want to talk about what I know you won't want to talk about."

"I'm so confused." Lena stood up. "Can I at least wish you a happy birthday?"

He folded his hands on the table. "Typically, I would say no. I haven't celebrated a birthday since I was a child. But it's you asking, so...my answer is yes."

Lena lowered onto his lap and wrapped her arms around his neck. "Happy Birthday," she whispered and placed a light kiss on his lips. He was shocked. This was the last thing he thought Lena would feel comfortable doing after receiving her ex-fiancé's secret trust. Ever since they'd entered Florida, nothing had made sense, however, so what was one more thing to add to the list?

"You're almost forty," she mumbled with a laugh. He went to poke her, but she darted away.

"Your ankle has been doing better since the hotel bet, I see," he said.

Lena returned to her seat. "It has. Thank you for the push."

"Hold on to that thought," he said. "I'd like you to consider something, but it's an option, nothing more." He licked his lips. The decision would be hers, of course. It had to be. But damn did he hope she would agree to his wild idea. "First off, I have to fly back to Illinois tomorrow morning."

Her face fell before she nodded. "Then I'm definitely buying you a birthday cake and singing you 'Happy Birthday' while you blow out some candles. It's not up for discussion! You're leaving. Consider it a birthday slash going away gift."

His heart swelled in his chest. He loved this woman. Plain and simple. There was no point trying to bury it any longer. "Well, that's where number two comes in. I'm going to open up my own shop in the downtown space we saw before we left. Mateo is on board with the rough business plan I drafted last night, too. Which won't leave much room financially for me to purchase my father's business, but he doesn't know that quite yet." He tore at the edges of a napkin. The decision to break free from the family business had finally found a resting place in his mind, allowing him to say what he had to say out loud—which, in turn, provided all the confidence he would need to do it again tomorrow when he met with his father.

Lena's eyes rounded. "Really? This is huge!"

He took her hands in his. "I want you to turn the front entrance into a coffee shop, *your* coffee shop, just like you said."

Lena's face fell. "You want me to...you trust me enough to do that?"

Palmer squeezed her hands. "It's your dream, isn't it? To run your own coffee shop?"

Her eyes darted around like there was a wasp in the room. "It was. It is. It will be again." Her eyes landed on the papers in front of her. "But the thought is so far from what I need to focus on right now."

"You don't need to decide until you're ready," he said, meaning every word while ignoring his urge to convince her. She had his offer. He wouldn't embellish it any further.

"I don't know when that will be, or what or who I'm supposed to be after all of this," she said. She took her hands away and waved at the papers. "And I cannot get caught up in you—" Her voice cracked, and she squeezed her eyes shut. "I have to remain grounded," she half whispered, half shouted.

"I understand," he said, even though it felt like he had just jumped out of a building without a parachute.

"If you did, Palmer, you wouldn't have brought up your grand idea at a moment like this, so no, I don't think you do understand."

His stomach clenched. "Since I'm leaving tomorrow and you're busy today, I didn't see any other option."

"Why wouldn't you speak with your father first or actually buy the space before talking to me? You're the planner, right? Where's the planning here?"

"I was excited, I guess," he said, which was the truth. He wasn't going to apologize, though. He had acted in the moment, which needed to happen more, just with some fine-tuning. "You're right. I should have waited."

"No, I mean, yeah, clearly I'm at capacity for surprises, but at least yours wasn't a secret for years and years and—" A knock on the door cut Lena off. "That better not be more unexpected news, I swear to god."

"At this rate, it'll be my father knocking." Palmer's heart jumped into his throat as Lena's eyes grew ten times their original size. "I'm kidding," he said.

"Are you, though?" Lena asked as another knock sounded. *Kind of.*

Palmer stood up and opened the door. Eliana's purple-tipped hair and bright smiling face looked up at him. She held out a box of muffins. "A morning-after gift! Because all gifts should be edible, in my opinion. And all mornings should come with a gift!"

"Double-chocolate or lemon poppyseed?" Lena asked from where she sat at the table.

Eliana gave Palmer a friendly shoulder-tap as she walked by him and said, "Both, of course!"

Palmer returned to the table while Lena worked on opening the lid of the box. Eliana placed a few paper napkins on the table and let out a low whistle.

"I see you got Seth's trust. Pretty wild, right? He never touched the money his grandfather left him, even though he could have years ago."

Lena froze with a muffin held in midair. Palmer wanted to

rush to her side as much as he wanted to rush out the door. Eliana had just dropped a huge bomb without realizing how nuclear it was.

"His grandfather left him money," Lena said. It wasn't a question. It was a fact said in an eerily calm manner.

"Yeah. An inheritance that went into a trust since Seth was like, what, nine or something when his grandfather passed away." Eliana tore off a piece of muffin and popped it in her mouth.

Palmer watched Lena like a hawk, ready to swoop in if needed. Lena placed the muffin down and slowly stood up.

"I'm going to...I need to..." She didn't finish what she was saying.

"Are you feeling unwell?" Eliana inspected the muffin Lena had just set on the table.

Lena walked into the hallway and quietly closed the bedroom door. Eliana turned to him.

"Did I miss something?"

Palmer cleared his throat. "He never told her about the trust."

"Oh, shit." The last word came out long and low.

Lena reappeared with a baseball cap on. "I'm going for a drive."

"What about your ankle—" Palmer started.

Lena held up a stern finger. "I *need* to go for a drive." She swiped the keys off the shelf by the front door, slipped on her sandals, and walked out the door without looking back.

"She'll be okay," Eliana said.

He wasn't so sure, but what choice did he have? He had to let her go.

25

Lena

Within seconds of stepping outside, Lena was damp with sweat. The humidity was so much worse than yesterday. She looked up at the sky and frowned. Ominous clouds were moving in quickly from the west. She hadn't planned on leaving one storm to enter another.

Douglas gave her a knowing look as she walked up to him. The moment she opened the driver's door, she immediately regretted not cracking his windows. He was an oven. She almost went to check the emergency chocolate in the back, but stopped herself. It was likely a puddle by now, another mess she would have to clean up later.

She smoothed her hands on the steering wheel, then buckled her seat belt. After adjusting the driver's seat so her feet touched the pedals, she started the engine. Douglas hummed to life as the scent of sun-kissed skin, leather, and vanilla circled around her.

"All right, old friend, take me somewhere pretty." She pressed on the brake, the pressure of the movement spiraling around her ankle. "We won't go far," she said, shifting into reverse. She turned onto the sand-dusted road and wound through rows of high-rise apartments until the view opened to reveal the sky and ocean. Up ahead was a small parking lot overlooking a public beach.

Just in time. Her ankle had gone all but numb. The parking lot was empty. The waves in the distance were huge and white-capped, reminding her of the temperamental waters of the Pacific. Coupled with the darkening sky and gusty winds, her time would be limited. She leaned her head back and closed her eyes.

Later today, she would meet with Seth's parents to discuss his trust. Tomorrow, Palmer returned to Illinois. Eliana knew about Seth's trust. Palmer had asked Lena to live out a dream with him. What was Palmer thinking, asking her to move to Illinois? Eliana *knew* about the trust. Lena squeezed her eyes tightly, as if to stop the truth from fully sinking into her mind. Why? And why did Seth's trust have to be reviewed in the first place? Her eyes flew open as she shouted up at the roof.

"It's not like we were legally married!" A low rumble of thunder sounded in the distance. "Oh. Was Seth not allowed to touch the trust until he got married? Is that it?" She strained to hear another rumble of thunder, but nothing came. "What do you think, Douglas?" Lena sat up straight and twisted in her seat. She would miss this old van and all the places he had taken her. The open road had opened her, too. She had rolled down the windows in her heart and let the fresh air in. And here she sat at the edge of the ocean—a place where she could start over again.

Just then, a gust of wind whipped through the driver's window and rocked the van on its wheels. Lena yelped, her hair flying around her as the glove compartment fell open with a startling *pop*. Placing a hand over her chest, she leaned to close the door. A thick musty smell rose from the compartment. Squinting, she noticed a slice of silver, a box perhaps, tucked away in the back, partially covered by papers. Thunder rolled overhead as Lena unbuckled her seat belt and scooted into the passenger seat. The angle from where she sat made the box disappear from sight. She leaned closer to the driver's seat and there the box sat, winking at her. No wonder she hadn't noticed it before; it hadn't been visible because she had been in the wrong seat.

She removed the box and flipped it over in her hand. It was surprisingly cool given the temperature outside. She wanted to open it, but at the same time, she didn't. How many surprises could she take in one day?

"Guess I'm about to find out," she said, then lifted the lid. Inside sat an exact replica of Douglas, down to the evergreen paint and chrome wheels. She placed the model in the palm of her hand, the weight of it heavier than she'd anticipated. Turning the model over, she noticed a switch on the bottom.

"No way." Her hands shook as she moved the switch to the *on* position. The inside of the little van illuminated.

"Look, Douglas!" Swiveling out of the driver's seat, she moved into the back of the van and rooted for the switch on the side of the double-range burner. The string lights lit up. "It's just like you!" She held mini Douglas to her chest while staring up at real-life Douglas. "Incredible," she said. A tear slid down her cheek and dropped off her chin. Lightning streaked across the sky as thunder boomed overhead. The wind was growing stronger. It was time to go.

Lena retrieved the box and flipped the lid open but stopped short. There was writing at the bottom. An inscription of some sort.

"What the—" She squinted and read it out loud, because Douglas deserved to hear what was engraved: "And so the adventure begins. I love you. Seth." Rain plinked on the tin roof. The storm was minutes away, but she couldn't move. She could barely breathe. Here it was, Seth's final *I love you*. She had it in her possession, finally, along with the wish for new adventures ahead.

"You're a clever one, Seth Cruz." A jolt of lightning startled her into the driver's seat.

"Thank you, we're on our way," she said. She placed the silver box between her legs and reversed out of the parking spot. By the time they reached the condominium, the rain was coming down in sheets. Lena tucked the newfound treasure underneath her shirt and ran, as best she could, to the front entrance. She was almost to the door when her ankle rolled. She clutched the box with one hand, while desperately trying to remain upright. A burst of wind wrapped around her, followed by a rattling crash of thunder. She regained her balance and ascended the remaining two stairs. Once she entered the lobby and caught her breath, she turned to look outside. She caught a glimpse of Douglas and his smile through the rain. Awareness grounded her to the floor. She grasped the silver box and walked down the hallway. If Douglas could weather the storm, then she would too.

After stumbling in from the rain, and reassuring Palmer that she was fine, Lena retreated to her bedroom. She was peeling off her rain-soaked clothes when a message came in from Seth's father.

No barbecue today due to the severe weather. We will bring dinner to you once the storm passes. Stay safe!

She lowered onto the bed, half-dressed but mostly naked. She wanted to dance in relief and cry in frustration. Did Mr. Cruz mean dinner for tomorrow or later today? How long did it take for severe weather to pass in Florida? A wave of fatigue washed over her. Maybe she would take a nap instead. Except, the windows were clattering, and Douglas was out there with no protection.

Her head hit the soft pillow. Laying down for a few minutes wouldn't hurt, though, right? The room was too dark for twelve thirty in the afternoon. She should be worried. She should put on shorts and return to the living room where Palmer was waiting for her. Her eyes drifted closed.

A knocking sound echoed inside Lena's dreamless mind.

"Lena?" Was that Seth's voice saying her name? She blinked as the room came into view. It was dark, like it was nighttime. "Lena? Mr. and Mrs. Cruz are here."

Lena shot up. That was Palmer's voice, not Seth's, because

Seth was no longer alive. Why was her mind the most forgetful after a nap? Was it because it had already done the task of remembering once and didn't have the energy to do it twice? Lena looked down at her bare legs right as the door began to crack open.

Shit!

She swung off the bed and dove for her shorts on the floor. With an impressive *oomph* and a carpet-burn belly flop, she managed to cover her underwear before Palmer's head rounded the corner.

"What are you doing down there?" Lena was flat on her back.

"Don't ask." She offered a small shrug, knowing full well he had, in fact, just asked.

Palmer moved into the room as she tightened the drawstring on her shorts.

"I already did." He offered his hand. Her smile grew tenfold.

This man.

She took his hand and stood up. "What am I going to do if I fall again and you're not around?" She had stumbled a lot during this trip, but Palmer had been there, offering his hand more than anyone else in her life. It had annoyed her at first—she was capable of getting up on her own. Now she understood his gesture was his way of comforting her.

"Oh, that's easy." He pulled her into his chest. "Keep me around."

His hold on her was so deliciously firm, and *oh*, how she wanted to give in to his lure and pick up from last night. Except, he had stopped her and—

Oh, crap.

She took a step backward, feeling shameful for forgetting so quickly. "Seth's parents are here!" Rushing to the nightstand, she tapped her phone and watched as a series of messages from Seth's father popped up.

"Yeah. They brought dinner," Palmer said.

"How long was I asleep?" Lena whipped her head around.

Why wasn't there a clock in this room?

"A few hours. You were out cold. I checked on you a few times when the storm got really noisy." Palmer tilted his head. "Douglas is okay," he said, reading her mind like he had since the very beginning.

"Douglas is okay," she said and slumped onto the bed. He had weathered the storm. It was her turn now. "Did they bring pizza?"

"You really do love pizza," Palmer said with a laugh. The mattress dipped as he sat next to her. "They brought tacos."

Lena dipped her head. Of course, Mr. Cruz made his famous tacos. They were savory and crunchy and disarming in the best way possible. "Prepare to be ruined by the best homemade tacos."

"I'm already ruined," he mumbled and scratched his cheek. "So, I'm invited to stay?"

"Where else would you go?"

He gave her a sheepish look. "Good point."

She ran a hand down his wrinkled sleeve. If she were capable of soothing his anxieties right now, she would. But Seth's parents were in the other room and most likely wanting to discuss the trust. She hoped Palmer understood. "We'll eat and go from there, yeah?"

He nodded. "Let's do it."

It was awkward. There was no other way to put it. Mr. Cruz talked with his hands, just like Seth, and Mrs. Cruz wore the same curious gaze as Seth. It was like returning to a home Lena would never live in. The tacos, however, were delicious. She tried to eat slowly and delay discussing the trust, but to no avail.

Mrs. Cruz cleared the plates while Seth's father began to thumb through the papers. Palmer offered to take out the trash, leaving Lena alone with Seth's parents.

"Were you able to look over some of the trust?" Mr. Cruz asked.

Lena nodded and folded her hands in her lap. Why beat around the bush when they all knew the purpose of this dinner?

"I'll admit, it was overwhelming to read," she said. "I'm not sure I understood a lot of it."

"The legal jargon can be cumbersome, but it's not overly complicated, although since Seth wasn't allowed to tell you, I understand how you may be feeling." Mr. Cruz licked his thumb and pulled a page out for her to read. "There was an NDA Seth had to sign, which seems odd for a trust. Then again, my father was an odd man. Basically. Seth couldn't reveal the trust to any potential long-term partner until they were legally married."

Lena stilled. Seth had no choice but to keep it a secret. What else had the trust prevented him from sharing? "So, let me get this straight, Seth wasn't allowed to talk about his trust at all?"

"Seth was able to speak about his trust freely to anyone not romantically involved with him." Mr. Cruz pointed to a paragraph. "My father included his definition of what he considered a romantic partner."

Lena's stomach churned. Had Seth consulted the trust to ensure she had met the required bullet points? "With all due respect, I'd rather not know."

Mrs. Cruz placed a platter of brownies on the table and patted Lena's hand. "Oh dear, no, it wasn't like that. Once Seth turned eighteen, the money was his, to do as he wanted. He never touched it, though."

Was she supposed to feel relieved? Because she didn't. She was angry, not for herself but for Seth. At the age of eighteen, he had been taught to withhold information from the most important people in his life. Any future partnership would be built on a cracked foundation, and without knowledge or consent.

"Did you two have a say in any of this?" she asked. Surely, Seth's parents would advocate for their only child, right? Secret-keeping seemed like a good enough reason to speak up.

Seth's mother placed a brownie in front of Lena. "Seth's grandfather was steadfast in his decisions. Especially when he found out he had cancer."

"My father adored Seth. He was his only grandchild. His intentions were out of love, but he wouldn't consider any other option." Mr. Cruz removed another page and placed it in front of Lena. "Lisa and I were...are the benefactors to Seth's inheritance."

Mrs. Cruz wiped away a tear. "My son loved you, Lena. There was a reason he didn't touch that money. He was waiting to have a family. With you."

"We want to give you half of it," Mr. Cruz said as he took his wife's hand.

Lena pulled at her right earlobe. She must have misheard. "I'm sorry, I don't know if I understand..."

Seth's father grabbed his messenger bag from the floor. "Since you and Seth lived together for longer than two years and were engaged for longer than one year, you are Seth's final romantic partner. Technicalities aside, this is what he would have wanted for you. To be taken care of." He handed her an envelope. "I had my lawyer draw up additional documents for you to review and sign."

"But, wait a second—" The room was closing in on her. Were Seth's parents not aware of her breaking off the engagement? "I'm not entitled to his money. I don't know if you know but you probably should know." She gripped the edge of the table as tears burned behind her eyes. "I broke off the engagement two days before he—"

Nope.

If she said it, she would cry, a cry that might never end. She took a deep breath. "I'm so glad Seth was doing what he loved for a living. I want you to know I am so proud of him. Had I been more patient, I like to believe I would have found my place in his dream. But I can't accept his money. He and I were in a weird place, and I... I can't accept his money. I'm sorry."

Mrs. Cruz scooted her chair closer to Lena and wrapped her arms around her shoulders. "My dear girl. When we love, we love messy. Everything in us scatters when love comes around. Our deepest wounds, and insecurities, and traumas, they all bubble to the surface. Love makes us vulnerable. It's supposed to." Mrs. Cruz pinned Lena with her deep blue eyes, just like Seth's. Lena's shoulders lowered as she softened into the familiar embrace. Seth was gone, but those who made him were still here. "You cared deeply for our son, and I know you always will. All the other stuff is the mess of true love. This is what he would have wanted."

Lena glanced over at Mr. Cruz, who nodded in agreement. It was then Lena noticed Palmer standing by the front door. He gestured, asking if he should leave. She shook her head.

"Thank you both," Lena said. It was all she could come up with. "When will you need an answer?"

"We'll head out after these brownies and give you some time to digest everything," Mr. Cruz said.

"Did you say brownies?" Palmer approached, his smile wide. Lena wasn't sure how much he had heard but was grateful for his upbeat reentry into the room.

Mr. Cruz walked to Palmer and shook his hand. "Thank you for your assistance in bringing the van here."

Lena's stomach dropped. Were they planning to take Douglas tonight? All of these moving parts, and her emotions could not latch on to any one of them. Her head began to throb.

"Douglas is a mess," she said, "but I promise I'll have him cleaned and ready for you by tomorrow."

Mrs. Cruz gave her a curious look. "Douglas?"

"That's the name of the van," Palmer said.

"Well, how strange." Mrs. Cruz took a bite of brownie and shrugged. Lena could feel Seth's father staring at her as she chewed. She noticed Palmer open his mouth more than once, maybe to alleviate the heavy silence. But maybe he realized, too, there wasn't much left to say. There were only things left to do. Things that required sensible decision-making, which Lena did not plan on tackling this evening. Except maybe one final decision before the night was over: to eat a second brownie.

26

Palmer

"It was nice of Eliana to offer to drive you to the airport today," Lena said as she handed Palmer a bottle of window cleaner.

He placed the bottle into an empty bucket. It would have been a nice offer if he had any desire to leave, which he didn't. Luckily the flight wasn't until later in the evening, so he had an entire day with Lena. Tomorrow would bring meeting after meeting. First with his father, then with Nancy about the property, and then a phone call with Mateo about their business plans. Gregor had insisted Palmer stay with him so he could take care of his immediate issues without the added stress of housing.

"Is Eliana helping us clean Douglas, too?" He mentally crossed his fingers that the answer was no. He wanted as much alone time with Lena as he could get.

Lena shook her head. "She's fundraising for her nonprofit at a nearby beach today. She seemed a little stressed, to be honest. I'm not sure she's getting the funds she needs." Lena handed him rags and cleaning wipes. "I think that'll be enough." She blew a piece of hair out of her eyes. "There's so much to do suddenly. I haven't even considered how I'll get around without Douglas and you driving me." Her laughter was strained. She released her hair from her ponytail, then refastened it exactly as it was.

"I'm sure Eliana will help, right?" Palmer said.

"Yeah. I'll figure it out. I need to find a doctor to look at my ankle, first. And I need my sister to mail my medical bills." She loosened her ponytail again. Her hair circled her face. "I wonder how long I can stay in this condo. The inheritance, too; what am I supposed to do?"

His heart jolted against his ribs. It sounded like she was planning to stay.

"I should just leave with you. I should, right?" Her eyes were wide, imploring him to what— Answer her?

"I can't stay with my sister. My parents are still with her. I have a doctor there, though. And a job, too. And, I have you—" Her head fell into her hands. "I can't think!"

Palmer set the bucket down and placed his hand on her shoulder. "One thing at a time."

She lifted her head, her crystal blue eyes piercing straight through him. "It'd be easier if you told me what to do."

"You know what I'll say," he said softly. "You have my offer."

"The offer that exists only in theory right now. You don't even own the building you want me to open a coffee shop in. You know that, right?"

"Well, that's what I would say to do. Come with me to help figure it out. We'll work through your issues together," Palmer said with a shrug.

"It's ridiculous, Palmer!"

He shook his head. Of course, it wasn't founded on logic. He was in love with this woman. He would do anything, say anything, be anything in order to keep her in his life. "It's completely reasonable. Wrinkles can be ironed out."

"Not owning a building is more than a wrinkle. That's like walking around in wet clothing thinking that they're dry."

"If the building isn't available, there are others around. The original showroom from my family's business, for example."

Lena sighed. "I thought you wanted to distance yourself from the family business. What happened to you going out on your own and releasing the family ties?"

She was pushing him, and he didn't like it. Having grown up with an unpredictable father with explosive outbursts, Palmer had done his best not to repeat the same behavior. But Lena was testing him.

"I do want to go out on my own, but I will always have ties to my family, and I will do what I have to..." He stopped himself. If he said more, a battle would ensue. One not meant to be fought.

"What do you mean *do what you have to?* You have the freedom to do whatever you want." Lena uncrossed her arms with an irritated sigh.

"I'm choosing to leave the cage I've been kept in. There's a difference," he said. She knew of his complications back home better than anyone else, or so he thought. Why was she being so difficult?

"Never mind," he said. "Let's get Douglas ready to go. Even though I don't agree with that, either."

Shit. He hadn't meant to say that last part out loud.

"Excuse me?" The color of Lena's face matched her hair. "Are there other things you don't agree with? This is my life." She jabbed a finger at her chest. "My choices. My decisions."

Palmer ran a hand down his face. Here was the stubborn woman he had met in the forest preserve, hell-bent on making her point.

She didn't need anyone.

He should have taken heed from the very beginning. "Then don't say you want me to make the decision for you."

"Seriously, Palmer!" Lena pointed at him. "You take everything so literally."

"You're right, I do take what you say literally. I also take it damn seriously. That's how I am with the people I care about." Palmer picked up the bucket. "You have my offer. Let's go clean Douglas."

"Fine." Lena swung the door open.

"Fine," he said and watched her stomp away.

Two hours later, Palmer was drenched in sweat and ready to jump into the ocean. Lena turned off the reggae station, which had been blaring the entire time, and stepped out of the van.

"He looks so empty," she said as she closed the sliding door.

"What are Seth's parents planning to do with him?" Palmer said.

Lena gulped down half of her water bottle. "I hope they still drive him around. The plan was to end the trip on the East Coast back when Seth was alive. Maybe they can go see the Appalachian Mountains, the lobsters in Maine, the tiny winding streets of Boston, the lights of New York City..." She rubbed her arms as if she were cold, which was impossible given the heat.

Palmer opened his mouth to state the obvious— *You keep Douglas instead!* Lena's steely gaze had him choosing different words. "I'm going to cool off in the ocean. You're welcome to join me."

She shook her head. "Mark called about twenty minutes ago. I should call him back."

Palmer nodded. After Seth's parents had left last night, Palmer had suggested Lena reach out to Mark about the trust before she made any decisions. She had puffed out her chest, telling him she had already, then wished him a brief good night. The soft click of her bedroom door closing had felt like a punch to his gut.

It sucked. Their last night together had been spent in different rooms. He understood the primal need to be alone after receiving startling news. But the hope that Lena needed him during those difficult moments burned in his chest all the same.

Lena pulled at her sweat-stained tank top. "I'm tempted, though."

"You are, huh?" Palmer took in her flushed cheeks and damp hairline. "Allow me to help you with this decision, then," he said and pulled his shirt over his head. He knew he wasn't playing fair, but their time together was ending. Last impressions were just as important as first ones.

Lena's lips parted. He thought for sure her gaze would bounce away from his naked torso. Instead, he caught a spark in her eyes. Was she up for the challenge?

"I know what you're doing," she said, wagging a finger at him. She then looped her finger underneath the hem of her tank top and removed it.

Palmer couldn't help but stare as she adjusted the straps of her tie-dye bikini top. He had no idea what she was up to but he was enjoying the view.

She lowered her arms. "Since I can't race you to the ocean, given your leg span and my ankle injury, I'm going to suggest we walk spritely toward the ocean."

He tried to gather his wits. "Did you just say *spritely*?"

"Listen, it's the best I got right now," she said. "I wasn't prepared to see your—you, this." She waved her hands up and down.

"Then spritely we shall walk," he said, aware his smile was most likely all teeth.

He tried not to rush ahead when they reached the scorching sand. Lena's pace had picked up, but he could tell she was pushing herself. At this rate, they would suffer third-degree burns.

"This sand is like walking on hot coals, my god!" Lena said, hopping on her left foot.

He held out his arms. Lena shook her head. He moved in closer.

"It's for the best. Otherwise, I'm leaving you here, and I won't feel bad about it," he said and wiggled his open arms.

"This is all your fault!" She rushed around him. "Bend down so I can get on your back! Hurry!" He did as he was told. Her legs wrapped around his waist as his arms looped underneath her knees.

"Hold on tight!" He ran toward the water. Every inch of Lena bounced against his bare skin. *Thank GOD* his bottom half would be covered by water any second. He splashed into the water and waded in with Lena still on his back. He could feel her breathing hard, too, as he lowered her.

Her fingers skimmed over the water. He followed her gaze

and focused on the horizon as rhythmic waves rippled around them.

"I don't mean to be moody with you," Lena said. "I have a lot on my mind, and with you leaving, it's just...a lot." Her body moved in cadence with the gentle swell of water.

"I know you have a lot to sort out. I wish I didn't have to leave so soon, so I could be there for you."

"I'm used to handling things alone. It'll be all right." She moved further ahead and dipped her shoulders underneath the water. "This was a great idea, by the way."

"Sometimes I have good ones," he said with a smile. "I hope you won't write off my less straightforward idea. Or at least that you think about it once I'm gone."

"There isn't much more to think about. You need to sort things out on your end," she said. His smile slipped. She flicked water at his face. "You'll keep me updated on your progress, right?"

"Of course," he said. "I'm gonna do a quick swim. I'll meet you by Douglas."

"Oh, right. Sure." She rolled her lips inward as if to stop herself from saying more. "That storm should have blown through today instead of yesterday. It would have given us one more night."

"Don't say that," he mumbled. The pulsing water moved them closer together.

"Why?" She gazed up at him through her lashes. He should have dived in already. Now he was stuck with his drenched emotions.

"Lena." He captured her from behind and pressed into her so she felt every inch of him. "Are you asking me to stay?"

She let out a soft gasp. "You can't."

"I would."

There was pressure on his chest. She was pushing him away. "I can't."

"We can," his voice cracked.

Lena gave him a sad smile. "The last thing I expected to find on this trip was what you and Douglas showed me—that life is worthy of joy and happiness."

"It is, Lena, especially yours," he said. All of that was possible *with him*, too. "Why won't you come with me then? Am I not enough?"

"Oh, Palmer, it's not about you. There are still too many days where I'm convinced happiness means I'm forgetting Seth." A powerful wave rolled up from behind and separated them. Lena was a few feet away and closer to the shoreline.

"I'll meet you at Douglas?" she asked, her expression apologetic. He nodded. As his pleas for her to reconsider dissolved like the salty water on his shoulders, he dove underneath an oncoming wave. When he resurfaced, Lena was at the shore. He turned and dove into another wave.

Lena was wrong. To some degree, it was about him, and he did have a stake in this game. She had rejected his offer—mostly—and now he feared that once he was out of sight, he would be out of her mind, too. There was so much yet to be explored. Why did he have to give her up so soon?

He swam underneath a few more waves, hoping the water would absorb his frustration, then surfaced and blinked at where the ocean met the sky. The colors were so similar, they erased the horizon line. It was beautiful, the way the earth and sky appeared as one. But the earth and sky were not one, no matter how much they relied on one another.

He had to focus on the task ahead. Facing his family and speaking his truth wouldn't be easy. It would be damn difficult, in fact, but it was necessary, like the clouds and the rain. He would build out a dream he hadn't dared to pursue until now—and leave the rest to the stars or universe or whatever else that was out of his control.

He turned and saw Lena on the beach. She waved. And kept waving. She was urgently waving. He couldn't tell if she was smiling or crying from this distance. Since he wasn't the strongest swimmer, he bounded through the water like a moose and met her within seconds.

"I can't believe it! You're not going to believe it. This is unbe-lievable!" Lena was shouting and smiling and appeared to have tears in her eyes. "Mrs. Cruz just called and said I could keep Douglas if I wanted. Can you believe it? And all it took was you and me talking about Douglas like he was a real human. I guess it became obvious to them that Douglas was meant to stay with me." Lena twirled around with her arms open wide. "I get to keep Douglas!"

"No way!" Palmer rushed into her twirling frame and caught her at just the right moment. He lifted her legs off the sand and kept twirling. Her laughter circled around him. It was a sound he would miss hearing every day.

He set her feet down on the wet sand. "Now you gotta get yourself roadworthy so you can drive him." He refrained from asking if she planned to stay in Florida. Maybe she would take Douglas on another trip. And maybe that trip would be her return to Illinois. His stomach sparked at the possibility of it all.

"Mrs. Cruz referred me to a doctor, so once I get the all-clear, I'll be good to go." She gave a thumbs-up, then hitched it over her shoulder. "You might want to check your phone, though. It hasn't stopped buzzing."

Palmer groaned. "I'm sure it's my father calling to request my coordinates."

"Do you think he knows bad news is headed his way?"

"Absolutely." Palmer ran a hand through his wet hair. "He's too intuitive for his own good."

"Sounds like someone I know." Lena's face was plastered with a goofy smile. It was damn adorable.

"I have no idea who you're referring to," he said with a wink. Whatever his future held, he at least had these moments to hold on to, and maybe that was all the reassurance he needed from now on.

27

Lena

Two hours remained until Palmer had to leave for the airport. Once they stepped into the condominium, Lena excused herself to wash away the salt and sweat. She needed time to process the day's events. All of her morning and most of the afternoon had been spent together with Palmer, working on Douglas, sweating, flirting, touching, all while tiptoeing over questions neither of them could answer. With Palmer leaving, the unexpected news of Douglas, and her upcoming call with Mark, nerves were coursing through her body, reckless and directionless. Well, not totally without direction. She was purposely avoiding her growing feelings for Palmer.

A simple look from his brown-green eyes, even a gentle laugh from his baritone voice, and she was wanting, *needing* more of him before he left. It was such a natural feeling—and yet that same need was beyond what she was capable of handling right now, which made her want him even more!

She turned the faucet in the shower to *cold* and stepped inside. The shock of icy water on her burning skin focused her mind on her actual needs: A goodbye to Palmer. A call with Mark. A decision for her future. Taking a deep breath, she moved her entire body underneath the spray of water and exhaled.

"Eliana stopped by," Palmer said once Lena emerged from the bathroom. He sat on the couch with no shirt on. Lena's skin immediately heated. What a waste of a cold shower. Her focus certainly didn't last long in the presence of Palmer. *Damn*, she wanted to kiss him and run her hands through his hair as she straddled his lap and—

"She said we could go to her place for a bite before heading to the airport. We can leave from there," Palmer said, cutting into her daydream.

"Oh, sure." Lena pretended to look for her phone and not at Palmer. Her phone was in the master bedroom, but Palmer didn't know that. He also didn't know she wasn't going to the airport with him. "I hadn't thought about dinner plans, especially since I'm not sure how long my call with Mark will take." It sounded scripted even to her own ears.

"You're coming to the airport, though, right?" Palmer craned his neck.

Lena flinched when his eyes met hers. Saying goodbye to Palmer would happen here, behind closed doors. Eliana didn't need to witness the emotions Lena wouldn't be able to hide.

"The call with Mark is in an hour." It was a mostly true statement. She had told Mark she would call once Palmer was gone.

"Damn," Palmer said under his breath. "Well, I know that's been hanging over your head all day. I'm glad it's finally happening."

"That makes one of us," she said with a forced laugh.

"You're not tied to any one decision. No matter what Mark has dug up, the choice is yours." His gaze drifted up and down her frame. "In fact, you have more freedom than you probably realize. More than me, that's for sure. And with Douglas as your wingman—" Palmer slapped his thighs and rose to his feet. Tall and sturdy. She already missed his shade. "You're in good hands. Will you let me know what Mark says?"

She nodded. "Expect a frantic text while you're in the air."

He approached her, his chest still totally bare, and her desire still totally unreasonable. The smile on his face made her stomach jump into her throat. "I'd invite you to join me if you hadn't already showered."

"Don't say that." Lena gently pushed her closed fist into his stomach. It was soft with a hint of muscle, which suited him. What didn't suit her was her temptation to get wet again. She had to concentrate on her responsibilities, and remind herself why she was in Florida in the first place.

Palmer must have sensed her incoming guilt and squeezed her shoulder. "You don't need to detour around happiness anymore. You're ready."

"Ready for what?" she whispered.

"For this." His mouth was on hers before she realized what was happening. She should have been startled. Instead, she tried to ignore the road in front of her, the one clearly under construction, while Palmer's musky scent pulled her in. Palmer had his own life to sort out. She did, too. But one more kiss wouldn't hurt, right? Except, Palmer's kiss included his warm hands grazing along the waistband of her shorts and her fingernails digging into his back. Kissing Palmer was so much more than kissing, wasn't it? It was an all-consuming experience.

She broke away from him before it could go any further. *Focus.*

"You should—" She stopped and watched him back away.

"I know. I just want to make sure you remember me once I'm gone." His dimples appeared, genuine and irresistible.

She knew he was being flirtatious. Although, part of her wondered how much truth was hiding behind his smile.

"We'll see each other again," she said. She attempted a lighthearted punch to his shoulder. He snagged her hand and placed it on his chest.

"The sooner, the better," he said. She could feel his heart beating underneath her palm. "I mean it. Don't stay away for too long."

Lena swallowed. She wasn't staying away on purpose. The decisions she had to make required purposeful thought. Which meant intentional distance. Otherwise, she would second-guess her first choice in a series of many.

"Once I figure everything out here, I'll figure out everything else." She felt like she was on repeat at this point.

"One day at a time," he said.

She smiled in relief. There was no need to worry that Palmer wouldn't understand. Yes, he pushed her to consider all of her options, but he still respected her choice.

"I'm glad you agree," she said as her phone started ringing in the bedroom.

Palmer raised her hand to his lips and kissed it before releasing. He disappeared into the bathroom. Lena felt lightheaded as her phone continued to ring.

Shit!

She rushed into the bedroom and answered the call without checking the caller ID.

"Lena, you might want to sit down for this."

Twenty minutes later, Lena paced the bedroom. Her right ear was hot from the phone pressing against it, or maybe it was the adrenaline surging through her veins. Her door creaked open.

"Who was on the phone?" Palmer asked. His hair was wet, and his face was free of its five-o'clock shadow.

"Mark. He called to let me know he was going to be busy later." The lump in her throat threatened to wreak havoc on her tear ducts. "We reviewed the paperwork."

"Just now?" Palmer's eyebrows shot up. "That didn't take long."

"Turns out there wasn't much to go over. The amount of money from the inheritance is...too much." Tension bloomed across her forehead. She would rather have Seth alive than be in possession of his money. "Seth's parents also decided to tack on the condominium."

Palmer pointed to the floor. "As in, they're giving you this condominium?"

She nodded. "It's too much," she repeated. "I'm not supposed to be given a car, a home, and money because Seth is dead. I'm supposed to disappear, just as he has."

The room was spinning. Somehow she found her way to the bed. Palmer was next to her. He'd probably guided her here. Like always. Her face fell into her hands. "I don't know what's worse, being overwhelmed by his death or being overwhelmed by my never-ending guilt."

Palmer leaned over as if to console her but didn't touch her. "I won't pretend to know what you're going through, but if you don't mind, I'll offer you my perspective."

Lena gripped his hand resting on his thigh. She was beyond familiar with it by now. "Please."

His fingers laced between hers. "No one wants you to disappear. If anything, what has been given to you is a testament to how much Seth's parents cherish and care for you."

She hated how strongly her mind wanted to falsify the truth. "I'm so overwhelmed," she said.

"You're supposed to be, Lena."

"I am?"

He leveled her with his eyes. "There's no script for what you're experiencing. The only way out of it is to go through it."

She shook her head. He was making sense, but clarity was out of her reach. "Can't I sleep until this all blows over?"

He laughed. "Rest, yes. Sleeping with the intent to avoid, no."

"I know," she sighed. Her unresolved emotions would seep into her dreams, anyway, which would only create more problems upon waking.

"Are you packed and ready to go?" She turned into him and soaked in his smooth face and dimples. It was a must with him leaving.

"Yeah." Palmer looked at her. The air between them sparked as it had the night before. This time, however, Palmer was the one to lift her chin and say, "One more for the road?"

"You're not leaving yet." Her fingers found his shirt and fisted it into her palm. She wasn't sure why, but it felt necessary. "I thought we were going to Eliana's for dinner?"

"We are," he hummed. "I'd rather kiss you here."

"I would like that, too." She released his shirt and wrapped her arms around his neck. Their lips melted together in a crescendo of lust-filled hopes. This type of lightheadedness was manageable. It came with a buzzing feeling and a warmth between her thighs. Their kiss deepened, and a moan escaped her lips. Why did they have to find a resolution in everything else before living daily in this? Why couldn't they continue to be together while working through the challenges that faced them?

Sliding her hands through his hair, she crawled onto his lap. His hands squeezed her from behind as her lips moved over his, earnest and absent of patience. Their time was coming to an end. She didn't want him to leave. She didn't want to be alone. His fingers crept under the back of her shirt, his touch searing her skin.

She broke away from his mouth, her breathing shallow. Was it really necessary for her to focus on anything other than this? Happiness was within her reach. If she didn't grasp on to it now, it would disappear.

"Drive Douglas back to Illinois with me," she said, throwing caution into a fiery pit of hormones.

Palmer's arms stiffened around her. "What?" His eyes slowly began to clear as he removed his hands from under her shirt.

She slid off his lap, feeling as if a million sandbags were piling onto her chest. She was a traitor to logic and had asked Palmer to do the exact opposite of what they'd planned. Yes, she was terrified, but maybe this was the exact question she was supposed to ask.

"Say something," she said.

Palmer ran a hand through his hair. "What happened to you staying in Florida while you worked through the details of Seth's inheritance and what his parents have included?" His tone was neutral, which made her want to punch things.

"Who says I can't figure all of that out while on the road with you, like we have been already." She searched his face for any sign that she was making sense.

"Oh, Lena." Palmer shock his head.

Her chest was burning and her hands shook. So, this was what taking a risk felt like.

Good to know.

She stood up and glanced around the dimly lit bedroom, with its pastel-blue walls and sea-star decor. This wasn't home. Her home had become evergreen-painted steel on wheels, and the person standing next to her.

She froze.

No.

Those were unrealistic expectations not meant to be placed on anyone ever again. Perhaps, though, Palmer had helped her find herself again, which was why being with him felt like home.

"I'm not making sense." She refused to look at the pity in his face, or listen to the excuses he was about to give her.

Palmer remained seated. "I would drop everything to drive with you and Douglas again."

"You would?" Her heart galloped in her chest.

"But you were right before. I have to sort out the life I left, just like you have to sort through the life you want. The longer I stay away from home, the worse things will become for those directly and indirectly involved." He approached her with open arms. She took a step back.

"Okay," she said. But it wasn't okay. She wasn't okay. She should have known better than to take another chance on a man who had his own dream to pursue. "I mean, it's not okay. But I understand. Emotions are high, and I admit I am grasping at something that probably doesn't exist between us."

"Wait. This isn't a rejection, Lena." He tried to reach for her. She moved farther away.

"Oh, I know. I do. It's too complicated to consider this, you and me, all of it, any of it, as anything other than friends." It was a truth she couldn't deny any longer. "Let's eat and send you on your way."

"Lena. Don't be upset. Please. I cannot leave with you upset." His shoulders slumped. She straightened her spine.

"I'm not." To prove her point, she walked into his chest and hugged him. It was her own fault for letting Palmer jumble her insides. What she was experiencing was a bout of uncontrollable mind-hiccups. Once he left, she would begin to think clearly again. "I apologize for earlier. You and I have important decisions to make. Separately," she said as she stepped away. Her legs were weak but stable. No more second-guessing her decisions. "So—" She gave Palmer her best *I'm okay* smile. "Do you think Eliana ordered pizza?"

It took a few seconds for Palmer to return her smile. "I have my guesses, but let's find out before it's too late to eat any of it."

"Great." Her left eye twitched. The corners of her mouth were starting to ache. She was about to turn and walk out the bedroom door when Palmer said, "Come to the airport with me."

Her face dropped. "I already told you—"

"You've had your call."

"I know."

"So, you can come to the airport, right? I mean, if you want to."

She shifted on her feet. "I don't know what I want anymore, Palmer."

His dimples disappeared. "Other than pizza, I'm guessing."

She shrugged. "Pizza is easier to digest than saying goodbye to you."

"Unless you're lactose intolerant. Which you're not. You're also not coming to the airport with me, are you? So, what else is left but to eat pizza?" He opened the door wide. She didn't move. "It's okay, Lena. Truly. Give me a hug, and we'll get on with it."

She was pulled into him before she could cross her arms and stomp her feet and act like a child. A series of non-goodbyes raced through her mind: how she would see him again soon and would text him as often as she thought about him, which would be all the time; how she would call him in the middle of the night just to hear his sleepy voice; and that she loved him, but had no idea how to be in love after losing love. She wanted to say all of what she couldn't, but instead, she said, "I'll miss you."

Palmer's arms tightened around her. "The moment you plan to visit Illinois, you let me know."

She nodded, her eyes damp. Palmer had given her what she needed to hear just like that. Taking a deep breath, she knew what she had to do, what she owed to herself and to Palmer to say out loud.

"I'll see you again soon," she said.

"I know," he whispered.

28

Palmer

H e didn't know what to do. He had no idea at all. And no amount of planning could relieve him of what had to happen. After a long kiss goodbye with Lena, Palmer had flown back to Illinois with a plan. One built on dreams rather than obligations, which fueled his determination to do what was necessary. But now that he sat face to face with his father, he had *no idea* what to do.

"What about the legacy?" his father said around a bite of omelet. "Have you thought about how this will affect your future son? He won't have the same opportunities because you chose to end the family business."

Palmer took a measured sip of lukewarm diner coffee. What a low blow. Even for his father. "Dad, you're the one who shut down the business, remember? You also rejected my idea to keep the business running in some way, and now you're here, guilting me about my theoretical son *or daughter's* future because you want to live in a yurt. Is that right?"

"Basically." His father didn't even have the decency to acknowledge the absurdity coming out of Palmer's mouth.

"Well, *basically*, Dad, I'm starting my own business. So, unfortunately, the family legacy will end with...you." Palmer leaned back. The dissonance vibrating through his body was teeth-rattling. He would sit with it, though, and refused to second-guess his choice. This was the right one for his future, theoretical children included.

"Your mother was right." said his father, placing his elbows on the table.

Palmer narrowed his eyes. Was that a smile on his father's face?

"She told me you would come back a changed man. Travel can do that to you, though. Especially road trips. Your mother and I did a poor job of prioritizing those experiences when you and Gregor were younger." His father rubbed his gray-speckled chin. "Mom is convinced I want the yurt for that very reason, to make up for lost time. Now she's threatening to divorce me if I make her move. I don't want to lose her."

Palmer mirrored his father's position. It was rare, like dodo-bird rare, for his father to talk about feelings. "She supported you when the business declared bankruptcy, and you started painting, right?" said Palmer.

His father nodded fiercely. "Without question."

"Could you maybe support her now without question?" It seemed pretty obvious to him. And really, what was the big deal? So his father wouldn't get a yurt, *boo-freaking-hoo*.

"How can I?" The wrinkles around his father's mouth deepened. "I'm the only Eriksson who failed the company, and this town is a daily reminder of that. Your mother refuses to leave. Her roots are here...our sons are here. She has her clubs and her social circle, and her volunteer work, too. I'm a deadbeat businessman painting over his failures. I don't know if I can stomach staying in this town, son."

Palmer felt as if he had just been plunged into an ice bath. Hearing his father speak so openly and in a tone of regret was a shock to the system. Yes, the business went under, but really, in Palmer's eyes, it was a blessing in disguise. Maybe his father wasn't a self-centered old man at all, but a lost soul trapped in familiar surroundings. Maybe it was time for him and his father to set aside their misunderstandings and offer each other support.

"You raised a family in this town, Dad, and successfully ran a business for as long as it was meant to be run. I doubt anyone would take what you've done and call it a failure."

"The empty showroom down the street would suggest otherwise, son. Folks around here aren't likely to show up at an old man's house to see his amateur artwork."

Palmer sputtered on his coffee as an idea popped into his mind. A napkin was jerked into his hands.

"Thanks, Dad." Palmer wiped at his mouth. His heartbeat picked up speed as he considered his next words. "I'm curious. How many finished paintings do you have, now?"

His father exhaled a long breath. "Ten, maybe."

"Wow," Palmer said, impressed. "That's enough for a small showing, I would think."

"Ten is the minimum for an art show." His father's cheeks colored. "I'm not sure people want to look at a bunch of water landscapes and manatees."

"I met a woman in Florida who swims with manatees for a living," Palmer said. He was stalling. Repurposing the original Husky's showroom into an art gallery was a huge risk, but buttering up his father was vital.

"What a life she must live." His father sighed. "I would love to swim with them one day."

"I could make it happen," Palmer said. His father looked at him with childlike glee. "If you hear me out," he added. Withholding wasn't his usual tactic when it came to being persuasive, but he was still dealing with a master guilt-tripper.

His father cupped his mug. "All right. Tell me what's on your mind."

Once inside Gregor's apartment, Palmer was out of breath. Three trips up and down steep stairs would do that, though. Wiping sweat from his forehead, he pushed the guest-room door open. The space was empty, aside from a wrinkled curtain hanging over the window. He set his boxes on the floor. At least the air smelled clean. But the lingering burn in his lungs reminded him he needed to renew his gym membership. Exercise was his go-to stress reliever, an outlet he would likely need sooner rather than later.

As the front door slammed shut, his phone pinged. A message from Lena popped up.

I'm glad you made it back safely! Good luck with the rest of your day.

Palmer's thumb hovered over the phone's keyboard. Should he type a simple *thanks*? Or should he tell her about his breakfast with his father? He should just call. There was so much to tell her already, like the surreal feeling he couldn't shake since stepping off the plane. He needed to hear her voice. But was that more than he had promised her, more than she wanted him to share?

"You're a damn genius, Palmer!" Gregor shouted.

Palmer pocketed his phone—he would figure out a response later—and walked toward the main room. After this morning's events, a two-hour call with Mateo, and an unnecessary but essential meeting with Nancy at the downtown space, he needed an entire pot of coffee. Palmer entered the kitchen as Gregor pulled a bottle of whiskey from a cupboard.

"I could have used your help with my stuff just now," Palmer said. "Also, why am I a genius?"

"I just got off the phone with our parents. Dad's gonna do it," Gregor said with a smile the size of Lake Michigan. He splashed a generous amount of whiskey into Palmer's glass. "Mom is so happy." Gregor rounded the corner of the breakfast bar and slapped Palmer on the back. "Whatever you said to Dad, it stuck."

"Let's not celebrate just yet." Palmer swirled the liquid in his glass. His father would need to follow through with his promise before Palmer jumped for joy.

Gregor shook his head. "I've never heard Dad this excited,

well, except when he started painting, which makes sense why he's on board with your idea." Gregor snatched his glass and clinked it to Palmer's. "Cheers to Dad's soon-to-be art gallery." Gregor held up a finger as he took a quick sip. "In the original Husky's location, no less. My brother, everyone." He set his glass down and clapped as if there was an audience. Gregor was known for these types of theatrics. Some might read them as sarcasm, but Palmer knew it was a show of love and appreciation. "How'd you come up with the idea?"

"It just kind of popped into my head while I was at the diner with Dad. I think the trip opened me up to life's...flow, or whatever."

"The trip. Right." The corner of Gregor's mouth tilted upward.

Palmer reached for his glass. "Yeah. The trip. Why are you looking at me like that?"

"And maybe someone else opened you up, too?" His brother was full-on smirking now.

"Damnit, Gregor," Palmer grumbled. Just like when they were kids, Palmer's secret had been effortlessly plucked from its hiding place. He sighed in defeat. "She's a force."

"I know. I've met her." Gregor took a sip. "She's staying in Florida, then?"

Palmer wondered if Gregor still carried an unrequited curiosity for Lena.

"For the moment, yeah. You'll be happy to know Douglas will remain in her possession. They gave it to her."

Gregor slapped his hands on the counter. "This day keeps getting better! Douglas was always hers, even when she didn't realize it."

Palmer nodded and pushed his glass toward Gregor. "I'm meeting Mark later to talk through some legal stuff. I need to keep a clearish head."

Gregor leaned into the counter. "You're different. Aside from the lack of beard, that is."

"Dad said the same thing." Palmer drummed his fingers

against the laminate countertop. "I'm going to put an offer on the downtown space today."

"That's great!" Gregor's enthusiasm was expected, but Palmer couldn't bring himself to match it. "It is, right?" His brother's voice faltered.

"No, it is great. It's just..." Palmer stood up. Movement would distract him from the discomfort of vulnerability. He couldn't remember the last time he had a heart-to-heart with his brother. They would always have each other's back but, like their father, they rarely talked about their feelings. He sure could use another man's perspective right now, however.

"Lena was...is...someone I had a hard time leaving. I really thought I had a foolproof way to bring her home with me, too." He scratched his temple. "Obviously, that didn't go through. I understand why she refused, and I accept her reasons." He paused and looked out the window at nothing in particular. "She said she wanted updates. I agreed, but what does that mean? I would text her every hour if I thought that was what she wanted. I don't know what she wants. I thought I did, so I offered her the front area to open up her own coffee shop." Palmer scrubbed a hand down his face. "I have the space nearly secured. Maybe after all the papers are signed, she will be more open to coming up here."

"Maybe she will," Gregor said. "Or, instead of continuing to offer her a space that requires monumental change on her part, you actually just give her...space."

"Like...leave her alone?" Palmer's stomach dropped. It would be impossible to go no-contact if that's what Gregor was suggesting.

"You can't make her change her mind right now. Pressuring her will only make her annoyed with you. Just let her air out and gather her thoughts. She'll come around." Gregor stood next to Palmer by the window. "You're a man of your word, Palmer. You can provide her updates but leave it at that."

"You're supposed to tell me to go chase the girl, Gregor,"

Palmer grumbled.

Gregor laughed. "Don't take this the wrong way, but seriously, brother"—Gregor placed a firm hand on Palmer's shoulder—"go focus on your own shit for once. Not a girl you can't have right now, not a family you can no longer save—*you.* Go focus on you."

Palmer wanted to talk his way around Gregor's logic and get to the answer he wanted to hear. His brother had plucked the truth out of him just as easily as the secret from earlier.

"I'm supposed to chase the dream, my dream," Palmer said flatly. "The one before Lena."

Gregor squeezed Palmer's shoulder before releasing. "You already are. And I'm not saying Lena isn't a part of whatever...but ya know bro, it's okay to put yourself first. Okay?"

"Sure. Okay." Was his brother right? Was it okay to put himself first? And was his resistance a normal reaction to change?

"I remember when you started your business," Palmer said, "and how it took over your life. I'm guessing that's what I'm in for."

"There's no way around the demand of being an entrepreneur. It's probably a good thing you're not starting a new relationship, too." Gregor's phone pinged. "Speaking of. Your younger and more dashing bro has a date tonight, and I'm guessing that's her."

The last time Palmer witnessed a woman texting Gregor had been in this very kitchen, except that woman had been Lena. Back when she had still been a mystery. So much had changed and yet, here he was again, in his hometown, thinking of her all the time.

Palmer walked to the sink and washed his glass. Gregor was chuckling at his phone as Palmer turned to dry his hands.

"I'm gonna clean up before I head out to see Mark," Palmer said, tossing the towel on the counter. "Thanks for the chat. I know we don't do it often, but I appreciate your feedback."

Gregor looked up, smiling. "I anticipate many more of these

now that we're roommates. Speaking of, rent is due on the first of the month."

"Oh, right. Rent. Of course." Palmer had assumed crashing on an air mattress in a room fit to be a closet would come at no cost.

Gregor barked out a laugh. "I'm kidding, bro! We gotta work on that sense of humor next time, eh?"

"Maybe you need to work on your jokes, little brother, eh?" Palmer ribbed Gregor as he walked by him and out of the kitchen.

The next day, Palmer stood in the middle of the downtown space, staring up at the exposed wooden beams and dusty Edison lights. In his hands was a signed contract from the sellers accepting his offer. In three weeks, and if all went as planned, he would close on the property and begin the process of opening his own business.

He removed his phone from his pocket, held the papers in front of him, and took a photo. The front area—the same one where he had envisioned Lena bustling around with a smile on her face—was blurred behind the contract, his signature scribbled in black.

"Perfect," he said to himself. He pulled up Lena's message from yesterday. He had argued with himself last night as to whether he should send a good-night text. In the end, he decided to give her space, just as Gregor had suggested.

He attached the photo with a smiley face and hit *send*. This was what he had promised—not good-nights or good-mornings, but updates. Even if it felt wrong to give only the bare minimum, he would keep to his promise.

29

Lena

She'd thought this part of the grieving process was over. Yet, over a month of oversleeping, undereating, and excessively crying, had passed in a blur. The endless void from the early days of Seth's passing had opened up again, tempting her to live there permanently. She had burrowed into that darkness before, having no other option at the time. But she wouldn't again.

An unexpected confidant was by her side now—someone who could understand, better than most, her rolling emotions. Every morning over the last month, Eliana showed up at Lena's door to go to the beach. They walked along the shoreline while Eliana spoke of the healing powers of water, and creatures, and nature. Eli was the light Lena had been missing during the early days of grief.

When Lena insisted on canceling the lawyer and doctor appointments and silencing the calls from Seth's parents, Eliana was there, telling her to go to the water. Lena would have been crushed by the weight of responsibility—and the minimal communication from Palmer—had it not been for Eliana telling her, over and over, to go to the water. *It looks like a mirror, but it blurs it all.*

Her toes sunk into the wet sand as the waves receded. Lena had promised to keep up their morning walks while Eliana was in Miami for the week, fundraising for her nonprofit. And she had, even in this ridiculous heat.

Pulling at her shirt, sweat trickled down her back. It was the first week of September, but Florida didn't know. Or Lena wasn't used to September in the South. She missed the chilly winds off the Oregon coast and the cool shade in Illinois. Here, it was hot and humid, 24/7.

Lena watched the water as she tried to quiet her mind. Today was different, though. Today the inheritance money would transfer into the new bank account she had set up, a recommendation from Mark to *keep your affairs more manageable*. But who was she kidding? She had no idea what she was doing.

On top of that, Douglas's engine kept overheating, Seth's parents were waiting for her to sign the condominium deed, and Palmer was fading into the distance. Of the three, she was most consumed by the last. She couldn't reason with herself. Palmer was respecting their agreement: updates. Nothing more. Nothing less. Why, then, was she upset?

This was their new reality now—one or two texts every couple of days. If texting him hourly didn't come off as excessive or needy, she would happily do it—no question. But Palmer was busy with his new business and living a life she couldn't merge with her own. Not at the moment, anyway. Maybe it would never happen. Maybe he had already moved on.

"Go to the water," Lena said to herself. White bubbles circled around her feet and submerged the skin around her ankle—a bone no longer broken. She wished she could say the same about her heart.

Dark clouds were gathering in the west, an indication of an approaching storm. Seth's father's voice echoed in her head—*Hurricane season is upon us, dear.*

Lena waited for one more wave to splinter around her ankles, then turned toward the parking lot. She wished Douglas had a carport or a garage to keep him protected rather than a parking lot filled with palm trees. His overheating engine, however, was the bigger problem.

Within minutes of driving, the temperature gauge spiked into the red. She had checked the fluids, the oil level, and the undercarriage for leaks. Yet, she refused to reach out to Gregor or Palmer. She had to find a mechanic in Florida, today. No more delaying.

The wind whipped around her face, but she still had a ten-minute walk back. The street lights flickered on as she walked into the condominium parking lot. She repositioned Douglas in the middle of the lot, away from the swaying palms. Rain began to fall as she rushed toward the front entrance. She looked at Douglas one last time before entering the safety of her building.

Lena was toeing off her soaked sandals when her phone rang. There was a time, not too long ago, when her sister's calls would have gone to voicemail. Now, she clutched her phone with relief and answered on the second ring.

"What's with all the noise?" Shay said over the phone.

"All that noise is yet another Florida storm blowing in," Lena said as she opened the hallway storage closet. A severe thunderstorm warning had been issued during her walk, and it was coming in fast. Storms off an ocean were wildly different from those in landlocked areas. Lena needed to close the storm shutters on the windows, a habit she had grown used to, but, for some reason, the tool she needed to close the shutters was missing.

"Mom mentioned something about bad weather down there. Seems like a daily occurrence," Shay said. "All the more reason to come back here."

"To the land of seasonal tornadoes? I'm not sure that's any better." Lena walked into the spare bedroom and spotted the crank-handle lying across the bed. Why had she left it in here? *...Oh, right.* She had burrowed in this bed during the last storm because the sheets still smelled like— She shook her head. "How is my nephew doing?"

"Missing his Aunt Lena," Shay sighed. "I miss you, too. How are you holding up?"

Lena lowered onto the bed. "I'm one of those long-form figures in a Salvador Dalí painting surrounded by melting clocks."

"Not at all vague or cryptic."

Lena smoothed her hand over the wrinkled comforter. "I'm abstractly present and sweating too much."

"We're worried about you, Lena," Shay said softly.

Lena wasn't surprised. Worrying was a Sullivan family trait. So many hours were wasted weeding their garden of concerns—a garden where nothing bloomed. During a call with her sister last week, Shay had suggested Lena come visit them soon. The baby was growing, and Lena was missing it. She longed to see her family, but the logistics of leaving felt insurmountable. The change in scenery and routine would be hard for her unsettled mind, never mind the more obvious obstacle, seeing Palmer—if she saw Palmer.

"I'll be fine," she said. "Once I secure the windows."

"Of course. I'll let you get to it. I just wanted to check on those dates I mentioned. Were you able to find a flight?"

"I will look tonight if the power stays on," Lena said. The line went silent. *Uh oh.* Shay was known to go quiet before launching into a long-awaited lecture.

"I bought you a ticket already. I can forward you the details. You leave in six weeks."

Before Lena could respond, the call cut out. She looked down at her phone and caught her reflection on the blackened screen. Her hair was falling out of its clip, and she had a dark smudge on her cheek. Her phone's battery must have died. Lena rubbed absently at her face while silently applauding her sister's courage. Shay had put her money where her mouth was, as they say, and had shown Lena how important this was to her—how important Lena was to her. A loud knocking pulled her back into the present moment.

Lena opened the door to a dripping-wet Eliana. "Grab your rain jacket, quick!"

Lena's heart rate spiked. "Douglas?"

"It's not good. Come on!"

Lena darted out the door, not bothering to find her jacket. Eliana caught up to her, their feet pounding down the stairs.

A bolt of lightning greeted them as they rushed into the lobby.

"Oh, no!" Lena flew out the main doors and splashed through the flooded parking lot. The wind pushed against her as the rain spat in her face.

"Careful, Lena, there's broken glass!" Eliana shouted from behind.

"No. No, no, no, no!" A crack of thunder shook her from above. She wiped at her face, wet from the rain and tears. "This can't be happening!"

A giant palm tree had somehow landed right on top of Douglas. His beautiful white roof was caved in, the pop-up tent most likely crushing the small kitchen inside, the windshield completely shattered. The tree had also smashed the rear hatch, destroying the access panel to the engine, the damage undoubtedly substantial. Lena slammed her fist against the trunk of the tree. Pain radiated up her arm.

"How is this possible? He's in the middle of the parking lot!" Lena looked around. The entire lot was covered in downed trees. Eliana stood next to Lena.

"The winds can be unpredictable," Eliana said, lowering the hood on her jacket. The rain was starting to let up. "I had to pull over before I entered the parking lot. I couldn't see two feet in front of me for a few minutes. I'm guessing that's when all of this happened."

"I'm glad you're okay," Lena said, wrapping an arm around Eliana's shoulder. "My god, though. He has a tree on him." She moved to inspect Douglas further. Parts of the engine peeked through the damaged rear panel. Lena placed a hand on her chest. This hurt more than she thought possible.

"I should be used to this by now," Lena said numbly. "The sudden loss of something I love."

A low rumble of thunder sounded amongst the fast-moving clouds. After a moment of silence, Eliana spoke. "I read once that loss is love's souvenir. Without it, we wouldn't know the value of love." Eliana bent down and patted the chrome bumper. "Douglas is still smiling."

Lena's cheeks were wet with tears. In this light, his scratch resembled a dimple. She squatted next to Eliana and placed her hand over her friend's. "Seth never said this was his favorite part of Douglas, but I knew it was." Her knees cracked as she stood up.

She loved this van for many reasons. It was a tangible memory she could climb into and drive away in. It had also become a place to store her grief, like the melted chocolate in the rear cabinets. Maybe this was nature's way of showing her that loss wasn't meant to remain inside a van like a souvenir, but live inside of her, instead.

"I have some phone calls to make," Lena said.

Eliana nodded. "I can contact Seth's parents and ask them to call the insurance company to assess the damages. If you'd like."

Lena wanted to cry all over again. Eliana cared in such an easy way. "You're the best, Eli."

"Tell that to my last failed relationship," she laughed with a shrug, then looped her arm through Lena's. "Dry clothes, first. Cookies, second. Yes. I have cookies. Phone calls, third."

Lena felt herself smile. "Cookies first."

30

Palmer

Palmer rubbed his bare arms as he walked toward Gregor's shop. It was one o'clock in the morning, the air outside was crisp, and Palmer was dead tired. The first of October was in two weeks, and he was determined to finish the renovations in the showroom before the upcoming holiday season. But with the multiple setbacks—contractors were notoriously unreliable, as was the ancient plumbing—he was already way behind schedule.

Given the delay, Palmer was relieved he had pieces in storage ready to go. Once the showroom was up to snuff, he would pull his furniture, and stage the room lickety-split. But even in the midst of the hellstorm of problems, there were still bits of excitement. His business sign had arrived yesterday, the very one that would hang outside his front entrance, for all to see. Setbacks be damned, Revival Goods would open in time for the holidays.

That had been the plan, anyway, until earlier that day. He should have known better than to trust a project that kept testing him.

"Your current pieces will look wonderful in here, son, but I wonder what else you could offer. Why not a fresh look for a fresh start?" his father had said. He had stopped in on Palmer before heading to the art gallery a few buildings over.

"You're suggesting I build furniture on top of handling this?" Palmer waved his hands around the mess.

"Have you built any furniture since returning from Florida? And what about all the reclaimed wood coming from your new supplier? I bet a backlog of creative pieces is waiting to come out of you. You don't want to burn out for the wrong reasons, right?" Palmer's father gave a slight shrug. "The older pieces could be for special releases or promotional offerings."

The suggestion had floored Palmer. Mainly because it was a good one and mostly because his father had offered it freely. No strings attached. Somehow, Palmer felt invigorated by the prospect of taking on such a huge task.

So, the new plan was to spend two solid months building pieces with Mateo's wood, which would arrive in a few weeks. Sure, the extra work delayed his opening, but it would be worth it in the long run. After all, he wasn't sprinting toward a dream. He was walking alongside it now.

His pocket buzzed, startling him enough to trip on nothing. He hadn't checked his messages since lunch. Erecting a wall made of reclaimed wood had been more complicated than he anticipated and determinedly more time-consuming. He stopped in his tracks. A message from Lena stared up at him. Why was she texting in the middle of the night? It had been weeks since they last texted, when she broke the news about Douglas and the storm damage.

He'd wanted to check in, but had leaned into his excuses for why not to. She had a lot going on, and he did, too. Truthfully, though, the front area had become a glaring reminder of how unlikely it was that his vision would come true. With each passing day, it became more apparent that Lena would remain in Florida.

Remember when we watched fireworks on the side of the road because we both forgot it was the Fourth of July?

Palmer smiled a big, ridiculous, goofy grin only Lena could bring out of him. He remembered. It was one of the best Fourth of Julys of his life. They had laughed wildly into a dark night while the sky sparkled in all directions. Afterward, they pulled into a college town and ate a late dinner on picnic tables in the middle of a food-truck court. Palmer had never experienced such a thing—food trucks permanently parked next to one another. Lena had, however, in Portland.

He thought about calling her. They hadn't talked on the phone since he'd left and she'd asked for space. As much as he cared for her, he respected her demands. He had plenty of his own and his twelve-hour delay in responding to her messages didn't necessarily help matters. But, *damn*, he missed her voice, her laugh, her...everything. He tapped out a reply.

Don't forget the killer grilled cheese from the food truck court.

He watched the three dots appear, then disappear. Then a message popped up.

Goodnight, Palmer.

He stared at his screen, unsure how to respond. Too many questions surrounded Lena's message and abrupt good-night—questions not meant to be asked by a mind too tired to think.

He pressed the lock button and the screen went black. Almost immediately, he tapped the screen again. The light glared as his chest constricted, a pressure only her voice could alleviate. But with the time difference, she was likely dozing off already. He pocketed the phone. He would call in the morning. Surely, he could carve out time and make her a priority. Hell, she was on his mind constantly. It was hard to think she wasn't a priority already. But words left unsaid would never be heard, and actions spoke louder any way you sliced it. Damn. Now he wanted a grilled cheese sandwich.

The following day, Palmer woke up with a sore neck and a puddle of drool on his pillow. Bright sunlight streamed through his window as he rolled over to check the time.

"Perfect." He'd forgotten to set his alarm, like an overworked, sleep-deprived idiot. He kicked off the blankets, stood up, and threw on his clothes from yesterday. As he darted out the door, he typed a quick message to Lena.

If I can make it work, I would love to chat on the phone sometime today.

His thumb hovered over the send button. He could feel how thinly his time was spread and hated how sparse his efforts—and hers, to be frank—had been. But it was the best he could do. In ten minutes, his plumber would arrive, leaving zero minutes to consider whether or not he would have time for a call.

He closed out of the screen without sending the message. If a woman was constantly on his mind, she deserved more than his rushed time. Tomorrow, he would wake up early. Tomorrow, he would not be rushed. Tomorrow, he would brush his teeth and have a cup of coffee, and without asking, he would outright call her instead. Tomorrow.

"You got galvanized steel piping," the plumber said the next morning. The plumber, Joe, had taken his sweet time yesterday, poking around, running the water, looking outside, and banging holes inside the walls. You name it, Joe was there doing it. After nearly a full day of no coffee, peanuts for lunch, and a warm bottle of water for dinner, Palmer was exhausted by simply existing.

"Which means messed-up pressure, funky-colored water, pinhole leaks, et cetera." Joe readjusted his low-hanging pants. "And bigger problems later on if you continue to ignore them."

"Does it look like I'm ignoring the problem?" Palmer pinched the bridge of his nose. Poor sleep and another late start weren't doing his temper any favors. "What do you recommend?"

"Replace them with copper pipes."

Bad news without coffee was even worse. "How much are we talking?"

Joe surveyed the bathroom and workshop area. "These are the only two rooms with plumbing?"

"For now," Palmer said. The front area was a blank slate he would eventually have to address, whether it be the coffee shop he had envisioned all along or something else entirely.

"I'd say you're looking at anywhere from eight to ten grand if I had to guess."

"Right." The old building kept sucking up his lumber money. "Let me crunch some numbers, and I'll get back to you," Palmer said as he walked Joe to the front. The door opened with a loud squeak and a blast of wind.

"My goodness," said Carrie as she rushed in and patted her already-perfect hair. "You certainly do *not* need a bell above the door with a noise like that." She readjusted the strap to her purse and looked around. "So, this is where you've been hiding since Florida?"

Joe lobbed a thumb behind him. "I'll show myself out."

Carrie offered a small wave to Joe then walked toward Palmer, her eyes narrowed. "I'm fine, by the way, in case you were wondering."

"How've you been?" Palmer wrapped her in a bear hug, lightly messing her hair. She squeaked and shoved him away.

"Fine until you messed up my hair." Carrie smiled and looked around. "I can see why you haven't returned my messages. It's coming together nicely, Palmer."

Palmer tried to see it from his cousin's perspective, one without the constant problems. "It's a labor of love, no question," he said.

"Speaking of love..." She twirled on her heels and pointed her cherry red fingernail at him, like a fairy godmother readying to grant a wish. "How is Lena since you left her?"

He pursed his lips. "I didn't leave her. She chose to stay in Florida."

"Right. Right. Shay told me. It's too bad she couldn't find a way to come up here."

"Well, there could have been a way but it didn't work out," Palmer said. "So, I'm here, and she's there." The simplicity of the sentence seemed to intensify his complicated feelings on the matter.

Carrie inspected her fingernails. "You two are staying in touch, though, right?" She stared at him with an intense gaze. "With a trip like that, for days and nights on end, together. That kind of experience keeps people connected, I would think."

He looked down at his scuffed-up boots. "We keep different schedules. She has a lot to figure out down there." His stomach burned. It wasn't that straightforward, but he had to keep pretending it was.

Carrie snorted. "Never in my entire life have I heard so many stilted excuses come out of your mouth."

"It's been difficult, Carrie. We lead different lives. And she chose to stay in Florida. What more is there to say?"

Carrie grabbed Palmer's arm and shook it. "What more is there to say?!" She shoved his arm back at him. "Everything you *need* to say to her, Palmer!"

"I don't know what you're going on about." He flexed his hands at the admission. He totally knew what his cousin was saying.

"Yes, you do." Carrie crossed her arms. "Yes, I'm shooting from the hip here, but look at this." She spread her arms wide. "Look at what you've done since returning from your time with Lena. You bought a brick-and-mortar for your own business! And you're freaking doing it! This wall, Palmer!" Carrie ran her hand down a section of pieced-together wood. "And look at you! You're different." Carrie placed a gentle hand on his arm. "All I'm saying is, don't let a little bit of distance get in the way of something rare and special."

Palmer reached into his pocket for his vibrating phone, thankful for the interruption. "It's Gregor. I should take this." Gregor only called if it was necessary.

Carrie hugged Palmer quickly, telling him she would return tomorrow for an update.

"Gregor, what's up?"

"I just got off the phone with Lena."

Palmer's stomach jolted. Why was everyone talking about Lena today? And why did his stomach burn? His brother, not Palmer, had gotten to hear her voice just now. *That's why, you idiot.*

"Oh? How's she doing?"

"She's having a tough time finding a mechanic down there that she trusts, so she called to see if it was possible to bring Douglas up here."

"All right. Sounds like a reasonable request. Is there a reason you're calling me?"

"She got cold feet," Gregor said. "I talked her through some shipment options, and she kind of freaked out. I get it. Douglas either goes on an eighty-foot open-air trailer, or Lena pays four times the amount for an enclosed trailer. Not what she wanted to hear, I guess. She clammed up before ending the call."

"And now you think she's reconsidering," Palmer said.

Papers rustled on the other line. "I have a contact who uses box trucks to ship super high-end sports cars. It's crazy expensive, but he owes me a favor."

"Do you want me to talk to her?" Palmer eyed the holes in the adjacent walls. He had numbers to look at and an unfinished wall to complete, never mind the brainstorming he needed to do for the new furniture builds, all while finishing a woodshop so he could build in the first place.

"There's no one she trusts more with that van than you, Palmer," Gregor said, bringing Palmer out of his stress-thinking.

"We haven't spoken much since I've been back," Palmer said tightly. He wouldn't dare admit to Gregor his feelings had been hurt or that he was still licking the wounds of Lena's refusal. But *damnit*, was he ever.

"If we don't act fast, she'll pull the plug. I'm certain of it," Gregor said.

"I know," Palmer could hear the edge in his voice. "I'll call her, promise. I'll check in tomorrow with you." He gripped the phone as he ended the call. Today would not be a complete shitshow. He was determined to make this right.

It was midnight by the time Palmer sat down to check his phone. The day was over. Lena was likely asleep, and he had, once again, let Lena down without her even realizing it, which made it worse somehow.

He pulled up her phone number and pressed the call button. Maybe she would sleep through the call, and he could leave a voice message—

"Palmer," Lena said. "Is everything okay?" Her voice was tired, scratchy, and goddamn beautiful. Why hadn't he made it a point to hear this voice every day?

"Yes. Kind of. Well, I guess it depends on what you mean by *okay*." He shut his mouth. He hadn't experienced rambling like this since junior high when he first started talking to girls he liked. "Were you asleep?"

"I was reading with my eyes closed." Lena yawned. "I'm guessing you spoke to Gregor." Her tone was flat and uninviting.

Palmer tensed. "You guessed correctly."

"It was a last-ditch effort. The reality is Douglas is totaled. He's junkyard parts. The cost of shipping a ruined van to Illinois is exorbitant. Unrealistic." She sniffled. "It is what it is."

He scratched his chin stubble. Logically, it was an incongruent course of action. But Douglas was much more than some smashed-up metal. Didn't she realize this?

"This isn't any old van," Palmer said. "This is Douglas. *Douglas.*"

"I know it's Douglas, Palmer. I also know nothing about

restoring vehicles, salvaging parts, or fixing car engines. None of it."

"That's where Gregor comes in," Palmer said.

"No," Lena said sharply. "It's not. This is where I abandon the things I love because I don't understand them. That's what I do."

The anger in her voice shot straight into his chest. Why hadn't he realized how deeply this was affecting her? He should have paused to consider her reaction. Hurt feelings be damned. This woman deserved more than his whiny ego.

"I'm sorry I didn't call sooner," he said softly.

Lena was quiet. "It's the frame," she said eventually. "There are multiple cracks deemed fatal for driving. It doesn't make sense to salvage an engine when the frame is beyond repair."

"So, bring him up here for a fresh start. Let's see what he's capable of."

"You can't fix this." Her flat tone returned.

"I still think there's hope—"

"Palmer, with all due respect, you haven't been around, you haven't read the reports, you haven't even seen him. And now, weeks later, you're suddenly the voice of reason? You can't swoop in and rescue me. Okay? Just...let it go." Lena sighed. "Listen, I need to get some sleep."

He didn't want to hang up with her upset. "I'll try to check in tomorrow."

She sighed again. "Tomorrow. Right. I doubt you'll have time." Her muffled voice said, "Goodnight."

With her voice still ringing in his ears the next morning, he made it a point to call her on his walk to the shop, but got her voicemail. He almost hung up without leaving a message. Instead, he left an upbeat *call me when you can* before quickly hitting the end button. And she did call back, while he was in the middle of negotiating a ten-thousand-dollar plumbing bill. He silenced the call and waited for the buzz that she had left a message, but it never came. And now here he sat, in his mostly dark and empty shop, with his phone dangling between his legs. Maybe she hadn't left a message for a reason. It was too late to call her now. And tomorrow? What would tomorrow bring but another game of phone tag?

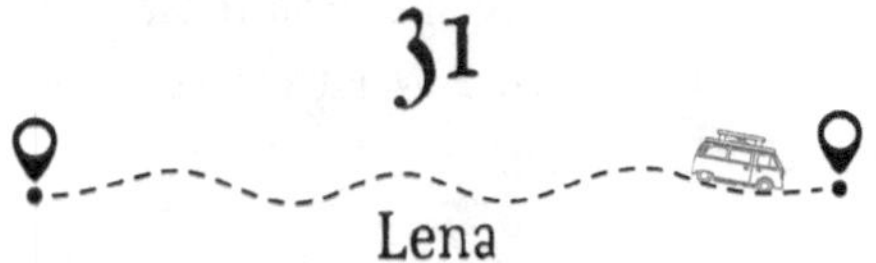

31

Lena

"I thought I'd find you here."

Lena turned from the horizonless sky to see Eliana's smiling face.

"You're home early," Lena said. The morning clouds had yet to burn off, which had kept her daily walk on the tolerable side of hot.

Eliana placed her hands on her hips. "No one showed up for the luncheon. I thought I advertised the crap out of this one, too."

"Are Fridays usually a good day for those things?"

"It's hit or miss. Fundraising should have a different name. There's nothing fun about it. Fun-*draining*." Water rushed around their feet. "I'll just keep busting my ass until I'm told to stop."

"I don't see you letting anyone stop you," Lena said.

Eliana squinted at her. "You're right."

"I spoke to Palmer last night," Lena said. Her thoughts mimicked the swirling water below her. Eliana remained quiet. "He called. Late. And tried to convince me shipping Douglas was the right thing to do. I got angry."

"As you should." Eliana nodded.

"I mean, what gives him the right to call at one in the morning and barge into something I've been processing for weeks?"

"That's rather presumptuous, considering his lack of communication."

Lena rolled her shoulders. "He called again this morning, while I was on the phone with my mom. I tried calling him back but it went to voicemail. I didn't leave a message. Maybe I should have. Maybe I should have pestered him with messages all along."

Eliana dug her toe in the wet sand and flung some in Lena's direction. "I don't see you as someone who begs for anyone's attention."

Lena wished she felt as certain as her friend sounded. "I keep replaying memories to the point that they're in my dreams now. The Fourth of July fireworks and the food trucks. It's messing with me. Why do our minds do stuff like that?"

Eliana considered her. "I think it's our brains' way of clearing out stagnant emotions."

"Aren't dreams supposed to be messy? And confusing? And amazing? Like, when I flew. I'd rather fly than clean my brain." Lena opened her arms to mimic wings as the wind blew across the water. She lifted her head and closed her eyes, inhaling the salty air.

Eli grabbed onto Lena. "You actually flew in your dream? I've always wanted to do that."

Lena lowered her arms with a laugh. When most people switched topics away from Lena's dream ramblings, here Eli was, envious of them. Just like Palmer's reaction back in June, when he'd returned with ice cream for her and Shay. *How wild it must be to wake up from something so vivid.*

Lena shook her head of Palmer's sparkling eyes. "It's what brought me here, essentially."

"Well, I'm jealous and happy all at once." Eliana smiled at Lena, then returned her gaze to the ocean. "Was it at least nice to hear his voice?"

Lena's whole body wilted. "Oh, Eli. It was so nice."

"I figured as much." Eliana looped her arm around Lena's. "So, what now?"

"The same thing I told Palmer." Lena took in a shuddering

breath. "Douglas goes to the junkyard, and I...go from there."

Eliana squeezed her closer. "Can I be candid with you?"

"Aren't you always?" Lena said. "But, yes, please."

Eliana squinted at the water. "You're letting go of what Douglas once was because you have to, but I'd hate for you to confuse letting go with giving up." Eliana's words softened Lena's defenses into a warm embrace. "For what it's worth, I still believe there's a place for Douglas, even if it's not an open road."

"I wish I believed that, too." Lena walked further into the warm water. A rolling wave crested her shins.

Eliana followed. "What do you believe?"

Lena sighed. "I don't know. Douglas is an old camper van meant to be driven and lived in while on the road. What could I possibly do with a forever-parked van—" Lena stopped abruptly. Flashes of grilled cheese, dimples, and scratchy picnic benches filled her vision like pages in a flipbook. "Oh my gosh." She turned to Eliana. "Oh, my freaking goodness!" Grabbing Eliana's shoulders, Lena shook her excitedly.

Eliana grasped Lena's shoulders and shook her right back. "Tell me what's happening!" she said.

"The food truck court. Food trucks. Douglas. Coffee. Truck. Van." Lena began to jump up and down in the water with her hands gripping Eliana's shoulders.

Eli jumped with her as salty water sprayed onto their shorts. "Douglas could be a coffee van!" said Eliana.

Lena released her. She smiled at her friend, the interrupter of manically said words. "I'm surprised you understood any of that, to be honest."

"You could say I have a talent for connecting one-worded dots."

Lena's toes sunk deeper into the ocean floor as thoughts flowed out in a rush of words. "I have no idea how van conversions work, but Gregor might. It's possible, right? Douglas could spend the rest of his days on a beach. Maybe. That's likely a lot of iced coffee." Her vision blurred as her mind dove into a memory of the day she sat with Palmer in Riverside Roasters with his notebook spread open. The same notebook he had brought on their journey together.

Do you ever drink your coffee cold?

I drink caffeine in all forms.

"Do you like iced coffee?" Eliana asked.

Lena shook her head. "I prefer my coffee hot." Lena sighed. How many future iced coffees would she have to serve? Would her quest for the perfect latte be replaced by ice cubes tumbling into plastic cups?

"Well, regardless of what coffee you'll serve and where, I really think you're onto something," Eliana said. "It won't be easy, but it'll be worth it."

"You think so?" Lena felt her heart expand to twice its size as the clink of ice cubes melted into a future worry. How long had it been since hope had welcomed her with open arms?

"With all the necessary doubts that come with a huge decision, I say it will absolutely be worth it." Eliana once again looped her arm around Lena's. "I guess I should ask again—What now?"

Lena squeezed Eli into her side. The logistics of where Douglas would go if he was capable of converting to a coffee van would fall into place. Or not. But she had to go for it.

"I'm calling the best mechanic in Illinois."

Three modestly sized cardboard boxes were stacked by the front door, taped and ready to be moved. Lena zipped her suitcase and shoved her pillow under her arm. The unsigned deed to the condominium rested on the kitchen counter. And an airline reservation to Illinois waited on her phone.

Seth's parents had been understanding of Lena's decision. Wherever she planted roots, it would be a result of her own hard work. Besides, she would be in Illinois with Douglas for the foreseeable future. Returning to Florida was still possible—she could envision Douglas on a beach clearly enough—but owning an empty condominium didn't fit into her life at the moment. Still, it was a choice that further separated her from Seth's family and those memories. Shay, on the other hand, was thrilled about Lena's return in five days. It wasn't clear how long Lena would stay, so she asked Shay to change her round-trip ticket to one-way. But it was another tough choice, taking her away from the support of her friend. Lena sure hoped this pain would find its way out of her soon.

With a heavy heart and full hands, she shuffled down the hallway toward Eliana's door. Lena's phone pinged as she set her things inside.

A message from one of the Eriksson brothers popped up. The only brother who had been in constant contact since *the big decision.* Granted, she was a paying customer, but still, every message from Gregor was a reminder of Palmer's continued absence. Which only continued to confuse her. It was as if she no longer mattered to Palmer unless he was actively helping her. Who helps someone so effortlessly and disappears just as easily?

She typed a reply to Gregor, confirming Douglas was in the truck and would arrive in three days.

Eliana had been with her the night before as the shipping company chained the broken van onto an electric ramp and raised him up. Lena reached for her friend's hand as Douglas disappeared into the back of the truck.

"This is going to work out. I can feel it," Eliana had whispered.

Now, a day later, Lena stood in her friend's condominium, where some of her personal items would remain for the time being. Various paintings of floating manatees and ocean landscapes filled the walls. Minimal furniture and loads of natural light filled the rest of the space. Eliana's free spirit was displayed perfectly. If only Eli could come with her. Lena could use the support, but the nonprofit needed Eliana even more. So, Lena would harness her friend's strength and bring it with her to Illinois. It was the best she could do.

After depositing her suitcase and pillow into the spare bedroom, Lena returned to Seth's parents' condominium for the rest of her belongings. It didn't take long. She didn't have much to move.

Exhausted, but too wired to rest, Lena lowered onto Eliana's couch and opened her laptop. A website for van conversions greeted her—research for next week. She had yet to share her idea with anyone other than Eliana. Gregor would be brought into the fold, eventually, if the idea was feasible. For now, Douglas would go to a trusted mechanic who wouldn't bleed out her funds with unnecessary work.

She closed her laptop with a sigh. Tapping her phone, she toggled to her messages, her finger hovering over Palmer's name. The last message from him was from a few weeks ago. Was she being too stubborn by not messaging him? Surely, he would want to know she was returning to Illinois. Hadn't he wanted to be the first to know? She tapped his name and began to type.

Hi stranger! Where have you been? Other than in my dreams?

She stopped typing and deleted the last question. What would happen after she told him the news? Would he respond with a thumbs-up emoji? A generic apology for being distant, followed by an empty promise to see her while she was in town? Her head fell backward as she groaned. Focusing back on her phone, she pressed the back arrow until all of her words were gone. The blinking cursor seemed to be laughing at her.

"Yeah. I know I'm being ridiculous," she said to the block of technology causing all the grief in the first place. She tossed her phone onto the cushion as a huge yawn took over. Maybe she would close her eyes for a few minutes and shut out these unnecessary thoughts.

Clattering dishes echoed in the distance as the room came

into focus. The light had changed. Manatees swam on the wall in front of her, and the air smelled of...pizza?

"Hey," Eliana said from the kitchen. "You were sleeping. I didn't want to wake you."

"I fell asleep upright?" Lena's neck felt like a kinked-up water hose.

"It happens." A beep sounded. Eliana's head disappeared behind the kitchen counter, then reappeared. She held a baking sheet. "I thought with the change in scenery and the upcoming travel, you would want some comfort food. Homemade."

"I slept through you making dinner?" Lena blinked. The kind words of her friend finally registered. "It smells fantastic."

"Is that your phone ringing?" Eliana asked. Lena swiveled her head from left to right.

"You're right. I hear it, too." She dug her hand between the cushions and extracted her phone. Why was she such a mess right now? Palmer's name looked up at her from the screen. She froze. The chimes kept signaling that Palmer was, for whatever reason, calling her.

"Are you going to answer it?" Eliana asked.

"If I don't right now, he'll go to voicemail," Lena said. She felt lightheaded. Her finger shook as she tapped *accept*.

"Hello?"

"Hey you, got a minute?"

32

Palmer

Earlier that day, Palmer stood inside Gregor's shop. He wasn't sure why he was here when he should be at the showroom. He also wasn't sure why he couldn't stop thinking about Lena. The last time they'd spoken was when he called her at midnight and she opened up about Douglas. He thought he'd done a good job of empathizing with Lena's struggle; the cost to ship Douglas *was* exorbitant. But, as he said to her, rarely did rational decisions leave room for emotional thinking, and this was meant to be an emotional decision. She hadn't agreed and made it clear he'd spoken out of turn.

He pulled out his phone. The urge to message her hit him twice a day, once in the morning, before his coffee, and another after leaving the showroom at night—and right now as he stood in his brother's shop wondering what was going on with her and her van.

I doubt you'll have time.

Damn, how he wanted to prove to her that he did. She was right, though. He didn't have time. Well, strike that, he did have time but it rarely aligned with hers. By the time he was done with his day, Lena was fast asleep. She deserved someone with energy left to give. He knew his circumstances were short-term, but *holy hell*, he was exhausted. And he missed Lena.

"Uh-oh. What's going on and why are you here in the middle of the day?" Gregor said as he strode into the shop, the thick soles of his work boots thudding against the cement floor.

"I was passing by," Palmer lied. He pointed to part of the shop that looked good as new. "Why is it so clean over there?"

"'Cause I cleaned it." Gregor put his hands on his hips. "What's going on? I've barely seen you, and now, suddenly, you're here inspecting my cleaning habits?"

Palmer shrugged. "It's a rare sight." He was stalling.

"It's for Lena's van. I thought you'd figure that was why."

Palmer's stomach dropped. "She decided to ship him after all?"

Gregor tilted his head. "She didn't tell you?"

Palmer shoved his hands into his pockets. "No."

Gregor opened his mouth, then closed it and tapped on his phone. After a few seconds, he cleared his throat and read, "*Douglas is in the truck and will arrive in three days*. She sent that an hour ago."

"Unbelievable," Palmer said. His chest tightened. What had changed her mind? *Who* changed her mind? And why hadn't she told him?

"I'm sure she assumes I'll tell you. We all know how busy you are," Gregor offered. Palmer didn't want to hear it. Gregor shifted on his feet. "Lena was surprisingly upbeat when we arranged his delivery. A complete one-eighty from our original call."

"Do you think she has something in mind for him?" Palmer asked.

"He wouldn't be on his way if she didn't." Gregor rubbed his stubbled chin. "I'll spend some quality time with him, keep Lena informed, and go from there."

"He's in the best of hands. That goes without saying, though," Palmer said.

"Thanks." Gregor patted Palmer's shoulder. "I'm sure she'll be in touch soon. Or, maybe send her a message. The phone goes both ways, right? She'll probably be up here soon enough anyway, checking on Douglas and whatnot." Gregor shrugged. "At least she made the right decision."

"Yeah. At least there's that." Palmer smiled at his brother.

Gregor was a good man with a big heart. A man who was lucky enough to have Lena in his good graces. Unlike Palmer, who had failed time and again at, well, managing his time. "Hey, speaking of the right decisions, how's that girl you've been dating?"

"Really, Palmer? You're gonna ask me about my love life before my afternoon coffee?" Gregor smirked and pointed to the corner office. "I just brewed a fresh pot."

"You make shit coffee, Gregor. No offense. I also never turn down caffeine."

"We can't all be superstar baristas like Lena, but I do what I can." Gregor opened the office door.

In a flash, a vision of Lena limping toward the counter at Riverside Roasters popped into his head. The jolt from seeing her had been more satisfying than any amount of caffeine.

Palmer poured a cup of coffee and took a seat.

"I've been ghosted," Gregor said.

"Ghosted? Like, you're being haunted?" Palmer took a sip and shuddered. "This isn't coffee. This is sludge."

"How do you not know what *ghosted* means? You're only two years older than me. She disappeared. Poof. Gone."

"What did you do?" Palmer inspected the thick liquid inside his paper cup. "Wait, I know. She drank your coffee."

"I may have gotten a wee bit defensive." Gregor lifted his mug to his lips and mumbled, "She wanted me to cut my hair, and I said, *Not happening, sweet cheeks.*"

Palmer sputtered into his coffee. "You called her *sweet cheeks*? Yeah, I'd ghost you, too."

"A woman who wants to change me is no woman for me." Gregor set his mug down. "On to the next."

"I'm not one to offer dating tips." Palmer set his cup down. Maybe he should keep his mouth shut. Gregor hadn't asked for advice, after all.

Gregor rolled his eyes. "But?"

"Well, take this with a grain of salt—"

"That goes without saying." Gregor smirked. His brother always had a witty one-liner up his sleeve.

Palmer cleared his throat. "I've learned that a person's mind reveals amazing things once you become curious about it instead of defensive." Palmer could do with taking his own advice, but instead downed the rest of his coffee. Well, "coffee".

"Says the man who thought I was being haunted." Gregor raised his mug in salute.

"I'll see you later tonight, smartass." Palmer checked the time as he walked out of Gregor's shop. He had two storage shelves left to assemble and then some number-crunching to do. Palmer jogged across the street as Mark came into view.

"Ah, there's Palmer," Mark said. He was standing at the front door with a man who was pacing back and forth on the sidewalk. "He'll know where the lumber goes."

The man handed Palmer a shipment slip. "Where to?"

Palmer stared at the paper. This couldn't be right. He wasn't expecting lumber from Mateo until next week. He didn't have the room, let alone the headspace, to organize such a large shipment. Right on cue, all of his stress dumped straight into every joint in his body. He flexed his aching fingers. "There's a loading dock in the back. I'll show you."

With Mark's assistance, transferring the wood from the delivery truck to the shop didn't take long.

"Bet you weren't expecting manual labor when you showed up." Palmer wiped sweat from his face with the bottom of his shirt.

"I needed the exercise," Mark said. A trail of sweat had soaked through the front of his shirt. "Dad-bod is a real thing."

"You're a string bean, Mark." Palmer surveyed the wood covering the shop's floor. "This is twice the amount of wood from Mateo, and he shipped it way ahead of schedule. Not a good start, if you ask me." Palmer was oscillating between excitement and irritation. Yes, he had an abundance of materials, but directions hadn't been followed.

"Mateo is probably eager for you to get started," Mark said, always the peace-keeping lawyer.

"Maybe. But bad habits are harder to undo later on." Palmer went to the mini-fridge. He was whining and needed to stop. "A problem for another time. Thanks for the help. I owe you one."

"Well, now that you mention it, Shay has been begging for a new set of bookshelves." Mark smiled and took the water bottle Palmer had handed him.

"Consider it done."

"You just made me husband of the year." Mark took a swig from the water bottle. "Hell, I should be already. Lena is going to be staying with us again for however long she's here for. Up-in-the-air plans are my favorite." Mark rolled his eyes to the ceiling. "One of these days, the spare bedroom in my house will be empty."

Palmer paused mid-sip. "She confirmed her travel already?" The tightness in his chest returned. Every piece of news today had felt like a dagger to his sternum. Why was he the last to know? He thought for sure she would tell him, even if it hadn't been her first call. Had Lena purposely kept her plans from him, or had she planned to share it next time he called? Was she planning to avoid him while she was here because of the lack of messages? Was this a sign she no longer wanted him in her life?

Maybe! You idiot.

"I didn't think Lena would follow through, but she is. Shay is in a cleaning frenzy while her parents watch the baby."

Palmer tried to play it cool, but deep down, he wanted to shake Mark's shoulders. Why wasn't he sharing *when* Lena was visiting? He fisted his hands. This wasn't him. This was a whiny, impatient, sleep-deprived imposter standing in his worn-out boots.

"Whelp, I'm off to see your dad about some contracts. Between Shay's family and yours, lately, I've been busy!" Mark readjusted his baseball cap. "At least I don't have to wear a suit."

"Maybe it's time for you to open up your own law firm."

Mark pointed his water bottle at Palmer. "Don't you plant those entrepreneur seeds in my brain. The baby is my start-up."

"Good point," Palmer said as he walked Mark to the front door.

"Hey, what's going on up here? It's so empty." Mark looked around the front area. It was the last item on Palmer's list and one he kept bumping down the line.

"I was thinking it could be an indoor artisan market for local crafters and small business-owners," Palmer said. Saying it out loud felt too serious.

Last night, he had been on his way out the door, when he stopped and sat on the floor in the middle of the front area. As he'd looked around, it had dawned on him—the coffee shop idea no longer felt right. How could it? He didn't want anyone but Lena running the shop and she had said no. Was it ridiculous to scrap an idea because it hadn't gone to plan? Sure. But he didn't care. After a few moments of brooding, he'd stood up and decided on an alternate plan.

"Maybe," he said to Mark. "Or maybe I'll park my truck in here during the winter." He opened the door with a light chuckle.

"You know, either one of those aren't half-bad ideas. Plus, street parking during winter is a nightmare." Mark smirked. "Oh, on Friday, Shay is doing a welcome-back dinner for Lena. You and Gregor are invited."

Finally.

"I'll be there," Palmer said without hesitation. In less than a week, Lena would be in his town once again. He waited until Mark was out of sight, then darted back inside to find his phone. What he had shared with Lena was too rare to toss away. He was a fool to believe the strength of their connection could survive without nurture. If anything, it knew its worth and demanded more.

Fumbling with his phone, he tapped her name. He hoped Lena felt the same and that she would answer his call. He hoped he wasn't too late for what he needed to ask. But more than anything he hoped Lena would say yes.

"Hello?"

"Hey you, got a minute?"

33

Lena

“There she is.”

Palmer's long arms circled around her while her rolling suitcase toppled forward. Resistance was futile. Palmer's hugs were all-encompassing.

Out of the frying pan, into the fire.

Lena melted into his embrace.

When Palmer's call came in last week, she had joked about good news traveling fast. Palmer had quickly agreed—*the news was great*—and then, in a shy voice, asked if he could pick her up from the airport. Surprising herself, probably even more than Palmer, she said yes without hesitation. Why go to war with her heart when her mind was barely working?

A blaring whistle jolted her out of Palmer's arms.

“Let's go, people!” the traffic guard barked. The pickup area at O'Hare airport was overwhelmed with vehicles, exhaust, and noise.

“Yes, ma'am,” Palmer said. “I had to get one in before the drive. You understand.”

The traffic guard flicked an unimpressed look in their direction, then darted to her next victim. Lena gave Palmer an amused expression as he opened the passenger door to his truck. The scent of evergreen surrounded her.

Palmer hopped inside and turned on his signal. “It's good to see you,” he said. He glanced at her and smiled. His beard was short enough to still show his dimples, but his hair was much longer.

Lena stopped herself from sighing in appreciation. He looked good. Too good. And she was a mess. She smoothed her wrinkled shirt and reminded herself Palmer was doing her a favor, nothing more.

"Thanks for coming to get me."

"No problem." Palmer checked the mirrors, then merged into bumper-to-bumper traffic. "I get you to myself for a little bit. It's a treat." He gave her a cute but not-so-innocent side glance. Her heart skipped a beat.

Definitely into the fire.

As Palmer navigated onto the expressway, he asked how her flight was—turbulent and packed—and Lena updated him on her status in Florida and her move. Her stomach ached. Palmer had missed so much.

"Where are you storing the rest of your things?" Palmer asked.

"Eliana's place. I don't have much, just clothes and my pillow. It's almost embarrassing," she said, trailing off, her nerves clawing at her heart. She had left a set of honorary parents and a struggling new best friend in Florida.

"How's her nonprofit going?" Palmer asked. Before she knew what was happening, Lena had revealed an idea she hadn't seriously considered until now.

"Do you think it's crazy?" Lena asked after telling Palmer what she intended to do to help Eliana.

Palmer's hands flexed on the steering wheel. "I think it's amazing." He glanced at her. "You're amazing."

Her neck heated as her insides melted ever so slightly. "It's not like the money was mine to begin with. The donation will be made in Seth's memory, too. He would have wanted to help her nonprofit. The rest of the money will go to Douglas. If that's the best option." Lena clasped her hands in her lap. What was it about sitting in a passenger seat with Palmer driving that opened her up so much? She shook her head. "One thing at a time."

"I'm all ears for whenever you need someone to listen."

Palmer turned off the expressway and onto a four-lane highway.

She shifted in her seat as her mind shouted warnings, one after another. His willingness to listen was a consequence of proximity. This was the secret to keeping his attention! She unclasped her hands and gazed at Palmer. Or was it because he was helping her again?

"When will you tell Eliana?" he asked.

Lena's body warmed without her permission. She always felt the most seen when talking with Palmer. And the most invisible in his silence. "I'm not sure. I want to tell her in person, but I'm not sure when I'll return to Florida. So, it might have to be a phone call."

"Or she comes up here to enjoy some snow, and you tell her then," he said.

Lena bit her lip. Palmer's suggestion was effortless and on point. It was hard to believe weeks had passed without hearing his voice. A voice that made her feel excited and alive. But this was how he treated everyone in his life. He was caring and helpful; she was part of his typical protocol. She had to remember this.

"Eliana told me before I left how much she missed the snow. I'll consider it. Thank you." Lena wanted to squeeze his hand in gratitude. Instead, she clasped them in her lap and stared out the passenger window.

The sound of the truck's blinker filled the quiet. "Are you needed at your sister's right away?" Palmer asked.

"I have some free time before the big dinner." Lena lowered the zipper on her jacket. His question had ignited something inside her. What exactly, she wasn't sure. "You're coming, too, right?"

Palmer nodded. "I'd like to show you what I've been working on before we head over to your sister's. If that's okay?"

More alone time with Palmer was more than okay with her. But was that more than she should say?

"As long as the plumbing is working. My bladder is about to

burst." She crossed her legs.

"The plumbing is, in fact, working," Palmer said with a laugh. "As of three hours ago." He glanced at her with a gut-punching smile. "Let's get you to your porcelain throne!"

Lena looked up at the exposed wood beams and Edison lights. "It's beautiful, Palmer."

Natural light spilled through the once foggy and dirt-ridden windows. The dusty concrete floor was lined with rows of glossy, distressed hardwood now. An intricate wooden wall separated the front area, with delicate spotlights shining onto the showroom.

She could envision the showroom filled with Palmer's furniture, gleaming in the natural light while showing off under the spotlights. One part was missing, however.

"Dare I ask what's going on over there?" Lena inched toward the front area. Palmer tilted his head, indicating she could walk in. Aside from the wood wall, the entryway area remained unchanged. Palmer stood next to her with his hands in his pockets.

"I guess you could say I hit a wall when I put up that wall." He laughed. It sounded forced.

"You've been working nonstop." She bit her lip. Was he hoping she would agree to his offer now that she was here? If her plans for Douglas were feasible, it would make Palmer's offer obsolete. The van's conversion had brought a new sense of purpose, which she was committed to seeing through.

Palmer tucked a piece of hair behind his ear. "Too busy to even get a haircut."

Lena looked up at him. "I like it."

"Good." He had inched closer to her. Or she had moved into him. It was hard to say. His fingers brushed her forehead. "Your hair is longer, too."

"Same problem as you." She swallowed as her eyes drifted to his mouth. After many seconds of staring, a buzzing noise registered. Palmer licked his lips and reached into his pocket.

"Hey, man. Yep. Okay. Yeah, we're headed there now." Palmer clicked off. "That was Mark. It's time to go." Palmer looked around. "He wondered the same thing, by the way, about this area. There's one idea I was playing with, but I don't know."

"It'll come together when it's meant to," Lena said. The air between them had grown heavier with each word uttered. Or maybe that was her imagination adding weight to their undeniable connection.

"I hope so." Palmer cupped the back of his neck. "I joked with Mark that I would park my truck in here. Not likely the idea that will stick but it was fun to imagine."

Lena froze as her eyes darted around. "You said what?"

Palmer gave her a funny look. "That I would park my truck in here."

"Your truck," she repeated. Could a vehicle fit inside the front area? Maybe against the wall with no windows, leaving plenty of room for café tables and wrought iron chairs for patrons to sit and enjoy a cup of coffee. She stifled a nervous giggle as her mind raced along a path of what-ifs.

"Are you all right?" said Palmer. She could feel his concerned stare. "Did you see something? A mouse? I still need to contact the pest company."

"No, not a mouse." Lena's eyes landed on the glass door. She spotted the faint lines etched on the outside glass, remembering the first time she saw the manatee—not so long ago, when she'd sat on the city bench with a broken ankle, back when random images of manatees popped up everywhere—in her dream, in Drew Eriksson's artwork, and right here. But they weren't random, were they? This image had guided her to Douglas and his glove compartment, which took her to Florida and Seth's secret, to Eliana and a true friendship, and right back here, to her family. And to Palmer. Her gaze returned to the man beside her. Eliana's voice rang through her ears. *Go to the water.*

Was this where she was meant to go? Was it possible? Could a permanently parked coffee van find a new home inside Palmer's showroom? Hope began to spread through her chest, trickling down to the tips of her toes and onto a million grains of possibility. Palmer would have to agree to it, though, and Douglas would have to be up for the challenge.

"Are you going to replace your front door?" she asked.

Palmer stood next to her. The warmth of his body radiated onto her arm. "The night of the sale, Mark and I went out for celebratory drinks. Afterward, I came here. As I was unlocking the door, I noticed the manatee." He smiled at her. "There's no way I'm replacing this door."

Lena returned his smile as every detail in the room came into focus: the dust particles floating in the air, the sound of traffic on the street outside, and Palmer's gentle voice, asking her if she was ready to go. She was ready. Ready to live in the dust that looked like sparkles and ready to take a chance on an idea that felt impossibly possible.

"Let's go," she said.

"The weather is too glorious for October. So, we're eating outside!" Shay waved her arms around. In the middle of the backyard stood a long, rectangular table, the top dotted with various tea candles, white plates, and gold cloth napkins. A canopy of twinkle lights were strung above, swaying in the open-air tent as the scent of roasted beef and garlic lifted off the gentle breeze. The ambiance was whimsical and cozy. A vast difference from the heat and water in Florida.

"This is amazing, Shay. Thank you." Lena wrapped her arms around her sister's shoulders. Shay had outdone herself and Lena felt overly loved by the gesture.

After many hugs and hellos, dinner was served, a menu fit for a five-star restaurant, thanks to Carrie's expert hand in the kitchen. With a full belly and a glass of whiskey, Lena ambled to the firepit. Her mom sat in an Adirondack chair, sipping wine while Hugo rested in her arms.

Lena lowered onto a chair, her knee bouncing at a rhythmic pace. She wanted to relax and lose herself in mindless fire-stares. But she couldn't. What she'd envisioned in Palmer's showroom earlier was far more interesting than the fire before her and the dancing shadows beyond. How could she avert her gaze from all that could be?

She glanced at Palmer who stood nearby talking with her father. Gregor hovered with a beer bottle in hand.

"How's the showroom coming along?" her father said in his signature booming voice. Mark offered Lena a commiserating glance as he walked by. *Good.* He could run interference and save Palmer from the Sullivan inquisition.

"It's getting close," Palmer said.

"The holidays will skyrocket your sales," Lena's dad said.

"They will, yeah, but I'm in no rush."

Lena shifted in her seat and took a sip of whiskey. Since when did Palmer forgo deadlines? Didn't planning revolve around end dates?

"What about that indoor artisan market you mentioned? Such a great use of the front area," Mark said.

All of the air in Lena's lungs left her body. She turned her head toward the men.

"Genius!" Lena's dad patted Palmer on the shoulder.

"News to me," Gregor said.

"It's a recent development." Palmer's eyes locked with Lena's. She wanted to look away. She wanted to run. Earlier, he had admitted to hitting a wall while building a literal wall. This sounded like the opposite of that. Palmer returned his attention to her dad.

"I'm not certain it'll come together the way I want it to," he said. His eyes darted toward her as he took a sip of whiskey. The same whiskey she was drinking.

Why hadn't she asked more questions earlier? Better yet, why hadn't she realized? His life was marching on without her.

She turned her attention to the flames dancing off the crackling logs. There was so much beauty in the courage of nature, wasn't there? In the way earth and fire collided, in the way the tides morphed in and out of sandy beaches. Could she follow suit and light a fire from within? Could she find the courage to rise up like a cresting wave and tell Palmer her idea? Would he be willing to hear her out in the first place?

Lena stood up. She had to do something or he would slip away for good. Walking toward Palmer, she cleared her throat. "Sorry to interrupt," she said to the group.

"Hey, sweetie," her dad said, his smiling cheeks rosy as Santa Clause. "Palmer was telling us about his showroom. Exciting stuff!"

"It is." She turned to Palmer. "Would you mind driving me to see Douglas?"

"Right now?" Lena's dad said.

"I can take you," Gregor added.

Palmer moved closer and said, "Of course."

Gregor grumbled while her dad shrugged and told them to come back as soon as possible.

"It won't take long," Lena said as her gaze locked with Palmer's again. His brows knitted together. She offered an encouraging smile. Everything was fine. Other than the fear waging a war inside her, but that didn't matter. She had to tell Palmer. She had to try.

The two-minute drive to the auto shop felt like twenty. The windows were dark, and the neon *Open* sign was turned off.

"It's locked." Lena pulled on the handle as if it would open magically. In her haste to leave, she'd forgotten to ask Gregor for a key.

Palmer jingled his keys. "The perks of living above an auto shop. Full access."

Lena stepped inside and waited, while Palmer found the main lights. She heard a crash and swearing, followed by, "I'm okay!" The lights blazed overhead.

There Douglas stood, with no roof, no windshield, and an

empty rear interior. She moved cautiously toward the van, her heart beating wildly. She ran her fingers along the bumps of a crack. It looked like Gregor had welded some of it.

"I got you, buddy," she whispered.

"Got him what?" Palmer said.

She yelped and spun around. "I just meant I'm here for him."

"You mean you have a plan for him." Palmer's eyes were bright and eager. He wanted her to tell him.

"Right, like, you know, *I got you*. It'll be okay, or whatever." Why was she hesitating? This was why they were standing in front of Douglas. But would Palmer be on board? He had his own dreams to nurture now. Her idea would find a way to survive outside of her. She had to start talking.

"Do you remember our phone call, however many weeks ago, when I was upset, and you urged me to bring Douglas here?"

"Of course," he said.

"I guess you could say a wild idea ignited in me the next day. Eli is the only one who knows. I held back telling you because I was angry with you. And hurt, if I'm being honest. But after seeing all that you've accomplished since you left, I can't be upset with you. We did our best."

Palmer reached for her hand, his palm scratchy and warm. "I'm sorry I wasn't there for you more."

"It's okay." She swallowed the lump in her throat. "I wasn't either. But we're here now. Together." She took a steadying breath. The flames of her courage would either be tended to by Palmer or not. She wasn't going to burn from within any longer. She had to let go. Now.

"Driving Douglas is no longer an option. He needs a foundation to keep him together—a place that will keep him permanently. As a refurbished coffee van."

Palmer dropped her hand as he looked at Douglas, then at her, then back to Douglas.

"A coffee van," he said as a dimple formed. She bit the inside of her cheek. "Douglas is going to be a coffee van." He turned so she could see his other dimple. He was grinning from ear to ear. "You're converting Douglas into your own coffee shop!" He whooped and wrapped his arms around her waist, spinning her in a full circle before setting her down.

It was the reaction she had hoped for, even though there was more.

"There's more.' Lena pushed her hair out of her face and straightened her shoulders. "I just need a minute to find the words."

Palmer nodded. "No rush."

Out of all the risks she had taken so far, this was the biggest one. Maybe it was for the best that she couldn't ruminate over the offer she was about to make. An offer Palmer could very well refuse. And she wouldn't blame him if he did. She half expected him to say no. After all, he had moved on, hadn't he? A local indoor artisan market made more sense than a van serving coffee. But life didn't come with a reverse switch— Douglas had taught her that back in the trailhead parking lot, where she'd first met Palmer.

"It seems," she started, then stopped. She could do this. "It seems I have a business partner now. You know him well, actually. He's right over there.' She pointed to the van. There was no turning back now. "I haven't decided where we'll end up. Maybe a beach in Florida. Maybe somewhere less warm. Maybe—" Lena took a steadying breath. *Maybe here with you.*

"Florida. Oh boy. I see a lot of iced coffee in your future," Palmer said with a small laugh.

Lena stilled. He remembered. It was now or never. "The front area of your showroom and the joke you made to Mark about parking your truck inside— What if we found a way to park Douglas inside there for real."

"You want to park Douglas inside the front area...for real?" Palmer repeated.

"Yeah. So, the showroom would have a coffee shop. Well, coffee van. But, coffee. There would be coffee. And lattes. And pastries."

Palmer looked like a zombie, unblinking and barely breathing. "When I left Florida, you were adamant we figure things out separately."

"I know. And I did. You did, too, right? With your workshop and showroom. I think I've done as much as I can without you. We're here together, now, and, I don't know, this feels right. You have a manatee on your front door." She shook her head. "I sound nuts."

Palmer surveyed Douglas then pinned her with a look that filled her with both excitement and dread. "There are a ton of what-ifs with Douglas."

She nodded. "I understand. You're using the space for something else now. It's a great idea, by the way." The need to run had returned.

Palmer inched into her. "Why do you think I haven't touched it?"

Her heart felt as if it was going to jump out of her chest. "You've been too busy?"

He shook his head as he continued to close the space between them. "Not quite."

She bit her lip. "You were waiting for more materials."

"Closer." He smiled. "I wasn't waiting for materials, though."

His fingers found hers and laced them together. "Third time's a charm?"

It couldn't be. The words sitting on the tip of her tongue were too perfect to be the answer to everything.

She squeezed their hands then took a deep breath. "You were waiting for me." She looked up.

His eyes locked with hers. "I was waiting for you."

And just like that, she was falling all over again. It was an incredible sensation she allowed herself to feel completely this time—no guilt attached.

He placed their hands against his chest. "Are you sure this is what you want?" he whispered.

She focused on the warmth of his skin, the roughness of his palm, and the certainty in her heart. "I found a way to keep Seth's dream alive while honoring my own at the same time. I can't see any other way to make this a reality than with you." A million dandelion seeds danced inside her stomach, joyfully floating on the breath of her wish. "If you'll have us."

Palmer pulled her into his chest, his chin resting lightly on the top of her head. "Give me a second," he said, his voice barely above a whisper. "My dream just came true."

Epilogue

Fluffy snowflakes swirled around Lena as she rushed into Revival Goods. A delicate tinkling bell had replaced the squeak of the front door. Why Palmer delayed the repair until the last minute was a mystery. But at least it was done.

They had bigger concerns right now. The snow was falling hard and fast, and the open house was scheduled in just a few hours. Nibbling her bottom lip, she pulled off her gloves.

"Eight to ten inches of snow, Douglas. And it's not even December yet!" Lena shoved her knit wool hat into her jacket pocket. Douglas stood off to her left, the side of his chrome bumper smiling at her, proud and gleaming, while his interior glowed from the white twinkle lights.

The van conversion had come together seamlessly—Gregor had been more than eager to take on a new project—and the end result was better than Lena could have imagined.

"You're right. Chicagoland weather is known for snow," she grumbled as if Douglas had stated the fact himself.

"Lena!" a muffled voice shouted. "The door!" Lena pivoted on her right heel and pulled the door open. A stack of pastry boxes greeted her. Lena took three off the top, revealing Carrie's pinkish cheeks and perfectly painted red lips.

"Thank you." Carrie blew at her blonde bangs and beelined to Douglas, her heels clicking on the recently finished wood floors.

"I just pulled these out of the oven." Carrie's head disappeared underneath the serving window. Lena had spent a lot of time with the new version of Douglas, but she was still adjusting. The sliding door was now the window Carrie had vanished behind. The back end was the entry point to the interior now. The floor of the van had been removed, exposing the shop's distressed wood planks, but the wheels remained. Lena had insisted the front end, dashboard, and steering wheel also remain, with the glove compartment intact.

Once Gregor and Palmer mapped out how to transfer Douglas into the building, a process Lena refused to witness, Carrie made it a point to stop in whenever she could. *All hands on deck!* had been Carrie's slogan throughout the process. She and Carrie had fashioned the van's interior together, and thanks to Carrie's experience in professional kitchens, the small space flowed perfectly.

"They're the most fluffy, flaky, perfect, and gooey cinnamon-apple Danishes ever to exist." Carrie's arm popped up, a massive Danish in hand. "Try it."

Lena never said no to baked goods, especially Carrie's creations. "Pull my arm, why don't you?" Lena said. Carrie snorted. "You really should consider doing a side hustle or something, Carrie," Lena mumbled around her bite. Gooey apple and flaky crust melted in her mouth.

Carrie's head reappeared. "I can't work full time and have a side hustle if I'm trying for a baby."

A chunk of apple lodged into Lena's throat. Coughing, she stammered, "That's wonderful, Carrie."

Carrie shrugged. "I'm done waiting for Talon to be ready. It's now or never. You know?"

Lena didn't know. She hadn't thought about having children with Palmer. Yet. The thought of thinking about it had her lips curving upward.

"It's coming down out there!" Palmer entered in a burst of snowflakes, his hair covered in white, his arms filled with more pastry boxes. "Hey, babe."

Lena swallowed the last of her Danish as her stomach danced

at the sight of him. It had only been eight hours since she saw him last, but the butterflies in her stomach were terrible timekeepers. He had trimmed his beard at some point, and the collared shirt underneath his gray wool coat was a vast departure from the various T-shirts he usually wore. But Palmer was just as tall, and his smile was just as heart-melting.

"Hey, handsome," she said.

He leaned into her and pressed his lips to her cheek. Her eyes fluttered against his familiar scent.

"You look amazing. If Carrie wasn't here right now..." Palmer licked his lips.

Her face warmed. She didn't often wear makeup, but she had spent extra time on her reflection this morning. Tonight was special. Shay had also insisted Lena wear her gold mesh shirt and black sequined skirt for the opening.

Before leaving the house, Lena had paused by her nightstand to tap the Douglas figurine three times. It was a ritual she'd performed daily since returning to Illinois. The tiny fairy lights inside the figurine had blinked in approval.

It's time.

Palmer's lips found hers over the stack of boxes and— Was that a tongue?

"Did you just lick me?" She laughed, pulling back.

"I couldn't resist." His eyes were dark and lovely.

Carrie snickered from the van. "You had Danish flakes on your mouth, Lena. You can't blame him for wanting a taste."

Lena's face was an oven. "Here, let me take one of those."

"Thanks," Palmer said. "And it was because she called me handsome, Carrie," Palmer called over Lena's head. "Your Danish preview was just a bonus."

Lena's face broke into the same grin that had shown up since she moved here. She rose to her tiptoes, stole a second kiss, and then pushed Palmer toward Douglas.

Once the holidays were behind them, she and Palmer would search for an apartment together. Or a house. Palmer wanted a house. Lena wanted to wake up to his dimples every morning, with or without his beard, in a house or a cardboard box. She didn't care. They both agreed there was no rush. For now, it was enough that their businesses shared a roof.

Carrie set a platter on the counter, then clapped her hands together. "Okay! Snow be damned, this opening is going to be the best opening ever!"

"Damn right!"

Lena turned to see Gregor, the owner of the booming voice. He held Eliana's hand as she navigated over a puddle of melted snow.

"This one has already slipped three times," Gregor said. Eli swatted at his hand.

"I'm a Floridian." Eliana straightened the hem of her leather miniskirt.

"Your leather skirt and stilettos suggest otherwise, m'lady," Gregor said with a smirk.

One of Eliana's legs shot out in front of her. "These are ankle boots."

"I must have gotten stuck on those legs and assumed you had heels on," Gregor said with a wink.

Lena's eyes bounced to Palmer; he rolled his in response.

"Hey guys! Let me grab a mop." Palmer darted around the wood wall and into the main showroom.

"Thank you for coming!" Lena bounded over to Eli and wrapped her into a huge hug. She had missed her friend.

Eliana laughed and squeezed Lena tightly. "I wouldn't miss it for the world. Besides"—she pulled back, her eyes glazing over—"I haven't seen snow for over twenty years."

"Oh, you don't need to tell us. We know," Gregor said as he passed the two. "Carrie, where's your husband? I have a bone to pick with him."

"Hey, Lena," Carrie said, her head poking out from the window. "Where did Palmer put those boxes?"

"Behind you on the coffee bar," Lena said.

Gregor waved his hand. "Earth to my dear, sweet, beautiful cousin. I asked you a question."

Carrie flipped open the lid and placed a cinnamon roll into Gregor's hands. "This should keep your mouth busy while the rest of us organize for the opening."

Eliana elbowed Lena softly and leaned closer. "He's wildly different from Palmer, isn't he?"

"He's a character. But wait until you see what he did with Douglas."

Eliana's eyes sparkled. "Show me."

Palmer stood in the middle of the showroom. Laughter sounded through the wood wall as the front door's bell chimed. This was it. After many sleepless nights, it was finally time. Each piece on the showroom floor was new, with its own story. Each piece had been crafted with love. There could be no other way. Lena was here with Douglas in the very spot he had dreamed she would call home. Thank god stubborn old Douglas knew all along what was meant to happen. His resurgence was Palmer's and Lena's reconciliation.

Resurgence Coffee inside of Revival Goods.

Palmer planned to reveal the new sign today, a reimagined rendering of his original concept. *R&R*. A simple logo designed by none other than Drew Eriksson.

Behind him, he heard the quick cadence of heels. "Palmer. There you are!"

His heart surged. "Hey, you," he said. Lena was beautiful any which way, and tonight was no exception. Her beauty was amplified, and his knees were all the weaker for it.

Lena tugged on his hand. "Come here. You have to see." Her face was flushed and glowing.

She pulled him toward the front, her hand trembling in his.

"Where is everyone?" Palmer asked. Café tables were

scattered throughout the space with golden tablecloths that sparkled underneath the luminescent twinkle lights. But the best part was the smell of freshly brewed coffee.

Lena pointed outside as she pulled him closer to the frosted windows. The snow had stopped, and a long line of people had formed outside the entrance. Mark was laughing outside as Shay waved excitedly. Lena's parents stood behind, her mom holding what looked to be a marshmallow in baby form. Gregor stood between Carrie and Eliana and was staring at his parents, who were standing at the front of the line, hand in hand.

Lena wrapped her arms around his waist, excited giggles rising to his ears. He pulled her closer and kissed the top of her head.

"Unbelievable," he murmured into her hair. He closed his eyes, breathing in how lucky he was.

Lena gasped. "Palmer."

Blinking, Palmer opened his eyes as a ray of setting sun filtered through the windows and onto one of Douglas's mirrors. Orange light shot across the room and landed directly on the front door. The manatee etching glowed.

Palmer gazed at Lena, her eyes swimming with emotion. "Unbelievable is right," she said.

He kissed her tenderly. "I love you, Lena."

Her smile was all he needed. *I love you*, she mouthed.

"I know," he said with a ridiculous smile, straightening his shoulders. "So, what do you say? Are you ready to open the door to our dreams?"

She took his hand in hers and squeezed it. "I'm ready."

Acknowledgements

As with my first book, boundless thanks go to those who offered their time and support to me during the daunting process of writing and publishing another book. It's one thing to turn a close-to-my-heart dream into a reality, but it's an entirely different beast to keep dreaming within this new reality created, to *Dream for a Second* time ... if you will.

Thank you to Mike for protecting my creative time at home as diligently as the first time and for supporting my pursuit of the new and exciting opportunities that have come up since the publication of *Time for Once*.

To Elliott, thank you for your curiosity and thoughtful little gestures, like the sticker of a VW van you brought home from your book fair, "for your second book, Mom!"

Thank you to my editor, Sophie, for polishing yet another manuscript of mine into a shining gleam, this time with far less accidental poetry for you to comb through.

To my critique partner, Nik, thank you for being on board without hesitation, even with the mixed feelings you originally held for Palmer. Your keen eye and male perspective transformed Palmer's white knight syndrome into a much more relatable and authentic character.

To my family and close friends, thank you for listening to me babble on and on about this book and for buying into my persuasive excitement! I hope I did not lead you astray and that you loved this story as much as I do.

Thank you to those who reached out to say hello, asked about my writing, read my writing, or held a genuine interest in the process of self-publishing. This simple interest is where subtle inspiration transpires.

And finally, to those who read my first book, you gave me the courage to offer a second one. Thank you from the bottom of my heart. I hope you'll stick around for more!

Author's Note

The heartbeat of *Dream for a Second*—Douglas, the van—was inspired by a real-life burnt orange 1983-in-a-half VW van with a Subaru engine named "Ginger." While in the frenzy of outlining a new story idea, I reached out to a close friend who had adventured in Ginger many times since we had first met. She and I had developed an easy friendship through fitness, personal growth, positivity, and family. I asked her about her experiences in the van; the smells, the views, everything. Luckily for me, she was a writer at heart, too.

Camping in her! A dream. The backseat folds down into a full-size bed. On cool crisp nights, your sheets are warmed from being over the engine while you drive.

During revisions, my family received news of the tragic loss of her life and two others. It has been an incomprehensible mix of confusion, sadness, anger, and grief. While grappling with the loss of lives taken too soon, I sought healing through continued vigilance in revisions. It was in the last pages of the book I recognized Douglas embodied more than I had set out to accomplish.

Douglas supports Lena, provides light in her darkest times, pushes her, challenges her, makes her grow, welcomes those who care for her, and, eventually, transforms alongside Lena.

Perhaps, without me realizing it, I had fashioned Douglas not just from the real-life rendering of Ginger, but from my friend's beautiful soul. She loved hard and embraced those who crossed her path with open arms, and with admirable fierceness—be it a lover or an old van, her animals, silversmithing, a far-away friend, her family, or the mountains.

I envision her traveling through the mountains in an old van filled with her most cherished loved ones, windows down, red hair wild and free, surrounded by love and held by *"the smell of when the sun warms your skin, vintage- in a good way. A hint of vanilla."*

You will be missed, my dear friend. I hope you know that the parts of this book that shine are because of, and for, you.

About the Author

Jes Smyth is a Chicago-area native with a degree in Psychology from the University of Iowa and the author of *Time for Once*. From a young age, Jes has been an avid reader, writer, and dreamer. She's also a small artist appreciator, a budding bourbon connoisseur, an accidental poet, and a lover of fuzzy socks. She says she writes every day and hopes the stories she creates will resonate with those who find curiosity in the changes life throws our way.

PRAISE FOR EMERALD CITY

I enjoyed reading book one but I gotta say this second book is just fantastic -It's got more surprises and twists at every turn, it's so unpredictable I'm in love! and the writing is so refreshing that I'm officially out of my book reading slump.

—@pinkbibliophile

Should you grab a copy if this book is up your alley? Yes yes you should. Pick up the first on Diamond City then Emerald City. Now I'm going to sit and count the days till I get the 3rd book in my hands.

—@booklovermarissa

As someone who doesn't usually read sci-fi, this book had me hooked. I started second guessing my trust in certain characters, and was not ready for the twists and turns this took.

—@mouses_smut_hut

Astrid Cole! I need the third book ASAP!

—@valeryarchaga

I cannot wait for the next book so that I can understand more about next steps and see a resolution. This book gripped me from page one and held me until the end. If you love adventure and sci-fi, run for this series.

—@hannahshardcovers

This book is full of action and jaw dropping scenes that you will NOT want to stop reading!

—@lostinthebooks_byk

💀 <—this is me when I finished this book. Dead. The twists and turns of this insane rollercoaster took me all over Diamond City and the Outskirts with Sage as she fought for her life, her family, her friends, and her people.

—@nbbookery